~ DREAM WITH ~

JENNY COLGAN

'A quirky tale of love, work and the meaning of life'
Company

'A smart, witty love story'
Observer

'Full of laugh-out-loud observations . . .
utterly unputdownable'
Woman

'A chick-lit writer with a difference . . . never scared to
try something different, Colgan always pulls it off'
Image

'A Colgan novel is like listening to your best pal,
souped up on vino, spilling the latest gossip –
entertaining, dramatic and frequently hilarious'
Daily Record

'An entertaining read'
Sunday Express

'Part chick lit, part food porn . . . this
is full-on fun for foodies'
Bella

Also by Jenny Colgan

Amanda's Wedding
Talking to Addison
Looking for Andrew McCarthy
Working Wonders
Do You Remember the First Time?
Where Have All the Boys Gone?
West End Girls
Operation Sunshine
Diamonds Are a Girl's Best Friend
The Good, the Bad and the Dumped
Meet Me at the Cupcake Café
Christmas at the Cupcake Café
Welcome to Rosie Hopkins' Sweetshop of Dreams
Christmas at Rosie Hopkins' Sweetshop
The Christmas Surprise
The Loveliest Chocolate Shop in Paris
Little Beach Street Bakery
Summer at Little Beach Street Bakery
The Little Shop of Happy Ever After
Christmas at Little Beach Street Bakery
The Summer Seaside Kitchen

A Very Distant Shore

By Jenny T. Colgan

Resistance Is Futile
Spandex and the City

Jenny Colgan is the author of numerous bestselling novels, including *The Little Shop of Happy Ever After* and *Summer at Little Beach Street Bakery*, which are also published by Sphere. *Meet Me at the Cupcake Café* won the 2012 Melissa Nathan Award for Comedy Romance and was a *Sunday Times* top ten bestseller, as was *Welcome to Rosie Hopkins' Sweetshop of Dreams*, which won the RNA Romantic Novel of the Year Award 2013. Jenny was born in Scotland and has lived in London, the Netherlands, the US and France. She eventually settled on the wettest of all of these places, and currently lives just north of Edinburgh with her husband Andrew, her dog Nevil Shute and her three children: Wallace, who is twelve and likes pretending to be nineteen and not knowing what this embarrassing 'family' thing is that keeps following him about; Michael-Francis, who is ten and likes making new friends on aeroplanes; and Delphine, who is eight and is mostly raccoon as much as we can tell so far.

Things Jenny likes include: cakes; far too much *Doctor Who*; wearing Converse trainers every day so her feet are now just gigantic big flat pans; baths only slightly cooler than the surface of the sun and very, very long books, the longer the better. For more about Jenny, visit her website and her Facebook page, or follow her on Twitter @jennycolgan.

~ DREAM WITH ~

JENNY COLGAN

The
Endless
Beach

sphere

SPHERE

First published in Great Britain in 2018 by Sphere

1 3 5 7 9 10 8 6 4 2

Copyright © 2018 by Jenny Colgan

ISBN 978-0-7515-6482-2

Typeset in Caslon by M Rules
Printed and bound in Great Britain by
Clays Ltd, St Ives plc

Papers used by Sphere are from well-managed forests
and other responsible sources.

MIX
Paper from
responsible sources
FSC® C104740
www.fsc.org

Sphere
An imprint of
Little, Brown Book Group
Carmelite House
50 Victoria Embankment
London EC4Y 0DZ

An Hachette UK Company
www.hachette.co.uk

www.littlebrown.co.uk

To my cousins Marie and Carol-Ann Wilson,
for their amazing work in fostering
babies and children

A Word from Jenny

Hello!

I first wrote about goings-on on the tiny Scottish island of Mure last year and had such a good time doing it I really wanted to go back. There is something very special to me about the communities in the Highlands and Islands of Scotland, where it is so very beautiful – but life can be tough up there too.

Let me quickly get you up to date from the last book, in case you haven't read it – which doesn't matter, by the way – or just so that you don't have to rack your brains remembering who is who, because I hate having to do that and I have a terrible memory for names. (I am also saying this as a get-out clause in case we meet and I forget your name!)

So: Flora MacKenzie, a paralegal in London, was sent up to the remote Scottish island of Mure – where she was raised – to help her (rather attractive and difficult) boss Joel.

Reunited with her father and three brothers, she realised how much she had missed home, and, quite to her own surprise, decided to stay and make a go of it, opening the Summer Seaside Kitchen, which sells the amazing local produce from her family farm, as well as making old recipes from her late mother's recipe book.

To absolutely everybody else's surprise, her boss, Joel, decided to relocate too, giving up his crazy rat race life for something calmer and more grounded. He and Flora are just taking their very first faltering steps into a romance.

They were both working for Colton Rogers, a US billionaire who wanted to buy up half the island, whereupon he (Rogers) fell in love with Flora's talented cheese-maker brother Fintan. With me so far? There's definitely something in the water up there (and dreadful Wi-Fi and long winters, both of which help) . . .

The other two people you need to know about are Saif and Lorna, both of whom appeared in *A Very Distant Shore*, the short book about Mure I wrote for the Quick Reads series.

Saif is a doctor – a Syrian refugee – who endured incredible hardship to make his way to Europe and was granted asylum in the UK, as long as he took his medical skills where they were most needed – the remotest parts of Britain. He has now had no news of the rest of his family for over a year. Lorna is the local primary head teacher, and Flora's best friend.

Okay, I think that is us! Oh no . . . there is one more thing. In my Rosie Hopkins series of novels, there is a baddie who is a social worker, and several social workers wrote to me to complain that they do an underfunded and undervalued job in very difficult circumstances and they didn't think the portrayal was very fair.

So I had another look at the character and decided this was a good point. I hope the social workers in this book help mitigate this, and go some way to showing a little of the genuine respect I have for the dedicated people who do this really tough job day in, day out.

Anyway, I very much hope you enjoy *The Endless Beach*, and have a wonderful day wherever you are. And if you are on holiday, one, I am very jealous as it is statistically raining where I am, and two, send me a selfie! I'm on Facebook or Twitter: @jennycolgan!

With love,

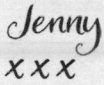

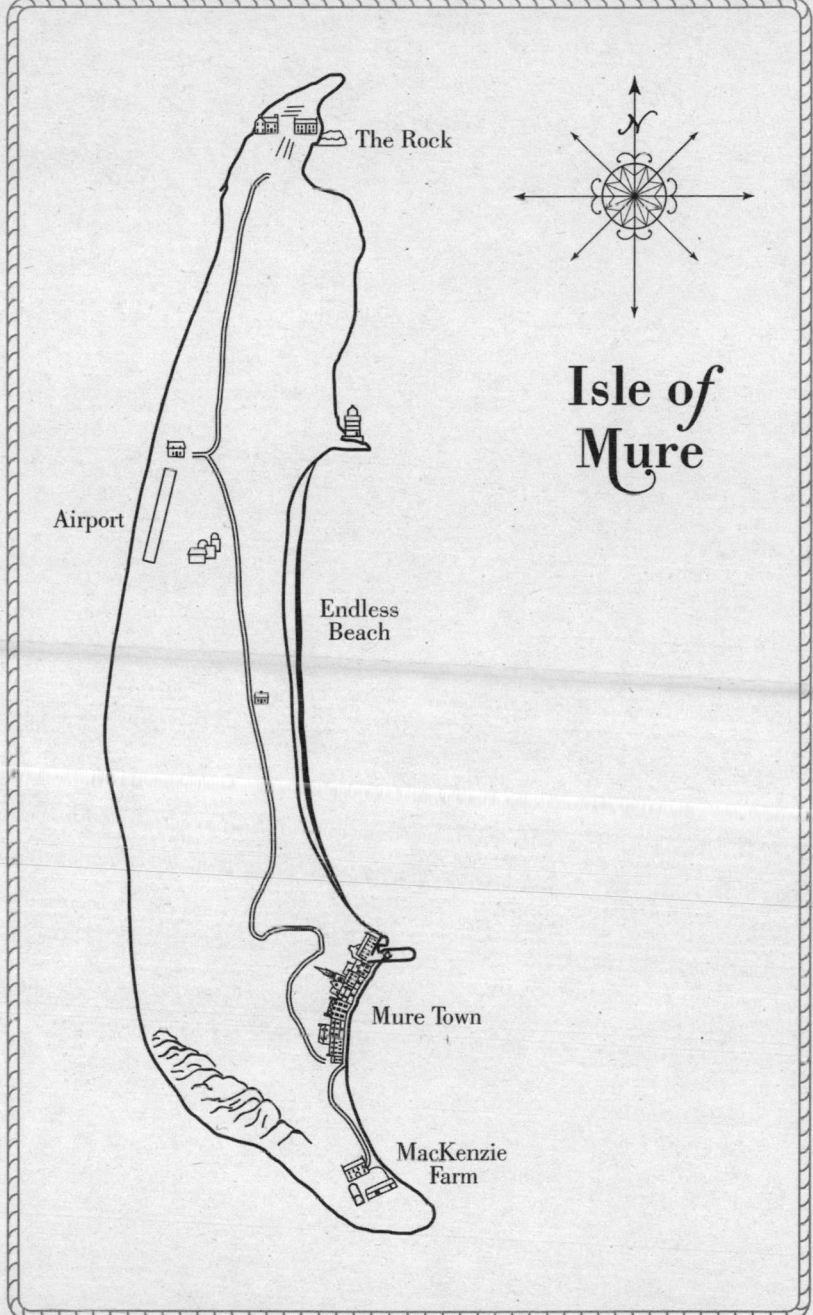

The Rock

Isle of
Mure

Airport

Endless
Beach

Mure Town

MacKenzie
Farm

A Quick Note on Pronunciation

As well as saying 'ch' like you're about to cough something up, here's a quick guide to pronouncing some of the more traditional names that appear in this book:

Agot – *Ah-got*
Eilidh – *Ay-lay*
Innes – *Inn-is*
Iona – *Eye-oh-na*
Isla – *Eye-la*
Saif – *S-eye-eef*
Seonaid – *Shon-itch*
Teàrlach – *Chèr-lach*

cynefin (n): *one's place of true belonging; the place where one feels most fully at home*

Once upon a time there was a prince who lived in a high tower made entirely of ice. But he never noticed, as he had never seen anything else, nor been anything else, and to him, being cold was simply the way of things for he had not known anything different. He was the prince of a vast wasteland; he ruled over bears and wild things and answered to nobody.

And wise advisers told him to travel; to take a bride; to learn from others. But he refused, saying, 'I am comfortable here,' and eventually the tower of ice grew thick and impossible to enter and nothing grew and it could not be climbed and dragons circled the tower and it became perilous and still the prince would not leave. And many people tried to climb the tower to rescue the prince, but none succeeded. Until one day ...

Chapter One

Even in early spring, Mure is pretty dark.

Flora didn't care; she loved waking up in the morning, curled up close, together in the pitch black. Joel was a very light sleeper (Flora didn't know that before he had met her, he had barely slept at all) and was generally awake by the time she rubbed her eyes, his normally tense, watchful face softening as he saw her, and she would smile, once again surprised and overwhelmed and scared by the depth of how she felt; how she trembled at the rhythm of his heartbeat.

She even loved the frostiest mornings, when she had to pull herself up to get everything going. It was different when you didn't have an hour-long commute pressed up against millions of other commuters breathing germs and pushing against you and making your life more uncomfortable than it had to be.

Instead, she would rake up the damped peat in the wood-burner in the beautiful guest cottage Joel was staying in while working for Colton Rogers, the billionaire who owned half the island. She would set the flames into life – and the room became even cosier in an instant, the flickering light from the fire throwing shadows on the whitewashed walls.

The one thing Joel had insisted on in the room was a highly expensive state-of-the-art coffee machine, and she would let him fiddle with that while he logged on to the day's work and made his customary remark about the many and varied failures of the island's internet reliability.

Flora would take her coffee, pull on an old jumper and wander to the window of the cottage, where she could sit on the top of the old oil-fired radiator, the type you get in schools but had cost Colton a fortune. Here she would stare out at the dark sea; sometimes with its white tips showing if it was going to be a breezy day; sometimes astonishingly clear, in which case, even in the morning, you could raise your eyes and see the brilliant cold stars overhead. There was no light pollution on Mure. They were bigger than Flora remembered from being a child.

She wrapped her hands round her mug and smiled. The shower started up. 'Where are you off to today?' she shouted.

Joel popped his head out the door. 'Hartford for starters,' he said. 'Via Reykjavik.'

'Can I come?'

Joel gave her a look. Work wasn't funny.

'Come on. We can make out on the plane.'

'I'm not sure ...'

Colton had a plane he used to get in and out of Mure, and Flora was absolutely incensed that it was strictly for company business and she'd never been allowed on it. A private plane! Such a thing was unimaginable, really. Joel was impossible to tease where work was involved. Actually, he was quite difficult to tease about anything. Which worried Flora sometimes.

'I bet there is absolutely nothing the stewardesses haven't seen,' said Flora. This was undoubtedly true, but Joel was already scrolling through the *Wall Street Journal* and not really listening.

'Back two weeks Friday. Colton is consolidating literally ... well ...'

Flora wished he could talk more about his work, like he could when she was still in the law trade. It wasn't just confidentiality. He was guarded about everything.

Flora pouted. 'You'll miss the Argylls.'

'The what?'

'It's a band. They tour and they're coming to the Harbour's Rest. They're really brilliant.'

Joel shrugged. 'I don't really like music.'

Flora went up to him. Music was in the lifeblood of everyone on Mure. Before the ferries and the aeroplanes came, they'd had to make their own entertainment, and everyone joined in with enthusiasm, if not always too much talent. Flora danced well and could just about play a bodhrán if there wasn't anyone better around. Her brother Innes was a better fiddler than he let on. The only one who couldn't play anything was big Hamish; their mother had just tended to give him a pair of spoons and let him get on with it.

She put her arms around him. 'How can you not like music?' she said.

Joel blinked and looked over her shoulder. It was silly,

really, a small thing in the endless roundabout that had been his difficult childhood, that every new school was a new chance to get it wrong: to wear the wrong thing; to like the wrong band. The fear of doing so. His lack of ability, or so it seemed, to learn the rules. The cool bands varied so widely, it was absolutely impossible to keep track.

He had found it easier to abdicate responsibility altogether. He'd never quite made his peace with music. Never dared to find out what he liked. Never had an older sibling to point the way.

It was the same with clothes. He only wore two colours – blue and grey, impeccably sourced, from the best fabrics – not because he had taste, but because it seemed absolutely the simplest. He never had to think about it. Although he'd gone on to date enough models to learn a lot more about clothes: that was something they had been helpful for.

He glanced over at Flora. She was staring out at the sea again. Sometimes he had trouble distinguishing her from the environment of Mure. Her hair was the fronds of seaweed that lay across the pale white dunes of her shoulders; her tears the sprays of saltwater in a storm; her mouth a perfect shell. She wasn't a model – quite the opposite. She felt as grounded, as solid as the earth beneath her feet; she was an island, a village, a town, a home. He touched her gently, almost unable to believe she was his.

Flora knew this touch of his, and she could not deny it. It worried her, the way that he looked at her sometimes: as if she were something fragile, precious. She was neither of those things. She was just a normal girl, with the same

4

worries and faults as anyone else. And eventually he was going to realise this, and she was terrified about what would happen when he realised that she wasn't a selkie; that she wasn't some magical creature who'd materialised to solve everything about his life ... She was terrified what would happen when he realised she was just a normal person who worried about her weight and liked to dress very badly on Sundays ... What would happen when they had to argue about washing-up liquid? She kissed his hand gently.

'Stop looking at me like I'm a water sprite.'

He grinned. 'Well, you are to me.'

'What time's your ... ? Oh.'

She always forgot that Colton's plane left to their schedule, not an airline's.

Joel glanced at his watch. 'Now. Colton has a real bug up his ass ... I mean ... There's lots to do.'

'Don't you want breakfast?'

Joel shook his head. 'Ridiculously, they'll be serving Seaside Kitchen bread and scones on board.'

Flora smiled. '*Well*, aren't *we* fancy?' She kissed him. 'Come back soon.'

'Why, where are you going?'

'Nowhere,' said Flora, pulling him close. 'Absolutely nowhere.'

And she watched him leave without a backwards glance, and sighed.

Oddly it was only during sex that she knew, one hundred per cent, that he was there. Absolutely and completely there, with her, breath for breath, movement for movement. It was not like anything she had ever known before. She had known selfish lovers and show-off lovers, and purely incompetent lovers, their potential ruined by pornography before they were barely men.

She hadn't ever known anything like this – the intensity, almost desperation – as if he were trying to fit the whole of himself inside her skin. She felt utterly known and as if she knew him perfectly. She thought about it constantly. But he was hardly ever here. And the rest of the time she wasn't any clearer about where his head was than when they'd first met.

And now, a month later, it wasn't so dark, but Joel was still away, busy on one job after another. Flora was travelling today but nowhere quite so interesting, and alas, she was back in the farmhouse.

There was something Flora felt as an adult about being closeted in the bedroom – in the single bed she grew up in, no less, with her old highland dancing trophies, dusty and still lining the wall – that made her irritable, as well as the knowledge that however early she had to get up – and it felt very, very early – her three farmworking brothers and her father would already have been up milking for an hour.

Well, not Fintan. He was the food genius of the family and spent most of his time making cheese and butter for the Seaside Kitchen and, soon they hoped, Colton's new hotel, the Rock. But the other boys – strong, dim Hamish and Innes, her eldest brother – were out, dark or light, rain or shine, and however much she tried to get her father, Eck, to slow down, he tended to head out too. When she had worked down in London as a paralegal, they had joked that she was lazy. Now that she ran an entire café single-handedly, she'd hoped to prove them wrong, but they still saw her as a light-weight, only getting up at 5 a.m.

She should move out – there were a few cottages to rent in Mure town, but the Seaside Kitchen wasn't turning over enough money for her to afford to do something as extravagant as that. She couldn't help it. They had such amazing produce here on Mure – fresh organic butter churned in their own dairies; the most astonishing cheese, made by Fintan; the best fish and shellfish from their crystal-clear waters; the rain that grew the world's sweetest grass, that fattened up the coos. But it all cost money.

She immediately worked out in her head what time it was in New York, where Joel, her boyfriend – it felt ridiculous, she realised, calling him her boyfriend – was working.

He had been her own boss, sent up with her to work on some legal business for Colton Rogers. But being her boss was only a part of it. She'd had a massive crush on him for years, since the first moment she'd set eyes on him. He, on the other hand, spent his life dating models and not noticing her. She hadn't ever thought she could get his attention. And then, finally, when they had worked together last summer, he had thawed enough to notice her: enough, in the end, to relocate his business to work with Colton on Mure.

Except of course it hadn't quite turned out like that. Colton had assigned him a guest cottage, a beautifully restored hunting lodge, while the Rock was preparing to officially open, which was taking its time. Then he'd shot off all round the world, looking after his various billionaire enterprises – which seemed to require Joel with him at all times. She'd barely seen him all winter. Right now, he was in New York. Things like setting up home – things like sitting down to have a conversation – seemed completely beyond him.

Flora had known theoretically that he was a workaholic; she'd worked for him for years. She just didn't realise what that would mean when it came to their relationship. She seemed to get the leftovers. And there wasn't much. Not even a message to indicate he was aware she was going to London today, to formally sign her leaving papers.

Flora hadn't been sure if they could keep the Seaside Kitchen going over the winter, when the tourists departed and the nights drew down so low it was never light at all, not really, and the temptation was very much to stay in bed all day with the covers over her head.

But to her surprise, the Kitchen was busy every single day. Mothers with babies; old people stopping to chat to their friends over a cheese scone; the knitting group that handled spillover Fair Isle orders and normally met in each other's kitchens who had decided to make the Seaside Kitchen their home, and Flora never got tired of watching the amazing speed and grace of gnarled old fingers producing the beautiful repeating patterns on every type of wool.

So much so that she'd realised: this was her job now. This was where she belonged. Her firm in London had originally given her a leave of absence to work with Colton, but that was over and she had to formally resign. Joel had too: he was working for Colton full time. Flora had been putting off going to London, hoping they'd be able to go together to sign off the paperwork, but it didn't seem to be very likely.

So she helped Isla, one of the two young girls who worked with her, open up the Seaside Kitchen for the day. They'd repainted it the same pale pink it had been until it had gone to seed and started to peel. Now it fitted in nicely with the black-and-white Harbour's Rest hotel, the pale blue of the tackle shop and the cream of many tourist shops that lined the front, selling big woollen jumpers, souvenir shells and stone carvings, tartan (of course), small models of Highland coos, tablet and toffee. Many of them were shut for the winter.

The wind was ripping off the sea, throwing handfuls of spray and rain into her face and she grinned and ran down the hill from the farmhouse, the commute that was all she had these days. It might be freezing – although she had a huge Puffa jacket on that basically insulated her from absolutely everything – but she still wouldn't swap it in a second for an overheated, overstuffed tube carriage; a great outpouring of humanity pushing up the stairs; hot, cold, hot, cold, pushing past more and more people; witnessing shouts and squabbles and cars bumping each other and horns going off and cycle couriers screaming at cabbies and tubes roaring past, free sheets being blown by the wind up and down the street with fast-food wrappers and cigarette butts ... No, Flora thought, even on mornings like this, you could keep your commute. She didn't miss it.

Annie's Seaside Kitchen was lit up and golden. It was plain, with ten mismatched bric-a-brac tables scattered artfully around the large room. The counter, currently empty,

9

would soon be filled with scones, cakes, quiche, homemade salads and soups as Iona and Isla busied themselves in the back. Mrs Laird, a local baker, dropped off two dozen loaves a day, which went fairly speedily, and the coffee machine didn't stop from dawn till dusk. Flora still couldn't quite believe it existed, and that it was down to her. Somehow, coming back to her old stamping ground and finding her late mother Annie's own recipe book – it had felt like a happy choice, not a desperate one, or a sad one.

It had felt like a great, ridiculous leap at the time. Now in retrospect it felt entirely obvious, as if it was the only thing she should have done. As if this was home, and the same people she remembered from her childhood – older now, but the faces were the same, handed down the generations – were as much a part of her world as they ever were, and the essential things in her life – Joel, the Seaside Kitchen, the weather forecast, the farm, the freshness of the produce – were more important to her somehow than Brexit, than global warming, than the fate of the world. It wasn't as if she was in retreat. She was in renewal.

So Flora was in an unusually good mood as she removed the MacKenzie family butter from the fridge – creamy and salted and frankly capable of rendering all other sorts of spreads redundant – and glanced to see all the locally fired earthenware ready and in a row. There was an English incomer living up past the farms in a tiny little cottage who made it out the back in a kiln. It was thick and plainly fired in earthen colours – sand, and grey and off-white – and they were perfect for keeping your latte warm with a thin, slightly turned-in top and a much thicker base. They'd had to have a polite sign made saying that the mugs were for sale, otherwise people kept nicking them, and the sales had provided a rather handy sideline and a completely unexpected new lease of life for Geoffrey from up off the old Macbeth farm road.

As soon as she turned the CLOSED sign to OPEN, the clouds parted, making it look as if they might get a ray or two of sunshine with their gale-force winds, and that made her smile too. Joel was away, and that was sad. But on the other hand, once she'd got this stupid London trip out of the way she could maybe get Lorna over to watch *TOWIE* on catchup and split a bottle of Prosecco with her. She didn't make much but they could still go halfers on a bottle of Prosecco, and truly, in the end, what more was there to life than that?

A song she liked came on the radio, and Flora was as full of contentment as anyone can truly feel in the middle of February, when a shadow passed in front of the doorway. Flora opened the door to their first customer of the morning who stepped back slightly from the arctic draught, blinking as they blocked out the light behind them. Then her good mood dissipated slightly. It was Jan.

When Flora had first arrived on Mure, she'd met a nice man – a very nice man – called Charlie, or Teàrlach. He led outdoor activity holidays on Mure, sometimes for businessmen and lawyers and organisations, which paid the bills, and sometimes for deprived children from the mainland, which he did for charity.

Charlie had liked Flora and Flora, resigned to the idea that she was never going to get together with Joel, had flirted with him a bit – well, more than a bit, she thought. She was always embarrassed to look back on it: how quickly she had gone from one to another. But Charlie was a gentleman and had understood. The other thing was, though, he had been on a break from his girlfriend, Jan, who worked with him. Jan had subsequently decided that Flora was a feckless tart and that it was all her fault that she'd led him astray. She had never forgiven Flora, but instead did her down fairly loudly and publicly whenever she got half a chance.

Normally this wouldn't bother Flora terribly much. But on an island the size of Mure, it could be quite tricky to avoid bumping into someone fairly regularly, and if that person didn't like you, it could get a little wearing.

Today, however, Jan – who was tall, with short sensible hair, a determinedly square jaw and a constant conviction that she was saving the world (she worked with Charlie on the adventure holidays) and everyone else was a feckless wastrel – had a smile on her face.

'Morning!' she trilled. Flora looked at Isla and Iona, both of whom were as surprised as she was at Jan's jolly mood. They both shrugged their shoulders.

'Um ... Hi, Jan,' said Flora. Normally Jan ignored her completely and ordered from the girls, proceeding to talk loudly the entire time as if Flora didn't exist. Flora would have barred her, but she wasn't really a barring type of person and had absolutely no idea how she'd have done such a thing. Anyway, barring one person who worked with the adventure programme while simultaneously funnelling food near its sell-by date to the children who came to visit, via Charlie, seemed a little self-defeating in the end.

'Hello!' Jan was swishing her left hand about

ostentatiously. Flora thought she was waving at someone across the street. Fortunately, Isla was slightly more up on this sort of thing.

'Jan! Is that an engagement ring?'

Jan flushed and looked as coy as she could, which wasn't very, and shyly displayed her hand.

'You and Charlie tying the knot then?' said Isla. 'That's great!'

'Congratulations!' said Flora, genuinely delighted. She had felt bad about Charlie; the fact that he was happy enough in his life to pop the question to Jan was wonderful news. 'That's just great. I'm so pleased!'

Jan looked slightly discombobulated at that, as if she'd been secretly hoping Flora would throw herself to the ground and start rending her garments in misery.

'So, when are you doing it?' asked Iona.

'Well, it will be at the Rock, of course.'

'If it's ready,' said Flora. She didn't know what Colton was prevaricating about.

Jan raised her eyebrows. 'Oh, I'm sure some people know how to get things done around here ... Do you have any raisin splits this morning?'

And Flora had to admit, annoyed, that they didn't.

'Well, it's wonderful news,' she said again. Then she didn't want to push too hard in case it looked like she was angling for an invite. Which she very much wasn't. More than a few people had seen her and Charlie about town last summer and remembered Jan's meltdown after she'd found them kissing. The last thing she needed was gossip sprouting again, not when things were finally calm and quiet.

13

So she went back behind the counter. 'Can I get you anything else?'

'Four slices of quiche. So. I know normally your stuff is too full of sugar and you waste a lot . . . ?'

Supreme happiness hadn't dented Jan's love of stating the worst possible take on practically everything, Flora noticed.

'Sorry, what was that?'

'Well,' said Jan, a smile playing on her lips. 'We thought you might like to cater the wedding.'

Flora blinked. She was desperate to get into catering; there was no news on the Rock, and she really did want to turn over some more money. She'd be able to pay the girls a little more. She'd rather not have to watch everyone watch her watch Charlie get married. But on the other hand, she didn't really care, did she? And they could really, really do with the money. And she'd be backstage all the time, looking after things in the kitchen. Actually, this might be the best possible solution.

'Of course!' she said. 'We'd be delighted!'

Jan frowned again. It struck Flora that Jan had had some kind of scenario playing out in her head in which she, Flora, would be rendered somehow humiliated by this. She didn't quite understand where the benefit was, but she certainly wouldn't give Jan the satisfaction of thinking that deep down, Flora was anything other than pleased.

Jan leaned closer. 'It would make a lovely wedding present,' she said.

Flora blinked.

A silence fell, broken only by the bell above the door ringing, as their morning regulars started to file in, and Isla

14

and Iona scuttled along the counter to serve them, judging a safe distance between being away from the difficult conversation and still being able to eavesdrop.

'Ah,' said Flora, finally. 'No, I think ... I think we'd have to charge. I'm sorry.'

Jan nodded as if in sympathy.

'I realise this must be hard for you,' she said finally. Flora could do nothing but look ahead, cheerfully. 'You'd think with that rich boyfriend of yours you'd want to do something good for the island ...'

Flora bit back from mentioning that that wasn't how it worked, not at all, and she wouldn't have dreamed of taking a penny from Joel, ever; in fact, the idea of ever asking him for anything filled her with terror. They'd never even discussed money. She was conscious as she thought this that they hadn't discussed anything much, but dismissed it.

Joel, who didn't understand this kind of thing particularly well, found it something of a welcome relief from the women he had dated in the past who pouted and always wanted to go shopping. But he also assumed that Flora didn't actually need or want anything, which wasn't true either.

But more than that, it was the idea of Jan and her wealthy, well-fed family tucking into one of the Seaside Kitchen's famous spreads – lobster, and oysters on ice, and the best bread and butter, and local beef, and the best cheese to be found around, glistening pies, and freshly skimmed cream. That they would take that, guffawing among themselves that they hadn't paid anything for it ...

Flora bagged up the pieces of quiche and rang it up on the till without another word. Jan counted out the money very, very slowly, with a patronising smile on her face, then left, Flora gazing hotly behind her.

Iona watched her go. 'That's a shame,' she said.

'That woman is a monster,' growled Flora, good mood almost entirely dissipated.

'No, I mean, I really wanted to go to the wedding,' said Iona. 'I bet there'll be loads of good-looking boys there.'

'Is that all you think about – meeting boys?' said Flora.

'No,' said Iona. 'All I think about is meeting boys who aren't fishermen.'

'Oi!' said a party of fishermen who were warming their freezing hands around the large earthenware mugs of tea and tearing into fresh warm soda bread.

'No offence,' said Iona. 'But you are always smelling of fish and having not enough thumbs because you got them tangled in a net, isn't it?'

The fishermen looked at each other and nodded and agreed that that was fair enough, fair enough indeed, it was a dangerous business mind you.

'Right!' said Flora, throwing up her hands. 'I have a plane to catch.'

Chapter Two

Flora drove the battered old Land Rover past her friend Lorna MacLeod's farmhouse on her way to the airport, but missed her by moments. That morning it was very windy, with a breeze off the sea and white tips of the waves beating against the sand, but it was definitely brightening up – the tide was in, and the beach known as the Endless looked like a long, golden path. You still needed a stout jacket, but in the air you could sense it somehow: something stirring in the earth.

On the way down from the farm, Milou bounding joyfully at her side, Lorna, the local primary school head teacher, and in fact teacher (there were two: Lorna took what was commonly known as the 'wee' class which covered the four- to eight-year-olds, and the saintly Mrs Cook covered the others) saw crocuses and snowdrops and daffodils beginning to push through their snaked heads. There was a scent in the air; over the normal sea-spray, which she never even noticed, there was an earthier scent – of growth, of rebirth.

Lorna smiled to herself luxuriantly, thinking of the months ahead, of the longer and longer days until the middle of the summer when it barely got dark at all; when Mure would be full and joyfully thronged with happy holidaymakers; when the three pubs would be full every night and the music would play until the last whisky drinker was happy or asleep or both. She put her hands deep into the pockets of her Puffa jacket, and set off, her eyes on the horizon, where the last rays of pink and gold were just vanishing and some cold but golden rays of early spring sunshine were pushing over.

She was also feeling cheerful as she now awoke when it was light, for starters. The winter had been mild, comparatively speaking – the storms had of course swept down from the Arctic, cutting off the ferries and causing everyone to huddle inside, but she didn't mind that so much. She liked seeing the children charge around in their hats and mittens, pink-cheeked and laughing in the school yard; she enjoyed cosy hot chocolates in town and curling up beside the fire in her father's old house. She'd inherited the house – to share, technically, with her brother. He worked the rigs and had a cool modern apartment in Aberdeen though, and he didn't care really, so she'd sold her little high-street flat to a young couple and set about trying to build a home in the old farm-house in a fit of spring exuberance. In fact, it was a shame she'd missed Flora, as Flora could have done with a good dose of Lorna positivity, for what came after.

She did, however, see Saif.

Saif spotted her at the same time from the other end of the beach. He lived in the old manse – the smaller, crumbling one, not the one Colton had lavishly updated – up on the hillside, empty since their vicar had moved to the mainland, the ageing population here no longer large enough to justify a full-time padre, on an island which, even though it had strong overtones of religious severity and Knoxism, had never torn itself away entirely from its earlier roots: the many, fierce gods of the Viking invaders; the green earth gods of its primary inhabitants. There was something on the island that was deeply, utterly spiritual, whatever your beliefs. There were standing stones on the headlands – the remains of a community that had worshipped heaven knows what – as well as an ancient, beautiful ruined abbey, and scattered stern plain churches with stubby steeples standing stiff against the northerly winds.

The house was rented to Saif as he did his two years' service to the community in return for which, it was promised, he would receive his permanent right to stay. He was a refugee, and a doctor, and the remote islands desperately needed GPs, although his promised right to stay of course was not guaranteed. Saif had given up reading about British politics. It was a total mystery to him. He was unaware that it was an equal mystery to everyone else around him; he just assumed this was how things had always been.

He had been having the dreams again. He wasn't sure he'd ever be free of them. Always the clamour, the noise. Being in the boat again. Clutching on to his leather bag as though his life depended on it. The look on the face of the little boy he'd had to stitch up without anaesthetic after a fight had broken out. The stoicism. The desperation. The boat.

And every morning, regardless of the weather, he woke up determined not to sink beneath his own waves – his own waves of waiting: waiting to hear about his wife and his two sons, left behind when he went to see if he could forge a passage to a better life for them all in a world that had got suddenly, harshly worse.

He had heard nothing, although he called the Home Office once a week. He was unsure if the distant neighbourhood he had left behind – once friendly, chatty, relaxed – even existed any more. His entire life was gone.

And people kept telling him he was one of the lucky ones.

Every morning, to shake the night horrors from his head, he would go for a long walk down the Endless to try to get himself into an appropriate state of mind to deal with the minor complaints of the local population: their sore hips, and coughing babies, and mild anxiety, and menopauses, and everything that he must not dismiss as absolutely nothing compared with the searing, apocalyptic misery of his homeland. A couple of miles normally did it. Through the winter, he had walked as the sun barely rose, half by instinct, welcoming the handfuls of hail that felt like rocks being thrown into his face, a phenomenon he had never experienced until he had come to Europe and which he had found almost comically inconvenient.

But at least the weather allowed him to feel something other than dread, and he let it scour out his head. When he was chilled to the bone – and exhausted – then, he felt clean. And empty. And ready for another day in this half-life – an eternal waiting room.

And he was thinking this when he saw it, and he threw up his arms in surprise.

Lorna saw this happen from the other end of the beach, and her brow furrowed. It was not like Saif to be enthusiastic. If anything, you had to work pretty hard to draw him out. Life on Mure was chatty – there was no way around it. Everyone knew each other and everyone used gossip as the lifeblood of their community. It wasn't unusual to know the goings-on and whereabouts of three generations of Murians at any one time. Of course, everyone was a millionaire in America or doing fabulously well in London or had the most brilliant and amazing children. You just accepted that as a given. Still, it was nice to hear, regardless.

But Saif never, ever spoke about his family. It was all Lorna knew that he had – or had had – a wife and two sons. She couldn't bear to ask anything more. Saif had landed on Mure stripped of everything – of possessions, of his status. He was a refugee before he was a doctor: he was something pitied – even, in some quarters (until he stitched up their injuries and tended to their parents), despised for no reason. She couldn't bear the risk of upsetting him, of taking away the last bit of dignity he had left, by prying.

So when she saw him waving, the bright empty Mure morning full of whipping clouds and promise, her heart started to beat faster immediately. Milou caught on to her excitement and bounded cheerily up the beach. She ran to keep up with him, arriving panting – the Endless was always much longer than you thought it was; the water played tricks on your concept of distance – and trepidatious.

'Look!' Saif was shouting. 'Look!'

She followed his pointing finger. Was it a boat? What was it? She screwed her eyes up.

21

'Oh. It's gone,' said Saif, and she looked at him, puzzled, but his gaze was still fixed out on the water. She stared too, trying to get her heart to calm down. Just as she was about to ask him what the hell he'd been going on about, she saw it: a ripple at first, not something you could be sure of, then, straight out of the blue, a huge body – vast, vaster than it had any right to be, so big you couldn't believe that it could possibly propel itself. It was like watching a 747 take off – a huge, shining black body leaped straight out over the waves and, with a vibrant twist of its tail, shaking off the droplets of water, plunged back underneath.

Saif turned to her, eyes shining. He said something that sounded like 'hut'.

Lorna squinted. 'What?'

'I don't know the word in English,' he said.

'Oh!' said Lorna. 'Whale! It's a whale. A weird ... I've never seen anything like that before.'

'There are many of them here?'

'Some,' said Lorna. She frowned. 'Some normal whales. That one looks weird. And it's not good for them to be so close to shore. One got washed up last year and it was a heck of a palaver, remember?'

Saif didn't understand whether a 'heck of a palaver' was a good thing or a bad thing, and did not remember, so he just kept looking. Sure enough, after a few moments the whale leaped again, and this time the sun caught the droplets dropping from its tail like diamonds, and what looked bizarrely like a horn. They both leaned forward to see it.

'It's beautiful.'

Lorna looked at it. 'It is,' she said.

'You do not sound so happy, Lorenah.'

He had never been very good at pronouncing her name.

'Well,' she said. 'For starters, I'm worried about it. Whales beaching is a terrible thing. Even if you can save them once, sometimes they just do it again. And the other thing . . .'

Saif looked at her quizzically.

'Oh well, you'll think this is stupid.'

He shrugged his shoulders.

'For Murians . . . on the island, I mean. They're seen as unlucky.'

Saif frowned. 'But they're so beautiful.'

'Lots of beautiful things bring bad luck. So we'll welcome them in,' said Lorna, her eyes fixed on the horizon. 'We need Flora. She can handle these things.'

Saif looked doubtful, and Lorna laughed. 'Oh, it's just silly superstition though.'

And the whale leaped again through the breaking waves, so strong and free, and Lorna wondered a little why she didn't feel joyous; why she had, unexpectedly, an ominous feeling in the pit of her stomach, quite at odds with the blowy day.

Chapter Three

Flora alighted at Liverpool Street from the airport and came up from the warm bowels of the subway, reflecting, briefly, how shocking London is when you've been away and aren't used to it; how there are more people, probably, on the railway concourse than live on her entire island. Then she realised that she'd been standing on the escalator a microsecond too long because somebody barged into her and made a loud tutting sound.

It seemed very strange to her that she'd only been away a few months, as the London commute used to feel as natural to her as breathing. Now she couldn't imagine why anybody would put themselves through this if they didn't absolutely have to.

Now, this morning was something she was not looking forward to. Not at all. It was ridiculous: all she had to do was go in, pick up her stuff, sign some forms for HR to tell them she was leaving and promise not to work for any more high-flying law firms in the next three months, which wouldn't be difficult, seeing as there weren't any high-flying law firms on Mure. There was no high-flying anything. That's what made it so nice.

So she shouldn't be nervous. But she was. The trouble was, Flora couldn't help herself remembering, now she was back in London. She remembered what it was like here, when Joel was constantly dating ridiculously beautiful models; when he used Tinder and hook-ups and all sorts of things Flora had never been particularly good at; when you would never, in your wildest dreams, have put a senior partner – a handsome senior partner too – together with some pale paralegal.

Flora was unusual-looking, she knew, but not traditionally lovely. Her hair was a very pale strawberry blonde, almost fading away to nothing, and her skin was white as milk. Her eyes were the colour of the sea; they changed almost constantly from grey to green to blue. She was the product of generations of island folk and Vikings.

But she wasn't like the gorgeously, beautifully made-up Instagram girls of London, with their amazing clothes – everyone in Mure just wore a fleece every day – and blow-dried hair – there was never any point doing this in Mure, for windy reasons. Here, everyone seemed so self-assured and busy and rushing and glamorous. And she felt herself shrink. Whereas Mure felt like her home, her place to be. It didn't, however, stop London making her feel like a failure.

Focus, Flora told herself. Focus on the good stuff. Their life together. She blinked.

There was no doubt that being with someone as driven, as tough as Joel was, was as her best friend Lorna said, difficult. A pickle. He had grown up in foster care, in and out of other people's homes. Flora wasn't exactly sure he'd ever managed to properly attach to anyone. She worried, genuinely, how much it was her he loved, how much her family – she and her three brothers adored each other, mostly through the medium of slagging each other off – or how much the island itself, with its calm atmosphere, where everyone knew each other. That it gave his anxious heart a berth, which was all very well. But Flora wondered if that was enough; if she, herself, were enough.

Because they had worked together, in this building, for four years, and he'd never noticed her. Not once. Never even known her name. Even though she'd spoken to him several times, when he first called her up to discuss Mure, he'd acted as if they'd never met before. Kai, her best friend in the office, had found it absolutely astounding that they had got together. And Kai was someone who cared for her. What on earth the rest of the office must be thinking she couldn't bear to imagine.

She steeled herself. In, out and it would be over. And she could get on with the next, massive stage of her life, whatever it was going to be.

Chapter Four

Fintan MacKenzie, the youngest of Flora's three elder brothers, blinked awake to the sight of his boyfriend, Colton Rogers, stretching in the sun.

'What are you doing?' groaned Fintan. They'd been finalising possible whisky suppliers for the Rock the night before – the development was coming on at an extremely leisurely pace – with fairly predictable results, and the early spring sunshine coming through the huge paned windows of the hotel room was messing with his head.

'Sun salutations!' said Colton bouncily. 'C'mon, join me?'

Fintan put his head back under the covers. 'No thanks! Also, you know, that is not your most flattering angle.'

Colton grinned and carried on. 'You won't say that when you see how bendy it makes me. Come on, get up. I've got green juice and green tea on the go downstairs.'

'The only thing green around here,' complained Fintan

as he headed off to the bathroom, 'is me. What have you got planned today?'

'Seeing my lawyer this morning to go over a few things,' said Colton.

'Is that the weird American guy?' shouted Fintan from the bathroom.

'Weird guy would suffice,' said Colton, 'seeing as you are talking to an American. Anyway, you should know. Isn't he marrying your sister?'

Fintan groaned and popped his head out of the bathroom. 'Don't ask me, for God's sake. Flora is a law unto herself. And anyway, marrying? Really?' He made a face.

'What have you got against marriage?' said Colton, stretching himself out again like a cat and bending his back.

'Only that it's for idiots,' said Fintan. 'Look at Innes.'

Innes was the eldest MacKenzie brother, who had married the beautiful Eilidh. It had ended badly, she had raced back to the mainland and now he saw his gorgeous, wilful daughter Agot not nearly as much as he would like.

'Mmm,' said Colton. He changed position and didn't say anything more, and there was a slightly odd silence between them. Then Fintan disappeared into the shower and promptly forgot all about it.

Colton kissed him when he got out.

'That's your "going away for ages" kiss,' grumbled Fintan. 'I don't like it.'

'Neither do I,' said Colton, a smile playing on his lips.

'What?'

'Nothing.'

'What?'

'Well, now I've got that tame lawyer working for me . . . '

'Can we stop talking about him please?'

' . . . I thought I'd go, maybe close down a few things – make it easier for me to spend more time here.'

'Seriously?' said Fintan, his face lighting up. Colton looked at him for a while, just enjoying the effect it had. 'That would be awesome,' said Fintan.

'I know,' said Colton. 'I'm going to . . . well. I have some ideas.'

Fintan embraced him. Then he looked up. 'Can we still go to the Caribbean in February though?'

'Yes.'

Chapter Five

Adu on reception smiled happily to see Flora and she was grateful to see a friendly face.

'You're back!' he said.

'Oh, no, I'm off,' she said. 'I'll turn in my pass later. I'm leaving.'

Adu looked surprised. 'You're leaving the firm?'

'Uh-huh.'

'Why?'

'To . . . um. I'm running a café in Scotland now.'

Adu blinked. 'But this is . . . this is the best law firm in London.'

Flora tried to smile. She tried to make herself think of all the punishing hours she'd put in here, the early mornings, the late nights, the endless tedious paper-work she really hated. She'd done everything her mother had wanted her to do – get a degree, get a career – and then, she'd been forced to go home, thinking she didn't want to – and realised she'd loved it all along. It was the strangest feeling.

And somehow, in an awful way that sometimes felt like a betrayal, it also had set her free.

It wasn't Adu who worried her. It was Margo, Joel's high-powered assistant, who had protected him from the outside world and run his life and diary with exceptional ruthlessness. Suddenly Flora wished they hadn't decided that it would have been ridiculous for them to turn up together. She wanted Joel there, his quiet presence calming her, her amazement every time she felt him by her side, as if every hair in her body lifted when he entered a room, like a sunflower gravitating towards him. She knew, deep down, it wasn't right to be so amazed, to be so bowled over.

She had handed him her heart in her hands without truly knowing whether this quiet, enclosed man could be trusted with it. But it had gone; it had flown from her as if it had always been his, regardless of what he wanted to do with it. She sighed. Maybe she wouldn't see Margo. Maybe she wouldn't see anyone.

'SURPRISE!'

Flora blinked. Her old desk, situated in an open-plan space and now occupied by a slightly insultingly young-looking girl called Narinder, was covered in balloons, and standing behind it, looking jolly, was her best work friend, Kai. Never one to let things pass undercelebrated, he had covered her desk with cakes and bottles of fizz, and everyone she knew (and many she didn't: things moved fast at the firm, but who cared when cake was involved?) was standing round, looking pink and cheerful.

'Hooray!' shouted Kai. 'You're making it out of here alive!'

Everyone cheered, and Flora also went pink. 'Och, I'm only . . . I mean, I'm in the middle of nowhere,' she muttered.

Kai said, 'Listen to you, you've gone all Scottish and you've only been away five minutes.' He popped a cork and poured fizz into plastic cups, and more people arrived every minute. Flora had kept her head down and worked incredibly hard for the four years she'd spent there, and she was touched by how many people came up to thank her for what she'd done or to say how much they'd miss her.

'See?' said Kai. 'You think no one ever notices you.'

'Come on, serve free cake and they could be saying bye to a pencil sharpener,' said Flora, but she was pleased nonetheless.

One older woman, one of the senior lawyers, who Flora had always looked up to as almost impossibly suave and glamorous, took her aside. She was on her second glass of fizz.

'Tell me about Mure,' she said. 'Are there jobs there?'

'Well, tourism mostly,' said Flora. 'Catering, always. Farming if you like. It's not easy up there to make a living. Doctors and teachers always welcome.'

The woman nodded. 'It was my dream, you know,' she said. 'To move away. To make money here, then go somewhere beautiful where I could . . . ' She smiled. 'This sounds silly, I know. But where I could set myself free.'

Flora nodded. She knew what she meant.

'You could,' said Flora. 'You could go any time. It's not

expensive to buy a house or anything. The people are nice. And there are lots of English people there,' she said, encouragingly. 'I mean, we have shops and everything. Well. Three shops. Okay, forget what I said about the shops.'

The woman smiled sadly. 'Oh, I'm too old to start over now, I think. Everything I know is here, and, well ... But you doing it ... amazing. I think it's amazing. I look at your Facebook.'

'Oh,' said Flora.

'And it's so beautiful and ... well. I'm jealous. That's all.'

And she patted Flora on the arm, rubbed briefly at her eyes and sashayed off on her amazing high heels which cost more than Annie's Seaside Kitchen turned over in a week. Flora watched her go.

'So,' said Kai. 'There's something else people want to know.' He leaned in conspiratorially. '*Spill!*'

Flora blushed. 'What do you mean?'

'Shut up! You know exactly what I mean.'

Flora's skin was so pale that she couldn't possibly hide a blush. She went scarlet.

'Seriously,' said Hebe, an incredibly beautiful girl with polished skin and long braids. She was pretending to be joking but Flora didn't think she was really. 'I mean, why you? I mean, obviously you're awesome and everything ... '

Her voice trailed off.

'Who are you talking about?' said a voice. It was Narinder, her replacement.

'She somehow pulled Joel Binder,' said Hebe in the same tone of voice. 'Basically, she held him hostage on an island until he gave in.'

'That's it exactly,' said Flora, determined not to take the bait.

Narinder shook her head. 'I never met him.'

'You never did?' said Kai. He googled the company's home page and brought up the picture of him. It was an image Flora knew incredibly well – his smart suit, the thick brown curly hair, the horn-rimmed glasses, the strong jaw and slightly disconnected expression. It was all him. She couldn't deny what she felt for him. Couldn't downplay it.

'Look at her!' said Kai. 'She's off in a dream. Are you choosing wedding dresses?'

'No!' said Flora furiously. 'Shut up! I don't want to talk about it.'

'Why, is it over already?' said Hebe. 'Has he definitely resigned too?'

'He's coming in next week,' said Flora defiantly.

'Are you a hundred per cent sure about that?'

Kai sensed the situation was getting a little out of hand. 'Come on,' he said, steering Flora away. 'Early lunch. Bye, everyone. Tell my clients I'm on it.'

'Bring back the real story!' shouted Hebe.

'Actually, I hate her. She can't have any cake,' said Flora as Kai ushered her along, picking up her bagful of belongings – which included a pretty pair of spare shoes in a ballerina style that would be rendered instantly useless by the mud of the farmyard in almost any season Mure had to offer and some expensive Chanel lipstick she'd bought to cheer herself up once following a disastrous Tinder date. It felt like another life.

She was pondering this as they waited for the lift and

34

then, just when they were nearly out of danger, Margo strode up to her. Flora's heart sank. Which was ridiculous. Margo had been the closest thing to an intimate Joel had ever had at the company. He had lots of acquaintances but hardly any friends as far as she could tell. He'd had a million girls, which she tried not to think about too much, but very few girlfriends who'd lasted longer than a week or so. He had no family, or at least not the type she would recognise. He may carry on talking to Margo. He might even – and Flora felt a momentary panic at the thought – want to continue working with her once they'd sorted out his move.

'Hello.'

Margo looked at her as if she hadn't recognised her first off. Then she smiled. 'Flora MacKenzie,' she said.

There was a long pause. Where the hell was that stupid lift? Kai suddenly was very interested in his phone.

Margo cleared her throat. 'So, how's Joel?'

Flora again went bright pink. 'Um, he's great.'

'And is he . . . in *Scotland* right now?'

She said 'Scotland' like someone might say 'Candyland': a ridiculous and temporary concept.

'Um, no,' said Flora. 'He's in New York at the moment, working for Colton.'

At this Margo's face brightened. 'Of course he is,' she said. 'I knew he wouldn't be able to stay in the country for long.'

She sniffed as the lift finally arrived and Flora and Kai went to step inside.

'No, but, he's, but . . . '

Kai jostled Flora into the lift as she stumbled over her words.

'Very nice to see you,' said Margo, walking on. 'Good luck with everything!'

'She's just jealous,' said Kai, two cocktails later.

Flora stuck out her bottom lip. 'No, she's just like everyone else! She doesn't think it's possible for people to change!'

There was a delicate pause. Kai had known Joel's self-obsessed, diffident ways for as long as Flora had.

'And he has, right? I mean, of course he has.'

Flora bit her lip. 'Yes,' she said stiffly. 'Of course he has.'

Chapter Six

Flora got home the next day feeling rather chastened. She was pleased to slip back onto the island, into the farmhouse kitchen where she arrived about five seconds after Fintan, who had travelled in rather more style than she had, and straight into an argument.

When Flora had arrived home months before, the farmhouse she'd grown up in had been a tatty thing, uncared for and unloved since their mother – the centre of their home and thus, really, their lives – had died, in the bed they all had been born in.

Fintan had locked himself away. He was almost unrecognisable these days from the bearded recluse he'd become. Innes, the eldest, and jolliest, had just about run himself into the ground through overwork, trying to hold the farm together. Her father had ploughed on, looking neither to right nor left, and that had nearly ended very badly too. Only big, sweet Hamish, who was generally believed to have been dropped on the head as a baby, was relatively unchanged. Although the first thing he'd bought with the money they got from the farm changing hands was a bright red convertible, so who could say?

Innes and Fintan were arguing about when the Rock was going to open – there was no point in them running the farm ragged for a clientele that hadn't arrived, and the summer season was bearing down on them at full speed. Fintan was saying sulkily that it had to be right; Innes was sarcastically pointing out that if Fintan and his lover boy ever stopped kissing for long enough they might be able to get something done, which was going down about as well as could be expected, especially when Hamish started making kissy noises.

'Hi, everyone!' said Flora, putting her bag down on the old kitchen table. Her father, Eck, awoke with a start.

He'd been taking an afternoon nap. Even stopping some of his work hadn't been quite enough to prevent him waking at 5.30 a.m., up with the milking, and that would never change now. They had been farming in the MacKenzie family for as far back as anybody knew. It was hard, sometimes, to think that this generation might be the last to do it.

Innes's daughter Agot, who'd just celebrated her fourth birthday, was there too, and now she clambered up and down Eck's armchair and all over his legs and shoulders. He looked up with pleasure at seeing Flora; partly, Flora knew, because of the distraction she would bring to the only MacKenzie grandchild. And so it proved.

'ATTI FLOWA!'

Agot had the famous selkie hair, not just colourless like Flora's, but a great rippling mane of silvery white. It looked as if it would glow in the dark. She was, too, a bewitching thing, full of confidence and the absolute belief that whatever she said was very important to everyone. Sometimes Flora caught herself looking at Agot and wondering what happened to girls when they grew up.

Flora gladly lifted her into her arms. 'Hello, my darling.'

'She's being a fiend,' said Innes. 'Can you distract her please?'

'I need to test a new recipe,' said Flora. 'Agot, do you want to help?'

'AGOT DO IT.'

'You can help.'

'ME DO IT. ALPING.'

Flora gave her a wooden spoon and took out the absurd tiny apron Colton had had made for her niece for her birthday. It was the same design as Annie's Seaside Kitchen – yellow on a pale-blue background, like the sun and the pale-blue sky – and it made Agot more certain than ever that she actually worked for the organisation – or, possibly, owned it.

'AGOT SPOON!'

Flora glanced at Innes and wandered across the kitchen. Bramble, the fat retired sheepdog who was snoozing by the fire, got up in case she was doing anything interesting, then went back to his busy day job of sleeping, farting and looking for pastry.

'You know,' Flora said quietly, 'doesn't Agot speak quite a lot like a baby? I mean, she is four . . . '

'*CHAN E ENGLISH A'CHIAD CANAN AGAM GU DEARBH!*' hollered Agot across the kitchen.

'Oh yes, sorry,' apologised Flora. She forgot Agot lived on the mainland, she was on Mure so often: English was her second language.

'Joel still away then?' said Innes, raising an eyebrow. Flora didn't look at him. It was exactly the wrong question. She didn't want to talk about it. Yes, he was away a lot. She realised other people saw their relationship as strange. In London, they couldn't see what he saw in her. On Mure, it was the other way around: people couldn't see what she saw in this tall, unsmiling, taciturn man. To be taciturn on Mure – it really stood out. There were a few hermit types here and there, of course: one or two more distant hill farmers; some confirmed bachelors.

But for most, island living meant sharing. Community. Knowing your neighbours when the snow swept down from the high north and the nights were dark and you'd run out of sugar, or you'd lost some sheep on the high crags, or your tractor was stuck in a bog, or you just needed some simple human contact in this world. A cup of tea and a wee dram and the gentle passing of the seasons could heal most things.

Someone whose head was always in their phone, who zoned in and out, who always seemed in a hurry, was not polite, did not ask after people's children and didn't even try to join in with their community – Flora disliked remembering the quiz night. Well. He was definitely seen as not quite right.

She couldn't explain – how could she? – how different he was in the small hours of the morning when he clung to her like a rock in a wild sea, their sweat and tears intermingling, far, far out to sea beyond the need of words at all. That wasn't a conversation she was about to have with anybody. So maybe they would just have to think that he was odd, that he didn't really care for her. And she would treasure those moments deep in her heart, even though there were precious few of them.

'Yup!' said Flora. 'Gives me a chance to get on with stuff.' Innes nodded and went back to looking at his books. 'Eilidh was always desperate to get back to the mainland too,' he said quietly. Eilidh was his ex, mother of Agot, who had fallen in love with handsome Innes when he was studying at the Scottish Agricultural College in Inverness, when there were parties and gigs and all sorts of things going on. But she hadn't at all acclimatised to a place where the social highlight of the month could be a golden eagle sighting, and they had eventually separated, which had broken both of their hearts. Agot seemed fairly sturdy about the entire thing, but, as Innes had confessed once to Flora after a couple too many whiskies, who knew? He hated being Island Daddy.

'Where is he?'

'New York,' said Flora. 'It's minus-twenty apparently. Makes Mure look like the Bahamas.'

They both listened to the barn door banging in the distance.

'Does it now?' said Innes dryly. 'You should go with him.'

'He won't let me,' said Flora. 'Says it's all work and stuff and wouldn't interest me. Plus I have the Seaside Kitchen.'

'Yes, but it can be pretty quiet round about now, can't it?' said Innes. 'I mean, it's really going to get crazy in the summertime, when the Rock opens up. We'll all be 24/7. I've heard New York is nice in the spring.'

41

'"I've heard New York is nice in the spring"?' mimicked Flora. 'Oh my God, who are you, Woody Allen? Anyway, I just got back from London. Look at me. I actually smell of London. It's a town; they have pavements and everything. Ooh, and they have staircases that move. You'd find it quite frightening.'

Innes shrugged and looked back at the accounts. 'No need to be so arsey just because your boyfriend keeps leaving the country every time he remembers that you have a nose like a piglet.'

'I do *not* have a nose like a piglet!' said Flora.

'PIGLETS NICE, ATTI FLOWA,' came a small voice. Looking round, Flora saw that Agot was attempting to pull an old blackened saucepan out of the cupboard that was twice the size she was.

'Agot!' she yelled, dashing forward, as the entire pile of pots and pans came clattering down on the flagstone floor. Bramble started up from his nap in front of the fire. Their dad started up too, both man and dog glancing round with remarkably similar whiskery expressions.

'AGOT NOT DO IT!' shrieked the little one, her face red with defiance.

'It's okay,' said Flora, starting to pick them up. 'Help me?'

But Agot had fled to her beloved father and had buried her face in his neck as if she had somehow been gravely insulted.

'You are such a monkey!' said Flora. She glanced over. Agot was slyly peering out of her father's cuddling arms to see if Flora was looking at her. As soon as she saw that she was, she buried her face again. Flora smiled briefly to herself, pleased it wasn't she who would be dealing with Agot's teenage years.

Fintan came in, carrying a vast bunch of fresh flowers. There were huge peonies; white roses; all sorts of things you couldn't possibly find on the Scottish islands in March. Flora stared at them as Fintan hummed around and looked for a vase.

'What are those?' she said crossly.

'Oh,' said Fintan. 'Colton sends them every day while he's away. God, I love that man.' He set about snipping the stems carefully.

'Well, that's not very sustainable,' said Flora, in a mood.

'Oh, I don't know,' said Fintan, arranging them carefully in an old earthenware pot of their mother's. 'I think we are.'

Chapter Seven

'*Oh yes.*'

'This,' said Flora, 'is one of the many, many reasons we are friends.'

She and Lorna were sitting in Lorna's front room on Saturday night. Flora had brought the food; her experimental leek and cheese twists were absolutely melt-in-the-mouth tremendous, particularly when accompanied by a rich red wine. The weather was throwing handfuls of rain against the windows out of a deep, pure blackness while they sat on a cosy sofa in their PJs and best woolly socks with a roaring fire in front of them and no work tomorrow.

Flora told Lorna about Jan's catering request and Lorna burst out laughing, which made Flora feel better immediately.

'Did she actually say that it would also be a charitable gesture?'

'It would,' said Flora. 'It would be a charity gesture towards the expansion of her gigantic bloody gob.'

Lorna shook her head. 'Some people are never satisfied. Have you spoken to Charlie about everything?'

'No,' said Flora. 'Should I? I mean, that would be dickish, wouldn't it? Like I somehow was implying he'd settled for second best.'

'He didn't,' said Lorna. 'He settled for ninetieth best. On Mure alone.'

'Oh, she's all right really,' said Flora, feeling bad. She picked up her phone. 'OMG.'

'What?'

'There's a message on it from her. Maybe she's standing outside the door listening to us!'

'No more wine for you,' said Lorna.

Flora looked at it. 'Oh no. Now I feel bad. She does want us to cater after all – wants me to give a quote.'

'Who are you competitively tendering with? Inge-Britt making greasy sausage sandwiches?'

'That's probably what I'd like at my wedding,' said Flora.

'She really wants you there to see Charlie and her getting married,' said Lorna.

'Well, that is totally fair enough,' said Flora. 'And it'll be a good test for when the Rock opens. Then we really will be swept off our feet. Hopefully.'

She and Lorna chinked glasses.

'How's Saif?' asked Flora, which was a question she could only really ask after a couple of glasses of wine.

Lorna shrugged. 'He got excited when he saw a whale.'

'Oh God, they're not back?'

Flora frowned. Her grandmother had always said she had a way with them – part of the daft old family lore she ignored about how the female line were all selkies who came from the sea and would go back there. But it was true in part: she felt an affinity for the great creatures, and worried about them when they were in danger.

'Anyway,' sighed Lorna. 'Apart from that, the usual. Sad. Bit foggy.'

'He's foggy?'

'No, it's foggy . . . He says it got really cold in Damascus in the winter. But, to quote, "You couldn't see your hand in front of your face at ten o'clock in the morning."'

Flora grinned. 'I quite like it. It's just nature telling you to get indoors and be cosy and have a slice of cake and sleep for a long time.'

'I told him that,' Lorna said. 'He said he was going to start prescribing vitamin D supplements to literally everyone on the island. I still don't think he's used to the NHS.'

'Any news about . . . ?'

Lorna shrugged. 'I assumed he'd tell me. But the way he looks out to sea . . . I mean . . . Surely he'd have heard something by now?'

'It's such a mess over there. Jesus, his poor family. Wouldn't he have heard if . . . if they were dead?'

'They had . . . have two boys, you know,' said Lorna. 'Two sons. One of them is ten. At that age . . . you know, if they're captured by the wrong side. They train them up, you know. Train them to fight. And nothing else.'

Flora shook her head. It was beyond imagination, the torment of their tall, gentle GP. She had thought Joel and Saif might get on, but when they'd met they had little to say to one another. 'God,' she said. 'I can't even think about it.'

She sighed. 'What do you think he does with his Saturday nights?'

In fact, two kilometres up the road, Saif was spending his Saturday night like he spent every Saturday night, even though as a doctor and a clinician this was exactly what he would have told himself not to do. Amena had had – oh, years ago now, so many years – a YouTube account they'd uploaded little films of the boys onto for their grandparents. But in fact neither set of grandparents had ever learned to use the internet, so it had in the end been a pointless exercise and there were only two: Ibrahim's third birthday, and Ash at four days old. Thirty-nine seconds of the first – a confused, serious-looking Ibrahim spitting over some candles, his long eyelashes casting shadows on his cheek. To Saif's utter frustration, Amena was behind the camera. He could hear her voice, encouraging and laughing; he could not see her face.

In the second, the focus was all on Ash, but it was just a baby's face – just a baby, and his own stupid voice. There was a half-millisecond of Amena, as the camera moved up and then what . . . how . . . what had he done? Cut it off, in the full expectation that he would be able to see that face every day for the rest of his life. What had he done . . . ? He watched it. Froze it. Watched it. He glanced briefly at the counter of views. Four thousand nine hundred and fourteen. It was a habit he had to break. He had absolutely no idea how.

'Tell me more about the whale.'

Flora was refilling their glasses and steering the conversation away from boys, as it seemed to be dangerous territory at the moment.

'Not sure what type,' said Lorna.

'Oh, for goodness' sake!' said Flora. 'Call yourself a teacher?'

'We're not all sea creatures in human form,' said Lorna. Flora smiled, but her face was pensive.

'I don't want another beaching,' she said. 'They're so horrid. Sometimes you're lucky, but sometimes . . . '

'I know,' said Lorna. 'I think the sea is getting too warm.'

'Are you sure you didn't see what kind it was?'

'Does it matter? It looked like it had a funny horn thing.'

'Really?!'

'Yeah, on its nose. Or maybe it was eating something pointy.'

Flora waited for the internet to slowly download a picture of a narwhal – a large whale with a unicorn-style tusk on its snout. 'Did it look like that?'

Lorna squinted. 'A nar-what? Are those real?'

'What do you mean, are those real? Of course they're real! Where do you think Scotland's unicorn symbol comes from?!'

'Um, I've never thought about it,' said Lorna.

'What do they teach in schools these days?' said Flora, grinning. 'The unicorn. On the union flag. The lion and the unicorn. Three lions on the chest for England. A unicorn for Scotland, described in ancient texts. Of course that's not what they saw.'

'That's the thing I just saw?' said Lorna.

'That's the thing you just saw. Incredibly, incredibly rare.'

'Is it lucky?'

Flora paused. 'The myths say ... well. Opinion is divided. Could be either.'

'I don't believe in luck,' said Lorna.

'I'm not sure if it matters whether you believe in it or not,' said Flora. 'But we'd probably better alert the coastguard and Whale Rescue anyway. A narwhal is a very special thing.'

'Yeah, all right, fish-whisperer.'

And they refilled their glasses, put a film on and finished the leek twists, and felt, for two girls in by themselves on a Saturday night, pretty contented with their lot.

Chapter Eight

Saif normally welcomed the distraction of work after his empty weekends, but today he was having a particularly trying morning. Old Mrs Kennedy was in with her bunions. The waiting list on the mainland was over eighteen months but she could have got it done privately in a week. She owned a croft and four holiday cottages. He couldn't explain to her that, in terms of her remaining lifespan, eighteen months represented probably quite a large percentage of it, and she really ought to spend the money.

'Aye, och no, I don't want to be a bother,' she'd said.

'But wouldn't you be less bothering if you could walk properly, Mrs Kennedy?'

Lorna had once told him, to his considerable surprise, that his normal timbre of speaking voice could sound aggressive to the locals, particularly the older ones, who'd watched too many American films where anyone who sounded Middle-Eastern was automatically a terrorist. Even though he found this profoundly annoying, he had tried to soften his voice and follow the gentle sing-song pattern characteristic of the island speakers. His English now, in fact, was both strange and very beautiful, a wonderful mix of both accents, with a music all of its own. Lorna loved to listen to it. When he was frustrated, however, it tended to sharpen up again.

'Aye, but you never know when that money might be needed!'

Saif blinked. What Mrs Kennedy did with her own money was, of course, absolutely none of his business. But the difference between being able to walk and not . . .

He shook his head and wrote her out another prescription for painkillers. She was putting weight on too which meant she'd need cholesterol checks and could possibly develop gout . . . Still. Next!

Straight after was Gertie James, an incomer from Surrey who'd given up a high-pressure dual-income lifestyle to come and do weaving and fire her own pottery and grow her own vegetables. Her husband had lasted about fifteen minutes, then given up and decided to rejoin the rat race. Now she was raising three completely assimilated and semi-feral island children, who were happy as clams running around muddy streams all day, knowing every single person on the island, building their own kites, speaking a mix of two tongues and eating tablet. They were no more likely to take to living back in a small Guildford semi with an au pair and after-school Mandarin, lacrosse and Kumon maths lessons than they were to fly to the moon.

'I just feel ... I just feel so ... '

Saif had learned over the last few months that, in the West, going to the doctor and saying you were 'feeling ... ' and just kind of letting the sentence run out was considered a totally acceptable and viable reason for accessing health-care. This was new to him. Even before Syria had turned into a warzone, going to the doctor cost too much money for you not to be very clear that there was a distinctly pressing reason for you being there.

He didn't deny for a second that mental health issues were real and overt and almost certainly underdiagnosed in his home countries. He had been born in Syria and raised in Beirut; the irony of his moving back to Syria after medical school for a brighter future had never once been lost on him.

But he found trying to guess the subtleties of people's malaise a little tricky still. He was not an unempathetic doctor – not at all. There wasn't a child who arrived scared and anxious who didn't leave with a lollipop, a jolly plaster and the sense of being taken seriously. But in some areas, he was less tested than others, and the 'I've just been feeling a bit ... ' symptoms he did find tricky.

He looked up at Gertie, who, in common with more than a few of the single or divorced women on Mure, found the plight of the tall, handsome, lightly bearded doctor terribly romantic. Alas, despite the lasagnes that regularly turned up on his doorstep (he had, truly, no idea why people did this) and invitations to the town's many social activities, he remained separate – a little distant, entirely focused on the old phone that was never far from his side. This only made him more attractive in many people's minds. Gertie sighed.

'I just . . . I just feel I've lost my sparkle.'

'I do not know if the NHS does sparkle,' said Saif. This was a joke on his part, but like many people Gertie was unclear when he was joking and when he wasn't, and simply looked concerned.

'I mean,' he said, trying to look professional, 'are you sure it isn't just the time of year?'

This was undeniably true. The very end of March was difficult for everyone; the winter had been long and dark, but Christmas had been wonderful. There was something cosy about the depths of winter. Now the evenings were meant to be getting longer; the equinox had been and gone; surely spring should be on its way? But lambs were being born into fierce storms and wet grass, into a world that still felt cruel, when it should start to feel welcoming and new. There were daffodils, yes, and crocuses, and the hardy little snowdrops; and green was beginning to wreathe its way across the land – but when you still had to scrape the ice off your car in the morning, when you still had to run across the road in howling gales and lashing rain, when it felt as if you were holding your breath, waiting for the year to begin, even as days of your life passed you by . . .

Yes. He understood what the half-sentence meant. He did. It was hard.

He looked up at Gertie. 'Spring will come,' he said. 'Things will get better.'

'Do you think?' said Gertie, her voice a little quavery. 'The winter is just so long.'

'The spring makes it worth it. Now, I could put you on the strong drugs, I suppose, but you have children, yes?'

Gertie nodded. Everyone knew Gertie's children. Lorna up at the school had wanted to tell Gertie this was actually a functioning modern island, not an Iron Age settlement, but she was slightly worried that Gertie would immediately withdraw them and attempt to home-school which, as well as making for a dangerous outlook for Mure's cats, would lower the school roll yet again. It was a constant balancing act to keep the island's only school open, but without it the island would die, and that was that, so Lorna was going to protect it to her dying breath.

'You want to be present for them, yes? Feel their joys and sadnesses? Because it is not like that for everyone, but for some people ... these drugs, they take away the lows but they can take away the highs too. They can isolate you from the world, you know? Wrap you in cotton wool ... remove you a little. For people whose pain is unendurable, of course. But can you wait, maybe for ...?'

Gertie looked out of the window. That day, for what felt like the first time in so long, the sun was out again. It felt as if the world was coming alive. 'Do you think?'

'I do think,' said Saif. 'I am old-fashioned doctor. If I could prescribe, I would say get dog. Take walk every day.'

Gertie smiled. 'Do you think that would help?'

'I think that helps most things. But get outside. See the world. See how you are. And if you are still ... no sparkle. Well. Then we have a problem. Please come back then.'

Gertie nodded. 'I'll try it,' she said. 'But I'll blame you if it goes wrong.'

Saif allowed himself a smile. 'But of course.'

He stood up politely as she left.

54

He wasn't feeling any better though, and he tried to figure out why, as he considered wandering along to the Seaside Kitchen for lunch. Flora had tried her hand at falafel for him. They were terrible, absolutely awful, but she had tried so hard and so sweetly that he had told her they were great. Now she made them all the time and he felt slightly duty-bound to eat them as everyone looked at him expectantly. Old Mrs Laird, who 'did' for him, would nudge him and say, 'Ooh look, there's Flora's flannels,' which was, to be strictly accurate, more or less what they tasted like. He'd much rather have one of her cheese scones, which were heavenly.

He wasn't in the mood for it today. He would stay here and finish off his paperwork ... He swung round to the computer. And that was when he saw it.

He didn't know why. It must have been to do with how the dates looked so different on his computer – or in his mind, maybe? Because they were in English and not Arabic? Because and this made him swallow – perhaps because he thought all the time now in English? He even dreamed in English; he dreamed sometimes that his family could not understand him, that he was shouting at them, shouting at them to come, and the only reason they did not was because he could no longer change his voice to the only language they understood. That had been a nightmare from which he had awoken sobbing, on damp sheets – sobbing even harder when he remembered, once again, that the nightmare was true. There was no respite from the nightmare that went

55

on every day: he did not know. He did not know what had happened to his family.

But now, as he glanced down at the phone, he realised. That he had missed it. That he had known on some level that it was today.

The venetian blind on his window, with which Saif was not particularly familiar and usually got tangled horribly, was thankfully already down. He got up and locked the door, even though he knew he was never meant to lock the door from the inside. He glanced around one last time. The morning surgery was finished and the afternoon house calls were not due for an hour.

Then he pulled down a roll of hospital paper, crouched down behind the examination bed, made himself as small and quiet as possible and wept, quiet racking sobs that felt more painful the more he tried to stifle them, conscious that he must be making the oddest of noises. Ash, his youngest, was six years old. Today. Or would have been six. He didn't even know that. Didn't even know.

And he had forgotten the day. And suddenly, once again, everything was too much to bear.

Chapter Nine

'Mwah. Just one more kiss.'

'Fintan!'

Flora was trying to do the Seaside Kitchen accounts at the table, and listening to Fintan on the phone was too much.

'Homophobe,' said Fintan, not looking remotely sorry.

'I'm a show-off-o-phobe,' said Flora. 'And you are *showing off*.'

'She's on her period,' said Fintan down the phone. 'No, I don't know either. Some girl thing.'

'FINTAN! Hamish, eat the phone.'

Hamish glanced up from the corner, looking quite happy at the prospect, but Fintan flicked them all two-finger Vs.

'That's it, I'm telling Dad,' said Flora. She looked around. 'Where is he?'

He wasn't dozing in the armchair as usual. Bramble was gone too. Flora got nervous when her dad wandered off. She stood up from the accounts – she tried to tell herself she needed a break, but really it was because they were just such bad news – and went off to stretch her legs.

'Colton says bye!' shouted Fintan jovially as she left. She would have slammed the door if it hadn't been warped.

She found her father round the front of the farmyard. He was leaning on the stone wall at the front of the property, over the wide mouth of the road that led down. It was quite the view: low-slung clouds across a wide sky, all the way down to the cobbled streets of Mure below; the beach beyond. He wasn't doing anything. Flora thought he was from the last generation that were content just doing nothing – not fiddling with their phones, but simply standing, waiting, watching. When she was little, he used to smoke roll-ups, but that had stopped a long time ago. His ruddy face was perfectly still, contemplating the only world, really, that he'd ever known.

Bramble's tail thumped on the cobbles.

'Hello dair, dhu,' he said. His voice retained the ancient speech patterns of his homeland.

'Daddy.'

He smiled.

'Fintan getting a bit much for you?' Flora asked.

Eck sighed. 'Ach, Flora. You know.'

Flora looked at him.

'Don't think of me as an ancient dinosaur.'

'I don't,' said Flora. She didn't. She thought of him as a rock, deep set in the soil, immovable; reliable and strong.

'It's just . . . it's very new to me, all this.'

'I know,' nodded Flora.

'I mean . . . do you think they'd get themselves married, do you?'

58

This hadn't occurred to Flora. She felt something of a little stab when she realised that Fintan would probably get married before she did. 'I don't know,' she said. 'We haven't really discussed it.'

'I mean, it would have been all right for your maither.' His pale-blue eyes scanned the horizon. 'But, you know. I mean. What would the Thurso boys make of it?'

Flora shrugged. 'I think you might find these days there are more Thurso men with gay people in their families than you'd expect.'

'You think that, so you do, do you?'

'You might be surprised.'

'I might at that.' He shook his head. 'It was simpler when me and your ma were young.'

'For you it was,' said Flora. 'For other people it was impossible.'

'Aye yes, that, right enough.' He sighed again. 'I just want you all to be happy.'

'Well,' pointed out Flora, 'Fintan's the happiest of all of us.'

Eck's eyebrows rose. 'I suppose he is at that.'

They both watched as Innes and Agot came marching up the hill from the ferry port. Agot was jumping up and down noisily at something. With her white hair she looked exactly like the new lambs bouncing in the fields.

'Ach, that girl wants a maither and a faither,' said Eck. We all do, thought Flora, but she kept it to herself, kissed her dad on the cheek and went down to try and get Innes to help her with the accounts, which he did with the highly disappointing outcome that she'd been right all along about how badly she was doing.

Chapter Ten

Colton was coming home for the evening – one evening! –
and not bringing Joel. That was what really did it.

He jetted in on Thursday, looking slim and a little drawn
from working too hard, but nonetheless he threw a huge
dinner at the Rock for everyone and they all went and had a
rip-roaring time. Hamish tried to chat up Catriona Meakin,
who was fifty-six if she was a day, a part-time barmaid, full-
time sweetheart, comfortably upholstered and very kind and
welcoming on the whole; he looked unbelievably delighted
when he succeeded.

The Rock had been opened up; from the jetty there was
a great red carpet leading up the steps, where braziers were
lit to show the way to the old wooden front door. Toasts had
been made and plans had been drawn up for when the venue
would be open – all very speculative, it seemed.

Flora had finished work and gone back to the farmhouse
to find it empty; no one had thought to tell her where they

all were. Eventually she'd figured it out and gone stomping down to the jetty, where Bertie Cooper, who helped Colton with transportation, beamed happily to see her (he'd always had a soft spot for her). He took her round the headland to save her walking the length of the Endless. It was a chilly night and Flora dug her hands into the sleeves of her jumper. She'd heard nothing about the lightning visit. But maybe, she thought, just maybe, Joel had come as a surprise . . .

Colton was sitting holding court in the warm corner of the bar, next to the crackling fire, Fintan on his lap. Lots of people from the village had spied the lights on and 'popped by' to see what was occurring; there was laughter and merriment and young Iona was singing in a corner, hardly pausing when she saw Flora except to wave cheerfully.

Flora scanned the room slowly. No sign of Joel.

'Hi, Colton,' she said, going over and kissing him, and he hugged her back.

'You didn't bring your lawyer with you?' she said, trying to sound playful and failing mightily.

'He's too busy,' said Colton, 'doing good things for me.' He saw Flora's face. 'Aw, hey, listen. He just wants to get everything done. Sorry. I gave him a lot to do. I decided at the last minute, okay? I haven't even seen him.' At least he had the grace to look ashamed of himself. He ruffled Fintan's hair. 'Sorry, Flora. I've had a lot on my mind.' He kissed Fintan lightly. 'I just . . . I just had to get home, even for one night. I dropped everything.'

Flora nodded. 'Sure,' she said.

She wandered back to town. It looked like being a jolly rowdy night, but she had to be up at the crack of dawn. And somehow, she just wasn't in the mood. She picked up the phone to call Joel, then put it back down again. There was no point in starting a fight, even if he picked up at all.

The next time Joel was home they'd talk. They had to talk. She'd said this the last four times he'd come home, then he'd walked through the door and pulled off all her clothes and somehow the moment had gone. She sighed and pulled out her notebook to see if there was anything she didn't have organised for the wedding of the . . .

Speak of the devil, for Charlie himself was walking up the high street pursued, as usual, by a long line of mites – wan, thin children from deprived areas of the big cities of the mainland. Flora waved to him. 'Well met, Teàrlach,' she hailed him cheerily. 'I haven't seen you since I heard the good news. This is great!'

Charlie didn't say that he had been deliberately avoiding her. He had had a very soft spot for Flora the previous summer, and had hoped that they might be able to start something. But as soon as he'd set eyes on the handsome, square-jawed lawyer up from London, he'd realised he didn't have a chance.

And he had known Jan for a long time. They worked together. She had a good heart. They were a good match. All would be fine. It was only for a millisecond, watching Flora's pale hair flutter in the breeze, that he felt a tiny twinge for what might have been. And what was even more difficult, if he was honest with himself, was the sense that she genuinely was very happy for him and Jan – that she was not thinking about what might have been at all.

'Thank you,' he said, going up to her and accepting her kiss on each cheek, although they got it slightly wrong and

Flora remembered about halfway through it was only people from London who did this and it might look a bit weird. It was too late to extricate herself even though both of them separately wished that actually people still just shook hands.

'And where are you all from then?' she said, deflecting attention onto the boys.

'Govan!' said one, and the rest all cheered.

'And how are you liking it here?'

They shrugged. 'There's nae PlayStation,' said one and they all nodded.

'And nae Irn-Bru.'

Flora looked at Charlie mock-crossly. 'I can't believe you're depriving them so badly!'

'Och no, it's all right, it's good, it's all right,' said one of the boys, a tiny mite dwarfed in the orange waterproofs they wore in the hills. He looked terrified, as if Flora had the power to send him home.

'Yeah, it's fine,' chorused the others rapidly.

Flora smiled. 'Well, you can stay then.'

She glanced at Charlie. 'We have some leftover raisin scones tonight – Isla was on Snapchat and let them burn a little bit. We can't sell them, but if you'd like them, they won't kill you.'

Charlie smiled gratefully as the boys jumped up and down in delight. 'Thank you,' he said, and she darted in to get the bag.

He turned to go with the boys. 'I am really pleased for you, you know,' Flora said as he walked away. He glanced back. His blond hair glistened in the evening sun, and his kind face looked a little conflicted.

'I know you are,' he said. 'I know.'

But Flora was already looking back down at her phone. Maybe she should call him after all.

➤   ↗

Lorna passed by five minutes later, seeing Flora still trying desperately to get a signal. 'Are you not coming up to the Rock?' she said. 'There's a hoolie on.'

'I know,' said Flora crossly.

'Well, why don't you just go there?' Lorna was saying. 'For the weekend. Can't Colton take you back?'

Flora blinked. 'But there's so much on ...'

'There's always a lot on,' said Lorna.

'Fly to New York for the weekend?' said Flora. 'Don't be mad. I might as well fly to the moon. Plus, I'd still have to get a flight home. Anyway, Colton wouldn't take me in case I distract Joel.'

'Come on,' said Lorna. 'Just buy yourself a ticket then. Joel is absolutely minted.'

'Well, that's got nothing to do with me,' said Flora stiffly. She didn't like discussing Joel's money; it felt grubby, like it got in the way. She didn't even know how much he made. 'And I've got a wedding to organise.'

'Don't be daft. Four vol-au-vents per head and a few sausage rolls and they'll be delighted. You could do it standing on your head. Haven't you got that farm money?'

Flora looked uncomfortable. Last year the farm had been sold to Colton, who was using it entirely to supply his own enterprises. Her share, obviously, hadn't been as big as her father's or her brothers', who'd worked on it and run it. But she had got a share nonetheless.

'I was saving it,' she said. 'This place ... it doesn't give me a pension or anything, and I didn't save a penny from London, even though I had a big salary.'

Lorna found this astonishing. 'Why not?'

'Because rent is insane and travel is insane and lunch and going out and ... '

'Could you not have gone out less?'

'No,' explained Flora patiently. 'Because all your money goes on renting a horrible place, so you want to be out as much as possible.'

Lorna nodded like this made sense.

'Anyway. I should probably keep it. For a rainy day. I don't think the Kitchen is going to make me rich.'

'But if you're as worried as you say ... ' Lorna let the sentence tail off. 'I mean, are you in a relationship or not?'

'Possibly not if I turn up by surprise.'

'Well, tell him you're coming.'

Flora looked up, and Lorna was amazed suddenly by how unhappy her friend looked. 'What if he says no?' she said simply.

'Is it really that bad?'

'I don't know,' admitted Flora. 'I don't know if he's playing at being here, or what. He emailed me yesterday to say he's going to be away another full month. I mean, for God's sake ... '

'Well then. I don't think you have any choice. Come back to the Rock with me.'

'No,' said Flora. 'But I will think about it.'

Chapter Eleven

Colleen McNulty, of Liverpool, England, did not talk about her job. It made people act weirdly towards her, either overly empathetic or massively racist – and both were, she didn't really like to admit, quite equally tiresome.

'I'm a civil servant,' she would say coolly, in a way that discouraged further conversation. Her grown daughter (she'd been divorced for a long time) was always interested, but otherwise the line between interest and prurience was hard to navigate sometimes, and she certainly had no interest talking to those who'd never known a day's hardship in their entire lives but thought that desperate people should be allowed to drown in the Mediterranean Sea for want of a little humanity.

She was equally dispassionate in the office, a featureless building on a forgettable industrial estate with only the tiniest of Home Office logos on the signage. She carried out the wishes of the government of the day, that was all. It wasn't her fault or her responsibility; she did it or she didn't. This wasn't cruel: there was simply no other way to deal with it without being overwhelmed – in the same way battlefield doctors kept up a black sense of humour. You had to distance yourself, otherwise it became unbearable. You couldn't get involved in individual people's stories – individual families – because then you couldn't do your job, couldn't function, and that was useful to precisely nobody.

If you had to deal with her, you might have thought her rude, curt and unfeeling. In fact, Colleen McNulty thought being efficient was the very best way to get through her day, and to please the God she fervently believed in.

As she took off her large, practical anorak that morning, hung it on the back of the door where it always went, checked that no one had touched 'her' mug and murmured good morning to her opposite number, Ken Foley, with whom she'd shared an office for six years and had never had a personal conversation, she expected little as she powered up the computer and looked down to see what the day would bring. It would be numbers on a page, that was all, boxes on a spreadsheet: not people but problems to be organised and sorted out and arranged until she left promptly at 5.30 to heat up her M&S pasta sauce carefully at home and watch YouTube videos about crafting.

She glanced at the header of the first email. And for the first time in six years, Ken Foley heard the very upright Mrs McNulty let out a tiny gasp.

'Colleen?' he said, daring to use her first name.

'Excuse me,' said Colleen at once, recovering her composure.

Every Friday, regular as clockwork ... You could set your watch by it, month after month, every week, the English growing more confident – even the accent coming in, the doctor she'd placed miles and miles away, up on that tiny island, asked if she had any news. She didn't get involved, ever, with her clients.

But he had always been so polite. Never ranted or raged like some family members (and indeed, of course, who could blame them?). Never accused her of being unfeeling or being responsible for the government's policies. Never beseeched or begged. Simply asked politely, his gentle voice calm, with only the slightest quiver betraying the desperate angst behind the question. And every week she reassured him that if they had any news, they would contact him immediately, of course, and he would apologise and say that he knew that, of course, but just in case, and she would politely shut him down. But she didn't mind him calling – she never did.

She took a peek at the email again, but she knew the boys' names off by heart. One of them, she noticed, had just had a birthday.

Colleen made it a rule never to look into circumstances – it was prurient, and not her job.

Today she found herself making an exception. Found in a military hospital. Sheltered in a school by what looked like a clutch of rebels and some leftover nuns, of all things. No mother, but the brothers together. Alive.

Colleen McNulty, who never displayed emotion over the exceptionally hard task she did day in, day out – well ... She swallowed hard.

She wanted to enjoy this call – to savour it. She really,

truly did. She glanced over at Ken and did a most uncharacteristic thing.

'I would like to make a private phone call,' she announced
pointedly. 'Would you mind?' And she indicated the door.

Ken was delighted to go down to the little kitchen area
and announce to all and sundry that the buttoned-up and
silent Mrs McNulty was almost certainly in the throes of some
tumultuous affair, probably with Lawrence the stock boy.

Chapter Twelve

The woman in the surgery was crying. Saif handed over the box of tissues he kept for when this happened, which was regularly, although not normally for this reason.

'I was just so sure,' she was saying. It was Mrs Baillie, who had four enormous dogs currently all baying their heads off outside the surgery. Mrs Baillie herself was a tiny woman. If he had had to put money on why Mrs Baillie would have to visit a doctor, he would have suggested that one of the dogs had fallen on her. He hoped she remembered to feed them on time.

'I was just so sure it was a tumour,' she said again.

Saif nodded. 'That is why we tell you not to look up things on the internet,' he said.

She sobbed again, repeating her grateful thanks. 'I can't believe what you've done for me,' she said again. 'I just can't believe it.'

'It was my pleasure,' said Saif, standing up. Lancing boils

wasn't his favourite part of the job, but this level of gratitude was both unusual and pleasant.

'I'll make sure to drop you in a wee cake!' Mrs Baillie smiled up at him through her tears as she got up to go. Saif privately wondered how much dog hair would get into a cake mix in Mrs Baillie's house but smiled politely and stood up as she went to exit. His phone rang, and he frowned. He had at least one more patient before lunch, and he wanted to check back on little Seerie Campbell's whooping cough. He pressed the intercom.

'Jeannie, I'm not done,' he said to his receptionist.

'I know,' she said apologetically. 'Sorry. It's the Home Office.'

Saif sat back down. They rang from time to time to check on his paperwork. It was routine, nothing to get excited about. Although he couldn't help it; he always, always did.

The voice was calm on the phone. 'Dr Hassan?'

He recognised the voice; it wasn't his London caseworker.

It was Mrs McNulty at the Complex Casework Directorate.

He found his eyes straying to the blood pressure sleeve on his desk. He wouldn't, he found himself thinking ridiculously, want to try that at the moment. 'Hel- . . . hello,' he stuttered.

'This is Mrs McNulty.'

'I know who you are.'

His heart was racing, incredulous.

'I believe I have some good news for you.'

Saif's breath caught in his throat.

'We have managed to locate two children we believe may be your sons.'

There was a long pause. Saif could hear his own heart-beat. He felt slightly disconnected, slightly out of body; as if this were happening to someone else.

'Ibrahim?' he said, realising that he had not said the name out loud in so long. Whenever he had spoken to her, he had always said 'my family'.

'Ibrahim Saif Hassan, date of birth twenty-fifth of July 2007?' said Mrs McNulty.

'Yes!' Saif found himself shouting. 'YES!'

Outside, Jeannie glanced up from her notes, but the remaining patient hadn't turned up, so she carried on tidying up morning surgery.

'Ash Mohammed Hassan, date of birth twenty-ninth of March 2012?'

Saif found himself simply saying thank you over and over again. Oddly, he sounded not entirely unlike Mrs Baillie. But he was babbling, and he realised he had to say something.

Mrs McNulty smiled to herself and let it play out.

'I'm going to email you through all the details, Dr Hassan. The nearest centre is in Glasgow. They'll be taken there ... there are various protocols ... '

Saif couldn't hear any of this.

'And ... ' he said when he'd managed to wrest back control of his breathing. 'And of my wife?'

'There is no news,' said Colleen. 'Yet.'

'Yet,' said Saif. 'Yes, of course. Yet.'

And they both pretended that it was simply a matter of time.

'Oh my goodness,' said Saif suddenly, astounded anew.

'The boys! The boys are here! My boys! My boys! My boys ...'

'I am,' said the unemotional Mrs McNulty, 'very, very pleased for you, Dr Hassan.'

And she made herself put the phone down on his over-enthusiastic thanks, as there was a team briefing at 11 a.m. and she had to redo her make-up because she was chairing the estates sub-committee.

'Good luck to you,' she said quietly.

Five hundred miles north-north-east, a tall, slender man with a neatly trimmed beard jumped up and punched the air, shouting so loud a flock of magpies took off into the nearby field, up across the scarecrows and into the clouded sky.

Chapter Thirteen

Lorna continued on down the harbour, enjoying a bit of sun on her lunch break even as work was piling up back at school, relishing just a tiny break from the sticky clatter of tiny hands, however fond of them she was.

She headed back to the farmhouse to pick up some of the leftover marking she'd forgotten. Unusually, someone was waiting for her there; she heard the shout before she made it up the track.

'LOREN-AH!'

She blinked. She knew immediately it was of course Saif.

'Lorenah ...!' Saif stopped short when he realised she was right there. He hadn't even known what he was doing. Jeannie was away on her lunch break; he had had to get out, do something before he burst.

The email had come through but the details had swum in front of his eyes. Lorna was the obvious solution. He'd run fleetly through the town to worried looks from passers-by who assumed there was a medical emergency in progress, but he noticed none of it.

The chickens pecked noisily around his feet as he stood there, panting. Lorna lifted her eyebrows. In his agitation, his tie was loose around his neck, his top buttons undone. She looked away quickly from the smooth skin beneath it. He was out of breath, and wild around the eyes, and in his hand he was waving something frantically.

'Where were you?'

'At school, of course! What is it? What's the matter? It's just a whale!'

Saif shook his head. 'Read this! Read this! Um . . . Please. Please to read it. Thank you.'

He proffered it. Lorna squinted at him. 'You can read English perfectly,' she said reprovingly.

'I need . . . I need to be sure,' panted Saif.

Only the noise of the birds in the trees and the chickens crooning and looking for their breakfast broke the surrounding silence. Lorna looked down.

It was an official email. From the Home Office. Lorna checked the stub of the sender address first. There were so many scams around these days; she got emails from fake iTunes accounts practically every day. But it was legit.

Then she read down slowly, aware of Saif's agonised trembling a metre away from her. Then, to check, she read it again.

'Do you need to sit down?' Lorna said, keeping her voice very calm in order to be understood by someone in a highly strung emotional state, something she was well trained in.

Saif nodded, feeling as if the blood were rushing to his

head, as if he were somehow outside his body just for a second. He staggered over to the wooden bench outside the farmyard door. Lorna went straight inside the house and brought out two glasses of water. Saif hadn't moved. She handed him the water and he took it without thanking her, just staring straight ahead.

'Yes,' said Lorna simply and softly into the clear air. Saif's gaze was still rigid. 'Yes,' she said again. She grew worried about him; his face was completely frozen. Then she realised, a millisecond too late, that he was trying with every fibre of his being not to cry. 'Your boys are here. They're coming home. Um . . . Here . . . They're coming here.'

She jumped up.

'I'll go and make some tea,' she said, and vanished back into the house.

Then she stood over the kitchen sink and, very quietly, sobbed her heart out.

Chapter Fourteen

After a little while, Lorna emerged from the farmhouse, able to speak again, carrying two fresh cups of tea. She'd boiled the kettle three times over to give them both time to gather themselves.

The sun had burned off nearly all the fog now and it had a fair chance of being a lovely afternoon – for the next half-hour at least, which was as far ahead as anyone could forecast on Mure.

'Ibrahim,' said Saif. 'Ash.'

'Your boys,' said Lorna, warmth in her voice.

He nodded. Then looked down at his hands. 'Amena ...'

Amena, Lorna knew, was his wife. There was no mention of her in the letter. 'No news. That doesn't mean ... it doesn't mean there isn't hope,' said Lorna softly.

Saif shook his head. 'She would never have left the boys,' he said fiercely. 'Never.'

'Maybe she had no choice. Maybe they were … taken,' said Lorna.

It was bad enough tormenting herself with what Saif had endured to reach safety. What had happened to those he had left behind was even worse; what had happened to two children, no older than her own pupils, beyond imagination.

Saif glanced down. 'It doesn't say anything.'

'Well, they'll need to check … There's an official process. Look, you have to go to Glasgow for a blood test,' she pointed out.

'I don't need a blood test to know my sons,' growled Saif.

'I know,' said Lorna. 'But probably best to go along with it, don't you think?'

'Authorities,' sighed Saif. He took the paper back from her, his hands still trembling, then folded it very carefully and precisely, once, twice, and tucked it into an old battered wallet he carried in his back pocket. Lorna privately predicted, correctly, that he would carry it there for the rest of his life.

Flora was restocking the cheese counter with a rather sensational marbled cheese Fintan had concocted when a sixth sense caused her to look up. Lorna and Saif were approaching. They both looked … She couldn't tell. She thought, not for the first time, how natural they looked together, like they were meant to be seen side by side. They just fitted somehow. Flora reminded herself that Saif was married and that it was none of her business anyway, and tried to look busy.

Just outside the shop, Saif stopped.

'What?' said Lorna.

Saif shook his head. 'I don't ... ' He looked at Lorna. 'Please, don't tell ... Don't tell anyone.'

'I think they're going to find out when two children arrive who look exactly like you,' pointed out Lorna.

'I ... I realise that.'

Saif looked down. For the first time since he'd arrived, nine months before, he'd begun to feel a part of the community; no one, any longer, stared at him when he shopped in the village, or took much notice of him down on the beach in all weathers. No longer did the old ladies insist on waiting an extra hour to see the 'other doctor' rather than deal with someone foreign with an accent. Now he was just Dr Saif (most people had simply given up the Hassan), as much a part of Mure as anyone else.

The idea of voluntarily going back to the whispers behind hands, the stares in the bakery, the speculation, because of his boys ... It would come, of course. But until then, perhaps he could enjoy being normal, just for a little longer.

Also, he did not want to share it. It was treasure: impossible, dusted gold that he wanted to clasp, to hold inside, to deal with the immeasurable astonishment of how this might come to be. It was close to overwhelming.

Lorna blinked. 'Okay.'

'Can you keep it to yourself?'

'Of course.'

And she truly meant it when she said it, and Flora watched as they swerved and, after all, didn't come in. She thought it was peculiar but, caught in dreams of New York, promptly forgot all about it until the day she was due to leave.

Chapter Fifteen

Flora couldn't sleep with excitement. She was going to see Joel! She was going to see him! And New York too, which she'd never been to before. She knew which hotel he was staying in, and had vague plans of simply going to meet him in the lobby – he would be so surprised! She packed her best new bra set, ordered specially from the mainland, and the best of her old London wardrobe. Her Mure wardrobe mostly consisted of fleeces, big jumpers and a variety of hats, and she wasn't sure it was quite the thing for New York.

Fintan came round in the morning to take her to the airport, smiling all the time and giving her a long list of things he wanted her to bring back from Dean & DeLuca, now he considered himself quite the international globetrotter from being at Colton's side.

'And if you see Colton, give him a big smooch from me,' he added.

'I bloody will not,' said Flora. 'He's the one keeping my boyfriend from me.'

Fintan beamed cheerfully. Flora had no idea how her brother's relationship seemed so uncomplicatedly happy. She wouldn't admit to being jealous. But she was.

They bumped into Lorna at the airport, who was waiting for her brother, back from the rigs.

'I'm doing it!' Flora shouted.

Lorna grinned. 'Woah, I wish I was too.'

'Come!'

'What, and watch you guys make out all over Manhattan? No, thanks!' Lorna smiled. 'It's great you're going to see him on his own turf.'

Flora winced at that. 'Don't forget I saw him on his own turf in London for years. He never noticed me once. Don't all the girls look like fashion models in New York?'

'How would I know?' said Lorna. 'I'm doing Ancient Egyptians with the primary threes . . . '

They called the flight; the half-dozen passengers stood up and shuffled forwards. It wouldn't take long to board.

Flora remembered something. 'Hey, what was with you and Saif the other day?'

Lorna looked up, immediately guilty. 'What do you mean?'

Flora had been merely trying to distract herself from panicking about New York by focusing on something else, but Lorna's furious blush and quick answer piqued her curiosity immediately. 'Ooh . . . ' she said.

'Flight's leaving,' said Lorna. She could see her brother Ian, who'd come on the inbound, crossing the tarmac.

'Something's up! Something's up! I can tell!'

'No, it isn't. Shut up.'

'This is why you want to get me out of the way. Are you planning a night of seduction?'

'No!' said Lorna, going a very dull shade of red.

Flora blinked, concerned. 'What's up?' she said. 'What's the matter? Did you ...? Something happened, didn't it? Did you come on to him or something?'

'No!'

'Well, what then?'

'I can't ... I can't say. I can't tell you.'

Flora looked at her for a few seconds more. There was a last call for the flight.

'Oh God,' she said. 'It's something. Is it about ... is he leaving? No, he can't, can he? Oh my God. Have they ... have they found his family?'

'I can't talk about it!'

'Shit! Oh my God! Really?! Oh my God! Mrs Hassan! I bet she's, like, super-beautiful. Not as beautiful as you though, of course.' She put her hand on Lorna's arm. 'God. I'm sorry. I really am.'

Lorna was choked up. 'It's not that. It's not her they've found.'

Flora blinked. 'Not the boys?'

'Flora MacKenzie!' Sheila MacDuff, who ran the airport, knew her family well. 'Did you no' hear the bing-bongs? Get on that aeroplane before I tell your da'!'

Lorna's face betrayed her.

'Oh my God. Oh my goodness.' Flora was frozen to the spot.

'You can't tell anyone,' said Lorna. 'Please. I promised

I wouldn't. Not until he's got everything sorted out.'

'Well, I shan't,' said Flora. 'Because I am off to New York!'

Lorna smiled weakly.

A thought struck Flora as she hoisted her bag and Sheila hustled her away. 'They'll go to your school.'

'They will,' said Lorna.

'They won't speak any English.'

'I'm sure Saif will teach them pretty quickly.'

'Oh, Lorna,' said Flora. 'It's great. It's wonderful news.'

'It is,' said Lorna. 'It is. It's wonderful.'

And neither of them said what was both true and unutterably awful: that as wonderful as the news was, it was yet another reason added to the great big pile of reasons that already existed as to why Lorna would never – could never – be close to the man she was absolutely, indubitably in love with.

Flora ran back across the concourse to give her friend a huge hug, even as the propellers had started turning.

'You can't,' said Lorna. 'You can't tell a soul.'

But her voice was lost in the noise of the plane.

Chapter Sixteen

The little hopper plane to Iceland went twice a week, stopping in the Shetlands, the Faroes and on up to Reykjavik. It was more of a bus than an aeroplane, but Flora was too excited – particularly at going north, instead of south – to mind the stopping and starting. She couldn't even read her book. She was going to see Joel! She'd sent him a brief text last night to say goodnight but she hadn't called him in case she betrayed her excitement. She just wanted to be with him. That was all, and she couldn't concentrate on anything else.

The Norwegian flight was nearly full and she settled excitedly into her seat. She'd never travelled like this before, casually hopping on a plane. It felt very grown up. And New York! She wondered if Joel would mind doing some sightseeing. Or whether he'd just want to stay in the hotel room all the time. Either, she thought, would suit her perfectly well. No! She would grab him as he came in from work and he would be amazed and he could take her out, to some fancy glitzy bar like she'd seen in the movies, and they would catch up properly and it would be amazing. Yes. She was happy now she had a plan.

She dozed off slightly just as they were coming in to land, and missed the swirling heights of the skyscrapers; then, slightly confused and more nervous than ever, she bumped through customs and found a taxi to take her into the city.

It was late at home on Mure, but at six o'clock in the evening, the sun was still shining brightly down on the gleaming sky-scrapers. The sight of Manhattan after the great expanses of emptiness of her home island felt very strange; it gave her an oddly dissonant feeling, on top of the jet lag. This wasn't just another town; this was another world. Even years of working in London hadn't prepared her for its hyperreal appearance nor, as she got down from the cab, the full sensory overload of the hot dog stands on the corners of the blocks, the steam from the subway, the vast number of people, the honking of the yellow cabs or the height of the great towers.

She stood, for just a second, on the pavement – on the sidewalk, she thought – and took it in. Here she was. In New York. In America. Joel's America.

Her heart beat incredibly fast. She looked around her. It was full of people streaming out of buildings for rush hour, moving quickly, smartly dressed, slim, on the move. She felt intimidated, even though of course once upon a time she'd thought herself just like this: catching the Docklands Light Railway; moving through Liverpool Street. But these people! Their teeth were so white, their clothes so expensive. They wore sunglasses and carried juice and barged past the obvious tourists in a clear two-speed system, and Flora, trundling with her carry-on bag, knew she wouldn't be mistaken for one of 'them' for a moment. And she knew equally that Joel absolutely would, that he would be a part of their slipstream without even thinking about it.

She entered the hotel cautiously. It was extremely grand, with high ceilings and columns and expensive fresh flower arrangements. It was filled with incredibly rich-looking middle-aged people, obviously there from out of town: well-fed, well-dressed types, as well as a smattering of beautiful young things. The reception staff, in chic black uniforms, were beautiful too, with small badges on their chests indicating how many languages they spoke. They all spoke at least three. Flora felt like addressing them in Gaelic to give herself a boost, but didn't dare.

'Hi,' she said. 'Joel Binder's room?'

It was only 6.30. Of course he wasn't back yet. It occurred to Flora suddenly that maybe he wouldn't be back until late after staying at work then going to a dinner or something. Maybe she could call him, find out. But then wouldn't she give it away? Wouldn't it come up as a local call? She wasn't sure at all.

The receptionist looked at her, Flora thought, with doubt. Then she dismissed the doubt as her just being paranoid.

(Actually, it wasn't in the least bit paranoid. The receptionist had been madly in love with Joel since he'd checked in and wandered in and out looking Byronic, distracted and completely lonely – but with lovely manners – ever since.

She'd had her hair recoloured, tried to be on duty whenever he came in, always had a sweet smile and a friendly word for him – he was working too hard, she speculated, and how amazing that he lived in Scotland – and had entertained several private fantasies about simply letting herself into his suite to be waiting there for him, naked, one evening.)

The receptionist was nothing but professional. She didn't know who this bedraggled person with the strange hair was, but she wasn't someone she'd have put with him in a line-up. I mean, if this was the competition . . .

'I'm afraid he's not in, ma'am,' she said in a slightly accusatory fashion. After all, if this person, or stalker, or whoever she was, couldn't even work out his movements, she barely deserved to be here.

Flora meanwhile suddenly felt overwhelmingly tired and desperately jet-lagged and grimy and in need of a shower and thirsty all at the same time.

'Um, could you let me in to wait for him?' she said. 'I'm kind of here as a surprise.'

The receptionist looked at her. 'Well, obviously not, ma'am,' she said. 'I mean, you could call him . . . '

'That kind of does for the surprise . . . ' said Flora.

'Yes, ma'am.'

Flora sighed. She looked around. There was a bar in the lobby. 'I think I'll just sit down for a little while,' she said. 'Wait for him.'

The receptionist was curious to see how this would play out. 'Of course,' she said, nodding.

Flora looked at the prices on the menu and tried to do the mental arithmetic to convert them, but found it difficult. She sighed. Whatever it was, it was very, very expensive. She ordered a cup of tea, then realised when it came (and was awful) that actually she didn't want tea, she wanted wine, but she felt too awkward and uncomfortable to call the waiter back. Suddenly, all the great hope and excitement that had propelled her across the Atlantic – and left her, she knew, very, very, very skint – seemed to be draining away.

She went to the bathroom. The flight had left her skin blotchy and dry, her lips chapped and her hair frizzed. She wanted to go out and see if she could find somewhere to buy some new moisturiser – probably not a Tesco Express but there'd be something, surely? – but what if he showed up when she was gone? She'd have to ask that eye-rolling receptionist again, and Flora wasn't a hundred per cent sure she trusted her to tell her the truth.

Flora sighed and did what she could with the body lotion the expensive hotel had sitting by the side of the sink. It smelled of lavender and didn't really do the job properly. As she was doing her best with the feeble contents of the make-up she still had in the plastic freezer bag she'd taken through customs, an enormous girl, like a huge blonde giraffe, came into the bathroom, talking loudly on her phone about, crap, no way was she going to Loopy Doopy you idiot, what are you, twelve?

She didn't even notice Flora was there – she towered about a foot above her, it felt like to Flora – but instead examined herself critically in the mirror next to her. She was utterly gorgeous: flawless skin, a long aquiline nose, clear blue eyes and pulled-back, silky blonde hair. The girl frowned at her perfect features in the mirror, then dabbed at a non-existent blemish on her chin. Then she realised Flora was there and rolled her eyes, as in, aren't we all girls together, what can you do?

'You look great,' said Flora impulsively. It was impossible, really, to say anything else when faced with such fabulousness.

'Oh, so do you,' said the girl unconvincingly, reapplying lip gloss as someone barked down the phone. 'Well, have a nice day . . . No, Sebastian, no, I don't *want* to go to Ann Arbor . . . '

She left a light, expensive scent on the air. That, Flora thought, looking back in the mirror after the goddess had gone, feeling dumpier and more washed out than ever, that was what Joel should be with. That was what New York girls were like: pulled together, groomed, fabulous, confident of where they were going and what they wanted. Everything she had seen Joel with in London, over the years, everything she remembered so well. What was she doing? What was she thinking? Was this all a ridiculous mistake? She looked at herself, sighing. Then she realised she'd better get out there, in case she missed him. And would there be disappointment in his eyes when he did see her? Was it only on Mure where there was only her, and a lot of seabirds and some sheep to look at?

Stop being ridiculous, she told herself. Stop being ridiculous. She came back out and sat down again and tried hard not to worry and to remember back a few months, midwinter, just the two of them, back on Mure, in the pitch black of January when it never really got light and they had stayed in for a whole weekend, spending the entire time wrapped up on the sofa, in blankets, watching old DVDs because they couldn't stream Netflix, eating hot buttered toast, with salted butter from the farm on bread Mrs Laird had made that morning, nutty and golden brown and simply heaven on the old earthenware plates, and the noise of the fire crackling upwards and the scent of the browning bread and the nearness of Joel and his body and . . .

Joel stalked straight past her. He didn't even glance around at the seated or milling tourists who wandered in and out of the hotel lobby at all hours of the day and night: jet-lagged, confused, stressed out or just plain lost.

He moved smoothly over to see if the contracts he was waiting on had been delivered. The same receptionist always seemed to be on duty, he had subconsciously registered, but not actively thought about. She looked at him now with something important to impart on her face. He hoped it wasn't hassle, like a room change. He just wanted a shower, some work, some food and, even though he had blackout curtains, a high-up, soundproofed room and almost silent air conditioning, he was hoping for sleep, although it was doubtful: he was grinding out the days and making his billable hours for Colton up until he could get home.

Home. The word felt so strange and tentative whenever he thought about it. Was it even possible that there was somewhere he thought of as home? Somewhere he could keep, treasured, secret in his heart even as he walked through boardrooms and hotel lobbies a million miles away; somewhere special, just for him, that was waiting for him at the end of this city, and all the other cities exactly like it . . .

The receptionist nodded her head. 'Are you expecting someone, sir?'

'No,' said Joel, his face wrinkling with distaste. He didn't want to deal with any of Colton's clients face to face if he could possibly help it, particularly the way Colton kept pulling out of their marketplaces without warning. Plus they were blowhards that went on about clean eating too much. He sometimes wanted to make them try some of Mure's very best carbs and fats, just to see their faces recoil in horror. The receptionist of course knew fine well he wasn't; she'd just wanted to see the expression on his face. It gave her some satisfaction.

'Well, there's someone here to see you. Maybe it's a surprise?'

When Joel first told Flora about his upbringing she never really realised its import.

He had told her in such a matter-of-fact way and felt no need to expand on the issue. There had been no tears, no histrionics. He had simply told her that his parents couldn't look after him and he had been brought up in the care system. Flora had always, looking at him, found it difficult to imagine that of Joel, who was so sorted, so handsome, so confident, so seemingly impregnable. He didn't seem broken about it, didn't seem even particularly fussed. It was his reality, and that was all it was.

In later years, Flora was to realise how naïve – how dangerously naïve – she had been to think like this. Of course, her upbringing hadn't been perfect – whose was, when you thought about it? Nobody's. But she'd had two parents, who had stayed together, who had loved her and encouraged her to the best of their abilities, sometimes successfully, sometimes less so. That was what family was: everyone muddling along.

She didn't get it. Not really. Not properly. She felt the sadness in the abstract, of course – not having a family, how awful. But she had had Joel on such a pedestal for so long, had seen him always when he was her boss as a great epitome of triumph and success and everything she longed for.

He had told her, but she had not understood, and would not for a long time.

If you have ever known a child in care, the one thing you do not do – you *never* do – is spring surprises. They have known surprises. They have known all the surprises they ever need to know. Surprises like: you won't be seeing your parents again. Or you won't be staying here any more. Or you're moving schools. Or we're so sorry, this placement hasn't worked out quite as we'd hoped.

If you want to show your love to a child of difficult fostering, be entirely predictable. In every way. Tediously and relentlessly. For ever.

Flora didn't realise this even as she started awake, not knowing at all where she was or what time it was. She was surprised, in fact, to find herself in the lobby of a very upmarket New York hotel, still in her Mure overcoat on this hot day, feeling bleary and completely discombobulated, only to find Joel looking down on her with an expression of abject horror on his face – the sum of her worst fears.

Chapter Seventeen

'Hey,' Flora said weakly.

She rubbed her eyes. He didn't say anything. Behind him, Flora gradually realised the receptionist was watching, hungrily.

'Hey,' said Joel eventually. There was no embrace. He was staring at her like he didn't know what the hell she was doing there. And she didn't either, she realised. She didn't know what the hell she was doing there. Why hadn't she obeyed her first instincts? Suddenly she wanted to cringe, to fold herself up or vanish into the ground.

'I thought I'd surprise you,' she said timidly.

'Consider me surprised,' said Joel shortly. He cursed himself for the look in her eyes: so disappointed in him. What the hell did she expect him to do? He was at work, trying to get through it, so he could come home. He wasn't over here playing up with other women or whatever she seemed to think if she was checking up on him.

'I just thought ... I've never been to New York.' Flora couldn't believe how lame she sounded, like she wanted to be his girlfriend so she could go on a school trip. 'So here I am!'

'And you're staying here?'

Joel said it without thinking. He was very tired, at the end of a long couple of weeks, and as soon as he'd said it he could have kicked himself. He didn't even know what he meant, but even so.

Flora's face went very white and very still. 'I'm sorry I inconvenienced you,' she said, and she went to grab her bag and leave.

After a second, Joel realised that she meant it and headed after her. The receptionist wished she could follow him. This had to be the end; he was absolutely furious with her. Obviously this was nothing serious. She definitely had an in.

'Flora!' he shouted as she headed through the bustling lobby. 'Come back. Sorry. I'm sorry. You just ... you just took me by surprise that's all. I hate surprises.'

Flora's voice was trembling and her eyes were full of tears. 'Well, I hate being an annoying idiot so I guess we're even,' she said.

'Don't ... I'm the idiot,' said Joel. 'I am. I'm sorry. Please. Please. Come upstairs. Let's get a drink. Let's ... I just wasn't expecting to see you here.'

'Really?' said Flora. 'Well, you dealt with it very gracefully. I'm going. I can stay somewhere else and I'm flying back on Sunday.'

'Don't be ... don't be ridiculous. Come on. Please. Come on. Come upstairs.' Joel glanced around. They appeared to be making a scene, which he absolutely could not bear. 'Please,' he whispered urgently under his breath.

All the way up in the elevator – the receptionist had huffily made up a spare key for Flora, her displeasure very clear – they were silent. Neither of them wanted to talk about what had just happened. It was as if the first – of how many? – barriers had been held up in front of them. And they had both failed, in ways that weren't clear to either of them. And now they were like strangers.

Flora almost unbent when she saw the suite – not one of her nobler instincts, as she would have been the first to admit. It was large, with a huge sitting room overlooking the whole of Manhattan, glowing pink in the early evening spring light: south to downtown and the new spaceship of the World Trade Center site; east to Brooklyn.

All the furniture was cream and grey: sofas and cushions, floor-to-ceiling windows and, oh my goodness, the terrace . . . Flora was drawn towards it. It was utterly entrancing.

She thought of how it was exactly what she'd dreamed it might be like . . . and how she and Joel would be sitting on that terrace, laughing at how brilliantly secretive she'd been, ordering cocktails . . .

She rubbed stubbornly at her eyes. 'I'm tired,' she said. 'It's 1 a.m. for me. Can I go to bed please? I'll sleep on the sofa.'

Joel didn't like crying women and he didn't like being emotionally manipulated. He'd drawn back; she was here. That was enough, wasn't it? Or was he going to have to feel guilty the entire evening? He was sick of feeling guilty. Feeling guilty was his default. 'Fine,' he said, going over to his desk and setting down his briefcase. 'Are you hungry? You can order something.'

Flora was starving. 'No, I'm fine.'

'Good.' His fingers strayed towards the briefcase.

'Are you ... are you *working*?' said Flora.

'I have a major conference with Colton. There's a lot he needs done. That's why I'm here.' His jaw was set.

Flora looked out at the lights popping on one by one over Manhattan – an amazing, astonishing world of amazing things out there she'd never experienced – and wanted to cry even more in frustration. Everything was out there and she was going to miss it all. Again. Because she wasn't really Joel's girlfriend. She'd wanted to find out and now she knew. She was just his ... what. His bed and breakfast? His country retreat?

Ignoring him, she went to the minibar, and pulled out a vodka and tonic without looking at the prices. She dumped her coat on the back of a chair, pulled off her big jumper – she'd been absolutely stifling – pulled the bobble from her hair, then poured her drink and took it out on the balcony, letting the mild spring breeze blow away the plane and the cobwebs and the jet lag.

Here, even twenty floors up – or perhaps especially – she could feel the city coming at her in waves. The honking of the cabs, impossibly distant below; the setting sun slanting shadows of enormous buildings, one on top of another; the width of the bouncing boulevards and avenues all heading in the same direction, unlike the little winding paths of her home; the hundreds of lighted windows across from her. She eyed up roof gardens and balconies enviously; people out on fire escapes and terraces on such a mild night; parties and friends and lovers and the oddity of a life lived far more closely and intimately with each other than she knew back in Mure, but at the same time distinct and anonymous and different. It was the oddest feeling. And, she thought, with a strange sadness, anyone looking her way right then would just have seen a girl with pale hair standing by herself. She might have been local, might have known New York like the back of her hand, might have been coming here all her life.

Flora found she quite liked this thought and, if this was to be – and here was a thought so frightening she put it to the back of her mind – but if this was to be her first and last trip ever to New York, she vowed to enjoy it. She would go and see everything tomorrow. She had thought Joel might accompany her, or take her to places he liked, but no matter. She would visit the Empire State, and the Guggenheim, and Ellis Island and everywhere she fancied, and she would stop in nice areas and eat at places recommended on the internet and ...

Well. She needed to have a plan. She had made a mistake ... and one, deep down, that she thought on some level she'd been making all along. He was out of her league. She was all right for what the Scots called a 'bidie in' – Flora MacKenzie, sitting at home, weaving and keeping the fires burning while the man went out and did whatever it was he was going to do in the great wide world. The bigger world beyond their quiet beaches and churning tides. Out there. Without her.

She drank her drink and tried to think calmly about it. It wasn't as if she hadn't been warned. By Margo. By her friends. It hadn't been as if she hadn't known.

Music drifted up to her from some bar or concert far below and she listened to it gently swaying on the warm wind, trying to feel, at least, in the moment; trying to salvage something in fact. She was in New York, and the stars were popping out at the purple edge of the skyscrapers and, as the tears rolled down her cheeks, she thought: Isn't that something? Doesn't that count for something? Maybe, one day, she could say: Well, once I listened to music at the very top of New York on a warm spring night, and I was young, or young-ish, and it was beautiful, and very, very sad . . . and she wondered who she might even be telling that to.

And she didn't hear the door slide open silently behind her, and she was unaware of anything until she felt on her bare shoulders the softest kiss, the sense of his presence behind her, and she squeezed her eyes tight shut and when she opened them again he was still there, saying nothing, this time putting his arms right around her, sheltering her from the wind, holding her, and he leaned his head against her back, just laid it there. And she thought of an old story of her mother's – of the sea sprites that came in the night, and you couldn't look at them to break the spell, even though they were the most beautiful, the most extraordinary of all the faerie world, but you could not look at them in the day. Not until the sun had gone down could they reveal themselves, and if you could not help yourself, if you took even the faintest peek, then they would vanish for ever into the mist and you would spend the rest of your life on the lonesome road, searching for their traces in all the world up and down but never would you find them or see them again. And that weeping and wailing was the sound the wind made through the rushes at night. So, her mother had said. Do not be afraid of the noises you hear at night. But never, ever look at a faerie if you love them.

So Flora stood, frozen, staring out still, her heart a waterfall, not daring to move, barely daring to breathe as Joel held on to her as if his life depended on it, kissing her softly up her shoulder. She shivered, and, thinking she was cold, he took off his jacket and put it round her, until gradually, reluctantly, as the moon rose behind the buildings, she turned round to face him.

Chapter Eighteen

Lorna pulled out her pad and paper.

'Okay,' she said. 'Blood test.'

'Check,' said Saif.

They were sitting on the harbour wall, preparing for Saif leaving, which he was doing the following week. His locum was the scattiest person either of them had ever met, so Saif was just privately hoping everyone avoided getting frightfully sick until he got back. And when he got back, well . . .

'Toys?'

'Wait and see what they like.'

'Good call. I will tell you that as of ten past three this afternoon it was Shopkins and Fidget Spinners. Which means it's now something else completely.'

'I don't understand what you just said.'

'Oh, Saif, you are so in for a . . . No, it'll be fine,' said Lorna. 'New clothes.'

'Waiting to see sizes.'

He had shown Lorna two screengrabs from the videos. His original wallet, with photographs, had been lost to the sea a lifetime ago.

'They are very handsome boys,' said Lorna.

Saif had smiled. 'They are.'

'Here.' Lorna handed over a parcel. 'Don't get over-excited. And I think this will just be the start of a deluge of gifts when everyone finds out.'

'Don't tell them,' said Saif urgently. Lorna felt slightly uncomfortable, but didn't say that Flora already knew.

He looked at the parcel.

'It's buckets and spades,' said Lorna, indicating the Endless Beach, where the hardiest toddlers were already marching up and down busily to the waves, making dams and digging holes, despite the chill breeze. 'They never go out of fashion. And you can't live on Mure without them.'

Saif blinked. 'Thank you,' he said. He clutched the parcel. 'They're really coming,' he said. 'They're really coming.'

'And it's wonderful,' said Lorna gently.

'I am as scared as I have ever been,' said Saif.

Innes came by. He was walking freely and Hamish was carrying vast loads of boxes: supplies for the Seaside Kitchen. Lorna was quite impressed by the division of labour.

'Hey!' She waved. 'Hey, Innes, how's Agot?'

He grimaced. 'She's a fiend. Bit her entire nursery class because she doesn't want to go to school on the mainland.'

'Good!' shouted back Lorna. 'We need her for the school roll.'

101

Innes shook his head. 'I'm not sure wolverines should get enrolled. Have you heard from my gallivanting sister?'

'Nope,' said Lorna cheerfully. 'I'm taking that as a good sign.'

She turned back to Saif as the boys marched on. 'And wellingtons,' she added when they were out of earshot. 'Don't forget wellingtons! Buy all the wellingtons!'

Chapter Nineteen

Flora turned round to face him.

'No more surprises.'

'Thank you.'

They stood there, frozen.

'I shouldn't have come,' she said after a long pause. 'I thought you'd want to see me.'

'I do,' he said. 'That's why I want to ... to get my head down, to get finished, just to work. So I can get home. That's all I do. That's all I care about. I thought you'd see that.'

Flora blinked. 'But ...'

'But what?'

'But I'm not just for ... for coming back to when you're tired of doing other stuff.'

Joel squinted. He really was very tired. 'What do you mean?'

'I mean, you go to all these amazing places and it's all

right to take me sometimes ... you know, I'm not just a scullery maid.'

'I never thought of you as a scullery maid. Also, what's a scullery maid?'

'You never take me out to nice places like this!'

Joel screwed up his face. 'I'm working fifteen-hour days in a windowless conference room fuelled by American coffee, the world's most disgusting drink. All I think of is getting through it, so I can get home to you. That's all I think about.'

'But I'm here.'

'I know. And I hate it here.'

Flora looked around. 'How can you hate it here?'

She was weak, and put up with too much, and all of those things, probably. But oh my God, here she was, under a purple New York sky with a man, the very smell of whom made her want to turn herself inside out – with so much love she felt she would die from it. It was all she wanted to do ...

Joel shrugged.

'Come on,' she said, shaking herself awake suddenly. 'No, I have a plan. Let's go out.'

She couldn't, she knew, just let him take her to bed. That was what always happened. And it was amazing, but nothing got fixed or moved on at all.

All Joel wanted – he so desperately wanted – was to take her to bed, tear that dress off her, lose himself in the pale beauty of her curves and her skin, then finally, blessedly, find some sleep because she was near him. Just being so close to her again was bewitching, almost made him forget his cases, his workload, the strangeness of being back in America, the pace of it all.

'Can I take you out tomorrow?' he said.

'Aren't you working tomorrow?' she said, teasing.

'I want you so much.' He pulled her very close to him on the terrace, so she could feel it.

'Tough,' said Flora, smiling at him. 'You get me into bed, I'll fall asleep. You need to take me somewhere noisy. With dancing.'

'I don't dance.'

'I don't care.'

❧ ❧

But Friday night in bustling New York, with a reluctant Joel and a clueless Flora, was a mistake, to say the least. Anywhere that looked nice had a two-hour wait for a table and rude, beautiful girls on the doors, looking doubtful when they hadn't booked, while anywhere else was full of tourists. Avoiding the ridiculously fake Irish bars that Flora absolutely had no wish to go into, they ended up in a dark oak bar full of lawyers – exactly the type of people Joel had absolutely no wish to see – and their gorgeous dates, obviously picked up from Tinder or just around and about the place. And Flora, exhausted and strung out, misjudged completely the strength of the cocktails. She drank two and ordered another at top speed and was, not to put too fine a point on it, drunk in half an hour, while Joel was not. And every time she tried to bring up the subject of the two of them, she realised she was repeating herself and not making any sense at all.

Drunk people horrified Joel – too many memories – and

he tried, gently, to convince Flora to go back to the hotel. She argued against it and told him he was a dreadful guy who didn't really care about her at all and was never any fun, and while Joel disagreed profoundly with the first accusation, he couldn't help seeing that she probably had a point about the second. On the other hand, they had come out to have fun and hadn't had the slightest bit of fun at all, and now Flora was the worse for wear and he was concerned about bundling her into the lift at the hotel in case she started yelling at him inside.

'Need any help, sir?' said the receptionist, smiling perkily at him in what she considered to be an unthreatening way. He tried his best to smile bravely back while Flora muttered unpleasant words in Gaelic under her breath about the receptionist, and kept trying to press the down button and stumble off to the bar as Joel was doing his best to encourage her upstairs. Finally back in the room, Joel went to use the bathroom. He came back prepared for a diatribe about how dreadful he was. Instead, fully dressed, Flora was lying diagonally across the bed, fast asleep.

Sighing, he drew the blackout curtains, gently took off her shoes, put a glass of water and two ibuprofen by her bedside and rolled her carefully under the duvet – then, knowing sleep had no interest in coming anywhere near him that night – put on the desk light in the main room, ordered up some coffee and returned to his files.

Flora woke incredibly early, woozy, with a headache and not a clue where she was in the pitch dark. She rolled over, remembered, then groaned heavily. She had messed things up ridiculously. She remembered being rude to Joel last night, yelling at him. She realised to her horror that of course he'd put her to bed. Oh God. And then . . . what? Where was he? He wasn't in the bed. Had he left in disgust? When she hadn't immediately gone to bed with him . . . then had gone out and rolled around like a loony. Oh God. She thought of him, all buttoned up and restrained and her wanging on like a drunken harpy. She saw the glass and the ibuprofen next to her bed, and dropped her head in her hands. Oh Christ. She had never had a worse idea in her entire life. What on earth had she been thinking? What an utter idiot she was.

Her eyes were getting more used to the dark room and she saw the line of golden light coming from next door. She got up to use the loo and brush her teeth, then glanced through the door. He was sitting, staring at his files, hadn't noticed she was there, and he took off his glasses and put them down for a second, and rubbed his dry eyes. He looked so young and so lost with this little gesture that Flora wanted to go to him, but she was afraid of his judgement, could not face him quite yet, she was feeling so bad, so she went back to bed and lay there in the dark, unable to sleep because of the time difference. Eventually, when he finally came to bed, she still lay there and did not move towards him, nor did he move to her, even though neither of them was sleeping, and it felt like the dawn would never come.

Chapter Twenty

Joel was up early the following morning to go into the office. Flora apologised and Joel said stiffly not to worry about it, it was nothing. They had still not even made love, and this was terrifying Flora because it was in that space they had together that nothing was ever wrong, and nothing was ever misunderstood; it had always felt like their bodies could talk to each other in a way that their brains could not: directly, with total honesty and utter mutual understanding. Whereas this . . . this was just a mess. And she had absolutely no idea how to fix it.

Still feeling utterly dreadful, she made coffee and sat in front of some strange American television, finding it odd to think that this was normal for everyone who lived there. It was going to be a beautiful day, she realised eventually, after trying to convert Fahrenheit to Celsius. And there was the city at her fingertips . . . once she felt a little better. She had a long shower, which felt like being pummelled by water, in the amazing rainforest bathroom, and that definitely helped. Then she looked through her hastily packed suitcase to see if anything was suitable. Nothing was. She could go and buy some light, pretty dresses, she thought suddenly. But when would she wear them? It wasn't like they got many hot days on Mure, or that they'd be suitable in the Seaside Kitchen.

She felt homesick, suddenly. It would be afternoon there; the trade would be coming in – the walkers, hungry for big sticky slices of millionaire's shortbread and raisin pies and steak bridies and everything they needed to refuel; the wee old ladies down from their grocery shopping who wanted scones and cups of tea; the farmers, in for their weekly look around the bright lights of Mure Town, who would take big sides of fruitcake back home to sit on their dressers all week to be consumed with small glasses of whisky and large hunks of cheese.

Then she told herself to stop being ridiculous; to buck up. They would fix it tonight. Definitely. Wouldn't they?

She looked around the sitting room, which Joel had left incredibly tidy, as was his wont. Then she opened the cupboard, where his row of suits was hanging. She found a jumper, the only thing there not freshly dry-cleaned, that still smelled of him, and buried her face in it, trying not to cry.

Suddenly the phone rang in the suite. Flora blinked. It must be Joel! Maybe he'd be free to meet her for lunch! Maybe he'd got to the office and changed his mind, realised he should take a day off to spend with her! Realised he loved her even if she was a ... well, a sloppy drunk with a loud mouth, she reflected, with another stab of agony. Oh God.

Tentatively she picked it up. 'Hello?'

'Hello? Joel?' It was a woman's voice. Flora bit back her inevitable disappointment and tried to ignore her growing fear.

'Um, hi, no,' said Flora stiffly. 'This is Flora. Can I take a message?'

There was a pause. Flora's heart was beating painfully quickly.

'Sorry, who is this?' she said. She couldn't stop thinking of that blonde girl in the bathroom, or even those girls in the bar last night, what she remembered of it, the ones Joel had thought were cookie cutter, but she had thought were beautiful.

'Oh my, sorry ... Are you *Scottish*?' The voice seemed older now to Flora, who was wrong-footed. 'Mark!' The voice on the other end was talking to someone else now. 'Mark! It's the Scottish girl!'

'Excuse me?' said Flora again.

'Oh, I am *so* sorry,' said the woman's voice. She sounded nice: mumsy and friendly. 'We had ... we had absolutely no idea you were in New York.'

'He never tells us anything!' came a voice from a distance behind her.

'I thought we'd just leave a message! Well, my dear. It is *so* nice to speak to you.'

Flora blinked. If she hadn't known ... or thought she knew ... she'd have thought these were his parents.

She suddenly felt how little she really knew about this man and it chilled her.

Chapter Twenty-one

'Sorry,' said Flora. 'Sorry if this is rude, but ... who are you? Can I take a message?'

'Of course ... I'm Marsha Philippoussis and ... Has he really never mentioned us?'

'No,' said Flora, more and more worried.

'Well, Mark – that's my husband – he ... he used to be Joel's ... Well, I'm not sure if I can say. We're friends.'

'Friends.'

It wasn't that Joel didn't have friends, Flora knew. He had squash buddies and lawyer buddies in most cities in the world and everyone was always pleased to see him. But he didn't have best friends, or intimate friends as far as she could tell. He didn't have a friend like she had in Lorna. But then, maybe most men were like that.

'You can tell her,' shouted the voice.

'Oh, okay. Well, dear. Mark was Joel's psychiatrist. When he was younger. But now we're ... friends.'

'Friends who never call each other when they're in the city!'

Clearly Marsha and Mark were quite the double act.

'Well … yes. We were hoping, since he's in the city, we might have dinner … Would you like to come, dear? Tonight?'

'Um, I don't know what he's got planned.'

Marsha laughed. She remembered what Joel's plans used to be – head for the nearest bar; pick up the most beautiful girl in the room; walk out with her. So she was very keen to meet the girl who had finally – at last – apparently tamed the odd, serious, driven boy she'd known since he was a child. She was hard to imagine; in Marsha's head she looked like a will-o'-the-wisp: a strange, exotic, bewitching creature.

'I'll call his cell,' said Marsha. 'It'll be turned off, but usually if you call four or five times he'll pick up eventually.'

Flora wondered how relaxed she would have to be with Joel to call him four or five times in a row. She didn't know many people who'd dare.

She left the hotel tentatively, relaxing instantly in the warm spring sunshine. Oh, it was glorious after the long dark months on Mure. She checked she had enough sunscreen in her handbag (island skin and hot sunshine did not normally work together too well), then, despite everything, she felt herself unfurl luxuriously as she moved between the long shadows on the busy pavement, getting in people's way but not even caring. The first hit of sun after a long winter made, she decided, everything about a long winter totally worth it. She breathed in the hot scent of New York pavements – hot

112

dogs, pretzels, fuel, perfume, bodegas – and loved it. She let the sun tickle the backs of her arms; felt it soak through her dress and warm her back. She wanted to lift up her hands and twirl in it, to take a bath in sunshine.

It was hard to feel so down. Okay, last night had been . . .

It had been awful, she couldn't deny it. Absolutely the opposite of everything she'd hoped it would be. There had been no delighted sweeping her up in his arms. There had been no impressed head-shaking at her amazing appearance. No happy astonishment and brutal kisses in the shadows of the world's greatest buildings, him showing her round the sights, taking some time off for the weekend so they could behave like . . .

She was honest with herself. Like a proper boyfriend and girlfriend. Not what she sometimes felt they were: shipwrecked sailors thrown together on a desert island, clinging together for sanity and safety amid the wreckage of their own hearts.

That was not what they were, she vowed. They could do better.

She quenched her hangover with an enormous freshly squeezed juice in a huge cup and a pepperoni pretzel – which was utterly delicious, larger than her head and couldn't possibly be good for her, although she did consider appropriating the recipe – then set off to walk to the Empire State Building even though she realised quite early on that walking the huge blocks of the city took rather longer than she'd expected, and that there was rather more of Broadway than any street she'd ever been on before.

It didn't matter though. She was so entranced by looking at everything: the people; the shop windows; the little apartments perched in the sky; the business of everything. Maybe, she thought, she even fitted in. Well, at least until she got to the Empire State Building and had to join the enormous line of other tourists just like everybody else, but even so. She looked thoughtfully at her phone. What if he didn't call her? What if she'd come all this way not to see him? She tried to think of a way to spin this to Lorna, who'd sent her several envious texts already, telling her it was hosing it down and asking for pictures. There wasn't one. She glanced at Fintan's Instagram – yes, Fintan had an Insta now for when he and Colton were flying about places having an amazingly romantic time. She tried her best not to be jealous of her brother's relationship but there seemed to be absolutely no doubt who was having all the fun now, even if he had done nothing but sit in a barn by himself making cheese in the freezing cold for three years after their mother had died.

She sent Joel a message:

Sorry about last night – not used to NYC drinks!!!

She had added too many exclamation marks, then she reckoned they looked a bit desperate and took them away, then decided the message looked too downbeat so she added one and then one more and decided that a) this was definitely it and b) she was going crazy. Then she sent it and held her breath and tried not to check her phone every ten seconds while the queue inched forwards.

'Joel! You didn't tell us you'd brought someone to New York!'
Marsha just launched into the conversation; she didn't

114

give him a chance to say anything or tell her he was too busy or use any of his usual deflection techniques. She just bulldozered over him. Normally Joel would freeze up or become rude when faced with someone behaving like this. But he didn't mind Marsha doing it. Quite liked it even. It showed how well she knew him, deep down.

'So this is her? This is the girl?'

Joel thought back to Flora ranting at him on the pavement last night outside the hotel and groaned. He really didn't want to see the look on the Philippoussises' faces if something like that happened again. He knew they would want to meet her, but he had absolutely no idea what they were expecting. Someone more model-like, maybe? More chicly dressed? Marsha was always immaculately turned out. But that was just New York women. Would they see that there was more to Flora – that maybe she didn't have perfectly manicured fingernails but underneath it all was a good heart and a spirit and a fire?

And it felt private to them as a couple – something only they shared – and he didn't feel entirely comfortable exposing that to daylight. But, he realised, it was time. He hadn't really had conventional relationships, but this had to be one of them. This is what he would have to do. It was what Flora wanted, of course it was. And Mark and Marsha were ... well, they were the closest thing to family he had. It would have to be done. So Marsha was extremely surprised – she had a list prepared of nine reasons as to why he should agree to bring Flora to dinner – when he said laconically, 'Sure. Can I bring her to dinner?'

Marsha was so taken aback she could hardly speak. But

she rallied pretty fast. 'Joel,' she said. 'You are being nice to her?'

And the pause told them both what they needed to know. 'Leave work,' said Marsha. 'It's a Saturday.'

Joel looked down at the papers. Colton had loaded so much on him it wasn't even funny. Something was up and he was being expected to handle all of it.

'And I'll see you later,' said Marsha, hanging up.

Flora was on the top of the Empire State Building, looking out at one of the most iconic views in the world, doing something she had dreamed of her whole life since she'd watched *Sleepless in Seattle* four times in a row one weekend. And all she could do was check her phone.

This wasn't right, she thought to herself. These endless nerves. He was her boyfriend. Okay, he'd never said the word – but on the other hand, he'd moved hundreds of miles to a tiny dot in the middle of the North Sea to be with her. If that wasn't commitment, what was? He could have moved and not lived with her if it was just the island he liked, couldn't he?

She tried to take in the stunning surroundings, the amazing ability of New York to be so strange and yet so overwhelmingly familiar at the same time; she took photos for other, happier couples and tried not to look bitter as she did; she googled where to go for lunch, for which she got thousands and thousands of responses, and glanced down at the list of amazing-sounding restaurants and wished she felt remotely hungry.

She was just turning round to head back when she heard

a ping on her phone. Somehow she knew straightaway that it was him – for good or for bad.

'Hello?'

'How are you feeling?'

Joel's detached, amused tones made Flora shut her eyes with overwhelming relief. She had been sure that he would find an excuse to withdraw even more, upset at her drunken rantings. Instead he sounded just like normal.

'Awful,' she said honestly.

'Good,' he said. 'I should have warned you about American drinks. Although on the other hand, you probably shouldn't have four cocktails in half an hour anywhere.'

'They don't do a lot of cocktails at the Harbour's Rest,' muttered Flora.

'They don't,' said Joel. He took a breath. 'Anyway ... tonight. Would you like ...? There are some people I'd like you to meet.'

Flora straightened up. It must be the lady who rang.

'I'll check my schedule,' she said, and Joel laughed.

Flora then spent most of the afternoon in something of a panic, looking up and down and around Fifth Avenue – completely paralysed by the sheer choice and range of things on offer – to find something appropriate to wear. She got lost in Sak's, wandered through Bloomingdale's far too overwhelmed to even approach anything, got shoe blindness, and realised that in her life she had rarely needed to buy summer apparel and didn't appear to have the knack.

Joel stared at the phone. Stared at the laptop. Thought

about what Marsha would say that night, then swore mightily and went to meet Flora.

He worried briefly about what Marsha and Mark would think, but they'd never met any of his girlfriends before; they rarely lasted long enough, and even so he seldom had the slightest bit of interest in sharing his upbringing. He hated – despised – the tilted-head look girls had often given when they heard about his past, as if they immediately saw him as some wounded bird only they could heal, so often he didn't mention it at all. It had been different with Flora; she was so wounded by her own mother dying that it felt they were sharing in something they both understood. Even though she couldn't understand it, not really. Losing a mother you had loved was not at all the same as never having known one.

But Marsha and Mark … There was no hiding there. Mark had read all his childhood files; Marsha, he surmised, had intuited the rest.

He hoped they'd like Flora. He hoped they'd think he was good enough for her.

He came across her panicking in Zara on Fifth, carting large amounts of clothes into the changing rooms. She looked hot and red-faced – sunny days didn't exactly suit her – and her hair was hanging damply from a ponytail. She had a huge pile of coloured dresses in her arms, none of which, he could tell, would suit her.

'Having fun?' he said mildly.

'Not really,' said Flora crossly. 'American sizes are weird and everything makes me look pale.'

'That's because you're translucent.'

'And nothing suits me and absolutely everyone else looks

118

amazing in these colours and I just look like a peely-wally washout.'

Joel wasn't sure what this was but guessed it wasn't good. He glanced around. There was no doubt about it: Joel was good at clothes, Flora reflected. He wore suits every day, that was what he did, but they were subtly different – better – than other people's suits: the slim lines of them, the positions of the buttons, the crisp shirts. He wasn't a dandy; he just got it effortlessly right. That life he used to have ... Everyone dressed well. She wouldn't have dared buy him so much as a tie. She sighed. Now he was eyeing her, frowning.

'What?'

'I'm not sure this is the right place for you,' he said. 'Zara is Spanish. It's designed for beautiful tanned señoritas who don't eat till 11 p.m. each night. Come with me.'

She followed him out and he guided her expertly to a very quiet corner of Bergdorf's, up on the fourth floor. She eyed him suspiciously.

'What?' he said. 'I dated a lot of models.'

'Well, *that* makes me feel better,' she said.

'They're very, very boring. Do we need to go through this again?'

Flora looked at the shop assistant, who had skin as pale as her own, but topped with a severe black bob and bright orange lipstick. 'No,' she said.

'Okay.' A smile played on Joel's lips. 'Let me do this.'

And Flora watched in mild amazement as he quickly blew through the racks, picking out some clothes, eyeing her, and putting most of them back. Finally he came up with three.

There was a deconstructed dress in the palest of

millennial pinks, with a soft Lycra top and a parachute silk skirt in softest teal that looked far too floaty and strange for anything Flora would ever have picked up. It swirled with her as she walked and made her look, with her pale hair and white shoulders, like a mermaid.

There was a very pale-silver see-through dress with tiny, almost invisible sprigs of flowers embroidered on the outer layer. The inner layer was a heavenly comfortable silk sheath, and the outer layer hung to the floor. From the second Flora put it on she found herself walking differently; it made her willowy and elegant, rather than slightly too tall and Viking-ish – it was a vision of a different type of person than she thought she could be, particularly as Joel came over and untied her hair carefully until it fanned out over her shoulders.

'Now you're a sprite,' he said.

The final dress was of palest green, in grosgrain, off the shoulder, slightly tighter and designed to be worn with heels. It was definitely a sexy dress.

'Oh yes,' said Joel appreciatively. He was sitting in a large armchair leafing through a magazine and glanced up as she left the changing room.

'Really?' said Flora, turning around. She blushed bright pink and Joel got an enormous jolt simply watching it happen. How he loved to raise that colour in her. He looked around to check how private the changing rooms were. The snotty-looking shop assistant immediately looked up as if she could sense what he had in mind.

'Let's go,' said Joel in a hurry, glancing at his watch. 'You've got time to go home and change.'

Flora checked the price tag. It was astronomical. 'Ah,' she said. Joel waved his hand.

'Stop it, please,' he said. 'All of them,' he said over his shoulder to the assistant.

'No, Joel, don't.'

He shook his head. 'I want to.' He pulled her close. 'You are literally the only woman I've ever met who hasn't asked for a thing.'

Flora swallowed. She knew he was complimenting her. But it felt like he was warning her too.

She shook that thought out of her head as she got changed, and the shop assistant bagged everything up for her, all wrapped in tissue, and they ran through the crowds as quickly as they were able. Joel started kissing her before they were even in the lift, and Flora looked around guilt-ily, then realised of course she didn't know anyone here so who cared, and she kissed him back with abandon and he practically carried her into the lift and they were completely oblivious, even as the receptionist watched them jealously.

Marsha and Mark lived uptown. Flora and Joel were still rather giggly when they turned up, a little late, Flora with her hair still wet at the ends but glowing in her silver dress. Joel made a mental note to buy her some earrings to go with it.

The Philippoussises lived in a fancy apartment building with a doorman on the Upper East Side, and Flora was intensely impressed by the old oak lift and the beautiful parquet flooring, as well as the views of the park.

Marsha answered the door, and Flora liked her

immediately. She was tiny, with short brown hair and a round figure dressed in something obviously expensive. There were large jars of lilies in the hallway and soft lighting all around. She had dark, beady eyes that took in everything – including the fact that the poor girl, she thought to herself, was obviously wearing a new dress. She wondered if Joel was up to his old tricks again, trying to control every environment he was in.

Joel leaned forward and kissed Marsha lightly, but he didn't get away in time as she stretched her arms up and insisted on giving him a hug.

'I swear you are still growing,' she said.

'Marsha, I'm thirty-five years old.'

'Yes, well, even so.'

Mark came through, holding a wooden spoon with a tea towel over his shoulder. Flora felt Joel relax beside her.

'Hello, sir,' said Joel respectfully.

'Come in, come in,' said Mark, beaming. He had a trimmed grey beard and his eyes twinkled. Flora immediately felt their warmth and intelligence and felt envious of them both. 'You must be Flora, our Scottish friend.'

He did not attempt a shot at the accent, as many Americans did, for which Flora was grateful.

'You look lovely,' said Marsha. Flora wasn't at all what she'd expected. She'd assumed she would be another of Joel's favoured willowy blondes. Although she had always suspected that it wasn't that Joel had a type as such, just that those kinds of girls were considered by the culture to be particularly desirable so he had made his choice in the same way he chose his watch or his apartment or anything else: by what appeared to be the best available to him at the time.

But this girl wasn't like that. She didn't look like anyone else Marsha had ever seen, and she lived in New York where eventually you saw everyone, more or less. Her pale hair; her skin was practically albino; those strange silvery blue-green eyes ... You didn't quite notice her at first glance; she was average ... then you took a closer look and she was extremely striking. Her voice when she spoke wasn't always easy to understand, but it sounded to Marsha like music. Please, she thought to herself. Let her be kind. But not too kind.

'So, how are you finding New York?'

'Amazing,' said Flora. 'It's weird – it feels like I know it already. And also: hot.'

Marsha looked puzzled. 'Oh, I think it's quite a cool spring.'

'It's hot compared to where I'm from.'

'Well, don't come back in July ... Would you like a Martini?'

'A small one, please,' said Flora, as Joel smirked. 'Stop it!' she whispered to him, as they followed through into the large kitchen-diner with its extraordinary city views. 'This is amazing,' said Flora as they moved back out to the terrace. Joel had stopped in the kitchen, where Mark was making a moussaka, and was updating him on his new job. Mark was nodding solemnly.

'So,' said Marsha, drawing her in. Flora remembered what she'd heard about Americans: that they were perfectly upfront in asking direct questions. 'You're the one.'

'Oh, I don't know about that,' said Flora, although she was thrilled by the statement, secretly – especially while sipping her Martini, which was incredibly strong but also rather delicious. She watched the long lines of the lights of cars, up and down the park.

'You're the only person he's ever brought to meet us,' said Marsha. 'And we've known him since he was eleven years old.'

Flora kept staring out. 'What was he like then?'

Marsha thought back. 'Clever. Sad. So tightly closed in on himself, you couldn't have peeled him open any which way. I'm not sure anyone ever has.' She left the unspoken question in the air.

'What happened ... I mean, he told me he was raised in care. Why? What happened? He's never said and it felt a bit strange to ask.'

Marsha shrugged. 'I haven't seen the files, of course. So I don't know. I will tell you this. With other wards, when they turn eighteen, Mark legally asks them if they want to be reunited with their birth family.' She sipped her drink. 'In this case, never.'

'And he never got adopted? Did no family want to keep him?'

Marsha shook her head. 'The system doesn't always work, alas.'

'What about ... do you have children?'

'Yes,' said Marsha. 'Of course, we couldn't have adopted Joel. Professionally, it's unconscionable. And our own children were too young at that time. But we ... we tried to do what we could for him.'

'He is very grateful,' said Flora.

Marsha grimaced. 'I don't want him to be grateful. I'd

really like him to take us totally for granted, fling his washing down and turn up whenever he feels like it. I'd love a world in which we don't have to beg to see him.' She looked up.

'But, Flora,' she said. 'You shouldn't have to be asking me. You know that, don't you?'

Flora nodded.

'That's all love is, you know. To know someone: to be fully known.'

And Flora couldn't speak as they headed back into the kitchen, where Joel and Mark were deep in a discussion of the intricacies of potential impeachment trials which, both the women intuited immediately, was their way of telling each other how much they loved each other. The evening passed pleasantly as Mark and Marsha talked about a disastrous trip to Italy that appeared to include a tour of the country's craziest hotels; about how Mark was refusing to retire, pointing out that half the people he saw were miserable because they had done so and had lost their purpose in life, plus he loved what he did; Marsha talked about her interior design course and the awfulness of the women who went on it; Joel did not talk much, as usual, but he laughed in the right places, and neither of their hosts did the thing Flora had been most excited about while also dreading: asking the couple what their plans were or where they were headed.

At 10.30, Flora let out an involuntary jet-lag yawn and Mark jumped up to get the coats. Joel went to the bathroom and they left, both thinking that it had gone as well as could be expected. Flora fell asleep against Joel in the car, Marsha's words ringing in her ears. As she nodded off, she swore to herself she would do it – she would know him.

Chapter Twenty-two

Flora tried to act nonchalant but she was fundamentally terrible at it. She sat on the huge bed, still staring out at the sensational view – she wondered if the people who lived here ever got tired of it, even as she wondered whether Paul Macbeth's lambs had been born yet and hoping she didn't miss their first days of bouncing cheerfully about. She was looking forward to going home tomorrow. She wished Joel was coming with her. She watched him untie his tie and he looked so alone, suddenly, standing in the dim light of the bedroom, and she walked up to him and put her arms around him.

'So they knew you as a child,' she said. 'What were you like?'

Joel shrugged. 'I don't know. That's the problem with psychiatrists. They never give you an end-of-year report.'

'Did you like being a child?'

He stiffened. 'Not terribly,' he said. Then he pulled her

round swiftly and hard up against him and looked straight at her, his hands locked on to her back in that way that made her gasp.

'Last night in New York,' he said. 'Let's make it count.'

He was up early on Sunday morning and she sat up and wrapped her arms around her knees, watching him. She told him about Saif's children coming back, and was gratified by his happiness at the news, and concern for how they would be. She lay back, faux casually.

'So was it mostly in New York you were brought up?'

Joel eyed her. 'Why do you ask?'

'I'm interested,' said Flora. 'It's quite a normal thing to want to know, isn't it?'

Joel shrugged. 'Well. Here and there.'

'You said that before.'

Joel looked at her, his dark eyes unblinking. 'I told you about my childhood.'

'You didn't,' said Flora, hating herself for sounding like she was nagging at him. 'You told me you grew up in care. You didn't tell me anything else about it.'

'There's nothing else to tell,' said Joel, glancing at his watch. 'I was fostered. I moved around families. Then I escaped and went to boarding school. Right, I have to shoot.'

'Do you . . . do you know what happened to your parents?' said Flora gently. Joel's face closed up tightly.

'I have to go,' he said again.

Flora looked around in dismay. 'You can't have brunch or anything before I go? It's Sunday.'

'Colton doesn't recognise Sundays. It's the big meeting today. For which I am not remotely prepared, thanks to being distracted by you. And the faster I'm done, the faster I can leave this place!'

And he kissed her and left, and that was that.

Chapter Twenty-three

In truth, although he'd tried to shake it off, Flora's visit had bothered Joel far more than he could bring himself to say. That he'd had a message from Marsha saying how much they'd liked her made matters worse. It felt like she was a cop, moving closer and closer to the truth about him. And he couldn't bear that. He wanted the soft-skinned girl who sat in the firelight, whose presence soothed his tortured soul, who acted as a balm to his troubled mind.

Not someone else like all the others – like all the legions of others whose hands he had passed through, who had wanted a full history, who had wanted to hear the whole story again and again and again, and you would think it would lose its power but it didn't. And the one decent thing he had in his life . . .

He had had to leave the hotel room as quickly as he could in the faint hopes that this would not be spoiled too.

He was under no illusions that she hadn't noticed.

Had the meeting with Colton gone well, then he might have been able to smooth it over; deflect it. The meeting did not go well.

The room was closed and private. There was nobody else there. This was very unusual. When Colton did business, he usually had a massive entourage around him, even if they were just there to laugh at his jokes. No Fintan, which was rarely a good sign. Fintan had done Colton Rogers nothing but good. He had toned down his abrasive side and made him laugh.

But here, in this huge conference room on the eighty-sixth floor of a midtown skyscraper mostly owned by Colton, was nothing but a vast table, a pot of coffee and the two men.

Joel took out the paperwork. 'I just . . . I realise it's not for me to question your decisions. But consolidating absolutely everything . . . I mean, what does Ike say?'

Ike was one of Colton's local money men.

Colton waved his hand. 'Doesn't matter,' he said. He pulled out a sheaf of paperwork from his hip backpack. Joel furrowed his brow; this was new.

'Here,' said Colton, hurling it across the table. 'Look at this.'

'You want me to take it away?'

'You can't take it away,' said Colton. 'You read it and redraft it and I get it typed up. Now. Today.'

Joel blinked, then put his head down and started to read. Colton watched him intently. There was absolute silence in the room.

After half an hour, Joel raised his head. 'Colton, you can't do this.'

Colton shrugged. 'I can do what I like.'

Joel looked at it again. 'But ... but, Colton. It's wrong. What it'll do ... ' His voice trailed off. 'I mean. Seriously. Are you sure?'

Colton shrugged. 'Well, it's my money.'

'But ... '

There was silence. Colton's face became mutinous. 'Joel, you're my lawyer.'

'Yes, but ... '

'No buts about it. You're hired. You're my lawyer. I don't want anyone else. You do what I ask. Or I can fire your ass and you can leave the island and break that sweet girl's heart and wash up fuck knows where, like I give a shit. Or a reference.'

He stared at Joel, very hard.

'But ... '

'Joel, you're a *lawyer*. You get murderers out of jail.'

There was a long silence.

'You gotta do it. Or I'm just going to find someone else, and you'll just make this whole thing take longer. Oh, and by the way, you breathe a word of this and you'll find yourself in more trouble than you can possibly imagine. I will dedicate the rest of my life to making yours a misery. And don't you forget that.'

There was a very long silence. Then Joel spoke up. 'I can redraft from these notes.'

'Good,' said Colton. 'Do it. And hurry up. I'm getting out of this hellhole.' He gesticulated to the stunning Manhattan views outside his window. 'And getting back to where things really matter.'

Chapter Twenty-four

'Are you absolutely, totally, one hundred per cent sure he isn't just a dickhead?'

Fintan was doing his best to be encouraging.

Flora thought back to how Joel had been as her boss in London: squiring a selection of models; never even glancing at people he considered his inferiors; his rude manner.

'Well,' she said, as Fintan parked the car. She was jet-lagged and exhausted. 'Well, I can see how people *might* think he was a dickhead.'

She looked up. 'He likes dogs.'

'Mate,' said Fintan. 'Only psychos don't like dogs. I didn't accuse him of being a psycho. Just a dickhead.'

They turned onto the little soil path up the hill to the farm. Bramble and the other family dogs immediately went utterly bananas. Flora almost raised a smile at that.

'Don't upset Dad,' said Fintan.

'Why?' said Flora, instantly stricken. Her father had

been very down after the death of her mother three years ago.

'No reason,' said Fintan. 'Only, he's so happy that you're settled – and Joel's someone Mum would have liked.'

'Unless she thought he was a dickhead,' said Flora mournfully.

'Well, yeah, that's possible too,' said Fintan. 'Anyway.'

Innes and Hamish came wandering in from the fields cheerfully. Since the farm had been bought out, the cushion of a little money, plus a new, guaranteed home for their organic produce, had taken a lot of the strain and worry from their lives. Farmers' lives were never without worry, of course – but even so, you could see a lightness in Innes's happy face as he took off his big boots and waved at them. Agot was inside the farmhouse.

'ATTI FLOWA!' She jumped up.

'You are not still watching *Peppa Pig*,' said Flora, smiling, and she picked the girl up in her arms and whirled her round.

'I'S LOVES PEPPA.'

'Well, I'm glad to hear it.'

Agot looked around mischievously then leaned towards Flora's ear and announced in a loud stage whisper, 'YOU GOT PRESENT FOAH AGOT?'

'Agot!' said Innes. 'Literally that was the exact and precise thing I told you not to say when Flora walked through the door.'

The imp looked utterly unrepentant. 'BUT LIKE PRESENTS,' she said, as if this was a ridiculous demand to have placed on her.

Flora smiled and sat down. 'Well,' she said, and drew out

133

of her bag a snow globe that had all the New York landmarks underneath it. She shook it for the little one, who gave a great gasp.

'SNOWZING!'

'It is snowzing, yes.'

Agot snatched it from Flora's hands, eyes wide.

'Be careful with it,' said Flora. 'Don't drop it.'

'NOTS DROP SNOWZING,' agreed Agot, nevertheless waving it about in a highly dangerous fashion, her eyes fixed on it.

'What do you say, Agot?' said Innes, watching happily.

'THANK YOU, ATTI FLOWA.' Agot's little face looked up, then creased into a frown. 'WHAT WRONG?'

Flora blinked. 'There's nothing wrong,' she said.

'YOU CRYING? SAD ATTI FLOWA? YOU SAD? YOU SAD? NOT CRY.'

Agot scrambled up into Flora's lap and started using her little hands to wipe away the remnants of tears from Flora's eyes.

'I'm fine!' said Flora, slightly desperately. 'Just a bit tired, that's all.'

'Are you missing Joel?' said Innes.

'Neh, he was being a dickhead,' said Fintan.

'Shut up, Fintan!'

'DOAN BE SAD.' Agot was unswervable on the topic.

'I'm not sad,' said Flora. 'I am very happy. Why don't you play with your snow globe?'

Agot looked at it. Bramble was trying to eat it.

'SNOWZER WAN WATCH PEPPA,' she said, snatching it back.

'Well, good,' said Flora. 'I think that's an excellent idea.'

'WAZ A DICKHEAD, ATTI FLOWA?'

The boys had already started squabbling about who was making dinner, and suddenly Flora felt overwhelmingly tired.

'Actually, I think I'm a bit jet-lagged,' she said. 'I think I'll just go to bed.'

Chapter Twenty-five

Dear Colton,

I regret to ...

Joel stared at the blinking cursor in frustration.

He couldn't think straight. He could barely think at all. He had messed everything up so thoroughly ... Maybe he should resign. Resign and leave Mure and stay here in New York or Singapore or anywhere else ... He would always be in demand.

The thought of leaving all of it behind: the only place that stilled his restless damaged heart; the only place he could breathe, away from the wretched air conditioning and the constant traffic noise and the beep-beep-beeping of everybody's phones and the endless lines of people and issues and problems all jangling up against him and crackling across the air ...

Christ. He deleted the email.

Dear Flora,

He flashed back suddenly to that weekend they'd spent together in the depths of winter: Flora pretending to be reading even though she kept falling asleep; he was working. Every time he looked up, her head would be drooping, then she'd see him looking at her and smile and say, 'It's actually very interesting,' and he'd smile back as the flames crackled in the wood-burner. The room had felt cosy, and Bramble, who had appeared to become a permanent feature ever since Flora had returned and disliked leaving her side, had turned over with a groaning noise that sounded exactly like a seventy-year-old man – which is what he was in dog years. Joel had suddenly found that he had completely lost interest in the work he was doing. He had pushed aside the folders and got up and put her book down. He had pulled her up towards him in the firelight and kissed her ferociously and she had leaned into him with such hunger, instantly and completely awake, those pale eyes of hers taking on a characteristically misty distant look he had learned to recognise very well. Then they had fumbled as she tried to take off the four layers of ridiculous clothes she was wearing and they had laughed – which was strange for Joel, as he rarely laughed – and they had locked Bramble in the bathroom and the flakes of snow had swirled around outside and settled on the harbourside so prettily as the heat of their bodies was magnified by the licking of the flames that threw their shadows against the wall. And he thought he had never been so happy – no, that he had never been happy at all.

And what had he done afterwards? He had slept. He had slept for nine hours.

Joel never slept anywhere. He had learned not to early in life: in foster homes, with children of the family who might make their displeasure at your appearance obvious in different ways, at unpredictable times of day; at boarding school, where one was never entirely safe from a master looking for miscreants, or older boys looking for trouble. His entire life was lived on guard.

Except for Mure. There, he was . . . there he was safe.

New York wasn't safe. It was confusing and busy and made him anxious. It made him have to keep a tight lid on himself, and what had he done? He had looked at her and seen in her eyes not the clear gaze of trust she gave him when they sat on the harbour wall; not the calm, focused look she had when she was working in Annie's Seaside Kitchen, perfectly following recipes handed down from her mother; not that clouded, melting look whenever he placed a hand on her, cheeks reddened, every time, her hands trembling in a way he found utterly irresistible . . .

No. She had looked at him in pain and confusion and disappointment, and in all the kinds of terrible ways Joel couldn't bear to be looked at – that triggered the panic, so deeply buried, of a little boy who, if he wasn't pleasing people, couldn't be certain of a roof over his head and food to eat, never mind someone to love him. And to make matters worse, now Colton was working to destroy it all.

There was no connection in Joel's life that you could screw up and still be loved. None. It simply had never happened to him. That was why he had fought so hard to be the best: to be the most successful, to turn in the most billable hours, to always beat the other guy, to seduce the most beautiful women, to always succeed.

To fail in Flora's eyes felt like the worst failure of all and he wasn't sure if he could bear it. And he didn't know what to do about it.

He deleted the email, cursing. He was no good for anyone or anything, it seemed.

Joel paced the suite, trying to distract himself. Something occurred to him – something that, even if he had screwed everything up, even if he had to move, he could do. One useful thing.

The country may be different, the context might be strange, but there was one thing that nobody knew more about than Joel: child services.

He reopened the laptop.

Dear Saif,

I just wanted you to know I have heard your wonderful news, and would be delighted to represent you, pro bono, for anything that may lie ahead.

Chapter Twenty-six

Sometimes a good night's sleep can solve everything. Sometimes you get two seconds before you realise that, no, everything is still pretty rubbish. Flora blinked at the ceiling and sighed. She hadn't called Joel. She didn't know how. She didn't know how she felt or where she was going to go, or where they were. She stared at the ceiling. Oh yes. And she had a wedding to prep for that she'd completely ignored while dashing off to the other side of the world.

The wind was coming in off the sea but it was salty and fresh and helped get the jet-lag cobwebs out of her brain as she opened up the kitchen door and let the dogs out, their huge tails wagging cheerfully in the morning light. She headed into the kitchen. 'Ta-da!' said Fintan. He held up some freshly made sausages in a paper packet. 'Haggis and herb.'

'That sounds gross.'

'And that is where you are wrong,' he said, turning up the Aga. 'Just you wait. These will cure all ills.'

Flora smiled sadly. 'How's Colton this morning?'

Fintan's face lit up. 'He's great! He's in LA shouting at share-holders. If it wasn't for this stupid wedding I'd be there too.'

Flora smiled. 'Ah, good.'

Fintan leaned over. 'If he's not making you happy . . . '

'Don't start,' said Flora. 'I can't think about it just now.'

'That means you'll just stay in the same place for ever, if he thinks doing this kind of thing is okay.'

'I know,' said Flora. 'I do know that. It's just . . . I met his psychiatrist.'

'He took you to meet his *psychiatrist*?'

'It's an unusual situation.'

'Does he have literally no friends? Did he have to pay him?'

'It's not like that,' said Flora, going pink. She had never mentioned Joel's past to anyone, which was difficult, as it made it harder to excuse him. 'He's had a rough time of it.'

Fintan paused and turned the sausages, which were spattering in the pan. 'He's a rich, handsome lawyer who can travel the world.'

'Rich, handsome lawyers have problems too.'

Fintan looked at his sister. 'I think . . . ' he said slowly. 'I just think . . . he should be treating you like a princess.'

Flora smiled. 'Cinder-bloody-ella, you mean. The jobs list for tomorrow is insane.'

'I know,' said Fintan. 'Isn't it brilliant?'

Charlie and Jan's wedding was booked in the ancient chapel that overlooked the headland, the lines of ancient graves standing sentinel against the waves. It was old – *old* old. By the time the missionaries had arrived, there had already been people living on Mure for thousands of years. Conversion had been swift – too swift, some said. The people had accepted the new religion, but had never quite forgotten the old, layered stories of sea gods, of seals and of Viking gods and princes in ice towers that were brought over the cold sea and told down the generations round the fire and out of earshot of the minister.

The reception was to be in the Harbour's Rest, slightly to Flora's surprise – she had expected a marquee in Jan's rich parents' garden, rather than the old, slightly slovenly hotel on the edge of town. Still, it would be handy that you could just leave when you'd had enough rather than waiting for the entire town to go, and the Rock of course still wasn't open. There was a guest list, obviously, but it was accepted that locals – and particularly the town's elderly residents – might well just turn up anyway at the church, weddings being rare on Mure in their small community (although outsiders came to get married there all the time for the picturesque backdrop and as a bit of one-upmanship, wedding-style, in terms of how complex they could make getting there for their guests). These extra guests would probably tag along to the reception too, so Jan had requested a buffet rather than a sit-down, and a reasonable limit on the cash bar.

But for the food, she wanted everything. Flora cursed her, under her breath, and tried to think of the money as she rolled out hundreds of individual sausage rolls; miniature scones, all light fluffy and perfect, to be served with local cream and bramble jam; tiny immaculate simnel cakes; pies

142

of every description; jellies and possets, even though Flora had had to dig deep into her mother's recipe book even to find out what they were. But not the wedding cake, of course, Jan had said smugly. That would be sent over from the mainland, the implication being that of course they wouldn't entrust Flora with the really important stuff . . . Flora had just smiled and bitten her tongue and said that was fine.

There was – she could not fail to admit – a tiny bit of her thinking: what if?

Could it have been her waking up this bright and breezy spring morning, not with a sense of dread, but with a secure sense of happiness? Knowing that she was going to marry a handsome, kind, upstanding man with whom she could build a life, straightforwardly and happily? With whom she could raise children who would speak Gaelic and English and who would go to Lorna's school? Seeing each other every day; working reasonable hours . . . ?

A very simple kind of happiness . . . That had been offered. But Charlie had seen the doubt in her eyes, the way her head turned whenever that damned impossible American had entered the room; he had seen it and known it and left her alone. She was doomed – never to have a simple, happy life like everyone else.

Flora felt incredibly sorry for herself – even as she fired up soda bread to be served with plenty of butter and island whisky, smoked salmon and local roe, and iced ginger buns that popped in the mouth with crème pâtissière squirting out, and endless eclairs, as Isla and Iona cut cucumber sandwiches in the back kitchen with the radio turned up loud and talked about what boys they hoped were going to show up and how short they could wear the black skirts Jan had requested.

By eleven o'clock, however, when the ceremony was going on – she didn't know if Jan thought she might have tried to crash it – she surveyed the room in pleasure. The carpet was faded (and a little dusty around the edges) and the ceiling was still tobacco-stained after all these years, but the long tables were absolutely stuffed and groaning with food around the centrepiece of a cake (which was very plain and unadorned and nothing Flora couldn't have knocked up in the Seaside Kitchen). There were heavy jugs of cream, two sides of locally smoked salmon and little hot bowls of Cullen skink, and it really was quite beautiful.

Flora allowed herself a little smile. So . . . A bride she was not. But she was definitely edging closer to being able to call herself a cook. Fintan stuck his head round the door, and gave her two thumbs-up.

They heard the wedding party before they saw it; it was a lovely bright and windy shining day and there were no wedding cars on Mure, unless you wanted to put flowers on a Land Rover (and some people did), so the entire party simply walked down the main street, to shouts and congratulations from holidaymakers and passers-by, delighted to find themselves in the middle of a wedding procession, as the bells rang out from the church. Flora steeled herself a little. This was Jan's day, and there weren't many people who didn't know that she and Charlie had had something of a flirtation the previous summer. She wished just for once that Joel could be by her side for something that mattered to her. Fintan, as if he could sense this, moved closer to her and squeezed her arm. He also dusted off some of the flour that had fallen on her apron and in her hair.

'Don't worry,' said Fintan. 'You have nothing to feel bad about.'

Flora didn't think that was true for a moment. But she stuck a smile on her face and did her best.

To be fair, Jan looked nice. Okay, she hadn't dyed her hair, so it was short and rigidly quite grey, or removed her glasses. But it was the first time Flora had ever seen her out of a fleece, and for sure, she had the most tremendous legs. She wore a chic, straight knee-length dress that showed them off nicely and a slightly 1980s-style but somehow appropriate white jacket. No veil, but she looked like herself. Charlie of course was in his kilt, as were the other men, with a black tie for once and a Bonnie Prince Charlie short black jacket with a black waistcoat underneath it.

Flora ducked out of sight as he came into view, back in the kitchen like Cinderella, while the plates with the hot canapés on them were rolled out – scallops, and neatly cut venison, and little haggis bonbons, piping hot with a horseradish cream. Inge-Britt, the manager of the Harbour's Rest (and one-time amour of Joel's, which Flora tried uncomfortably to forget and Inge-Britt, who had a fairly healthy Icelandic attitude towards this kind of thing, already had genuinely forgotten), was laying out glasses of ordered-in Prosecco, some of which had been poured too early and was already going flat – although Flora didn't like to mention that.

Flora squinted at the crowd coming through. There really

did seem to be an awful lot of people ... Jan had been insistent that there was catering for a hundred people, which was plenty, obviously, but there were far more than Flora had been expecting showing up.

Not only that, but there were lots of children. Jan had definitely not mentioned children ... Many of them, Flora assumed, were part of Jan and Charlie's outreach groups that they ran together, taking children from the mainland in difficult situations out on adventure holidays. While this was an entirely laudable aim and a wonderful thing to do, Flora sometimes wished that Jan didn't show off her moral virtue quite so regularly.

But the problem with these children was they couldn't wait for a buffet. They didn't know they were meant to hold off until everyone had a drink and was settled and organised so the speeches could begin and everyone could behave reasonably. They went straight to the heaving buffet table and immediately began stuffing their faces with whatever they could find.

'No!' said Flora, horrified, as her lovely display was being ruined before the guests had even got in to see it.

She came out of the kitchen, not even caring that she hadn't cleaned up or put some lipstick on. The boys, startled, looked up at her guiltily and a hush fell on the room. Jan turned round with an expectant look on her face. Flora immediately felt herself blush bright pink.

'Um. I mean, hello. Would you like to wait until everyone is here and everyone can start the buffet together?'

She put on her most ingratiating face and was aware how fake her voice sounded. In fact, she sounded like she'd been chasing away hungry children from food. This was not really the look she'd been after.

Jan bustled over, a pitying smile on her face. 'Not to worry, Flora ... Everyone here is our guest.'

Flora tried to pull her aside. 'But ... but we've only got food for a hundred guests! You said a hundred!'

The room was now absolutely packed, and the boys had gone straight back to stuffing their faces.

Jan tinkled a little laugh Flora hadn't heard before. 'Oh, it's hardly difficult, what you're doing, is it? It's lovely to welcome *all* our friends to celebrate our marriage ... '

Charlie came up behind Jan, grinning nervously and looking rather sweaty.

'Oh ... yes ... Congratulations,' said Flora. 'I'm very ... I'm really pleased for you.'

Jan tightened her grip on Charlie's hand proprietorially. 'Well, of course you would have to say that,' she said. She looked around. 'I see the American appears to have left.'

Flora blinked. There were even more people slipping in through the door, including a few disreputable Harbour's Rest drinkers that she was reasonably certain wouldn't have received an invitation in a million years. 'So, anyway ... Do you know how many you're expecting?'

'Flora,' said Jan. 'This celebration is important in our community. It's important to all of us. Obviously you moved away from the islands.'

And then I moved back, thought Flora mutinously.

'But for those of us who've always stayed here, who believe in the island as our home ... this is an important day for all of us.'

'So ... how many?'

'Everyone is welcome,' said Jan. She glanced over at the rapidly diminishing buffet table. The boys were throwing vol-au-vents at each other and crumbs were getting underfoot. 'Oh dear, it's looking a little thin.'

And she glided across the floor as if the situation were nothing to do with her.

Flora turned, grabbed Isla and Iona into the kitchen and hooked Fintan, who'd been heading over for a gin and tonic.

'Everything,' she hissed. 'We get everything we've got in stock.'

Fintan frowned. 'Well, she's not having the ageing range.'

Fintan had started to lay cheese down, like wine, in preparation for the Rock reopening. It was extraordinary stuff, really beautiful, and Flora sometimes wished they could sell it on the open market. It would make a fortune.

'Anything,' she repeated. 'Anything that's in the freezer, anything lying about, and everyone start baking. The quickest thing – Iona, you do sandwiches. Run down to the Spar.'

She was sad; up until now they'd used the best of everything.

'Buy up whatever ham they have. All the cucumbers.'

She thought about the local shop's cucumbers. They could be a little tired, to say the least. Cucumbers had to travel a long way to reach the Northern Isles.

'Put loads of butter on everything. Oh Christ,' she moaned. 'We won't have time to make any more bread. See what Mrs Laird has.'

The girls, to their credit, worked at lightning speed with what they had. They found every piece of fruitcake – Flora stockpiled them for the kitchen, did them in huge batches. They also found a vast pile of frozen gingerbread Flora had forgotten she had, and ended up microwaving it into a pudding and adding custard. They scraped every crumb out of Annie's Seaside Kitchen and served it up to an increasingly drunken and demanding crowd, even stooping, eventually, to ransacking Inge-Britt's stock of crisps simply to give Jan's guests something to eat.

Finally, after what seemed to Flora about twenty hours of rowdy people and dancers and bar bores and singers, and after the speeches were made, the cake was cut and the free bar was shut, there was not a crumb to be found, and people, sensing the main affair was over, started to drift off.

In the kitchen, the girls were working like Trojans washing up, and Fintan had pitched in like a good one. Flora was flat out, her hair pulled back in a ponytail, sweat on her brow. She looked around. There wasn't a scrap left; they'd even used the sausages Inge-Britt served in the morning, and the eggs, to make a last-minute frittata they'd cut into slices. There wasn't a single thing left untouched. The mess, though, was everywhere.

Flora wanted to weep. She barely knew what people had eaten. All the lovely, delicately handmade little cakes and hors d'oeuvres she'd had ready at the start had been shovelled carelessly into the mouths of boys who couldn't have cared less what they were eating. People had been looking around with hungry looks on their faces until they got drunk enough not to care or were happy enough with a bag of crisps. The idea of anyone wanting to book her after this was unthinkable. Plus they'd spent all their petty cash in the local shop and probably owed Inge-Britt money for the crisps.

As the straggling members of the wedding party headed outside to watch Charlie and Jan go to pick up the night ferry to the mainland – they were going to Italy, Flora had heard Jan say a million times – Flora laid her exhausted head against a doorframe and let a tear run down her cheek. Then she told herself not to be so silly, there were still hours of clearing up to do. And she didn't even want to think about the envelope that had been pushed into the kitchen by Jan's taciturn father.

It would contain, she knew, a cheque for the precise amount that they had agreed in advance – to feed a hundred people. It would be nowhere near enough to cover the extra food and extra hours or the use of Inge-Britt's kitchen. The wedding was meant to make them money – launch them. Instead, all that people would remember were the empty plates; the messy sandwiches.

Oh, there was no point, she told herself. No point in worrying about this or dwelling on it too long. Perhaps she had been getting complacent; the Seaside Kitchen had been running so well she had taken a weekend off. She had taken her eyes off the prize and forgotten what it was actually like to run a catering situation, day after day. Well. Now she knew. She rolled up her sleeves and filled the sink, and tried to chalk it up to experience. But her teeth were definitely gritted.

There was a quiet knock at the swing doors of the kitchen. Flora glanced up wearily. There wasn't, truly, a single soul she was terribly desperate to see at that precise moment, and that in itself made her sad. The woman standing there was a stranger, although Flora had glimpsed her in the wedding party. She was wearing a flowery dress and white sandals; she had thick glasses and long black hair and an apologetic look.

'Um, hello?'

'I don't work here,' said Flora. 'You need Inge-Britt. Hang on.'

'No, no,' said the woman. She had a Glasgow accent. 'I just wanted to say ... I'm so sorry ... I'm the youth worker. With the boys. I'm so sorry – I realised when I came in what they'd done to the buffet ... I was caught behind them at the church.'

'That's okay,' said Flora. 'They did quite a lot of stamping, though.'

'They were over all week doing Outward Bound and they just had such a wonderful time, and I was meant to be escorting them back when they found out about the wedding and just pestered and pestered to be allowed to stay.'

She looked down.

'You know ... they get so few happy events like this, some of them. A lot of them, they barely go out at all. And there certainly aren't a lot of weddings in their backgrounds. Some of them.'

At this, Flora felt absolutely stricken with guilt. All she'd thought about was the boys making a mess of her lovely

151

spread. She had forgotten completely about who they were, and where they'd come from. She tried to think about what they would be like teasing Charlie, who, despite his size, was the softest lump ever to walk the earth, and the hope in their little faces and how on earth you could turn that down.

'I meant to come out and control them, obviously.' The woman twisted her fingers nervously. 'But I got caught up in the pews, and one of them had to go to the loo and by the time I'd showed him the rest had kind of pelted down the street and ... I'm really sorry.'

'That's okay,' said Flora. Weirdly, just saying that, and getting the apology, did somehow make it feel a bit better.

The woman glanced around. 'Do you want me to send them over to help clear up?'

'Oh gracious, no,' said Flora. 'No. I want them to enjoy their holiday.'

The lady smiled. 'They're on the same ferry over as Jan and Charlie, so I don't know how much of a wedding night they're going to have.'

Flora grinned. 'I'm glad they managed to come.'

'So are they,' said the woman. 'Thanks for being so understanding. I thought you'd be writing furious letters to the council demanding my head on a platter!'

'I would not be doing that,' said Flora. 'Although I might have served it if I'd thought of it earlier. Do you want a cup of tea? Or, sod it, there's some leftover Prosecco here ...'

Kind Inge-Britt had secreted away a bottle for her.

The woman looked guilty. 'Oh, I shouldn't. I've got to see the boys back ... okay. Half a glass. Don't tell anyone.'

'I shan't. Where are they?'

'They're all early for the ferry. Charlie's arranged a kick-about match for them on the green.'

Flora shook her head. 'On his wedding day?'

'He's a good man.'

'He is,' said Flora, musing. 'He really is.'

They sat together in the kitchen.

'Can I ask you something?' said Flora.

'Sure.'

'These kids ... They're in care, aren't they?'

'Some of them ... Some of them are sometimes with a parent. Often the best situation is when you can get them with a grandparent.'

'What makes care places fail?'

'Aggression usually. If there are other children in the family, and the child can't handle sharing the attention ... sometimes they kick off if that's all they know.'

Flora frowned. This didn't sound like Joel at all. He could be distant, but she couldn't imagine him being violent or having uncontrollable rage. If anything, he was far too controlled.

'Any other reasons?'

The youth worker took another sip from her glass. 'Well,' she said. 'Sometimes kids just don't fit. It's not their fault. Trauma at home knocks them off-kilter, but they're a little unusual to begin with. Asperger's syndrome can be difficult to place. Or, weirdly, sometimes the opposite. A lot of our foster families come from lower to middle incomes. We had a child once who was a genius, more or less: unbelievably clever, really unusually good at maths, a bit of a prodigy. We couldn't settle him in foster care at all. Either his foster family thought he was too snotty or showing off or they just didn't know how to deal with him.'

'How is he now?' said Flora, breathless. This was more like it.

'He was lucky. We found him a scholarship, parachuted him out of the care system. To boarding school.'

'Wouldn't he be lonely there?'

The woman looked sad. 'That's the deal with my job,' she said gently. 'They're all lonely, dear. So lonely. Something a child should never know how to be.'

She got up to go and poured the last of her glass down the sink.

'One more question!' said Flora. 'I have a friend. A friend who ...'

And she explained the situation with Saif and his boys.

'It will probably be fine,' said the youth worker. She handed over her card. Her name was Indira, Flora saw. 'But, any problems, you call me, okay? I won't forget you feeding the five thousand today. I owe you one.'

Chapter Twenty-seven

Saif didn't mean to yell. He had never been the yelling type. But Lorna was so damned enthusiastic, as if this was a school project, not his life.

Lorna hadn't been able to think of much else, was desperately full of ideas of what they would be like and how it would be, and what she could do to welcome them, and how troubled they would be – would they be violent? Brainwashed? So traumatised they upset the other children? She would have to work out a strategy for dealing with the other children – she would possibly need help from refugee resettlement groups which meant people coming from the mainland – and, gosh, it was exciting, of course it was, but so complicated too.

So she was spilling over with plans and thoughts when she went to meet Saif that morning for an early walk. It was a windy day and fun to feel blown down to the Endless Beach, the breeze waking her up, making the waves dance – although going back would be harder – only to find him there, staring out to sea, his face absolutely set in stone.

He had turned round slowly, and it was only then that she realised his eyes were full of rage.

'Are you all right?'

'I trusted you!' he shouted furiously. He was brandishing something; he'd obviously expected to see her. 'I trusted you with the biggest . . . I trusted you with my entire life. My life and my family's life in your hands. And . . .'

Lorna felt her heart drop to her stomach, that awful way when you begin to suspect that you have made a terrible, terrible mistake.

'What?' she said, trying to sound breezy but hearing the tremor in her voice.

'You tell everyone! You tell everyone on this island now and they know!'

'I didn't!' said Lorna, panicking. She'd told Flora, but she'd sworn her to secrecy, hadn't she? 'I didn't!'

'Joel! He knows!' He showed her the email. Lorna read it in silence.

'Flora guessed!' said Lorna. 'I didn't tell her.'

'And now she tells everyone!'

'It will only be Joel.'

Surely, thought Lorna to herself. Please. But she could understand the impulse completely – the joy of spreading good news, for once, was powerfully strong. Of course Flora wanted to make people happy and rejoice in something good happening – for Saif, for the island, for the world – out of the desperately awful situation.

'There is no such thing as "only" here,' said Saif, who

found the tight-knit community very like the world he had left behind in Damascus with its extraordinary combination of it being both delightful and infuriating that everyone knew about every step of your life before you'd even taken it half the time. 'It will be in the papers and in the grocer shop and whispered round my surgery and you will turn my children into zoo animals before they even arrive and you will give me no chance to prepare and we will be overrun …'

'Overrun by people who mean well – who care,' said Lorna, stung. 'Who want to do the best for you and your family. Why is that a problem? Joel is offering you free legal advice! I want to make the school ready and appropriate for the boys. Everyone will want to help!'

Saif shook his head. 'No,' he said. 'Everyone wants to gossip and be nosy and find out what it was like and poke at the little brown boys. And take pictures and talk about them.'

He turned his face to the sand.

'What if they are injured, Lorenah? What if one of them has lost a hand, an arm … You still want everyone looking, asking? Huh?'

Lorna didn't say anything for a long time.

'I'm sorry,' she said eventually. 'I'm sure Flora hasn't told anyone else.'

Saif shook the paper furiously. 'Are you?' he said. 'I … I am not sure.'

And he turned round and stalked off down the beach and Lorna watched him go in absolute dismay, wanting to be cross with Flora but knowing full well deep down that the fault was entirely her own.

It was odd. Saif was to remember every second of the next two weeks in the same way as he remembered the very first night of his eldest son Ibrahim's life: in the house, every second weighing upon him with the enormity of how his world had changed for ever as he gazed down at this tiny, tiny being, while Amena slept in the back room, torn and utterly wearied.

That first night had been quiet. He remembered every sound the cicadas made in the courtyard; the distant rumble of Damascus traffic that didn't permeate into their pleasant suburb; the little bundle, with bright red cheeks, tiny fists, a wobble of black hair. It wasn't crying exactly, just snuffling and twisting slightly crossly. Saif had been a doctor for long enough to know that he should of course leave him to settle and on absolutely no account lift him up. He lifted him up.

In that tiny yet huge new world and new dawn, he had walked Ibrahim up and down, out into the blessed cool of the courtyard, where the heavy scent of the hibiscus petals opening up in the night lay upon the gathering dew and mingled with the dusty smell of the city streets and the last remnants of the delicate scent of evening meals passing on the breeze. They had paced up and down, Saif and his baby, as Saif pointed out the moon and the stars above and told him how he'd love him to there and beyond, and the little thing had snuffled and nuzzled into him and fallen asleep on his shoulder and Saif had promised to protect him with his life.

He had not done that. He had failed. The world Ibrahim

had been born into – and Ash too – had slowly, then to their mounting disbelief very suddenly, crumbled around their ears. And worse: it had crumbled as the rest of the world had stood by, wrung its hands, prevaricated, wobbled.

But that first night. The heavy scents, the quiet rumbling; the tiny, snuffling, incessantly alive creature in his arms; where it had all begun. And now, did he have the chance to begin again?

'I'm sure he'll be fine,' said Flora. 'I am so, so sorry.'

Flora had closed the shop on the Monday. Partly because she was just so exhausted after the wedding and partly because they had literally nothing to sell and she was going to have to wait for supplies to be replenished – flour, and milk for more butter to be churned. There was a real problem when you promised to make everything locally. You couldn't just nip to the cash and carry and stick everything back in the cupboard.

'Oh, don't worry about it,' said Lorna. 'I shouldn't have told you.'

'You didn't tell me! I guessed!'

Flora had gone to fetch Lorna from school, where she had nervously covered over a book she was reading in her office.

'What's that?' Flora had said suspiciously, but Lorna had shaken her head and refused to answer. 'If it's *How to Leave Teaching*, I will kill you,' said Flora.

Lorna shook her head. 'God, no,' she said, waving at the collection of pupils who liked to stay behind in the playground for some fairly competitive inter-form football matches. It was easy to have inter-form matches in a school with only two classes, and sometimes the bigger ones would make up the numbers in the littler class.

The little school sat at the top of the hill overlooking Mure Town. Made of red sandstone, it still had the original carved letters over the doors for 'Boys' and 'Girls'. It was a windy spot in the wintertime, but in the summer the high vista with water on two sides of the hilltop, the town down in the sheltered harbour below, the boats steaming off to far-distant lands and the oil rigs on the horizon was a beautiful sight. Of course, the view was entirely unappreciated by the children who ran freely back and forth there, blithely unaware of their unfettered childhood – unconstrained by helicopter parents. Everyone knew all the other parents and the children roamed at will – the few cars on the island rarely travelled at more than twenty miles an hour anyway – up and down the lanes and in and out of each other's houses.

There was danger on Mure – in unattended burns; in climbing the fell in bad weather; or jumping in the sea on a day when the rip tide wanted to pull you out, and regardless of how warm the summer's day might be, the water was never going to be warm. But the normal dangers – of heavy traffic, of abduction and strangers and muggings – were not present. Children were free to play. In the long winter months, they had to hunker down, like everyone else, with books or video games. But as soon as the light returned, desperate to be free, they were outside as late and as long as possible. It was not unusual, in the height of the summer when the sun never set, to see children playing in broad daylight at ten o'clock in the evening.

'No,' said Lorna again. 'Actually, I want to do more of it. I just need more people to have some damn children.'

'Probably starting with us,' said Flora gloomily as they headed down to the Harbour's Rest. There was a pretty beer garden there, as long as you were wearing a fleece, and they sat outside, smiling happily at other friends coming past.

'Hahaha,' said Lorna. 'God, there's more chance of Mure getting the Olympics.'

'Tell me about it,' said Flora. 'Oh God, can you imagine? All those *rowers*?'

'You're going to fix it, aren't you, Flores?'

'I don't know,' said Flora soberly. 'I seriously don't know where his head is. He'll be back soon. And meanwhile, I don't dare look at the accounts.'

'Just send Jan another invoice.'

'I would,' said Flora, 'except I know exactly what will happen: "Ooh, Flora, I know you're so jealous of our amazing happiness but I would have thought you could have spared a thought for penniless orphans, blah, blah, blah ... "'

'Can't you talk to Charlie on his own?'

'Oh God, no, he's terrified of me now, like I'm suddenly about to cast my womanly wiles and try to ensnare him, like I *totally* didn't do last time. Gah.'

'Maybe it's Mure,' said Lorna. 'Maybe it's being on this island makes our love lives totally suck.'

'Has to be,' said Flora. 'Can we go drinking on a school night more? I mean, if you can pay ...'

'Seriously?'

'Yes,' said Flora. 'Yes. It really is that bad.'

Chapter Twenty-eight

Saif had had a flurry of checks. A woman had come to check the house, and as he looked at it through the eyes of a stranger – the first person apart from Mrs Laird who had stepped over the threshold since he'd moved in the previous year – he realised how unsuitable it was for children: still full of the last occupant's heavy dusty furniture; an ancient creaky fridge; no television.

He tried to cheer up the bedrooms upstairs by ordering some stencils from the mainland – boats and rocket ships, who knew what boys liked? But they made the old sofas with their antimacassars and the damp, sagging beds somehow look rather worse. The woman, however, simply checked a bunch of boxes on a form and said nothing either positive or negative. Evidently he had passed as he soon got an email requesting that he present himself at an address in Glasgow on a certain date – and to expect to book lodgings for a fort-night. His young, rather ditzy-seeming locum had arrived from the mainland, and tried to slip away without anyone noticing. He also tried to sleep at night, a million questions swirling around his head. It was not, he thought morosely, the best of times to fall out with his only friend, who also worked with small children every day. But his pride stopped him from calling her – he never called her anyway; their relationship was much more casual. To call her felt like it would be crossing a line. And his thoughts were so overwhelming he couldn't bring himself to do it.

At last the day came.

He tried to slip into Annie's Seaside Kitchen without attracting attention – which is actually quite difficult when you are a six-foot-one Middle-Eastern man on a small Scottish island where you are one of only two doctors.

'Hello, Dr Saif!' chorused Iona and Isla as he walked through the door. He looked nervously around for Flora – he was reasonably sure Lorna would have told her everything – but she wasn't out front yet. She was still finishing off some chive and herb focaccia out the back with the expectation that in today's mild but windy weather something that could be eaten by the harbourside but wouldn't blow away might be just the ticket, and trying to balance the accounts, which was an upsetting job at the best of times.

'Um ... can I have some kibbeh?' he said. He had absolutely no idea that Flora had finally got wise to the falafel catastrophe and put the hot spiced lamb sandwich on the menu purely for him. It had never even occurred to him. Now they had become instantly wildly popular in the village and were beginning to be seen as quite the speciality, excellent lamb being something Mure had no shortage of.

'Of course!'

The bell tinged, and old Mrs Kennedy and Mrs Blair came in together, quite flustered.

'That whale is back! Look! It's not safe!'

'It'll block the ferry.'

'Flora, you need to do something!'

'No, I don't,' said Flora immediately.

Iona immediately grabbed her phone.

'I'm going to stick it on my Insta.'

'It always just looks like a blob,' said Isla.

'Well, I'll zoom in then. Whale selfie.'

'It's not a whale,' said Mrs Kennedy seriously.

'Okay, well why did you just say, "The whale is back"?' said Iona petulantly, shuffling with the camera on her phone.

'It's a narwhal,' she said. 'It's very wise, very rare, very beautiful, and absolutely is going to overwhelm this entire island before they sort it out.'

'What do you mean?' Saif couldn't help himself asking.

'Oh hi, Saif. Now, I really am having a terrible bit of trouble with my ...'

Saif was used to this kind of thing and brushed it off.

'Make an appointment with Jeannie ... I mean, why will we be overwhelmed?'

'Tourists,' tutted Mrs Kennedy, as if tourism wasn't the lifeblood of absolutely everything they did. 'Everyone wants to see one. Then the authorities will want to tow it away. Then the Greenpeace campaigners will turn up.'

'What do they want with it?'

'They don't know either. I think they just like their

pictures being taken next to it. Flora, just go talk to it.'

'It's not like that!' said Flora. 'I'm not a seal! And you're being . . . seal-ist!'

'All the women in your family can talk to whales.'

'Is this true?' said Saif.

'Yes, Man of Science, it is,' said Flora, rolling her eyes. 'Do you want coffee?'

'Yes please.'

Flora passed him his customary four sugars. 'I need to catch the ferry,' said Saif. Flora blinked. She wanted to ask why but didn't dare.

'The ferry won't go if it's in its way,' said Mrs Blair.

'I am trapped,' said Saif, trying to sound casual but actually panicking. His meeting in Glasgow was at 4.30. He had to make this ferry – he had to – and it had to be on time. He hadn't slept a wink. He had spoken constantly out loud to Amena as if she were there, but he'd felt stupider than ever. He was terrified. He wished Lorna and he were still friends, that she could come with him; he knew what she was like with children. But of course she didn't speak Arabic and the children would be even more confused, and, no, that was a terrible idea too. Oh God, why couldn't they have found his wife?

But no. This was his to do alone. But on what should be the happiest, most amazing day of his life – the day he had dreamed and dreamed would come when his babies would be returned to him – he was filled with terror and foreboding. If he said the wrong thing, would they refuse to let him take them? Would they think they'd been radicalised? Surely not – they were only little.

As a rule, he tried to avoid the sensationalist headlines – most people on Mure read the local news and little else. The passing crazes of Edinburgh and Westminster and Washington meant little to people whose lives were measured by the changes in the weather and the length of the days, not Twitter and politics and shouting on television debates.

But still, he knew it was out there: ugly, ill feeling that infected people whether they wanted it to or not; every terrible tragedy; every spitting, postulating right-wing and left-wing and all sorts of crazy given air time. He just kept his head down, tried to do his job as well as he was able. And of course, as people got to know him they knew what was more or less intrinsic to human beings: everyone was pretty much all right, just bumbling along trying to make the best of it like everybody else, although he disliked it when people felt the urge to point out to him that he was all right, you know? Because he knew it meant 'for one of them', however kindly said.

He accepted his coffee and bade everyone a good morning.

'Why are you going to the mainland?' said Mrs Blair suspiciously. She hadn't been to the mainland since her daughter had married an Aviemore snowboarder, and, well, look how *that* had all turned out. It had confirmed to her absolutely that going off the island was pretty much a bad idea, and why would anybody have to, seeing as everything anyone could ever possibly want was here, in her opinion?

Saif hadn't thought about people asking him this, although he had a brief moment of relief that she didn't know already.

'Um, bit of shopping?' he tried vainly. It was a reason he'd heard from people before, which was specific enough to give a reason and vague enough to discourage speculation, so hopefully it would do. It would be all round the village by nightfall that he was some kind of crazed shopaholic, but there wasn't very much he could do about that. Flora didn't catch his eye.

Mrs Blair nodded. 'Well, be careful on that mainland,' she said. 'It's not all it's cracked up to be.'

'Thank you,' said Saif.

By the time he reached the harbour and nodded to the other passengers – there were more than usual as the flight had been cancelled – the narwhal had, he assumed, moved on. There was no hold-up and soon the mate was unwinding the thick rope from the harbourside, and the pastel-coloured houses of Mure, jolly and sparkling in the windy sunlight, started to recede from view. The water grew choppier and the puttering noise of the boat tilted them up and down in a way that reminded Saif unpleasantly of another journey across the sea – memories of which faded into dimmer images in the daytime but were never terribly far from him in dreams that were filled with the weeping women and, somehow worse, the silent children who had learned how to stay very quiet and still as their world was torn apart around them. He remembered the rough shouting of the smugglers, who would send a swift kick to those they didn't think were moving fast enough, and the freezing cold of the waves – he had never known such cold as they broke over the side – and the strong smell of cheap diesel infiltrating everything, even over the unwashed bodies and fear of the people crammed together inside. It had been a glimpse of hell.

Saif shut his eyes briefly and tried to dispel the memories and focus on the task ahead. His heart was glad, but still so fearful. He wished ... Oh, how he wished Amena was there. He imagined – let himself imagine briefly as he stood with his hands gripping the railing far too hard – walking into a small windowless room, like the many he had passed through as he'd been singled out and processed into the new world of the British Isles. He imagined himself walking through the door, and Amena there, her long hair shining, smiling at him, as beautiful as she'd been on their wedding day, her face lighting up, the boys as beautiful and loving as ever, saying, 'It's okay! It's okay! I took care of them! They're fine! And now we shall all be happy!'

His eyes shot open. This was a ridiculous fantasy and it would not help him in the slightest to deal with the real world: to deal with things as they were. Spray splashed up against the side of the boat. And then ... He squinted. Surely not. Surely ... Was he still dreaming? Was that ... ?

He stood alone, most of the other passengers having decided the wind was just a little too bracing so they had taken happy refuge in the cafeteria or the bar below. He stared straight ahead, but his brain couldn't make sense of what he was seeing. It was a whale – the whale he had seen, he was sure of it, the same deep belly, the white tinge to the skin, the same beautiful twist of curves, as if a child had drawn parabolas on the sky.

But there really was something different he could clearly

make out now. This whale had ... There was no denying it ... It had a horn, like a unicorn's. It was huge, twisted like barley sugar, and it protruded from the animal's mouth. It was the single strangest thing that Saif had ever seen: stranger than the phosphorescence on the Greek shore, or the scarab beetle his brother had once kept in a matchbox, marvelling over its jewel-like brilliance.

But this ... This must have beamed in from space, or from some other magical realm. It really was quite the most amazing thing Saif had ever seen, and it frolicked in the wake of the big ferry as the water churned up behind it. Saif was worried it would get sucked underneath the great propellers, but it seemed perfectly happy, swimming under and over the bouncing wake, curling itself up and down.

Was this a symbol? A message, even, from Amena? Saif was not the holiest of men: he was a scientist and had been trained to be rational. But surely it would take a harder heart than his not to think it possible, as the great, impossible beast tossed in the sunlight glinting off the waves ... If wonderful, amazing things could happen ... Well ...

Meanwhile, five hundred miles south, in Liverpool, Colleen McNulty looked sadly at her packed lunch and wondered if there was any way to find out what was going on today. But she only sent out the letters after all. She was only a clerk. As soon as Ken was out of the room, disappearing for an overlong toilet break as he did every day at around 10 a.m. (it was, she sometimes mused, all the unpleasant bits of marriage without any of the nice parts), she reached down into her bag and double-checked the two little parcels – a stuffed bear and a fluffy dog she'd been unable to resist. She knew the boys were older, possibly too old for stuffed toys, but she couldn't think of anything else children might like. They were simply addressed to the doctor's office in Mure – no signature, just a little note saying, 'From a well-wisher'. She'd be in big trouble in the office if she was suspected of interacting with any of the unit's clientele in any way. She would slip out at lunchtime and go to the post office and hope that, in some tiny way, it might help, just a little.

Chapter Twenty-nine

The interview room was exactly as Saif had predicted. Two women were there waiting for him.

'Now,' said the obviously senior caseworker. She was slightly taller and thinner and better-dressed than other people, though not in a way you could necessarily put your finger on straightaway. She had high cheekbones and her hair was a short flat top, and Saif was impressed and a little intimidated all at once. 'I'm Neda Okonjo. Would you like to speak in English or Arabic?'

'English is fine,' said Saif. He had got so used to living his life in English, it felt like speaking Arabic again would be a challenge. Arabic was his old life; English was his new. Here, in this anonymous bunker somewhere on the outskirts of the huge grey city of Glasgow ... Here they were about to collide. 'Can I see them please?'

'I'm sorry,' said Neda. 'You understand we have to ... '

She introduced the other woman, who was a doctor, and

who took the swab. He obediently opened his mouth as she scraped around. He had sent a blood sample already; this was just to check that he was the same person the sample had come from.

'You realise it's just a formality.'

'Of course. And then I can see them . . . '

The two women exchanged a glance.

'We need to fully debrief you.'

'Of course . . . Are they . . . are they all right?'

'Be right back,' said the doctor, and Saif and Neda sat in pained silence, Saif staring into space, Neda tapping on her phone. Presently the doctor returned, and nodded gently at Neda.

'Good,' said Neda, leaning forward.

'Can I see them?'

Neda pushed the full notes across the table. Saif read them incredibly quickly, his heart racing. It was hard reading.

'You should know. When we found them . . . '

'My wife . . . ?'

'I am so sorry. We simply don't know.'

'She would never have abandoned them.'

'I realise that. The area they were found in . . . It was basically shredded. A bombsite. Anyone who could have fled had fled.'

'She would never have left them!' He scanned all the papers again. She wasn't mentioned at all.

'Please, Dr Hassan. Sir. Please keep calm. I'm not insinuating that for a second.' She frowned. 'You didn't have anyone you wanted to bring with you?'

Saif shook his head, terrified suddenly that if he showed displeasure or anger she would somehow prevent him from reuniting with his boys. 'I apologise.'

Neda nodded and went on. 'They were living with a group of other children . . . effectively feral . . . Some deserting soldiers helped them with food, found them things to eat, but there wasn't much.'

Saif shut his eyes.

'Ash . . . Ash, we believe, broke his foot at some point and it wasn't reset properly. We'll be looking into doing the procedure here before you leave.'

Tears immediately sprang to Saif's eyes at the idea of his baby hurt, limping, getting around on his wounded leg with no mum and no dad.

'I realise this is upsetting,' went on Neda. 'And Ibrahim. We have reason to believe he spent a lot of time with the soldiers. There's psychological help available – not as much as I'd like, I'm afraid. Austerity. But we will be here for you, as much as we can.'

Saif nodded, but he wasn't really listening. He needed to have his arms around them immediately. 'Can I . . . can I see them now, please?' he asked as calmly as he could.

Neda and the doctor looked at one another. They passed over several pieces of paper, all of which he signed.

'Follow me,' said Neda.

The second room, down a long corridor, had windows in it, and, Saif noticed through the window in the door, toys of all kinds. His heart felt like it would stop. He wanted to go to the bathroom, was slightly afraid he was going to be sick. Kindly, the doctor put her hand on his arm.

'It will be fine,' she said softly. 'It might take a while, but it will be all right.'

But Saif, blinded by the tears in his eyes, could hardly hear her as he blundered through the door, then stood there, trembling, blinking in the natural light, in the middle of the low-ceilinged room. Two thin boys, barely taller than the last time he had seen them nearly two years before, turned round, their huge eyes wide in pinched faces, both in terrible need of a haircut, and Ibrahim shouted loudly, and Ash whispered, tentatively and wonderingly . . .

'*Abba?*'

Chapter Thirty

Saif held his breath. Ibrahim had, after the first time saying his father's name, been silent. He had retreated to the corner table of toys, where he had been banging pegs into a wooden board with a toy hammer – a game far too tiny for a boy of ten, although he looked younger.

Ash, however, who was six now, wouldn't let his father go. He had shrieked and raced towards him and clambered onto his lap and refused to budge. The last time Saif had seen him, he had been a round-faced babyish angel of a boy, only just four, still with the folds of the baby he had been on his knees and elbows.

Now he was so thin it was heartbreaking; his eyes were huge in his face, his cheekbones hollow and his legs and arms like sticks. When Saif picked him up, he weighed about as much as the well-fed Mure four-year-olds he treated in his surgery. He frowned and looked at Neda, who glanced at her notes.

'They're both on high-calorie meal drinks as well as food,' she said. She read down further and smiled. 'Apparently neither of them like them.'

Saif buried his head in Ash's shoulder, so he couldn't see him cry. 'I'm so sorry,' he whispered in English so Ash wouldn't understand him. The child replied, 'Abba's back!' in Arabic, as if he'd been away for a day.

Ibrahim's head shot up at his father speaking this strange language, and his brow furrowed in a way that reminded Saif painfully of his mother. He indicated for him to come closer, and said, 'Come here, my darling boy,' in Arabic. But Ibrahim still regarded him warily.

'Don't worry,' said Neda quietly. 'This is all totally normal.'

'Stop talking the way they talk,' Ibrahim hissed quickly at Saif.

'My darling,' said Saif. He walked over and knelt down beside his boy. He put his arm around him. Ibrahim flinched at his touch, and he backed away.

'That is how we are going to speak from now on. It is not so difficult. You're very clever. You learned some already at school, remember?'

Ibrahim blinked. Of course, thought Saif. He hadn't been in school for so long. He thought of the report again. Hiding out with resistance soldiers. What he had seen ... He couldn't bear it.

'Have the people who speak English not been kind to you?' he asked. Ibrahim shrugged.

'They brought you home to me,' said Saif.

'This isn't home.'

176

'No,' said Saif. 'But you'll like where we're going.'

'Going home to Mama,' muttered Ash, his face still buried in his father's neck, even though Saif's beard tickled him. Saif closed his eyes.

'I keep telling him,' said Ibrahim, his face still cross. 'Mama is gone. Everyone is gone. Everything is gone.'

He hit the block in the children's game very hard with the hammer. Silence fell in the room.

Neda stepped forward. 'There are new homes,' she said. 'You will have a new home now. Tell them what it's like.'

'Well,' started Saif. 'It is very windy. It's fresh and blowy and sometimes you get blown right across the street.'

He could see Ash looking up at him, interested.

'And it is very old, and there are lots of green hills and . . . boats . . . and sheep and . . . Oh, you will like it, I'm sure. Lots of dogs!'

Both the boys stiffened. Saif immediately realised what a mistake he'd made. They knew about the border crossings, when the soldiers would appear, their snarling beasts sniffing vans and lorries, looking for stowaways: looking for problems. He realised suddenly how much he'd changed and even relaxed. The island felt so safe, so much a haven for him, that dogs no longer scared him, and he couldn't even remember how this had come about. He thought of Lorna's daft dog, Milou, who rushed up to him every morning when they were on the shore at the same time. He had definitely helped. Then he remembered that Lorna wasn't his friend any more and that God knew what was round the island by now. Then he thought, bitterly, none of this mattered. All that mattered now was in this room.

Mrs Cook peered in to where Lorna was, once again, working late.

'Don't stay too late!' she said. Lorna looked up. She'd just received an official confirmation from the refugee resettlement council. It wasn't a secret any more: the boys were on the school roll. She showed it without comment to Mrs Cook, who'd have Ibrahim in her class.

Sadie Cook read it slowly, then took off her glasses. 'You knew about this?'

At least someone knew she could keep a secret, Lorna thought. She nodded.

'Good God. I mean, this is going to be huge . . . Can they speak English?'

'Those Galbraith children can't speak English!' pointed out Lorna.

'Good God, yes,' said Sadie. 'They'd have to go some to be worse than that lot of ferals.'

'Well,' said Lorna. 'Quite.'

Sadie looked at the paper. 'And the mother?'

Lorna shook her head. 'No news.'

'Christ. It's awful. Just awful.' Even so, a slightly mischievous twitch played around her mouth. 'Oh my goodness, that poor man isn't going to know what hit him.'

Chapter Thirty-one

Over the next several days in Glasgow, there were numerous psychological evaluations, the beginnings of some English lessons and many, many forms to fill in and go over.

Neda was patient and useful throughout, and the doctor, whose name Saif never learned, was on hand to make sure the boys had their vaccinations and to build up red books for them – the British medical history they would need throughout their lives – as well as testing them for everything possible. They were malnourished, obviously: small for their size and underweight. They had internal parasites from eating God knows what, and lice, and Ash had his foot reset under a local anaesthetic. While he clung onto his father the entire time, he was so heartbreakingly quiet and brave Saif couldn't bear to think of what else he'd had to endure.

But apart from that, they were fine; there was no lasting damage, on the surface at least. Saif's graver nightmares, of lost limbs and head injuries, were not coming true.

Psychologically, things were quite different. Ash had not left Saif alone. Neda had counselled that it might not be a good idea to let him sleep in the same bed, but he had howled so piteously – and in the hotel room too – that Saif had given in, and the hot restless figure had tossed and turned next to him all night. It was like carrying about a small koala bear. Ibrahim, on the other hand, was distant and cold; not overtly aggressive, but sullen and wary. He point-blank refused to look at the English storybooks or repeat basic words. He would not touch his father, and he endured the vaccinations and endless blood tests with a stoic look on his face and a refusal to be comforted. Ash started to go the other way. It was as if he'd learned, belatedly, that if he cried he'd be rewarded with some attention or a sweet, which Saif was also very unsure about. But it must have been so long since he'd had any attention at all.

At the end of the first week, Neda somehow sourced a DVD of *Freej*, let one of the other charity workers babysit and took Saif out for coffee in a little Lebanese restaurant she knew in Glasgow.

'How are you doing?' she asked.

Saif shook his head and answered honestly. 'I haven't slept. I'm ... It's ... I mean ... I thought it would be like getting my boys back. These ... They've changed so much.'

Neda nodded. 'Don't worry,' she said gently. 'It will just take time. But it *will* take time. It won't happen fast. But kids ... they have a lot of resilience. They've been through a lot. Routine, good food, fresh air ... Plenty of that, and they'll start to heal. They need to be out of this centre, stop

180

being poked and prodded by grown-ups. They need to be around other kids.'

'But Ibrahim . . .'

'It's very common.' She smiled. 'If it helps, I've got a twelve-year-old, and he's like that all the time.'

Saif smiled. 'It does actually.' He played with the sugar bowl. 'I wish Amena were here.'

'You've heard nothing your end?'

Saif shook his head. 'Ibrahim must have been the last to see her . . . I mean, I haven't heard from my cousins, or anyone . . .'

Neda looked at him, so full of pain. 'You have no family left at all?'

Saif shrugged. Yes, he did, but they were fighters, and he never mentioned this to the authorities. 'Not really,' he said quietly.

Neda changed the subject. 'So you're going to be a single dad?'

He smiled. 'Yes, I suppose . . . There's a lady who helps out who said she'll babysit while I'm at the surgery, and they'll be at school and . . . It is a lot to take in.'

Neda glanced at her watch. 'Well,' she said. 'Don't forget to enjoy it.'

And Saif hadn't the faintest idea what she meant.

Chapter Thirty-two

Tentatively Saif took the boys out, shops on Mure that didn't sell bagpipes or whisky being rather thin on the ground. He kitted them out with big fleeces and waterproofs, which were comically large, and treated them to a burger, which turned out to be a terrible idea. Ibrahim remembered drinking cola with a group of soldiers and turned terrified, and Ash wouldn't let Saif put him down even to pick up the order, and everyone looked at them and someone tutted, and Ash started screaming and in the end Saif just left everything behind and scurried back to the refugee centre, his heart beating wildly, convinced that he wasn't up to it, that he couldn't possibly deal with the two traumatised little lads.

But Neda was perfectly stark about it: either he took responsibility for his boys or they would have to go into care, or, even worse, back. (This wasn't remotely true, but she was cross with Saif for being so scared of taking up his responsibilities and was trying to scare him straight.)

'I'll be up to visit very soon. Any questions, night or day, you ring me. Except for night, if you love me at all.'

And she smiled to show she forgave him for the disastrous outing.

'Look,' she said finally. 'You'll be fine. All over the world, mothers do this every day. Fathers do it every day. You'll be fine.'

And Saif, with a finally sleeping Ash clinging onto his arms, hoped she was right.

Meanwhile, he'd called Jeannie, the receptionist at the surgery. And, realising it was ridiculous not admitting what he was coming back with, and how it would be, he explained the situation and confessed everything.

Jeannie's shocked silence made him realise, with a start, that the news wasn't around the entire village at all. He'd just assumed Lorna and Flora would have told the world between them. Realising they had not, humbled him.

'Ah,' he said. Then added, 'Can you explain to everyone?'

'Of course!' said Jeannie, who would, Saif knew, be delighted to be the bearer of gossip, knowing, as she did, more about the health and medical history of every single person on Mure than anyone else and unable to breathe a word of it. 'Don't worry. I'll tell them not to bother you. Hang on, does the school know?'

'Of course,' said Saif. 'They're enrolled, ready to go.'

'And what about childcare?'

'Well, I'm their father.'

'Yes, but you'll be working ... You know school finishes before surgery, don't you? And you'll be on call still.'

Saif blinked. Why hadn't he thought of all this before?

He knew why. Because until he'd held them in his arms, he couldn't let himself believe that they were real.

'Could you ...?'

He could hear the smile in Jeannie's voice.

'Let me ask around. Mrs Laird will have some hours for you. She's very fond of you, you know. There'll be plenty of help. Oh, Saif, this is wonderful. Such wonderful news. Lorna must be delighted.'

'Why?' said Saif instantly.

'Well, you know ... to fill up the school, of course!'

'Oh yes, of course.'

'How are things?' said Jeannie, changing the subject. 'I can't imagine. You must ... Oh, you must be so happy.'

Saif glanced around their little room at the cheap hotel. Ibrahim was in the corner, furiously playing a war game on the iPad Saif had thought at the time would be a good thing to buy him and was already deeply regretting. Ash was sitting staring at nothing, his arm tight around Saif's ankles, twisting a lock of his hair around his finger over and over again.

'Oh, it's, ahem, fine,' he said.

'Must be hard for them.'

Saif couldn't say it was hard for all of them. So he simply thanked her profoundly and hung up the phone. Ibrahim was still refusing to speak English and said he didn't have to go to school – school was for losers, for people who didn't trust in God to see them through – and Saif had absolutely no idea

184

how he was going to win this one. Ibrahim had always been a sensitive child: curious and questioning. How he used to make them laugh with his complex questions about how the world worked, and his desire to get things figured out.

Now as he sat, obsessed with the game on his lap, Saif wondered what answers he'd found out there on his own, tossed on the seas of a war.

He had thought the overnight ferry might be a fun treat for them. Once again, of course, he had thought wrong.

They had said goodbye to Neda, Ash clinging to her and sobbing like his heart would break, which made nobody feel at ease, and Ibrahim shrugging as if he didn't care, which was equally bad. They both balked at the boat, even though they'd been flown to Britain originally. They were fearful of the way it bucked and rolled; a swell had risen up and the crossing was difficult. Ash was sick sporadically and Saif ended up spending half the night with him bent over the toilet; Ibrahim refused to glance up from his iPad, which Saif made a promise to himself to get rid of as soon as was humanly and psychologically possible, and by the time they finally got in sight of Mure, Saif was incredibly anxious about the days and weeks and months ahead.

Would they be accepted? How on earth would they learn English? How would he peel Ash off him every day? How would he manage to work too? – and there was absolutely no way he couldn't work; that was the condition of his visa. How could he mother two motherless boys?

Saif had felt powerless before: in the war; on his long

journey. But he had never felt quite so low as this, and the weather mimicked his mood, black clouds glowering down over the top of Mure. There was a crack of thunder and Ash screamed and hid his face up his father's jumper. Even Ibrahim notably tightened his grip on the video game.

'It's just thunder,' said Saif. 'Come on, let's go up on deck and take a look at your new home.'

Up on deck it was freezing, incredible for April, with winds blowing straight down from the Arctic, screaming across the sea. Bouncing raindrops mixed with the high spray from the huge arching waves; vast seagulls screeched round the port. Ash immediately burst into tears. Ibrahim stared at his feet, sulkily refusing to look at the view.

'So, this is going to be your new home,' said Saif, trying to put on a cheerful face although he hadn't slept properly now for weeks. 'See the jolly houses on the front? All different colours? And round the harbour there's a beach that goes on for so long people call it the Endless Beach! And in the summer there's a festival down on the beach! And all the children come and celebrate the Vikings and . . . '

But neither were listening. As the CalMac made monstrous noises going into reverse, Ash was sobbing his heart out and Ibrahim simply turned round and re-entered the body of the ship, and Saif had to run and get him back before he got lost, even though the boy shook him off as soon as he got there.

The amount of luggage that both the lads had was pitiful, even with the new clothes he'd bought in Glasgow. They were two lost souls, washed up here, and Saif was as scared as he'd ever been in his life as the little, terrified, broken family disembarked the large boat into the freezing grey morning of Mure.

Saif was busy trying to carry all the bags and Ash at the same time, and he didn't look up until they'd fought the wind to the end of the jetty, past the terminal building and towards the car park. Then he did look up and saw them.

Lined up, frozen and wriggling, along with a large number of townspeople – particularly the older ones, who always liked to see anything that was going on – was Lorna, wearing a huge anorak, with a group of her schoolchildren. As soon as they saw them, the little ones waved wildly and she ordered them to lift up the sign she'd had made, painstakingly and probably, she thought, only being able to get what she could from the internet, entirely wrong.

WELCOME, ASH AND IBRAHIM.

مرحباً آش و إبراهيم

Saif prodded the boys to look. Ash blinked, and Saif remembered that although he was six, he hadn't yet been to school or learned to read. It was perfect that there were

187

only two classes in the school here: he could be in with the little ones, starting from the very beginning, even though he would be eighteen months older than many of them. He was, though, about the same height.

Ibrahim, on the other hand, looked up, and Saif saw the first glint of hope in his eyes since he'd arrived.

'They speak Arabic?' he asked, his expression desperate. Saif winced.

'No,' he said. 'We speak English now.' He repeated it, as gently as he was able, in English, just as Lorna raised her arms, and the children started to sing the Arabic alphabet song, quite dreadfully.

At this, Ash lifted his head from his father's jacket and turned to watch in amazement as they sang a song even he knew.

Saif tried to smile. He knew – and could see from Lorna's anxious face – that they were trying the best they possibly could. And when they came to an end, he and the other adults who'd gathered round to watch clapped as hard as they could.

Lorna looked up at him with a hopeful expression on her face, and Saif immediately forgot their row, or any disagreement they had had. How on earth could he not have realised that it would be far better to tell the people here about this, the hardest challenge of his life? Why did he think they would stand and point? His own people would have welcomed him and helped look after him and his family when things had gone badly wrong. What made him think the people here would be any different?

'Thank you,' he said.

'بالحب و السعادة,' said Lorna.

Saif looked up, surprised. 'You speak Arabic now?'

'قليلاً,' she replied. 'I'm trying to learn.'

Then she blushed, and did not want to betray how she had done little with her evenings since she'd heard the boys were coming other than swotting up and being addicted to Babbel, which was better than being addicted to watching Netflix, although it still, she did not like to reflect, left her sitting alone in her late father's house night after night as her youth slipped away.

Flora came running down to the jetty as the friendly policeman, Clark, came up and seriously shook Ibrahim's hand (Ash wouldn't turn round) and beamed kindly in the absence of having anything to say. Flora had a large care box of food, including as much baklava as she'd been able to put together. And Saif took it and wondered, standing there in the howling gale, overwhelmingly grateful, whether this could possibly, possibly be enough.

Chapter Thirty-three

The storm had passed in a flash, as weather so often did in the high islands, and a glorious afternoon had arrived from nowhere. Fintan was rushing to the airport. He knew Colton didn't need picking up – one of his staff could drive him – but he didn't care.

He hadn't seen the same thing at Charlie and Jan's wedding as Flora had at all. He'd seen happiness and the amazing sight of the entire community there, celebrating together. Since his mother had died, he'd felt so frustrated living on the island, doing the same thing day in and day out. Meeting Colton had changed all that so much; he saw things now through Colton's eyes. He appreciated more and more the beauty of the landscape, the peace and tranquillity they found there, the privacy and peace and quiet of mind. He saw what Colton saw. And he loved his clever, mercurial boyfriend more than ever.

Colton beamed as he got down from the plane. He

looked thin and a bit overtanned. The US always did that to him. 'Oh *God*, I wanna kiss the ground,' he said. 'You know, if you ever don't come and meet me, like one tiny time, I'm going to reckon we're in real trouble.'

Fintan kissed him. 'Then it'll never happen,' he promised. 'How was New York?'

Colton frowned. 'I think I have a very depressed lawyer. On the other hand, that makes him a highly overworked and busy lawyer, so in that sense it's not going so badly.'

'Ugh,' said Fintan. 'Flora is doing nothing but mope around too.'

'Honestly,' said Colton, with the happy confidence of someone who thinks other people's emotional problems will never happen to them, 'I don't know why they just don't figure it out.'

Fintan smiled happily.

'Seriously. My sister is a pain in the arse, but she's not that bad really.'

Colton sighed. He knew he was partly the cause of Joel's unhappiness, and that he was about to make a lot of other people unhappy too with what he was proposing. But he wasn't going to think about that right now. When it came to Joel and Flora . . . well. He had dated a lot of different people down the years, and had come to some conclusions: one, that there was no single person for everyone; and two, if you found someone you were crazy about, who liked you in return, you were the luckiest goddam son of a bitch in the world. He'd spent plenty of time in love with people who only saw him as a friend, or were in denial about their own sexuality and feelings, or were simply wrong place wrong time.

Now he was in his mid-forties, he knew: waiting for what you wanted, waiting for something perfect, was a disaster. It would never work. You had to jump. If you jumped and it went wrong, well, that was that. You could fix it. But if you wouldn't commit, wouldn't settle, kept waiting for the next thing, the thing that would take absolutely no effort, that would be incredibly easy. Well. That was not going to happen.

Fintan had made a meal, but Colton shook his head. 'Neh,' he said. 'I'm not hungry. I think I want to stretch my legs, shake off my jet lag, rebalance my melatonin, you know?'

Fintan did not know, as he rarely went anywhere, but he nodded regardless. 'Sure,' he said.

'Let's walk one of those stray dogs you always have,' said Colton.

'They're not strays!' said Fintan. 'They're loyal working dogs! Who happen to have a lot of freedom.'

This was true. Bramble was in the habit of ambling down the high street to go and visit the Seaside Kitchen from time to time. Residents and visitors had got used to him marching down the street, and Hamish had trained him to pick up the paper and bring it back to the farmhouse, so everyone was happy with the arrangement – except for Bramble, who smelled all sorts of awesome things around Flora, but was never given any of them. All the cuddles he got en route kind of made up for it, but not entirely. However, he was a wise dog, and lived permanently in hope.

'Whatever,' said Colton. He was just so happy, so pleased

to be back on the island again, and it made Fintan happy just to look at him.

'So, apart from your miserable lawyer, how was New York?'

'Shithole,' said Colton. 'Too hot and sticky and I hated it. Can't breathe there. LA was even worse.'

'I brought you something.'

'Is it cheese?'

'Colton!' said Fintan. 'Shut up!'

'I love your cheese,' said Colton. 'I'm just saying.'

There was a silence as they headed automatically through the town to park up at the Endless.

'So,' said Colton.

'It's not cheese!'

'Okay, so what is it?'

'I forgot it,' said Fintan sullenly.

Colton sniffed in the car.

'Stop it.'

'It's just ... it smells a bit like ...'

'This car always smells like cheese.'

'Well, that's true. You could still surprise me. Soft cheese? Blue? Hard?'

'Shut up!'

'Because I got something quite hard for you ...'

They got out of the car, grinning, and sure enough, there was Bramble, trotting up the high street, the newspaper between his teeth.

'Good timing,' said Fintan, patting him and retrieving it.

'He maybe smelled the new cheese,' said Colton.

'Shut up about cheese!'

They set out. It was evening, but the sky still looked like a studio set: a blue that faded to white, or rather, to a colour you couldn't quite put your finger on, a little like Flora's hair, something that faded into itself, that was hard to look at.

Near the harbourside, the beach was busy with brave toddlers paddling in the shallow freezing water, little crab-catchers with their nets and fishermen on the jetty. (There weren't so many fish close in to shore; it was more of an excuse to get out of the house on a fine evening, and chat to their companions and share a nip or two in friendly silence than a genuine activity.)

But as they walked on, the weather changed: the sun swept out again and they both took off their shoes, letting their feet sink into the soft, warming sand, the crowds enjoying the beauty of the evening fall behind them and, sheltered from the wind by the rock behind, they felt the sun on their necks and the soothing noise of the waves and little more.

After a few hundred metres, Colton stopped, a serious look on his face.

'*Okay*,' said Fintan. 'Okay, it was cheese. Sorry.'

Colton shook his head. 'I don't need any gifts from you,' he said, rubbing his greying goatee.

'I know,' said Fintan stubbornly. 'That's why I wanted to give you something anyway. Nobody ever does. They just assume you have everything.'

Colton blinked, surprised. It was true. In his life, Fintan was practically the only person who as much as bought him a drink. He was just so used to paying all the bills it hadn't even occurred to him. He smiled to himself. If he'd had a moment's doubt, it had just been assuaged.

He glanced around. Some sea peeries were circling, far out over the waves, and a heron was lifting off from the rocks. Apart from that, they were completely unobserved, at the far end of the Endless Beach. It was a perfect evening. Colton held his breath and it felt for a second that everything except the waves was still – everything in the entire world. Time was not moving on, the world was standing in place and nothing had changed or ever would, which meant that either you could think that nothing was particularly impor-tant – or everything was.

Colton dropped down on one knee.

Fintan's mouth dropped open.

'What . . . what are you doing?' he said, glancing round in case anyone was behind them. Colton suddenly felt a bolt of fear. Had he completely misjudged the situation? Fintan had spoken about men in the past, but nothing remotely serious; he hadn't even come out until last year. Was it possible that he was just practice for the younger man? Before he moved on? He started to panic. Colton was not traditionally one of life's panickers.

Fintan was still staring at him. Then, thank God, to the mournful calling of the peerie above, he bit his lip, and tried to stop a smile of pure delight spreading across his face.

'Fintan MacKenzie,' Colton said slowly. 'I have never done this before, and seriously I never want to do it again as I am getting old and my knees can't really take it, and the sand is actually quite wet when you get down here.'

Fintan's hand had flown to his mouth.

'But I can't imagine being happier with anyone, anywhere on earth, than I am with you. And your . . .'

Bramble thought they were playing a game. He came and sat down next to Colton on the sand and was now pawing him, thinking he was going to throw something for him. Colton giggled. 'Stop it, Bramble!'

Bramble threw his paws over his arms.

'Aw, for goodness' sake, Bramble. I don't want to marry *you*.'

Fintan gasped audibly.

'Shit, what did you think I was doing down here?' said Colton.

There was a pause.

'Is that it?' said Fintan finally.

'What do you mean?'

'My proposal. Is that it? You proposing to a dog instead of me?'

Bramble was now jumping up and down, licking Colton's face delightedly.

'Stop it!' said Colton. 'That's it, I'm getting up. Hang on, I can't get up until you give me an answer . . .'

'I haven't had a question!'

'This is much more uncomfortable than it looks when people do it in the movies.'

'Right, fine. Come on, Bramble,' said Fintan.

'No! Wait. Right. Okay. My darling. Baby. I . . . I adore you. Have done since the first time I met you, all sulky and a bit drunk.'

'That's very much me at my best,' said Fintan.

'And . . . and the rest of my life is going to be here. It is. I've decided. I've been, hell, everywhere. And nowhere is better than this. Fact. I want to be here, I want to be with you, and time . . . time. Well . . . ' He winced. 'It's always later than you think.'

Fintan smiled down at him. Bramble let his tongue loll out and panted from his exertions. Colton wobbled.

'FINTAN! FOR FUCK'S SAKE!'

'Okay, okay, okay. Yes! YES!'

Chapter Thirty-four

No sleep. Endless work. Nothing from Flora. Nothing from Colton except more work, of the worst kind.

The hotel was bearing down on him oppressively, and he no longer felt he could call Mark ever since both he and Marsha had made such a massive point about how much they adored Flora, of course, and how much they felt this girl was the one for him and how he should settle down and so on and so forth. So he cut himself off from that.

He exercised relentlessly, which normally worked to quell his restlessness, but pounding the city sidewalks for hours didn't help; didn't tire him out enough to sleep; didn't switch off the endless, clouded panic circling in his brain. He tried more work, but the more he did, the more Colton fed him. He tried drink and realised that in the past he would have gone to a bar and found an incredibly attractive woman and tried to screw it out of himself . . . but he didn't . . . He didn't want to do that any more. There was only one thing he wanted, only one person, and he couldn't seem to get through to her at all – couldn't seem to get it right. He was worried that she would want more and more and more, and all sorts of things that weren't in him to give.

And now that place – the place he thought he'd found, where the endless, self-doubting torment, the desperate running and fleeing wasn't necessary – now was that still there for him? Colton was about to change it irrevocably. Was he even still welcome there? He had no idea, truly, what was going on in Flora's head; he felt merely that he had been locked out of paradise, that Flora's careful, non-committal chats echoed precisely the language he had been used to all his life, when a well-meaning but nonetheless determined social worker had explained, yet again, why he wasn't welcome at this place, that they would try and find somewhere else for him.

He went to the balcony. The heat and noise of the city rose up to meet him. Christ, he hated it here. He hated it. He wanted to be cool, and quiet, and walking a long beach, and smelling the freshest of sea wind, just letting the air blow out every cobweb in his head. No. They weren't cobwebs. They were more like twisted snakes, coiled around the inside of his brain, squeezing tighter and tighter, and if Flora knew ... If she only knew, if she got close enough, if she suspected what was beneath the carapace of him; what it contained ... It was a writhing, choking mass of slithering monsters that tightened every synapse, the great coiling insides of him that he could conceal with a smart suit; with a charming manner; with a fit body; with spending money; with everything like that. For as long as that worked.

He couldn't risk letting her get closer. But if he didn't, he would lose everything. And Colton was taking a sledgehammer to it all.

His head hurt, as if the monsters in there were trying to burst out, trying to escape. He couldn't ... If he ever let them out, if he ever did, he worried that he would start to scream and never, ever be able to stop.

He staggered along the balcony, peered over the top and stared down to the ground. The suite wasn't on the street side; it simply led down to the roof of another building.

Why was it so fucking hot? Hot everywhere. He'd turned on the air conditioning, but then he'd started to shiver uncontrollably. He didn't know how long he'd been in this room, in this hotel. His brain was cloudy. None of his clothes fitted; he didn't know what the hell was wrong with everyone. He couldn't remember the last time he'd eaten. He blinked; sweat was dripping down his forehead. He staggered forward again.

➤ ➤

Flora was closing the Seaside Kitchen and had dismissed the girls and was making Lorna a cappuccino. 'This we can afford,' she said. 'Well done today.'

'Thanks,' said Lorna, blushing. 'Was he pleased? He was hard to read. I think he was pleased.'

'I can't believe you studied Arabic for a month.'

Lorna blushed more. 'It's a beautiful language.'

'You're a dark horse.'

'You're not. God, but those boys are tiny.' Lorna sighed. 'He's going to need a lot of help.'

Flora gave her a look. '*Sexy* help?'

'Oh Christ, of course not,' Lorna said. 'Trust me, I've given up in that department. Can you imagine? Not in a million years.'

'Things that shouldn't happen in a million years do actually happen, you know,' said Flora, licking the foam off the cappuccinos she'd made them. 'I mean, look at this place.'

They looked around at the lovely painted homely café.

Lorna smiled. 'True. But I think he has quite enough on his plate, and I'm hardly going to impinge upon his image of his missing and perfect wife, am I? Anyway, it's inappropriate. I'm going to be looking after his boys. Christ. That's a job ahead. Poor wee mites, they looked miserable. It would be disgusting weather this morning.'

'I know. Want me to send up some buns tomorrow?'

'Nothing in the budget,' said Lorna gloomily.

'Nothing in the charity fund,' said Flora equally gloomily. 'Jan takes it all.'

'Any news from Joel?'

'Um, I'm playing it cool.'

'*You?*'

Flora went pink. 'I know, I know. Shut up.'

'You literally pursued him for four years . . .'

Flora ran her finger round the rim of her cup. 'Seriously, I'm desperate enough to try anything.'

Lorna nodded.

'And, by the way, you're *learning Arabic* . . .'

'To help the children,' said Lorna piously. 'So, you're giving him the cold shoulder . . .'

'Nothing . . .' Flora shook her head. 'Not a thing. I haven't heard from him at all.'

Lorna grimaced. That didn't sound good. 'I mean,' she said. 'You know what those friends of his told you in New York.'

'Yes,' said Flora, 'but they didn't say, "Keep on making a fool out of yourself. For ages and ages and ages."'

Lorna looked sympathetic but glanced at her watch. 'Sorry,' she said. 'I have to go. I have nine miles of marking.'

'I know,' said Flora. 'I've got accounts.'

'Isn't it great, being awesome women completely in control of our lives and destinies?' said Lorna, getting up and giving Flora a hug. 'Look,' she said. 'You love him. Put your cards on the table. If you want him, I don't think waiting is going to do it.'

'Me either,' said Flora. 'But what if he brushes me off and says he's too busy?'

Then she sat, staring at the telephone, pondering and weighing up what to do, without the faintest idea, not the slightest, about the tumult that was taking places thousands of miles away. She had a romantic notion, or had done in the past, that if you were with the person you truly loved, you would pick up on how they were feeling, 'tune in' to their vibes; even if they were far away, you could pick out a star or sense from a passing cloud how they were or when they were thinking of you.

There was every possibility, she now realised, that this was total and utter crap.

On the other hand, as she stared at it, her phone started to ring ...

Flora grabbed the phone and picked it up.

'Hello?' she said, registering with some disappointment as she did so that it was Fintan, not Joel.

'YAYYYYYY!' came a noisy roaring sound down the phone. It sounded battered and windy.

'Fintan? Where are you? Are you drunk?'

'No!' came the ecstatic voice. 'Actually, now you mention it, that sounds like a totally fabulous, fantastic idea. Let's go and get drunk!'

'Yes, doing my accounts always goes better when I'm drunk,' said Flora. 'What's up?'

'Tell her,' came Colton's unmistakably growly voice behind him.

'*What?*' said Flora.

'We're getting married!' screamed Fintan joyously down the phone.

Flora paused, only for the very briefest of milliseconds, before she screamed 'Yay!' down the phone too.

It wasn't fair, it really wasn't at all fair to be jealous of her brother for getting married first. She was fine about it. Great, in fact. She loved Fintan; she loved Colton; this was all brilliant. Brilliant. And she would be happy, she told herself. Plus, it really *was* a good excuse for not doing the accounts.

'That's wonderful!' she said. 'Who proposed?'

'The one with the grey hair,' said Colton. The phone was now obviously on speaker. 'Obviously. Come join us up at the Rock for some fizz.'

'What did Dad say?'

'He's the next call,' said Fintan. Flora bit her lip. He'd

called her first. Without Mum, he'd called her first. That meant so much.

'He'll be ...' She thought for a moment. 'Well. He'll handle it.'

'Do you think he'll walk me down the aisle?'

They both burst into fits of hysterical laughter.

'Oh, Fint,' said Flora suddenly. 'Oh, Mum would have loved it.'

The boys fell silent on the other end of the phone.

'Aye,' said Fintan. 'Reckon.'

'Oh my God,' said Flora. 'Who's going to break it to Agot? She'd better be flower girl.'

'Oh yes,' said Fintan. 'Come on, come on. I'll pick up some food from home. We'll get the fires lit up at the Rock. Come on.'

And that is how Flora didn't get around to phoning Joel until much, much later.

Joel hadn't realised he'd emptied the minibar: it just suddenly was empty, and he was staring at it, slightly dumbfounded. Everything seemed very off. He tried to remember when he'd last eaten, then realised he couldn't. He eyed a wobbly Toblerone but decided he couldn't face it. He looked at his phone. Nothing. Nobody to call, nobody to ... He looked at his computer. The words swam in front of his eyes. Christ, he was tired. He was just so damn tired. Of holding it together. Of doing well. Of needing nothing, and nobody.

And he didn't. He didn't need anybody. He got up, staggered to the terrace again, fell down. Perhaps he should go out. Perhaps he should see if they had any whisky downstairs. They had to have whisky, didn't they? In Mure they served the best whisky in the world … What was it called again? Something weird and Gaelic and unpronounceable and you sat round the fire and got cosy and mixed it with a tiny bit of water and the first time Flora had bought some for him he'd mentioned ice and she'd looked utterly horrified and …

The next thing Joel knew, he was back on the balcony. Perhaps he'd blacked out for a second. He didn't know where he was. He didn't know what was happening. Only that everything was too much.

The champagne cork popped and everyone cheered, their faces bright in the evening light after the sun had made its late appearance. A huge fire still crackled in the grate – you could always do with a bit of insurance on Mure. Everyone was laughing and Fintan was sitting on Colton's knee, occasionally glancing up at him as if in wonder that all of this had come to pass.

'Have you got a ring?'

Fintan nodded and leaned over. Flora gasped. It was exquisite: two bands of silver, between which was a carved metal design of little cogs slotted together. 'Like a butter churn,' said Fintan.

Flora shook her head. It was utterly beautiful, unique and absolutely them. 'It's lovely.'

'What did Joel say?' asked Colton lazily, who was not really listening to the MacKenzies' chatter. When they all were yapping en masse, he found the accent got thicker and became difficult to follow, but he rather liked this. He simply leaned back and let it all wash over him like birdsong – sipping whisky rather than champagne, the man he loved on his lap, the fire flickering in the fireplace, still light past nine o'clock – and felt that a happy life had nothing much more to offer.

Flora froze. You would have to have known her rather less well than her brothers not to notice. 'Um, I haven't . . . '

Innes frowned. 'Are you two . . . ?'

'Sssh,' said Fintan quickly.

'No,' said Flora. This was ridiculous. Of course she would phone him. They were normal people. If he was out in a bar or too busy to talk to her or . . .

Suddenly her heart started to race. This. This was a reckoning. She would call him. She would tell him the loveliest, happiest news that had happened to the MacKenzies in a long time. And if he was truly her boyfriend – a part of her family, her community – he would be delighted, thrilled, interested.

And if he was too busy, if he passed over it . . . Well. Then she would know.

She felt cold inside. But after the disastrous trip . . . There had to be limits. There did. She didn't need a perfectly designed engagement ring that cost a fortune. She didn't need a big wedding or a fancy declaration. But she needed to know where she stood. She needed to know she meant something.

She stood up, excused herself from the table, knowing full well the boys would watch her go then gossip about them. She couldn't think about that just now.

Outside it was colder than it looked. The sun was making a full high arc of the sky, the wide light the palest yellow, almost leached of all colour; the sea, unusually, as still as a millpond as far as the eye could see, a perfect flat calm. It was an utterly ravishing evening, and up here at the Rock, with its manicured gardens and walled terraces – with its red carpet leading down to the jetty where guests would arrive by boat – the fiery torches were lit, a merry path although it was not dark at all.

The air was heavy with the scent of the last of the spring bluebells, neatly serried in rows by the Rock's army of gardeners, the very last of the daffodils fading away.

Flora looked around, took in the beauty of the evening, terrified that everything was about to change so much and spoil and leave her. She thought of Joel, his beauty, his set face, his unexpected flashes of humour which, she now suspected, he had used all along to keep her from getting close. The sex.

Maybe. Maybe she could live like this. Maybe she could handle it. Being ignored. Undervalued. Left on her own for months on end. Waiting around for some crumbs from her lover's table. Or maybe she couldn't.

Joel was sitting down on the terrace when the phone rang, although he wasn't quite sure how. He'd been standing up, hadn't he? Trying to get cool? Or had he? Everything was quite jumbled in his brain.

At first, he didn't realise what was making the sound; his head was full of noises and everything sounded like

207

the scream of a phone, but it persisted and persisted then it stopped – did it? Or did he pass out? – and then it started again and then it stopped.

Flora stared out at the sea, furious. She wouldn't leave a message. This was too important. He would see it was her on the caller display, even if he was out. He was never more than two feet from his phone, not even at night when he used it as an alarm clock. He walked about with his life in the palm of his hand, wrapped in plastic. The phone was important to him. Whether she was was a different matter.

She hung up and phoned again, hung up and phoned again, realising this was bordering on craziness but so wound up and anxious and angry she no longer cared how she seemed or came across. If he thought she was some kind of disposable, cool, non-interested girl, well . . . she wasn't, and that was how it was.

She glanced back at the beautiful building of the Rock, tranquil in the evening light: the grey stone so comforting; the glories of the garden just beginning to come to fruition; the small group inside laughing convivially in the soft light. It looked so happy. She felt so on the outside looking in.

She dialled again. Dialled again. Last time, she promised herself. She would dial one last time.

Joel half-opened an eye. He felt like a shipwrecked man, clinging to a world that turned round and round and tipped him up and down again until he no longer knew which way was up. And still that persistent sound in his ears. He had to make it stop. He *had* to make it stop.

He grabbed the phone, which had skittered nearly to the very edge of the balcony. There was a gap between the glass protective wall and the floor. He was tempted to kick the phone over. See how it fell, first. See how it soared and twirled through the air; see if it was the right . . .

He squinted at it, realising he was seeing double, that he couldn't make sense any more of the words that were there. F . . . l . . .

'What?'

'Joel!'

'What is it?'

Flora was taken aback. 'Um. Does there have to be a reason?'

'No, of course not. Tell me . . . Is it nice there? Not too hot? Christ, it's fucking hot here . . .'

'Joel . . . I just wanted to call you with the news. Colton and Fintan got engaged! They're getting married.'

Flora waited anxiously for his reaction. There was a long pause, over thousands of miles. Then she heard a massive exhalation of breath.

'Of course they fucking are,' said Joel. And he hung up.

Flora slowly put down the phone. Enough. She stared out over the sea. Enough was enough now. She turned to go. She wouldn't say goodbye to the boys; their evident happiness was a little much for her right at the moment. She knew they'd be all right. In fact, better, she'd pop in on her dad in the morning and try and do some good. He hadn't wanted to come out that evening – he slept in the farmer's way, always had: 8 p.m. to bed, 4 a.m. rising. Not that she'd get much sleep tonight.

Bertie, who ran a boat around when they were at the Rock, was waiting at the jetty. He jumped up.

'Hello, Flores!' he said, going bright pink as always.

'Can you take me home, Bertie?'

'Aye, of course! Love to! Boat or car? Come on, take the boat. It's a lovely night!'

'Why not?' thought Flora. It was hardly like it mattered and the fresh air might help her get some sleep at least. So she nodded and followed him to the jetty.

Chapter Thirty-five

Joel realised he was in a mess. But he didn't know how to get out of it. Everything had come to a head suddenly, and he didn't know how to cope. He couldn't control his breathing.

Gulping, he felt a sudden skip in his heartbeat – a massive electrical jolt. He grabbed the phone like a lifeline. Before he knew what he'd done, he'd pressed the callback button, although in his confused, twirling state he wasn't sure why, or even whom he was calling. His breath came in great shuddering gasps.

There was no signal out at sea, and Flora found a queer sort of quiet and contentment staring out over the wide ocean, feeling alone and facing the world by herself. Whatever happened, she knew, she wasn't the same girl she'd been a year ago: timid, scared, upset to the point of paralysis by the death of her mother; angry at having to come back to the island.

Now, this was home, and despite its many inconveniences she loved it. She had a little business – well, okay, they were pretty much running on empty at the moment, but it was her business and she could manage. She was doing all right. She'd never be rich, but then she'd spent some time with rich people. She wasn't sure it made them remotely happy. And there wasn't that much point in having fancy dresses on Mure.

The worst feeling, she thought, was that she'd failed. She'd known Joel, she thought, as closely as anyone could know him. As close as anyone could get. And still she couldn't crack it. She couldn't get through; she couldn't fix him. Everyone had been right. He wasn't tameable, simply because he didn't know what it was to be tame. But she had tried her hardest. She had.

It wasn't until she got closer to shore, back into the range of Mure's single lone mobile phone mast, that she realised her phone was ringing. She'd taken the voicemail off when she'd left London, not wanting to be a slave to her phone any more.

If anyone had ever checked the records, they would see that it had rung 138 times.

Flora stared at it as Bertie looked at her, a hopeful expression in his eyes that turned to disappointment as she answered it. 'Joel?'

There was a short pause. Then just two words.

'Help me.'

Chapter Thirty-six

Flora burst through the door of the Harbour's Rest.

'I need to use the hotel phone and the computer,' she said. 'Sorry, the signal is just too shitty. It's an emergency.'

'It is,' said Inge-Britt as Flora scrolled desperately through the internet until she found a listing for the psychiatrist Mark Philippoussis in Manhattan and explained the situation to his receptionist, who patched her through. She remembered the room number and Mark got down there in record time, Marsha following on, plus a police officer in case they couldn't get into the room. Flora had also called the hotel management and caught the receptionist who was in love with Joel and who had, too, been increasingly concerned by his weight loss, his late nights, his odd hours and habits and the glazed look in his eye whenever she tried to flirt or say hello. She could not have been kinder or more helpful to Flora then, and Flora was half glad and half absolutely distraught that she wasn't there when they finally got through the door and found him, sitting on the balcony, looking over the edge, as if he wasn't sure where he was, even with the huge pinkening city spread beneath his feet.

Chapter Thirty-seven

'Well, fuck that, man.'

Flora couldn't help but be impressed. Having not really contemplated, beyond the buying of holidays and possibly a little flat one day, what money could do, it was quite incredible to watch Colton in action.

He was talking to Mark Philippoussis, or rather shouting at him.

'Let me talk to him!'

Mark was entirely calm about the whole thing. 'One of your staff appears to be suffering from nervous exhaustion,' he said politely, 'while also being tremendously drunk. I think the last thing I'm going to do is let you talk to him.'

'He's my employee and I have a duty of care and if I have to fly him back, I will.'

Flora went up. 'Please can I speak to them? Please?' She grabbed the phone and moved to another part of the hotel. 'Mark?'

'Flora? Is that you?'

'Yes ... What's happened?'

'Did you know he was working so hard?'

Flora gulped. 'He always does that.'

'I know. It looks like ... He's dropped a lot of weight, Flora. I think he's just exhausted. Did anything stressful happen to him at work?'

'He never talks to me about work.' Flora shot a look at Colton, who turned away.

'What about you two personally?'

Flora paused long enough for Mark to pick up on it.

'Listen, Flora. Why don't you let me and Marsha take him to our place? Let him sleep it off?'

'Then will you send him home, Mark?' said Flora anxiously.

'Do you think that would be the best thing for him?'

Flora wished she knew. 'Yes,' she said. 'Can I speak to him?'

'He's passed out, Flora.'

'Jesus,' said Flora. 'What is it? What's wrong with him?'

'I'll need to talk to him, but I would say panic attacks and overwork. I don't know what's made him so anxious; he's normally so controlled. As soon as he wakes up, I'll call you.'

'Are you taking him to hospital?'

'Not tonight.'

'Good,' said Flora, relieved. He'd sounded so ... so very desolate.

Colton snatched back the phone to make it very clear to Mark that he would pay for anything required and could have a jet on standby, but Mark was short with him and the call ended.

Flora sat by the window as, after ten, the evening finally began to darken, the moon at last to rise.

'Did you know something was wrong?' said Fintan gently, twisting the brand-new ring on his finger.

'I ... I just thought he was like that ...' She looked around, stricken. 'He got further and further away. But ... you know ... Men do that.'

Fintan nodded. 'I know.'

He placed a reassuring hand on Colton's knee, even as Colton stared outside as they sat and waited the night through for news.

Chapter Thirty-eight

Saif's boys hated his house, their new home. It was freezing cold and draughty. A flat handsome grey house made of expensive stone, it had beautiful outlooks, slightly out of the town.

But the previous owner had had little spare money for its upkeep, and the window frames were peeling and cracked, draughts blew in everywhere and the thick curtains Saif used to keep the light out during the long summer evenings were heavy with dust. It was cold and spooky, and as Saif looked around he wondered anew how this had never occurred to him before.

This house had only ever been a place to eat and sleep. He left at the crack of dawn, usually to walk the beach, and to hope and wait for his family; then he was busy at the surgery all day and on call most nights. Mrs Laird came in a couple of times a week to do for him, and she would leave him a casserole or a lasagne – he'd got used to her bland cuisine eventually; the children ate quickly and without comment – and then he'd just make some soup or eat at the Seaside Kitchen and have a sandwich in the evening. He barely thought about food at all.

Now, looking around, he realised how bleak the house really was, even with the pathetic stencils he'd bought to try and cheer things up. It had never been a family home, had never felt like one.

He felt even more the idiot. If he hadn't got so irrationally cross and silly with Lorna, she'd have helped him before to make up nice rooms for the boys – there was plenty of space in the house. All he needed to have done was to buy bright covers and curtains – or whatever it was boys liked. He felt sorry and ashamed.

'I'm scared, *Abba*.'

Ash was still clinging to him. He'd had his foot X-rayed and reset in Glasgow, but he was really meant to be walking on it to strengthen it. Instead, he still refused to be put down at all, not even for a moment.

'That's okay.'

'I sleep in your beb?'

Saif really wasn't in the mood for another night of being kicked in the head by a small boy in a plaster cast. On the other hand, what were his options? He well remembered the first night he'd spent here, freezing, alien, sobbing.

'Of course,' he said, putting on the lamps. 'Bed. It's pronounced "bed".'

'Bib?'

He looked at Ibrahim. 'Do you want to sleep with us too?'

Ibrahim shrugged. 'I don't care.'

Saif nodded. He knew this meant yes. 'Okay. Well, let's stay together tonight, okay? I'm sure the storm will have moved on tomorrow.'

He was not remotely sure about this at all.

His phone rang, and he cursed. All out-of-hours calls were still directed to the locum service, surely? Who could want him this late? He glanced down and saw it was Flora MacKenzie. That was strange.

'Hello?'

'Saif? It's Flora ... I'm so sorry to bother you.'

'That's all right, but ... Sorry. Is this medical?'

'Yes.'

'You know, I'm on ... It's the on-call doctor ... '

'I know, I know. I'm so sorry, Saif. But ... ' She explained the situation.

Saif nodded. 'That sounds like ... It sounds like a nervous breakdown, Flora.'

He could hear her swallow. 'He shouldn't stay there?'

'I don't know.' Saif thought about it carefully, even as Ash kept trying to pick his fingers from the phone. 'I think ... ' he said eventually. 'I think this kind of thing is best treated with care. And peace and quiet.'

'But can you treat it?'

'Yes. I can.'

There was a pause.

Chapter Thirty-nine

Joel was always very hazy on what happened next. He dimly remembered Mark asking him lots of questions, but wasn't too sure exactly how he'd answered them. Colton had organised a plane to bring him home, and Mark sobered him up with a large amount of coffee and a drip – the hotel was not unused to such scenarios.

'What do you want, Joel?'

And he had found that oddly funny, and then he was so exhausted and Mark's voice was so kind and soft and he just said, 'Can I go home?'

And he got on the plane, and that was the last thing he remembered.

Flora didn't sleep at all. She paced the Endless through the night when it didn't really get dark, just a kind of twilight at midnight, the sun immediately rising again. Colton and

Fintan dozed off together in armchairs, but Flora refused to rest all through the five hours the flight was in the air. It was a light and bright 4 a.m. when the tiny dot appeared in the wide white sky, slowly circling downwards, the only manmade object for miles, above the tin shed that housed the tiny airport. Sheila MacDuff emerged. She would normally be furious to be woken at this time, but was feeling rather pleased this morning because the reason was so big and gossip-worthy. Her husband, Patrick, who worked as air traffic controller and gift shop operator, waved from the little control tower as the plane made a perfect landing in the glimmering dawn.

Colton and Fintan woke up and came out with Flora to greet the flight. Flora leaned her head on Fintan's shoulder as the door opened on the tarmac and a thin, stooped figure, with Mark by his side, limped down the steps. Everyone watched Flora to see what she was going to do, but she just stepped forward, carefully, worried – as if he were fragile.

Mark's cheerful New York tones as he scanned the gravel and the windswept fields around the airfield broke the ice.

'Where the hell is this place? The moon?'

Joel was woozy and quiet in the Land Rover. Flora took his hand and he looked at her. 'I'm sorry about the fuss.'

She shook her head. 'Don't be ridiculous. This is Colton's fault for working you too hard.'

Colton, in front, was uncharacteristically subdued.

'Yeah,' he said, turning round. 'Yeah. I'm sorry. You can sue me if you like.' And he smiled weakly.

Joel didn't take the olive branch. Instead he stared at

Colton, his eyes burning. Flora noticed the look, but didn't understand it. It was like Joel hated him.

'You need sleep, man.'

They parked up at Joel's cottage at the Rock. Mark had a room down the hallway. Joel had never been so pleased to see anything in his life.

He walked in by himself. 'I'm not sick,' he said and turned around at the door. Colton was looking at him. 'Thanks,' Joel muttered. 'Thanks for getting me home.'

'You're welcome, man,' said Colton, and once again something passed between them. Joel had hardly looked at Flora at all.

She followed him into the bedroom. He looked up at her, and she was deeply troubled by how thin and haunted he appeared. How had she not noticed when she'd seen him? Why hadn't she questioned the evasiveness, the way he had stopped coming home?

They looked at each other. Then Flora moved into the beautiful bathroom, with its old claw-footed tub, and started running a very hot bath. Joel screwed up his face.

'Come on,' she said quietly, unbuttoning his shirt. 'Get in.'

And carefully, gently, she put him in the bath and climbed in behind him, and tenderly washed him and held him and kissed him gently and every time he started to woozily say something she would hush him and say tell me tomorrow, and he let her. Then he climbed into bed and was instantly asleep. She stood there, gazing at him, wondering what the hell she could do now, until, after five o'clock, she too became overwhelmed with exhaustion, and lay down beside him and drifted off to sleep.

Chapter Forty

Once again, Annie's Seaside Kitchen did not open on Monday morning. Mrs Cairns waddled down looking for her first cheese scone of the day (Saif had warned her about her weight many times, and she had looked at him and said, quite clearly, 'Doctor, I am seventy-four years old, my husband is dead, my children live in New Zealand and you are seriously telling me I can't have a cheese scone?' Saif had said uncomfortably, 'Madam, I think you can have one cheese scone but you cannot have four cheese scones,' and Mrs Cairns, who had, after huge initial reservations about whether the brown doctor was there to blow up the island, rather overestimating the island's political interest to ISIS as a target, had grown to like him and the way he gravely called her madam, and actually he was rather handsome when you came to think about it, a bit like Omar Sharif . . .) and she sighed heavily when she found it shut. The gaggle of her friends and relations, many of whom she had hated for murky reasons for almost half a century, joined her slowly as they pondered where they could go to discuss their latest ailments and who may or may not have died.

Charlie's face fell as he cheerily led his latest bunch of troubled youngsters off the boat for their early morning sausage roll. It had been a difficult crossing: the ones who weren't throwing up were, frankly, going bananas on the boat, charging about here and there, and the stewards, who knew him pretty well and were usually very tolerant, were raising eyebrows left, right and centre. He'd promised them all the best sausage rolls in the country if they'd behave, and now he was stuffed.

Isla and Iona had been absolutely delighted by the news of an unexpected day off, having not yet caught up with the gossip, and had decided to go sunbathing, even though it was fourteen degrees with a wind that felt like somebody was spinning a fan over some ice, but Isla had waited a very long time for her new bikini to arrive from the mainland and was absolutely not going to miss the opportunity to wear it.

Hillwalkers and holidaymakers, excited by the amazing TripAdvisor reviews (except for 'Very disappointing lack of Chinese food – one star' and 'Couldnt understand wot they was saying, theys shood speek English up here – one star') and in the mood for something delicious to set them off for ten hours' hard walking in goodness knows what weather, realised they were going to have to make do with whatever the supermarket felt like offering them, or the beer-smelling Harbour's Rest. They tried, and failed, to put a brave face on it, particularly the dragged-along hikers, there to make up the numbers but who were now clearly going to do nothing but moan all day. It was not working out very well for anyone.

If Flora could only have seen it, it would have cheered her up immeasurably to see how, in such a short time, the Seaside Kitchen had become such a mainstay of their little community.

But she couldn't.

The confusion in Joel's head as he awoke around ten-ish was hard to deal with. First, he had the mother of all hangovers. He also had absolutely no idea where the hell he was. He glanced around, his eyes scratchy and sore, his brain still furled up in cotton wool, muggy. What? What the hell had just happened? Argh, oh God, oh God, his head . . .

He tore to the bathroom and threw up. He looked at himself in the mirror; he barely recognised himself. Where the hell was he? What was this?

Finally, gradually, he pulled himself up, found a huge fluffy white towel and pulled it around himself. He was so light-headed he staggered against the doorframe. When was the last time he had eaten? He couldn't remember. Oh God, he felt awful.

It was only then, clutching the door, trying to work out what the hell had happened, that he caught sight of the room beyond, and his brain exploded.

Wasn't he in New York? His heart skipped in panic. The panorama in front of him . . .

His first thought was he had died. He had jumped – suddenly it scissored back into his brain: the balcony, the heat, the height. He clutched again at the doorframe, his head trying to focus on what he was seeing.

Instead of the bright reds and oranges of the New York sunset, ahead of him was a palette of washed-out pale greys: a huge glass window looking out onto a dawn that precisely reflected the room they were in, huge grey vistas, clouds and sea, soft white sands, pale flattened grass, deep blues. He blinked. And there, on the bed, stretched out, pale, her hair around her like sea grass . . .

And then he remembered. And he was so grateful he nearly burst into tears. Okay, his career might be in ruins . . .

But she was still here. The worst had not happened. He sat on the bed for a little while, making his breaths go in and out with hers. She shifted slightly in her sleep and he leaned over and kissed her on the forehead and headed out to blow the cobwebs away – to breathe the fresh air he had missed for so long.

Chapter Forty-one

Lorna turned up at school early and nervous. The news hadn't reached her about Joel yet; she was worried about their two new arrivals. The children wanted to sing their alphabet song again – they had, to be fair, spent an awful lot of time practising it – and it was a fine day, so Lorna decided to let them. Neda Okonjo had sent over the briefing notes on both the children, which she had to keep locked in a filing cabinet. Both gave her cause for concern. She'd had children from difficult circumstances before, of course – there were divorces on Mure like anywhere else, and Kelvin McLinton's father had fallen under the wheels of his tractor one awful stormy day.

But this was something she was worried she wasn't fully equipped to cope with. She'd read as much as she could online about dealing with post-trauma in children and infants. Much of it was reassuring – as she kept telling herself, as long as babies were loved and looked after, they possessed so much resilience. She reminded herself that her grandparents' generation had lived through evacuation and war. But this was a challenge she was desperate not to get wrong, for Saif, and for the boys themselves.

'Just do your best.' Neda had been cool, clear and reassuring on the phone. 'Nobody's going to expect perfection. Just keep to what they can do, and don't worry too much about their English – basically to get that they need to do the opposite of what we recommend for most children, and watch about six hours of TV a day. Just try and make sure the other children are as nice as possible, and let them draw lots of pictures. Did you know children's drawing is universal?'

Lorna did.

'Well. Appreciate that. Every neurotypical child has a way of building up the world through their hands. Let them do it and they'll slot right in with the rest of the class. And keep your Google Translate on.'

Lorna stood. She'd chosen a long skirt, hoping in some odd sense that she might look more like women they were used to seeing, although she didn't really know much about that at all, and she plastered another big smile on as she saw Saif arrive.

He greeted her, trying his best to smile in return. He looked exhausted. Lorna thought it suited him.

'I am so sorry,' he said. 'I had an emergency last night. They haven't had much sleep.'

Indeed, Ash was sleeping on his shoulder, having not quite woken up in the car. Ibrahim was trailing sullenly behind, the sleeves of his blazer hanging down past his fists, kicking the fronts of his new black shoes against the gravel.

'Hope it was okay,' said Lorna, and Saif figured he would leave her to find out for herself; he was on his way to the Rock now anyway.

He shook Ash awake, who instantly started to cry, then held both the boys close.

'It's just school,' he said firmly. 'Ash, you'll like it. They have lots of toys to play with and things to draw. Ibrahim, there'll be other boys to play with.'

Ibrahim shrugged.

'And I'll be back at lunchtime.'

They were starting with some half-days. If they had to come back to the surgery with him, they just would.

Ash set up his shrill, one-note yell again, and Saif tried not to let his irritation show too much.

'أهلاً بالمعلمة,' said Lorna. 'Come in and welcome.'

Saif looked at her. 'One year here and there was a fluent Arabic speaker all along,' he said with a half-smile.

She flushed. 'I'm terrible!'

'Your effort,' he said, 'is the biggest compliment and kindness anyone could do me ... I am sorry I ever ...'

She shook her head. No apology was needed between them. He nodded.

Then he indicated Ash, whom he had to peel off himself again.

'No, I really am sorry,' he said.

'Happens all the time,' said Lorna with a smile, and looking in Lorna's pretty freckled face, the warmth of her reassuring, slightly nervous smile, Saif felt his world stop spinning, just a little. He was not alone.

'لعب. Toys,' she said to Ash, who stopped screaming for

a second, then shook his head and started again. 'Well, we have toys.'

And, holding him to her as if he were a much younger child, and in direct contravention of about forty health and safety regulations, she took him inside, Ibrahim glancing sullenly at Saif before reluctantly trailing after her. Saif stood and stared in amazement that it had been, in the end, easier than he'd been expecting.

Flora awoke to an empty bed and a knock on the door. She blinked as it all came rushing back, and sat up. Jesus. What time was it? Where was he?

Where was he?

There was another knock on the door, and she jumped, startled. As she looked around, Joel appeared at the French windows that led to the garden, thin as a wraith, frightening her even more. He passed through the room without looking at her and opened the door to Saif.

'Excuse me!' said Flora, pulling up the covers.

She was horrified. Saif looked equally disconcerted. 'Ah,' he said. Flora rolled her eyes.

'Sorry,' said Joel.

'Shall I come back?'

'No, it's . . . ' started Joel.

'Actually, could you give us five minutes?' said Flora. 'You can get a coffee at the lodge?'

Saif nodded and beat a hasty retreat. Flora felt her heart in her mouth as Joel turned round.

'Um.' She cleared her throat. 'Hello.'

'Hey,' he said.

'How are you feeling this morning?'

'A hell of a lot better than I felt last night.'

She yawned and got out of bed and went towards him. 'What happened?'

Joel shrugged. 'I spoke to Mark. He says stress and panic attacks. Brought on from overwork.'

'Is that all?' She looked up at him.

'He doesn't think so.'

'And what do you think?'

'I think you look absolutely ravishing and we should tell Saif to stay away for a bit . . . '

Flora shook her head. 'That doesn't solve things.'

'It solves some . . . '

'JOEL!' shouted Flora. 'This is not the way! You were blind drunk and falling apart. Why? Okay,' she said. 'I think I'm going to have to hand this over to Saif and Mark. I'm here for you, Joel. But I'm not helping you. I'm not making you better. I'm making you exactly the same. I hoped . . . I hoped I'd be able to help, to do something for you. To be with you. But I can't.'

Joel stared, gutted, helpless, unable to move.

'I am here for you. But I am not doing you any good, Joel. And you are not doing me any good either. All I think about is you, and it's torpedoing my business and torpedoing my life and I can't . . . I can't do this to myself either . . . '

She found herself choking up.

'I'll be at the farmhouse. But I am here for you whenever you want me. Not for sex. Not just for sex. I am here when you are ready to be here with me. If you want me. Not Mure,

232

not a home, not an island, not some dream of a sea creature. Me. Just me.'

'Flora, this is ridiculous. It's fine. Everything's fine.'

'One doctor is standing outside this door with heavy medication and another doctor is waiting for you in the lodge,' said Flora. 'That is nobody's definition of fine. If it wasn't for Colton, you could have woken up this morning in a damn hospital.'

'If it wasn't for Colton, I wouldn't be in this mess in the first place.'

'He didn't make you work with a gun to your head.'

'He might as well have done.'

Flora walked up to him and gently stroked his face. 'I love you,' she said, quietly. She had never said this before, not to him, and she wasn't sure if she'd ever get a chance to say it again. She needed to know that she'd done it. Even if nothing happened from now on. Even if this really was it.

There it was. It hung in the air. The very last card she had to play.

He looked at her, stricken, unable to answer, his head desperately trying to make sense of the situation. She couldn't love him just because she felt sorry for him; he couldn't bear it. 'It's ... This is just a misunderstanding,' he said.

There was a very long silence after that.

'It is,' said Flora. 'It is, Joel. And the person who has misunderstood it is you.'

And she kissed him and turned to go. She picked her top up off the pillows where she'd left it the night before.

The pillow under her hand was soaking wet. Someone had been crying into it. She turned around and walked away, a pale ghost down the paths of the beautiful gardens of the Rock.

Chapter Forty-two

Saif came back in again, having taken the opportunity to call the school and check on the boys, but Lorna had had her hands full and hadn't answered, so he was full of trepidation.

He blinked again at Joel being up and about. It wasn't at all what he'd been expecting. He hadn't had much experience in mental health issues, and not as much time as he'd have liked that morning to catch up on the reading, but he wasn't expecting someone greeting him courteously and asking if he'd like more coffee. He focused on Joel's right hand. It was trembling, even as he put his other hand on it to try and make it stop.

'Do you know where you are?' said Saif gently.

'Does anyone?' said Joel, then shook his head. 'I'm fine. Sorry. I got very overstressed and . . . combusted. It was good of Colton to fly me home.'

'Now there are several options suggested in this case . . .

I think we should start you off on benzodiazepine and see how you react to that ...'

Joel held up his hands. 'Wait ... wait. I mean, there's nothing wrong with me. I had a bad night, that's all. Overworked.'

'That's right,' said Saif. 'You were also dehydrated and you're underweight. This doesn't seem to be a new issue for you.'

'I'm fine.'

Saif blinked. Usually he was trying to keep people off antidepressants. This wasn't one of those cases.

'Joel, there is no shame in asking for help if you need it. It's just an illness.'

'It's not,' said Joel. 'It's a natural response to an intolerable situation. Dammit.' He looked around the room. 'What else would you recommend if you weren't prescribing?'

Saif shrugged. 'Rest. A good diet. Peace and quiet. Gentle exercise.'

'Well, I'll get peace and quiet,' said Joel. 'Nobody's speaking to me.'

Saif nodded.

'And the food here is pretty good. If I can get my hands on some.'

'And you need to keep talking,' said Saif. 'Find someone to talk to.'

'Oh God,' said Joel.

There was another knock at the door. It was Mark.

'Jesus Christ, man, this place is stone-cold awesome,' he said. 'Have you even drunk the water? It doesn't taste like any water you've ever tasted. I don't think it is water. It's like

236

drinking cold light. And that air! It's like you get a detox just by walking about! Right. Let's get you sorted out.'

He shook Saif's hand. 'Did you get him to take anything?' Saif shook his head.

'Me neither.' Mark rolled his eyes. 'Ornery bastard. Thanks for trying, Doc. And you and I,' he went on, pointing to Joel, 'we have work to do. Like, a *lot*.'

'Good luck,' said Saif, and slipped out. He hadn't even started morning surgery yet, and he had the boys to pick up later. This was turning into a very challenging day.

Saif was late up the hill to the little school at lunchtime, which wasn't strictly speaking Mrs MacCreed's fault. In the normal scheme of things, he didn't mind at all when she went on about her bunions. She came as often as their appointment system would allow, told him cheery stories about her grandchildren and how well they were doing, brought him a pie and beamed at him as he gave her foot a cursory examination. Then he reissued her prescription. He'd told her it could be done automatically either at reception, or, even more simply, delivered straight to the pharmacy, but she had got a very hurt look on her face and he realised that he was simply part of Mrs MacCreed's social rounds. Her children were on the mainland and her husband was long in the ground – the men worked themselves to death; the women, small and wide and wiry, somehow carried on, bent into the wind, for an incredible length of time – and she was lonely, and he hadn't mentioned it again. Today the pie was venison. There was meant to be an official cull on the deer but it was best not to ask where it had come from. Saif had been astounded deer were on the island at all, until he was informed the Vikings had imported them a thousand years ago. He felt sometimes like he was walking through a world of long ago. This pleased him.

But there really was no hurrying Mrs MacCreed.

His long legs stretched out as he sprinted the last few yards up the hill. It didn't occur to him to drive; he very rarely drove on the island, only to night calls, and it wasn't until he was halfway up that he thought he should probably have brought the car so he wouldn't be carrying Ash down the hill, but it was too late.

Lorna watched him, standing with a silent, trembling Ash by her side and a sullen Ibrahim, fists balled, a little further away. They were going to have to talk, but first she had to squeeze out of her head the sight of his strong powerful body in motion. For many, many nights she had lain, pondering on whether his chest was smooth or hairy; wanting to trace the dark hairs on the back of his hand up through his cuffs; wondering about his golden skin and how it would contrast so strongly with her pale . . .

She shook herself. This was completely pointless and entirely inappropriate, particularly so considering she was holding one of his offspring by the hand. She flushed bright red. Saif, looking up, thought she was angry.

'I'm so sorry,' he said. 'I'm genuinely so sorry. I got held . . . '

She shook her head, feeling obscurely that she should be apologising to him for the disgusting pictures of him she'd plastered all over the inside of her head while standing next to his children. They didn't warn you about this in teacher training college.

'No, no, it doesn't matter. It's only lunchtime. We're not late.'

Saif bent down and opened his arms. Ash flew to him, dragging his bad foot behind him. Ibrahim stayed exactly where he was.

'So, uh, how did it go?' Saif asked desperately. It was a parental look Lorna recognised very well, although here it was slightly more important than usual. She bit her lip.

'Don't forget, it's just the start,' she said. 'Nobody expects this to be smooth straightaway.' She didn't know how to put it so she started with the positive. 'Ash mostly stayed very close to me.'

He hadn't unpeeled his fingers from her all morning. There were eleven children in the class; she still had to attempt to work with all of them. She had called in Seonaid MacPherson from the other class, who was eleven and big for her age, and she had managed to get Ash sat on her knee. Seonaid had very kindly gone through a baby book Lorna had dug up, pointing out 'cat', 'dog', 'ball' and so on and trying to get Ash to repeat the words. He hadn't repeated any of the words, but it was a start.

Ibrahim, on the other hand . . . She'd encouraged him to go play shinty with the other boys at playtime, and to her delight he had joined in, the boys making room for him willingly.

That had been until one of them, little Sandy Fairbairn, had tackled him, fairly gently, to take the ball, whereupon Ibrahim had leaped on top of him and started punching him hard in the face while screeching at him.

She had separated them immediately – shamefully, given her lack of Arabic, only able to yell, 'Stop, stop!' at Ibrahim – and comforted Sandy, who was more shocked than seriously hurt. She was dreading confronting his mother at home time. There was understanding and then there were cuts and bruises. And she wasn't enjoying this either.

Ibrahim was staring at the ground, refusing to meet his father's eyes.

'There was ... an incident,' she began, glancing at him. He looked up. He might not understand the words, but he knew she was dobbing him in, that much was clear, and his eyes burned with hatred.

Saif's face fell. Ibrahim looked frightened. Saif and Lorna shared a thought neither could voice. When they had been looked after by soldiers, how had that worked, exactly? What had the boys seen? Ibrahim had been two years in a world of war and violence and still didn't want to open up. Saif flashed back to Joel earlier that morning, all buttoned up. The boy became the man.

'I'll talk to the other child's mother,' said Lorna. 'But I'm afraid you'll have to make it clear ... '

She was worried she was sounding too teacher-like.

'Please,' she said. 'Please make it clear. They are both very welcome here. So welcome. But there are some things that could make it difficult, and violence is one of those things.'

Saif nodded. 'I understand. What they have been through ... '

'I know,' said Lorna. 'I realise that. Everyone does, I promise. But they can't hurt other children.'

Saif nodded again. 'I know. I know. I am sorry.'

Saif ended up taking the afternoon off – much to Jeannie's smirking lack of surprise, as she'd raised four kids and knew exactly what was going to happen – and he tried to bring lunch out into the garden, but the boys refused to eat the food and complained that it was too cold, even though the sun was shining. The boys were shivering and Saif realised in amazement how he'd got used to the weather. He ended up admitting defeat and opening the packs of fig rolls he'd stockpiled, which they ate silently. There had been three casseroles left on the doorstep, but he couldn't imagine them eating any of them. There was also a mystery package of teddy bears that was postmarked somewhere in England. Not a clue as to the sender, Saif had been entirely puzzled and considered throwing them away in case they were from racists or someone who wished them harm. However, Ash had caught sight of the parcel and had grabbed the small bear and was refusing to let it go, so he just had to apply Occam's razor and assume nobody had actually stuffed a bear with anthrax and sent it to a refugee child.

They sat back down inside.

'So,' he said tentatively. 'What do you think of school?'

'I stay with you, *Abba*,' said Ash decisively, from his place on Saif's knee. He was licking out the figs and discarding the biscuit. Saif wasn't sure this was as successful a weight-putting-on strategy as it might be.

'But you're a big boy now who goes to school!'

Ash shook his head.

'No. Me stay with *Abba*.'

It was as if he'd been frozen on the day his family disappeared: crystallised as a toddler. He held his son closer. He wanted to say, Of course. I will turn you back into a baby and we shall start over.

But he couldn't start over. The days had ticked relentlessly past – the months, the years – and they would never ever get those days back again. And there was no point wishing things could have been different. Everyone wished things could have been different.

He held the boy tight. 'You are my big boy,' he said and kissed him hard. 'And I will never ever leave you again except for school, I promise.'

The boy's little body relaxed a little.

'When Mama coming?' he said, sleepily.

Chapter Forty-three

'No!' Mark said, shooting out a hand. 'I mean, this place! It's awesome! It's just ... I mean ... I thought living in the middle of nowhere ... It sounded like Alcatraz or something. I could never get my head round it. But *this* place ...'

Joel half-smiled. The Rock was perched at the very northern tip of the Endless Beach, and they were walking down it, slowly. He still felt a little fragile.

'It's not always like this,' he said, as two tiny puffs of cloud chased each other across the sky, and the water lapped far up the beach. It was high tide, and it was as if someone had filled up a bath between Mure and the mainland.

'I mean it's just ... it's just so ... clean. So pure. Look at the water!'

Joel nodded. 'Yes.'

'I can see ... I can see why ... Shoot, is that a heron?'

Joel let him walk on some more.

'Joel. Forget me being your friend. I'm not your friend right now, you have to understand that?'

Joel looked up and sighed. 'I just need sleep.'

'You need a lot of things.' Mark glanced around. 'This is better than any yoga class I've ever been to,' he said, mostly to himself. 'I have to bring Marsha out here. She thinks she'll evaporate if she ever leaves the island of Manhattan, but I think this would surprise her.'

'So, what's going to happen?' said Joel.

Mark sighed, and took his glasses off for a moment. His eyes were light brown: clever and penetrating. He looked much more direct and sharp without the spectacles, which gave him a distracted professorial air. Joel wondered briefly how much he really needed them, or how much they let him set up a barrier of professional affability.

'Well,' said Mark. 'That's really up to you, isn't it?'

'Saif thinks I had a nervous breakdown.'

'I agree with him.'

Joel blinked. 'That's . . . Professionally I had some bad news.'

'Well, that will happen,' said Mark. 'Most people develop some resilience to that kind of thing.'

Joel nodded. 'You also made a series of major life changes.'

'I move about a lot.'

'And this move was meant to be the opposite of that.' Mark looked at him carefully. 'This isn't a placement, Joel. You're not being judged on whether you can stay.'

Joel halted. 'Of course I fucking am,' he said. 'By every single last person here. Who don't think I'm good enough for their local princess.'

'Can you be?'

'You want me to be better.'

'I want you to get better,' said Mark. 'That's not the same thing at all.'

They walked on again.

'Is this what you want, Joel?' said Mark. 'Because until you're sure and until you're sorted, I don't think you should be breaking that nice girl's heart if you're going to flee again.'

Joel sighed. Everything he had wanted Mure to be felt like it was falling down around his ears. 'You think I should leave her alone . . . '

'I just think you need a break from all distractions.'

'Flora's not a distraction.'

Mark didn't answer that. 'I think you just need some time to heal yourself first.'

Joel hated the neediness in his own voice as he said, 'Will you stay?'

'Everyone needs a holiday,' said Mark, beaming as the harbour came into view. 'Now, is there anywhere good to eat around here?'

'Oh God,' said Joel.

Chapter Forty-four

Almost imperceptibly, a routine developed. Joel was forced to stay in bed until late, even though he protested he was a poor sleeper. He'd be made to eat a huge breakfast, then he and Mark would play Scrabble or read quietly in the empty hotel, before taking huge long walks covering the length and breadth of the island via its many hidden byways and long quiet roads. Mark had bought a sturdy stick and a large straw hat and looked ridiculous but incredibly happy, and both men grew brown under the sun. He kept trying to persuade Marsha to come out, but she refused, pretending she didn't want to leave Manhattan. In fact, Manhattan in summer was sticky and unpleasant, but she intuited that what the two men were doing together was incredibly important, and she wanted to give them every chance to get on with it by themselves.

Mark kept in touch with Flora – and spent plenty of money in the Seaside Kitchen – but kept her and Joel apart.

Joel was either going to come round and face up to things, he figured, or he wasn't, and he wanted to spare Flora as much pain as possible.

In fact, Flora was already in pain. She threw herself into where she knew she was needed: work. Annie's Seaside Kitchen was in very real danger of going under, and Flora was trying to solve its money problems by working harder and longer hours. She wasn't going to add to anyone else's worries by discussing it, but it was constantly on her mind. The holiday crowd was in full swing now, and she spent all day feeding people freshly baked cakes and scones; pies and pasties; endless coffees and thank goodness it got hot enough for them to sell a lot of cold drinks, a major source of their mark-up. She also decided she needed something else to do; Lorna was incredibly busy with the school end of term, and everything had been so tough for everyone.

Then Fintan wanted an engagement party, and how could she deny them that?

'Family rates,' Fintan had said. 'You'll give most of the food for free. I don't want it to look to Colton like we'd take advantage.'

Flora hadn't answered that. She desperately needed to take advantage of Colton Rogers, but she saw Fintan's point.

'Everyone tries to rip him off,' explained Fintan. 'I want him to see ... to realise ... that's not why.' He blushed.

'I know,' said Flora, wincing slightly. But of course they could do it. Of course she could, couldn't she?

'To be honest,' said Fintan, 'I've hardly seen him since we got engaged. And he looks really worried all the time. Do you think he thinks he's doing the wrong thing?'

'I think all American men are completely and utterly fucking useless,' said Flora, scattering flour to roll out dough. 'Next question?'

➤   ⌁

Colton in fact had finally agreed to meet up with Joel, who was feeling awkward about the fact that he was still living at the Rock.

Colton was looking thin and drawn as Joel knocked and let himself in.

'How are you?' Colton said.

Joel shrugged. He was aware he was the topic of conversation on the island, but he felt insulated from it, somehow. And putting down his laptop and his phone (Mark had threatened to flush it) was also doing him the world of good.

'How are you?' he asked in return. He still couldn't quite believe what Colton was planning.

Colton shrugged. 'Who cares?' he said. 'It might amaze you to know that you managed to finish all the paperwork before you had your ... little turn. I didn't realise I'd hired such a sensitive flower.'

Joel blinked. He didn't want to give Colton the satisfaction of showing him how awful he'd felt.

Colton shuffled his papers. 'So, let's cut the crap, Joel. This is happening whether you want it to or not. You've been with me this far. It's practically finished. There's no more work to be done ... for now.'

Joel nodded.

'But ...' Colton's face suddenly looked uncharacteristically vulnerable. 'I'd still like you to be my lawyer.'

There was a pause.

'Come on, Joel. Someone has to do it. I'd rather it was someone I trusted. Completely.'

Joel looked up at that.

'Please.'

Joel heaved a sigh. 'I can't ... I can't work much.'

'That's okay. Do a little bit as and when. Stay in the Rock. Eat a lot of cream. You know I don't care about the expense.'

'Thank you.'

'No problem,' said Colton. 'All you have to do is back me.'

Joel closed his eyes. That was, indeed, a problem.

Chapter Forty-five

The days continued to lengthen – and every single one of them, Saif dreaded once again going to school pick-up. Ibrahim was refusing to play at all with the other boys, who had done what children do naturally in such situations and withdrawn from him, even for shinty.

Ash was still showing no signs of becoming less clingy, although he had begun to say a few English words – 'dog' had come up, and 'sweeties' (Saif suspected major bribery on Mrs Laird's part, which would be correct). Saif was still so worried though. He was up all night doing paperwork he didn't get round to in the day and he barely thanked the old ladies who brought casseroles, even though he couldn't do without them. He also couldn't do without Mrs Laird, who, between looking after his boys and making her incredibly popular bread for the Seaside Kitchen, was working more hours than her arthritic knees could strictly handle. But he still couldn't get a smile out of either of the boys.

Ibrahim was only happy on the iPad, which was a terrible dependence Saif didn't have the first idea how to break. He'd taken them for their counselling classes on the mainland but they had just sat there, completely mute, Ash with his head once more in Saif's armpit. The psychologist had nodded and suggested that they meet by Skype from now on, which wasn't particularly making anything better.

Neda was coming in a week to check up on them. Saif was terrified she'd see what a pig's ear he was making of everything and take the little ones away. And his early morning walks of course had ceased, and he missed them. Now Lorna was his children's headmistress, it felt even harder to have her as a friend, and he was privately amazed by how much he missed her.

There had been one saving grace. The locum covered his on-calls several nights a week when he couldn't get babysitting. One wet and windy night, when she was meant to be on duty, she'd called him, having just half-severed one of her fingers in a bolognese incident.

The boys were both asleep; he didn't know what to do. Mrs Laird was visiting her sister in the Faroes. He tried Lorna first, then Flora, only to discover that apparently they'd gone to the pub together.

'I'll come down if you like,' said the friendly voice from the farmhouse, and Saif hadn't even known which brother it was until Innes turned up five minutes later, apologetically with Agot who'd caught wind that something was up and insisted on coming with him, whereupon both the boys had instantly got up too.

'Thanks so much for this,' said Saif, throwing on his coat and grabbing his bag.

'Aye, no worries,' said Innes.

Ash had been fascinated by the little girl instantly, and put out his hand to touch her white-blonde hair. Agot in her turn tried to grab his incredibly long eyelashes, which made him cry. Agot immediately started rubbing his back suspiciously hard, saying, 'THEAH, THEAH, DOAN CRY, DOAN CRY,' until eventually, to Saif's surprise, Ash repeated 'DOAN CRAH' and Innes and Saif swapped a thumbs-up.

'I'll stick on some cartoons,' said Innes.

Saif looked at him, genuinely touched. 'Thank you,' he said.

'Agot will watch anything as long as it flashes enough to give you a seizure.'

'I'm worried Ash will get a little . . .'

Indeed, seeing that Saif had put his coat on had made Ash very anxious, and he ran over to his father and put his arms around his knees.

'I'll be back very soon,' said Saif, trying to peel him off gently.

'NOT GO.'

'I'm coming back. I have to do my job.'

'*ABBAAA!*'

Saif looked at Innes apologetically.

'Ach, he'll be fine,' said Innes. 'We have plenty of lambs who are exactly the same.'

'Whom you then kill,' said Saif, then stopped when he saw Innes's face.

'I am joking,' he explained.

'Oh,' said Innes, who genuinely hadn't been sure.

'I have to stop joking in English,' said Saif.

'No, you should joke. It's good,' said Innes, smiling even as Ash started to yell and panic-breathe.

'There, there, young man, don't worry.'

'DOAN CRY!' Agot was back. 'DOAN CRY, BOY!'

There was a moment when Saif was minded to tell the locum to stitch up her own hand or basically just go anywhere where he didn't have to leave his family.

Innes nodded. 'They'll be okay,' he said roughly. 'You have to go sometime.'

'They need a dad.'

'The island needs a doctor. You're going to have to be both.'

❧ ❧

Saif did the fastest stitching job of his life and handed over some painkillers to his wildly embarrassed locum, then drove at eighty miles an hour along the deserted country roads to get back to the house, his heart beating. How would Ash have coped? Would Innes have managed the screaming? What would they have done without him? Would they feel abandoned all over again? How much would this set him back? And the horrible, clawing thing at the back of his mind: could childhood trauma turn a grown man into . . .

Well, there was no point focusing on that now. None. He just hoped things weren't too . . .

As he entered the gloomy, foreboding house, a strange noise met his ears. Was it screaming? His heart rate surged and he ran forwards into the sitting room ... There was nobody there. He turned round, in full flight or fight mode. Where was he? Where were they?

He followed the noise to the top bedroom, the spare room he'd earmarked for the boys, and entered.

There they were, bouncing furiously on the beds: Ash, on his injured foot, and Ibrahim, throwing himself about in an ungainly way, and Agot, who was screaming, amid fits of laughter from all three of them, 'BOUNCE, BOUNCE, BOUNCE!' and the boys were shouting 'BOUNZ! BOUNZ!' and then Ibrahim fell off and they all collapsed laughing.

Saif looked around for Innes, who was sitting in the corner, half asleep even through the racket.

'Hey,' he said, as the three noticed him.

'*ABBA!*' Ash was back in his arms immediately – but panting, out of breath. Ibrahim looked up, then his face shut down as he saw his father. Agot carried on bouncing.

'Well, I am guessing you are all fine,' said Saif, half cross, half delighted.

'MIDNIGHT FEAST?' suggested the little pagan Agot, but Innes carried her, complaining madly, down the hill, and Saif tucked the boys back into bed, and he lay sleepless until morning time contemplating the school uniforms he'd bought them that hung over the chair, which were made for ten- and six-year-old Scottish children, and made them look as if they were wearing sleeping bags.

Flora and Lorna had missed all this, propping up the bar in the Harbour's Rest.

'Crap,' said Flora, necking a gin and tonic. 'And now I'm apparently throwing a huge party I can't afford for Fintan and Colton to celebrate their perfect love.'

'He's still here though,' pointed out Lorna. Flora nodded. 'He is. Mark doesn't think it's a good idea we have a relationship till he's ... well. Till he's recovered.'

'Do you recover though?'

'Dunno,' said Flora. 'I think I shall also eat some peanuts. You know, Lorna, you can't miss what you never really had.'

'I do,' said Lorna crossly, accepting a handful of peanuts. They sat closer on their chairs.

'How are the boys doing?'

'Also awful. I am failing in every conceivable way.'

'You're fabulous!'

'I am getting older and older every single second, waiting for something to happen. And nothing's going to happen. I have to snap out of it.'

'More gin ... ' Inge-Britt sorted it. 'Ooh!' said Flora.

'What?'

'You know who else is brilliant and single at the moment who isn't Saif?'

'This better not be one of your brothers.'

'It's ... Oh.'

'Seriously?'

'Come on. Innes is handsome. Apparently.'

'*Innes?* Seriously, Flora. I've known him since I was four.'

'So, you know he's a decent guy.'

'It's icky. Like Joey and Rachel in *Friends*.'

'Or maybe Ross and Rachel in *Friends* . . . '

'Which is also icky.'

'Oh yeah. Come on, let me marry off my brothers.'

Lorna thought about it. 'Flora. I've lived on this island thirty-two years. Innes has lived here thirty-five.'

'Ooh, you know how old he is! You must like him!'

'No, I've just been at every single birthday party he's ever had.'

Flora blinked.

'My point is: don't you think if we fancied each other, we'd have done something about it by now? There's nobody else here!'

'Well, maybe that's it. When you've been through everyone in the world and there's nobody left . . . '

'Seriously?' said Lorna.

'He's been single for ages! Agot and the business take up all his time.'

'What if we got together and broke up and you had to take sides?'

'I'd take yours,' said Flora. 'I've got loads of other brothers.' Lorna smiled. 'Oh, come on, are you telling me you find him disgusting?'

'I've just never thought of him that way,' said Lorna. Innes had been the heart-throb at school but she'd always spent so much time with Flora he'd just been the guy who'd teased her and called her Freckles and touched her plaits. She hadn't liked it one bit. But there was no doubt he was pretty much the pick of what was on offer.

'Plus it'd be weird,' she said. 'Agot will be coming up soon.'

Flora shook her head. 'She'll go on the mainland with her mother.'

'Are you sure? She's here a *lot*.'

'I know,' said Flora fondly. 'I will miss the little wildebeest.' She glanced at Lorna. 'Of course, if you snared her father ... '

'Stop it, you big weirdo!'

'I just want someone to be happy! Except for Fintan and Colton: they're *too* happy.'

'So you want people to be happy but only to a certain Flora-acceptable extent?'

'This is why I will never run for parliament. Inge-Britt! Tell me what you do for men!'

'Are you stupid?' said Inge-Britt. 'What about the nuclear submarine out in the loch?'

'The what?' Lorna and Flora both said at the same time.

'Whoops!' said Inge-Britt serenely. 'I forget it's top secret.' She picked up the empty glasses. 'Those Russian sailors,' she whispered. 'Wowza.'

And she sashayed off, leaving Flora and Lorna looking after her in confusion and not a little envy.

Chapter Forty-six

Joel squinted through his glasses as he and Mark took their constitutional. After the first day, they never spoke about Joel's health again. They spoke about books they'd read or baseball. Not a single thing that touched on what was happening or the future, what Joel would do or where he would go. Mark felt he had to decompress the boy within the man, and give him enough breathing space to figure out what to do after that. He was well aware this was a rich man's cure. He was equally well aware that he and Marsha both blamed themselves for not taking the boy in when he was young and raising him as their own. They should have done. If he wasn't having such a nice time, this would have felt like penance.

Up on one side of the fell on a bright breezy day, they came across a group setting up tents. Joel remembered the name in time. Charlie: Flora's ex, the one he'd met before. He was with a grumpy-looking woman with short hair and a large collection of young boys. He looked at them curiously. They were unkempt, many of them, with razor-short hair done cheaply and quickly; bitten fingernails and missing teeth and surly expressions.

Joel recognised them with a start. The hand-me-down T-shirts from goodwill stores. The slightly aggressive stance in children who had been just as likely to receive a blow as a kiss. A belligerent look on their faces that said that they didn't care what you were going to say to them; they'd heard worse. He looked at Mark, and Mark understood wordlessly and nodded at him to go forward.

Joel had heard Flora mention Charlie's work of course, and something about a wedding, but he had been in full work mode then and not paid attention. No. He was trying to be more honest with himself: he had heard perfectly well, but hadn't wanted to listen. Other lost boys were not his concern, and he'd suffered just as badly at the hands of other foster children as he had in other homes; they jeered at him for his bookish ways. There was always that ongoing sense of competition between them: who would get adopted? Who was getting too old to be charming?

Now it was as if he was seeing them for the first time, as he stood, alone in the world, scowling at it, just as the boys did.

Charlie smiled, his wide-open, uncomplicated face simply friendly and welcoming, and Joel suddenly wished savagely that Flora had married him after all so at least one of them could be happy. If she'd married him, he wouldn't have to worry about her any more, could be sad by himself.

'Morning!' said Charlie. 'Say hello to Mr Binder, everyone.'

'He-lloww, Misterr Binder,' chorused the boys sullenly.

Charlie came close. 'I heard . . . I heard you'd been having a tough time of it.'

Joel shrugged. 'Honestly, it's nothing. I'm fine. Bit of overreacting.'

'Um, right,' said Charlie, rubbing the back of his head awkwardly. 'I must have got the wrong end of the stick.'

Joel could feel Mark looking at him, and took a deep breath.

'No,' he said. 'In fact, you didn't. I have been finding things pretty rough. Thanks for asking.' Mark beamed approvingly. 'This is my friend, Dr Philippoussis.'

The fierce-looking woman marched up. 'Who's this?' she barked.

'Um, this is Joel and Dr . . . ' Charlie was not used to Greek names and rather let it peter out. 'And this is my . . . uh, my wife, Jan.'

Jan looked him up and down.

'You're Flora's American,' she announced. 'I thought you'd have had a bit more meat on your bones. Like my Charlie,' she said smugly. Joel remembered now that Flora didn't like her, which was puzzling, as Flora generally liked everyone, like a Labrador. But he was beginning to see her point.

'Are you off?' she said. 'You're on mental health leave, aren't you?' She could not have picked a worse term. Joel's face tightened. 'Excellent! We can use you round here. Get your DBS check, and come and join us. Here, I'll drop the forms in.'

'Excuse me, what?'

'We need volunteers! We always need volunteers! Come and help us with the boys.'

'Oh, no, I . . . I don't think so.'

Mark coughed meaningfully.

'Everyone else on this island has two jobs. You have none. Seems about right, don't you think? Don't worry; we won't make you do anything mentally taxing or stressful. Just put up some tents and cook some sausages.'

'I don't think it would be appropriate.'

'Or maybe it's your moral imperative,' said Jan in that direct way of hers that brooked no argument.

'This is Joel, who's going to come and help out,' she announced to the boys, all of whom cheered.

'Oh, I really don't . . . I really don't . . .'

'I'll drop the forms in to the Rock. Bye!'

Jan marched on. Charlie looked at Joel apologetically.

'Is she always like this?' Joel couldn't help asking.

'She gets stuff done,' said Charlie.

'I like her,' said Mark, rubbing his beard.

Chapter Forty-seven

'Do you know who fancies you madly?'

Flora was in one of those moods when she got home, and she'd had another gin and tonic. She was meant to be cooking for all the family but it wasn't working too well. Hamish was off again in his ridiculous sports car, it being a Friday night, and her father had decided that if she was to come up to the house smelling of gin in a way that would make her mother's eyes roll in her head (it would not have done this), then he was going to have a whisky.

Innes had just arrived, Agot marching ahead. It was true, Flora thought, a little fuzzily. Agot was here a lot more now. She realised Eilidh was busy with her full-time job on the mainland and Innes being his own boss made it easier for him to have her around – plus she'd been raised on the farm, and Mure was the kind of place where everyone kept an eye on everyone else's children. Even so.

'I BORED,' announced Agot. 'I WAN SISTER.'

'You've got me,' said Flora ingratiatingly. Agot looked her up and down.

'YOU ATTI,' she said crossly. 'AND YOU OLD ALSO.'

'Also' was Agot's new word. Flora wasn't sure she approved.

'Agot,' said Innes. 'Behave.'

'AGOT NOT BEHAVE ALSO.'

Flora deftly cut her a piece of the new bread and spread it thickly with butter. 'I think *Robot Wars* is on,' she said optimistically. *Robot Wars* was Agot's new favourite show as she now felt *Peppa Pig* was for unsophisticated babies.

'KILLBOT LIVES!' shouted Agot, marching into the underused front room to turn on the old television set. Innes watched her go.

'So anyway, back to this person who fancies you madly,' said Flora, chopping onions for curry, which her father disapproved of. She thought about adding extra chillies, then thought of an evening of Agot complaining and decided against it.

'Who?' said Innes, with a puzzled look. It was true: in his youth he'd been through half the island. 'I mean, someone I don't "know"?'

Flora smiled annoyingly.

'Stop being annoying.'

'Flora being annoying?' said Fintan, coming through the door wearing a new, incredibly expensive-looking man bag, which he placed reverently down on one of the ancient threadbare armchairs. 'That doesn't sound like her, except for every day.'

'Shut up, Fintan,' said Flora, kissing him on the cheek.

'Oh God, hark at the metropolitans,' said Innes, rolling his eyes.

'Someone fancies Innes, and he's so old now he's forgotten what it's like,' said Flora, embracing Colton who'd come in just behind. He was looking tired, but was clutching a bottle of wine a client had given him as a parting gift that they would drink that evening without checking the label – and none of them would ever find out that it was an incredibly rare vintage worth approximately £8,000.

'Well, I'm not surprised,' said Colton.

'HEY!' shouted Fintan, batting him on the lapels.

'What? I'm being gentlemanly. You don't want me to say, Christ, your family look like raccoons.'

'I want you to say everyone in the world looks like a raccoon next to me,' said Fintan, mock-crossly, then they kissed and everyone rolled their eyes.

'Stop it!' said Flora. 'Or I'm cancelling your party.'

'A lady fancying Innes,' said Fintan. 'How strange and unusual.'

He came over, tasted Flora's curry sauce and stuck a heap of extra chilli in it. She hit him on the hand with a wooden spoon.

'Who is it? Mrs Kennedy? Apparently she can take out her false teeth.'

'Shut up, Fintan,' said Innes.

'Well, you are getting on a bit. Mrs McCreedie? If you like a sheepskin bootee, she's the one for you.'

'Actually,' said Flora. 'It's someone you know very well.'

Innes grimaced. 'It's not one of your crazy friends from the mainland again, is it?' he said. 'They're all completely weird and they talk total shit and have stupid hair.'

'I think what you mean there is they're contemporary and fashionable,' said Flora.

Innes snorted. 'Aye, that'll be right.'

'Fine,' said Flora. 'Don't find out.'

'Just invite her to the barbecue,' said Fintan. 'And we can spot her then.'

Chapter Forty-eight

'Are you sure you're really going to throw an actual barbecue for the party? I don't know anyone who even has one.'

There was a superstition on Mure and indeed many of the islands that to buy anything deliberately intended for outdoor use was simply tempting fate: storms, power cuts and torrential rain. If you wanted to barbecue something, you could use bricks and an old grill like everybody else; you were mad to try something different. It was arrogance that would simply invoke the wrath of the gods.

'Colton's bringing one over. Apparently he has a top-of-the-range, blah, blah ...'

'Colton is bringing a barbecue to your house?' Lorna frowned. 'Why don't you just go to Colton's? *And* he's got flunkies and things.'

Flora shrugged and Lorna remembered that Joel was up there, and changed the subject. 'It will hose it down.'

'It might not.'

'You're planning something for two days away. You're a crazy person.'

'I know,' said Flora. 'But on the other hand ... Come to the barbecue. Toast the happy couple. Have a couple of beers. Stand close to Innes. Eat a sausage in a suggestive manner.'

'Flora!'

Lorna couldn't deny it though. She was so lonely. The idea of dressing up nicely to go and do something glamorous ... Well, not glamorous, but something ...

'What were you going to be doing?' asked Flora annoyingly.

'Bundle up in my raincoat, watching the rain pound against the windows,' said Lorna. 'That is exactly what I'm going to be doing.'

'See you there,' said Flora. 'Wear something sexy.'

'My pink fleece or my brown fleece?'

'Just make sure you've unzipped the top bit as far down as you can.'

'To reveal my other fleece underneath?'

'Something like that.'

'Don't let me stop you going,' said Joel.

'You're not going? I know I said you should be careful of Flora, but this is a big event.'

'I said I'd help out with the boys today.'

Joel couldn't face seeing Colton and Fintan so happy. He just couldn't.

Mark frowned. 'And what might Flora say to that?'

267

Joel shrugged.

'Don't you think you should tell her?' Mark's tone was gentle, but firm. 'I think you've had enough time apart now. Don't make her wait for you, Joel, if you can't be there.'

Joel knew he wasn't just talking about the barbecue.

Saif was just so damned tired. All the time. It was just one thing after another. He hadn't really thought about how much Amena and his mother had done for the children at home; hadn't really appreciated how much they'd tended to their needs while he'd at first gone to work, then later worked hard constantly on figuring out how to get them away and to safety. He thought of those long days in the market square; the low voices and misinformation; the selling of everything they had to sell. The planning and the fear.

But it was the day-to-day stuff he couldn't figure out now. He'd thought he was prepared for the mental anguish, the pain and the difficulty. He wasn't at all prepared for Ash sitting on the corner of his bed, refusing to get up and instead pulling the Velcro on his tiny trainers to and fro, every noise like a wire brush on Saif's brain, no matter how often he told him to stop, or threatened to take the trainers away. Which he couldn't, of course: Ash's huge eyes would fill with tears, and the idea of depriving him of anything, or making him unhappy in any way at all suddenly seemed utterly unbearable.

So they would start over. And he also faced an internal battle about tearing Ibrahim away from his iPad, when it was the only thing he wanted to do ... He had succeeded, though, in switching it to English, which was something, he supposed. But every day he approached the school hoping for better news, and every day Lorna was too kind to tell him that he would have to stop carrying Ash everywhere, for everyone's sake, and that the boys still weren't accepting Ibrahim, who lashed out when anyone went anywhere near him, and how she wished she knew what to do, she really did, and it must only be time, mustn't it?

The Thursday before the barbecue was a glorious evening and Saif decided to walk the boys down to the harbour front and buy them some chips and Irn-Bru. He couldn't personally stomach Irn-Bru, even without knowing what was in it, but he understood that it was part of Scottish religion, and respected that. Hot vinegary chips, though, reminded him of the spiced fried potatoes they used to get at home, and he had developed a fondness for them and wanted to introduce the boys. Ibrahim mooched down the hill, looking as if going for a treat on a beautiful day was the single worst thing that could possibly happen to him.

Outside in the queue – for plenty of Murians had had the same idea on such a glorious evening – was Innes, holding Agot by the hand.

'Hey,' said Saif, wondering how Innes, who looked to be a single father to all intents and purposes, managed everything – his job and his daughter – while still looking so at ease in his own skin. Perhaps it just came naturally to some people. Perhaps he had just been a fool for thinking it would come easily to him. 'Thanks again for the other night.'

'ASSSHHHH!' yelled Agot.

And then, in the queue, Ash did the most unexpected thing. He clambered out of Saif's arms of his own volition.

He limped over to where Agot was jumping up and down.

'CHIPS, CHIPS, CHIPS!' Agot was yelling in excitement.

Ash grinned. He'd lost one of his front teeth, which made him look very comical. Then, all of a sudden, 'CHIPS, CHIPS, CHIPS!' he shouted, in a perfect imitation of her broad islands accent.

'KETCHUP ALSO!' hollered Agot.

'KETCHUP ALSO!' echoed Ash.

'Goodness,' said Saif, completely taken aback. Innes smiled distractedly. Agot bossing around other children she'd met was hardly a new experience for him.

'Oh, it's nice they're getting on ... Things going better then?'

Saif was overwhelmed with the desire to say, 'Awful, unbearable, how does anyone cope?' Then he glanced at the two children, Agot a little hopping imp, Ash desperately trying to imitate her.

'Well, you know,' he said weakly.

'We were just heading to the harbour wall,' said Innes in his easy way. 'Want to join?'

Innes never knew how much that simple invitation meant to Saif. A simple outstretched hand of friendship, meant without expectation, neither intrusively nosey, nor desperately worried about saying the right thing. It was just one chap to another, with no agenda. Saif had lived with nothing but other people's agendas for so long: the sheer banality of the invitation made him want to weep.

'Sure,' he said.

So they bought chips and Irn-Bru, except Agot wanted something called Red Kola, so of course Ash wanted it too, and got it, and Saif offered some to Ibrahim too, who shrugged and said he didn't care, which Saif realised meant he desperately wanted some, and they all took the steaming paper-wrapped parcels and crossed the cobbled street to the sea wall. They sat, watching the children on the little harbour beach, shouting at Agot every time she tried to feed the seagulls who swooped around the children and looked entirely huge and alarming enough to carry them away.

'I'S WANTS SEAGULL CARRY ME!' shouted Agot, holding up her arms, whereupon Ash did so too, the chips fell to the ground and there was quite the kerfuffle getting everything sorted out again and drying tears and replacing the chips. But it was, Saif realised, a normal sort of fuss – the kind of thing that would happen to any family, any parent, out with children – and he was deeply and profoundly grateful.

'We're having a barbecue on Sunday,' said Innes casually. 'To celebrate my brother getting engaged. Bring them if you like.'

Something struck him.

'Oh, but also he's getting engaged to a big hairy American bloke so I don't know if . . . '

Saif smiled tightly. He knew people meant well, but he didn't like the implication that because he wasn't from there he was automatically a bigot. Innes registered this immediately.

'Sorry, I mean, some of the old buggers around here have been very weird about it.'

Saif nodded. 'How is your father?'

'Oddly cheerful,' said Innes, eating a chip. 'I think he just wants us to get out of the sodding house.'

'YOU COME MY HOUSE?' said Agot to Ash. Ash nodded.

'Yes,' he said.

'Did you understand that?' said Saif in Arabic, crouching down. 'Did you?'

'He's not stupid,' said Ibrahim.

'Did you?' said Saif.

'YES!' shouted Ash in English.

Saif blinked in amazement. This was ... this was amazing.

'Well, uh, well, I'll be off,' said Innes.

'Oh, yes, sorry,' said Saif, immediately reverting to English. 'Thank you.'

And he meant it more than he could convey.

Chapter Forty-nine

Annie's Seaside Kitchen was quiet, the girls gone, everything cleaned and polished and put back, ready for another day tomorrow. Flora was sitting alone at a rickety table in the corner of the room with a calculator and a mounting sense of panic. She put down her tea and glanced up as there was a knock on the door. Sometimes a hopeful wet tourist would swing past after closing time, and sometimes, if she was in a better mood than this, she'd whip them up a quick coffee and piece of flan and send them on their way happy.

But not tonight. She shook her head, then the visitor knocked again. It wasn't until she looked up that she realised it was Joel.

'Hey,' she said, swallowing hard as she turned the old Yale key. Her heart was beating. Was he here to declare himself? To tell her how much he missed her, how he just wanted to devote himself to her, how he'd made a mistake?

He was looking better, she realised, with something of a

pang. There was some colour back in his cheeks. Fresh air was obviously doing him good. She wanted more than anything to run her fingers through his curly hair. He leaned in to kiss her and she did too, but they both aimed badly, and he ended up half on her cheek and half in her ear and she went bright red immediately and jumped back.

'Uh, hi,' he said.

Flora stood aside to let him come in.

'What are you up to?'

Flora shrugged. 'Just looking at . . . accounts and things.'

She wished she had some make-up on. She hadn't had a second all day, that was the problem. She never stopped.

Joel looked at the dusting of flour she had across her forehead and wanted more than anything to gently wipe it off, take her head in his hands . . . but no. As Mark said, he had to get himself well.

'How . . . how are the accounts?'

Flora suddenly wanted to burst into tears. She was so tired getting everything ready for Sunday, and the one person she wanted was standing in front of her like an accountant giving her an audit.

'Awful, if you must know.'

Joel blinked. 'But you're always so busy!'

'You can talk . . . Sorry,' Flora added quickly.

'It's okay . . . ' He glanced at the computer. 'Can I take a look?'

Flora's eyes widened. He'd never shown much interest in the business before. 'Um, sure,' she said.

'How old is this laptop? Do I have to wind it up at the back?'

'Joel . . . '

'It's heavier than you.'

'Glad something is.'

Joel smiled, and it shot through Flora like a dart. Then he wiped his glasses on a clean white napkin, and bent his head.

Flora went through the back to the kitchen, finishing the last of the day's chores and the first of the new day's prep. She made them a coffee, not because she wanted one but because she couldn't think of anything else to do. Then she went back into the main room. It was gently lit. The evening was light but grey, and the round old-fashioned lamp posts on the harbour were glowing softly from beyond the window panes. She briefly leaned her head against the window frame and looked at him. He was as engrossed as ever – as far away, she thought, as ever.

'Here.'

Joel looked up and smiled. 'Thank you. But I'm off coffee.'

'Oh. Really?'

'Coffee, wine, processed food ... Basically Mark's got me eating grass and animal fats and that's about it.'

'Okay ...'

She fetched him a glass of water, just as he took his glasses off and sighed.

'Flora ...'

Her heart leaped. 'What?'

'Flora ... this can't go on. It isn't ... It can't work.'

Flora steadied herself against the counter. Everything was coming tumbling down. Everything was over. Just as she had known it would, just as she'd suspected all along.

'Look,' he was saying. 'Look at your inventory. Look at

your stock control. You can't ... I mean your portion control is a disaster. Look at this.'

He beckoned her over, but she couldn't trust her limbs to move. 'I thought you were a lawyer,' she said.

'Yeah, good luck to corporate lawyers who can't read a profit and loss account,' said Joel. He looked up at her. 'I mean, you could get cash in, but it would be like putting water in a leaky bucket.'

Flora nodded, biting her lip.

'I mean, you make far more pastries than you sell every week. Why aren't you just making fewer?'

Flora stared hard at the ground. She didn't want to tell him: because she needed something to give Teàrlach's boys.

'And why are you even paying near market value for produce from your family farm?'

'Because your bloody boss hasn't opened the hotel yet, which would allow us all to make a living,' said Flora, her face hot. Joel blinked but didn't comment.

'I mean, you're just charging far, far too little. For everything. Do you really need three different types of sausages?'

Well, she did, Flora thought crossly, because not everyone on Mure ate pork any more, and he should know that.

'But ... but people are spending their pensions in here,' she said. 'There are young mums ... and you know what farming is going through.'

'Yes, but you're packed out with rich holidaymakers. Presumably they could spend a bit more.'

'We can't do that,' said Flora. 'We can't have one price for local people and one for tourists.'

Joel arched an eyebrow. 'I don't see why not.'

'Because it's illegal, Mr Lawyer-person.'

'Well, there are ways around that . . . '

'I just want to run a good business!'

'I want you to do that too, Flora. I just . . . You know I want good things for you.'

And? thought Flora desperately. And? And what else?

'Listen, I'll . . . Can I send you an email with some thoughts?'

'I don't need rescuing.'

He stopped short at that, and half-smiled. 'I can't even rescue myself,' he said. 'But there are things you could do. Lots. Positive things. Think about it. Please?'

Flora nodded mutely as he stood up to go.

'Oh,' she said at the door, yearning to take his hand and bury her head in his chest, even though Mark had made it delicately clear that they both needed space. 'Why . . . why did you come by?'

Joel put his coat back on. 'I . . . I can't come to the party on Sunday,' he said. 'Sorry.'

Her face fell. She had hoped . . . just a little . . . that he would turn up, see how brilliantly everything was going and what a happy time everybody was having and he'd want to join in and . . . Joel joining in. That was a stupid thought, for starters.

'Okay,' she said. 'Thanks for the tips.'

'You're welcome,' he said, and ducked out into the pale-grey foggy evening, and she lost sight of him before his footsteps faded from earshot.

Chapter Fifty

Saif was still anxious, but not quite as terrified as he had been, when Neda showed up later that week.

His optimism, as they went down to the harbour to collect Neda from the ferry, faded fast. She emerged, tall and glamorous-looking, by the quayside next to the bearded walkers and excited Americans clutching their bumbags. She stood and looked around.

It was a glorious morning, cold and breathtakingly fresh, like a glass of iced water. The chilly waves danced in the light. She blinked, pulled on a large pair of sunglasses and walked up the jetty towards them, her heels clacking loudly on the cobblestones.

Instantly Ash was trembling in Saif's arms, and Ibrahim turned away, back to his iPad.

'It's Neda!' said Saif encouragingly. 'She's nice!'

Ash was still shaking.

'What is it?'

The little boy muttered something that Saif strained to hear, even as Neda leaned over. She shook her head.

'No,' she said. 'Listen to me, Ash. I'm not here to take you back.'

Saif gasped that he would think that. Ash was still flinching, and the tears were running down his face as Neda straightened up again.

'I'm just visiting! I have presents for you!'

But Saif couldn't hear her. He had turned his face away. It felt ridiculous now he was even thinking about it, but nonetheless it was true. There was a tiny part of him that had also worried that maybe they would want to go back. That anywhere would be preferable to living with him. He suddenly felt overwhelmed and grabbed Ash close. Neda glanced at him shrewdly, then smiled.

'Look at this amazing place!' she said. 'Now, is there anywhere you can get a cup of coffee? We need to sit down to unwrap presents!'

Ibrahim lagged behind as Saif showed her up the harbour walkway towards Annie's Seaside Kitchen, where many of the grateful disembarkees – the ones who were home and the ones who'd been warned of poor food on their journey – simply couldn't believe their luck. She turned to Saif and smiled broadly and spoke in English.

'Did you seriously think they'd rather come back with me?'

Saif blinked twice. 'Only for a second.'

She shook her head. 'Honestly. Did you really think they'd be here for five minutes and everything would be rainbows and fairy tales?'

Saif's shoulders sagged. 'But it's so, so hard.'

'Welcome to parenting,' said Neda.

Saif smiled weakly. 'But I can't put Ash down, or get Ibrahim off his iPad.'

Indeed, the boy was walking, staring at the screen, oblivious to everything around him.

'What do you mean, you can't?'

Saif looked at her.

'Just put Ash down.' They had crossed the quiet road and were walking up the pavement towards the Seaside Kitchen, in its little pink building. Neda looked at him. 'Do it!'

'Um, I don't think he wants to go down.'

'He doesn't want to eat his vegetables either, am I right?'

Saif winced. 'One thing at a time.'

Neda shook her head. 'Doesn't work that way I'm afraid, my friend. You can't fight every battle. Just fight one.'

'Which one?'

'The "do as I say" one.'

Saif laughed. 'I don't think so.'

They headed up the road, Saif aware everyone was looking at them.

'Well, you're a doctor. What would you recommend?'

'I would recommend people do not come and visit me for child-rearing advice.'

Neda tutted. 'Come on. What would you say?' Saif shrugged. Neda lowered her voice. 'What would Amena say?'

It was a low blow, and Saif winced a little. 'There is no news?' he said quickly.

Neda shook her head. 'I'm sorry, Saif. But if she were here . . . '

'She would say, "Ash, you are a big boy, you have to walk."'

'Mm . . . ' said Neda.

They took another couple of steps. Then Saif whispered in Ash's ear. 'Darling. I'm going to put you down, so you can walk and make your leg all nice and strong.'

Ash's little jaw jutted out and he immediately got a steely look in his eye. 'No, *Abba*.'

'I'm afraid so,' said Neda. 'We're going to the coffee shop to get treats and presents. Want to come?'

She indicated to Saif, who put Ash on the ground. Ash immediately started to scramble back up his trouser leg. For an underfed six-year-old with a damaged foot, he was surprisingly strong. Neda watched Saif to see what he would do, and Saif found himself red and conscious that this was a test – not for Ash, but for him.

Saif uncurled the little fingers, even though it felt unbearably cruel. Ash screamed all the louder. This was great, thought Saif, growing red, Ash having the mother of all crazed screaming tantrums in the middle of the high street, on the thronged harbour, on an early Friday morning. The number of people on the island who wouldn't have heard about the doctor's deranged child by lunchtime was practically negligible.

'Right, let's go,' said Neda. She smiled cheerily at Ash. 'We'll see you in there. I hope they have buns. I love buns, don't you?'

Ash continued howling, his face bright red, his good leg hitting the pavement. Neda kept smiling.

'Am I just supposed to walk away? When he's upset?'

Neda shrugged. 'It's up to you, Saif.' She lowered her

voice. 'It might make things trickier, you know, in the long run, if you can't treat him like a normal kid.'

'He isn't a normal kid.'

But Neda was already marching on. Saif felt torn, looking at the little boy having a paddy on the pavement and the tall, confident woman striding ahead of him.

Saif took a pace towards Neda. There was a pause and suddenly, just for a moment, the screaming let up, as Ash glanced up to take in the new situation. Then he resumed, louder. Saif looked pained.

Neda pushed open the door of Annie's Seaside Kitchen, which dinged loudly.

'MMM,' said Neda loudly in English. 'LOOK AT ALL THESE CAKES.'

This time, the pause in the screeching was much longer. Ibrahim blindly followed Neda. Saif allowed himself another step.

'What kind of muffin are you going to have, Ibrahim?'

Well, this was too much for any six-year-old to bear. The idea of Ibrahim being allowed to choose a big cake all to himself while he was left out on the pavement was an injustice too far. Ash picked himself up and ran, tearfully, to the door.

Flora was regarding them with a slightly puzzled expression on her face, particularly as Neda was holding the door and blocking the way out for three backpackers and their gigantic backpacks, which were now getting in the way of Mrs Blair's new shampoo and set which she'd come down to show off, so that was pleasing absolutely nobody.

Then Flora looked through the window and saw the

boys – she'd seen them in passing of course, but hadn't met them officially. She broke into a grin and beckoned them in. And even with Joel's dire warnings echoing in her ears, she couldn't help but bring out a couple of lollipops she had secreted away.

'Welcome,' she said. 'Welcome, all of you.'

Ash's sobs had slowed to the occasional whimper by the time they were all sitting down, and Mrs Blair's shampoo and set had been patted back into position, but, to Saif's astonishment, Neda didn't let up at all.

'I know how you feel,' she said, as Isla brought over two flat whites. 'Wow,' she added. 'Thanks!'

Flora was always faintly insulted by the patronising way people reacted to the fact that she sold good coffee – she resented the assumption that everyone who lived in the islands was some kind of hunkering rube who thought instant was a treat.

Neda continued, 'And I don't want to lecture, but for the moment, at least, you have to be mother and father to those boys.'

'You mean tell them off.'

Neda shrugged. 'Again, it's up to you.'

'You say "it's up to you" when you mean "do as I say",' said Saif, smiling.

'Do I?' said Neda, biting into an iced finger. 'Oh my goodness, this is terrific.' She turned to Ibrahim, who was slouching in his seat and, as usual, staring at the iPad in front of him, then looked back at Saif.

Saif sighed and leaned over. 'Ibrahim. I need to take your iPad.'

Ibrahim went wide-eyed. 'You can't,' he said. 'It's mine.'

'While we're in the café.'

'Until she goes?'

'She is Neda, please.'

'Until Neda goes?'

'Just give it to me now.'

Everyone sat looking tense at the table, except for Ash, who had a bun in one hand and the lollipop in the other and had quite forgotten his bad mood.

'What lovely boys you are,' said Neda cheerfully. 'Now, are you going to show me your school?'

Flora smiled as she watched the boys leave. Saif made them turn and lisp awkward thank yous to her. Ibrahim was his double, she saw. He had the exact same furrowed brow and grave expression on his face. Ash was a beautiful child, with long eyelashes. But both the boys were too thin. She would fix that, she vowed. A few more cheese scones. Ugh, no, she had to make the scones smaller ... Oh, why was it so hard?

~ ~

Ash managed to make it halfway up the hill before collapsing in dramatic fashion and declaring himself utterly exhausted. Neda asked him to say it in English, which to Saif's amazement he absolutely could. She laughed at his face and said, not to worry, she knew plenty of full-time fathers who also found this kind of thing incredibly tricky, which made Saif relax a little and find his own smile at Ash's dramatic over-acting, which is why the first time Lorna saw them approaching from the staffroom window, the two boys walking, Ibrahim without his iPad, and the beautiful, tall woman walking next to Saif, her heart dropped right into her boots.

She certainly never made him smile like that, or laugh so his white teeth showed. They were a good-looking couple too, she thought. Who was she? It couldn't be ... It wasn't as if Saif couldn't have found a girlfriend, was it? After all, he'd meet someone one day, right? But she had comforted herself so much by thinking that he was just too loyal, too respectful to his wife, to ever ...

'Hello!' said Saif. He was definitely in a better mood than he had been the last few weeks when he'd been exhausted and strung out, picking up his furious, uncommunicative children, watching with a parental heartbreak Lorna recognised very well as his children were left out of playground games, unpicked, alone in the corner of the school.

Today his face was sunnier, more open, and Ash – was that child walking? Lorna had never seen him on the ground before. She waited for him to try and cling to her as he usually did, but instead – and this stung frightfully – he held the tall woman's hand.

'Lorenah. Miss MacLeod,' said Saif, smiling. 'This is Neda Okonjo. She's the social worker who's helping us ... She looked after the boys in Glasgow.'

'Hello,' said Lorna, more stiffly than she meant. She hadn't realised social workers were quite so glamorous these days. Saif wondered why she was being weird.

'Hello,' said Neda. 'Hey, I think you're doing a great job with the boys.'

Lorna blinked. She, personally, had not been thinking that at all. She'd been worried she was failing them desperately. She couldn't get them to say a word of English, or join in, or respond to anything.

'They understand everything we're saying already!' said Neda. 'Great job.'

Lorna frowned. 'Do they?'

'Look at Ibrahim,' said Neda, grinning. The boy immediately flushed and stared at the ground.

'He's pretending he doesn't understand. But he does. He's a very handsome boy.'

Ibrahim blushed even more. Saif couldn't believe it.

'And he's much better at football than he thinks he is.'

'You're a miracle-worker,' said Lorna.

'No. You are,' said Neda. 'Trust the process. Both of you. Trust how clever the boys are and how much they're taking in, even when they don't realise it. Treat them like the other boys. Please. No more carrying.'

Lorna nodded.

'No letting Ibrahim on computers. If he can manage not to hit anyone – eh, Ibrahim? No hitting?'

Ibrahim shrugged.

'Let's make a deal. I bet if you stop it, you'll be playing football with everyone in a week.'

'Don't care.'

'In English.'

And he did. 'I don't care,' he said, pink to the ears.

'You don't have to care,' said Neda softly. 'You just need to play.'

And the bell rang, and for once the children disappeared

inside the school building on their own, getting caught up in the little stream of boys and girls, getting lost in it – just like normal children going about their day. And Saif and Lorna stared at each other in disbelief.

'Right,' said Neda, turning round. 'Let's have a look at the home set-up. Don't worry, I'm just ticking boxes. You're obviously going to be fine.'

'You're amazing,' said Lorna, glancing back towards her classroom.

'Well, it was nice to meet you too,' said Neda and she turned round and marched off down the hill, Saif turning to follow her, in awe, and Lorna reflected that she'd fallen in love with Neda in ten seconds flat, and she didn't blame Saif in the slightest if he'd just done exactly the same thing.

Chapter Fifty-one

Joel woke up early, feeling trepidatious, like it was his first day at school. Of course it was already light outside. He realised it was at least a month since they'd had to put any lights on at all. Such a strange sensation.

He clambered into the 'rugged' clothes his secretary Margo had bought him last year. They didn't feel right at all – he preferred a well-cut suit, as armour, something that allowed him to vanish subtly into the background of any room he was in. The moleskin trousers and the rough-hewn pale checked shirt with a waterproof lining felt odd. Also, putting them on, he became conscious of how much weight he'd lost and grimaced. Then he set out into a misty morning, the grey haar obliterating all distinction between land and sea; the kind of morning, in fact, that often burned off into a glorious afternoon, but it made heavy weather of the first part of the day. He took the piece of paper which had arrived the day before.

Grabbing a coffee, he set out up the hill. That he was working with Flora's ex-boyfriend, and her arch-enemy, hadn't escaped him. He was aware he hadn't mentioned it in the café. She had looked so disappointed that he wasn't going to the party, he didn't want to make matters even worse.

Not knowing the way, as it turned out, was no problem: the bright orange tents and screams and yells of the boys were visible and audible from miles away, as was the scent of sizzling sausages on the fire.

Charlie was there, on his own third cup of coffee, typically weary as he always was. Every group of troubled youngsters had a bedwetter and some tiny fiends who liked to tell horror stories, although many of them had already lived through their own horror stories. He nodded to Joel, taking in – in a way that surprised Joel mightily – the expensiveness of his outdoor clothing.

'Morning.'

'Hey.'

Joel felt awkward. He held out his envelope. 'I brought this.'

Charlie just tipped his head. 'Give it to Jan. She handles all the paperwork.'

'Who are you, mister?'

A small boy of about eight or nine was standing in front of him. His head, which might have been blond, was shaved down to the wood, his body was skinny and none too clean-looking and there were dark hollows under his eyes. His posture was defensive; he had the look about him of a kid that was always waiting for a telling-off.

'I'm Joel,' he said mildly. They looked at each other. Joel wasn't about to say anything else. Adults asking questions was probably more than this kid ever needed.

'Are you American?' said the boy, eyes widening. 'You sound weird.'

'Yes, I'm from America originally.'

'What are you doing in this shithole then?'

'Caleb,' said Charlie, but in a relaxed way. 'What did we say about swearing?'

'Shit isn't swearing,' said the lad. 'Fuck is swearing.'

'No, shit definitely counts.'

'Oh. Sorry.' He readdressed his question. 'Why are you in a poo-hole like this?'

'I happen to like it,' said Joel.

'Like it more than America? With like sunshine and guns and cars with no tops on and California and skyscrapers and stuff?' The kid's eyes widened further.

'It's not all like that.'

'It's naaat allll laaak that.' The child tried out a dreadful imitation of Joel's drawl, then called the others. 'Aye! Ye gadgies! Yon mon here's a Yank!'

Other shaved heads emerged. Joel knew on one level that small boys having short hair simply made practical sense. But his hair was always shorn when he was a boy because nobody loved him enough to comb it. He'd worn his dark curls longer than was usual for a lawyer, long enough to flop over his high forehead, ever since. Flora adored it, and would have loved it even more if she'd known the reason why.

The boys gathered around Joel as an object of

curiosity, and Joel wished he'd brought some sweets to hand out. They all wanted to know about gangs and guns and the streets and all sorts of notions and appeared to have picked up most of their American assumptions from playing *Grand Theft Auto*, but he helped as much as he could. He noticed Charlie watching him, not in a disapproving fashion.

Jan arrived, looking scrubbed down as usual.

'Hand over that,' she said, gesturing at the envelope in his hands, and he did so. 'Right,' she said, studying it carefully. 'You can take down the tents and wash up while we start our forest walk. Has everyone got their squirrel charts?'

'Can he no' come with?' said Caleb, the boy who'd first spoken.

'Not this time,' said Jan. 'You can stay and wash up if you like.'

There was a pause.

'Aye, all right,' said the young lad.

'You'll have fun on your walk,' said Charlie.

'Neh, he wants to stay behind and get felt up by yon teacher,' said a huge overgrown lad, bulky of shoulder, his voice already breaking, to an outbreak of laughter from the others. Joel went puce.

'You want to go home, Fingal Connarty?' shot Jan, sharp as you like. 'I don't want to send you home, son. I want you to stay. Can you stay?'

The huge boy shrugged.

'Then you keep a civil tongue in this place.'

Caleb, however, heard none of this. He had turned bright

red, and went charging up towards Fingal, fists outstretched, and despite being several inches shorter than the other lad, still managed to get a reasonable uppercut into Fingal's pudgy nose.

'Oi, you little fucker!'

Fingal rugby-tackled Caleb, bringing him down to the ground, and was about to start pounding on him when Charlie and Joel managed to pull them both apart.

Jan then did a surprising thing. She went to both of the boys and put her arms around them.

'It's OKAY,' she said. 'It's okay. Can you apologise?'

'He called me names!'

'So what?' said Jan.

'I've got a bleeding nose! I'm going to kill you!'

It was decided, fairly speedily, that Caleb would in fact stay behind with Joel and help with taking down the camp. Joel was starting to worry he'd made a terrible decision.

Charlie gave him a walkie-talkie, as phones didn't work up the hill, and told him they'd be back in two hours, if he wouldn't mind organising their main breakfast.

'How many are you?' said Joel.

'Thirty,' said Charlie. 'See you later!'

Caleb said that the night before they'd taken the dishes to a nearby stream, so they decided to do so again. As Joel had thought, the haar began to burn off, and from up here the sheep on the farm were tiny fluffy dots, and the sailing boats and great steaming tankers were toys on the horizon.

It was quiet away from the sea, only the birds calling and chirruping to one another.

Joel answered Caleb's questions about America as entertainingly as he could, even into the second half-hour about *Avengers Assemble*.

But oddly, he didn't mind. It was the first time in a long time that he'd spoken to anyone who wasn't telling him terrible news; or trying to ferret information out of him. Caleb was the first person he'd met since he couldn't remember when who didn't want anything from him, who didn't care who he was.

'I want to go to America,' said the boy eventually.

'Well, there's no reason why you shouldn't,' said Joel. 'Just work hard at school and get a job.'

Caleb laughed. 'Ha. What's the point?'

'Well, I wanted to travel.'

'Yeah,' said Caleb, kicking the dirt. 'You're not from where I'm from.'

Joel looked at him. 'I grew up in a children's home.'

The boy blinked. 'Aye?' he said cautiously. They were scrubbing the frying pan, neither of them particularly well.

'Aye,' said Joel, rather clumsily.

'And you went to college and that?'

'Yes.'

'And you still came *here*?'

Joel laughed and splashed him with bubbles. 'Watch it,' he said.

But Caleb still stared at him curiously.

Joel set about making breakfast without too much

clattering. It was odd how he found that the simple chopping up of mushrooms and tomatoes was exactly what he needed: calming and meditative. He could see straightaway what Flora got from it. It was pleasant to be out here, in the breezy early morning air, rather than stuck inside an office staring at a screen. He glanced up and found himself being regarded by a large hare, who flattened its ears then bounded off across a field of wildflowers. Joel found himself doing something uncharacteristic: he was smiling.

He turned round then at a sound. At first, he thought it was just one of the birds, but as he listened he realised it sounded more like a stifled sob.

He walked over to behind a copse and found little Caleb, his face absolutely filthy, desperately trying to stifle sobs. As soon as he saw Joel, he turned his face away fiercely, wiping his nose on his grubby sleeve.

'Hey,' said Joel, as casually as he could. 'Are you hiding to get away from helping with breakfast duties?'

Caleb shrugged. Joel wanted to go and sit beside him but didn't feel that would be the right approach. It was like dealing with a terrified animal.

'I'm sorry,' said Joel, realising. 'I didn't mean to splash you with bubbles. I was trying to mess about, that was all. It's my first day.'

'It's no' you, mister,' came the small voice.

'Are the other boys being assholes?'

Caleb shrugged.

Joel sat down, pretended to be very busy looking at his cup of coffee and didn't say anything for a moment. In the distance, two cormorants circled the cliff at the end of the beach.

'They're stupid,' said Caleb. 'Anyway, their mas are rubbish. Hoors the lot of them.'

'Don't say that,' said Joel gently.

Caleb rubbed his face again.

'Were they talking about mothers?'

Caleb shrugged. 'I don't care.'

Most of the boys had mums, whom they lived with on and off; many were with their grandparents; nearly all had some kind of family contact. Only Caleb was truly alone, it transpired: in a residential home, for as long as he could remember; never adopted. He wasn't cute, with his scrawny rattish features and embittered expression. Oh, Joel knew it all so well.

'Everyone wants girls, don't they?'

He didn't even know why he said it.

Caleb nodded fiercely. 'They want the cute ones. Blah, blah, blah, ooh, kissy cuddle face.'

He scowled again.

'In my day, they wanted boys to work the land,' said Joel. 'I didn't look like I could do that either.'

Caleb looked up. 'Did they make you?'

'They tried,' winced Joel, remembering one particularly long summer on a cotton farm in Virginia. There had been a lot of shouting. He had been so tired he had fallen asleep every night at the dinner table. Theo the farm hand had thought he was useless and bullied him endlessly. The smell of the fields had haunted him for years. Mind you, he'd had no problem with insomnia then, he found himself thinking.

Caleb sat up and they both threw rocks into the stream

for a bit, not speaking even as they could hear the other boys, returning to the camp, shouting things.

'It sucks,' said Caleb.

'It does,' said Joel, throwing a stone with exceptional force. 'It sucks ass.'

Caleb shot him a sideways glance. 'Does it get better?'

And Joel thought about it. 'Yes,' he said, 'it does. Now wash your face and we'll get to breakfast.'

Chapter Fifty-two

Saif was definitely on a post-Neda high when he decided that a Saturday afternoon walk in the blowy mountains might be quite the thing – it would help Ib forget about his iPad for one.

It had also occurred to him, as Neda had told him, that he would have to talk about their mother at some point. And possibly being high up in the hills might provide ... well ... a safer space. A space for all of them that wasn't just tiptoeing about the house, with the constant sound of computer games and Ash whimpering in his sleep. He didn't want to carry Ash up the hill – one good thing since they'd got here was that he was filling out and putting on some weight. There weren't quite the hollows under his eyes that there had been before, and he was getting heavier to carry everywhere. Though his hollows had transferred themselves directly to his father.

Nonetheless Saif tried to be jolly as he got them, grumbling, into waterproofs and wellingtons. It was cool and breezy outside, and the grass bent in the wind. Ibrahim moaned and complained the entire way. Ash was bouncier, particularly when he saw a hawk that Saif pointed out to him.

Annie's Seaside Kitchen was busy as he popped in for some rolls to take with them, and Flora was looking slightly distracted.

'How's Joel?' said Saif casually. Joel hadn't come to see him to ask for drugs, and Saif was unsure as to whether this was a good or a bad thing.

Flora stiffened. 'You'd have to ask him,' she said, and Saif regretted mentioning it immediately. Ash was pointing at the big jam and cream scones at the front of the display and Saif made a promise he could have one if he climbed to the top of the hill, which Ash immediately did, whereupon Saif bought it for him and Ash immediately dissolved into tears and demanded it now and Saif eventually gave in and gave him a little bit, which brought on more tears and a full door-slamming stomp-out from Ib and the same sinking feeling in Saif's stomach that nobody – nobody – could be doing a worse job with the boys than he was, and he was their father. He was conscious not just of the loss of Amena, who would surely know what to do in that beautiful smiling way of hers, but his own mother, long dead, and the way she could soothe him when he was upset and the way she seemed to move . . .

He shut it down and pasted on a smile, trying to channel Neda.

'Come on! Let's go! Last up is a loser!'

The boys stomped grumpily behind, Ash moaning that he had a stomach ache, Ib pointing out every five minutes that he was bored. Saif thought for a second what would have happened if he had ever spoken to his own father like that, but again, it wasn't worth bothering about right now.

And the view from high up really was worth it, as they finally reached it and threw themselves down, complaining even though they could see all the little boats in the bay and the grey slate of the roofs of all the houses of the town.

Saif pulled out sandwiches and cans of juice and the boys picked at them listlessly. It had heated up a little bit up here, and he stretched out on the grass and let it tickle his nose. When you got close, you could see the beetles scuttle here and there, a busy world beneath the world they lived in. Were they as concerned? Did such awful things happen? How many bugs had he trodden on just to get here, and did they even notice when children, wives, parents got lost – vanished off the face of the earth?

Even so, it was pleasant up in the hills. Even Ib had lost his characteristically guarded look. Saif stared at him.

'Do you guys . . . ?'

He tried to start casually. It had been the last thing Neda had said to him before they left. They had to discuss Amena. Don't make a big deal out of it, she'd said. Just talk about her. Just let it flow naturally so they didn't feel that anything was their fault, or not up for discussion. It would be hard at first, but the more they talked, the better it would get. He had nodded when she'd said that, thinking how reasonable she sounded.

'Do you think about Mama a lot?'

Ash shot up immediately. 'Mama is coming? She's here? Mama's back?'

Ib read Saif's expression better. 'Of course she isn't,

you idiot. She's probably dead. And even if she wasn't, why would she want to come here?'

The crushed look on Ash's face made Saif more furious with Ibrahim than he'd ever been with anyone in his life. He did his best to swallow it down. He was so upset he could have . . . No. No. It was a child he was dealing with. A sad, wounded child without a mother.

He did his level best to keep his voice calm.

'We don't know where Mama is,' he said softly. 'But lots of people are looking for her. I just want you to tell me a bit about how you think about her and how you feel.'

Catastrophe unfolded. Ash collapsed into hysterical tears, like those of a two-year-old: endless, sobbing until he was hyperventilating. He cried until he threw up the sandwiches and scones all over the grass, whereupon Ibrahim called him a disgusting baby, which made him cry more and Ib stormed off in disgust.

Saif tried to hold on to Ash and move him away, even as a large column of ants came to investigate the spew, and grabbed his phone to call Neda, cursing when he remembered, yet again, that there wasn't a bloody mobile signal in the middle of one of the most peaceful, technologically advanced countries in the world – and he swore again.

'I just want Mama back,' Ash was howling and Saif rocked him like a baby, while shouting for Ibrahim, at first crossly, and then more and more worriedly. The fell was trickier than it looked; there were plenty of gullies and precipices one could easily get lost down.

'Come on,' he said to Ash. 'We need to go find Ibrahim, right?'

Ash just howled harder. 'Now Ib has gone too!'

'He hasn't gone. We just need to find him.'

Saif's head was instantly filled with horror stories of children drowning in gullies and tripping and falling over rocks.

'IB!' he roared, but the wind carried his voice away. He swore massively and rapidly in English, which he didn't think counted as proper offensive swearing, even though Ash looked up at him as if he totally understood what he was saying.

'Where's Ibrahim? Where's my brother?'

Ash's hysteria seemed to be taking on an even higher pitch. To make matters worse, the black clouds that could appear out of nowhere on even the sunniest days, like a speeded-up film, were gathering overhead. That's all they needed, a quick drenching.

He stood up and gazed around. Nothing stirred, except for the wind through the straw and the lambs hopping through the lower fields. Oh goodness.

➴ ➶

Joel was following behind the boys as they walked in a crocodile, finding an odd sense of recognition – even though the dialect they spoke was different – of the memories; of boys together. They bawled and hollered and laughed out loud and Jan and Charlie let them – as long as they were roughhousing and not being cruel – shake the kinks and the wiggles out, bay at the moon, tire themselves out, expend their energy without feeling that they were being troublesome; without having to conform to an institutionalised Victorian style of behaviour that so many boys simply weren't designed for. There was some singing of songs, including one that got abruptly halted for reasons Joel didn't understand, as it couldn't possibly be worse than the filthily rude rugby song they'd been on a moment or so before. Jan made a face and said 'sectarian' which left him no wiser than before.

The clouds were coming in, but Joel had learned fairly early on that weather was simply a condition of clothing – nothing to revel in or complain about, but merely to be got through with a song and a lot of shouting. The boys had bird-spotting manuals, which Joel had thought they would ignore, but they were actually very officious about spotting the various breeds, and laughing at one another when they made mistakes. They were just about to stop at the top of the river, where there were gentle rapids that Charlie let them kayak down, when he caught a flash of a waterproof out of the corner of his eye.

At first Joel thought it was one of their boys, but when he looked closer he caught sight of a thin, darker-skinned lad ploughing blindly through the trees, tripping and stumbling up the hill. Charlie caught his eye and nodded and Joel peeled off and headed towards him.

He hadn't met Saif's children, but he guessed pretty quickly that this was who this must be. There was something almost transfixing in the boy's misery and rage, and he wished he spoke a few words of Arabic.

As he drew closer, the threatening rain began to fall, and the boy, who still hadn't seen him, grabbed for a tree root, didn't make it and stumbled down the hill, tumbling over the too-large and unfamiliar wellingtons he was wearing.

Joel leaped down the copse and grabbed him by the shoulder just in time to stop him tripping back even further. The boy lashed out.

'It's okay,' said Joel. 'It's okay, it's okay. I can help you.'

'NO ONE HELP ME!' shrieked the boy, and Joel didn't know whether he meant no one ever had or that he didn't want anyone to, and realised of course that it could easily be both.

'NO ONE HELP ME!' the child cried out again piteously. 'NO ONE HELP ME!' and Joel looked at him, and he saw himself, and he saw little Caleb, and he saw a gulf he didn't know how to cross.

He saw all of those things before the boy, to Joel's utter surprise, collapsed into his arms, and Joel stiffly put his arms around him and said, 'There, there,' although he didn't know why people said that, or whether it helped, or maybe it did, and then he said, because he knew this much was true: 'People want to help you. They do.'

🐦 🐦

Saif was soaked and bedraggled by the time he'd carted Ash halfway across the damn mountain and found Joel and Charlie and a bunch of other people with his boy, warm and dry in a vast tent, a fire crackling outside. Ib wasn't saying much, but the other boys didn't seem to care about that. They'd met plenty of quiet ones in their time too. Caleb was sitting right next to him.

'Oh, thank goodness,' said Saif. He wanted to be cross, to ask the boy what the hell he thought he was doing, but he was just too relieved. Actually what he wanted to do was cry.

'Do you want to stay and have some sausages?' said Charlie jovially. 'They're veggie.'

'Are they?' said one of the lads. 'Chuff's sake.'

'You'll have to pay for them,' interjected Jan. 'We're a charity.'

'Um. Yes. Yes, I think we would,' said Saif.

'You know,' Neda said on the phone when he finally got a signal again, with a smile in her voice that made Saif think that perhaps everything hadn't been quite as dreadful as he'd expected. 'This is a good start. Tears, anger, shouting, pain . . . These are all feelings. Letting them out. It's a good starting point.'

'Are you serious?' said Saif. 'I nearly lost one of them.'

'Yes, but you didn't,' said Neda.

Saif glanced over to where the two boys were snuggled up to one another back in the house, drinking hot chocolate and watching television – in English, hallelujah, even though it appeared to be some strange adult drama full of people confronting each other in public houses; however, in his state of mind he'd take it. And of course Neda was right: nobody had ever said this would be easy.

Then he took a deep breath and went and turned the television off.

'Let's talk about Mama,' he said, and he brought out the pictures he had stored on his phone, and they looked at every single one of them.

There was no need to talk about the last thing the boys remembered, that Neda had shown him on the transcripts,

304

that he couldn't allow himself to dwell on, not yet, possibly not ever: that one morning, after a night of heavy shelling around Damascus, Amena had gone to fetch bread, leaving the boys at home for safety, and had never been seen again.

Instead, they talked about the food she had cooked and the songs she used to sing until both the boys had inched closer, and Ash curled across his lap, which he'd expected, but Ibrahim fitted himself under his arm, which he had not, and they talked into the night, gradually quieting, until all three of them fell fast asleep on the sofa, tangled up like puppies.

Chapter Fifty-three

In a funny way, seeing Neda had fired Lorna up too. She had to stop with this ridiculous pining: Flora for once was right. She was going to go to this barbecue on Sunday and she was going to dress up and have fun and stop feeling like a dowdy spinster schoolmarm.

And Flora was right about another thing: come Sunday, the weather was once again kind. The rest of the UK had been battered by the storms, but they had passed through and now the country was bathed in a funnel of high pressure, and the sky was a deep and cloudless blue. Already, the teenagers swigging cider by the harbourside were turning a deep shade of pink for skin unused to the bright rays of a sun that never set.

Lorna took a bottle of Prosecco from the fridge. She wore a pretty flowered dress she'd bought for a wedding down south three years ago – if she breathed in and stood up really straight, she could still get into it – and she curled her red hair round her shoulders and put on lashings of mascara and some light lipstick. As she looked in the mirror, she reminded herself: she was a young woman. She should enjoy it. Especially on a beautiful day like today.

It seemed that the MacKenzies had invited pretty much everyone to the engagement barbecue. To be fair, when you got weather like this, which was quite rare, you just wanted to follow the smell. There were the Morgenssens, all the dairy boys, who got precious few days off and were going to make the most of this one, so they were already quite far into the local ale. The boys had pulled hay bales out so everyone could sit around the farm courtyard, and had set up not just the underused barbecue, but they had dug a pit too and covered it in woodchips Fintan had set smoking the night before. Innes had sniffed and told him he was just showing off, but Fintan was adamant. If they were throwing a party, they were going to do it right. And just as well, as everyone brought engagement gifts, properly gift-wrapped and everything.

Fintan tried not to show how touched he was. In public, he was defiant that this would be the first gay wedding Mure had ever seen. Deep down, he was as keen to be accepted as anyone ever was. It was all right for Colton, who didn't give a toss what anyone thought about him, and hadn't grown up here. But being welcomed meant a lot to Fintan, who, more than almost any of the MacKenzies, desperately missed their mother's comforting ear. She would have had a good time today, he thought, looking around: the musicians tuning up;

307

the beer cold in the bins full of ice; dogs and children already starting to lark through; Flora's spectacular chocolate mousse chilling in the fridge.

Innes came over. 'Mum would have liked this,' he observed, and Fintan started.

'Yeah,' he said. Innes passed him an already open bottle of beer, and they toasted.

Saif wasn't sure what time to show up and what to bring. He didn't really get invited to many social events on Mure – partly because he kept himself to himself and didn't join the golf club or the pub quiz team; partly because he was foreign; but mostly because he'd seen absolutely everyone's private parts, and nobody likes that. So he was excited to go, and dressed the boys in clean white shirts.

When he'd woken up – very cricked and cold and uncomfortable on the sofa with a dead arm and broad daylight outside, even though it was 4 a.m. – he'd had a sense that things were changing. Not quickly, but changing they were, and for the better. And now, he had the inclination to believe Neda. He'd see her again in a month; he wanted to show her how much they'd improved. He thought, for the first time, that it might be possible. Then he looked back into the bedroom and sighed.

'I DON'T WANT TO GO!' Ibrahim was shouting. He'd returned to his bedroom and was lying full-length on the bed.

'There'll be other kids there.'

'I hate them!'

'Agot will be there,' said Ash happily.

'Exactly.'

'She's a baby.'

'She's not a baby! Just play nicely.'

Ibrahim sighed in a very teenage way. 'Can't I just play on the iPad today? When there's no school?'

'No,' said Saif. Saying no did not come easily, but he was trying it out for size. 'If you're polite and speak English, then I will let you play on it tonight.'

Ibrahim weighed this up and declared it officially acceptable.

'But not with that baby Agot.'

'Deal,' said Saif.

They walked through the farm gates – late, obviously: he'd got it wrong again. A group of people were in the corner playing a piano they'd trundled out of the house, and there was a fiddle, and various already quite drunk people were standing up to do a song. Huge numbers of children were tearing round and round the house playing with the dogs. The smell of grilled meat went all the way down the drive and was driving the dogs potty. He felt suddenly nervous as they walked through the gateway, feeling that awful party feeling when you think you won't know anyone or that everyone is looking at you, and he realised that bringing a bunch of flowers when the field in front of the farmhouse, which was lying fallow this year, was absolutely teeming with poppies and wild daisies, was perhaps a little unnecessary. Agot came tearing up to them, her almost-white hair glinting in the sun. She was wearing a medieval princess dress of velvet with a long train, goodness knows how or why. But, oddly, it rather suited her.

'MY FRENS!' she yelled.

From Agot's point of view, she had been feeling most out of it, as all the other children went to the local school and had been ignoring her, and she had been on at her father to let her attend simply by calling it 'MY SCHOO!' whenever they drove past it. Eilidh's parents were elderly, and on the mainland. When she was with her mother, Agot got farmed out to a succession of babysitters and, it seemed to Innes, anyone who could take her. It wasn't that Eilidh was a bad mother – she was a wonderful mother. But trying to keep together the fabric of family and home and work when her ex lived a body of water away was so tough on both of them. It gladdened his heart to see so much of his daughter; he knew many divorced fathers didn't or couldn't. But he had no idea what to do with Agot's apparently implacable will to move.

Ash lit up. 'AGOT! PLAY!' he demanded. His small vocabulary of English words tended towards the imperative.

'YES!' said Agot, equally happy to respond in shouts, and the six-year-old and the four-year-old took themselves off. Saif looked for Ibrahim, who was staring rather longingly at a rowdy football game that was going on at the end of the low field, consisting of several boys, a couple of girls, some drunk dads and some dogs.

'You could go and play,' said Saif.

Ibrahim shrugged. 'They won't want me.'

'This is a party. It's different from school. You're good at football.'

'I'm not,' said Ibrahim.

'Well, you can't be worse than that dog there.'

The ball came soaring towards them. Saif nudged him. 'Go on.'

'*ABBA!*'

'Just return it. Then you can come back to me.'

'You are *so* embarrassing.'

Saif found himself grinning. That was all he wanted to be. An embarrassing dad.

He straightened up as Ibrahim slouched off, handed back the ball and was ushered in by one of the fathers. He smiled once more to himself and moved forward.

Two things struck him, almost simultaneously. The first was Lorna. He would barely have recognised her. Gone was the fleece she wore for cold walks in the early morning, hair pulled back. Instead, she was wearing the prettiest summer frock – Saif didn't know a lot about women's clothes, but he could see the tumbling flowers and the way the long skirt swayed in the light breeze, and it looked pretty to him. Her hair was loose and glorious – that shimmering red that looked so exotic and foreign – and tumbled down her back. She was wearing a little make-up, and her eyelashes were long, and she was laughing in the sunshine, and Saif felt a jolt of something he hadn't felt for a long time, and he remembered suddenly last year, when they had nearly, just for a moment, kissed at the town ceilidh. Suddenly he found his throat was dry, and his cheeks were pink, and as the sun glinted off her hair he felt a way he hadn't felt for a long time. It was several seconds before his reflex guilt kicked in, before he told himself, I am married, I am, I am, in the eyes of God and the world, to a woman I love, even though every day brought less and less news; even though even the boys now only asked at night.

Then Lorna turned and saw him and her heart leaped, and every idea she'd had of playing it cool or not reacting or ignoring him in favour of Innes . . .

She stopped, frozen, caught in mid-smile, unable to disguise her delight at seeing him, her heart lurching. Oh, he was exactly the only person she wanted to see and they gazed at one another . . .

'Hey, beer?' Saif blinked, and tried to focus on the person handing him a drink. It took him a moment to realise it was Colton, and he was about to make his excuses and move towards Lorna when he stopped and looked twice, and suddenly everything changed.

Chapter Fifty-four

Colton wasn't Saif's patient – Saif presumed he had a private doctor elsewhere – so Saif hadn't seen him for a long time.

Probably it wasn't as noticeable if you saw him day to day.

But Saif knew. In his country, where medicine could be expensive, many people put off going to the doctor until as late as they could. Often far too late. And when they came into his surgery, they had a look about them. It was experience that taught you, and Saif knew it very well.

Saif stared at Colton, who was looking at him cheerfully, beer still outstretched.

Gradually, Colton took in the look. Saif glanced around to make sure nobody was standing too close to them. He didn't see Lorna's face fall rapidly into deep disappointment, as he had seen her and then immediately snubbed her to talk to Colton.

He did not see her tip the rest of the glass of wine down her neck in double-quick time, grab a huge refill, then march off, face hot, to look for someone – anyone – else to talk to, and to stop herself bursting into tears.

'What is wrong with you?' Saif said quietly and urgently. He never realised how direct and rude his English could sound sometimes. The English language not having a formal tense meant he just assumed nobody minded how you spoke to them.

'What are you talking about?' said Colton. 'Have a beer, enjoy the lovely day. You drink beer, right?'

Saif rolled his eyes and didn't answer, taking the beer. 'You have not been to see me.' His voice was barely louder than a whisper.

Neither was Colton's. 'Why would I have to do that?' he said uncomfortably.

'You have lost a lot of weight.'

'I'm getting married. That's what people do.'

Saif shook his head. 'I do not want to alarm you. But I would like very much for you to come in and see me. In fact, I would like to send you for some tests. I do not want to scare you or spoil your party. But I would highly recommend that . . .'

Colton grabbed Saif by the arm and marched him over to the quiet side of the barn, where there was no one else around. 'Shut up,' he hissed. 'I don't want to hear it. And I don't want you shooting your mouth off either.'

'What would I be shooting my mouth off about?'

Colton spat on the ground. Saif looked into his clouded eyes and heaved a sigh. 'Doesn't he know?'

There was a long pause. Colton stared at the ground.

'You're getting married! You should tell him! Where is it?'

There were so many options now. Treatment in the West was astonishing to Saif. For all the complaints about the NHS, he found it passionate and compassionate and mind-bogglingly successful.

'Pancreas. Well. It started there.'

Saif never swore, as he was never sure which taboo words in his new language were mild and which were unfathomably insulting. But now he did. There was barely a worse prognosis.

'Fuck,' he said.

'You sound funny when you say that,' said Colton.

'Stage?'

Colton held up four fingers. 'You're a doctor, right? You can't tell anyone.'

'You should perhaps tell your husband.'

'After the wedding,' hissed Colton.

They glanced round. The scene under the wispy clouds in the sky was idyllic. The football match; the dancing; the laughter in the air; the children running; the fiddle music; and the green hills stretching down, dabbed with lambs and wildflowers and bright waving poppies all the way to a deep blue sea that went on for ever.

'There is nothing they can do . . . ?'

'You think I can't afford the best doctors, Doc? No offence. You think I haven't checked this shit out? That that hasn't been my full-time job for months? I have my own morphine supply, my own whisky distillery . . . Hell, I'm just happy it isn't dementia.'

Colton's bravado was touching, but he wasn't even fifty.

'Doc.' Colton leaned over. His voice was slightly slurred. It seemed impossible Fintan hadn't noticed.

'I have one. Last. Summer. I want to spend it here, on this place I love. I want to get married to the boy I love, without everyone giving me fucking puppy dog face. I want to be happy, and then I want to drift away. Chemo will give me an extra six months of throwing up in a fucking bucket. It doesn't matter anyway, because this shit is spreading to my brain and you know what that means.'

Saif did. Delirium. Hallucinations. Mental incapacity. The full checklist of horrors.

'I'm not having it,' said Colton. 'I control my life. I control what I do. I always have. And I am telling you. I'm not having it.'

'Don't say any more,' said Saif. This was perilously dangerous, legally speaking. 'Please don't say any more.'

Colton swigged from a paper cup of whisky. 'I find I worry less these days,' he said. 'About how much alcohol is good for me.'

He pointed at Saif.

'Vow of silence, right? Hippocratic oath.'

'Who knows already?'

'That piss-ant lawyer of mine,' said Colton, sighing. 'I sure wish I'd never told him. He fell apart. That is the one thing I feel bad about.'

Agot suddenly appeared, her little witchy face sly.

'UNCO COLTON! UNCO COLTON, IS AGOT YOUR BRIDESMAID?'

'Yes, of course you are, Agot. Always.'

'WE NEED HORSIE! ME AND ASH NEED HORSIE!'

Ash was jumping up and down, pretending he knew what was going on.

'AND YOU, ASH DADDY ALSO,' said Agot indignantly.

Which was how, after receiving the devastating news, Saif and Colton, after another slug of his whisky, ended up on all fours in the long, sweet-smelling green grass, riddled with tall daisies and dandelions, each with a child on their backs, roaming the garden and making appropriate noises.

And Lorna gave up, and drank another too-large glass of wine, and decided to go and see what Innes was up to.

Flora was going crazy in the kitchen, bustling about, taking cling film from the tops of salads and things people had brought, sending Hamish out with bottles to top people up. Anything, in fact, to save her having to smile and answer questions about Joel. She sighed heavily just as Mark walked in, carrying the most expensive bottle of wine the little supermarket sold (which was not very expensive), and with a huge pile of hog roast on a roll. He looked as happy as a clam, but his face fell when he saw her.

'Ach, my Flora,' he said, putting his arm around her. 'I know. I know.'

'I haven't even seen him,' said Flora. 'I haven't seen him at all.'

'You need to let him recover. Let him get there on his own.'

'What if he doesn't?!'

Mark patted her on the shoulder. 'Life is difficult,' he said. 'Your food, on the other hand . . . it is amazing. And it is a wonderful afternoon, and the sun is shining and there is wine . . . Life could be worse.'

'Yes, it could. But, Mark. Why can't . . . why can't he just let me in?'

Mark sighed sadly. There was so much he could say. But he couldn't say any of it.

'It's very difficult for him,' he said.

'It's difficult for everyone,' said Flora. 'Can I ask you one question?'

'Um, I don't know.'

'If you were me, would you wait?'

Mark rubbed his neck. 'Come on, Flora. There's only one person who can answer that.'

'No, there are at least three, and two of them won't talk to me. By which I mean you and Joel, by the way, in case it wasn't obvious.'

'It was quite obvious, thank you,' said Mark amiably. 'But that only leaves one person to answer the question.'

Chapter Fifty-five

Saif finally managed to persuade Agot and Ash there was ice cream in the kitchen if they went and asked Flora nicely. He looked closely at Colton, pulling himself up. His face was grey, and he was sweating and breathing heavily. Saif didn't say anything.

'There you are!' Fintan came up to Colton and slung an arm casually around him. 'You look hot. Are you too hot?'

'I'm fine!' said Colton. 'And a man in need of a beer.'

Fintan kissed him. 'Your wish is my command,' he said. Then he added, 'Don't expect it to be like this after we're married,' and headed off to the kitchen.

'I won't,' said Colton, watching him go. Away from the noise of the musicians, the afternoon suddenly felt quiet: the sun not so warm; the sky not so bright; the music slow and getting slower as the two men stood there in silence.

Saif badly wanted to go home, but he couldn't. Agot was showing Ash *Frozen* in the back parlour, and to Saif's total surprise when he'd wandered in to check, Ash knew all the songs in Arabic. When he asked him how, Ash, not wanting to tear his eyes from the screen, had muttered something about the soldiers having it, leaving Saif wondering precisely what had happened then, and whether Ash would ever really remember. He would have asked Ibrahim but the boy had finally – *finally* – got himself insinuated into the football game and there was absolutely no way Saif was going to mess with that. So he watched with the little boy and girl for a bit – Agot having decided she wanted to sing the same words as Ash – rubbing his beard, then reluctantly went back outside.

Lorna had definitely found her courage from somewhere, somewhere being a chilled glass of rosé on a warm summer's day. Innes was standing watching the football, talking hay prices with some of the farmers who'd driven their tractors here from over the hill. She walked over to him, feeling the sun warm on her back, her dress fluttering around her legs.

'Hey,' she said, handing him the beer she'd picked up for him on the way.

Innes blinked at her, took in the dress, the pretty hair ... Oh my God! This was Flora's mystery woman! Of course it was: those two were thick as thieves! He'd rather assumed Fintan and Flora had just been teasing him, but now here she was ... He'd never given Lorna a second thought; she was his annoying little sister's best friend after all, always closing the door and giggling and smelling the place out with what he had learned was nail polish (with the occasional undercurrent of cider and black in their teenage years).

'I'm here to persuade you to enrol Agot,' she said, grinning.

He looked at her. Her face was smiling.

'I think you could persuade anyone to do anything,' he said frankly. His blues eyes crinkled in his suntanned face, and Lorna felt her insides suddenly turn a little watery. She felt defiant too. Why shouldn't she have some fun? Why shouldn't she stop moping after some ridiculous, completely out-of-reach man she was never going to be with? Was she going to sit on a shelf for ever?

'Well, that's fortunate,' she said, moving closer. 'But we don't have to talk about school.'

Lorna wasn't very experienced at flirting, and not particularly good at it. But suddenly, there was something in the evening that made them both not care.

'We don't need to talk about anything,' said Innes, taking a grateful swig of the beer. The fiddlers had started up a fast jig. 'Dance?'

Lorna held out her hand.

Joel glanced at his watch. The streets of Mure were empty. Every single person on the entire island was up at the barbecue. And he should go, he really should, even if it was the last thing he could handle right now.

Joel took the hill road, expecting to see the boys – it was their last day today; they'd catch the morning ferry back, but Jan had said they didn't need him. He had watched, genuinely surprised as the boys had complained less, laughed more, seemed to stand up straighter by the end of their stay. They had gone brown as nuts in the sun, laughing and splashing about in the stream. He was going to have to have a word with Colton, make sure they didn't lose their funding, as Jan kept threatening they were about to . . . No, he wasn't going to think about Colton.

He wandered up and the boys crowded around him.

'Well,' he said. 'Nice to meet you all.'

They cheerfully chorused a goodbye and Joel had the pleasant sensation of doing something positive, something that wasn't just for him.

Before he'd got too far, Caleb had caught up with him. 'Oi! Mister! Joel! Mister!'

Joel turned round. He glanced up, expecting to meet Jan's disapproving face, but she just smiled.

'He wants to come into town with you!' she yelled.

As usual, Jan didn't ask whether this would be all right or not. She said what was happening and you had to deal with it.

'Okay then,' said Joel.

They walked in reasonably companionable silence. Joel stopped at the grocer's and asked the boy if he wanted anything, expecting an order for sweets, but Caleb shook his head. 'That's all I get,' he said quietly. 'Can I have proper food?'

And Joel's heart sank and he wanted to take him to the Seaside Kitchen to buy him something wholesome, but of course it was shut for the party, so then naturally Caleb wanted to know where everyone was and when he found out they were at a party his eyes got very wide and he rushed back and told everyone. Almost before Joel knew it, they all appeared to be marching up the hill road to the MacKenzie farm, where the boys could smell the most delicious barbecue. Caleb gleefully slipped his hand into Joel's, as the other boys congratulated him on his magnificent scheme. Joel looked down at him and grinned.

Caleb gazed at him wonderingly. 'Can I see your watch? I won't steal it.'

Joel unstrapped the heavy Jaeger-LeCoultre he always wore, which had been knocking the boy's slim wrist. He had bought it when he got his first bonus, solely because Mark had one and it seemed a nice, heavy, centring thing to have. Caleb looked at it in awe.

'How much is this worth?'

Joel smiled. 'It really doesn't matter.'

'Can I have it then?'

For a moment, Joel was tempted to give it to him, before he realised the horrendous amount of trouble they would all get into if he let this happen.

He looked at Caleb. 'When you finish school,' he said. 'If you get all the way through and pass your exams – because you're obviously smart – then you come and find me. And I'll help you in any way I can. And then you can have the watch.'

'Whoa! That's going to be my watch!'

'If you get your head down,' said Joel. 'And ignore all the crap. And just get on. And try your best. Caleb ... '

The boy was staring at him as if he held the meaning of life.

'There is a way out. I promise there is. You just have to work harder than the next person. Which doesn't seem fair and it doesn't seem nice and you'll think nobody will care, and you might be right. They might not. But then it doesn't matter, because you'll be old enough and out of there and you can make the world care about you. It just takes time.'

Caleb nodded. 'Well, I'll have time,' he said cheekily. 'Because I'll have your watch.'

'You'll have my watch,' agreed Joel, feeling very nervous as they approached the farm gates, and very unsure of the welcome awaiting him.

Chapter Fifty-six

Flora walked out into the courtyard, glass in hand. She noticed to the side that Innes now had his arm around Lorna's waist and, across the room, that Saif was trying very hard not to look at it. She saw her father, happily oblivious to all of this, beaming at everybody there, obviously quite surprising himself with the speed with which it had become completely normal to him that his son was marrying another man – a foreigner at that. Amazing. Almost as amazing as Hamish, who was sequestered in a corner with a girl Flora had never seen in her life before – busty, and incredibly overdressed for a Sunday barbecue, in a low-cut top and a very short skirt. Hamish wasn't saying much, but he looked utterly delighted.

Flora cleared her throat.

Colton and Fintan were holding each other closely, looking expectantly at her as the crowd quietened. God, Colton had lost a lot of weight. She thought only brides did that.

Joel was nowhere to be seen.

'Um,' she said, her voice growing quieter.

'I just wanted to say ... thanks for coming. To celebrate the engagement of Colton and Fintan, even though obviously that's very annoying as two people shouldn't get married whose names sound exactly the same ... '

There was some appreciative laughter.

'But we are so happy that they are and that they're going to be staying here on Mure ... '

A cheer went up.

' ... and Colton will be getting the drinks in. Hopefully.'

Colton raised a glass with a half-smile.

'So. Eat, drink, be merry, everyone ... and here ... '

There had been a collection box in the Seaside Kitchen for weeks, hastily hidden if either of the happy couple came in. Flora didn't think anyone hadn't contributed. She lifted the cloth she'd had underneath the trestle. There it was. A swing.

She didn't know when it had occurred to her that a swing would make a nice gift. It was for the tree just outside the Rock before you got to the walled garden where the vegetables grew. It just seemed the perfect spot for it. It was a large swing, built for two by the endlessly talented Geoffrey, and inscribed carefully by old Ramsay at the forge: 'Colton & Fintan, September 2018' in immaculate letters.

The men knew immediately where it was for. Fintan jumped up, grinning and pink. Colton didn't move for a little bit, and when she glanced back up at him – this guy who had received honours and prizes his entire life, who had done little but win acclaim and awards wherever he'd been – she saw tears in his eyes, and suddenly, for the first time, he looked his age.

Fintan held it up.

'This is beautiful,' he said wonderingly. 'Geoffrey, was this you?'

The old man, who rarely said more than was strictly necessary at any given moment, nodded shyly.

'We'll treasure it,' said Fintan. 'Outside the Rock, don't you think? On all those freezing evenings! We can swing on it to keep warm.'

Colton did his best to smile, but still didn't seem quite able to trust his voice.

Fintan embraced Flora. 'Thanks, sis,' he said and she hugged him back.

'I'm so glad you came home,' he added under his breath, and Flora grinned.

'That's not what you said at the time.'

'I'm an older, wiser man now,' he grinned back.

'No, you *have* an older, wiser man,' corrected Flora, and watched as Fintan put the swing down – very, very carefully – and went back to embrace Colton, who still hadn't moved. He seemed very overcome by emotion, she thought.

Everyone else was clapping and turning back to their drinks and the fiddles were starting up again, and as she stood there she realised that everyone had turned away. And she was still there, alone, her brothers engulfed.

'That was a nice idea, lass,' came a voice, and she realised her father was by her elbow, surrounded, of course, by the omnipresent dogs. 'Very nice.'

He clasped her arm. She could never quite get used to being taller than him.

'That chap of yours?'

Flora winced. How could she say it? Joel had let her down. Or she hadn't been enough. Either way ... There was to be no excusing it. No understanding it, even. If even her father had noticed ...

She just shrugged.

'He's over there,' her dad said.

Chapter Fifty-seven

Joel stood, looking awkward, holding a small boy by the hand.

'Uh, hi,' he said.

'You came!' said Flora, unable to conceal her delight. He looked so much better: much, much healthier than he had a few weeks ago, stumbling off the plane. Then her eyes travelled to the little mite next to him.

'Hello,' she said kindly. 'Who are you?'

But then the entire party traipsed up behind them, and she clocked the entire band of boys, with a smug-looking Jan and an oblivious-looking Charlie bringing up the rear.

'HELLO, FLORA,' shouted Jan loudly. 'So lovely to have your ex working for us now! He's just wonderful; I can't believe you let him go.'

Flora blinked twice and turned round and headed straight into the house.

This was her home – the place she had lived most of her life, in happy times and sad. But there was nothing here for her tonight. Her hands scraped the corridor wall, covered in old pictures of her and the boys: riding ponies; blowing out candles. Her parents, getting married in black and white, nervously beaming at each other, looking like children dressed up in wedding clothes. Rosettes from long-forgotten dancing shows; small trophies here and there. The detritus of a long family life in an old family home.

She picked over the various people having loud, slightly pissed-up but very intent conversations in the kitchen, and glanced again out of the window at happy couples dancing in the golden early evening light, including Innes and Lorna.

Even if you took away the fact that Innes was her stupid big brother, you couldn't deny they made a good-looking pair: his hair blond in the sun, hers a shimmering red-gold glinting in the light; both laughing; dancing with practised ease, Innes from many nights seducing girls on and off the island and Lorna because she had to teach all the little ones for the Christmas party. They were lovely together, and Flora felt a mixture of happiness and sadness all at once. She caught a glimpse of Saif suddenly, sitting to the side sipping a beer while getting his ear bent by Mrs Kennedy, who thought that her medical woes were of interest to everyone, and probably took this even further with the doctor. But his eyes were watching the dancers too, and his face was sad.

Flora slipped out of the side door and walked down the hill, not even turning to say goodbye to her father, who was now happily ensconced in an old chair they'd pulled outside, chatting to his cronies. She wouldn't be missed, and even if she was, she certainly didn't want to draw attention to herself leaving, or spoil anyone else's fun.

The harbour was uncharacteristically quiet. The campers had obviously retired, finding that Sunday trading laws were still very strict on Mure, and that there really was nothing open, particularly in the afternoon. They'd all be on the Endless Beach, Flora assumed, making the most of the glorious day. Or, if local, it seemed that everyone on the entire island was up at her house.

She stared out to sea, desperately looking for the narwhal dancing – anything to lift her spirits. She wondered briefly why Colton had been so emotional. It was sweet really; he'd never seemed like a terribly emotional man.

But seeing Joel again. That's what had really set her off. When he hadn't even come to see her.

The realisation was like a wave breaking over her head. He was getting better – it was obvious. And still he didn't want her. And she couldn't keep kneeling at the edge of the table for crumbs. She couldn't survive off closed minds and turned backs and things – so many things – left unsaid. It was like trying to love a rock. No, she thought bitterly to herself. At least rocks were solid and stayed put. Joel was a law unto himself. She felt horrible deep down in her stomach.

The tide was high, lapping against the harbour wall. The Endless Beach had disappeared almost completely; it must be a lea tide, that rare mystical confluence of moon and water that made the world feel entirely enslaved to the gentle deep blue.

She knew now. The Seaside Kitchen was leaking, but summer was coming on strong. She could do it. They were going to make it up, she knew they were. She could keep it together. She could make it on her own, after all these years of yearning so much for Joel. She was still here. And the tide would still come in and go out, and the sun would still rise – well, until the clocks went back, at any rate – and she would persevere. And sustain. She could.

'Flora!'

She squeezed her eyes tight. She didn't want to talk to anyone and she certainly didn't want to talk to him, not here, not now.

'FLORA!'

Joel couldn't get her to turn round. She was walking away from him. How many other people had he seen walking away? He couldn't bear it. He ran ahead of her across the walkway to the harbour, as she kept walking, head down, not looking at him.

'Go away, Joel,' she hissed. He dived up in front of her on the wall, and she blindly put her arms out to move him out of the way. He stumbled, surprised for a moment, as Flora looked up, also surprised, and without warning he found himself off balance and slowly, and entirely without cere-mony, he fell sideways off the harbour wall into the water.

'JOEL!'

Flora's face was a picture as she peered over. The water was shallow but utterly freezing, about knee deep, and he immediately tripped in the rip. He had managed to hurl himself into a forward roll as he fell – and landed rather beautifully, Flora was unsurprised to note – but he was choking and coughing and utterly drenched, and completely shocked by the sheer temperature. He stood up, his brown hair dripping and curling more now it was wet, falling over his glasses.

Flora couldn't help it. She burst out laughing.

'Why do we live in the Arctic?!' shouted Joel, and Flora couldn't help noticing the 'we'. But she was too helpless to respond. His trousers were utterly ruined.

'Thank you for your sympathy and kind help,' said Joel. 'Oh my God, I'm going to die of hypothermia.'

'It's only up to your knees,' pointed out Flora. 'Also . . .'

She pointed to the far end of the Endless, where the sand backed into the dunes and the tide never took over completely. You could just see a family playing there, the children in swimming costumes splashing in the water.

'Oh, for Christ's sake,' said Joel. 'Okay, I get it; you're all Nanook of the North.'

He waded towards the wall and tried to scale it, but without success. Flora watched him but didn't follow him, as he waded round to the slip. Her heart was beating incredibly fast.

'Please,' he said, hands out as he approached, dripping all the way. 'Can we talk?'

'I don't know,' said Flora. 'Can you?'

Chapter Fifty-eight

Feeling distinctly hazy, Lorna clocked somewhere that Saif had left – without saying goodbye; without speaking to her at all. Fine. If that was what he wanted, Innes was looking handsomer and handsomer in the bright early evening; the noise was growing louder and everyone was having an absolute ball; Colton and Fintan were dancing together, completely wrapped up in one another; a few midges were circling, but lazily, as if even they didn't want to ruin the perfection of the day.

Innes checked that Agot was busy – she was, climbing up Hamish, who happily pretended not to notice she was using him as a climbing frame. Or, possibly, he hadn't actually noticed . . .

'Come for a walk?' he said to Lorna. Lorna, giggling and none too steady in her heels, agreed and Innes pinched a bottle of fizz from the big bin full of ice and two plastic glasses, and they set off.

Saif had not gone; he had been rounding up the children, amazed that they appeared to have had a good time. He just caught sight of Lorna, still laughing, her gauzy dress floating behind her, following that handsome brother of Flora's. He shouldn't feel anything, he knew.

He felt a lot. He refused to admit it to himself, pressed it down. This was ridiculous. He was a married man. He was.

Innes and Lorna headed off, by mutual consent, not down towards the town and the Endless, where partygoers were staggering up and down, but behind the farm, climbing up the stony hill. Lorna abandoned her shoes, which they both decided was quite hilarious, and they clambered up over the grass and the moss, as the view expanded in front of them.

Finally, they came to a rock with an outlook over the top of the farm, tiny below them now, sheep dotted about like cotton buds. You could see for miles, right across, Lorna felt, the top of the world. Innes passed her the bottle and she drank, and they laughed nervously, and then Lorna giggled some more and then Innes laughed too, both of them conscious that they had known each other since childhood. He moved over and tentatively put a hand around her shoulders and she flushed.

'So,' said Innes, who, Lorna knew already, was incredibly practised at this kind of thing. She, on the other hand, was definitely a bit rusty.

Innes moved closer.

'You look pretty in that dress,' he said.

Lorna realised that he was about to come in for a kiss. And simultaneously she realised that she was sitting here, feeling the pleasant weight of a man's arm around her and pretending – desperately fantasising, even, as they sat out on a hillside overlooking the most beautiful bay in the world – that he was somebody else. Oh, to hear those words – but from Saif. Innes was great, but . . .

He moved closer again. She told herself, just go for it. For goodness' sake, she was a living, breathing woman, wasn't she? She liked sex, didn't she? It was a beautiful summer night and there was a handsome man sitting right next to her and she had absolutely no other prospects on the horizon of anyone quite so nice, and she should enjoy it. She should . . .

Then she turned, and realised again it was Flora's brother – *Flora's* brother, of all people – and she realised she was laughing again and it wasn't polite and Innes was actually looking a bit wounded.

'What's wrong?' he said.

'Oh God. Sorry. Innes, I'm sorry. I'm just remembering that time you came home from Cub camp and you'd got into a fight defending Hamish because he'd eaten all the sausages . . .'

Innes smiled at that too.

'Well, he did eat all the sausages. But the other kids weren't very understanding about it.'

'You had this bloodied nose and you were so furious!'

Innes smiled. 'Maybe I'm the patron saint of lost causes.'

He passed over the bottle.

Lorna smiled back and took it. 'You were cute.'

'Cute.' Innes's brow furrowed. 'Not a word any man ever wants to hear, if I can be totally honest with you.'

Lorna leaned her head on his shoulder.

'I know. But now we're here ... I mean, it's ridiculous. I remember you eating that slug.'

'Hamish ate one first!'

'Yeah, and he liked it.'

They both smiled.

'I remember when you got all those spots on the end of your nose and locked yourself in Flora's room for the evening,' said Innes.

'Yes, and none of you were remotely helpful,' said Lorna, screwing up her face in mortification.

'Oh, come on, you were my wee sister's annoying friend! Of course we weren't.'

'But did you have to make up a song about me?' She smiled at the recollection. 'Except for Fintan. He lent me his tea tree oil. Where did he even get tea tree oil?'

'How did we never suspect?' said Innes, shaking his head.

'I think what I'm saying is ... '

'We're family,' said Innes. He nodded his head. Then he looked at her.

'You do look good in that dress though. Compared to, you know. Spotty Muldoon face.'

'Thank you.'

Innes frowned. 'Flora totally told me you had the hots for me.'

'She told me the same thing!'

'Oh my God! Let's kill her!'

'She was trying to promote incest!'

'No,' said Innes. 'Let's pretend we had a massive outdoor session.'

337

'Abso-bloody-lutely not!' said Lorna. 'There are parents down there!'

'Come on, I have to tell them something. Tops?'

'Tell them we really appreciated Colton's champagne. Or don't tell them anything!'

'I'm sure everyone's too pished to notice we've even left.'

'That,' said Lorna, watching the remains of the barbecue waltzing crazily around the farmyard far below, 'is absolutely right.'

And they toasted each other with the little plastic glasses and smiled – at an accident averted and a friendship renewed – and everyone went to bed alone, although some felt more alone than others.

➴ ➴

Back at the Manse, Fintan was still shaking his head.

'Quite a gift, eh? And you thought the pitchfork-wielding locals would set us on fire.'

Colton scratched his neck.

'I don't remember putting it quite like that.'

'Remember when you arrived . . . ? Ooh, I'm in Mure to keep private . . . I can't speak to any locals or hire them . . . '

Colton smiled. 'Well, that's before I got to know you.'

'You sound so dodgy. Come here.'

Colton smiled sadly as Fintan widened his arms, and came in for a reluctant hug. Fintan started kissing him.

'Ah, babe, I'm exhausted.'

Fintan blinked. 'Are you sure? I thought it was after the wedding you were meant to start going off me.'

'It's not that,' said Colton. His painkillers were in the

338

locked cupboard behind the bathroom door. He needed to get to them and quickly. How many weeks to the wedding? he calculated. Could he hang on until everything was signed and done?

Well. He had to.

'I'm just exhausted. It's been a great day. I love you.'

'Are you sure?' said Fintan suspiciously. He started to kiss up Colton's neck.

'No, baby, honestly.'

'Fine,' said Fintan, slightly insulted, but too good-natured to take it personally. 'Hey, did you taste that new cheese?'

'I did,' said Colton, relieved to be back on safe ground. 'You've done a terrible thing to cheese.'

'It's Mrs Laird who pickled the onions. All I did was put them into cheese.'

'A terrible, terrible thing.'

Colton's hand shook as he opened the cabinet. He couldn't bear, couldn't deal with the idea of the fuss and upset that would be unleashed if what Saif had unearthed – and Joel already knew – got out. It would be horrendous.

All that pity, and people thinking Fintan was only marrying him because he felt sorry for him, or worse, because he wanted his money, and all those hospitals, and tests, and being forced into shit he didn't want.

If he could just make it through the wedding then Fintan would be his next of kin – without being suspected of being in cahoots with him – and they could make the right choices. Together. That was all he had to do. In Colton's life, he'd always done what he needed to do. Normally by just working harder than other people. By gritting his teeth and getting on with it. He was going to grit his teeth and get on with it for as long as he was able.

'Are you still taking all those vitamins? You're going to rattle, you big Californian freakbag,' came Fintan's voice from the other room.

Colton washed them down, wincing.

'Yeah,' he shouted back. 'On the other hand, they might also make me more in the mood . . . '

'Yeah, baby!'

Chapter Fifty-nine

Back at the Rock and somewhat drier, Joel wanted to drag Flora to bed immediately. He felt, for the first time in so long, good and positive and suddenly – as soon as he'd seen her face – so much more sure. About everything.

Flora was having none of it.

'You have to talk to me.'

'About what?'

'About you. About your life. About what makes you be like this.'

'Like what? Come on, Flora . . .'

'No,' said Flora. 'Otherwise we'll start up again and it will be just the same and you won't let me in, and it'll end. Badly. And you'll go off and work for my evil arch-nemesis so she can sneer at me.'

'What?' said Joel, bamboozled.

'I'm not kidding,' said Flora. 'I want to know. All of it.'

'There's nothing to know,' said Joel. 'I told you. I was brought up in care. Get over it.'

'You can't get over it!'

'I'm fine!'

'You're not fine!'

'This isn't your business.'

'It is!'

'It isn't! Goddammit, Flora! I just wanted ... I just wanted to have something pure. Something that isn't part of that life. My selkie girl.'

He couldn't have picked a worse thing to say.

'That's not me, Joel! That's not me, some easy-going water bloody sprite that comes and goes and asks for nothing. For *nothing*. Because I'm not a real girl; I'm some stupid fantasy you have of an island and a life that just does nothing but sit around and wait for you and takes care of all your needs but doesn't get anything in return. Because I get *nothing* from you!'

He was suddenly furious. 'You have *all* of me. You have everything I have ever had to give.'

'IT'S NOT ENOUGH!' screamed Flora.

Suddenly, in his fury Joel threw the chair on the floor. Flora stared at it, then up at him.

And then he was right in front of her, breathing hard, and she was staring back up at him, her heart pounding furiously, and, even as she cursed herself for her utter stupidity, she couldn't help herself: she grabbed his face and before she knew it he was kissing her, furiously hard, almost painfully, and she was tearing at him, half from frustration and rage and everything she felt overspilling as if she didn't know how

342

else to express herself. Every word she had spoken had been pointless. Everything had been a waste. What did she have left, after all? And she grabbed him and pulled him tight towards her and they fumbled their way to the door, both of them aware that Mark might be back at any moment. They opened the door. A cleaner was at the bottom end of the corridor wielding a duster and pushing a trolley full of towels.

Both still breathing heavily, Joel tucked his shirt back into his trousers, Flora's hand went to her burning face and they tried to half-walk, half-run as normally as possible down the corridor.

Joel fumbled with the electronic key in the door of the guest cottage, and looked incredibly close to kicking it in before the green light finally showed, and they collapsed through it, without words, letting it slam loudly behind them. Joel immediately turned to Flora and pushed her hard against the wall, as she found herself absolutely frantic: ripping the expensive shirt buttons when she couldn't unfasten them; tearing at them to get through to the smooth chest; pulling off her own top so he could bury his face in her breasts. All the sadness, all the anger and grief and frustration needed to be swept away, the only way they knew how. He stopped briefly, looked at her with furious lust in his eyes and dragged her over, throwing her on the high bed. As she pulled back the crisp white sheets, he was already on her, pushing down her jeans, and she responded with equal fervour, grabbing him as if she wanted her body to swallow him up, to rip through her skin, to become a part of her and she didn't want him to stop. She didn't recognise the noises they were making; she was screaming at him and he was responding, furiously, tumultuously, as it burned through them like a purifying fire. Flora wasn't sure if it was love or rage or both, and they shouted, both of them, as he collapsed finally on top of her, a maelstrom of sweat, breathless, with items of clothing they hadn't managed to remove from the bed all round them. Joel swore, uncharacteristically, and rolled off and lay facing the wall. Flora tried to get her breath back and felt her heart rate slow, very gradually, and stared at the ceiling, trying to come back down to earth – trying not to think, What now . . . ?

Eventually, Flora had to get up and go to the bathroom. Joel still hadn't moved. She hadn't touched him or spoken to him; his broad back was motionless beside her on the bed. She moved, slowly, her muscles aching. As she got out of bed, he flinched beside her. She turned her head.

'Come back to bed.'

His voice was low, almost imperceptible. The mood had changed completely, like all the fight had gone out of him. Flora blinked. He was still lying facing the wall.

There was a pause. Outside, somewhere, a lost lamb baaed loudly, repeatedly, looking for its mother.

Joel still wouldn't turn around.

'Well,' he said. She stared at the back of his head.

He heaved a great sigh. When he spoke, his voice was very low and calm.

'When I was four years old. My father,' he said finally. 'When I was four years old, my father killed my mother. In front of me. He would have killed me too, but my mother . . .

My mother screamed and ran to the doorframe and there was a lot of blood and noise everywhere and he tried to run away.'

Flora was utterly winded.

She found herself kneeling on the bed, but didn't want to go any closer.

'I remember everything. I remember being there very clearly. My father killed my mother. The police took him away. He died in jail. I never saw him again. I didn't speak at all for two years. The government tried to foster me out but none of the placements ever worked out for me. I did well at school, got a scholarship and the government paid for me to live there until I got a full scholarship to college. Dr Philippoussis was the guidance counsellor connected to the school.'

'He is,' said Joel very slowly, 'the only person who knows.'

Inside, the snakes were writhing, coiling themselves more tightly around his brain. Sex had stopped them, shut them up for long enough, allowed him to break through and speak out. But now, he could feel them moving again.

'Did you love your mum?' Flora's soft voice was like balm.

'I don't know,' said Joel, his voice faltering. He had to, he knew. He had to push on through, defeat the things in his head. 'I don't remember. I found out later she and my father . . . They took a lot of drugs. They got in a lot of trouble. She was a dropout.'

'Their families?'

'I didn't ever know my father's family. I don't know if he even did. He was just feral, through and through.

345

My mother ... she was from a wealthy family. Gave up everything for him. They cut her off completely.'

'But what about you? What about when you were left all alone?'

'They didn't want to know. Didn't care. I was some mistake by the daughter who'd gone bad. She had a lot of siblings, I know. Maybe they were worried about their own kids' inheritance, that kind of thing. Who knows? I don't, and I don't care.'

'But ... your grandmother?'

'That's right,' said Joel. 'I come from a long line of absolute bastards on both sides.'

The snakes in his head tightened their grip, as Flora shook her head in disbelief, but he was too far in to stop now.

'That's ... '

'It happens all the time,' said Joel. 'Four times a week in your country, did you know? A man kills his partner. Leaving God knows what chaos behind.'

Flora blinked. 'Jesus ... '

'So,' said Joel. 'Now you know.'

'Now I know,' said Flora. 'And I don't care a bit.'

And then she pulled up the bedsheets and she dived right underneath them and crawled over and found him in the dark and held him – pinned herself to him from behind – held him fiercely tightly and neither of them wanted to talk any more, not then, and so Joel turned around and once more took her fiercely on the large bed. They turned off their phones, and made love, and slept, and held each other, and ordered room service and said as little as possible, to let the detonation and the dust settle – to see if they could deal with the new reality now that it was out there, now it was a part of their existence, now Joel had brought the wolf through the door, the violence unleashed; the boy become man, and the damage it had wrought.

Chapter Sixty

'No more secrets,' Flora had whispered lying next to him on the bed, and she had never been so happy in her entire life.

'You say that while I can't see your selkie tail.'

'Stop talking like that,' she said, kissing him in a warning fashion. Then she got up, groaning. 'Argh, wedding planning day.'

'Did you give any thought to the finances?'

Flora didn't want to confess that she had found his email almost incomprehensible and grimaced. 'One nightmare at a time.'

'Quite,' said Joel, who was dreading the wedding more than Flora could possibly have imagined.

Flora sat in the Rock with Colton, looking at her ring binder. Fintan and Colton were going big. Really, really big. She wasn't a hundred per cent sure she was up to it, not after the

Jan controversy, but she was doing her best – the barbecue had been a success after all, although a lot of that had had to do with the farmers' cask of ale and their incredible luck with the weather.

Colton was flying in champagne from a small vineyard, which would be completely wasted on the local residents but presumably not on the investors and rich Americans she assumed must be coming. But she'd assumed wrong, it turned out. Apart from a handful of friends – both his parents were dead – from college there was almost nobody coming for Colton at all. He'd shrugged it off cheerfully.

'Billionaires don't have friends,' he said. 'Or else they have to buy them. And my family are a bunch of tightass Republican birther homophobic bastards.'

'All of them?' said Flora.

'Every single last one. I just want people I love. Actual people I really love.'

'And all the drunks from the Harbour's Rest who'll want to come,' pointed out Flora.

'Collateral damage,' said Colton.

Flora looked at him critically. 'Stop losing weight for the wedding. You're not trying to get into a Kate Middleton dress. Are you? *Are you?*'

Colton shook his head. 'Neh. It's just being fed properly by your brother.'

'Well, that's odd,' said Flora. 'Because every time I eat Fintan's latest batch of cheese, I put on half a stone.'

Colton smiled weakly and changed the subject. 'Okay, so, anyway, the cloudbusters.'

'The what?'

Colton shrugged. 'I know, I know. Sometimes it's beautiful. But sometimes it isn't.'

He gestured outside, where it didn't look remotely summery. A sideways sweep of rain had appeared from nowhere and the Seaside Kitchen was pleasantly full of steamed-up tourists in cagoules sitting out the storm and finishing all the cheese scones and moving on to the potato scones.

'Yes, and?'

'Well, I want to have the wedding outside. I want it to be perfect.'

'You can't control the weather though.'

'Ah,' said Colton. He pushed over a brochure to Flora, who took it in amazement.

'"Cloudbusting Services",' Flora read in puzzlement. She looked up. 'You're joking, right?'

Colton shook his head. 'Nope. They seed the clouds with silver and it clears them away.'

'Where do they go?'

'I don't know. Science,' said Colton.

Flora leafed through. 'So they guarantee you a clear day on your wedding?'

'Yup.'

'That's *insane*!'

Colton looked serious. 'You know, Flora, I'm only planning on doing this once.'

'You'll have to,' said Flora. 'I don't care how rich you are: how much is this costing?'

'Never you mind,' said Colton. 'Just remember that I give a lot to charity.'

'I can google it, you know.'

'I give a lot to charity. Right, I have to go. Do you think you know what you're doing?'

'Making the most amazing meal anyone's ever had ever?'

'Great! Thanks.'

'I'm googling cloudbusting, you weirdo.'

'Can't wait to welcome you as a sister.'

'And please,' Flora genuinely was begging. 'Please, when are you opening this place up for business?'

Colton looked shifty. 'Ah, don't you like having it just for us?'

'Yes,' said Flora. 'But I like paying my staff even more.'

➤ ➤

'Okay, here's a thought,' Flora said, testing out yet another wedding cake recipe on everyone as they sat at the kitchen table in the farmhouse. Joel looked up, desperate to get out of unsuccessfully attempting to have a conversation with her father about farming.

'What if I change everything that needs butter to margarine?'

Joel winced.

'Not likely,' said Fintan.

'Yuck!' said Hamish.

'Come on, you guys, you're not helping. Hamish, come work for me for free.'

'Look,' said Innes. 'Running a business is hard. Maybe you're just not cut out for it.'

'Shut up, Innes! You're the one who nearly lost the farm.'

'Hey, don't have a go at Innes,' said Fintan. 'I was the

one who nearly lost the farm. There must be other things you could try.'

Flora looked at him. 'I could marry a billionaire. Where is he, anyway?'

Fintan shrugged. 'He's up to something secret on the mainland. I hope it's buying me a really large present.'

Flora caught Joel looking dismayed at that remark, but thought little of it.

'Do you need more investment?' said Innes.

'No,' said Flora. 'It's just pouring money down a black hole. Oh God. The only thing I can do is whack the prices up.'

'You should do that,' said Joel. 'It's absurdly cheap.'

'But I don't want to gouge everybody in the neighbourhood!'

'Can't you gouge the tourists then?' said Innes, who was cross because someone in a hire car had beeped his tractor as he'd been driving up the hill. 'They're bloody annoying buggers.'

Flora thought about it. 'I suppose ... What if I had a discount card?'

'What do you mean?' Joel took off his spectacles.

'Well ... We talked about this ... I can't charge my locals more.'

'You could ... '

'I shan't!'

Joel smiled to himself.

'*But*,' said Flora, 'what if I bumped up all the prices then gave every single local person a discount card that brought it back down to what it was and only took extra money off the tourists? And Jan ... '

The boys stopped what they were doing.

'Hang on,' said Innes. 'Did our Flora just have quite a good idea?'

Fintan shook his head. 'Flora, are you sick?'

'And every time you're rude to me,' said Flora, 'I'm adding another hundred quid on to your wedding bill.'

'Shut it!'

'Two hundred!' She smiled gleefully. 'That could work, couldn't it?'

'You'd have to explain it four times to Mrs Blair,' said Innes thoughtfully. 'And get the cards printed.'

'I can do that. Agot, draw me a card.'

'I DO THAT ALSO.'

Joel put his glasses on and grinned at her wolfishly. 'You might just have cracked it,' he said, glancing at his watch. 'C'mon, let's go home.'

'WOOOO!' said Fintan.

'Three hundred!' said Flora as they walked out of the door – Flora blushing, Joel practically pulling her along.

'And,' she said as they walked down the cobbled road to town, even though he kept trying to smother her with kisses on the way, 'your boys owe me one by the way. Well, not those exact boys. But even so. Do you think they'd fancy helping me out as wedding staff?'

'I'm not sure child slavery is as good an idea as your other one about the cards.'

'Work experience?'

'I'll ask Jan.'

'Ask Charlie.'

Chapter Sixty-one

Saif was surprised to see him there in the waiting room. He was running desperately behind: the children had had to get dressed up for Viking day and Ash had run up and down the stairs brandishing a sword and refusing to answer to any other name than Storm Cutter.

But he welcomed him in politely.

Colton sat down and took a deep breath. 'I need my medication increased.'

Saif stared. 'I haven't got your medical notes. I can't just do these things willy-nilly.'

Colton made a quick phone call, and the notes appeared on Saif's computer ten seconds later as if by magic. He sat in silence while Saif read them. The prognosis was very grim indeed. Pancreatic cancer was not one of the sexy high-profile ones that got celebrity campaigns. And Colton was very far along. It was so clear when you looked at him, but what was obviously jaundice had been covered up with

354

Colton's heavy Californian tan. He'd had his teeth whitened, wore sunglasses permanently and absented himself on business. Even so.

'How are you keeping this from Fintan?'

'A lot of effort and lying.'

'I haven't read much but ... I mean, there are experimental treatments ...'

'None of them worth a dime, Doc. The one thing I do know a bit about is where to put my money. And none of them are worth a nut.'

Saif frowned.

'And it says here you've turned down chemo?'

'Chemo is fucking barbaric, man,' said Colton, shaking his head. 'I throw up and fall apart and feel like crap so I get an extra three months.'

'Three to six ...'

'Yeah, but that's the winter anyway ...'

Saif blinked at Colton's dark humour and decided to risk responding to it. 'Won't that feel longer?'

Colton's laugh turned into a coughing fit. 'Thanks, Doc. It's nice to talk to someone who gets it. That lawyer of mine completely fell apart.' He leaned forward. 'Morphine and whisky,' he said. 'That's how I'm doing this.'

'I can't prescribe whisky,' said Saif.

'That's all right: I bought a distillery.'

Saif raised his eyebrows, unsure if Colton was joking. (He wasn't.)

'I'll get my prescriptions filled on the mainland. Don't need any busybodies around. But you make sure it's generous.'

'There are guidelines,' said Saif.

'Fuck 'em,' said Colton.

Saif stood up. 'Mr. Rogers,' he said. 'If you are looking for me to do something I should not do . . . You know where they would send me back to.'

Colton blinked. He hadn't thought about it. 'Gee,' he said. 'Sorry.' For sure he'd find a pharmacist he could bribe somewhere. Things weren't that hard when you were rich. He stuck out his hand. 'I shouldn't have asked.'

'It's your right to ask,' Saif said. 'Believe me, I am sorry to refuse.'

'Just give me as much as you can.'

Saif had given him as much as was possible without an alarm being raised. 'Done.'

'And . . . you'll be here for me, right?'

Saif nodded. 'Any time,' he said. 'But please, please get the support of your family. I can't do a thing without them, you know that.'

He couldn't understand the need for secrecy when more than anything, surely, you needed love and support around you. Pretending everything was fine wasn't going to make this go away.

Colton grimaced. 'Soon,' he said. 'Let me just get through my wedding day.'

Chapter Sixty-two

The wedding day dawned pale and clear. Flora never found out if Colton had used the cloudbuster or not, but it couldn't have been more perfect. The ceremony was being held in the back garden of the Rock, its green lawn trimmed within an inch of its life. There was a marquee, but it looked like people were going to be able to spend the entire day outside. An orchestra was playing.

Flora was wearing the green dress Joel had bought her in New York and almost all of the work had been done: Isla and Iona were busying themselves and, to her amazement, Jan and Charlie's group of boys were making themselves incredibly useful fetching and carrying.

As well as the Mure spread, there were lobsters in tanks and a special sushi chef flown in from LA, an edible flower salad and a green juice cocktail bar Colton had insisted on and presumably everybody else was simply going to ignore. There was a cascade of macaroons and an ice sculpture – but nothing, Flora thought, looked quite as lovely as the long board of Fintan's magnificent cheeses, laid out with fresh green grapes, Flora's best oatcakes, Mrs Laird's bread, local apples and imported white peaches amid chilled pitchers of rosé. It looked like a painting.

Innes and Hamish were both the best men for Fintan. Innes was in charge of the stag night, which had ended with fourteen young farmers jumping off the end of the dock at midnight, thirteen young farmers landing in the water and one young farmer landing on a fishing sloop and breaking his wrist. Saif, who had been invited but was trying to save up his babysitting, tried not to be too disapproving when woken by loud singing outside his window at four o'clock in the morning and instructed to get his plastering kit out.

Innes was also in charge of the transport, the rings, the bridesmaid, the speeches and making sure everyone had the right tartan on. Hamish was just to stand there and look handsome in the photographs, Flora said, patting him on the hand. Colton didn't want a best man; he said he already had the best one. Flora had mentioned to Joel how odd she found this, but he had been completely uninterested; he didn't seem to care to hear about the wedding at all. Flora wondered if he was secretly prejudiced, although she hadn't noticed anything like that about him at all, but in the business of the day had put it to the back of her mind.

The MacKenzies were of course getting dressed at the farmhouse and Flora went up to fetch them.

She stopped at the farmhouse door, looking in at the scene. Innes was straightening their father's bow tie. Hamish was trying to smooth down the bit of hair that wouldn't ever smooth down, and already looking hot and uncomfortable in his tight collar. Fintan was putting on just the tiniest bit of mascara. Agot was standing in a great heap of tulle and flowers and bounced up.

'ATTI FLOWA!'

Flora smiled and the boys turned to her, and with the sunlight behind her, suddenly she looked so like the one person missing from the room, and they all knew it. And she stepped forward and they all gathered in a group hug.

Hamish wanted to drive his sports car down, but of course they wouldn't all fit. Instead, on such a glorious day, Flora swapped out her shoes, and they decided to walk, arm in arm – Agot and Flora in the middle, Fintan and her father at their sides, Innes and Hamish making up the ends – and everyone who saw them marching straight through the centre of Mure, the four kilts swishing, waved and honked and sent good wishes and followed them as they walked the full length of the Endless, up to the Rock. The church bells pealed them on their way, and Fintan was nervous and giggly and they told old stories and made old jokes that only siblings could ever understand. They talked about their mum, and it wasn't until they drew near the Rock, which already was full of cars and people milling about, that Fintan's nerves really kicked in.

Flora took him aside, as she had to just check on the food one last time.

'Amazing,' she said. 'You look gorgeous.'

Fintan shook his head. 'You know,' he said, his voice cracking slightly. 'When Mum was sick ... it felt like I'd never be happy again.'

'I know,' said Flora. 'Now, give me a hug before you ruin your mascara.'

Innes, hand in hand with Agot, saw Eilidh, Agot's mother, waiting by the gate. She smiled nervously. Agot pulled Innes over and took her mother's hand in her free one, joining them.

She looked good, thought Innes. Really good, in fact. He smiled, and she smiled back, and he asked her if she would like to sit together and she said she would. Lorna, passing by, also smiled when she saw them and resolved to corner Eilidh and drone on about how wonderful her school was. Just in case.

Hamish darted after one of the new seasonal barmaids he'd had his eye on to ask if she liked sports cars.

And old Eck, ramrod straight, walked out into the sunny garden behind Agot, who was making a very careful and serious job of throwing rose petals out along the red carpet, and in front of all his friends and neighbours, walked his youngest son down the aisle.

Chapter Sixty-three

Flora looked closely at Colton standing at the altar. He didn't look terribly well; he must have real wedding nerves. Which was strange. Since he'd met Fintan, he hadn't seemed remotely in any doubt about it. Well, she'd never got married and probably never would. She glanced at Joel standing beside her. Oddly, he looked furious, his hands gripping the chair in front of him tightly. She squeezed his hand, but he didn't respond, so she concentrated on watching the service and lustily joining in the 'Hebridean Wedding Song' as Joel squinted at the incomprehensible words on the hymn sheet.

Finally, the vicar joined Fintan and Colton's hands together and produced the long white cords for purity; pink for love; blue for faith for the handfast.

'Will you love and honour and respect one another?' she asked.

'We will,' Colton and Fintan replied.

'And so the binding is made,' she said, tying the first cord.

'Will you protect and comfort one another?'

'We will.'

'And so the binding is made.'

'Will you share each other's pain and seek to ease it?'

'We will.'

'And so the binding is made.'

'And will you share each other's joy and laughter, every day of your lives?'

'We will.'

'And so the binding is made.'

And they kissed, and the congregation erupted, and a full pipe band (Colton had insisted, much to Fintan's eye-rolling) suddenly appeared from the depths of the grounds and led the grooms, followed by everyone in the wedding party, back down the aisle to a rousing march, and Mure's first ever gay marriage ('that you've heard about,' Fintan had sniffed whenever it came up) was ready to be properly celebrated.

Flora was in the kitchen when it happened. She had decided to make up a separate buffet for the boys so they could gorge themselves on sausage rolls and cheese sandwiches and crisps in the back of the catering tent. However, plenty of Murian residents had decided they actually preferred this to the sumptuous spread on offer outside and kept sneaking in, muttering about 'fancy food' and helping themselves to cheese and pineapple on sticks – and Flora had to keep chasing them out again.

At first, only catching a glimpse out of the corner of her eye, she thought it was one of the old geezers that haunted the Harbour's End, grey and wheezing. She could certainly spare a few sausage rolls, she was thinking, when she turned around and realised to her absolute horror that it was Colton.

It was as if he was hiding behind the door, leaning against the wall. His bow tie was looking rather wilted and he had a crumpled-up piece of paper in his hand. He was sweating and looked green and in pain.

'Colton?' She ran over. 'Oh my God! Are you okay? Aren't you meant to be having your picture taken? Do you need to sit down? Is it the heat?'

Anything above fifteen degrees counted to Murians as dangerously extreme temperatures.

He turned to her, momentarily confused, swallowing hard. 'Can I get a glass of water?'

'Sit down.' Flora studied him. He looked awful. She suddenly hoped it wasn't anything she'd served. Was the seafood all right in the heat? 'Are you okay?'

'Just ... just ...'

Colton was suddenly so desperate to tell her he could have cried.

'Just the heat.'

'Well, that's your fault!'

Flora whisked round suddenly at the voice to find Joel there behind her, his face grave. Next to him was Saif. They'd both noticed him slipping into the kitchen, and, for the first time, shared a glance of their common knowledge, then run to him.

'Excuse me,' she said, still thinking little of the situation. 'This is a working kitchen, *actually*.'

They both ignored her. Saif knelt down and took Colton's blood pressure.

'You should be in hospital,' he said quietly. 'Now. It's done. Come on. Enough.'

'I'm still doing this,' said Colton. 'It's my day.'

'You're nuts,' said Joel. 'You've signed the paper. Let us take care of it.'

'What the hell's going on?'

Joel glanced at Flora, who turned pink. 'Can you give us a minute?' he said.

'This is my kitchen and this is my brother-in-law, so no, *actually*, Joel. What's going on?' said Flora.

'Please,' said Saif, turning his liquid eyes on her, and after that, Flora could do little but retreat. Joel grabbed her wrist as she left.

'Everything's fine,' he said quickly. 'But could you waylay Fintan for a moment?'

'How is everything fine?'

Flora's heart was beating fast. Something was obviously terribly wrong. And Joel had that face on again. That closed-up face.

'Please, Flora, don't ask me.'

Flora, terrified, peeked out of the door of the marquee.

Fintan was there, looking gently buzzed on champagne in the glorious, ridiculous afternoon sunlight. He was handsome in his kilt, a smile and a word for everyone, as well as happily receiving compliments on the food and the sheer beauty of the day. He was surrounded by the locals, people who'd known him as man and boy, who had seen how troubled he'd been during their mother's illness and subsequent death and how Colton had brought him back to life. He stood in a pool of golden light. Very close by him, Agot was twirling round and round to make her ridiculous dress ride out, and next to her Flora noticed Ash was doing exactly the same with his little baby kilt someone must have unearthed for him; and they were both hysterical with laughter.

She stood, watching Fintan for a moment. He was so happy. He glowed with it, in the perfect sunlight, in Colton's perfect garden.

She glanced back at Colton – he looked sick, so sick. Why was Joel in there? What did he know? Saif made more sense but it was as if they knew something . . .

Her heart beat faster still, even as Fintan threw back his head laughing at something Innes was saying. She backed away. Speeches next, then lunch . . . Everything had a schedule, had been planned perfectly. She glanced round. Joel was heading back towards her, a concerned look on his face.

'What's the situation?'

'He's just overexcited . . . hot,' said Joel.

'He needed his lawyer to tell him that?'

'He'll be fine. He's coming out to cut the cake. Too much fizz on a hot day.'

'Well, that's his fault,' said Flora.

Joel blinked. 'Sure.' He looked at Fintan.

'He looks so happy,' said Flora. She turned round. 'You'd tell me if something was . . . '

Joel had already vanished back inside the marquee

though, and Flora signalled to Iona and Isla to start circulating with more canapés.

Back inside the tent, Saif was all but ordering Colton to get to the hospital, and Colton was absolutely refusing. This was his day and he was getting through it, goddammit. He drank another glass of water and asked Saif if he had anything he could give him. Saif had anticipated this moment, and he did. Ten minutes later, Colton was on his feet again, but Saif wasn't remotely happy about it.

'It's my wedding day,' said Colton hoarsely. 'Now I'm going out there before the bastards notice I'm not actually there.'

Saif and Joel both gave him an arm, helped him up and walked him to the flap of the marquee, where he shook them off and walked over to Fintan, putting on a wide and unconvincing smile.

All eyes turned to Colton as he tinked his glass for attention. Amid the exquisite gardens, the green of the lawn and the blue backwash of the sea, he looked almost translucent, and as he stood there he shook. Flora glanced at Fintan, who looked confused, suddenly, as if this was just dawning on him too. Then, with a sudden horrible cold feeling in her heart, she went and linked arms with Innes, as Joel was nowhere to be seen.

'What's up with . . . ?' Innes began, but Flora shook her head and shushed him. The speech was beginning.

'I just wanted to say . . . thank you to all of you, those of you who have come a long way and those of you who just wandered round the corner . . . to all of you in this place who have done so much to make me feel welcome, make me feel at home . . . '

'That's because you bought us all champagne!' shouted a wag in the crowd and there was a welcome ripple of laughter.

'I have never . . . I have never been so hap—'

Colton's eyes were brimming with tears and he grabbed hold of Fintan, whose eyes were also moistening. Flora frowned. He wasn't cuddling Fintan. He was leaning against him.

Fintan realised something was wrong and turned round, just as Colton mouthed '. . . happy' once more and collapsed onto the ground.

Chapter Sixty-four

Immediately there was pandemonium. Fintan leaped down straightaway, calling Colton's name. Saif and Joel ran from the marquee straight past Flora, who stood watching them open-mouthed. Saif cleared a way and put Colton in the recovery position, gently persuading him to come round. More water was brought. Joel pulled his phone out and the helicopter, which was there ready to take the boys off to start their honeymoon, was pressed into rather more urgent service to take Colton to the hospital. And all around, people fanned themselves and said, after all, he hadn't looked well, and hadn't he got thin, and they tutted and tried to shelter themselves from the ridiculous heat and worried together.

Flora went straight to find Joel and wanted to throw a tray at his head. 'He's sick!' she shouted at him.

'Flora, you know I can't talk about it. It's privileged. I can't say a thing.'

'So he's really sick! And you let him marry my brother!'

'Why? Would your brother have dumped him flat if he thought there was something wrong with him?'

'No! But don't you think he has a right to know?'

Joel was furious. 'Of course I do! It's not my decision to make! If it was me . . .'

'If it was you, you wouldn't tell anyone either,' snarled Flora. 'You'd keep it all locked up from everyone, just as usual. I thought we'd *finished* doing this.'

Joel stared at her, wounded. 'But. I. Can't. Say,' he said through gritted teeth. 'You know that, Flora.'

'But it is something they can cure?' said Flora in anguish. 'Can't they? Oh God. Just *tell me*! JUST TELL ME!'

'I. CAN'T. SAY.'

'You would screw up my entire family so you didn't lose a job?!' said Flora. 'You would literally risk the lives of people I love so that you could keep on making lots of money?'

'That's not how it works!'

'You let this happen,' said Flora. She was so white-hot with rage she couldn't see straight.

'Actually, I think I'm going to find out how a sick man is doing,' said Joel furiously, pulling out his phone and heading out of the marquee.

'Don't forget to NOT TELL ME, ONCE YOU KNOW!' screamed Flora after him in front of half of the guests. She turned round to also leave, but of course she then had to walk past everybody she knew in the gardens, all of them looking to her as if she knew. Innes and Hamish were approaching, and her father – oh Christ, her dad – was looking utterly confused standing next to the vicar. What a mess.

Joel reached the other end of the marquee. The

helicopter was still circling overhead, but oddly not landing on the clearly marked 'H' over to the side of the orchard. Colton was sitting on a chair, his head nodding a little, an obviously deranged Fintan sitting beside him, pleading with him, but Colton was, of all things, on his phone.

Joel moved forward, glancing at Saif who was shaking his head in disbelief. Before figuring out what would be best, Joel turned to the watching crowd.

'Would you mind . . . ?' he said awkwardly. Most people had never heard him talk and turned round. 'I'm sorry. Would you mind . . . leaving, or going back to the marquee please?' He looked at the disgruntled and concerned faces and had an idea. 'Actually, no, hang on – Inge-Britt – can we continue the party at the Harbour's Rest? Send Colton the bill? And we'll keep everyone updated. I'm sure it's nothing, just overexcitement.'

There were a few disappointed faces, but Joel looked smoothly authoritative and they had no choice but to turn away and head back up towards the house. Joel instructed the minibus driver, and let people tell Colton to get well soon, and hopefully they'd be back in time for the famous but terrible 1970s rock band he was rumoured to have flown in for the occasion.

By the time he got back to Colton, they were no further on. The helicopter was still circling without landing. Fintan was still shouting in a way that couldn't be heard over the din.

Joel moved quietly over to Colton's other side. 'What are you doing? You need to get on the helicopter.'

'I'm not getting on any fricking helicopter, dicks, and I don't know how to make myself any more clear,' hollered

Colton. He was sweating and looked dreadful and spoke into the phone again.

'Back off, Jim. I won't tell you again. Get back to the mainland before you run out of fuel.'

'Please,' said Saif. 'Please.'

'SOMEBODY, JUST TELL ME WHAT'S GOING ON?!' Fintan yelled in pure frustration.

'JOEL KNOWS!' shouted Colton suddenly. The helicopter at that moment chose to peel off to the side, its blades whirring against the blue, taking off over the sea. The men watched it go for an instant. Then they switched their attention to Joel.

'What?'

'Joel knows,' said Colton again, wild-eyed.

Joel froze. Fintan was looking at him, eyes wide with incomprehension and fear.

'Knows what, Colt? What do you know?' he asked, his voice bitter and low.

Flora came out from the marquee to see how the boys were; she'd seen everyone else head back to town, but she was damned if she was going. She folded her arms, ready for the fight. Her hair had escaped the bun she kept it in for catering, and it was flapping in the wind behind her back, the pale dress Joel had bought her, what felt like a million years ago in New York, blowing out in the breeze. Joel, glancing up, almost lost his breath. She looked like a fury: a beautiful, alluring avenger.

'Tell them.' Colton sounded husky. Saif folded his arms too, absolutely furious even as Flora stepped forwards and Joel found himself surrounded by accusing eyes. All the

MacKenzies: Innes, who'd sent Agot back with Eilidh and Saif's boys; big Hamish, who wasn't quite sure what was going on but was standing with his family anyway; Eck, trembling a little and quite confused. Everyone was staring at him, except for Colton who was resolutely looking away and out to sea, ignoring Fintan's hand on his shoulder.

'What?!' said Fintan, looking petrified.

'For God's sake, Colton,' Joel swore under his breath. He closed his eyes. For a moment, nothing could be heard except the rasp of Colton's laboured breathing.

All of this stuff. All of this stuff he had been carrying about for so long. All of this pain. His head tightened and twisted. He felt the snakes again, writhing, squeezing in his head.

As he stood there, Colton stretched out a gnarled hand, the skin tight over the knuckles, took Joel's long fingers and squeezed them. His watery eyes stared into Joel's.

And Joel nodded in resignation.

'Uh,' he said, standing up straighter. 'I have legally signed papers in my possession indicating the wishes and living will of Colton Spencer Rogers ... '

'The *what*?' said Fintan. And before Joel could get any further he burst into tears and flung himself on Colton.

Flora watched Joel in disbelief. The entire day had cracked like an egg. She saw his hands trembling, even as Colton held on to him with one hand and tried to cover Fintan's sobbing head with the other.

'It is his recorded wish that he remain on the island at all times, regardless of his health situation.'

372

Joel's voice sounded robotic. Flora looked at Saif. He looked sad, but not at all surprised, and she realised with a jolt that of course he must have known all along too. Her fury rose even further.

'And you were going to tell me when?' shouted Fintan in disbelief. 'We're married! We just got married!'

Colton looked up at Fintan with terrible sadness in his eyes.

'Oh my God. You're sick. You're sick. You didn't tell me. You bastard. You absolute bastard. How sick are you?'

Colton sniffed. 'About a hundred per cent, as it happens.'

'And you weren't going to tell me?'

'No,' said Colton.

'Why? So you could trick him into being your carer?' shouted Innes suddenly, unable to contain himself. Everyone looked at him. Fintan looked up at Colton, tears falling down his cheeks.

'Did you not think I'd look after you? Did you think I'd walk away if I knew? Did you think I'd ever walk away from you?'

There was silence.

'Of course not,' said Colton eventually. He stared at Joel again, who cleared his throat.

'Mr Rogers ...' he said carefully. 'Mr Rogers has made it very clear in all of his paperwork that there was absolutely no evidence of coercion or weakened resolve when you agreed to marry and indeed when you did marry.'

'What? Why?' said Fintan.

'So that there wouldn't be potential complications ... later ...'

'Nobody,' croaked Colton. 'Nobody could say you married me for money, knowing what you know now.'

'But I don't know anything now!'

'Saif?'

Saif stepped forward, very unhappy to be singled out. 'The prognosis with this type of cancer . . . '

Fintan let out a howl of animal misery and buried his head in Colton's lap. Colton stroked his brown hair.

'Sssh, it's all right. Listen to the man. Don't make him say it twice.'

But Fintan was muttering, 'I can't do this again, I can't do this again,' and did not respond.

Saif had done harder things than this. ' . . . is . . . We don't like to talk in terms of time, but months. Depending on what types of treatment are used.'

'Months for some and years for others?' said Innes.

'Some or more months.'

'But where is the cancer?'

'It is widespread.'

Fintan raised his head. 'You said you had the flu!'

'I had that too.'

'And when you were always away . . . and you didn't open the Rock?'

Colton nodded. 'I had to . . . finalise a few things.'

Fintan looked at him. 'How can you be so calm? This is the worst day of my life.'

Colton cradled his head to him closely once more. 'It can't be,' he said quietly. 'Because it's the happiest of mine. And from now on, every day has to count.'

Chapter Sixty-five

Joel had backed away, but Flora followed him.

'What have you done?' she said, her voice icy. 'What have you done to us?'

'I was following his wishes. Someone would have had to have done it.'

'So what exactly is the stupid fucking plan? What?'

'Well, he didn't want anyone to know.'

'For fuck's sake! He's going to die? But there must be treatments ... new experimental stuff they let you have if you're very rich?'

'Apparently nothing that'll work longer than a couple of months. And he said he doesn't want that. He doesn't want to go to hospital. He wants to manage it at home, fly anyone in he needs to. Sit by the beach, watch the tide go out. Here. Home.'

'Oh God,' said Flora, her voice cracking. 'Poor, poor Fintan.'

'Poor everyone,' said Joel, staring at the floor.

Flora looked at his exhausted face, the stress the last few months had put on him, carrying all of this around, and could have wept for him. 'You've carried this around all this time? You made me think it was all my fault!'

Joel was bamboozled. 'How could it have been your fault?'

She turned and walked away. She glanced around at the remains of the feast, of the washing-up the boys had done so diligently, but still there remained half-eaten crumbling pieces of cake, birds on the grass looking for crumbs, everything falling and decaying away.

Outside it was growing dark. Finally, the light summer nights were beginning to come to an end, reminding her that the long dark winter was coming, when the sun never rose at all, and everything was collapsing around her – and would get worse and worse.

She walked slowly back towards Fintan and Colton, still entwined in one another down by the water's edge, even as the sun was setting and the stars were starting to appear behind their heads. As she did, a little figure moved towards her.

'UNCO FINTAN SAD?'

Flora turned round. Oh my goodness, why was Agot still here? Everyone was meant to be at the Harbour's Rest; Agot must have run back on her own. She was such a minx.

'I'S HELPING!'

And she ran towards the two figures, her white hair streaming out behind her, and clambered up onto them, pushing her way in, surprisingly strong for such a tiny girl, until she was sitting between them.

Both of them immediately closed their arms around her too, making a trio, and as she saw that, Flora started to run, and knelt down next to them and added her own arms, and Innes and Hamish did too, and Flora got up and grabbed her father, who was still confused, and they all stuck together like glue. Joel saw them there, and he turned around and began to walk away. Flora's head went up and she saw him, once more out on his own – once more alone of his own choosing, even in the very depths.

Chapter Sixty-six

Joel walked through the darkening night, down the path from the Rock towards the Endless. It grew cold, but he didn't care. Somehow, blundering around in the dark summed things up better than he could have predicted. Creatures scattered at his approach, as if he were some kind of incoming monster, and he pushed his way on through, completely and utterly unable to work out how his life had become such a mess.

He looked down the long stretch of pale sand, glinting now under the full moon rising.

Then suddenly at the end of the beach he saw something sparkling. And, simultaneously, out at sea, he heard a great thudding noise and saw a huge head tilt out of the water; it was unimaginably vast, a truly extraordinary-looking thing, with – Joel squinted – was that a horn? Did it have a horn on its nose? Like a unicorn?

Almost convinced he was dreaming, Joel moved forward

to where most of the town was standing, watching the beast as it moved irrevocably closer to the shore.

'It's going to beach itself!' someone yelled from further down the beach, closer to the Harbour's Rest. Joel looked at the poor creature, thrashing desperately about in the sea.

'No!' he said. He took out his phone and falteringly googled what to do about a beaching whale. For once the internet held, and he read, blinking, that you could lure a whale off a beach with fire. He glanced around to Inge-Britt, who had come up to see what was going on.

'Have you got anything we could set on fire?' he shouted. Then instantly he realised and turned around, running.

'Come with me!' he shouted to the group of Charlie's boys who were also clustered by the waves, watching intently. They ran towards him instantly, and they all rounded the head of the beach in a tearing hurry.

'The torches!'

Of course, all the torches were set up at the Rock, lining the steps between the jetty and the building.

'CAREFUL!'

They grabbed as many as they were able, and Joel shouted for them to be handed over to the grown-ups (although a couple of the older boys demurred and followed him anyway), and, without thinking, he ran headlong into the sea, waving madly.

The creature was coming closer and closer as more and more of the islanders ran into the sea. It felt like the entire town was there now. One of the boys, who had done some fairly excellent cat burglary back in the city, had found the gardener's hut where the torches were stored and had broken more of them out.

This alerted everyone at the Rock. There was a good view from there, up high.

Colton and Fintan were still sitting there with Agot between them. Now she wriggled out from underneath them and began dancing excitedly on the grass, shouting, 'ALLO, WHALE! ALLO! DOAN GO, WHALE!'

The entire town now waded in deep, under the starry sky, frantically waving their flaming torches in the air, moving closer, shouting furiously at the huge beast who tossed and turned this way and that.

Flora moved down towards the waves, worried someone might get hurt. And then, and only then, did she see the person who was furthest out and deepest in, waving his torch so desperately in the air.

A quietness stole over her. It was a sense she had always had when close to the creatures of her island: the island of her ancestors, deep back into Viking lore and further even, back to the myths and dreams of selkies, and the people who came from the sea. It was a sense that this was something she understood.

She kicked off her shoes and walked slowly down to the water's edge. The people with torches – she didn't take one – parted to let her through. Fintan sat up to watch, wiping his eyes. The water was freezing but she didn't notice or mind; the waves parted for her as she left the land behind; the noise of everyone screaming and shouting was drifting away and still she walked deeper and deeper into the water, feeling the cares of the island fade behind her, feeling the fear and panic of the huge animal even closer as she moved through the waves, her thin dress streaming behind her, her hair wet.

Finally, she was shoulder to shoulder with Joel, who looked at her, incredulous, but didn't say anything, just held his torch as high as he could.

'Don't say anything,' she said.

'My beautiful selkie girl.'

'I only wanted to be your girl, Joel.'

Her attention was caught by the huge beast, and suddenly a change came over her as she stepped further into the water. '*Much-mhara adharcach*,' she called out softly. Joel couldn't make out a word she was saying, but she wasn't talking to him. She seemed, although it was absolutely crazy, to be talking to the huge creature. Certainly it looked as if it were looking straight at her – at them – but that couldn't be right, could it?

The thrashing tail seemed to quieten somewhat and Flora moved forwards, even though the water was up to her neck, and he wanted to grab her and hold her and keep her safe. He glanced back towards the beach. The flames – scores of them – roared high above the waves, the noise reaching them, but Flora was still talking quietly to the creature and, as he watched her, she put her hand out and touched the beast on its grey-blue flank, just once, and as she did so, quick as anything, the creature's tail shot up and hit Flora on the side. It knocked her clear out of the water and through the air, and there was a bounding and a massive churn of the waves, and a huge splash and noise, and Joel felt himself almost slip under the water as he yelled and pushed forwards. He tripped and his head went under, and everything was churning beneath him. When he pulled it up again, he couldn't see anything at all; his glasses had gone and he'd lost sight of the whale and lost sight of Flora and he could see nothing and hear nothing except the roar of the ocean and the cries of the lost.

Chapter Sixty-seven

Joel washed up on the shore.

By the time he had recovered his footing – if not his glasses – and started to fumble around, looking for Flora, calling her name, realising how freezing the water was, he saw that the sky was already lightening in this ridiculous place at the top of the world. A dawn was somehow coming. He looked around. The narwhal ... The narwhal was gone. The great creature had somehow managed to turn itself around and get away from the island it had haunted all summer.

'FLO-RAAAA!'

Nothing. The sea ahead was just starting to glow with the first rays of light of the morning.

'FLOOO-RAA!'

He could hear nothing above the waves; his teeth were chattering. Then there was a noise behind him. He turned around, incredibly slowly.

All along the beach of the Endless stood a line of island-ers, still brandishing their torches. And they were cheering and applauding.

In the middle of all the people was a pale figure with long hair the colour of the sea, and a green dress that clung to her like a mermaid's flesh, and she stepped forward, looking as if she didn't feel the cold in the slightest, and she opened up her arms. And he pulled himself back and away from the waves, looking out into the open sea one last time, thinking he could just – could he? – make out the shape of a fin in the very far distance.

He waded in to shore, utterly soaked, utterly freezing, straight into the arms of Flora, who wrapped them around his neck, equally soaked, and kissed him in front of the entire town.

Chapter Sixty-eight

'Oh God,' said Lorna, who had been waving a torch next to Saif, who'd wisely decided to stay on shore and try and persuade the more elderly and drunken residents not to get in the sea. 'Oh God.'

Lorna was a little over-emotional and had been up all night.

Saif shook his head. 'I know.' He glanced up. 'Would you mind coming and helping me with Colton?'

'Of course not,' said Lorna. Wild rumours had already been running riot around the Harbour's Rest, unfortunately most of them correct. Together, with Fintan stumbling along behind him like a child, they managed to load him up onto one of the Rock's golf carts to take him back to the Manse.

'Is he going to be all right?' whispered Lorna. Saif shook his head in a warning that she shouldn't ask him about it.

'Oh goodness,' said Lorna and she helped him get the

sleepy Colton down and undressed and into his pyjamas. Saif gave him a shot that should make him feel better and told the maid what to do.

It was fully light by the time they took the cart back across the island, but it didn't seem like anyone was going to bed any time soon.

'Well, that's not how I usually expect weddings to turn out,' said Lorna, making conversation.

Saif was tired and not concentrating and blurted out the first thing that was on his mind. 'I thought you'd be with Innes anyway.'

Lorna turned to him in shock. 'Of course I'm not with Innes! Why would you think that?'

Saif shrugged. 'He's very popular. Why wouldn't you be?'

He wished he could keep the infernal tone of jealousy out of his voice. He couldn't be jealous: it was ridiculous. Absolutely ridiculous.

'Why wouldn't I be?' said Lorna. 'Why wouldn't I be?'

She clambered down and stood on the beach, the early rays of the sun hitting her bright hair. Saif got down onto the beach beside her.

'Well, one, he's practically my brother, and two . . . '

He stared at her. 'Two? What is two?'

Lorna reached out her hands and said, as if he were a complete idiot, 'Saif . . . two . . . is you.'

'*ABBA! ABBA!*'

And then Ibrahim and Ash found their father and over-whelmed them both. They were overexcited, both of them babbling in a mixture of Arabic and English, had he SEEN it, had he SEEN the huge *hawt*, had he seen it, *Abba*? It was huge, it was amazing and it was night-time and only dark for a little bit, and the water was so cold, and there was a BIG MAGIC WHALE ...

Lorna melted into the shadows, wishing the ground could swallow her up, but somehow, deep inside, glad. At least she'd said it. At least she didn't have to go through the rest of her life turning down opportunities – Innes might not be the right thing for her, but it was definitely a start – or wishing for what might have been. Because she knew, she knew one hundred per cent, that it absolutely never could have been and never could be, and there was – even as she watched her friend walk up the beach in a daze, hand in hand with Joel – a satisfaction in that, if nothing else.

Chapter Sixty-nine

'You saved her,' said Flora.

'How do you know it was a girl?' said Joel later, as they were warming up in the huge bath at the Rock.

'I just do,' said Flora, but wouldn't be drawn any more on what had happened.

'You did it,' said Joel. 'With your magic powers. That are totally made up and I totally don't believe in them . . . '

'Good,' said Flora. 'Oh Christ. I should call Fintan. Maybe I'll just go up there.'

Joel put his hand out. 'You should probably give them a bit of time.'

Flora shook her head. 'I can't . . . I just can't . . . '

'There'll be plenty of time to be with Fintan. In the weeks and the months . . . '

They had got into the bath together. Somehow it was the most vulnerable position imaginable: the two of them, back to chest.

'The last time,' said Flora, staring down at the water. 'The last time ... He looked after our mum. When I was ... well. When I was working for you. But when I was too scared.'

She swallowed.

'This time, I can be there for him. At least.'

He soaped her shoulders gently, marvelling once more at their pale shapely perfection, kissing her tenderly, wondering how close he'd come to nearly losing her.

'Very close,' said Flora suddenly.

'What?' said Joel, startled that she'd read his mind.

'I like it,' said Flora. 'When we're very close.'

She in turn couldn't believe how different it was from the last time he'd been in this bath, at the very lowest ebb.

'I need ... ' She took his hand and placed it over her heart. 'I need you to feel for me. And let me feel for you. I need to know you, and I need you to know me. And that is all I have to say.' She took a breath. 'Tell me everything about Colton.'

He half-smiled. 'I can't,' he said one last time.

Then, slowly but deliberately, he turned her round. She stared into his eyes fearfully.

'But if you like,' he said, 'I can tell you everything about me.'

She held his gaze for a long moment.

'I would like that,' she said.

Chapter Seventy

Fintan was standing, silent and brooding, by the window, the dawn light shining in.

Colton stirred.

'Please,' said Colton. 'Please come and lie down with me.'

Fintan took off his kilt, put on that morning with such joy and expectation. He pulled off his shirt, sighing deeply, shaking his head.

'How could you?' he whispered. 'How could you keep it from me for so long?'

'Because ...' growled Colton. 'Because every time you mention your mother you tear up. Because every time I think about what you've been through – what I'm about to put you through – I feel like the biggest son of a bitch on earth. Because I love to see your smile and I love to hear your laugh and, right now, the biggest fear I have is that I'm never going to see those things again, and I knew it would start right the moment you found out. Because ...'

He let out a great sigh.

'Because as soon as I got the diagnosis I should have broken up with you. I'm a heel. An absolute heel not to do that for you. I should have treated you so badly you hated me and were absolutely delighted when I walked out the door.'

Fintan shook his head. 'You couldn't have done that.'

'Well, if I'd been a half-decent man, I'd have given it a shot.' Colton covered his face. 'Man, I am so, so sorry.'

Fintan crawled up on the huge, luxurious bed. It was to have been their marriage bed. No: it was.

'Is there nothing left to try?' he said. His voice was a rasp.

'Let me tell you,' said Colton. 'There is nothing you or anyone else could do about this disease. You could hate me or love me or divorce me or whatever you like. Stage four pancreatic cancer gives no shits about what you do at this point, what I do, what anyone does. You got that?' He put one arm around Fintan. 'Please?'

Fintan looked up at him. 'This isn't fair!'

'I know, baby, I know.'

Fintan crept under his arm. 'Other people get everything they want.'

'I did,' said Colton.

Fintan blinked.

'Now, listen. You're protected,' said Colton. 'I'm not leaving you much. It's all going to Cancer Research. Obviously. But if anyone tries to dispute the will, it's all on paper and it's all known: you didn't coerce me to marry you; you had no idea I was sick; you had no idea what was going on. A hundred witnesses there today. That's why I did it, you understand? You have no idea what hard-asses my family are.'

'Well, they produced you,' said Fintan.

'Yeah.'

Fintan blinked again.

'And you will have the Rock, and the Seaside Kitchen, and the Manse. That's for you. And some years' running costs – not loads. Not enough so you can lie on that gorgeous little ass of yours. And nobody will ever, ever dispute it or try and take it from you. You got the best lawyer in the world protecting that. And you are well within your rights to storm out, or to break up with me, or hell, I don't even care what you do.'

'What will you do?'

'I'm going to stay here. On my beach. In the most beautiful place on God's earth. Eating good food. Drinking good whisky. And if you would keep me company I would be very, very happy. But if you can't, I understand.'

Fintan didn't say anything.

'But right now, whatever Saif brought me is making me want to sleep like a baby. God bless that man.'

Colton looked at Fintan. 'Will you be here when I wake up?' he said.

'I don't know,' said Fintan.

Chapter Seventy-one

The spell of good weather continued right through August. Saif started walking the Endless in the morning again, but now with the boys to give them a bit of a blow before school, and he did what Neda told him to and talked about their mother every day. They looked for the boat, of course, but more as a ritual: more of a chance for them all to be together; more as force of habit.

It was a few weeks before Lorna and Saif ran into each other.

Lorna came down later than usual with Milou that day, and Ash and Ibrahim were there, bouncing up and down delightedly as she appeared. Ash was desperate to know if she'd seen his picture that Mrs Cook had pinned up, and Ibrahim told her shyly, and to her utter delight, that he'd finished the *Horrid Henry* book she'd given him, and could he possibly have another? She was pleased to see them, but she'd managed to avoid Saif at school pick-up since the new term had started, and had absolutely no wish to see him here. She couldn't avoid him for ever, after confessing everything – but she wanted to give it a very good try. But here he was, and they were both walking in the same direction.

They stood, looking at one another, as the boys ran far away, playing with Milou, all three kicking happily in the chilly sea.

Lorna couldn't bear to look at him now. It made her tremble, with hope, with despondency, with such utter desire as she felt the reality of the two of them, alone, no other Murians for miles. It was just the feel of him on the salty air; the huge sky above them; the pale sand. And nothing for her. She opened her mouth to make small talk about Colton – nobody on Mure could talk about anything else – but then he turned round suddenly, stricken, eyes wide with his desire, his overwhelming yearning – and nothing came out.

What would it be like? he thought with a sudden shiver. He had thought of little else since the wedding. What would it be like? That red hair, coiled around his fingers, that had haunted his dreams. To count every freckle on her pale skin. He shut his eyes tightly. When he opened them she was still standing there, and the air between them felt wavy and charged, and time had stopped. Lorna realised she was holding her breath, as if there were no need to move on to the next stop, the next second, the next bit of the universe, when everything in it, everything she was and had ever wanted to be, would be changed by what was going to happen in *this* moment, in *this* instant, and after it nothing could be the same. She wanted to hold it, before she slipped and moved and changed, and she needed to bring her eyes up to meet his but she was terrified of what she might see there; the desperate desire she herself felt; the melting sense of recognition, the same wanting.

But what if it were not? Could she bear it? Could she wait? Could she not?

And she did not look into his eyes. Which was a shame because she would have seen all of those things there, and she might have tipped him over the edge, caused him to abandon everything he had planned – everything he believed and ever wanted – had she grabbed him and pulled him to her.

But Lorna was not like that. And there were children on the beach. And she did not raise her head until he started, with great difficulty, to speak.

'Lorenah . . .'

She closed her eyes. Trying to work out his tone.

'There is . . .'

He stopped. Then he took a deep breath. Because if he could not have what he wanted, he needed to explain why. He was not a man for lengthy speeches, and the phrases swirled in and out of Arabic in his head, in a more ornate and old-fashioned style, and he was reminded of the ancient formal language of the *Grimms' Fairy Tales* his mother had read to him as a child.

'There are . . .' he went on stiltedly, his accent making him slow down to be as clear as he could.

'There are worlds. There are so many worlds and so many times for you and me. If you were born in my village and we had been children there. If my father had moved to Britain, so long ago, and not Damascus. If I had come here to study. If you had travelled and we had met . . .'

Lorna shook her head. 'Those things would never have happened.'

'They could have happened, a million times,' insisted Saif. 'And I would have passed you in a marketplace or we would have been laughing in a coffee shop or on a train somewhere.'

Lorna smiled painfully. 'I don't think you would just have swung by Mure.'

'If I had known you would be here, I would have.'

They both stared out to sea.

'Had we but worlds enough, and time,' said Lorna ruefully. Saif glanced up.

'لذلك من حين لآخر ... إذا كان لدينا وقت,' he said softly.

'You know it!' said Lorna, the lump in her throat making it difficult to get the words out. Of course he knew it. Of course he knew poetry. Because the perfect man had walked straight into her world, shaken it up, ruined it, she felt sure, for anyone else she could ever possibly meet, especially on the quiet island.

And she had barely ever touched him, couldn't even look him in the face, had to live side by side with him, in each other's pockets – she had to look after his children – all the while knowing that they could never be together.

'Of course,' said Saif with what sounded to Lorna like kindness in his voice, although it was not.

It was the deepest of sadness, and an ocean of regret.

She wanted to take his hand, hold him, just once. But when she moved a little closer, he flinched, and she backed away, horrified, her hands at her mouth.

'I need to go,' she said, her voice sounding strange to her own ears.

'Lorenah,' he said, but she had already turned away and it was too late and he could not say to her that he had flinched because he knew the second she put her cool hands on his skin he would not be able to resist, for all his brave words, for all his love and devotion for Amena, for all that he wanted to think of himself as a good man; he would throw all of that away without a second thought; he would have grabbed her and held her and taken her home and never let her go.

Saif had been through many hardships in his life. But to watch for the second time, after first leaving his family, to watch the chance of happiness slip through his fingers, seeing somebody he loved walk away from him once again, was unbearable.

It was as raw as the bitterest of aloes, the deepest of cuts, as her footprints made a larger and larger arc away from him in the sand.

Chapter Seventy-two

And the young knight climbed and climbed and slashed through many roses that grew up the tower of ice, and broke down the walls and fought his way inside through many hardships and much pain. And he saw the beautiful prince there. And he tried to slay the dragon that circled the tower, flapping its green decayed wings, the flesh tearing off its bones; but each time he thought the dragon must be speared, the dragon screeched once again, through its jaws that smelled of death; and escaped and circled the tower once more until the knight was exhausted.

And the prince said, 'You too cannot succeed; none can; you have failed and now you must also leave me.'

And the knight said, 'Sire. May we not fail together?'

And as the dragon screeched and roared around the castle, he crept in the slit of the window of the tower of ice from which there is no escaping, and he knelt down by the bed.

'Your mum told you some weird stories,' said Colton.

'Wherever you are I will stay with you.'

And the prince said, 'But there is no way out.'

Colton sleepily raised his head. 'What happens next?'

'I forget,' said Fintan, leaning his dark head against Colton's grey one. He entwined his fingers with Colton's. 'I don't think it matters. Not any more.'

'I have something to tell you,' said Joel as Flora burst into the house, happy after the most successful day's takings the Seaside Kitchen had ever had. *And* there was a huge crowd of visitors from London, and they'd all made a point of remarking on how reasonable everything was, which had vindicated her decision even more. Locals made a point of brandishing their loyalty cards so vehemently that tourists, who had fallen in love with the island and Flora's food, had started asking for one too. Of course she couldn't bear to refuse, and she'd issued a couple here and there, so the problem was going to raise its thorny head again at some point, but she didn't want to think about that right now.

'Really?'

'Yes,' Joel frowned. 'I can't believe I'm making a habit of this.'

'I can't believe you made Mark go home.'

'I know,' said Joel. 'I felt guilty about Marsha. I think he'd have stayed here for ever.'

'They'll be back,' said Flora smugly. 'So, did the doc say you're cured?'

'Ha!' said Joel. 'Psychiatrists *never* say that.'

In fact, the bear hug Mark had offered and Joel had accepted at the airport had told him way more than that.

'Well, what is it then?'

'Ah, come down the Endless with me. Grab Bramble.'

'He'll be snoozing.'

'That's because he's far too fat for a dog.'

'Stop calling my dog fat, you . . . doggist. Fattist. Whatever.'

'I'm not the one overfeeding your dog.'

They picked up the lazy creature, who was snoozing at Eck's feet as usual, and headed down to the beach. Ahead, Joel spied the most ridiculous contraption: a full Bedouin tent. Nobody could remember whose idea it was, but it meant Colton could come and sit out without getting too uncomfortable or chilled, as well as proving quite the draw to people. Rare was the evening, with a fire lit on the sand, that they didn't gather round, to chat, or chew the fat, or sit with Fintan if Colton was sleeping. When Colton was awake, Fintan did the best he could to smile and look happy and chat.

When he was asleep, Fintan felt like he was teetering on the edge of a very high cliff, and it was taking an island to help him hold on.

There was a sizeable crowd tonight, and Joel paused in a quieter section of the beach. Flora looked at him curiously.

'You have to understand,' he said in his quiet, under-stated way, 'I have never said these words. To anyone. Ever. Out loud. Okay. You have to realise that it might not mean very much to you, but it is very difficult for me.'

Flora looked at him curiously but knew better than to say anything. Joel swallowed nervously. He opened his mouth. Started. Failed. Tried again.

'Ach,' he said.

Bramble came bouncing up, holding a ridiculously long stick. Joel looked at it, then took it off him (as a very benign creature, Bramble didn't mind at all).

'Okay,' he said. 'Give me a minute.'

And he took the stick, and gently traced

in the sand.

'Will that do?' he said, glancing up at Flora.

She looked back at him, heart bursting, grinning from ear to ear, and she saw that small, shy smile – the one only she ever saw, and even then not very often.

'Absolutely not,' said Flora. 'That "o" looks like an "a" to start with. And everyone knows it doesn't count if you don't say it. And ...'

She realised he didn't know she was teasing. So she did the best thing she knew how, and kissed him.

'I love you,' she said.

He covered his face with his hands and looked embarrassed.

'Say it!' said Flora.

'Don't make me!'

'Okay, well, just start with ... just say the "I".'

'"I", I can say.'

'Okay, and now try the "you" part.'

'"You".'

'See, you're already 66.666 per cent there . . . '

And they made their way together down the Endless Beach hand in hand.

'How about you say, "I love strawberries" then just put "you" in at the end instead?' tried Flora.

'I'm not . . . I mean, I don't really care much about strawberries either way . . . '

'Okay, well pick something you really love.'

'Avocados. I love avocados.'

'You can say, "I love avocados" and you can't say you love me? What's *wrong* with you, man?'

'Also, why can't you get avocados on this island? This is a real problem with this island . . . '

'I'm glad our lack of avocados is the worst thing about living here.'

'It truly is,' said Joel. 'How about I write it every day?'

'Every day?'

'Every day. Tide comes in, washes it away, tide goes out, I write it.'

'That's twice a day, you div.'

'Twice a day then.'

'I like that,' said Flora. 'Sounds committed. Low tide gets pretty late in the winter . . . '

'Well, I'm a very committed person now, apparently.'

'Apparently you are,' said Flora, biting her lip and smiling.

And they wandered on, hand in hand, Bramble's huge tail wagging lazily behind them, up towards the rest of their family at the top of the Endless Beach.

Acknowledgements

Grateful thanks to: Maddie West, David Shelley, Charlie King, Manpreet Grewal, Amanda Keats, Joanna Kramer, Jen Wilson and the sales team, Emma Williams, Steph Melrose, Felice Howden and all at Little Brown. At JULA huge thanks to Jo Unwin and Milly Reilly. Thanks also Laraine Harper-King and the Board.

Recipes

Here are some true Scottish recipes I have collected together for you. I realise some of them have appeared in other books, but this is a proper local edition. ☺

CHEESE SCONES

You will find these in every café in Scotland, for very good reason. Scottish cheese is among the best in the world (and I lived in *France*), and a good sharp hard cheese works wonderfully with soft warm scones. And salty butter, I insist. This should make you a dozen.

250g self-raising flour
A pinch of salt
Dried chillies *to taste* (i.e. absolutely none is also fine)

50g butter (make sure this is cold and cubed)
60g cheese (a mature Cheddar is good)
A splash of tonic water
80ml milk (or to consistency – add slowly)

Heat the oven to 200 degrees Celsius – cold butter, hot oven is always my mantra when it comes to scones.

Mix everything together, dry first, then rub in the butter and add the liquids until you have a nice sticky ball. You can roll it out if you're neat and cut out little scone shapes or just stick it into smaller random balls if you're in a hurry – trust me, they're going to get eaten really fast.

Brush the tops with a little extra milk and stick in the oven – ten to fifteen minutes should do it; they should be a lovely golden colour.

Some maniacs split them and put *more* cheese inside, but honestly, all you really need is some lovely salty butter to ooze out of them. Oh goodness, I can't even type this recipe without wanting to run off a quick batch.

TABLET

I know, I know: Scotland has a reputation of being a country that eats a lot of sugar. And this recipe does nothing to counter that. Hey, if you like sweet things, tablet is DELISH DELISH DELISH and that is all I have to say about that. Except once, when we were living in France, I sent it in with my son for 'tastes of the world' day, and when I went to pick him up, one of his little classmates came up to me and tugged me unhappily on the sleeve, saying *'Madame! Madame! C'est trop sucré!'*

With that in mind, the recipe does start with:

    1kg granulated sugar
    1 large tin of condensed milk
    125g butter
    A drop of fresh milk to dampen the sugar

Turn the hob on to six or medium high. Butter and line a baking tray.

This is a stirring game. Put the sugar in a pot, dampen with milk, and add the butter and the condensed milk and get going. After ten minutes, it should be coming to the boil – once it is boiling, turn down the heat but keep stirring! The calories you expend doing this *totally* balance out the tablet, I promise.

When it's ready, it should be a beautiful dark gold colour, and a ball of it (use a teaspoon) will solidify in cold water.

Then take the pan off the heat and – stir faster! When it's thickened, pour into the tray and leave to cool – cut it into slices before it sets completely though. It is also nice chopped up into squares in a little tartan bag as gifts.

SHORTBREAD

You can't make Scottish recipes without making shortbread, and this one is nice for kids to join in with as it's so simple. If you can't get your hands on Fintan's unsalted butter, buy the highest quality you can afford.

150g *very good* butter
60g caster sugar
200g plain flour

Pre-heat the oven to 180 degrees Celsius and line a baking tray.

Cream the sugar and butter well, then add the flour until you get a paste. Roll it out to about one centimetre in thickness, then cut it however you like – be creative (or lazy, like me, and just use the top of a glass ☺)!

Sprinkle some extra sugar on top, then chill the dough in the fridge for at least half an hour otherwise they won't bake nicely.

Put it in the oven for twenty minutes, or until golden brown and delicious.

HAGGIS PAKORA

This has become so popular and widespread over the last few years that it's rapidly passing into 'classic' status. It's also ideal for kids if you're having a Burns Night supper and are a little tentative about going the whole hog (although haggis is lovely, it's just spicy sausage, just try one bite, etc., etc.).

1 haggis
150g chickpea flour (plain flour is okay if you can't find chickpea)
1 tsp turmeric
1 tsp cumin
1 tsp paprika
1 chopped-up spring onion
250ml buttermilk (again, you can use plain yoghurt if you can't find buttermilk)
2 tbsp chopped coriander
Oil for deep-frying

Cook (microwaving is fine) and cool your haggis and cut it into chunks, then mix with the other ingredients.

Deep-fry – carefully! – and place on paper towels to soak up the oil.

Serve with chilli sauce or mango chutney.

CRANACHAN

This is so easy for pudding but delicious and really almost healthy (for Scotland).

150g raspberries
150g oatmeal
150g double cream
Drambuie to taste

Toast the oatmeal *lightly* (otherwise it will catch fire). Line the bottom of pudding glasses with the raspberries mixed in with Drambuie. Then whip up the cream and mix it and oatmeal together with, yes, more Drambuie, and pour over the top.

Leave to set in the fridge for an hour or so before serving if you can. And I like sprinkling mini meringues on top of mine but apparently that makes me a heathen, so I shan't mention it.

Loyalty Card

~ DREAM WITH ~

JENNY COLGAN

Keep in touch with Jenny and her readers:

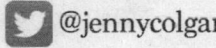 JennyColganBooks 🐦 @jennycolgan
📷 JennyColganBooks

Check out Jenny's website and sign up to her newsletter for all the latest book news plus mouth-watering recipes.

www.jennycolgan.com

LOVE TO READ?

Join **The Little Book Café** for competitions, sneak peeks and more.

 TheLittleBookCafe 🐦 @littlebookcafe

IF YOU LIKED
The Endless Beach

YOU'LL LOVE
The Summer Seaside Kitchen

Flora is definitely, absolutely sure that escaping from the quiet Scottish island where she grew up to the noise and hustle of the big city was the right choice. In the city, she can be anonymous, ambitious and indulge herself in her hopeless crush on her gorgeous boss, Joel.

When a new client demands Flora's presence back on Mure, she's suddenly swept back into life with her brothers (all strapping, loud and seemingly incapable of basic housework) and her father. As Flora indulges her new-found love of cooking and breathes life into the dusty little pink-fronted shop on the harbour, she's also going to have to come to terms with past mistakes – and work out exactly where her future lies…

If you liked *The Endless Beach*, you'll devour Flora's first outing in *The Summer Seaside Kitchen*.

'Gorgeous, glorious, uplifting'
MARIAN KEYES

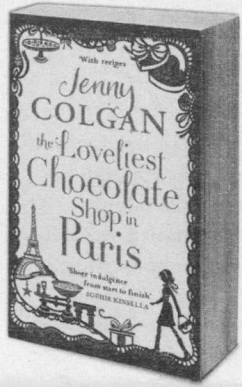

Life is sweet!

As the cobbled alleyways of Paris come to life, Anna Trent is already at work, mixing and stirring the finest chocolate. It's a huge shift from the chocolate factory she used to work in back home until an accident changed everything. With old wounds about to be uncovered and healed, Anna is set to discover more about real chocolate – and herself – than she ever dreamed.

Can baking mend a broken heart?

Polly Waterford is recovering from a toxic relationship. Unable to afford their flat, she has to move to a quiet seaside resort in Cornwall, where she lives alone. And so Polly takes out her frustrations on her favourite hobby: making bread. With nuts and seeds, olives and chorizo, and with reserves of determination Polly never knew she had, she bakes and bakes and bakes. And people start to hear about it ...

'Sheer indulgence from start to finish'

SOPHIE KINSELLA

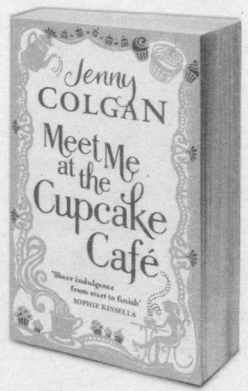

Meet Issy Randall, proud owner of the Cupcake Café

After a childhood spent in her beloved Grampa Joe's bakery, Issy Randall has undoubtedly inherited his talent, so when she's made redundant from her job, Issy decides to seize the moment. Armed with recipes from Grampa, the Cupcake Café opens its doors. But Issy has absolutely no idea what she's let herself in for . . .

One way or another, Issy is determined to have a merry Christmas!

Issy Randall is in love and couldn't be happier. Her new business is thriving and she is surrounded by close friends. But when her boyfriend is scouted for a possible move to New York, Issy is forced to face up to the prospect of a long-distance romance, and she must decide what she holds most dear.

'An evocative, sweet treat'
JOJO MOYES

Remember the rustle of the pink and green striped paper bag?

Rosie Hopkins thinks leaving her busy London life and her boyfriend, Gerard, to sort out her elderly Aunt Lilian's sweetshop in a small country village is going to be dull. Boy, is she wrong. Lilian Hopkins has spent her life running Lipton's sweetshop, through wartime and family feuds. As she struggles with the idea that it might finally be time to settle up, she also wrestles with the secret history hidden behind the jars of beautifully coloured sweets.

Curl up with Rosie, her friends and her family as they prepare for a very special Christmas...

Rosie is looking forward to Christmas. Her sweetshop is festooned with striped candy canes, large tempting piles of Turkish Delight, crinkling selection boxes and happy, sticky children. She's going to be spending it with her boyfriend, Stephen, and her family, flying in from Australia. She can't wait. But when a tragedy strikes at the heart of their little community, all of Rosie's plans are blown apart. Is what's best for the sweetshop also what's best for Rosie?

'A fun, warm-hearted read'
WOMAN & HOME

There's more than one surprise in store for Rosie Hopkins this Christmas...

Rosie Hopkins, newly engaged, is looking forward to an exciting year in the little sweetshop she owns and runs. But when fate strikes Rosie and her boyfriend, Stephen, a terrible blow, threatening everything they hold dear, it's going to take all their strength and the support of their families and their Lipton friends to hold them together.

After all, don't they say it takes a village to raise a child?

Meet Nina

Given a back-room computer job when the beloved Birmingham library she works in turns into a downsized retail complex, Nina misses her old role terribly – dealing with people, greeting her regulars and making sure everyone gets the right books for their needs. Then a new business nobody else wants catches her eye: owning a tiny little bookshop bus up in the Scottish highlands. Out all hours in the freezing cold, driving with a tiny stock of books ... can Nina really make it work?

'A natural, funny, warm-hearted writer'
LISA JEWELL

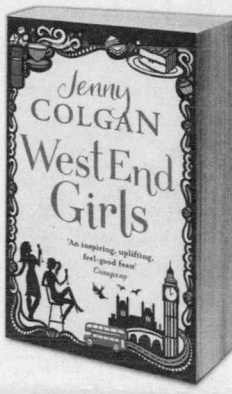

The streets of London are the perfect place to discover your dreams...

When, out of the blue, twin sisters Lizzie and Penny learn they have a grandmother living in Chelsea, they are even more surprised when she asks them to flat-sit her King's Road pad while she is in hospital. They jump at the chance to move to London but, as they soon discover, it's not easy to become an It Girl, and West End boys aren't at all like Hugh Grant ...

Sun, sea and laughter abound in this warm, bubbly tale

Evie is desperate for a good holiday with peaceful beaches, glorious sunshine and (fingers crossed) some much-needed sex. So when her employers invite her to attend a conference in the beautiful South of France, she can't believe her luck. At last, the chance to party under the stars with the rich and glamorous, to live life as she'd always dreamt of it. But things don't happen in quite the way Evie imagines ...

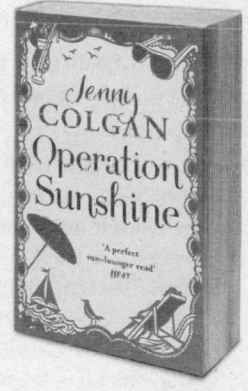

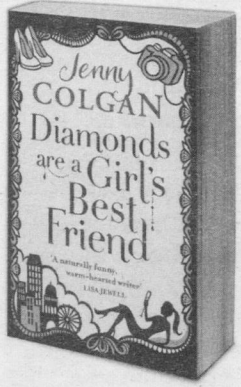

How does an It Girl survive when she loses everything?

Sophie Chesterton is a girl about town, but deep down she suspects that her superficial lifestyle doesn't amount to very much. Her father is desperate for her to make her own way in the world, and when after one shocking evening her life is turned upside down, she suddenly has no choice. Barely scraping by, living in a hovel with four smelly boys, eating baked beans from the tin, Sophie is desperate to get her life back. But does a girl really need diamonds to be happy?

A feisty, flirty tale of one woman's quest to cure her disastrous love life

Posy is delighted when Matt proposes, but a few days later disaster strikes: he backs out of the engagement. Crushed and humiliated, Posy wonders why her love life has always ended in disaster. Determined to discover how she got to this point, Posy resolves to get online and track down her exes. Can she learn from past mistakes? And what if she has let Mr Right slip through her fingers on the way?

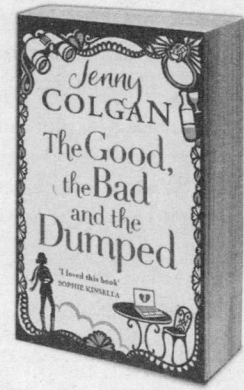

PRAISE FOR INTERNATIONALLY
BESTSELLING AUTHOR

JULIE KAGAWA

'Katniss Everdeen better watch out.'
—*Huffington Post* on *The Immortal Rules*

'Julie Kagawa is one killer storyteller.'
—MTV

Julie Kagawa is the internationally bestselling author of the Iron Fey, Blood of Eden and The Talon Saga series. Born in Sacramento, she has been a bookseller and an animal trainer and enjoys reading, painting, playing in her garden and training in martial arts. She lives near Louisville, Kentucky, with her husband and a plethora of pets. Visit her at www.juliekagawa.com.

For official Blood of Eden news and extras, visit www.BloodofEden.com.

Available from Julie Kagawa

ROGUE

The Talon Saga Book 2

JULIE KAGAWA

MIRA Ink is a registered trademark of Harlequin Enterprises Limited, used under licence.

Published in Great Britain 2015
by MIRA Ink, an imprint of Harlequin (UK) Limited,
Eton House, 18-24 Paradise Road,
Richmond, Surrey, TW9 1SR

© 2015 Julie Kagawa

ISBN 978-1-848-45382-1
eBook ISBN: 978-1-474-01890-6

47-0515

Harlequin (UK) Limited's policy is to use papers that are natural, renewable and recyclable products and made from wood grown in sustainable forests. The logging and manufacturing processes conform to the legal environmental regulations of the country of origin.

Printed and bound by
CPI Group (UK) Ltd, Croydon, CR0 4YY

To Laurie and Tashya

PART I

COUNTDOWN

GARRET

I stood before a silent, watchful table, six pairs of eyes on me, keen gazes ranging from suspicious to appraising as we waited for the charges to be declared. Men in uniforms of black and gray, with the emblem of the Order—a red cross on a white shield—displayed proudly on their jackets. Their harsh, lined faces reflected a lifetime of war and struggle. Some I knew only by reputation. Others I had trained under, fought for, followed commands from without a second thought. Lieutenant Gabriel Martin sat at one end of the table, his black eyes and blank expression giving nothing away. I'd known him nearly my whole life; he had molded me into what I was today. The Perfect Soldier, as my squad mates had taken to calling me. A nickname I'd picked up during the relatively short time I'd been fighting. *Prodigy* was another word that had been tossed around over the years, and *lucky son of a bitch*, if they were feeling less generous. I owed most of my success to Lieutenant Martin, for recognizing something in a quiet, somber orphan and pushing him to try harder, to do more. To rise above everyone else. So I had. I'd killed more enemies of the Order than anyone else my age, and the number would've been much higher had the unexpected not occurred this summer. Regardless of my situation, I had been one of the best, and I had Martin to thank for that.

But the man sitting across the table was a stranger, an impassive judge. He, along with the rest of the men seated there in a row, would decide my fate tonight.

The room in which I stood was small but Spartan, with tile floors, harsh overhead lights, low ceilings and walls with no windows. Normally it was used for debriefings or the occasional meeting, and the long table usually sat in the center surrounded by chairs. Except for the main headquarters in London, Order chapterhouses did not have designated courtrooms. While disorderly conduct among soldiers was expected from time to time, and desertion sometimes reared its ugly head, full-blown treason was unheard of. Loyalty to the cause was something every soldier of St. George understood. To betray the Order was to betray everything.

The man in the very center of the row straightened, eyeing me over the polished wood. His name was John Fischer, and he was a respected captain of the Order and a hero in the field. The left side of his face was a mass of burn scars and puckered flesh, and he wore them like a medal of honor. His steely expression didn't change as he folded his equally scarred hands in front of him and raised his voice.

"Garret Xavier Sebastian." He barked my full name, and the room instantly fell silent. The trial was officially under way. "For disobeying a direct order," Fischer continued, "attacking a squad mate, fraternizing with the enemy and allowing three known hostiles to escape, you are accused of high treason against the Order of St. George." His sharp blue eyes fixed on me, hard and unyielding. "Do you understand the charges brought against you?"

"I do."

"Very well." He looked at the men sitting in chairs along the far wall behind me, and nodded. "Then we will commence. Tristan St. Anthony, step forward."

There was a squeak as a body rose from a chair, then quiet footsteps clicked across the floor as my former partner came to stand a few feet from my side.

I didn't look at him. I stared straight ahead, hands behind my back, as he did the same. But I could see him in my peripheral vision, a tall, lean soldier several years older than me, his dark hair cropped close. His perpetual smirk had been replaced with a grim line, and his blue eyes were solemn as he faced the table.

"Please inform the court, to the best of your ability, of the events that led up to the night of the raid, and what conspired after."

Tristan hesitated. I wondered what was going through his head in the split second before he would give his testimony. If he had any regrets that it had come to this.

"This summer," Tristan began, his voice matter-of-fact, "Sebastian and I were sent undercover to Crescent Beach, a small town on the California coast. Our orders were specific—we were to infiltrate the town, find a sleeper planted among the population and terminate it."

The man in the center raised a hand. "So, to be clear, Talon had planted one of their operatives in Crescent Beach, and you were sent to find it."

"Yes, sir." Tristan gave a short nod. "We were there to kill a dragon."

A murmur went through the room. From the very first day the Order had been founded, soldiers of St. George had known what we fought for, what we protected, what was at stake. Our war, our holy mission, hadn't changed in hundreds of years. The Order had evolved with the times—firearms and technology had replaced swords and lances—but our purpose was still the same. We had one goal, and every soldier dedicated his entire life to that cause.

The complete annihilation of our eternal enemies, the dragons.

The general public knew nothing of our ancient war. The existence of dragons was a jealously guarded secret, on both sides. There were no real dragons in the world today, unless you counted a couple mundane lizard species that were pale shadows of their infamous namesakes. True dragons—the massive, winged, fire-breathing creatures that haunted the mythology of every culture around the world, from the treasure-loving monsters of Europe to the benevolent rain-bringers of the Orient—existed only in legend and story.

And that was exactly what they wanted you to believe.

Just as the Order of St. George had evolved through the years, so had our enemies. According to St. George doctrine, when dragons were on the verge of extinction, they'd made a pact with the devil to preserve their race, gaining the ability to Shift into human form. Whether or not the story was true, the part where they could change their form to appear human was no myth. Dragons were flawless mimics; they looked human, acted human, sounded human, to the point where it was nearly impossible to tell a dragon from a regular, every-day mortal, even if you knew what to search for. How many dragons existed in the world today was anyone's guess; they had woven seamlessly into human society, masquerading as us, hiding in plain sight. Hidden and cloaked, they strove to enslave humanity, to make humans the lesser species. It was our job to find and kill as many of the monsters as we could, in the hopes that one day, we could push their numbers over the brink and firmly into extinction where they belonged.

That was what I'd once believed. Until I met her.

"I've read your report, St. Anthony," Fischer continued. "It says you and Sebastian made contact with the suspect and began your investigation."

"Yes, sir," Tristan agreed. "We made contact with Ember Hill, and Garret began establishing a relationship, per orders, to determine if she was the sleeper."

Ember. Her name sent a little pulse through my stomach. Before the events of Crescent Beach, I'd known who I was—a soldier of St. George. My mission was to make contact with the target, determine if it was a dragon and kill it. Clear-cut. Black-and-white. Simple.

Only…it wasn't so simple. The target we'd been sent to destroy turned out to be a girl. A cheerful, daring, funny, beautiful girl. A girl who loved to surf, who taught *me* how to surf, who challenged me, made me laugh and surprised me every time I was with her. I'd been expecting a ruthless, duplicitous creature that could only imitate human emotion. But Ember was none of those things.

Fischer continued to address Tristan. "And what did you

determine?" he asked, speaking more for the benefit of the court, I suspected. "Was this girl the sleeper?"

Tristan stared straight ahead, his expression grave. "Yes, sir," he replied, and a shiver ran through me. "Ember Hill was the dragon we were sent to eliminate."

"I see." Fischer nodded. The entire room was silent; you could hear a fly buzzing around the window. "Please inform the court," Fischer said quietly, "what happened the night of the raid. When you and Sebastian tracked the sleeper to the beach after the failed strike on the hideout."

I swallowed, bracing to hear my betrayal lined out for everyone, play-by-play. The night that had brought me here, the decision that had changed everything.

"We'd found the target's hideout," Tristan began, his voice coolly professional. "A nest of at least two dragons, possibly more. It was a standard raid—go in, kill the targets, get out. But they must've had surveillance set up around the house. They were in the process of fleeing when we went in. We wounded one, but they still managed to escape."

My stomach churned. I had led that strike. The targets had "escaped" because I'd seen Ember in that house, and I'd hesitated. My orders had been to shoot on sight—anything that moved, human or dragon, I was supposed to gun down, no questions asked.

But I hadn't. I'd stared at the girl, unable to make myself pull the trigger. And that moment of indecision had cost us the raid, as Ember had Shifted to her true form and turned the room into a blazing inferno. During the fiery confusion, she and the other dragons had fled out the back and off a cliff, and the mansion had burned to the ground.

No one suspected what had happened in the room, that I'd seen Ember over the muzzle of my gun and had frozen. No one knew that the Perfect Soldier had faltered for the very first time. That in that moment, my world and everything I'd ever known had cracked.

But that was nothing compared to what had happened next.

"So the strike was a failure," Fischer said, and I winced inside at the word. "What happened after that?"

For the briefest of moments, Tristan's gaze flicked to me. Almost too fast to be seen, but it still made my heart pound. He knew. Maybe not the whole affair, but he knew something had happened to me after the failed strike. For a short time after the raid, while headquarters was deciding what to do about the escaped dragons, I'd disappeared. Tristan had found me a while later, and we'd gone after the targets together, but by that time, the damage was done.

What had happened after the raid, I'd never told anyone. Later that night, I'd called Ember, asked her to meet me on an isolated bluff, alone. I'd been wearing my helmet and mask during the raid; she hadn't known I was part of St. George. From the hurried tone of her voice, I had guessed she was planning to leave town, possibly with her brother, now that she knew St. George was in the area. But she'd agreed to meet with me one last time. Probably to say goodbye.

I'd been planning to kill her. It was my fault the mission had failed; it was my responsibility to fix it. She was a dragon, and I was St. George. Nothing else mattered. But, once again, staring at the green-eyed girl down the barrel of my gun, the girl who'd taught me to surf and dance and sometimes smiled just for me... I couldn't do it. It was more than a moment's hesitation. More than a heartbeat of surprise. I'd stood face-to-face with the target I had been sent to Crescent Beach to destroy—the girl I knew was my enemy—and I could not make myself pull the trigger.

And that was when she'd attacked. One moment I was drawing down a wide-eyed human girl, the next I was on my back, pinned by a snarling red dragon, its fangs inches from my throat. In that moment, I'd known I was going to die, torn apart by claws or incinerated with dragonfire. I had dropped my guard, left myself open, and the dragon had responded as any of its kind would when faced with St. George. Strangely enough, I'd felt no regret.

And then, as I'd lain helpless beneath a dragon and braced myself for death, the unthinkable had happened.

She'd let me go.

Nothing had driven her off. No one from St. George had arrived in the nick of time to save me. We'd been alone, miles from anything. The bluff had been dark, deserted and isolated; even if I'd screamed, there'd been nothing, no one, to hear it.

Except the dragon. The ruthless, calculating monster that was supposed to despise mankind and possess no empathy, no humanity, whatsoever. The creature that hated St. George above all else and showed us no pity, gave no quarter or forgiveness. The target I'd lied to, the girl I'd pursued with the sole intent of destroying her, who could have ended my life right then with one quick slash or breath. The dragon who had a soldier of St. George beneath its claws, completely at its mercy...had deliberately backed off and let me go.

And I had realized...the Order was wrong. St. George taught us that dragons were monsters. We killed them without question, because there was nothing *to* question. They were alien, Other. Not like us.

Only…they were. Ember had already shaken every belief the Order had instilled in me about dragons; that she'd spared my life was the final blow, the proof I couldn't ignore. Which meant that some of the dragons I'd killed in the past, gunned down without thought because the Order had told me to, might've been like her.

And if that was the case, I had a lot of innocent blood on my hands.

"After the raid," Tristan said, continuing to address the table, "Garret and I were ordered to follow Ember Hill in the hopes that she would lead us to the other targets. We tracked her to a beach on the edge of town, where she did indeed meet with two other dragons. A juvenile and an adult."

Another murmur ran through the courtroom. "An adult," Fischer confirmed, while the rest of the table looked grim. Full-grown adult dragons were rarely seen; the oldest dragons were also the most secretive, keeping to the shadows, hiding deep within their organization. The Order knew Talon's leader was an extremely old, extremely powerful dragon called the Elder Wyrm, but no one had ever laid eyes on it.

"Yes, sir," Tristan went on. "We were to observe and report if the target revealed itself as a dragon, and all three were in their true forms when we got there. I informed Commander St. Francis at once and received the order to shoot on sight." He paused, and Fischer's eyes narrowed.

"What happened then, soldier?"

"Garret stopped me, sir. He prevented me from taking the shot."

"Did he give any reason for his actions?"

"Yes, sir." Tristan took a deep breath, as if the next words were difficult to say. "He told me...that the Order was wrong."

Silence fell. A stunned, brittle silence that raised the hair on the back of my neck. To imply that the Order was mistaken was to spit on the code that the first knights had implemented centuries ago. The code that denounced dragons as soulless wyrms of the devil and their human sympathizers as corrupted, beyond hope.

"Is there anything else?" Fischer's expression was cold, mirroring the looks of everyone at the table. Tristan paused again, then nodded.

"Yes, sir. He said that he wouldn't let me kill the targets, that some dragons weren't evil and that we didn't have to slaughter them. When I tried to reason with him, he attacked me. We fought, briefly, and he knocked me out."

I winced. I hadn't meant to injure my partner. But I couldn't let him fire. Tristan's sniping skills were unmatched. He would've killed at least one dragon before they realized what was happening. I couldn't stand there and watch Ember be murdered in front of me.

"By the time I woke up," Tristan finished, "the targets had escaped. Garret surrendered to our squad leader and was taken into custody, but we were unable to find the dragons again."

"Is that all?"

"Yes, sir."

Fischer nodded. "Thank you, St. Anthony. Garret Xavier Sebastian," he went on, turning to me as Tristan stepped away. His eyes and voice remained hard. "You've heard the charges brought against you. Do you have anything to say in your defense?"

I took a quiet breath.

"I do." I raised my head, facing the men at the table. I'd been debating whether I wanted to say anything, to tell the Order to its face that they had been mistaken all this time. This would damn me even further, but I had to try. I owed it to Ember, and all the dragons I had killed.

"This summer," I began, as the flat stares of the table shifted to me, "I went to Crescent Beach expecting to find a dragon. I didn't." One of the men blinked; the rest simply continued to stare as I went on. "What I found was a girl, someone just like me in a lot of ways. But she was also her own person. There was no imitation of humanity, no artificial emotions or gestures. Everything she did was genuine. Our mission took so long because I couldn't see any differences between Ember Hill and a civilian."

The silence in the courtroom now took on a lethal stillness. Gabriel Martin's face was like stone, his stare icy. I didn't dare turn to look at Tristan, but I could feel his incredulous gaze on my back.

I swallowed the dryness in my throat. "I'm not asking for clemency," I went on. "My actions that night were inexcusable. But I beg the court to consider my suggestion that not all dragons are the same. Ember Hill could be an anomaly among her kind, but from what I saw she wanted nothing to do with the war. If there are others like her—"

"Thank you, Sebastian." Fischer's voice was clipped. His chair scraped the floor as he pushed it back and stood, gazing over the room. "Court is adjourned," he announced. "We will reconvene in an hour. Dismissed."

★ ★ ★

Back in my cell, I sat on the hard mattress with my back against the wall and one knee drawn to my chest, waiting for the court to decide my fate. I wondered if they would consider my words. If the impassioned testimony of the former Perfect Soldier would be enough to give them pause.

"Garret."

I looked up. Tristan's lean, wiry form stood in front of the cell bars. His face was stony, but I looked closer and saw that his expression was conflicted, almost tormented. He glared at me, midnight-blue eyes searing a hole through my skull, before he sighed and made an angry, hopeless gesture, shaking his head.

"What the hell were you thinking?"

I looked away. "It doesn't matter."

"Bullshit." Tristan stepped forward, looking like he might punch me in the head if there weren't iron bars between us. "Three years we've been partners. Three years we've fought together, killed together, nearly gotten ourselves eaten a couple times. I've saved your hide countless times, and yes, I know you've done the same for me. You owe me a damn explanation, partner. And don't you dare say something stupid, like I wouldn't understand. I know you better than that."

When I didn't answer, he clenched a fist around a bar, brow furrowed in confusion and anger. "What happened in Crescent Beach, Garret?" he demanded, though his voice was almost pleading. "You're the freaking Perfect Soldier. You know the code by heart. You can recite the tenets in your sleep, backward if you need to. Why would you betray everything?"

"I don't know—"

"It was the girl, wasn't it?" Tristan's voice made my stomach drop. "The dragon. She did something to you. Damn, I should've seen it. You hung out with her a lot. She could've been manipulating you that whole time."

"It wasn't like that." In the old days, it was suspected that dragons could cast spells on weak-minded humans, enslaving them through mind control and magic. Though that rumor had officially been discounted, there were still those in St. George who believed the old superstitions. Not that Tristan had been one of them; he was just as coolly pragmatic as me, one of the reasons we got along so well. But I suspected it was easier for him to accept that an evil dragon had turned his friend against his will, rather than that friend knowingly and deliberately betraying him and the Order. *You can't blame Garret; the dragon made him do it.*

But it *wasn't* anything Ember had done. It was just... everything about her. Her passion, her fearlessness, her love for life. Even in the middle of the mission, I'd forgotten that she was a potential target, that she could be a dragon, the very creature I was there to destroy. When I was around Ember, I didn't see her as an objective, or a target, or the enemy. I just saw her.

"What, then?" Tristan demanded, sounding angry again. "What, exactly, was it like, Garret? Please explain it to me. Explain to me how my partner, the soldier who has killed more dragons then anyone his age in the history of St. George, suddenly decided that he couldn't kill *this* dragon. Explain how he could turn his back on his family, on the Order that raised him, taught him everything he knows and gave him a purpose, to side with the enemy. Explain how he could stab his own partner in the back, to save one dragon bitch who..."

Tristan stopped. Stared at me. I watched the realization creep over him, watched the color drain from his face as the pieces came together.

"Oh, my God," he whispered and took one staggering step away from the bars. His jaw hung slack, and he slowly shook his head, his voice full of horrified disbelief. "You're *in love* with it."

I looked away and stared at the far wall. Tristan blew out a long breath.

"Garret." His voice was a rasp, choked with disgust and loathing. And maybe something else. Pity. "I don't... How could—"

"Don't say anything, Tristan." I didn't look at my ex-partner; I didn't have to see him to know exactly what he felt. "You don't have to tell me. I know."

"They're going to kill you, Garret," he went on, his voice low and strained. "After what you said today in the courtroom? Martin might've argued clemency if you'd admitted you were wrong, that you had a brief moment of insanity, that the dragons had tricked you, anything! You could have lied. You're one of our best—they might've let you live, even after everything. But now?" He made a hopeless sound. "You'll be executed for treason against the Order. You know that, right?"

I nodded. I'd known the outcome of the trial before I ever set foot in that courtroom. I knew I could have denounced my actions, pleaded for mercy, told them what they wanted to hear. I had been deceived, lied to, manipulated. Because that's what dragons did, and even the soldiers of St. George were not immune. It would paint me the fool, and my Perfect Soldier record would be tarnished for all time, but being duped by the enemy was not the same as knowingly betraying the Order. Tristan was right; I could have lied, and they would've believed me.

I hadn't. Because I couldn't do this anymore.

Tristan waited a moment longer, then strode away without another word. I listened to his receding footsteps and knew this was the last time I would ever talk to him. I looked up.

"Tristan."

For a second, I didn't think he would stop. But he paused in the doorway of the cell block and looked back at me.

"For what it's worth," I said, holding his gaze, "I'm sorry." He blinked, and I forced a faint smile. "Thanks...for having my back all this time."

One corner of his mouth twitched. "I always knew you'd get yourself killed by a dragon," he muttered. "I just didn't think it would be like this." He gave a tiny snort and rolled his eyes. "You realize my next partner is going to feel completely inadequate taking the Perfect Soldier's place, and will probably have a nervous breakdown that *I'm* going to have to deal with. So, thanks for that."

"At least you'll have something to remember me by."

"Yeah." The small grin faded. We watched each other for a tense, awkward moment, before Tristan St. Anthony stepped away.

"Take care, partner," he said. No other words were needed.

No goodbye, or see you later. We both knew there wouldn't be a later.

"You, too."

He turned and walked out the door.

★ ★ ★

"The court has reached a decision."

I stood in the courtroom again as Fischer rose to his feet, addressing us all. I spared a quick glance at Martin and found that he was gazing at a spot over my head, his eyes blank.

"Garret Xavier Sebastian," Fischer began, his voice brisk, "by unanimous decision, you have been found guilty of high treason against the Order of St. George. For your crimes, you will be executed by firing squad tomorrow at dawn. May God have mercy on your soul."

DANTE

Fifteenth floor and counting.

The elevator box was cold. Stark. A pithy tune played somewhere overhead, tinny and faint. Mirrored walls surrounded us, blurred images staring back, showing a man in a gray suit and tie, and a teen standing at his shoulder, hands folded before him. I observed my reflection with the practiced cool detachment my trainer insisted upon. My new black suit was perfectly tailored, not a thread out of place, my crimson hair cut short and styled appropriately. A red silk tie was tucked neatly into my suit jacket, my shoes were polished to a dark sheen and the large gold Rolex was a cool, heavy band around my wrist. I didn't look like that human boy from Crescent Beach, in shorts and a tank top, his longish hair messy and windblown. I didn't look like a teen without a care in the world. No, I had completed assimilation. I'd proven myself, to Talon and the organization. I'd passed all my tests and confirmed that I could be trusted, that I cared about the survival of our race above all else.

I wished my sister had done the same. Because of her, our future was in question. Because of her, I didn't know what Talon wanted from me now.

On the thirtieth floor, the elevator stopped, and the doors slid back with barely a hiss. I stepped into a magnificent lobby tiled in red and gold, my shoes clicking against the floor and echoing into the vast space above us. I gazed around, taking it in, smiling to myself. It was everything I'd imagined, everything I'd hoped Talon would be. Which was good, because I had plans for it all.

One day, I'll be running this place.

My trainer, who'd told me to call him *Mr. Smith* at the beginning of my education, led me into the room, then turned to me with a smile. Unlike some dragons whose smiles seemed forced, his was warm and inviting and looked completely genuine, if you didn't notice the cool impassiveness in his eyes.

"Ready?"

"Of course," I said, trying not to appear nervous. Unfortunately, Mr. Smith could sense fear and tension like a shark sensed blood, for his eyes hardened even as his smile grew broader.

"Relax, Dante," he said, putting a hand on my shoulder. It was meant to be comforting, but there was no warmth in the gesture. I'd learned enough to realize that all his overtures were empty; he'd taught me that himself. You didn't have to believe what you were saying; you just had to make others believe that you cared. "You'll be fine, trust me."

"You don't have to worry about me, sir," I told him, determined to show nothing but cool confidence. A stark contrast to the twisting bundle of nerves in my stomach. "I know why I'm here. And I know what I have to do."

He squeezed my shoulder and, even though I knew better, I relaxed. We turned, and I followed him down a narrow hallway lined with office doors, around a corner and finally to a single large door at the end of the hall. A simple gold sign hung against the painted wood: A. R. Roth.

My stomach cartwheeled again. Mr. Roth was one of Talon's senior vice presidents. One of the dragons who, while not so far up the chain that he was in contact with the Elder Wyrm itself, was pretty darn close. And he wanted to talk to me. Probably about Ember and what they planned to do about her.

Ember. I felt a brief stab of anger and fear for my wayward twin; anger that she would be so stubborn, so rebellious and ungrateful, that she would turn her back on her own kind— the organization that had raised us—to run off with a known traitor, consequences be damned. Fear of what those consequences could be. Under normal circumstances, a Viper, one of Talon's fearsome assassins, would be dispatched to deal with a dragon who went rogue. It was harsh but necessary. Rogue dragons were unstable and dangerous, and they put the survival of our race in jeopardy. Without Talon's structure, a rogue could accidentally, or even purposefully, reveal our existence to the humans, and that would spell disaster for us all. The human world could never know that dragons walked among them; their instinctive fear of monsters and the unknown would overtake them, just as it had hundreds of years ago, and we'd be driven toward extinction again.

I knew the measures Talon had to take against rogues were necessary. Though the loss of any dragon was a heavy blow to us all, those who refused to align themselves with the organization had already chosen their path, proven their disloyalty. They had to be put down. I understood. I wasn't going to argue that.

But Ember wasn't a traitor. She had been misled, deceived, by that rogue dragon. She'd always been hotheaded, gullible, and he had fed her a tangle of lies, turning her against Talon, her own race…and me. *He* was at fault for her disappearance. Ember had always had…problems…with authority, but she'd been able to see reason and listen to the truth until she met the rogue.

I clenched my jaw. If she just returned to the organization, she would realize her mistake. I would make her see the truth: that the rogues were dangerous, that Talon had our best interests at heart and that the only way to survive in a world of humans was to work together. *Ut onimous sergimus.* As one, we rise. She'd believed that, once.

I had never lost sight of it.

We stepped through the door frame into a cold, stark office. One entire wall was made up of windows, and through the glass, the city of Los Angeles stretched on to the distant mountains, towers and skyscrapers glinting in the sun.

"Mr. Roth," said Mr. Smith, ushering me forward, "this is Dante Hill."

A man rose from behind a large black desk to greet us, smiling as he stepped forward with a hand outstretched. He wore a navy blue suit and a watch that was even more impressive than mine, and a gold-capped pen glinted in a breast pocket. His dark hair had been cropped into short spikes, and his even darker eyes swept over me critically, even as he took my hand in both of his, nearly crushing my fingers in a grip of steel.

"Dante Hill! Pleasure to meet you." He squeezed my hand,

and I bit down a whimper, smiling through the pain. "How was your trip up?"

"Fine, sir," I replied, relieved as he loosened his viselike grip and stepped away. Talon had sent a car to take us from Crescent Beach to Los Angeles, but the drive had been far from relaxing, with my trainer drilling me on company policies, protocol and how to act in front of the regional vice president. I was an insignificant hatchling, meeting with an elder who was likely several hundred years old. First impressions were crucial. And a terrible faux pas was, of course, to complain in the presence of Talon's executives, especially if it was about the organization. "It was so smooth, I barely noticed the drive."

"Wonderful, wonderful." He nodded and gestured to the plush leather chair sitting in front of his desk. "Please, have a seat. Can I have my assistant get you something to drink?"

"No, thank you, sir," I said, knowing the drill. "I'm all right." I sat carefully in one of the chairs, feeling myself sink into the cool leather, careful not to slouch. Mr. Smith did the same and crossed his legs as Mr. Roth returned around his desk and beamed at me.

"So, Mr. Hill. Let's not beat around the bush." Mr. Roth clasped his hands on the desk in front of him and smiled over the surface. As I'd been taught, I politely dropped my gaze so I wouldn't be staring right into his eyes. Another social gaffe, and a very dangerous one: holding the stare of another dragon, particularly a male, was a blatant challenge or threat. In ancient times, the challenge between two alpha drakes would be settled via personal combat, with the contenders ripping, biting and slashing each other, until one of them either fled in defeat or was killed. Nowadays, two rival dragons obviously couldn't throw down in the middle of the city, but there were a thousand other ways to destroy a competitor without getting your claws dirty. Which was good, because that was something I could excel at.

"Your sister," Mr. Roth said, making my insides clench, "has gone rogue." He observed my reaction carefully; I kept my face neutral, showing no anger, surprise, sorrow, shock—nothing that would be considered a weakness. After a brief pause, Mr. Roth continued, "Ember Hill is now a traitor in the eyes of Talon, something we take very seriously here. I am sure you know our policy on rogues, but I have heard the organization wishes you to be in charge of retrieving her, Mr. Hill."

"Yes, sir," I replied, careful not to sound overeager. "Whatever it takes to bring her back, whatever you need me to do, I'm your man."

Mr. Roth raised an eyebrow.

"And yet, some have called into question your own loyalty, both to Talon and our cause. As the brother of a known traitor, we worry that your motivations might be…tainted." He offered a smile, even as his eyes stayed hard and cold. "So, I fear I must ask. Can we trust you, Mr. Hill?"

I smiled. "Sir," I began, as clearly and confidently as I could. "I know my sister. Ember and I have always had… different opinions, when it came to the organization. I know she can be reckless and stubborn, and that she has a slight problem with authority." A tiny snort from Mr. Smith was the only indicator of my massive understatement.

"But Ember isn't a traitor," I went on, feeling Mr. Roth's

hard gaze on me, assessing and critical. "She's gullible and hotheaded, and I believe the rogue dragon Cobalt took advantage of this to get her to leave with him. He lied to her about the organization, and he lied to her about me, otherwise she would have never turned on us like this."

Mr. Roth's expression hadn't changed. And neither had mine. "Ember tried to get me to come with her that night," I admitted, seeing no indication of surprise from Mr. Roth. "She begged me to leave town with her and the rogue, but I knew I couldn't do it. Not because of the consequences, but because I know my place." I raised my chin slightly, not enough to challenge, just enough to state my cause. "Sir, my loyalty to Talon has never wavered. I don't know why Talon is taking a less…direct approach to dealing with my sister, why the Elder Wyrm has chosen to spare her, but I do know that I am grateful. And I'll do whatever it takes to bring Ember back so she can resume her place in Talon, where she belongs."

Mr. Roth nodded.

"Excellent, Mr. Hill," he said in a bright tone of voice. "That is exactly what we want to hear." He picked up his desk phone and pressed a button on the machine. "Please send Ms. Anderson in," he ordered into the speaker. I blinked, wondering who Ms. Anderson could be; I'd never met her before.

Abruptly, Mr. Roth stood, which prompted us to rise, too. "Your words are commendable, Mr. Hill," the VP said, walking around to stand beside us. "Therefore, Talon is prepared to give you the best possible resources to locate and bring back your sister. In a moment, you'll be shown to your new office, but for now, there is someone I want you to meet."

I gave a pleasant nod, though my mind was spinning. *New*

office? And the best resources possible to find her? I was pleased, of course. It seemed the organization had recognized my potential, but at the same time, I knew this was abnormal. Talon was huge; its reach spanned the globe, and it had countless other developments, mostly of the multimillion-dollar variety, to worry about. The disappearance of a single hatchling, rogue or not, was barely a blip on its radar. *Why? Why are they going through all this trouble to find one hatchling? Ember, what have you done?*

The office door clicked softly as it opened, and Mr. Roth raised a beckoning hand.

"Ah, Ms. Anderson. Please come in. Have you met Mr. Hill?"

"Haven't had the pleasure," said a lilting, musical voice. I turned to face the newcomer. My brows arched a bit, and I straightened quickly. Not a human; this was another dragon, and on top of that, a hatchling. Except for my sister, I'd only ever met with adult and senior dragons, but this girl looked just a year or two older than me. She was fair and slender, wearing a light blue skirt and heels and looking faintly uncomfortable in them. Like she'd rather be wearing jeans and a T-shirt. Her pale, almost silvery hair was styled atop her head, the sides pulled back to accent her high cheekbones, and the large, crystal-blue eyes stared straight ahead.

"This is Mist," Mr. Roth introduced as she regarded me in silence, her gaze coolly remote. "Ms. Anderson, this is Mr. Hill. I expect the pair of you will get along famously."

I hid my surprise. By introducing her by her first name, Roth was subtly informing her—informing all of us—that I was in charge. That, although she was slightly older and had probably been working here awhile, we were not equals. I hoped the other hatchling wouldn't challenge my position, but Mist held out her hand as if this meeting was nothing out of the ordinary. "Nice to meet you, Mr. Hill," she said, her voice as cool as her face. I took the offered hand with a wide smile.

"Mist." I smiled, holding her gaze. "The pleasure is mine."

"Ms. Anderson is one of our newer operatives," Mr. Roth continued, seemingly unaware, or uncaring, of the tension as we sized each other up. "She comes highly recommended by her trainer, and we believe her skills are adequate for this situation. She will be aiding you in the search for our wayward Ember.

"Ms. Anderson," Mr. Roth continued. "Would you please introduce Mr. Hill to the rest of his team and then have someone show him his office? I would take him myself, but I have a meeting with your trainer in a few minutes. Mr. Hill…" He turned to me. "You say you have your sister's best interests at heart? Now is your chance to prove it. Bring her back to Talon, where she belongs. We will be keeping an eye on your progress."

I nodded politely, though I knew the meaning behind those words. *We'll be watching you* was the translation of that statement. *Don't disappoint us.*

I won't, I promised silently, and turned away.

As I followed Mist out of Mr. Roth's office, I nearly ran into someone coming in, and I stepped aside with a hasty apology. The person I'd almost hit barely gave me a second glance as she passed, but my stomach dropped as I met her familiar poison-green eyes. Lilith, Talon's elite Viper assassin, gave a short nod, recognizing me as well, before continuing into Mr. Roth's office and closing the door behind her.

Apprehension flickered. *Why is Lilith here?* I thought. *Is she...?* I glanced at Mist, walking beside me with her eyes straight ahead. *Is she Mist's trainer? Is that why she's here?*

Wary now, I followed Mist into the elevator, keeping her in my side view as she pressed a button, still not looking at me. The doors slid shut, and the box began to move.

"So." Mist's voice echoed in the tiny space, startling me. I'd been expecting her to stay quiet and distant, not speaking unless absolutely necessary. I'd been about to break the silence myself and was surprised that she'd beat me to it. "You're Dante Hill."

Her voice was a challenge. It seemed we were going to butt heads after all, unless I could win her over. I could've used my position to demand obedience; Roth had put me in charge, after all, but resentful employees did not produce fast results. If I was going to find Ember quickly, I needed her on my side.

Smiling, I leaned against the wall and put my hands in my pockets, adopting a pose of easy nonchalance. "I am," I agreed pleasantly. "Though you seem surprised, Mist. Let me guess—you expected me to be taller."

Mist's expression remained neutral. "A Chameleon in training," she remarked, raising a slender eyebrow, "using humor to defuse a tense situation. Classic disarming technique."

I kept the smile on my face. "Did it work?"

She blinked, and the other corner of her mouth twitched. "No," she replied, though her eyes said differently. "But thank you for trying. I am, unfortunately, well versed in the various faction trainings and techniques. Your Chameleon charm is not going to work on me, I'm afraid."

"Give it time."

The elevator had passed the first floor. And still, we continued to descend. Past the basement, and the subbasement, going even deeper underground. "Do you have something against Chameleons?" I went on, wondering how many sublevels this place had. The glowing numbers above the door had stopped moving altogether.

"Not at all," Mist replied. "Chameleons are a vital part of Talon. We all have our place." Her piercing blue eyes remained brutally honest as she looked me over, assessing. "What I don't like is having vital information kept from me, especially if I need it to do my job."

I gave her a puzzled frown. "You think I'm hiding something from you? That's a rather hasty conclusion. We haven't known each other very long."

"It's not you, Mr. Hill." Mist's tone remained coolly polite. "But you must know that this situation with your sister is not normal. Why is Talon so interested in her? Cobalt I can understand—he's a dangerous fugitive who has caused real harm to the organization, and his actions cannot be ignored any longer. The rogue must be stopped, that is very clear." Her piercing blue gaze sharpened, cutting into me. "But why is Talon so invested in bringing *her* back? Why go through all this trouble? Ember Hill is a hatchling who has done nothing for the organization." Mist's eyes narrowed even further. "Why is she so special?"

Her words were eerily familiar, as I heard my own suspicions parroted back at me. The situation with Ember *wasn't* normal. Talon was expending considerable resources to return her to the organization when they could have sent out a Viper and been done with it. Even bringing *me* on was puzzling. Yes, I was her brother and the person who knew her best, but why bother? What made her—*our*—situation so special?

However, I wasn't going to tell Mist that I shared her concerns. If I was going to bring Ember back, if I was going to make a future for us in Talon, then I had to appear fully in control of the situation at all times. I could not appear weak, or scared, or unsure, because Talon had no use for dragons who failed. I was not going to fail.

"I'm afraid I can't give you the details," I told Mist, who gave me a cold look but didn't seem surprised. Talon shared information only if they thought it was necessary; that much at least she understood. "I would," I went on, "if I were allowed. Just know that finding Ember is our top priority. The Elder Wyrm wishes that she be returned to the organization. The reasons are irrelevant."

The elevator stopped, and the doors slid open. Mist watched me a moment longer, blue eyes appraising, then gave a tiny nod. "Of course," she said, coolly professional once more, and motioned me into the hall. "This way, Mr. Hill. I'll introduce you to the rest of the team."

"Just call me Dante," I invited, a tactic to gain her loyalty, and followed her down a long, brightly lit corridor past several offices, until we came to a door at the very end. Without hesitation, Mist pushed it back, and we went through.

I gazed around, impressed. The room beyond was enormous, a sprawling floor of desks, computers, flashing screens, and people. Aisles of long counters snaked their way across the room, each holding numerous computers with glassy-eyed humans sitting in front of them. The entire back wall was one enormous screen divided into numerous parts that projected a dozen images of maps, satellite feeds, security cams and more. The murmur of voices, ringing phones, buzzing computers and clicking keyboards all blended into a general cacophony of noise that flowed over me as I stepped through the door.

"This is our operating center," Mist explained, leading me across the floor. All around us, humans hurried by or typed feverishly at their desks, avoiding eye contact. Mist continued as if she didn't notice or care. "Talon has dozens of these centers all around the world. It's where we monitor Talon's assets, keep an eye on St. George movement and track persons of interest to the organization. We're mostly in charge of the western region of the US, which is where we think your sister is right now."

She stopped at a desk where two humans sat across from each other, a pair of large screens separating them. When Mist's shadow fell over the desk, the overweight male and small bespectacled female looked up and gave her polite, fixed smiles, which she ignored.

"Mr. Davids and Ms. Kimura have been tasked with locating your sister," Mist told me, not even looking at the two humans. "They've been trying to pinpoint her location ever since she left Crescent Beach. Unfortunately, they've been unable to find any trace of her, or Cobalt, unless something has changed in the time I've been gone?"

She looked down at the humans as she said this, and both of them went pale.

"No, ma'am," the male said quickly. "So far, there have

been no leads on Ember Hill or the rogue dragon Cobalt. We know they're still in California somewhere, but other than that, we've been unable to get a lock on them."

"Where have you been looking?" I asked, making all of them glance at me. Mist raised her eyebrows in amused—or annoyed—surprise, but I ignored her. The humans paused, obviously wondering who I was, some bossy kid in a business suit come strolling into their affairs. I kept the smile on my face and held their gazes with my own, polite but expectant, and after a moment, they looked away.

"We've been able to uncover a couple of Cobalt's nests in the past," the male informed me, quickly turning back to the screen. "His so-called 'safe houses' for rogue dragons. We've been monitoring those areas, hoping he might return to one of them to hide. Unfortunately, when one goes down, he often moves the rest, so we haven't been able to pin him down."

"What about his network?" I asked. "If he has so many safe houses, he has to be able to communicate with them somehow. Have you tried tracing messages back to his location?"

"Of course," the other human said. "We've been trying to breach his security for years. But we've never been able to crack it. Whoever's on the other side knows exactly what he's doing to keep us out."

"What about St. George?" I asked. "Do you have ways of tracking them?"

All three stared at me, varying degrees of confusion and doubt crossing their faces. "Yes," the female human said slowly. "Of course, we have extensive systems for monitoring any movement made by the Order. But we already determined that the cell in Crescent Beach returned to their chapterhouse. When Ms. Hill and Cobalt fled town, their trail went cold, and St. George abandoned the search. There hasn't been any movement from the Order for days, at least not in this region."

"Do you know where this chapterhouse is?"

More puzzled looks. "We could probably find it," the male human said, furrowing his brow. "But, like we said, St. George activity has been quiet the past few days. We believe trying to find Cobalt's underground network is more important—"

"Stop looking for the safe houses," I interrupted. "Ember won't be there. If I know my sister at all, she won't be content to sit and hide. You're wasting your time looking for them." I glanced at the huge screen on the far wall. "Find St. George," I said, feeling Mist's curious gaze on me. "Start looking for the Order. The chapterhouse is a good place to begin. Find it, and tell me when you do."

The humans gaped at me, clearly dumbfounded but too polite to say anything. Mist, however, had no such reservations. "Why?" she asked is a low, cool voice. "You're telling us to abandon the search for the rogue's network when we have clear orders from Talon's VP to locate it, and your sister. Do you know something we don't, Mr. Hill?"

"No," I said, keeping my gaze on the far wall, on one of the many maps spread across the screen. I didn't have any concrete evidence. It was just a hunch, a suspicion, that had been plaguing me since before I left Crescent Beach. But my intuition was rarely wrong, and I'd learned to trust my gut, especially when it came to my sister. I only wished I had listened to it earlier. Much, much earlier.

"But there was…a human," I went on, as they all stared at me like I'd gone insane. "One of the people I met in Crescent Beach. He was a friend of my sister's. Really, I only saw him once or twice. But…there was always something about him, something that I didn't like. I saw him fight, once—he was definitely trained. And he just showed up out of nowhere one day, always hanging around my sister."

"That is not enough reason to suspect someone, Mr. Hill," Mist said in her calm, logical voice. "You can't expect us to drop everything and switch to a new plan of action simply because you have a hunch."

"The night Ember left Crescent Beach," I continued, ignoring that last statement, "she told me she was going to meet this human, alone. She said she wanted to tell him goodbye before she went rogue." I paused, my chest tightening with the memory. "That was the last time I saw her.

"I don't know if that human was part of the Order," I went on, looking back at Mist and the Talon employees. "But I suspect that he was. And both Ember and Lilith were attacked that night by St. George. Ember was close to that human. She…might've told him things, about us. About Talon. If you can find him, track the cell he belongs to, he might lead us to Ember."

"And if he doesn't?"

I narrowed my gaze. "Then you can blame it on me. But it's worth a shot. Better than searching for places where she *might* show up or trying to crack this impossible-to-breach network."

She gave me a long, appraising look. "All right, Mr. Hill," she finally said. "It's not like we have a choice. Mr. Roth did put you in charge, after all. We'll do it your way." She turned to the humans. "You heard him, then. Find that chapterhouse. Start monitoring all St. George activity in the region. If the Order so much as sneezes, I want to know." She looked back at me, crystal-blue eyes defiant. "Did you happen to catch this special human's name, Mr. Hill?"

I nodded. "Yes," I said, feeling a slow burn of anger in the pit of my stomach. Anger at the rogue, and St. George, and the human, for taking my sister away. At jeopardizing all my plans with Talon. I would find her, and nothing would stop me from bringing her back. "His name was Garret Xavier Sebastian."

EMBER

Three hours on the back of a motorcycle, the sun beating down on your shoulders and the wind whipping through your hair, though exhilarating, reminds you why flying wins every time.

"You okay back there, Firebrand?" Riley called over his shoulder. I peeked up from his leather jacket and caught my reflection in his dark shades. My hair whipped and snapped like a flame atop my head, too short to tie back but just long enough to be horribly tangled when we stopped. Before us, the highway stretched on, an endless strip of pavement heading east. Around us, the Mojave Desert provided much the same scenery: sand, scrub, cactus, rock and the occasional hawk or turkey vulture. The air shimmered with heat, but heat never bothered me. My kind was well adapted to dealing with blistering temperatures.

"My butt has gone numb!" I called back, making him smirk. "My hair is going to take hours to untangle, and I think I've eaten like four bugs. And I swear, Riley, if you tell me I should keep my mouth closed, you're going to be riding the rest of the way sidesaddle."

He grinned. "We're about forty-five minutes out. Just hang on."

Sighing, I laid my chin against his back, watching the eternal sameness flash by around us, and let my mind wander.

It had been three days since we left Crescent Beach. Three days since my world had been turned upside down, since I'd learned Talon was hiding things from me, since I'd fought the Order of St. George and discovered that Garret wasn't who I thought he was. Three days since I'd made the decision to go rogue and leave town with Riley, abandoning my family and my old life, and branding myself a traitor in the eyes of Talon.

Three days since I'd last seen Garret. And Dante.

I clenched a fist in Riley's jacket, my emotions churning with anger, sadness and guilt toward them both. Anger that they'd lied, that I'd trusted them, only to have them betray that trust. Garret was part of St. George; he'd been sent to Crescent Beach to kill me. Dante, the brother who'd promised to have my back no matter what, had turned me in to Talon when he'd discovered I was going rogue. But at least Garret had redeemed himself somewhat, saving me and Riley from a Talon assassin, then warning us that his own people were on their way. It was because of him that I was here now, on the back of a motorcycle with Riley, flying across the Mojave Desert. I didn't know where my brother was, but I hoped he was okay. He might've abandoned me to Talon, but I knew Dante. He thought he had been doing the right thing.

Idiot twin. He still didn't know the truth about the organization, the dark secrets they kept, the lies they told us. I'd make him see, eventually. I would get him out of Talon soon.

After I took care of this other thing.

The sun was beginning to drop toward the horizon when Riley slowed and pulled off the highway into a large, nearly empty lot on the side of the road. A sign at the edge of the pavement cast a long shadow over us as we cruised by, making me squint as I gazed up at it.

"'Spanish Manor,'" I read, then looked at the "manor" in question, finding a boxy, derelict motel at the end of the nearly empty parking lot. Peeling yellow doors were placed every thirty or so feet, and ugly orange curtains hung in the darkened windows. Exactly one car, an aging white van, was parked in the spaces out front, and if not for the flickering vacancy sign in the office window, I would've thought the place completely abandoned.

Riley cruised up beside the van and killed the engine, and we both swung off the bike. Relieved to be able to move around again, I put my arms over my head and stretched until I felt my back pop. Gingerly, I tried running my fingers through my hair and found it hopelessly tangled, as I'd feared. Wincing, I tugged at the snarls and tore loose several fiery red strands while Riley looked on in amusement. I scowled at him.

"Ow. Okay, next time, I get a helmet," I said, and his grin widened even more. I rolled my eyes and continued my hopeless battle with the tangles. Of all the human beauty traditions, I found hair the most time-consuming and obnoxious. So much time was wasted washing, brushing, teasing and primping it; scales never had this problem. "Where are we, anyway?" I muttered, separating a stubborn knot with my fingers, trying to ignore the dragon beside me. It was hard.

Lean, tall and broad-shouldered, clad in leather and chains, Riley certainly cut the figure of a perfect rebel biker boy leaning so casually against his motorcycle, the breeze tugging at his dark hair. He took off his shades and stuck them in a back pocket.

"We're about an hour from Vegas," he said, and nodded to the ramshackle Spanish Manor squatting at the edge of the lot. "Wes told me to meet him here. Come on."

I followed him over the parking lot, up a rusting flight of stairs and down the second-story hall until we came to a faded yellow door near the end. The curtains were drawn over the grimy window, and the interior of the room looked dark. Riley glanced around, then knocked on the wood, three swift taps followed by two slower ones.

A pause, and then the door swung open to reveal a thin, lanky human on the other side, dark eyes peering at us beneath a scruff of messy brown hair. He scowled at me by way of greeting, then stepped back to let us in.

"About time you showed up." Wes slammed the door and threw the locks as if we were in a superspy movie and there could be enemy agents lurking outside, hiding in the cactus. "I thought you'd be here hours ago. What happened?"

"Had to make a quick stop in L.A. for a few things," Riley answered, brushing by him. He did not mention the "things" in question, namely, a duffel bag full of ammo and firearms. Both he and Wes ignored me, so I turned to gaze around the room. A quick glance was all that was required; it was small, rumpled, unremarkable, with an unmade bed against the wall and soda cans scattered everywhere. A laptop sat open and glowing on the corner desk, nonsensical words and formulas splayed across the screen in neat rows.

"Riley..." Wes began, a note of warning in his voice.

"Where are the hatchlings?" Riley asked, overriding whatever he was going to say. "Are they all right? Did you find the safe house?"

"They're fine," Wes answered, sounding impatient. "They're holed up near San Francisco with that Walter chap, with strict instructions not to poke one scale out of the house until they hear from you. They're bloody peachy. *We're* the ones we have to worry about now."

"Good." Riley nodded briskly and walked across the room to the desk, then bent down to the screen. "I assume this is it, then?" he muttered, narrowing his eyes. "Where we'll be going tonight? Did you get everything you needed?"

"Riley." Wes stalked after him. "Did you hear a word I just told you, mate? Do you know how crazy this is? Are you even listening to me?" The other ignored him, and with a scowl, Wes reached across the desk and slapped the laptop shut.

Riley straightened and turned to glare at the human. In the shadows, his eyes suddenly glowed a dangerous yellow, and the air went tight with the soundless, churning energy that came right before a Shift. Riley's true form hovered close to the surface, staring out at the human with angry gold eyes.

To his credit, Wes didn't back down.

"Listen to yourself, Riley." The human faced the other in the dingy light, his voice solemn. "Listen to what you're trying to do. This isn't stealing a hatchling away from Talon. This isn't walking up to a kid and saying, 'Oy, mate, your organization is corrupt as hell and if you don't leave soon you'll never be free.'" He stabbed a finger at the laptop. "This is a bloody St. George compound. With bloody St. George soldiers. One slipup, one mistake, and you'll be hanging from some corporal's wall. Think about what that means, mate." Wes leaned forward, his gaze intense. "Without you, the underground dies. Without you, all those kids you freed from Talon will be helpless when the organization comes for them. And they *will*, Riley, you bloody well know they will. Do you even care about that anymore? Do you care that everything we've worked for is about to go up in flames?" He gestured sharply at me. "Or has this sodding kid got you so wrapped around her finger that you don't know what's important anymore?"

"Hey!" I protested, scowling, but I might as well have shouted at a wall. Riley clenched his fists, nostrils flaring, as if he might punch the human or Shift into his true form and blast him to cinders. Wes continued to glare, chin raised, mouth pressed into a stubborn line. Both of them paid absolutely no attention to me.

"What are we doing, mate?" Wes asked softly, after a moment of brittle silence. "This isn't our fight. This isn't what we said we would do." Riley didn't answer, and Wes's tone became almost pleading. "Riley, this is crazy. This is suicide, you know it as well as I do."

Riley slumped, raking a hand through his messy black hair, the tension leaving his shoulders. "I know," he growled. "Trust me, I know. I've been trying to convince myself I haven't completely lost my mind since we left town."

"Then why—"

"Because if I don't, Ember will go without me and get herself killed!" Riley snapped, and finally looked in my direction. Those piercing gold eyes met mine across the room, the shadow of Riley's true form staring at me. I shivered as he held my gaze. "Because she doesn't know St. George like I do," he went on. "She hasn't seen what they're capable of. She doesn't know what they do to our kind if we're discovered. I do. And I'm not going to let that happen. Even if I have to sneak into a St. George base and rescue one of the bastards myself."

I swallowed, feeling something inside me respond, a rush of warmth spreading through my veins. My own dragon, calling to Riley's, like he was her other half.

Wes scrubbed a hand down his face. "You're both completely off your rockers," he muttered, shaking his head. "And I'm no better, since it seems I'm going along with this lunacy." He groaned and plopped into the chair, then opened the laptop. "Well, since you appear to have lost your mind, let me show you exactly what we're up against."

Riley turned from me, breaking eye contact. I knew I should go see what Wes was talking about. But I could still feel the heat of Riley's gaze, feel the caress of the dragon against my skin. I needed to get away from him to clear my head, to cool the fire surging through my veins. Leaving them to talk, I slipped into the small, only slightly disgusting bathroom and locked the door behind me.

Wes's and Riley's voices echoed through the wood, low and urgent, probably talking about the mission. Or, in Wes's case, trying to convince Riley, once and for all, not to go through with this. I sank onto the toilet seat and ran my hands through my hair, letting the words fade into jumbled background noise.

I knew Wes was right. I knew what I planned to do was stupid and risky as hell. I knew I hadn't considered all the threats, didn't realize what I was getting into. What I was planning flew in the face of everything I'd been taught, and if I voiced it out loud, it sounded insane, even to me.

Break into a compound of St. George, the ancient enemy of our race, the Order whose sole mission was to see us extinct, and rescue one of their own. Sneak into a heavily armed base full of soldiers, free a sole prisoner who could be anywhere and get out. Without getting blown to bits in the process.

It sounded crazy. It *was* crazy. It was downright suicidal, like Wes said. I didn't fault him, or Riley, for being reluctant. They had no stake in this, no reason to want to undergo a mission that could get us all killed. They had every right to be afraid. If I was being completely honest, it terrified me, too.

But I couldn't leave him behind.

I went to the sink to splash water on my face but paused when I caught sight of my reflection. A skinny, green-eyed girl stared back at me from the mirror, red hair standing on end, eyes ringed with dust and dark circles. I didn't look remotely Draconian. I looked tired, and dirty, and very mortal. Nothing fierce or primal lurked inside my gaze to indicate that I was anything more than I seemed.

Was that why he'd hesitated that night on the cliff? When he'd pointed that gun at my head, and I'd finally realized what he really was? When he'd ceased to be Garret and became the enemy, a soldier of St. George?

He could've killed me. I'd been in my human form, taken off guard, and had been too stunned to do anything at first. He'd had me at point-blank range, alone and trapped on a bluff miles from anywhere. All he'd had to do was pull the trigger.

But he hadn't. And later, he'd betrayed his own people to save me and Riley from Lilith, my sadistic trainer and Talon's best Viper assassin. Lilith had come for Riley that night, and when I'd refused to leave him and return to Talon, she'd tried to kill me, too. She'd nearly succeeded. We'd survived only because of Garret's unexpected arrival and his help in driving off the Viper. Otherwise, Lilith would've torn us apart.

But, by helping us, Garret had damned himself. To aid a dragon was treason in the eyes of his Order, and the punishment for such betrayal was death. He'd told me that himself. Garret had known the Order would kill him, and he'd still chosen to save us.

Why?

I'd tried to follow him that night, hoping to somehow get him away from the soldiers who were now his captors. But there had been no opportunity for a rescue, and Riley had finally convinced me that falling back and planning our next move was the best option. So here we were.

I turned on the sink and splashed cold water on my face, washing away the dust and grime. When that was done, I attempted to tame the snarled bird's nest atop my head, wincing as I ran my fingers through the knots and tangles, finally combing them out. I had a brush in my backpack, along with a change of clothes and other essentials, but primping seemed like a giant waste of time right now. Besides, who was around that I wanted to impress? Wes hated me, and Riley... Riley was interested in my other half.

My dragon perked at this, sending a curl of warmth through

my stomach, and I squashed it, and her, down. I didn't know what I was going to do about Riley, but there were other things to focus on. Hopefully, Riley and Wes had come up with a brilliant plan, because other than knowing I couldn't leave Garret with St. George, I didn't have a clue what to do.

When I came out of the bathroom, Riley and Wes were bent over the laptop, talking in the same low, urgent tones. Riley glanced up, and our eyes met once more, making my skin flush. Then Wes snapped his name, and he turned his attention to the computer again.

Edging up behind them, I peered over Riley's shoulder at what looked like an aerial map on the screen. The surrounding area seemed barren—desert and dust and flat, open ground—but in the very center of the map sat a cluster of small buildings. No roads led to it; no other buildings or landmarks stood nearby.

"Is that where Garret is?" I asked softly. Wes shot me a dirty look. "That," he stated, narrowing his eyes, "is St. George's western chapterhouse, and it took me a bloody long time to find it, thank you very much. It's not like the Order advertises where they are—technically those buildings don't exist on any map or sightseeing brochure. But yes, the bastards that tried to kill us in California have likely returned there, your murderous boyfriend included." He snorted and turned away, and I resisted the urge to slap the back of his head.

"I had no idea it was so close," Riley muttered, staring intently at the screen, his face grim. "Right on the Arizona/Utah line. I'm going to have to relocate a couple safe houses farther east."

"There's nowhere completely safe, mate," Wes said quietly, slumping back in his chair. "Not since they caught on that Talon moved a lot of its business to the States. They're bloody everywhere now."

"Where were they before?" I asked.

"England," Riley answered without looking at me. "St. George's main headquarters is in London, where it's been for hundreds of years. They're very traditional, and they don't like change, so it took them a while to spread out. That's why Talon does a lot of business in the US and other countries— the Order doesn't have such a strong presence here. Or it didn't for a long time." He leaned over the laptop. "This is a fairly new base," he stated, staring at the tiny white squares on the screen. "It wasn't here ten years ago." One finger rose to trace the perimeter, his face shadowed in thought. "There's the fence, and that's probably the armory, barracks and mess hall, officer housing…so this big one has to be headquarters." He tapped the screen, tightening his jaw. "That's where he'll probably be."

"Bloody fabulous," Wes muttered. "The most heavily guarded building of them all. Tell me again why we're doing this? If it was a hatchling we were all getting ourselves killed for, I'd understand. I wouldn't like it, but I'd understand. That's more your type of loony." He continued to glower at Riley and ignore me, as if I wasn't standing not three feet away. Well within singeing distance, I thought. "Even if we do get this blighter out, what makes you think he won't run straight back to St. George to tell them where we are? Or shoot us in the back himself?"

"He won't," I snapped, glaring at Wes. "I know Garret. He's not like that."

Wes turned a disgusted sneer in my direction. "Really?"

he drawled. "Then answer me this, if you know the blighter so very well—how long did it take you to figure out he was part of St. George?"

I flushed. I'd never guessed the truth, never let myself think Garret could be the enemy, not until he'd aimed a gun at my head, and even then I hadn't wanted to believe it. Wes gave me a smirk. "Yeah, that's what I figured. You only *think* you know him. But the truth of it is he was lying to you that whole time. He would've told you anything to get you to reveal yourself, anything you wanted to hear."

"He saved us from Lilith—"

"He shot at a bloody adult dragon," Wes interrupted. "Because it was clearly the bigger threat. And when it was over and his squad hadn't arrived to back him up, he told you what was necessary for him to stay alive. He told you exactly what you wanted to hear."

"That's not true!" I remembered Garret's face that night, the intense way he'd looked at me, the remorse and determination and guilt. *I'm done,* he'd told me. *No more killing. No more deaths. I'm not hunting your people anymore.*

Wes snorted. "Leopards can't change their spots," he said with maddening self-assurance. "St. George will always hate and kill dragons because that's what they do. It's the *only* thing they know how to do."

I looked to Riley, standing silently beside the desk, hoping he would back me up. To my dismay, his mouth was pressed into a grim line, his jaw set. My heart sank, even as I turned on him, frowning.

"You agree with him," I accused, and his eyebrows rose.

"You think this is a huge mistake, even though you were there. You heard what Garret said."

"Firebrand." Riley gave me a half weary, half angry look. "Yes, of course I agree with him," he said evenly. "I've seen what St. George does, not only in the war, but to all our kind, everywhere. How many safe houses do you think I've lost to their cause? How many dragons are murdered by the Order every year? Not just the Vipers or Basilisks or the ones directly involved in the war." His gaze narrowed. "I've seen them slaughter hatchlings, kids younger than you. I once watched a sniper take out an unarmed kid in cold blood. He was on his way to meet me, riding his bike through the park, and the shot came from nowhere. Because I couldn't get to him in time." Riley's eyes flashed gold, the dragon very close to the surface, angry and defiant. "So, no, Firebrand, I'm not completely thrilled with the idea of rescuing one of the Order," he finished in a near growl. "Any excuse for another of the bastards to die is a good one in my book. And don't think your human is innocent just because he fought Lilith and let us go. He has dragon blood on his hands just like the rest of them."

I cringed inside, knowing he was right. But I still raised my chin, staring him down. "I'm not leaving him to die," I said firmly. "He saved our lives, and I won't forget that, no matter what you say." He crossed his arms, and I made a helpless gesture. "But you don't have to come, Riley. I can do this alone. If you feel that strongly—"

"Firebrand, shut up," Riley snapped. I blinked, and he gave me a look of supreme exasperation. "Of course I'm coming with you," he growled. "I told you before, I won't let you take on St. George alone. I'll be with you every step of the way, and I'll do my damnedest to keep us alive, but you can't expect me to be happy about it."

I swallowed. "I'll make it up to you, Riley, I promise."

Riley sighed, running a hand through his dark hair. "I'll hold you to that," he said. "When this is over, I fully expect you to do whatever I say, no hesitation, no questions asked. But first, let's concentrate on getting through the next twenty-four hours. Come here." He motioned me forward. "You'll need to see this, if you're planning on sneaking into the base with me. You *are* planning on coming, I assume? No chance of talking you out of it?"

"You know me better than that."

"Sadly, I do."

I eased in front of him and gazed down at the screen, suddenly very aware of his presence, his hand on my arm as he peered over my shoulder, the smell of his leather jacket. Wes grumbled under his breath, something that included the words *sodding* and *bollocks*, and Riley gave a grim chuckle.

"Yeah," he muttered, his deep voice close to my ear, making my skin prickle. "Just like old times."

COBALT

I slipped out the second-story window and dropped silently to the ground. Behind me, the office building remained dark, empty, as I leaned against the cement wall and dug my phone out of my pocket.

"It's done," I muttered into the speaker. "Everything is wired to explode. I just need confirmation that the building is empty before I detonate."

"Roger that" came the voice on the other end. "Building is empty, the only thing left is the security guard outside. You are clear to proceed when ready."

"Are you sure?" I growled, my voice hard. "I don't want a repeat of what happened in Dublin. Are you absolutely certain there are no civilians inside?"

"That's an affirmative. The building is clear. Waiting on your signal."

"All right." I stepped away from the wall. "Leaving the premises now. I'll report in again when it's done. Cobalt out."

Lowering the phone, I gazed across the empty parking lot,

thinking. It would be easy enough to slip through the fence, cross the street and vanish into the darkness without anyone knowing I was here. In fact, that was what Talon expected, what I was supposed to do. They chose me for these missions because I was damn good at my job—infiltrate a target, steal or plant whatever I was supposed to and get out again. All without being seen or leaving any evidence behind. I was probably the youngest Basilisk to infiltrate Talon's enemies, and I was here only because the last Basilisk sent out on assignment never returned. But I kept completing missions, and the organization kept sending me on more, regardless of danger, time or my personal feelings. I didn't know what this particular company had done to earn Talon's wrath, and I didn't want to know. Better not to ask questions; it was easier that way. But Talon required me to finish this assignment, and I knew what I had to do now.

Instead, I turned and headed toward the front of the building, following the wall until I found what I was looking for. A pudgy man in a blue-and-black uniform, silver flashlight dangling off his belt, sat in a chair near the front entrance. His arms were crossed, and his large chin rested on his chest as he sat there, eyes closed. I snorted.

Sleeping on the job, Mr. Rent-A-Cop? What would your employers have to say about that?

Bending down, I picked a pebble off the ground, tossed it in one hand and hurled it at the security guard. It struck his forehead and bounced off, and the human jerked up with a snort, nearly falling out of the chair. Flailing his arms, he glared around, then straightened as he spotted me, waiting in the shadows. I grinned at him and waved.

"Hey! Stop right there!"

I laughed and sprinted away as the guard scrambled after me. I jogged across the parking lot, making sure not to run too fast. Didn't want him to give up the chase just yet. Pulling out my phone, I clicked it on and began dialing a sequence of numbers, the gasping, panting voice of the guard echoing behind me.

"You there! Freeze! I'm warning you…"

Sorry, human. I reached the chain-link fence surrounding the property and leaped for the top, hitting the post and vaulting over with one hand. My thumb hovered over the final button as I walked swiftly away, hearing the guard reach the fence and pause, not bothering to pull himself up. *This is going to be a bad night for you. But at least you'll be alive. That's the most you can hope for when crossing paths with Talon.*

I pressed the button.

A massive fireball rocked the air behind me, blowing out windows, shattering walls, sending pieces of the roof flying as the building erupted in a gout of flame. I felt the blast of energy toss my hair and clothes, and didn't look back. Crossing the street, I slipped the phone into my pocket and melted into the darkness, leaving the structure burning behind me and one dazed rent-a-cop staring in dumbfounded amazement.

★ ★ ★

I reached my hotel room less than an hour later. Stripping out of my black work clothes, I changed quickly, then flipped on the news. The image showed the burned, demolished remains of the building I'd just left, surrounded by people and flashing lights. The words on the bottom of the television read: "Live: Mysterious explosion destroys office complex." I sank onto the bed, watching grimly as a reporter's voice filtered from the TV.

"…happened around 1:00 a.m. this morning," the voice announced, as the image flipped to a bird's-eye view of the demolished rooftop, gaping holes crumbling into darkness. "Thankfully, all the regular employees were gone, but we are getting reports that the janitorial staff was in the building when it exploded. Rescue teams are on the scene now…"

No. I clenched a fist on my leg, horror and rage flooding my body. Leaping upright, I snatched my phone from the bed, dialed a number and stood there, shaking, until someone picked up.

"Well done, agent," the voice on the other end greeted. "We saw the reports. Talon will be—"

"What the hell happened?" I snarled, interrupting him. "The building was supposed to be empty! They swore to me it was clear. No one was supposed to be inside."

A pause. "Talon weighed the information and decided that the assignment would go forward as planned," the voice said in a stiff, flat tone. "The loss of civilian life is…regrettable, but necessary."

"Like hell it was! They told me the building was clear."

"It is not your place to question the organization, agent." Now the voice sounded angry. "Nor is it your job to know the details. Your job is to obey. You've performed as Talon wished, and the mission was a success. This conversation is over."

The line went dead.

I lowered the phone, seething. Sinking onto the bed again, I stared at the television, watching humans and rescue dogs paw through the smoldering ruins, listening as a reporter interviewed the guard I'd saved. He credited himself with chasing the alleged bomber through the building and across the parking lot and made the pursuit sound much closer than it actually had been. But he did describe me as a young white male with dark hair, dressed all in black, and the police were on the lookout for anyone matching that description. They wouldn't find me, of course. I didn't exist in their systems; as far as the humans could tell, I was a ghost. By the time the authorities even got close to this hotel, I'd be on the other side of the country. Back to the war they couldn't see.

Back to Talon.

I ground my teeth, tempted to hurl the phone at the wall, or maybe the television so that I wouldn't have to see the aftermath of what I'd caused. *Dammit.* This wasn't the first time something like this had happened, but it was the first time Talon had outright lied to me. Before, there had been suspicious happenstance, crossed communications, orders that could've been misinterpreted or reasoned away. Not this time. Talon had *assured* me that building was clear; I would have never pressed that button if it wasn't.

And they knew it, too.

Sickened, I switched off the TV and flopped back on the bed, dragging my hands down my face. What now? How could I go on like this, knowing Talon would lie, that they would use me and more innocent people would get caught in the cross fire?

I could hear my trainer's thin, high voice echoing in my head, mocking me. *There is no such thing as an "innocent casualty," agent,* it said. *This is a war, and people will die. That is the ugly truth of it. A few human deaths should not concern you.*

But they *did*. A lot. Maybe I was the exception; maybe no other dragon in Talon cared if a few janitors were killed because they had been at the wrong place at the wrong time. But I did. And now more people were dead because of me.

My phone vibrated beside me on the quilt. Sitting up, I grabbed it as the screen came to life, showing a new message.

Stop moping, it read, indicating no one but my trainer, the Chief Basilisk himself. Brusque and to the point as always, but somehow finding ways to insult me. A car will be at your location in five minutes. You have a new assignment.

Another mission? So soon? Dammit, I had just barely completed this one, and I was *tired*. More than tired. Sickened. Numb. Furious. Both with myself and with Talon. I didn't want to go back. I wanted to lock myself in a room and drink an insane amount of alcohol, until the scene on the news faded out of my mind. I'd be equally happy to stalk into an office and ream someone out, possibly with fire and a lot of cuss words. The last thing I wanted was to be called back for another assignment.

But what else could I do?

Methodically, I rose and began packing my things. Talon's word was law; the opinions of a juvenile Basilisk agent didn't concern them. They would send me out on another mission, and they would continue to do so, regardless of what I wanted. But I had the ominous, sneaking suspicion that I was reaching the limit of how far I could be pushed, used, lied to. One word hovered at the back of my mind, constant and terrifying, appearing in my thoughts no matter how hard I tried to shove it back.

Rogue.

GARRET

Six hours till dawn.

I lay on my cot with my hands behind my head, staring at the ceiling of my cell, watching the cracks blur and run together. Around me, the jail block was dark, quiet. The only light came from beneath the door to the guard station at the end of the hall, and I was the only prisoner in the room. I'd been given my last meal hours ago—rations and water, as the Order didn't believe in final requests—and it had been delivered by a cold-faced soldier who had spit "dragonlover" at me before tossing it to the floor. Where it still lay, untouched, near the front of the cell.

Six hours till dawn. Six hours before my cell door would open, and a pair of soldiers would step through, announcing that it was time. I'd be handcuffed, escorted across the training field and taken to the long brick wall facing the rising sun. There would be witnesses, of course. The Perfect Soldier was about to be executed for treason; there would probably be a crowd. Perhaps the entire base would turn out. I wondered if Tristan would be there, and Lieutenant Martin. I didn't know if they would come; truthfully, I wasn't certain I wanted them to witness my final moments, as a traitor to the Order. There *would* be a line of soldiers standing in front of that wall, six of them, all with loaded rifles. I would be taken before them, offered a blindfold, which I would refuse, and then I'd be left standing there alone, facing them all. The countdown would begin.

Ready...

Aim...

Fire!

I shivered, unable to stop myself. I wasn't afraid to die; I'd prepared myself for death many times before. In the field, before a strike on a nest, or facing down a single dragon—we all knew that, at any moment, we could be killed. Soldiers died; it was a fact of life, one you couldn't predict or avoid. There was no tactical reason the soldier standing just inches away would take a bullet to the temple and I would be spared. I was alive because I was good at what I did, but sometimes I'd just gotten lucky.

But there was a distinction between cheating death and knowing the exact time it would come for you, down to the last second. And there was a difference between dying in battle and standing there with your hands behind your back, waiting for your former brothers in arms—the very soldiers you had fought with, bled with—to kill you.

Five and a half hours till dawn.

I didn't regret my choice. I'd meant every word I said in the courtroom. And if it came down to it again, and I stood on that beach with the dragon I was sent to kill, knowing that if I let her go I would die instead... I would still choose to save her.

But I *had* betrayed my Order, and everything I knew, to side with the enemy. I'd seen fellow soldiers die in front of me, torn apart by claws or blasted with dragonfire. I'd watched

squad mates throw themselves in front of bullets or charge
into the fray alone, just to give the rest of us an advantage.
I knew I deserved death. I'd turned my back on the Order
that raised me, the brothers who had died for the cause, to
save our greatest foes. I knew I should feel remorse, crushing
guilt, for family I'd betrayed.

But lying on my cot, mere hours from my own execution,
all I could think of was *her*. Where was she now? What was
she doing? Did she think of me at all, or had I been long forgotten in the flight from Crescent Beach with the rest of her
kind? Surely there'd be no reason for a soldier of St. George to
cross her mind; she was free, she was with her own, and I was
part of the Order. I was still the enemy of her people. Though
it made me sick to think of it now, the number that had died
by my hand. Ember should hate me. I deserved nothing less.

But I still hoped she thought of me sometimes. And as
the minutes of my life continued to slip away, I found myself thinking more and more of the moments we'd shared.
Wondering what would've happened…had we both been
normal. I knew that wishing was wasted energy, and regret
changed nothing, but for perhaps the first time in my life, I
wished we'd had more time. If I'd known what would happen, I would have spent every moment I could with her. I
would have done a lot of things differently, but it was too late
now. Ember was gone, and in a few hours, I was going to die.
Nothing would change that, but at least her face would be the
last thing on my mind before I left this world.

*I hope you're happy, Ember, wherever you are. I hope…you'll
always be free.*

Five hours till dawn.

EMBER

"Wake up, Firebrand." Riley's voice was soft and deep, and my dragon stirred to life at his touch. "It's 2:00 a.m. Fifteen minutes till go time."

I lifted my head from the pillow, fighting the grogginess pulling me down. The room was dark; only one lamp had been left on, and outside the sky was black. I hadn't thought I could sleep, but I must've been more exhausted than I'd felt. After the three of us had gone over the plan, Riley had told me once more to get some rest, and I'd drifted off almost as soon as my head touched the pillow.

The plan. I sat up as my heart began an irregular thud in my chest. It was time. This was it. Tonight we were going after Garret.

"Better get dressed," Riley said, nodding to my backpack on the bed. He had changed, too. No longer in dusty jeans and a white T-shirt beneath his jacket, he now wore a dark shirt that clung to his chest and arms, black jeans, gloves and a belt with several compartments and pouches on the side. At the desk, Wes was garbed in all black, too, a ski cap perched on his head. But he looked sullen and scared, like he'd rather be doing anything else. Riley, looming over me at the edge of the mattress, looked completely in his element, and my heart gave a weird little flip in my chest.

"Come on, Firebrand," Riley urged as I sat there, blinking at him. "We're sort of on a time schedule, here. Get your ninja suit on, and let's go."

"Right." Shaking the final cobwebs from my brain, I grabbed the backpack from the corner and hurried to the bathroom. Unzipping the top, I rummaged around until I found what I was looking for and pulled it out.

The sleek black bodysuit unfurled in my hands like a spill of ink, shaking free of wrinkles, creases, everything. It had been a final gift from my trainer when I'd "graduated" basic training and would've started my real education. The form-fitting suit was specifically tailored for me and would not rip or tear like normal clothes when I Shifted into my true form. The constantly warm, clinging fabric seemed to melt into my skin when I changed, and still covered my body when I turned back, so it was probably the coolest thing I owned.

It was, I'd discovered later, the outfit of the Vipers, Talon's deadly and notorious assassins, which was what they'd wanted me to become, too. Needless to say, I had issues with hunting down and killing my own kind simply because Talon ordered it. Talon's rule was absolute, and the Vipers were used to silence dragons who weren't loyal to the organization. Dragons like Riley who had gone rogue. I couldn't do it. And because Talon wouldn't accept no for an answer, I'd gone rogue, too. That was the main reason I'd left the organization. I would not become a Viper like my trainer, Lilith—ruthless and unmerciful, willing to kill without a second thought. I refused to turn into that.

But the suit definitely came in handy.

I slipped into the outfit, shuddering as the fabric sucked at my skin, melding to my body. Yeah, the magic ninja suit was awesome, but the way it felt almost alive was still creepy as hell. After putting on my shoes and shoving my normal clothes into my backpack, I left the bathroom and nearly bumped into Riley on the other side of the door.

He put out his hands to steady me, but quickly pulled them back with a grimace. I frowned in confusion.

"What? Do I smell or something?"

"No," he muttered, not meeting my gaze. "Sorry. It's not you, Firebrand, it's just…" He made a vague gesture at me. "That thing. Brings back fun memories, if you know what I mean."

I suddenly realized the problem. "I look like a Viper," I said, and he nodded.

"When you've been out of Talon as long as I have, the last thing you want to see is that outfit. Because it usually means you're fighting or running for your life."

"I'm a rogue now, too, Riley."

"I know." He reached out and brushed the base of my neck. A jolt of heat surged through me from that spot, as his fingers lingered on my skin. Riley's gold eyes almost glowed in the shadows. "I'm glad you're here, Firebrand," he said, his voice low and soft. "I'm glad I won't have to meet you down the road someday as a Viper. That would kill me, having to fight you." His mouth twitched in a faint smile. "You have no idea how relieved I am that you left the organization. That you saw Talon for what it really is."

I swallowed, the warmth spreading through my whole body

as the dragon rose to the surface, pushing against my fragile human shell. The Viper suit tightened, flattening to my skin until it felt like I wasn't wearing anything at all. I could Shift, I realized. Right here in this tiny hotel room. What did I have to lose? No one would see me but Riley and Wes. And then, if I Shifted, Riley would probably change, too. I wanted him to. I wanted to see his true self, his other self, the one who called to my dragon and who peered down at me with gleaming golden eyes.

Cobalt.

Get it together, Ember. I breathed deep to cool my lungs, to calm the fire spreading through me, and tried to grin back. "Yeah, well, I bet you didn't know what you were getting into," I said lightly.

"Doesn't matter." Riley dropped his arm and stepped back as if he couldn't bear to touch me anymore. Or perhaps, if he kept touching me, a large blue dragon would suddenly make a very explosive appearance in the middle of the hotel room. "But if we live through this, you owe me, Firebrand. Bigtime." He glanced at Wes, who was packing his laptop into a shoulder bag, his jaw set. "Everyone ready? Once we start, there's no turning back. Wes?"

"Piss off" was the sullen answer. "Like I have any sort of choice. When you're killed by St. George, don't expect me to babysit two dozen bloody hatchlings the rest of my life."

Riley ignored that. "We'll take two vehicles until we're a couple miles from the base. From there, we'll go the rest of the way on foot. Wes, how close will you need to be to pick up their signal?"

"Bloody too close," Wes muttered. "But it shouldn't be

hard to find, since they'll be the only ones within a hundred miles putting one out. The challenge will be jacking in without raising any kind of alarm."

"If you do have to move closer, don't go in the van. Last thing we need is for them to see headlights cruising toward them across the desert."

"Oh, really? Is that what I'll want to do, then?" Wes zipped his bag ferociously. "Silly me, here I was thinking we needed big neon signs that said Here We Are, Shoot Us Please on top of the roof."

Riley rolled his eyes but didn't comment. "ETA at the St. George perimeter will be zero three hundred. Once we're finished inside, we'll meet at the rendezvous and get the hell out of Dodge. Ember…" He turned, and his gaze met mine. "You're with me. Let's go."

★ ★ ★

The drive to the Arizona/Utah line was silent and mostly empty. Few cars passed us on the long stretch of highway across the Mojave Desert. Overhead, the moon peered down like a sleepy, half-lidded eye, surrounded by a billion stars that stretched on forever. Out here in the desert, many miles from cities or lights or civilization, the sky called to me. I thought of Shifting, of leaping off the bike, changing forms midair and soaring through the empty sky. Annoyed, I pushed all tempting thoughts to the back of my mind, willing my dragon to settle down. In a couple hours, we would be sneaking into a heavily armed base filled with soldiers whose main goal was the complete genocide of our species. There were more important things to focus on than midnight flights in the desert heat.

Garret. I hope you're okay. Hang in there, we're coming for you.

It felt like a thousand tiny snakes were writhing in my stomach, and I breathed deep to calm them down. Was the soldier going to be there when we came for him? Was he still alive? What would he say when we finally found him? I would think that a dragon showing up at a St. George base in the middle of the night wasn't something that happened often, if ever. Would Garret be happy to see me? Would he accept help from a dragon, the creature he'd been trained to kill on sight?

Or would he turn around and alert the rest of the base to our presence, having concluded that dragons were the enemy after all and needed to be destroyed? It had been days since that lonely night on the beach where I'd almost died, attacked by my own trainer. Garret had saved us, but he was also a soldier of the Order. According to Talon doctrine, St. George couldn't be reasoned with, accepted no compromise and showed no mercy to their enemies. Garret was back with his own people now. What if they'd convinced him that he'd been wrong after all, that dragons were the enemy, and the next time he saw one he'd put a bullet in the back of its skull?

Garret wouldn't do that, I told myself. *He's different than the rest of them. He saw that we weren't monsters. And he...he promised me that he was done killing. He wasn't going to hunt us anymore, that's what he said.*

I had to believe that. I had to believe Garret would keep his promise, that the soldier who'd helped fight off Lilith and let us go was the same person I'd gotten to know over the summer. The boy I'd taught to surf, who'd played arcade games with me, whose smile could make my stomach do tipsy cart-

wheels. Who had kissed me in the ocean and made all my
senses surge to life, who'd made me feel like I wasn't a dragon
or a human, but a strange, light creature somewhere in between. That person was not a soldier of St. George, a cold
ruthless killer who hated dragons and slaughtered without
mercy. No, when Garret was with me, he was just a boy who,
at times, seemed just as uncertain and confused as I was. I'd
seen a glimpse of the soldier on the bluff, when he'd pointed
a gun at my face, his eyes hard and cold. But even then, he
hadn't pulled the trigger.

Would he pull the trigger now?

I sighed and pressed my cheek to Riley's back, trying to
stop my brain from looping in endless circles. Rescue Garret
first. That was the looming issue at the moment, the thing I
had to focus on right now. We could deal with everything
else *after* we were clear of St. George.

Riley made a sharp left turn, pulled off the highway and
headed into the desert. Startled, I tightened my arms around
his waist, and we sped between rocks and cacti, following
the van ahead of us. Abruptly, Riley flipped off the lights,
as did the van, and we traveled in darkness for a while, only
the faint light of the moon guiding the way. Finally, the van
slowed and pulled behind a shallow rise, skidding to a halt in
a billowing cloud of dust. Riley swerved, cruising beside it,
and killed the engine.

Heart pounding, I sat up as the absolute silence of the desert descended on us like a glass dome. Except for my own
breathing and the soft creak of the motorcycle, the complete
absence of noise was chilling, and my dragon bristled. I didn't
like it. It reminded me of my old school in the middle of the

Great Basin, the place my brother and I had spent the majority of our lives, learning how to be human. Surrounded by desert, open sky and a whole lot of nothing. You could go outside and stand for hours in the same spot, the sun blazing down on you, and your ears would start to throb from the eternal, looming silence. I'd hated it. Sometimes, it had felt like the silence was trying to steal my voice; that if I went too long without making any noise, I'd become as still and lifeless as the desert around me. Dante had never understood why I was always so restless.

Dante. A lump rose to my throat as I clambered off the motorcycle, and I forced my thoughts away from him. One problem at a time.

"Still up for this, Firebrand?" Riley whispered, jolting me out of my dark musings. With a mental shake, I nodded as my heart resumed its painful thud against my ribs. Riley gazed at me, then turned and pointed across the desert to where a scattering of distant lights winked at us in the darkness.

"That's the base," he said quietly as I stared at the glimmers marking our objective. Garret was somewhere behind those walls, and with any luck, we'd get to him and be long gone before anyone from St. George knew we were there. "We're about two miles away," Riley went on, "but we can't risk driving any closer and having them see us. Stealth is our only chance to pull this off. From here, we walk."

Wes slipped out of the van, ski cap pulled low over his head, and stalked around the vehicle to yank open the back doors. Riley joined him and dragged a black duffel bag out from under the seat. My heart lurched as Riley casually pulled out a small black pistol, checked the chamber for rounds and holstered it to his belt with easy familiarity.

I swallowed at the sight of the gun. "Riley?" I ventured, suddenly terrified and angry about being terrified. "Tell me the truth," I said as he glanced over. "And don't think for a minute that I'm backing out, but...how dangerous is this really going to be?"

Wes snorted. "Oh, sure, *now* she asks. On bloody St. George's doorstep."

Riley sighed. "Truth, Firebrand? I wouldn't agree to do this if it was complete suicide," he said, holding my gaze. I blinked at him, surprised, and he gave a weary smile. "Wes might preach doom and gloom, but trust me when I say I know what I'm doing. We'll be going in when most of the base will be asleep. This particular chapterhouse is extremely remote and well hidden; they're using isolation to deter unwanted guests, so security should be minimal. If no one knows where you are, why bother with a ton of guards and patrols? And trust me, two dragons sneaking *into* a St. George compound doesn't happen often, if ever.

"But," he went on as I relaxed a bit, "that doesn't mean it won't be dangerous. These types of missions usually go one of two ways: without a hitch, or spectacularly wrong. Hopefully, we'll be able to sneak in, find what we want and tiptoe away without anyone knowing we were there. That's the best-case scenario. I think you can guess the worst-case scenario. So, on that note..." He held out a pistol to me. "Ever shot one of these?"

Numbly, I shook my head. I'd handled a gun before, both in my training with Lilith and then briefly when I'd disarmed the Glock aimed at my face, but I'd never fired one. Certainly not at a living creature.

Riley smiled grimly. "If it gets to the point where we're shooting at people, then the mission is FUBAR and we need to get out of there as fast as we can." He held up the weapon. "These are only to be used as the very last resort. But if the mission does go south, you're going to want something to defend yourself with. The problem with claws and teeth is that you have to get in close to attack, and that might be tricky if they're all firing M-16s at you."

"I've never fired a gun before, Riley. I don't even know if I could…shoot someone. Not for real. I've never killed anyone before."

Riley's lip curled in a hard smile. "Yeah, well, you're gonna have to get over that, Firebrand," he stated bluntly. "We might not be part of Talon anymore, but St. George doesn't give a damn about that little fact. To them, all dragons are the same. Rogue, hatchling or Viper, it makes no difference to the Order. They'll kill us regardless of faction or sympathies." He lowered the gun, his gaze almost accusing. "This is still a war, but we aren't just fighting one side anymore. Not only do we have to be on the lookout for St. George—Talon will be breathing down our necks, as well. We kind of got the shit end of both sticks, if you haven't noticed by now."

I blinked, stunned. I'd never heard Riley sound so bitter. Although, ever since we'd left Crescent Beach, he'd seemed… different. More serious and take-charge. This was not the cocky, insufferable, devil-may-care rogue I'd met before. He was not the mysterious lone rebel I'd thought he was, but the leader of an entire rogue underground, with who knew

how many dragons and humans depending on him. I suspected now that the dragon I'd met in Crescent Beach had
been putting on a show, a mask, the perfect identity for the
current situation. I wondered, yet again, if the Riley I faced
now was the real one.

At my silence, Riley gave me a weary, sympathetic look,
his voice going softer.

"Sorry, Firebrand. I didn't mean to jump down your throat
like that. I know you've never killed anyone, and I don't expect you to. Not tonight, anyway." He sighed and raked his
hair back. "I've just…seen a lot, you understand? From Talon
and St. George. I've lost friends and hatchlings to both orga-
nizations, and some days it feels like I'm pushing a boulder
up a never-ending cliff, and if I let up for one second, it'll roll
back and crush me." His brow furrowed and his eyes darkened
as he looked away. "One day it *will* roll back and crush me."

His gaze flicked back to mine. "What I'm trying to say is, if
you're going to stand against Talon, you have to do whatever
it takes to stay alive. And one day, that might involve shooting someone. Or incinerating them. Or tearing them apart.
Yeah, it's ugly, it's messy and it's not fair, but that's the truth
of it. This is our world, Firebrand. This is the world you live
in now." He held the gun out to me once more. "Unless you
want to go back."

I swallowed. "No," I said, and reached out for the weapon,
curling my fingers around the hard metal. "I'm not going
back." Riley tossed me a holster as well, and I slipped it around
my shoulder, feeling the weight of the gun, cold and deadly,
against my ribs. I hoped I would never have to use it.

"All right." Riley shut the van and looked toward the distant base. I saw him take a short, furtive breath, as if steeling himself for what was to come. "I think we're about ready. Just remember…" He shot a firm glare in my direction. "We do this my way. If I tell you to do something, don't question it. Don't even think about it. Just do it, understand?"

I nodded. Riley glanced at Wes, who watched him with the grave, resigned expression of someone who thought they might never see him again. "We're going. If I give the word, get out and don't look back. Wish us luck."

"Luck?" Wes muttered, shaking his head. "You don't need luck. You need a bloody miracle."

And on that inspiring note, we started across the desert.

RILEY

One mile to the gates of hell.

I shoved the thought away as I led Ember across the dusty plains, heading closer to that ominous glow looming ahead of us. Fear and second thoughts were dangerous now. This insane rescue was officially under way, and I had to focus on what was important; namely, getting us in and out without being discovered and gunned down. When I was a Basilisk, I'd been taught never to ask questions or think too hard about what I was doing. I didn't need to know the *whys*, I just needed to complete the missions.

Of course, it was when I'd started asking questions that I'd realized I couldn't be part of Talon anymore.

Ember walked behind me, silent in her black Viper's outfit, gliding over the sand like a shadow. She made no noise, moving like a Basilisk herself, graceful and sure without even realizing it. Lilith had taught her well. The only thing she hadn't taught her was the Vipers' ruthlessness, that apathy toward killing that Vipers were known and feared—for. I was glad of it, but at the same time, I knew it wouldn't last. Not in our world. There was too much at stake. Too many factions that wanted us dead, too many people to try to protect.

Eventually, the day would come when Ember would have to kill someone and when it did, she would have to make a choice as to what kind of dragon, and person, she really was. I just hoped it wouldn't change her too drastically.

"You're about two hundred yards from the fence." Wes's voice buzzed in my ear, courtesy of the wire I was wearing. Part of the package I'd picked up in L.A. "No security cameras as far as I can tell, but be careful."

"Got it."

We reached the perimeter fence, nothing heavy duty or unusual, just simple chain link topped with barbed wire. Signs reading Private Property and Trespassers Will Be Prosecuted hung from the links every thirty or so feet, but there was nothing to indicate that a heavily armed military compound lay beyond. St. George was nearly as good as Talon when it came to hiding in plain sight, as private armies were sort of frowned on by the United States government. The bases where the soldiers were housed used isolation and misdirection to stay off the radar of those that might take issue with a large number of armed fanatics squatting on US soil.

Good news for us: this base was counting on its remoteness to deter unwanted visitors, so the fence wasn't well patrolled. Bad news for us: if they did start shooting, no one would ever hear it.

Ember crouched beside me, peering through the barrier. We'd approached the base from the north, giving the fence a wide berth as we circled around, and I could see a cluster of squat buildings about a thousand yards beyond the fence. The space between was dark and shadowy, but terrifyingly flat and open.

No turning back now.

Pulling out my wire cutters, I began snipping through the links, silent and methodical. Oddly enough, the familiar task helped calm my nerves; how many times had I done this before? Ember pressed close, her shoulder brushing mine, and my pulse leaped at the contact, but I didn't stop until I'd cut a line just big enough for us to slip through.

"Stay close," I murmured, replacing the cutters. "Remember, don't do anything until I give the word."

She nodded. Reaching down, I peeled back the steel curtain, motioned her through, then slipped in behind her. As we passed through, the fence gave a soft, metallic slither, echoing the chill running up my spine.

Okay, here we were, on St. George soil. Still in a crouch, I scanned the layout of the base, noting buildings, lights, how far the shadows extended. Ember waited beside me, patient and motionless, green eyes shining with resolve. I sensed no fear from her, only stubborn determination, a will to see this through no matter what, and squashed the flicker of both dread and pride.

"We're in," I whispered to Wes.

"All right." I imagined furious typing on the other end. "Hang on, I'm trying to find the security system…there we go." More silence followed, as Ember and I huddled at the fence line, gazing around warily. "Okay," Wes muttered at last. "Looks like only headquarters and the armory actually have cameras. So you're going to have to get inside before I can walk you through."

"Got it," I muttered back. "I'll let you know when we're in. Riley out."

Staying low, we scurried across the open ground toward the buildings, keeping to where the shadows were thickest. It being the very dead of night, the compound was quiet; most soldiers were asleep, probably having to be up in a couple hours. I did spot a couple guards near the perimeter gate, but other than that the yard was deserted.

"It's so quiet," Ember whispered as we crouched behind a Hummer, maybe a hundred yards from the first set of buildings. "Just like you said. That's a good thing, right?"

"Yeah, but let's not get cocky." I nodded at the roof of the largest structure, straight ahead behind a clump of smaller buildings. "If this isn't exciting enough for you, wait till we get inside. All it takes is for one alarm to go off, and the entire base will swarm out like we poked a stick down an ant nest. So stay on your toes, Firebrand. We're not out of here yet."

Her eyes flashed, but she nodded. We continued across the yard in silence, even more wary for hidden dangers and sudden patrols. The base remained quiet and still, but I stayed on high alert. Ember might think this was a walk in the park, but I knew how quickly things could turn. And if they did turn, our chances of getting out were slim to zilch.

As we drew close to the first row of buildings, creeping along the outer wall, the door in front of us swung open. Biting back a curse, I dived behind a corner, pressing myself against the wall, as Ember did the same. I felt the heat of her body against mine and squashed the impatient riling of my dragon as a pair humans paused at the bottom of the steps, talking in low, rough voices.

"Damn kitchen duty," one growled, sounding sullen. "Of course, I'd have to pull it today. You going to the execution?"

"I dunno," the other replied as Ember stiffened beside me. "It seems…kinda wrong, you know? I saw him in the South American raid, when he charged that damn adult lizard by himself. Kid's completely fearless."

"He's a dragonlover." The other soldier's voice was cutting. "Did you not hear what he said at his trial? I personally can't wait to see his guts sprayed all over the ground. Better than he deserves, if you ask me."

They walked on, arguing now, their voices fading into the darkness. When they were gone, I blew out a quiet breath, slumping against the wall, then glanced at Ember.

Her face was white with horror and rage, her eyes glowing a bright, furious emerald in the shadows. Like she might Shift, here and now, and tear those two soldiers to pieces. Quickly, I put a hand on her arm, feeling it shake under my fingers, and leaned close. "Easy, Firebrand," I whispered as my dragon tried pushing its way to the surface again. I shoved it back. "This is why we're here. He's not dead yet."

Though that *was* the confirmation I needed. They were going to execute the soldier today, probably as soon as it was light outside. Not that I cared—I'd be more than happy if another St. George bastard kicked it—but that didn't give us a lot of time to work with. If we were going to get him out, it had to be now. But Ember's reaction to the news sent a flare of anger through my veins. Why did she care about this kid so much? He was just a human and, more important, he was St. George. I remembered the way she'd looked at him, the way she had danced with him, and my anger grew. Ember was a dragon; she had no business getting involved with a human. Once we rescued this bastard and were far enough from St.

George that I could breathe again, I would show her exactly
what it meant to be a dragon.

Ember took a deep breath and nodded. Carefully, we eased
around the buildings, hugging the walls and shadows, inching
steadily toward the large, two-story building near the center.
We avoided the brightly lit front, of course, sidling along the
back wall until we reached a small metal door.

Ember started forward, but I grabbed her arm, motioning
to the camera mounted over the steps. We shrank back into
the shadows again as I spoke into the mic. "Wes, we're at the
back door of the main building. No guards, but there is a
camera up top and it looks like you need a key card to get in."

"Hang on." Wes fell silent while Ember and I pressed
against the wall and waited. "Okay," he muttered after a few
seconds. "Just give me a minute to see if I can turn it off."

As he was talking, a body suddenly came around the corner. A human, wearing normal clothes, his dark hair buzzed
close. He jerked, startled, and for a split second the three of
us gaped at each other in shock, before his muscles tensed,
mouth opening to shout a warning.

And Ember lunged in, a black blur across my vision, hitting the soldier in the jaw right below the ear. The human's
head snapped to the side, and he collapsed as if all his bones
had turned into string, sprawling facedown in the sand.

I breathed in slowly, as Ember blinked and stared wide-
eyed at the fallen soldier, as if she couldn't believe what she'd
just done, either. My arms were shaking, adrenaline coursing
through my veins. It had happened so quickly; I hadn't even
had time to move before the soldier was unconscious. And
my reflexes weren't slow by any means.

"Firebrand," I breathed, and she looked at me, almost frightened. "That was…impressive. Where did you learn that?"

"I don't know." She backed away from the body, as if afraid she wouldn't be able to stop herself from doing something else. "I just… I saw him and…" Her eyes darkened, and she shook her head. "I don't even remember what I did."

Lilith's training. This was what the Vipers taught their students—how to be fast, how to be quick and lethal, and to strike without thinking. To recognize a threat and take it out. Immediately.

"Riley." Wes's voice crackled in my ear, wary and anxious. "You okay? What's going on?"

I shook myself. "Nothing," I told him, moving toward the fallen soldier. Ember had had to silence him, no question, but we still had to deal with him. Last thing we needed was for him to wake up and alert the rest of the base. "Small problem. It's been dealt with," I continued, kneeling beside the human and reaching into a compartment on my belt. "How's the unlocking the door part coming along?"

"What are you doing, Riley?" Ember asked suddenly, watching me with wary green eyes. "You…you're not going to *kill* him, are you?"

I shook my head, showing her the plastic zip ties I pulled from my belt, though I found it a little ironic. Had Ember been a full Viper, I doubted this human would be alive. And I wasn't going to snap his neck or slit his throat while he lay there, helpless. Even though I hated the bastards, and would gladly blast him to cinders if I had to, I wasn't a killer. Not like them.

Wes's voice continued to buzz in my ear. "I can get the door open," he said as I pulled the soldier's arms behind him and zip-tied his wrists together. "But if I start blacking out cameras, they might get suspicious. Best I can give you is a thirty-second feedback loop, but you'll have to get inside before the feed goes normal again. Think you can do that?"

I gagged the human with the roll of duct tape in my belt, then heaved the unconscious body over my shoulder. He hung like a sack of potatoes—a heavy, well-muscled sack of potatoes. "Do it," I grunted, staggering toward a Dumpster we'd crouched behind a moment ago. "Just give us fifteen seconds. Ember, get the cover, will you?"

She scurried to the Dumpster and pushed up the lid, releasing the stench of old milk, rotting things and decay. I probably shouldn't have felt so spitefully pleased as I dropped the body between reeking sacks of garbage and closed the top, but I did.

At the bottom of the steps, we hung back in the shadows, watching the door and the camera up top. "Gimme a moment," Wes muttered as I drummed my fingers against my knee, feeling highly exposed. Another soldier could come waltzing around the corner anytime. We might've gotten lucky once; twice would be pushing it. "All right," Wes finally said. "In ten seconds, the camera will go off and the door will unlock. Both will happen almost simultaneously, so you'll have to get up there fast. Ready?"

"Yeah," I muttered, feeling Ember tense beside me.

"Then…go! Now!"

I burst forward and raced up the steps, not daring to look at the camera peering down at me with its soulless black eye. My fingers closed on the handle just as there was a soft beep, and the light above the key-card slit turned green. Wrenching open the door, I motioned Ember inside, then ducked over the threshold myself. The door closed, shutting behind us with a soft click that seemed to echo down the long, brightly lit corridor ahead.

We were inside St. George HQ.

Now the real fun began.

EMBER

I should probably be terrified.

I *was* pretty nervous. I was inside the St. George complex, surrounded by a whole army of dragonslayers who'd kill me without a second thought if they knew I was here. We still had to find Garret and somehow sneak *him* out without being discovered. And that close call with the soldier... my nerves were still singing, my hands shaking with adrenaline. I hadn't even thought. I'd just seen him and...boom, he was on the ground. Would I do that again? *Could* I do that again, if I had to?

Was this what my trainer meant when she said I'd be an amazing Viper?

I pushed those thoughts away. *Focus, Ember. Find Garret. That's why we're here.*

"Where to now?" I whispered to Riley.

He huddled against the wall, speaking softly into his wire. "Wes, we're in." A few seconds passed with Riley listening to whatever the human was saying. Finally, he nodded. "Right," he muttered. "Heading there now."

"Did he find Garret?" I asked.

"No," Riley answered, making my heart sink. "But he's

jacked into the security system and says that there's a prison
floor somewhere below us. If your human is scheduled for
execution in a couple hours, that's where he's going to be."
Riley cast a wary look down the corridor. "There are still
guards wandering about. Be careful."

I nodded, and we started down the hall, which at this
time of night was empty and deserted, but way too bright for
comfort. Doors lined the corridor, most of them closed, but
a few sat open, showing office-type rooms with desks and
computers. I wondered what the soldiers and officers of St.
George did when they weren't killing dragons. It was hard
to picture them doing normal things like checking email and
IMing with friends.

As I passed yet another office door, a glint of metallic red
caught my eye. And, for some reason, the hairs on the back
of my neck stood straight up. I paused just outside the door
and peeked in, letting my eyes adjust to the dim light. At
first glance, it seemed like just another office, with standard
office furniture: chairs, metal cabinet, giant desk in the center. Nothing strange or out of place...until I saw where that
faint glimmer was coming from. For a second, I frowned, not
knowing what I was looking at.

Then it hit me like a punch to the stomach, and bile surged
up my throat, burning the inside of my mouth. I was frozen,
unable to look away, unable to do anything but stare at what
lay through the door.

On the wall above the desk, spanning nearly corner to
corner, hung the hide of a small red dragon. I could see the
long elegant neck, the lighter belly scales, the curved black
talons still attached to the feet. Its scales were a darker red

than mine, almost rust colored, and it had thin stripes down its back and tail. From its size, it had been a hatchling at the time of its death, my age or younger. At one time, this lifeless skin had been a dragon, just like me. And now...now it was a trophy decorating someone's office.

I think I made a choked, strangled noise, because Riley was suddenly at my side, pulling me away. "Shit," I heard him growl, almost yanking me from the door. "Don't look, Firebrand. Don't look at it. Come here."

I was shaking. Riley dragged me into the hall and pulled me to him, holding me close. I buried my face in his shirt and squeezed my eyes shut, but I couldn't forget the horrible image seared into my brain. I could still see that limp, empty skin hanging on the wall, and I knew it would probably show up in my dreams.

Riley's arms were around me, a shield between me and the rest of the world, a world that slaughtered teen dragons and nailed their hides to the wall. "You okay?" he whispered, his head bent close to mine. I wasn't, but I nodded without looking up, and he blew out a breath. "Damn St. George," he muttered, and his voice was slightly choked, too. "Murdering bastards. Damn them all."

"I'm...okay," I whispered, though I really, really wasn't. It was like something out of a horror movie, seeing someone's skin nailed to the killer's wall. I wondered what they'd done with the rest of the dragon once they'd peeled its hide away, then immediately wished I hadn't. "It's all right," I managed, drawing back, though his grip didn't loosen. "Riley, I'm fine. It's..."

A door squeaked somewhere in the mazelike hallway. We

tensed as footsteps echoed down the corridor, growing louder every second. Riley jerked up with a whispered curse. As the steps drew closer, we gazed frantically around for a hiding place, but, other than the open door behind us, there was nothing.

Sorry, Firebrand, Riley mouthed, and yanked me into the room with the dead dragon. I bit my cheek, feeling tainted, as if the ghost of the murdered dragon lurked in the room with us, and I might glance up to see a pale, bloody figure watching accusingly from the wall.

Pressing into the corner beside the file cabinets, we held our breath as the footsteps came toward the room. I turned my face into Riley's arm and clenched my jaw, trying not to look at the grisly symbol of death on the wall in front of us.

The footsteps passed the room without slowing down and continued down the corridor. Riley waited a long moment after they had faded away and silence fell once more, before finally leading us from the room. I kept my face down and my eyes half closed until we were out of the office, but I could still feel the dead dragon's presence at my back.

"Damn St. George," Riley hissed again, sounding almost as sick as I felt. "Depraved, murdering... Ugh. I'm sorry you had to see that, Firebrand." He put a hand on my arm, steady and comforting. "Sure you want to keep going?" he asked. "It's not too late to turn around. Do we keep looking for the human, or get the hell out of here?"

Frowning, I pulled back to look at him. He gazed back grimly. "This is the true face of St. George, Ember," he said, and his voice was almost a challenge. "This is what they do. What they *all* do." He nodded to the room behind us. "How many times do you think your soldier saw that hide hanging on the wall and thought nothing of it? It was just a skin, a trophy, not a living creature with thoughts and fears and dreams, like everyone else." His eyes narrowed. "We're not people to them, Firebrand. They don't see us as anything but monsters. And I know you don't want to hear it, but your human was raised to think exactly like them. He saw you in the same way he did that hide on the wall."

I shuddered, remembering the skin, tacked onto the wall in plain sight, and for a moment, my resolve wavered. Was I making a mistake? Was it really possible for someone to change his entire perspective? Garret had grown up in St. George, where these awful tokens of death and murder were considered trophies. Decorations to hang in someone's office, like a stag head or a tiger pelt. Because to St. George, we were monsters. Animals. What if Garret still thought like that?

What if he doesn't?

I swallowed hard. Regardless of what Garret believed, I couldn't leave him. If I didn't get him out tonight, he would die. Even if he saw me as a monster, I wouldn't abandon him now.

"No," I told Riley, turning from the office door and the horrible trophy hanging within. "We don't stop. We keep looking. I'm not leaving him to die."

Riley shook his head. "Stubborn idiot hatchling," he muttered, though one corner of his mouth curled up. "All right, we keep going. Wes, you there?" A pause, and Riley rolled his eyes. "Yeah, she did. Of course not, have you met her? How far are we from the stairs?"

We crept through several more hallways, passing more

darkened rooms and offices that I was careful not to peek into, until we came to a door that opened onto a stairwell. Here, Riley stopped us, saying there was a camera on the other side, and we had to wait until Wes shut it down. Once he did, I darted through the frame and started down the cement stairs, feeling Riley close at my back. The steps didn't take us far; just one loop around to an identical metal door, which we pushed through and stepped into yet another hallway.

At the end of the hall stood a door, lonely and unguarded. There were no cameras or humans around, but Riley grabbed my arm when I started forward, pulling us to a stop a few feet from the end of the corridor.

"Got it," he muttered, speaking to Wes, I figured, and turned to me, his face grave.

"What's wrong?" I whispered. "Is Garret not here?"

"Oh, he's here, Firebrand," Riley said, his voice matching the look on his face. "Wes confirmed it on the security feed. But he's not the only one." He nodded to the door. "That's a guard room. You need to pass through it to get to the jail block beyond. One problem, though. Guard rooms tend to be guarded."

My skin prickled. "How many?" I asked.

"Two." His expression darkened. "Both armed. They won't be expecting us, but we're going to have to be fast if we want to take them out before they sound the alarm. Think you can pull off another crazy ninja Viper attack? We're not going to get another shot at this. Once I open that door, there's really no going back."

My stomach dropped. After a moment, I took a deep breath, steeling myself. Whatever it took, I would find Garret. Even though these new instincts freaked me out. Even though I wanted nothing more than to be done with this place, with its armed humans and dead dragons hanging on the walls. We were almost to the soldier; his life depended on us reaching him, and I wouldn't let anything stop me now.

I glanced at Riley and nodded. "I'm ready. Let's do this."

GARRET

One hundred and twenty minutes till dawn and counting.

The hardest thing about waiting to die is being torn between wanting more time and wishing they would just get it over with already. You can't sleep, of course. You can't focus on anything else. Your mind keeps tormenting you with questions and memories and what-ifs, until you wish they'd just do you a favor and knock you senseless until it was time. Maybe that was a coward's way out, but I didn't want to show up to my execution looking beaten down and exhausted. I would not beg, or cry or plead for mercy. If this was my last day on Earth, I wanted to end it well, facing Death on my feet with my head held high. That was all a soldier of St. George could hope for.

As I lay on the cot, unable to sleep, unable to stop the relentless countdown in my head, my nerves suddenly prickled, making my breath catch. It was faint, but I recognized it instantly. The same feeling I got when I was about to kick down the door to a target's residence, or when I suspected an ambush lay just ahead and we were about to walk right into it. A soldier's instincts, telling me that something was about to happen.

Carefully, I swung my legs off the mattress and walked to the front of my cell. The room on the other side of the bars remained empty and dark, but I couldn't shake the feeling that something was wrong. Were they coming for me early? No, that wasn't right. The Order was nothing if not punctual. I still had another hour and fifty minutes before I was scheduled to die. Maybe the pressure was finally getting to me. Maybe I was having a nervous breakdown.

A sudden *boom* in the absolute stillness made me jump, the familiar crash of a door being flung open or kicked down, and I instinctively went for the gun at my belt, though of course I was unarmed. Shouts and cries of alarm rang out from the guard room beyond the cell block. Helpless, I clenched my fists around the bars, listening as a battle raged just a few yards away, muffled through the wall. There was a short scuffle, the scrape of chairs and the thud of bodies hitting the floor... and then silence.

I waited, holding my breath, my whole body coiled and ready for a fight. I didn't know what to expect, but whatever was coming, I was ready.

And then the door to the guard room opened, and I met a pair of vivid green eyes across the hall. Turns out, I wasn't ready at all.

The breath caught in my throat, and for a moment, I could only stare. *Not only a nervous breakdown, I'm also hallucinating.* Because there was no way she could be here. No sane reason she would show up in the middle of a St. George base, minutes from my execution. My mind had snapped; I was seeing things that weren't there. *The Perfect Soldier, unable to face his own death, goes crazy at age seventeen.*

Numb, I gaped at her, unable to look away. Bracing for the girl silhouetted against the light to writhe into shadows and moonlight and disappear. She didn't vanish but smiled, in a way that made my heart twist, and hurried to the door of my cell.

"Ember?" Still incredulous, I couldn't move as the figure drew close, gazing up at me. A hand reached through the bars, pressing against my jaw, and I drew in a shuddering breath. It was warm, and solid, and real. Impossible as it was, this was real.

My hand closed on her wrist, and I felt her pulse, rapid and steady, under my fingers. "What are you doing here?" I whispered.

"I came to get you out, of course," Ember whispered back, her breath fanning across my cheek, further proof that she wasn't a ghost or a figment of my imagination. Her gaze met mine through the bars, flashing defiantly. "I wasn't going to leave you, Garret. Not after you saved us. I'm not going to let them kill you."

"You came here for me?"

"Ember," growled a new, impatient voice, one that was vaguely familiar. I gazed past her shoulder and saw a second figure, dark haired and dressed in black, scowl at me from the open door of the guard room. With a start, I realized it was the other dragon, the one Ember had fled with when she left Crescent Beach.

"No time for this, Firebrand," he snapped, and tossed something to her, something that glittered as she caught it. "Come on. Those guards won't stay down forever. Open the door and let's get the hell out of here."

I was still reeling from the fact that Ember was *here*, that two *dragons* had shown up in the middle of the night to save me, but the second dragon's words jolted me out of my trance. As Ember shoved the key into the lock and wrenched the door open with a rusty creak, I suddenly realized what this meant, what was really happening.

"Garret," Ember said as I paused, staring at the open door. "Come on, before someone sees us. What are you doing?"

At the edge of the hall, the other dragon gave a snort of disgust.

"I told you, Firebrand." He gestured sharply in my direction. "You can open the monkey's cage, but you can't force it to leave. He's not moving because we're the enemy, and he'd rather stay and let them put a bullet through his skull than escape with a pair of dragons. Isn't that right, St. George?" The figure turned to me, mouth curled in a sneer. "Never mind that they sold you down the river without a second thought. But you know, I don't care one way or another about your loyalty hang-ups. You have three seconds to choose before I say the hell with it and leave you here. So what's it gonna be? Come with us, or stay here and die?"

Escape. Leave St. George with two dragons. With the enemy. I'd been fully prepared to die a moment ago, but now freedom was staring me in the face. If I did this, if I stepped through that door, there was no turning back.

For just a moment, the Perfect Soldier recoiled at the idea of accepting the help of our greatest enemies, even now. But I knew the truth, and it cast an ominous shadow over my thoughts. There was something wrong within the Order, something I'd never seen before I met Ember. It was treason to speak against St. George doctrine, treason to consider that the Order could be mistaken. No one in St. George was willing to hear the other side of the story, that a dragon, a creature whose race they had hunted and killed for hundreds of years, could be more than just a monster. No one was willing to accept the idea that the Order of St. George had slaughtered those who did not deserve it.

Regardless, the Order was no longer home. I'd already been sentenced to die, at the hands of the very people who had raised me. I wouldn't be any more of a traitor if I left this place in the company of two dragons who'd risked their lives to get me out. That made a pretty good argument, right there.

"I'm with you," I said quietly, and stepped through the door. The other dragon was still watching me, gold eyes assessing, but my gaze sought Ember's, and I saw relief spread across her face as I left the cell. I heard another disgusted snort from her companion, but I ignored it. I was a soldier of St. George no longer. I had no idea how Ember and her companion were going to get us *out* but, at least for now, I was free. If I was going to die today, I would go down fighting.

"Come on," growled the second dragon, gesturing impatiently. "It's almost dawn."

We hurried from the cell block, passing through the guard station, where two soldiers lay in crumpled heaps on the floor, out cold. One of them had what looked like a broken nose and the other's forehead was a mess of blood where, I suspected, he'd been bashed against the edge of the desk. I paused, kneeling down to grab the 9 mm from one of their side holsters, trying not to look at them as I checked the chamber for rounds. I might be with the enemy now, but they were still my former brothers, men I had trained with and fought beside. That couldn't be forgotten in a single night, or even in a single act of betrayal. The male dragon glared at me as I rose with the gun, obviously not pleased with the idea that I was armed, but didn't challenge me as we continued down the hall and up the stairs to the main floor.

The building was quiet as we exited the stairwell; it was still too early for most soldiers to be up and about, though I could see the sky had turned a disquieting navy blue, no longer the pitch-black of true night. Morning formations began at oh five hundred, which was less than an hour and a half away. The base would be stirring soon. Not to mention, we still had to get past security and the patrols around the perimeter fence. I didn't know how Ember and the other dragon had managed to get this far without being seen, but I was less than optimistic that we could waltz out again without trouble. Everything was quiet. This seemed way too easy.

The other dragon—Riley, I remembered his name was—stopped us at the back door and spoke quietly into what I presumed was a wire. A moment later, he nodded and pushed open the door, confirming what I suspected; they had an outsider hacked into the security cams. He had to be good; Order security was tight. He also had to be fairly close to pick up the signal.

Outside, it was still dark. We skirted the light and stayed to the shadows, moving low and silent across the barren yard. Once, a patrol passed us, talking in low voices, and we flattened ourselves against a wall until they disappeared. The buildings provided some cover, though we had to be wary of windows and doorways where someone could spot us. But what worried me the most was the last stretch to the fence line; flat and open, with little to no cover. If we were spotted and they opened fire on us then, we'd be gunned down in seconds.

I imagined the uproar this would cause. If the Order realized two dragons had been able to walk in, free a prisoner, and walk merrily out again, there would probably be several weeks of chaos as chapterhouses around the globe scrambled to tighten security, double patrols and lock down networks. Training would intensify. I imagined heads would roll higher up the chain of command. Dragons making a mockery of the Order? Sneaking in right under their noses? A few months ago, the idea would've angered and horrified me; right now I was severely disinclined to care. St. George was done with me. I didn't know *where* I would go from here; the Order had been my whole life. I didn't know what else was out there. But one thing I was sure of: dawn would not find me standing in front of the firing wall, about to be executed for saving a dragon.

But we weren't out of here yet.

Four hundred yards to the perimeter fence…and everything exploded.

As we huddled by a wall, ready to make that final dash over open ground toward the fence line, a siren blared, shattering the quiet. Ember jumped, and the other dragon cursed, pressing back into the wall as lights erupted all around us. Spotlights flashed to life, huge white circles gliding over the ground and scouring the sky. Doors opened, and soldiers began pouring from everywhere, looking confused but alert as they gathered in loose squads, gazing around warily.

"What's going on?" Ember whispered.

"They know we're here," the other dragon spat. "Probably found the empty cell and the guards." He swore again and peered around the corner, narrowing his eyes. "Wes, we've been discovered. Can you kill the lights?" A moment passed, and he shook his head. "Fine, then get out of here! Don't worry about us—we'll catch up at the rendezvous point." He paused a moment, then snarled, "I don't care, Wes, just go!"

Soldiers were everywhere now. I raised my gun, though I cringed at the thought of firing on my former brothers. "We're not going to make it," I told the other two quietly. And for a second, I felt a stab of regret that Ember had come. I'd wanted her to be free of St. George, to not live in fear of dragonslayers trying to kill her. Now, she would die here with me.

"It's too far," I told them as they glanced back. "There are too many between us and the fence line. We'll never reach it without being seen. Ember…" I looked into her wide green eyes. She stared back without fear or regret, making my heart twist. "I'll lead them away. They'll be looking for me. You and Riley get out of here, any way you can."

Her eyes flashed defiance. "Don't you dare, Garret," she almost snarled. "I didn't come all this way to free you just to leave you behind again. That's the most pointless thing I've ever heard." She stepped away from the wall, and her eyes were glowing now, a luminous emerald green. "We're getting out of here, all of us, right now!"

A searing white light swung around, pinning us in its glare. I winced and raised my arm to shield my face, just as the girl in front of me disappeared and a fiery crimson dragon reared up to take her place. Shouts rang out over the base, as the red dragon landed on all fours, dark wings outstretched, and roared a challenge that made the air shiver.

"Shit!" There was another ripple of energy as Ember's companion shed his human form, becoming a sleek blue dragon with a fin down his neck and back. My pulse spiked as the two inhuman creatures turned on me, eyes glowing. Even now, instinct was telling me to run, that they were the enemy and I had to gun them down before they attacked and tore me to shreds.

Shots rang out behind me, sparking off the wall. Ember snarled, flinching back, and I spun, raising my weapon. A patrol of two was rushing at us, guns drawn and firing on the dragons pinned in the spotlight. They hadn't seen me, or rather, their attention was riveted to the creatures behind me. I raised my gun, silently asking forgiveness, and fired at their legs. The soldiers cried out and pitched forward, crashing to the ground, but I could see more running toward us. The whole base was alerted now and knew dragons were inside the compound.

"Garret!"

A metallic red body lunged to my side, and I had to force myself not to leap away as a narrow, reptilian face peered at me. "Get on," the dragon said, lowering her wings. "Hurry! We have to fly."

Get on? *Ride* a dragon? For a split second, I balked. Talking with dragons was one thing. Accepting their help was another. But riding one? Especially if I knew the dragon was also a slender, green-eyed girl I had kissed on more than one occasion?

With a roar, the blue dragon reared up and blasted a cone of fire at a patrol that came around the corner, guns raised. The soldiers fell back with cries and screams, and Ember snarled, baring her fangs at me.

"Garret, come *on*!"

I shook myself and vaulted onto her back. Her spines poked at me as I wrapped my arms around her neck and settled between the leathery wings. I could feel heat radiating from the scales, the muscles shifting and coiling beneath me, and I repressed a shiver. This was not the Ember I knew. The girl had vanished, any hints of humanity disappearing as the dragon moved, savage, majestic and terrifying at the same time. She craned her neck to look back at me, long muzzle close enough to show rows of fangs, the scent of ash and smoke curling from her jaws.

"Hang on."

More gunshots rang out, and the blue dragon snarled something in Draconic, the guttural, native language of dragons. Ember spun, making me tighten my grip, took three bounding leaps forward and launched herself into the air. Her wing muscles strained beneath me like steel cables pulsing beneath her skin, and we rose into the sky. The spotlight followed, keeping us brightly illuminated even as we left the base behind. Gunshots roared; I heard a howl of rage from the blue dragon, and gritted my teeth, hunched low over Ember's back. She jolted suddenly, then her wings flapped furiously as we picked up speed, racing to get away from the spotlight and out of range of the compound. Very gradually, the spotlight disappeared, and the gunshots faded away, as we fled St. George and escaped into the desert.

★ ★ ★

We were out. We'd actually escaped St. George.

The wind whipped at my hair and clothes as I shifted on

Ember's back and cautiously sat up, gazing around in amazement. The desert stretched out before me, vast and endless, looking like an ocean of sand in the predawn light. Where it met the sky, a faint smear of pink was peeking over the horizon, though the land was still dark and shadowed. From this height, I could just make out the distant highway and the tiny glimmers of cars that followed it.

I drew in a quiet breath, wondering if all dragons felt this exhilaration. I'd gone surfing with Ember before, had felt that addictive rush of excitement and adrenaline while coursing down a huge wave.

It was nothing compared to this.

On impulse, I glanced behind me, at the compound I was leaving behind, and my blood chilled. Headlights speared the darkness from several vehicles, following us across the open desert. I counted three SUVs and at least one Jeep with a spotlight fixed to the roof, all straining to close the distance. There was no place to hide out here. If those vehicles got much closer they would start shooting, and we wouldn't stand a chance.

"There's the van!"

I looked at the blue dragon, then at the ground, where a large white van was speeding across the flat plain, trailing a billow of dust. Instantly, the blue dragon folded his wings and dropped from the sky, plunging toward the ground. I felt the subtle shift of muscles beneath me as Ember did the same, though a ragged shudder went through her as she glided after the blue. She was panting hard, sides heaving, and I hoped carrying me away from the base hadn't put too much of a strain on her.

The blue dragon plunged low to skim the ground, then wheeled hard so that he passed in front of the van, in full view of the driver. Instantly, the van slammed on its brakes, coming to a skidding halt in a writhing cloud of dust. As the blue dragon landed, the front door opened and a human jumped out, wild haired and skinny, shouting something at the dragon as he hurried forward.

I realized with a start that Ember had dropped low to the ground and was gliding toward the van at top speed. Alarmed, I tensed, wondering when she would slow, but another shudder went through her, and she abruptly dropped from the air like a stone.

At the last second, she flapped her wings and pulled up enough to slow her momentum, before we crashed headfirst into the ground. I was thrown clear, striking the earth and rolling several yards, the world spinning around me, before I finally came to a halt several yards from where Ember had fallen.

Wincing, I staggered upright. My head throbbed, my arms were bloody and the world was still spinning, but nothing seemed broken. I ignored the stab of pain from a bruised or cracked rib and stumbled toward the dragon.

"Ember…"

My stomach twisted. She lay on her side a few yards away, heaving in great, shuddering gasps. One wing was crumpled beneath her, the other lay limp on the ground. Her legs moved feebly, clawing at the loose sand and rock, and her tail twitched a weak rhythm in the dirt. But in the time it took me to reach her, she slumped and went motionless. Her wing gave one final spasm and was still.

"Ember!"

A dark-haired, naked human raced up to her, dropping to his knees beside the scaly neck. "Ember," Riley said again, putting a hand on her side. "Can you hear me? What happened? Are you—?"

He stopped, his face going pale. I limped up beside him just as he pulled his hand back, the palm and fingers covered in red, and my heart stood still.

"Oh, no." His voice was a whisper, and he surged to his feet, glaring back at the van. "Wes!" he yelled. "Ember's been shot. Help me get her in the van before St. George catches up."

"Bloody hell." The shaggy-haired human raced around the van, pausing to throw open the back doors. "I knew this was a bad idea, Riley. I knew the stubborn brat was going to get us all killed."

"Shut up and help before I rip off your legs and leave you for St. George."

"I'll help," I broke in, and he turned to glare daggers at me. Without waiting for an answer, I stepped around the unconscious dragon and knelt beside her, sliding my arm beneath a scaly foreleg. Ember stirred weakly, her claws raking the sand once, but she didn't wake up. Riley hesitated, then crouched on the opposite side, taking her leg.

"Wes!" he spat as we braced ourselves to lift the dragon off the ground. "Get over here. You're going to have to help, too."

"On three," I said as the other human dropped beside me, muttering curses the whole time. Over Ember's back and wings, Riley gave me a last baleful glare, but then his attention shifted to the dragon between us. "One...two...three!"

We lifted. Ember sagged, wings and tail dragging along the ground, her neck dangling awkwardly. She wasn't as heavy as I'd expected, considering this was a very large, armored reptile who was complete dead weight at the moment. Somehow, the three of us manhandled the dragon over the ground and into the back of the vehicle, grunting as we pushed and pulled her inside. She barely fit; her wings were crumpled against the sides, her neck bent at an awkward angle, and we had to loop her tail over her back. I ended up pressed against the front seat with her neck draped over my lap, curved talons pricking my leg through my jeans. Riley glared at me over Ember's motionless body, obviously hating how close I was, but there was no room to move. Nor was there room for the both of us to be back here, with an unconscious red dragon sprawled across the floor.

"Riley!" Wes snapped as the other hesitated, reluctant to leave me alone with Ember, I guessed. "St. George is coming! Bloody hell, put some pants on, would you? Let's go!"

Riley cursed and backed away, reaching out to close the back doors. His eyes glowed yellow in the shadows of the van as he stared at me. "If she dies," he said softly, "I'm going to kill you." It was not an idle threat.

The roar of a distant engine, not our own, echoed over the hill behind us, getting steadily closer, and my stomach lurched. St. George was not about to let us go. Wes shrieked at Riley again, and the doors slammed, cutting off my view of the outside world. Ember groaned and stirred, wings fluttering, but she didn't awaken. I swallowed hard and scooted aside so that the narrow, horned skull was pillowed against my legs. Her breath was shallow and hot against my skin,

and I put one tentative hand on her scaly neck, trying to ignore the rows of fangs hovering over my leg, the claws that
scraped close to my body.

The blood seeping across the floor, making my insides cold.

The van lurched forward, bounced once and gained speed
as it rumbled over the sand. We fled into the desert, the roar
of St. George behind us, the head of a dying dragon resting
in my lap.

PART II

ALL THAT GLITTERS

COBALT

Twelve years ago

"Agent Cobalt? They're ready for you now."

I stood and rolled my shoulders forward and back, trying to shake out the stiffness, then followed the assistant down the hall toward the room at the very end. I hated meetings like this: sitting in a cold office building, being polite and deferent, while the flat, appraising glare of a senior dragon bored into me from across the table. Normally, Talon didn't bother with face-to-face conferences, speaking to me directly only when they felt the assignment especially important. I'd rather the organization contact me the usual way: via an envelope or a folder left at a dead drop, where I could read through my assignment in peace. Where I didn't feel like I was being judged.

Especially now. Especially since I was still furious with the way the last assignment had gone down, the lives lost because of me. Because Talon had lied, and I'd believed them.

I strode into the meeting room, where a trio was seated around a long wooden table in the center of the floor. I recognized Adam Roth, a youngish-looking man in a perfectly tailored gray suit. One of Talon's junior VPs, though he was still older than me by at least a couple centuries. I held his gaze a split second longer than was probably safe, saw a flicker of something lethal go through that calm expression before I averted my eyes, glancing at the pair seated across from each other a few chairs down.

My stomach dropped. My trainer, the crusty old bastard himself, sat quietly with the tips of his fingers steepled against his lips, ignoring everything around him. Or appearing that he did. I knew better. Nothing in this room would have escaped his notice, not even the pigeons nesting on the sill behind his head. He was older than Roth, one of the oldest trainers in the organization; a tall, thin man with a sharp chin and even sharper black eyes that were never still. His dark hair was streaked with silver, and the jagged scar beneath his left eye only added to his mystique.

Not long ago, the sight of him would have filled me with both anticipation and dread, like a nervous schoolboy handing his report card to his parents. Now the only thing I felt was resentment. Why was he here? As if I needed someone else judging my every move, silently criticizing.

The last person in the room was barely noticeable, his presence overshadowed by the two adult dragons. A human, I realized when I finally studied him. Thin and gangly, with a mess of brown hair and a rumpled collared shirt half tucked into his pants. By human standards, I guessed he was fairly young; maybe eighteen or nineteen. I was surprised. If he was in this room with Roth and one of the oldest trainers in the organization, then he had to know what we were. Who was this human, and what did he do, to warrant such privileges? He didn't look like anything special to me.

"Ah, Agent Cobalt," Roth said, rising smoothly from his chair. "Thank you for coming. Please, have a seat." He gestured to the table, and I sat one chair down from my trainer, leaving the human on the other side by himself.

"Hello, Cobalt," the Chief Basilisk murmured without looking at me. One corner of his lip curled in that faint, amused smile I hated. It had been more than a year since I saw him last, but he could always make me feel like a bumbling hatchling again with just a look. "I hear you've been doing well."

"I'm sure you have," I muttered as Roth sat down, smoothing his tie, then folding his hands before him on the table. "I'm sure you've heard all kinds of things about me lately."

This was not smart, antagonizing my trainer in front of the VP. A few years ago, I could have expected a swat upside the head at best and a six-hour training session at worst. But the years of being cowed by him were over. I was a full-fledged Basilisk, and not only that, I was one of their best. This might be a dangerous game I was playing, but it was no more hazardous than the missions they expected me to pull off without a hitch. Let him know I wasn't happy; I couldn't do anything about Talon or my assignments, but I didn't have to be thrilled about them.

My instructor's thin mouth twitched—impossible to tell if he was angry or amused by my lack of respect—before he turned to the head of the table. The VP was watching us now, dark eyes intense.

"I have reviewed your previous assignments, Agent Cobalt," Roth began, dispensing with the pleasantries, which was a relief. I didn't have the patience for useless small talk about my trip and what I thought of my accommodations. "Your trainer speaks highly of you and, from what I can discern, with good reason. We have not had such a young Basilisk do so well in a long time. When we asked your trainer who was best suited for this assignment, you were his top pick. Congratulations."

"Thank you, sir," I said flatly, dredging up a polite nod and a stiff smile. "I do what I can for the good of the organization."

I almost gagged on the words. But it was what I was expected to say. I was not so crazy as to insult the organization itself; if I did, I probably wouldn't walk out of this room alive.

Mr. Roth smiled, though his expression was cold. Turning to the giant screen on the far wall, he pressed a remote, and an image flickered to life: a satellite feed of a snowy wilderness in the middle of nowhere. A scattering of plain gray buildings sat within a fence at the edge of the mountains.

"I am certain you know what you are looking at," Mr. Roth said, watching me across the table.

I gave a short nod. "It's a St. George facility," I replied, observing the image on the screen, committing the layout of the place to memory. "If I had to guess, one of their northern chapterhouses."

"Yes," Mr. Roth agreed. "A brand-new Order chapterhouse, in fact. We discovered this base last week and have been monitoring it heavily ever since. As their security system isn't online yet, we have decided this is a perfect opportunity to strike. Do you see this building, Agent Cobalt?" A red circle appeared on the screen, around one of the identical gray buildings in the center of the compound. "That is their data center. And your target." Roth's voice remained matter-of-fact, as if he'd just announced the time of the next conference call. "We need you to infiltrate their base, find the main computer and download a sensitive file from their network. After that, destroy the building so that no traces of us, or the information theft, can be found."

I kept my expression cool, but inside, my stomach dropped. I'd received dangerous assignments before, but this? Sneak into a St. George base? Break into a chapterhouse swarming with enemy soldiers? "What will I be looking for?" I asked. "I have some computer skills, but I'm no hacker. Even in a new base, their files are sure to be well protected, or at the very least encrypted."

Mr. Roth smiled. His cold gaze shifted to the person sitting across from me, and the human looked up from his laptop.

His eyes were sullen. As if sitting in a room with three dragons not only failed to impress him, he resented being here in the first place.

"Right. Hang on a moment." Somehow, his English accent didn't surprise me. I watched as the kid reached around his laptop, yanked something free, then slid it to me over the table.

I picked it up: a simple black USB drive rested between my fingers. Puzzled, I looked back at the human and raised an eyebrow.

"What is this?"

"A program that will let me hack into their system undetected, find the data we're looking for and download the correct file to Talon's network," the kid answered, not meeting my gaze. "Take back the drive, and the theft will be untraceable. They won't be able to follow it back to us. So don't worry about the technical stuff. I've got it covered. All you have to do is plug it in. You can do that, can't you, mate?"

Ignoring the challenge in the human's voice, I nodded, slipping the drive into a pocket. I wanted to ask what the data was for, what was so important that I was crossing enemy lines. But I understood that everything was on a need-to-know basis, and if Roth thought the information was important, he would tell me. If not, then he wouldn't answer the question regardless. I had my mission; I didn't need to know the whys.

I was, however, even more curious about the human across from me. He obviously knew what we were; Roth was making no attempt to hide it. Talon employed some of the brightest and most talented humans from around the globe, luring them with promises of wealth, power, security, whatever they desired. But most of Talon's human workforce had no idea who—or what—their employers actually were. They did their jobs, went home to their families and returned the next morning, completely unaware that the company they worked for was anything but normal. Only a few mortals were privileged with the truth, those whose silence had been bought with money, threats or blackmail. There were a few humans in Talon who were slavishly loyal to the organization, who truly believed dragons were the superior race and were proud to work for them. But every dragon knew that humans, as a whole, were gullible, weak and easily swayed. To bring one into the know, to reveal our true nature, was a massive risk and something the organization avoided unless there was a solid, undeniable reason the human would not betray us to the outside world.

So, what was *this* human's reason? I wondered. Why did he seem nearly as angry and resentful as me?

"When you are finished transferring the file," Roth continued as the kid dropped his gaze and went back to staring at his computer, "find the data storage center and destroy it. This will cripple their network and blind this particular base. They will be unable to recover quickly, making retaliation against us nearly impossible. But there is another reason we are sending you, agent."

He paused, and his gaze flicked to my trainer, who grunted and sat up in his chair before turning to me.

"The other reason," the old Basilisk said with one of his faint, evil smiles, "is to test what we hope will be a fun new toy for our side. So you're going to be a bit of a guinea pig for this assignment. We have something that we've been working on, and we believe it's nearly ready for use in the field. Congratulations, agent, you get to take it for its trial run."

I suppressed a wince. A hatchling or rookie agent might've been excited for this news, willing and eager to test out something new. I was not. I knew what kind of "toy" I'd be working with, and frankly, it scared the crap out of me. Talon had always been on the cutting edge of science and technology, knowing that keeping ahead of the times was not only profitable, it was essential for our survival. As a race, we had survived because we had evolved, and knowledge was power. Talon hoarded knowledge like they did wealth, turning everything into profit for the organization. Not only did they fund countless research centers, they had their own laboratories, where the most brilliant minds the organization could find worked tirelessly, uncovering secrets, pushing boundaries, experimenting with things best left alone.

Things like magic. Magic still existed in the world today, otherwise how could a fifteen-ton dragon shrink down into a two-hundred-pound human body? Just because nobody used it anymore didn't mean magic didn't exist. In the Elder Wyrm's time, at least according to the stories, magic was everywhere. There were witches and demons, monsters and ancient swords, wizards, the Good Neighbors and even the rare unicorn, wandering the deepest parts of the forest. But with the rise of civilization and technology, magic had been long forgotten. Even the Elder Wyrm didn't use it anymore, or maybe there wasn't a lot of the ancient power left in the world. Because we had lost the capacity for it—or perhaps because we really didn't need it anymore—Shifting into human form was the last bit of old magic we could do.

But, in recent years, the Talon laboratories had been coming out with strange, crazy, unexplainable things. Bodysuits that wouldn't tear when you Shifted, drugs that specifically targeted the dragon anatomy, weird crap like that. According to rumors, they were experimenting with blending old magic and science, mixing them together, though that should've been impossible. There were also whispers that these tests were just preliminary; that the scientists were working on something "big." Something that would change the dragon world forever. I didn't know how much of that I believed, but whenever the labs came out with a brand-new "toy," somehow my trainer was the first to get his hands on it.

I could feel the old Basilisk watching me, his gaze burning the side of my head, and stifled a sigh. "Of course, sir," I muttered, not meeting his gaze. "Whatever Talon needs me to do." Because that's what they expected me to say, even though my insides roiled with anger as I did. A pause and then, though I knew better, my curiosity got the better of me. "What kind of thing will I be testing out, exactly?"

My trainer chuckled. "Oh, I think you'll like this, Agent Cobalt," he said, his hard smile making me realize I would feel the exact opposite. And the old bastard knew it, too. "In fact, I believe it's right up your alley."

GARRET

"Bloody hell," the man beside me muttered.

I turned from the window and gave him a wary glance. We'd been traveling for nearly an hour, fleeing down dusty roads with the sun beating down on us, turning the inside of the van into an oven. Knowing St. George was still out there, we'd avoided the main strip of highway, taking back roads and constantly looking for vehicles that could belong to our pursuers. No one seemed to be giving chase, and with every mile, we drew farther and farther away from the St. George chapterhouse, but being out in the open like this made me nervous. The Order wouldn't stop hunting me, especially now that I was in the company of dragons. Dragons who had broken into their chapterhouse and escaped with a traitor. We had to find shelter soon. I hoped my rescuers had a place they could go.

The driver, Wes, I think his name was, pursed his lips at the dashboard before raising his head to call over his shoulder. "Running on fumes here, Riley," he said, his voice tight and sharp. "I'm going to need to stop for gas, or we'll be hauling a bloody dragon carcass across the desert on foot."

"Dammit," came the low voice from the back. "All right, pull off when you get the chance, but let's do this quickly."

Wes immediately made a right turn and hit the gas pedal, presumably heading toward the highway again. I turned in my seat to peer into the back. Riley crouched at Ember's side, fully clothed with a bloody rag in hand, pressing it to her ribs. We'd switched places not long after the van started moving, as I had no idea what to do with a wounded dragon, and Ember was bleeding all over the place. She now sprawled across the floor of the van, large wings brushing the windows like leathery curtains. Her scales gleamed metallic crimson in the sunlight through the glass and threw fragments of light over the walls. She was not, I realized with a chill, something small or subtle that we could easily hide. All anyone had to do was peek in the window to see a large red *dragon* curled up on the floor.

The smell of blood soaked the back of the vehicle, making my stomach turn. "How is she?" I asked, and the other dragon shot me a murderous glare.

"Not good." His voice was clipped, as if he was speaking to me only out of necessity. "She's lost a lot of blood, and that slug is still inside her somewhere. I've stopped the bleeding for now, but we have to get her somewhere safe before we can take care of the wound." He put a hand on a scaly foreleg, his forehead creasing with worry. "Probably a good thing she's unconscious, but she won't be able to Shift back until we get it out. It could tear something vital if she changes back with the round still inside her."

My stomach twisted with worry. Not only for Ember, but that we wouldn't be able to get somewhere safe without anyone noticing the large mythological creature in the backseat. As if reading my thoughts, Riley's gaze flickered to me and turned hard. "So you'd better hope no one sees her between then and now," he growled, "or we'll have the Order back on our tail faster than you can pull a trigger. And probably Talon, come to think of it." He snorted, lip curling with disgust. "It would be just like them to show up now."

I frowned, not sure I'd heard him correctly. "Why would Talon be after you? I thought all dragons—"

"Well, you thought wrong." He gave me a look of contempt. "There's a lot about us you don't know, St. George," he went on, an accusation and a challenge. "Maybe if you tried talking to us instead of blowing us to pieces, you'd realize that."

"Riley," Wes broke in before I could answer, "gas station in three miles. If we don't fill up now, we might not get another chance. And I need to visit the loo."

"All right." Reaching down, Riley grabbed the edge of the canvas Ember was sprawled on top of and began tugging it free. "Do it, but hurry up."

I turned in my seat and watched the desert flash by. Watched the pavement stretch on, until a lone gas station appeared on the side of the road, shimmering in the near distance. My apprehension grew. It was not a tiny little outpost in the middle of nowhere. It was a huge truck stop with a restaurant and mini-mart attached, and there was a crowd. I glanced back as Riley gently peeled one of Ember's wings from the wall and folded it carefully against her body before pulling the canvas over her. Her tail and the tips of her claws poked out, but at least she wasn't as blatantly noticeable as before. Still, if anyone got too close, they would immediately know something large, scaly and inhuman was sprawled on the floor of the van.

We pulled up to one of the pumps, and Wes leaped out and slammed the door behind him, leaving the keys in the ignition. I scanned the station warily, keeping an eye out for anything suspicious, but nothing seemed out of the ordinary; families wandering back to their cars, a couple large trucks sitting off to the side. No soldiers, black SUVs or anything that belonged to the Order. So far, so good.

Wes wrenched the pump off the handle, shoved it into the tank to start the flow of gas, then went hurrying into the store. I scanned the area once more before glancing at the two dragons behind me.

"You're not part of Talon," I confirmed, as Riley smoothed the canvas over Ember, covering the exposed parts as best he could. It was a strange concept. All dragons, we were told, belonged to Talon, the huge dragon organization that spanned the globe. Banded together, working together, to overthrow mankind. I'd never thought there could be discontents.

But then, I'd never thought I could befriend a dragon, either. Or that she would risk her life to save mine.

Riley, tugging a corner over Ember's front claws, gave a snort.

"No."

I waited, but he didn't offer any further explanation. But there was something there, an undercurrent of disgust that wasn't pointed entirely at me, but at Talon. Curiosity prickled. And guilt. Here was one more fact about dragons that the Order had gotten wrong. This dragon wasn't part of the organization; in fact, he seemed to despise it. How gravely was the Order mistaken when it came to our ancient enemies? And how many lives had *I* taken, because I believed we were doing the right thing?

"If you're not part of Talon," I ventured, "who are you with?"

"Myself." Again that clipped, brusque reply. Somehow, it didn't surprise me.

Something chirped close by, startling us both. Riley reached back and pulled out his phone, staring at the screen. His expression screwed up with disgust.

"Oh, for God's sake, Wes. Really?" He stuck the phone in his back pocket, shaking his head. "You and your damn nervous stomach. Perfect timing as always."

He straightened and peered out the window, scanning the surroundings just as I had a moment ago. I recognized that wariness, that caution for traps and enemies and hidden dangers. He had been a soldier, once. Or some kind of operative. We were parked at one of the farthest pumps, and no one was close by, but he still scanned the area for a good twenty seconds before glancing at me.

"I'm going inside." His glare was hard, his face taut with suspicion. "We'll need a few things if we're going to be holed up for a while, and my idiot partner is out of commission. I'll only be gone a minute, but…" His gaze flicked to the large canvas lump beside him, the tail and claws poking out from beneath. "Can I trust you with her, St. George?"

I met his glare, keeping my voice steady. "Yes."

His lips tightened like he'd swallowed something foul, but he didn't say anything as he made his way to the front door.

Snatching the keys from the ignition, he slipped out of the
van and slammed the door behind him, leaving me alone with
an unconscious dragon in the backseat.

Silence descended, throbbing in my ears, broken only by
Ember's slow, labored breaths beneath the tarp. I turned in my
seat to look at her fully. The canvas hid most of her body, but
her feet, ending in hooked black talons, stuck out of the bottom, as did the long, spade-tipped tail. I could see the points
of her horns and wings, the curve of her neck, the very tip of
her muzzle peeking from the edge of the cloth. She twisted
and curled a lip in her sleep, revealing a flash of very long,
very sharp fangs, and a cold knot formed in my stomach.

Ember... *This* was the real form of the girl I'd met in Crescent Beach. I'd seen her like this before, but only in passing.
When we were battling one another, soldier to dragon, each
of us fighting for our lives. And later, when I was urging her
to run before my team showed up to kill them all. I'd seen
her real form then, but it was a fleeting awareness, buried in
the urgency of the moment. I'd been too distracted to give
it much thought.

Now, though, it was staring me in the face, impossible to
ignore. Ember was a *dragon*. A huge lizard, with scales and
wings and claws and a tail. All my memories from Crescent
Beach, from the summer that had disappeared too quickly,
were of the girl. Surfing with her. Slow dancing at a party.
Kissing her in the ocean, feeling my blood sizzle and my
breath catch. The green-eyed girl with an infectious smile and
a fierce love for life. But Ember wasn't a girl. Ember wasn't
human. Ember was...this.

A car pulled off the highway and cruised to a stop at the

pump next to ours. The doors opened, and a family of four piled out, making me tense. But after a short squabble between two small boys and their mother, she managed to herd them toward the mini-mart. The father remained behind long enough to fill the tank and make me nervous, before he finally meandered into the store. I drummed my fingers on the armrest, wondering where Riley and Wes were.

A scraping sound jerked my attention to the back. The canvas lump was moving, shifting from side to side with confused growls. Ember tossed her head, flinging the cloth away and exposing a bright red dragon to the open air. She tried staggering upright, but lurched to one side and collapsed against the door with a loud thump, making the vehicle rock. Her tail lashed the sides of the van with metallic clanking sounds as she growled and clawed herself up again, the sunlight gleaming along her metallic crimson scales.

"Ember." Swiftly, I moved to the back, barely dodging a wingtip as it flapped against the wall. "Hey, stop. Calm down." Her head whipped toward me, and I instinctively threw up my hand, catching a horn as it smacked into my palm. "Stop!"

She froze at my touch, and I was suddenly holding the head of a groggy red dragon, her muzzle right at eye level. Her fangs gleamed as she stared at me, nostrils flaring, and for a second, I felt a jolt of fear, realizing how close she was. If she lunged or snapped or spit fire at me, I'd catch it right in the face.

Quickly, I released her. She didn't pull away but continued to stare at me, a puzzled expression in her reptilian green eyes. "Garret?"

My muscles unclenched at the sound of her voice. It was weak, confused and in pain, but it was *her* voice, Ember's voice. Though I didn't know what I'd expected. Those slitted eyes blinked again before she sagged weakly, struggling to stay upright. "Where am I?" she asked, her words slurred. "What's going on?"

I took a careful breath. "You need to lie down," I told her gently. She stumbled and fell against the side, and I winced as the van rattled. "Ember, look at me." I reached out, catching one of her horns again, forcing her attention back to me. "You have to relax," I said as she looked up, her eyes now bright with pain and fear. Her jaws parted as she panted, showing rows of deadly fangs, and I resisted the urge to yank my hand back. "We're out in the open, and you can't be seen right now. Please. Lie down."

She stared at me a moment, and I forced myself to breathe calmly. This had to be one of the most surreal moments of my life: pleading with a near-delirious dragon to lie still so that we wouldn't be discovered. With the exception of the flight from the base, I'd never been so close to a live dragon, not for this length of time. Never close enough to feel its breath, smelling of heat and smoke. Or the bony ridges of its horns under my palm. In the past, if a dragon had been near enough to touch, it was either dead or I was fighting for my life, trying to make it so.

A tremor went through the dragon in front of me and, to my relief, she sank down again, her head touching the floor with a muffled groan. Her wings fluttered once and her tail thumped the side of the van, before her eyes closed and she went limp, asleep once more. I let out a short breath, glancing out the side window, and froze.

A boy of maybe five stood a few feet from the van, clutching a fountain drink in both hands, his eyes huge as they stared at me. I gazed back, guessing that he'd seen everything, unsure of what to do, as his parents walked around the car, his mother reaching for his arm.

"Jason, come on. What are you looking at?"

The boy pointed. "The dragon."

"A dragon?" Her gaze rose, a puzzled look crossing her face as she spotted me. Heart pounding, I offered a feeble smile and a helpless shrug, and the woman frowned.

"Okay, that's nice, dear. Come on, Daddy's waiting." Taking the boy's wrist, she quickly steered him toward the car, and I started breathing again. As they piled into the car, the little boy's face peered through the window at me, eyes huge and staring, until the car pulled onto the highway and sped off toward the horizon.

Riley and Wes came out of the store, each carrying a couple plastic bags, and hurried toward the van. I pulled the canvas over Ember again, gently covering her head and body as much as I could, before slipping quietly into the front seat.

A moment later, Wes wrenched open the front door, tossed a couple grocery bags into my lap and moved aside to let Riley in. The other dragon climbed into the back through the front seats, not wanting to open the side door and risk exposing Ember to the world, I guessed. But he paused, his gaze flickering over the sleeping dragon and the obviously disturbed tarp, before shifting to me.

"Problems, St. George?" he asked, his voice suspicious. I shook my head.

"Nothing I couldn't handle."

He continued to glare at me, but at that moment, Ember flapped a wing in her sleep, throwing back the canvas again. A line of red spattered the window, making my insides curl. Riley muttered a curse.

"She's bleeding again," he growled, kneeling swiftly at her side. "Wes, grab the first-aid kit—she can't afford to lose any more blood. St. George, get us out of here."

I waited until Wes slid into the back with Riley, then moved to the driver's seat and turned the key in the ignition. "Where am I going?" I asked as the van roared to life.

"Vegas" was the snapped reply. "It's not far, and I have a place we can hole up for a few days." Ember twitched, kicking a back leg against the wall, and Wes let out a yelp. Riley cursed. "I'll give you directions when we get close, but right now, just drive!"

Throwing the van into gear, I pulled onto the highway, passed a dusty sign that read Las Vegas 64 Miles and sped off into the sun.

DANTE

"Mr. Hill. Do you have a moment?"

I looked up from my desk. Mist stood in the doorway, manila folder in hand, looking poised and calm and expectant at the same time. Her silver hair was pulled into a ponytail today, and it made her look younger, not quite so severe. It was hard to believe Mist was my age; she acted so composed and mature, I wondered if she'd had a normal upbringing. Or whatever was considered *normal* for us, anyway.

I sighed and put down my pen, where I'd been scribbling notes on a yellow sheet of paper. "Mist," I said, smiling as I beckoned her into the office. "How many times have I asked you to call me Dante?"

"Counting today, exactly five times." As always, there was a subtle note of challenge beneath the polite tone. "And I predict you will ask me at least twice more in the future. But that is irrelevant at this point." She stepped back into the hall, looking suddenly anxious. "If you would come with me, Mr. Hill, I think you should see this."

★ ★ ★

Back in the operations room, I gazed up at one of the enormous screens, watching a satellite map blip into view,

showing a swath of dusty brown, with patches of green inter-
spersed throughout. Mist stood beside me, also watching the
screen, while the two human workers sat at their keyboards,
typing furiously.

"This," Mist explained, leaning back against a desk, "is the
eastern Mojave Desert, close to the Arizona/Utah line. When
you told us to look for the Order's western chapterhouse, we
began directing our satellite feeds to the areas close to and
around Crescent Beach."

"Hold on," I said, holding up a hand. "We have satellites?"

Mist gave a short nod. "We own one of the largest satellite communication networks in the world," she said coolly.
"It isn't difficult to put in a few extras.

"Regardless," she continued, as if that was unimportant,
"when we started searching, we found...this."

The feed zoomed in, focused and showed a bird's-eye view
of a facility smack in the middle of nowhere. Even from this
height, it didn't look very impressive. I could see a fence with
two gates, several long rectangular buildings and the road that
cut through the vast, empty desert surrounding it.

"That," Mist announced, as if she could feel my skepticism,
"is St. George's western chapterhouse."

I frowned. "Are you sure? It doesn't look like much. Certainly not a heavily armed military base."

She gave me a look of veiled annoyance. "That's what
they want you to see, Mr. Hill," she said. "The Order uses a
combination of security and complete isolation to hide their
chapterhouses. Some of them, like the main headquarters in
London, are too heavily armed for us to do anything about.
Some of them, like this one, rely on isolation to keep them

secure. Talon knows of several large Order facilities around the world, but the smaller chapterhouses are good at concealing themselves and hiding in plain sight. The only reason we found this one was because we were actively searching for St. George movement in the region. At your request, Mr. Hill, and this took us all night."

I held up my hands. "Point taken. No need to bite my head off. I believe you." She sniffed, looking mollified, and I glanced back at the screen. "So, this is their western chapterhouse," I mused, crossing my arms. "I'm sure Talon will want to know about this. Have you informed Mr. Roth?"

"No," Mist replied gravely. "I figured you deserved that honor. After all, you were the one who pointed us in the right direction. But that's not all we found," she continued, before I could feel smug that I had been right. "Look at this."

The screen went dark as the scene faded to night, only a few points of light glimmering in a sea of black. Then one of the humans clicked a key, and the image switched to a grainy green color. I could see the buildings, blurry and indistinct, through the emerald haze, and the fence surrounding the base as the camera zoomed in. The time on the bottom left of the screen read 3:26 a.m., dated two days ago.

I blinked. Two small black dots were moving across the desert from the east, looking like tiny crawling insects from this height but definitely making a beeline toward the fence. They weren't coming in from the road; in fact, it looked like they were actively avoiding the gates, heading toward the most isolated corner of the compound. As I stared, amazed, they paused at the fence a few seconds, slipped through a hole they must've cut out and began creeping across the yard to-ward the main headquarters.

"What in the world?" I whispered, baffled as I watched their progress. "That can't be…"

"We believe it *is* Ember, Mr. Hill," Mist finished solemnly. "And Cobalt. None of our agents have received orders to move on a St. George facility in several months. Cobalt has the knowledge and the skills for this type of work, and he is bold enough to infiltrate even an Order chapterhouse. It's one of the reasons he is so dangerous to the organization."

"But why is Ember with him?" I asked, unable to tear my gaze from the two tiny figures, darting through shadows and around corners, avoiding the light. Anger and fear caught in my throat. She was inside a St. George base! What was she thinking? If anyone spotted her, she was dead. *Get out of there*, I wanted to shout, knowing it was futile. *Ember, you stubborn idiot, why are you doing this? Get out of there before you're killed.*

Mist didn't say anything. Turning, she nodded to one of the humans, who bent over the keyboard. A moment later, the screen jumped to fast-forward, with the time in the left corner accelerating rapidly, though nothing inside the base appeared to move.

"Stop," Mist commanded, and the screen froze. "Look at the upper left corner, Mr. Hill," she went on, nodding to the blurred image above us. "Behind the vehicle, near the main headquarters. What do you see?"

I followed her gaze and drew in a sharp breath. "Three of them," I muttered, squinting to make sure I was seeing correctly. No, I wasn't mistaken. There were the two figures in black from earlier, only now there was a third party member, huddled behind the car. "They were there to get some-one out," I breathed, trying to wrap my head around what it could mean. "But…why? St. George doesn't take prisoners, at least not with us. Who…?"

I trailed off, a cold lump settling in my stomach. "The soldier," I whispered, feeling the blood drain from my face. "The human from Crescent Beach. They were there to free the soldier of St. George."

My legs felt weak. This was not what I'd expected. I'd hoped that, by watching the chapterhouse Sebastian belonged to, he would lead us to Ember. Or that Ember would con-tact him, somehow, and we could follow when they moved on her and the rogue. I'd never expected her to breach St. George itself.

Mist's eyes were grave as she turned to me. "So, not only has your sister gone rogue, she is also fraternizing with the enemy," she said. Her voice was quiet, meant only for me and our team members. "What do you intend to do with this information?"

I took a deep breath. "I have to tell Mr. Roth," I said, feeling slightly ill, but knowing there was no other choice. "If Ember is associating with St. George, Talon must know immediately. She could unknowingly put the organization at risk, though I have no idea what she thinks she's doing." Anger flickered, and I scrubbed a hand down my face, trying to stay calm. Ember going rogue was bad enough, but to aid one of the Order? How was I supposed to advance my cause, convince Talon that my sister was being manipulated, if she kept pulling stunts like this?

Straightening, I looked back at the paused screen, at the

trio of figures huddled against the car. "Did they escape?" I asked, almost dreading the answer. Surely Mist wouldn't be showing me this footage if they hadn't. But if the worst had occurred, if Ember hadn't gotten out of that compound alive, I wasn't going to stand here and watch. Even after everything, I didn't think I could handle seeing my sister gunned down right in front of me.

Surprisingly, the other dragon's lip twitched into the faintest of smiles. "Oh, you could say that," she said, and hit the pause key on the computer.

Seconds later, with my heart in my throat, I watched the two dragons flee the compound amid a flurry of lights and gunshots. If I'd had any doubts that one of the figures in black was Ember, they were long gone now.

I took a slow breath as the two dragons soared offscreen, vanishing westward and out of sight. The soldier sat astride one of them, and a flicker of rage and disgust pierced my amazement. With a brisk nod, I turned on one of the humans.

"Send a message to Mr. Roth immediately. Let him know we've found her."

EMBER

"Ember," Dante said. "Get up."

I groaned. My bed was warm and comfortable, and the air outside my nest of blankets was cold. It was a Saturday, at least I thought it was a Saturday, and I was supposed to meet up with Lexi later this afternoon to go surfing. She didn't want to go early because of *reasons*, which meant I could sleep in today. Of course, that didn't account for obnoxious brothers coming into my room to bother me.

I peeked through the covers, intending to tell said obnoxious brother to go away, only to find I was no longer in my room.

I sat up, blinking. Moonlight filtered in from a window, casting hazy light over an assortment of shadows and unrecognizable lumps. I frowned in confusion, sliding out of bed, giving a little shiver as I stood. The floor beneath my bare feet was hard and icy cold.

"Ember."

I turned. Dante stood a few feet away, watching me with eyes glowing green in the darkness. Behind him, the labyrinth of crates hovered at the edge of the light, looming and ominous, casting Dante in their jagged shadow.

"Traitor," he whispered.

I growled, curling my lips back from my fangs. I didn't know when I'd Shifted forms, but tongues of fire licked at my teeth as I snarled and half opened my wings, facing my brother down. "You're one to talk," I said, my voice echoing weirdly off the rafters. "I thought we were leaving Talon together, but you had no intention of coming with me, did you? You were going to tell Lilith where I was all along."

He didn't respond and I slumped, tail and wings drooping, while my twin watched me without expression. "You lied to me, Dante," I said, feeling the cold flood of regret douse the flames within. "I thought I could trust you, but you sold me out to Talon."

"I did no such thing." Dante's voice was calm, though his eyes narrowed to shining green slits. "*You* were the one who betrayed us, Ember. When you left with that rogue." He slipped away, his voice growing faint as he faded into the black. "You made the call. It was your choice to leave, to abandon everything we had worked for. Sixteen years of preparation, gone in an instant. You walked out on Talon, and you walked out on me."

"Dante, wait."

He didn't stop but vanished into the darkness, the echo of his footsteps fading to nothing. Calling out, I started after him, but the shadows closed in, and everything went black.

★ ★ ★

Wincing, I opened my eyes.

I lay on the floor in a room I didn't recognize, curled up on something soft. It took only a second to realize I was in dragon form, lying in a nest of blankets, and this had been a bedroom at one point, because a bed and a dresser had been shoved up against the far wall. Apart from those two pieces of furniture, the room was unnaturally empty. No clothes on the floor, no pictures or posters hanging from the walls, nothing to give the room personality. It seemed to have been empty a long time.

My thoughts swirled sluggishly, like they were trapped in glue. I blinked hard, trying to focus as I raised my head, waiting for my vision to clear. What had happened to me? The last thing I remembered was flying away from something, and a sudden jolt to my side, like I'd been hit with a hammer. I didn't remember passing out, but I must have, because everything after that was a blur. How much time had elapsed since then? I wondered.

And where am I now?

Cautiously, I looked around, trying to get a sense of where I was, and froze.

A body was slumped in a chair a few feet away, sitting against the wall with his arms crossed and his eyes closed. Even through the confusion and sleep haze, I knew it was Garret.

My stomach tightened, and memory came back in a rush. I remembered everything that had brought me here; infiltrating the St. George base with Riley, freeing Garret, fleeing across the wasteland with the soldier on my back. There was also one very hazy memory of a voice that sounded exactly like Garret's, telling me to lie down, but that might've been from a dream.

But I wasn't dreaming now, and the soldier was here, in the very same room. Sunlight slanted through the blinds over the windows, glinting off his pale hair, painting bright bars over his clothes. He wore faded jeans and a white T-shirt, and in sleep, he appeared younger than he was. Less a hardened soldier and more like a normal teen. Like the Garret I'd known in Crescent Beach. Before he became St. George, the enemy, a soldier who had killed dragons his whole life.

I rose carefully, trying to be silent as I sat up, but Garret was either just dozing or a really light sleeper, for his eyes shot open as soon as I moved. Piercing metallic-gray pupils met mine across the room.

"Ember."

His voice made me shiver, low and soft with relief. Carefully, as if trying not to make any sudden moves, he stood, his expression teetering between wary and hopeful. "You're awake," he breathed. "Are you all right?"

"I…think so." I stood slowly, bracing myself for pain. There was a dull ache in my side as I moved, but nothing sharp or stabby, which was a relief. Cautiously, I eased myself upright, craning my neck, curling and uncurling my talons, testing muscles. Except for the subtle but persistent ache in my side, everything seemed to be working fine. I took a breath and let it out slowly. "Looks like I'm all here. What happened?"

"You were shot," Garret said quietly. "When we were running from St. George. We brought you here, and Wes managed to dig the slug out, but it was touch and go for a while."

"What do you mean?"

His gaze flicked to my side, where the ache was coming from. "You nearly died, Ember," he whispered. "We didn't know how serious it was until we got here. You lost a lot of blood, and if the bullet had gone a few inches to the left…it would've struck your heart."

"Oh," I said, as the gravity of that statement sank in. "Really?"

He nodded, his face tightening. "That first night," he said in a curiously choked voice, "I didn't know if you were going to make it. You didn't move the entire time, not to eat, or Shift, or anything. Riley said that…that you had gone into hibernation, that when the dragon body takes a lot of damage, it slows to almost nothing and falls into a near coma until it can heal itself. I had no reason to doubt him, but…you were so still. You've been out for three days, and I couldn't even tell if you were breathing or not."

"Hey." I stepped toward him, slowly, knowing I was still in dragon form and not wanting to make him nervous. "It's all right. Look." I half opened my wings, casting a dark shadow over the walls and floor. "I'm okay," I said, offering a smile. "I'm still here."

He gazed at me with an expression that made my heart turn over, before his eyes narrowed and he shook his head. "You shouldn't have come," he said, sounding almost angry now. I blinked and reared back in surprise as he turned on me. "Back at St. George. You shouldn't have risked it. You don't know what you've done, what the Order will do to your kind now. St. George won't let this stand. Word of the break-in has probably reached London. Every chapterhouse in the region will be looking for you. You'll never be safe."

I lashed my tail, nearly knocking over a lamp on the dresser. "Guess next time I'll just stand back and let you be shot to death."

Garret winced and had the grace to look ashamed. "I'm sorry," he muttered, and the anger vanished as quickly as it had come. "I don't mean to sound ungrateful. I owe you my life, and I'm glad you came for me. I just…" He paused, uncertainty creeping into his voice and stance. "I'm not entirely sure *why*."

"Why?" I cocked my head, peering down at him. "What do you mean, you don't know why? The answer should be obvious."

Hope rippled across his features, so fast I might've imagined it. Though his voice remained neutral. "I'm a soldier of St. George," he insisted. "All my life, I believed what the Order believed. I followed the tenets, and I killed when they told me to, what they told me to, without question. Every single time." He looked away for a brief moment, eyes darkening. "You know what I've done," he murmured, staring at the wall. "You know what I am. Why would you risk your life to save a dragonslayer?"

A lump rose to my throat. "You weren't a soldier of St. George to me." The words came out a near whisper, and I swallowed hard. "Not in Crescent Beach. I never hated you, Garret. Even after…that night." The night he'd pointed a gun at my face, and I'd seen what he really was for the very first time. The night we'd inevitably turned on each other, because what else could we be except lifelong enemies? A soldier of St. George and a dragon. "And after what happened with Lilith, I couldn't leave you to die. Even if it was the Order, I wasn't going to let them kill you."

Garret still wasn't looking at me. He stared at the far wall as if he couldn't bear to see a huge reptile standing beside him instead of a girl, and my heart sank. "So, what now?" I asked softly. "Are we enemies, Garret? Do you hate me for being a dragon?"

"No!" He looked over quickly, his face earnest. "I could never hate you, Ember. If anything, I should be asking *you* that question. If you really knew what I've done…" He sighed, bowing his head. "But no. I'm not your enemy. You risked your life when you went into St. George, you and Riley both. I'm in your debt."

I sat down, curling my tail around my legs as I gave the former dragonslayer an exasperated snort. "Yes, well, for future reference," I said, thumping the spade-tip of my tail against the ground, "when someone decides to save your life, for whatever reason, the proper response is *thank you*. Guilt and groveling optional but highly encouraged."

A tiny chuckle escaped him then, as if he couldn't help himself. "Point taken," he murmured, the hint of a smile finally crossing his face. "Would you like the groveling done now or later?"

"Oh, later. Definitely later. When I can get comfortable and enjoy it for a few hours."

"Hours, huh? I'll keep that in mind." He shook his head, meeting my gaze. "Thank you for coming after me," he said, quite serious now. "You didn't have to, but I'm grateful you did. I wasn't…quite as ready to die as I thought."

I nodded. The haunted look had not quite left him, but it was a start. At least he was talking to me like a normal person again and not walking on eggshells around "the dragon." For now, it was enough. "So, where is everyone?" I asked, gazing around. Garret nodded out the door.

"Riley was sleeping in his room, last I saw" was the answer. "Wes left a few minutes ago for supplies. The three of us have been taking watch in turns since we got here. We've been waiting for you to wake up before we decide where to go next."

"Where are we, anyway?"

"Vegas," replied a new voice from the door.

I craned my neck around to look back. Riley stood in the frame, his gold eyes intense as they met mine. He wore ripped jeans and a black T-shirt, and looked strange without his ever-present jacket. His dark hair was mussed and shaggy, his clothes rumpled. Half circles crouched beneath his lids, as if he hadn't slept in a while.

I forced a weak grin, even as my senses flared to life, sending heat through my veins. "Hey, you. I'm up."

"Dammit, Ember." Riley entered into the room and, without hesitation, strode to my side. Garret drew back, melting into the corner as the other drew close. Riley's hand came to rest on my neck, a searing spot of warmth even through my scales. "Are you all right?" he asked, his gaze flicking to my ribs, where the bullet had pierced through. "Why didn't you tell me you were awake?"

"It was on my to-do list."

He pressed his forehead to mine, skin to scales. "Don't scare me like that, Firebrand," he whispered, as my stomach danced and my wings fluttered restlessly. "If you had died, I don't know what I'd have done, but it would probably involve eating that St. George bastard over there."

"That's not very reasonable," I whispered back, knowing that Garret could hear us, and Riley probably didn't care if he did. "Then all our scheming against St. George would've been for nothing."

He snorted and drew back, rolling his eyes. "Have you eaten yet?" he muttered, an exasperated smile crossing his face. "You were out for three days. I imagine you're probably starving right now."

Food. I was suddenly ravenous, like a bear coming out of winter hibernation: skinny, starving and cranky. Food sounded wonderful. In fact, nothing else mattered right now except food. Riley chuckled.

"Yeah, that's what I thought. There's pizza in the fridge and— Whoa, hold on, Firebrand." He put his hands out, stopping me as I pressed forward. Impatient, I glared at him, and he smirked. "No dragons in the kitchen. The neighbors would have a fit." I blinked, remembering that I was still in the form that wasn't supposed to exist in normal society. The one that would cause a panic if seen. I repressed a sigh. It felt so natural to be in my real body again; I was reluctant to Shift back.

"Your clothes are in the dresser behind you," Riley said. "Get changed, and meet us when you're human again." His smile faded, a darker note creeping into his voice. "There are things we have to discuss."

RILEY

Ember exhaled, sending tendrils of smoke curling around me, and turned away, padding toward the dresser in the corner. I watched her a moment, the sweep of her neck and wings, the way the narrow bars of sunlight glinted off her crimson scales. The urge to Shift was almost painful, burning my lungs and making the air taste like ash. I turned away before it got too tempting and jerked my head at the soldier, motioning him out of the room.

We walked into the hall and shut the door behind us. "All right," I said, keeping my voice low, so Ember wouldn't catch it. "You've seen her. She's going to be fine now. Why are you still here, St. George?"

The soldier kept his gaze on the closed door, his voice low and flat. "I have nowhere else to go."

"Well, that's not my problem, is it?" I brushed past him into the kitchen, knowing Ember would be out soon and on the hunt for food. Except for a box of leftover pizza, there wasn't much to be had, and I'd sent Wes out for supplies a couple hours ago. Hopefully he'd be back soon. This wasn't the nicest neighborhood, miles from the glitz and glamour of the Strip, the stretch of giant casinos Vegas was famous for. If you looked out the back window, you'd see a bunch of small, ugly houses and beyond them, the flat, dusty expanse of the Mojave Desert, stretching away to the distant mountains. Crime and poverty ran rampant here, but that suited me just fine. No one asked questions, no one came poking around, and no one wondered why a white van was suddenly parked in the driveway of a previously vacant abandoned house.

The soldier followed me into the kitchen, sweeping his gaze around the room, like he always did. "They'll be hunting you," he stated, making me shrug.

"Nothing new there."

"You're going to have to move soon. It's dangerous to stay here, especially with St. George looking for us."

Irritation flared, and the anger that I'd repressed during the whole ordeal surged up with a vengeance. In the three days we'd been here, we had tolerated each other's presence in the most mature way possible: pretending the other didn't exist. St. George didn't talk to me, I didn't talk to him, and things were good. Sort of an unspoken truce between us while we waited for Ember to revive.

Now, though, all bets were off. I narrowed my eyes, wondering what would happen if I Shifted forms and bit the soldier in half. Ember might've forgotten that he was part of the Order. She might have forgiven him for hunting down and slaughtering our kind without remorse, but *I* wasn't okay with it. In fact, the only reason I hadn't shoved him out of the van and left him in the middle of the desert to fend for himself was the girl who'd convinced me to rescue the murdering bastard in the first place. She was also the reason I hadn't chased him out of the house with fire and told him not to come back. Right now that was a pretty tempting option.

"Don't tell me how to do my job, St. George," I said in a low, dangerous voice. "I've been at this a lot longer than you. I've been outsmarting your kind since before you could wrap your itchy little fingers around a trigger. I don't need some murdering dragon killer telling me to be careful of the Order."

"You've never broken into a St. George chapterhouse," the human countered, as if he knew anything about me and what I used to do. "I know the Order. They're not going to let that stand. Once word of this reaches London—and it probably already has—they're going to throw everything they can at us, and they won't stop until we're all dead."

"Oh, is that why you're still here?" I challenged, crossing my arms. "You want the dragons to protect you, now that you're the hunted one?"

"No." St. George glared at me, a flicker of anger crossing his face. "I don't care what happens to me," he said, sounding so earnest I almost believed him. "But I want Ember to be safe. I owe her my life, and I can't leave knowing the Order is hunting her right now."

"They were *always* hunting her, St. George," I snapped. "Every single day. The hunt never stops. The war never ends. Or did that fact slip your mind? The only thing that's changed is now the Order has a wasp up their ass because their pride has been stomped on, and they'll be desperate to save face. Never mind that they've been kicking down our doors and blowing us to pieces for years. But don't worry about Ember."

I smirked, as his face darkened. "The Order won't ever get that close. I'll take care of her."

"Also," came a new voice from the doorway, "she's quite capable of taking care of herself."

Guiltily, we turned. Ember stood at the edge of the tile, arms crossed, looking peeved with us both. Her red hair stuck out at every angle, and she was definitely thinner than normal, making my gut squeeze tight. But her green eyes were as bright as ever, and the fire lurking below the surface hadn't dimmed. I could see the dragon peering out at me, the echo of wings hovering behind her. She shot us—well, *me*—an exasperated glare, before marching to the refrigerator door and yanking it open.

"Ember," St. George began as she emerged with a flat white box. "I—"

"Garret," Ember interrupted. Her voice was a warning as she turned around. "Not to sound rude, but I am a dragon who hasn't eaten for the past three days. Unless you're about to reveal a stash of doughnuts hidden somewhere in this room, I would steer clear right now."

He blinked, and I snickered at his shocked expression as Ember moved past us, heading toward the counter. "Number one rule when dealing with dragons, St. George," I said, as the girl hopped onto a stool and opened up the box. "Don't get between a hungry hatchling and its food. You might lose a finger."

Ember glared at me, looking like she might growl something in return, but then decided food was more important and devoured half a slice in one bite. I went to the fridge for a soda, and St. George settled quietly against the wall, as the starving dragon went through an entire pepperoni pizza by herself. Two minutes later, Ember trashed the box, dusted off her hands and finally turned to look at us.

"So." She drummed her fingers on her arm, looking back and forth at each of us. "What now?"

Good question. "I guess that depends, Firebrand."

"On what?"

"You." She frowned at me, confused. Crushing the empty can, I put it in the sink and went to the fridge for another. "Let me ask you something," I said as I closed the door. "What did *you* think was going to happen, Firebrand? After you left Talon? After you went rogue?"

She cocked her head. "I...don't know," she stammered. "Isn't that where you come in? I thought you had this whole rogue thing worked out."

"Normally, I do. But my plans don't usually involve sneaking into highly guarded St. George compounds to rescue the enemy." I didn't look at the soldier as I said this, and St. George didn't give any indication that he cared. "This whole situation is a bit abnormal for me, Firebrand. Frankly, I didn't expect to have you around this long."

Anger flashed across her face and she raised her chin. "Well, if I knew you were just going to get rid of me, I would've saved you the trouble."

"Don't be thick. That's not what I meant." I shook my head, giving her an exasperated look. She glared back, and I sighed. "What did you think I was going to do after taking you away from Crescent Beach?" I demanded. "Toss you out on the streets and say, 'Good luck, have a nice life'? Give me some credit. I'm a little more organized than that."

She frowned. "Then…what *was* going to happen to me?"

I started to answer, then paused. I didn't like talking about my network so openly, especially with the human still in the room with us. Not that I was afraid he could go running back to the Order, but I trusted him about as far as I could throw him. Hunted or not, he had dragon blood on his hands, and that would never change.

As if reading my thoughts, the soldier raised his head and met my glare. "You can tell her," he said in a low voice. "It's not like I can take your secrets back to the Order."

I smirked. "If I thought you could, you'd already be a pile of bones in the desert, St. George," I stated. "That's not what concerns me."

"Riley!" Ember scowled. "You don't have to be a jerk. He's not with the Order anymore."

"Firebrand. You don't get it." I turned on her, narrowing my eyes. "It's not about me. This isn't just my life I'm risking, it's *all* the dragons I've freed from Talon. They look to me to keep them safe, keep them off Talon's radar and away from the Vipers. Not only do I have to worry about the organization, I have to worry about St. George, too, because the bastards don't know there's a difference between rogue dragons and Talon, and they wouldn't care if they did."

I shot another piercing glare at the soldier, who didn't reply. Though by the look on his face, he knew I was right.

"So, yes, Firebrand, I'm a little paranoid that there's an ex-soldier of St. George in the same room as us," I finished. "I believe the *last* time there was a soldier of St. George in the room with us, we were being shot at." I put a fist to my chest, glaring at her. "This is *my* network, my underground.

I've spent too many years getting dragons out of Talon to put their lives in danger now."

Ember stared at me, surprise and amazement reflected in her eyes. "How many dragons are we talking about?" she asked. "How many rogues do you have?"

I sighed again, feeling my shoulders slump in defeat. Too late to hold back now. "Over twenty this year," I admitted, and her mouth fell open. "And that's just counting dragons, not the humans working for me. The hatchlings I steal from the organization are all green and starry-eyed, so they have to have a human agent looking after them until they're ready to set out on their own."

"I had no idea."

I smirked. "When I said I'd take care of you, Firebrand, I wasn't joking. I already have a place set up and waiting. A quiet little town near the mountains. You'll be living with your 'grandfather' on a couple private acres of forest that butts up against a national park. No beaches, sadly, but it's green and peaceful and isolated enough that Talon or the Order will never find you. You'll be safe there, I promise."

"And what will you do?"

"What I've always been doing. Fighting Talon. Getting hatchlings away from the organization. Helping them disappear." I shrugged, feeling suddenly tired. "Maybe if I do this long enough, there'll be enough free dragons someday to take a stand against Talon," I muttered. "That's my pipe dream, anyway." Impossible, unattainable, but I had to hope for something.

"I'll help you."

Ember's response was immediate. No hesitation or fear, just

eager determination. I straightened quickly, alarm and exhilaration rising up at the same time. Part of me had known this would happen; after Crescent Beach, how could my brash, stubborn hatchling want to do anything else? But at the same time, I knew I couldn't subject her to this life. It was dangerous, terrifying, bloody and occasionally it was just soul crushing. I'd seen so many die, had been responsible for countless deaths myself. There had been nights when I wasn't sure I'd survive till dawn, when I'd wondered if the next hour would be my last. I'd seen the worst of Talon, St. George and the whole damn world, and it had turned me into a hard, cynical bastard. I couldn't do that to her.

And of course, there was that *other* reason. The one pounding through my veins, even now. The one snarling at me to say yes, to take her with me so we could be alone, no humans or dragons or soldiers of St. George to interfere. The reason I was an exhausted, cranky mess, because I couldn't sleep while she lay there, still as death. I couldn't focus, couldn't eat or plan or do anything. If St. George had kicked in the door, I would've burned the whole place to the ground before I left her behind.

I couldn't keep going like this. It was dangerous; for me, for Ember, for everyone in my underground. She was a distraction, a fiery, tempting, intriguing distraction, and I had too many people counting on me to keep them safe. I had to get away from her, for both our sakes.

Though, convincing *her* of that was going to be a challenge.

"I'm not going to your safe house, Riley." Ember's voice was final, as if she knew what I was thinking. Her eyes flashed, and she crossed her arms, staring me down. "Don't think you can get rid of me now. I'm not going to hide away and do nothing while you're running around dodging Vipers and dragonslayers and who knows what else. I'm not blind anymore. I've seen what Talon does, how they're willing to kill anyone who doesn't conform to their standards. I'm going to help you and all the dragons who want to be free. I want to get as many of us away from Talon as we can."

"Firebrand," I began, and she set her jaw, ready for a fight. "I know you're angry with Talon," I went on, "and you want to strike back at them somehow, but think about what you're doing. This is a dangerous life. We're constantly on the run, from the organization, and St. George, and the Vipers. Hell, you just woke up because you were *shot* three days ago. That's the kind of situation you'll be facing again if you come with me."

"I know."

"You'll never have a normal life," I insisted. "I can't suddenly decide I don't want to do this anymore. There are too many who are counting on me, too many I promised I'd keep safe. I'll probably be doing this for the rest of my life, or until something—either a Viper or a St. George bullet—kills me."

"That's why you need someone watching your back."

My temper flared. "Dammit, Ember—"

The door banged open, crashing against the wall. I jumped and spun around as Wes lunged into the room, turned and slammed the door behind him. His eyes were wild in his pale face.

"St. George!" he gasped, making us all jerk up. "They're here! I think they're right behind me!"

EMBER

They're here.

Fear crawled up my spine. St. George had come. Again. It didn't seem to matter where we went, what we did; they were always one step behind, seconds from kicking in the door and spraying us with lead. And now that I had so blatantly waltzed into their territory and given the figurative finger to them all, they would be eager for retribution. It was no longer a job, I suspected, no longer a routine slaying of faceless enemies. Now, it was personal.

"What do you mean, they're right behind you?" Riley snapped, stalking toward Wes, who had already locked the door and was peering through the eyehole. "St. George doesn't know who you are, they've never seen you before. How would they know you're even a target?"

"I have no idea, mate, but *someone* was staring at me in the parking lot," Wes snapped, spinning around. "And when I was driving back, I noticed I'd picked up a tail. That's why it took me so bloody long to get here. I was trying to lose the bastards, but they could still be out there."

Riley walked to the edge of the windows and peered

through the glass, keeping his back to the wall. "I don't see anyone," he muttered. "Maybe you lost them."

"They're out there." Garret's quiet voice cut through the tension. We all glanced at him, standing against the wall with his arms crossed. His stance was weirdly calm. "If this really is St. George, the surveyors Wes saw will be narrowing the houses down right now. The assault team is probably on its way. We don't have a lot of time."

"Then we need to leave." Riley strode out of the kitchen. "Right now. While there's still daylight. Wes, get everything together."

"Where are we going?" I asked as Wes hurried out of the room, muttering curses. Riley turned to look at me, frowning slightly.

"Into the city," he said. "Downtown, where there's lots of people. The Order won't try to murder us in a crowd. At least, I hope they won't resort to that." He stabbed a glare in Garret's direction before turning back. "Hiding in plain sight has always been a good tactic for us. We disappear into the crowds, and neither Talon nor the Order can come after us without arousing suspicion. Besides, there's someone there I have to see. We just needed you to wake up before we left."

I felt a brief stab of guilt. "You were all waiting on me?"

One corner of his mouth twisted up. "Kinda hard to hide a dragon in a hotel room, Firebrand. The fire marshal would blow a gasket." He brushed my arm, a brief, light touch that sent curls of heat through my insides. "Hurry and get packed so we can get out of here. I *really* don't feel like seeing St. George again."

We gathered everything, which took only a few minutes. I

didn't have anything except my backpack with some clothes and a couple small personal things. Wes had his laptop, and Garret had the gun he'd taken from the Order and the borrowed clothes on his back. Everything else fit into a single duffel bag, which Riley swung over his shoulder. The rogue traveled light and efficient, ready to pack up and move at a word. Everything was disposable; clothes, vehicles, places to stay. In fact, the only thing I knew he kept with him at all times was that dusty leather jacket.

"All right," he muttered, staring through the peephole in the front door as we crowded behind him. At my side, Garret pressed close, making my heart skip. I could feel his presence, burning across my skin, even as I tried to focus. "I don't see anything out there," Riley went on, his gaze scanning one end of the street to the other. "Looks like we're still in the clear."

"Don't be fooled," Garret murmured. "If St. George is out there, watching us, you won't be able to see them."

Riley snorted without turning around. "Well we certainly can't sit here until they kick down the door," he growled, and turned the knob. Bloodred sunlight spilled through the crack as he pulled the door open, and dying sun shone directly into my eyes, making me squint. For a moment, he didn't move from the frame, casting one final look around the empty street. Shielding my eyes, I peered past his shoulder, searching for anything out of place. The yards and streets were empty; no suspiciously parked cars, no "electricians" or "painters" pretending to be working nearby. Everything seemed perfectly normal. The van sat inconspicuously at the edge of the driveway, but it seemed an impossible distance away.

"Okay," Riley went on, pulling the door back and stepping into the open. "All clear. So far, so—"

A muffled crack rang out from nowhere, making my heart jump to my throat. A sharp hiss followed the gunshot, and the van jerked, then sagged to one side, its back tires deflated in an instant.

"Shit!" Riley lunged back inside and slammed the door, as the rest of us backed hastily away. "Dammit, they're already here." Another crack rang out, and the front window shattered with a ringing cacophony, sending glass raining to the ground. I yelped, covering my face as splinters flew everywhere, and Garret grabbed my wrist, dragging me away from the glass.

"Stay back from the windows," he ordered, pushing me against the wall beside the window frame. I grunted at the impact and scowled at him, but he wasn't looking at me. His gaze, narrowed and grim, was on the rows of houses beyond the broken glass. "Snipers," he breathed, as Riley pressed himself to the other side of the frame, his lips curled in a silent snarl. "They've found us."

"Brilliant," Wes spat from behind the couch. "Snipers, that's bloody fabulous. I am *so* glad we risked life and limb to rescue you, St. George." He glared daggers at Garret, as if wishing the next bullet would make the soldier's head explode. "I don't suppose giving you back will make them leave us alone?"

"Over my dead body," I snarled at Wes, my stomach clenching violently at the thought. "Try it, and I'll throw *you* through that window."

"It wouldn't matter, anyway," Garret replied in a serious

voice, as if Wes's suggestion was actually legitimate. He looked down at me, his expression pained. "I would surrender to them," he said, "if I thought the Order would spare you. But they're here for all of us, and they won't bargain with dragons. I'm sorry, Ember."

I glared back at him. "I wouldn't let you go, anyway. So you can stop being so damned fatalistic. No one is giving anyone up. We're getting out of here together, or not at all."

He blinked, a raw, almost vulnerable look passing through his eyes, and we stared at each other a moment. Outside, it was eerily silent. The sunlight slanting through the broken window caught on shards of glass and glittered red, like drops of blood.

Riley's low, frustrated growl broke the silence. "Dammit, where are they?" he muttered, peeking cautiously around the frame, careful to keep his head back. "Why don't they just charge in and shoot us already?"

"This isn't the full strike force." Garret stared out the window, his expression grave. "Not yet. When the survey team followed Wes back, they had to alert headquarters to let them know they found the targets. They have the sniper guarding the house just to pin us down, make sure we don't leave until the assault team arrives."

Wes swore again, peering around the sofa. "Right, then, if that's the case, I vote we not stand here and let them pick us off. And since the van is now shot to hell, who's up for sneaking out the back door?"

"No." Garret shook his head. "That would be a bad idea. The sniper will be positioned in a spot where he has a full view of the neighborhood. If we try to leave, he'll just as easily pick us off from where he is now. It's not worth the risk."

Riley snorted. "You've got it all figured out, don't you, St. George?"

Garret's voice was flat. "It's what I would do."

"Oh, that's right. You've done this before, haven't you? Shot kids in the back while they were running away?"

"Guys," I said in exasperation, glaring at Riley. "This isn't helping. Focus, please. Garret…" I glanced at the soldier, touching his arm. "You know St. George. You know how they think. What can we do?"

Garret nodded, looking thoughtful. "We'll need to neutralize the threat first," he replied, slipping into soldier mode, logical and calculating. "Find out where the shooter is, sneak around and take him out before the rest of the team arrives."

"Oh, is that all?" Riley frowned, gesturing to the broken window. "And how are we supposed to find where this shooter is without taking a hole to the head? I don't feel like playing whack-a-mole with a trained sniper right now."

Garret edged close to the window, keeping his back pressed to the wall. For a brief moment, he closed his eyes and took a deep breath, as if preparing himself. Then, before I could stop him, he straightened and peered through the frame, leaving his whole head exposed. Almost immediately, a shot rang out, slamming into the sill and tearing away chunks of wood in an explosion of splinters as he ducked back. I flinched, pressing close to Garret with my heart thudding against my ribs, but he wasn't even breathing hard.

"Jeez, Garret!" My voice sounded shaky, unlike the soldier beside me. He straightened, looking perfectly calm, like getting shot at by snipers was routine. I scowled and smacked his arm. "Are you crazy?" I demanded. "You want to get your head exploded? Don't do that again. We'll find the shooter another way."

"One block down," he murmured, making me frown with confusion. His eyes were closed, brow furrowed, as if recalling an image from memory. "Across the street on the corner. There's a two-story house with an attic window. Foreclosed, I think. The shots are coming from that direction."

I stared at him in amazement. "You got all that just now?"

"Partly." He peered out the window, keeping his back against the wall and his head inside this time. "But I observed the area when we first arrived, made note of all the places we might be attacked, where someone could set up an ambush. The house on the corner would be Tristan's ideal..." He stopped, his jaw tightening. "It makes the most tactical sense," he finished stiffly.

"Okay," I said. I wished I could peek out the window, see the house for myself, but I also didn't want to risk a bullet between the eyes. I didn't know if I'd be fast enough, especially now that the shooter knew where we were, and maybe had his crosshairs trained right at me. "So we know where the sniper is. What now?"

Garret drew away from the window, face grim. "Wait here," he said. "Stay inside, I'll try to get close enough to take him out."

"What? You're not doing this alone." He ignored me as he sidled past, keeping close to the walls, and I grabbed the back of his shirt. "What if there's more than one?" I insisted as he turned in my grasp, his face stony. "What if he has a partner and you get hurt, or shot? There'll be no one around to help. You need someone watching your back, at least."

"Firebrand," Riley warned in a no-way-in-hell voice, and I turned to glare at him, too.

"What?" I demanded, still keeping a tight hold of Garret's shirt. "I can do this. I've been *trained* to do this. Lilith taught me herself, or did you forget that I was supposed to be a Talon assassin?" He took a breath to argue, and I raised my chin. "I seem to remember sneaking into a heavily armed St. George base a few nights ago and doing just fine."

"Until you got shot!" Riley made as if to stalk forward, then jerked back, away from the window. His eyes glowed angrily as they met mine. "This isn't a normal bullet, Firebrand," he said. "This isn't something you can recover from. You get hit in the head with a sniper round, you don't have a head anymore."

"I won't get shot."

"You can't know that!"

"Ember." A strong hand closed over mine, gently prying me loose. I turned back to meet Garret's steely eyes, gazing down at me. His face was expressionless, and for a moment, I didn't know if he would tell me to stay behind or not. Which was too bad, because I was coming with him whether he liked it or not. But then he gave a small sigh and released my hand, his gaze flicking out the window.

"We'll have to move fast," he said, scanning the street like he was planning the best route to the sniper perch. "Stay low, keep your head down and don't stop moving. A moving target is much harder to hit. We'll have to circle around, and we'll stay in cover as much as we can, but don't panic if you're shot at. And don't freeze, no matter what. The sniper will likely have a partner guarding his back, too, so we'll probably have to deal with more than one. Do you have a weapon?"

I shook my head, ignoring the fear spreading through my insides, making my stomach curl. "I won't need one."

Behind me, Riley made an impatient sound and reached for something at his back. "Dammit, Ember," he growled. "Yes, you will. Here." He tossed the pistol at me, and my heart lurched as I caught it. "Just don't get yourself killed, all right?"

His eyes stabbed at me, and I couldn't tell if he was furious, worried, or absolutely terrified, before they shifted to Garret. "We're running out of time," he said, his voice clipped and matter-of-fact. "What do you need on our end, St. George?"

"We'll never make it to the house if the sniper sees us coming," Garret replied calmly. "Can you cause a distraction? Something that will take the shooter's focus off the surrounding area for a few seconds?"

"Yeah." Riley nodded, and raked a hand through his hair. "Yeah, I can do that. Wes…" He glanced at the human, still huddled behind the couch. "Get ready to move. You're in charge of finding us another car, now that the van's been shot to hell." There was a muffled curse behind the sofa, and Riley turned back to us. "Get going. I'll make sure their attention is elsewhere."

"What are you going to do?" I asked.

"Oh, you'll know it when you see it."

"Right." I took a breath and glanced at the soldier beside me. "Okay," I whispered, resolved for what I had to do. "Ready if you are."

"Ember."

Riley's voice was almost strangled. I looked back to find those piercing gold eyes on me, his expression tormented. "Don't get hurt, Firebrand," he said in a low voice, meant only for the two of us. "I don't think I could take it this time. Come back alive, okay?"

A lump caught in my throat, and I nodded.

Garret brushed my arm, indicating for me to follow. With one last look at Riley, I turned away, trailing the soldier through the living room and out the back door, stepping into a dusty, weed-strewn yard. We sidled around the house, keeping our backs to the wall, until we came to the corner and the edge of the driveway. Garret peeked around the wall, his gaze scanning the open street and the rows of houses across from us. I braced myself against him to peek over his shoulder, feeling the tension lining his back.

"When do we move?" I whispered, thinking that the distance from one side of the road to the other had never looked so far.

"We have to wait for the distraction," Garret replied, easing back. "Right now, we're right in the shooter's line of sight. We have to get across the road and behind the houses without being seen."

I swallowed. "I wonder what Riley's going to—"

There was a roar, a sudden inrush of air, and a window above us exploded into shards of heat and flames. Glass and splinters of burning wood showered us, making me flinch and press against the wall, as a massive firestorm erupted inside the house. As Riley launched his distraction in the most dragony way possible.

Garret tapped my leg. "Now."

GARRET

I darted from the house and sprinted across the road as quickly as I could, Ember close at my heels. I knew we were exposed; even with the rogue's distraction, there was a chance the sniper would see us. But it seemed the sudden firestorm was enough of a disruption; we reached the other side without any shots fired and ducked behind another house.

The building we'd left had quickly become an inferno, tongues of fire snapping from the windows and roof, as dragonfire burned hotter and fiercer than normal flame. It hadn't gone unnoticed by the rest of the neighborhood, either. Cries of alarm were beginning to echo through the streets as civilians spilled from their own homes onto the pavement, gaping at the fire. A crowd formed rapidly in front of the burning house, talking to each other or speaking frantically into their phones. Some were even taking pictures. The police would arrive soon with the fire department, and they'd likely shut down the whole block. We didn't have much time.

"This way," I told Ember, and we crept swiftly up the street, weaving between fences and ducking behind cover when we could, moving toward the house on the corner. Ember stayed with me, never hesitating or slowing down, following my lead without fail. No more shots were fired on the house; there were far too many people out front now, watching the building burn. St. George wouldn't risk firing into the crowd and hitting a civilian. But we didn't want the soldiers following us, either. Or alerting the rest of their squad to where we'd gone. The threat had to be nullified before we could escape.

Which meant I would have to fight St. George face-to-face.

For a moment, crouched with Ember behind a parked car in a driveway, preparing for the next dash to cover, I felt a stab of guilt. What was I doing? These were my former brothers, men I'd fought beside just a few short weeks ago. What if the sniper was someone I knew? What if I got up there... and it was Tristan facing me on the other side? And if it was my former partner, staring at me down the sight of his gun, could he make himself pull the trigger? Could I?

We approached the last house, slipping through a rotting privacy fence and across an overgrown yard, moving swiftly for the door. There was no time for regret. I had made my choice. Past friendships, memories, the camaraderie I'd always been a part of—none of that mattered. The Order would kill me and my companions if I didn't do something now.

We reached the back entrance, a simple wooden door that was probably locked from the inside. There was no time to pick the lock, no time for a quiet entrance. I drove my foot into the door, aiming for the weak spot right beside the handle, and it flew open with a crash.

The interior of the house was dark and empty, littered with trash and cobwebs. The windows were boarded up, and the air was musty and stale. A flight of wooden steps sat against the wall on our left, leading to the second floor. No St. George soldiers in sight, but they would likely be upstairs.

I jerked my head at Ember and started up the staircase, muzzle of the gun leading the way. The steps opened into a small corridor with two bedrooms sitting across from each other, their doors partially open to show empty, gutted floors and walls. A flight of wooden attic stairs had been pulled down and sat open in the middle of the hall.

As I started toward it, gun drawn, a flicker of movement in the corner of my eye gave me just enough time to react. As a soldier stepped out of the adjacent bedroom with his gun raised, I spun and struck his wrist, making him drop the weapon. Immediately, he lunged, grabbed my weapon arm and slammed me into the opposite wall. He was bigger than me, stocky and broad shouldered, with a shaved head and small black eyes. I recognized his face, though I didn't recall his name. A scar twisted one side of his lip down as he snarled and smashed my wrist into the frame behind me. Pain shot through my hand, and the pistol clattered to the floor.

"Fucking dragonlover," he growled, and threw a hard right hook at my temple, thankfully letting go of my wrist. I managed to block, ducking and getting my arm up, though the blow still rocked my head to the side. I lashed out with my other fist, throwing a body shot below his unprotected ribs. He grunted and slammed me back, cracking my head against the plaster, then smashed a fist at my face. I threw out my arm, deflecting the blow to the side, and spun with the motion, using the momentum to smash him into the wall.

He whirled with a back elbow at my face. I shifted, letting it graze my cheek, then drove my foot into the side of his knee.

There was a pop, and his leg crumpled beneath him. As he hit the floor with a howl of pain, I snaked one arm around his throat and braced the back of his neck with the other. He thrashed, beating at my arms, trying to loosen the grip on his neck, but I set my jaw and didn't move, counting down the seconds. At eight and a half, with no blood carrying oxygen to his brain, he shuddered and went limp in my arms.

I held him there a few seconds longer before I relaxed and let the body slump to the floor. One soldier down. But his partner, probably the sniper himself, had to be close—

A shot rang out in front of me.

I jerked, tensing to attack, then froze. Ember, wide-eyed and pale, stood at the top of the steps, a smoking pistol pointed at the ceiling behind me. Heart in my throat, I turned as a body dropped from the attic stairs and hit the floor with a thud.

A small hole pierced his forehead, right above his eyes, a near perfect head shot. Blood trickled down his face, over the bridge of his nose toward his mouth, open in surprise. One limp hand clutched his sidearm, a gloved finger still curled around the trigger.

Ember gave a tiny gasp and lowered her weapon. "I—I saw him through the hole," she whispered, sounding dazed. Her arm trembled as she gestured weakly at the attic steps. "He had his gun out...pointed at your back. I didn't know what else to do."

She was shaking, eyes glassy as she stared at the body on the floor, as if waiting for it to move. When it didn't, she looked up at me, almost pleading. "Did I...? Is he...?"

I blew out a long breath, closing my eyes. "He's dead."

Painfully, I bent to retrieve my weapon, reluctant to glance at the fallen soldier, in case it was someone I knew. Rising, I checked the firearm out of habit, feeling aches from new bruises start to bloom along my body. My head throbbed, and my neck and back were sore from where I was slammed against the wall. But I was still alive.

Finally, inevitably, my gaze strayed to the body crumpled at the bottom of the steps, the sniper who had been firing on us from the attic window. For a split second, I tensed, wondering if I would see a familiar face with short dark hair, glazed blue eyes now staring at nothing. But the body at the foot of the steps was older than Tristan, unfamiliar to me. Through the aching guilt of what I'd just done, I felt a tiny prick of relief. I was truly the enemy of St. George now. I'd fought beside our ancient foes and had struck down my former brothers in arms but, at least for today, I wouldn't have to face the person I dreaded fighting more than anyone else.

I hoped it would never come to that.

Ember was still standing at the top of the stairs, gazing down at the fallen soldier. Her skin was ashen, her bright hair a shocking contrast to her face. "I killed him," she whispered, her voice choked and horrified. "He's really dead. I didn't... I didn't mean to..."

"Ember." I took a step toward her, and she flinched away, wide-eyed and trembling. Sympathy curled my stomach. I remembered *my* first kill, several years back, though it felt like a lifetime ago. It had been a dragon, and though I'd received nothing but praise and admiration from my brothers, I'd never forgotten the way it had stared at me as it lay there in the grass. I remembered its gaze, confused and terrified, before its eyes glazed over and it passed into death. I'd never spoken of it, but the nightmares from that day had haunted me for weeks afterward.

I knew what Ember was feeling right now, and I wished I had the words to comfort her, or the time. Sadly, we had neither. "Come on," I said, starting toward the stairs. "Hurry, before the authorities arrive. We can't be caught here."

She blinked as I brushed past her, then followed me down the steps. "What about the...body?" she asked, stumbling over the word. "The police will find it. There'll be a murder investigation at the very least. If anyone saw us enter the house, they'll be looking for us, too."

"Not likely."

She frowned at my brusqueness. "How can you know that?"

"Because St. George has ways of covering this up," I explained as we left the house, easing around the faded walls. "That soldier you killed," I went on, gesturing back to the empty building, "he's a ghost. We all are. We have no background, no past, no family except the Order. We don't register in any system. When we die, we vanish, as if we never existed."

"Oh," Ember mused, though she didn't sound reassured. "That's...kind of sad. All that fighting, and no one even remembers you when you're gone."

I didn't have an answer for that, so I stayed quiet. We slipped through the fence and huddled on the corner of the street, keeping a wary eye on the crowd surrounding the burning house. The roof was fully engulfed, clouds of black smoke billowing into the evening sky. I hoped Wes and the rogue dragon had been able to get out safely. And that they had come up with a getaway plan.

Sirens wailed in the distance. I tensed, and Ember froze, gazing down the street. The authorities were on their way. I glanced at the burning house, debating whether to search for our companions or to vacate the area and hope they caught up.

A sleek black SUV suddenly rounded a corner, barreled across the road and squealed to a stop in front of us. The driver's window buzzed down, and Riley glared out at us, jerking his head at the back. "Get in!" he barked, as the sirens grew louder. "Let's go!"

Yanking open the back door, I ducked into a black leather interior, the smell of new car surrounding me. Ember followed and slammed the door behind her, and the tires screeched as Riley stepped on the gas and roared away, leaving chaos in our wake.

COBALT

Nearly there.

I pressed back against the office wall, holding my breath, as a pair of soldiers swept down the hallway just outside the door, their boots thumping in unison. They marched around a corner and out of sight, and I exhaled slowly in relief. Getting into this place had been a huge pain in the ass, with more close calls than I was comfortable with. It had taken all my considerable skills to make it this far unnoticed, and I still had to get out again once I was done. But one problem at a time.

A large wooden desk sat against the far wall, a computer perched atop the surface. Pressing into a corner, I hit a number on my phone and held it to my ear. One ring, and someone picked up.

"I'm in," I whispered. Slipping around the desk, I jiggled the screen to life and pulled the human's thumb drive out of my pocket. "Inserting the program now," I said, and stuck the drive into the side of the computer.

For a few seconds, nothing happened. Then, a bar flashed across the top of the screen, the tiny white numbers above the strip at 0 percent. As I watched, it flicked to 1 percent, then 2 percent as the numbers started inching upward. Very, very slowly.

Oh, don't rush or anything, I thought, peering around the desk at the open door. *No life-threatening situation here. Just me, a dragon sitting in the middle of St. George. Please, take your time.*

Footsteps echoed down the hall, coming gradually closer. I winced and ducked beneath the desk, shoving myself into a corner as voices drifted into the room, talking of meetings and drills and other boring things. Two humans passed by the door and continued down the hallway without slowing. I waited until they were truly gone before popping out and glaring at the bar on the screen.

Eighty-six percent. Dammit. How long did hacking a file take? Biting back my impatience, I waited, drumming my fingers on the floor, until the strip had completely filled and the numbers finally hit 100 percent. I yanked it out and stuffed the drive into my pocket then rose, relief and a strangely grim sensation stealing over me. One thing down.

But I wasn't done yet.

The backpack felt heavy against my shoulders, reminding me of what came next. I slipped out of the room and made my way through the building, on high alert for guards, until I found the stairs. According to the Chief Basilisk, my final objective was below me, on the very last floor.

The hallways were dark as I crept across the tile, though a light glowed near the end of one of the corridors, the murmur of human voices drifting through an open door frame. Thankfully, I didn't have to go far. My objective sat behind an inconspicuous white door at the end of a lonely hall, unguarded and exposed. The door was locked, but my skills got it open fairly quickly, and I cased inside.

A cold blast of air hit my skin, and my breath billowed in front of me as I gazed warily around. The room was windowless, stark and almost freezing. The walls were bare, the floor empty except for three metal towers in the center of the tile, blinking with dozens of green and blue lights. As server rooms went, it was pretty small, unlike the vast rooms with dozens of computer towers lining the floor that I had seen in other buildings. These servers would provide only enough information for this one isolated compound. I wondered why Talon was so keen on blowing it up. Still, I had my mission, and it wasn't my job to ask questions. The sooner I was done here, the sooner I could leave.

Shrugging out of my backpack, I knelt and carefully eased the padded black case out, then clicked it open. The incendiary device sat within, and my heart pounded as I stared at it. The new "toy" I was supposed to try out was a bomb, and not just any bomb. This one was much more powerful than a normal explosive, my trainer had said. A combination of science, magic and dragonfire, packed into this small, deadly package. Dragonfire was not like normal fire; it burned hotter, fiercer, and was capable of melting steel and turning flesh to ashes in minutes. It had the tendency to cling to whatever it touched, consuming any material until it was completely gone. Even now, with all the technology and tools and firearms dragons had adapted over the centuries, our breath remained our most lethal weapon. It was the main reason St. George feared us in battle. If this thing worked the way Talon expected, it would not only destroy this room and pulverize the servers, it would spread caustic, roaring dragonfire through the whole floor, blowing out walls, weakening supports and bringing the whole building down on top of it.

And of course, anyone caught in the blast would be nothing but a smoking, blackened skeleton when they were found, an image that made my gut clench. More killing. More deaths. But at least this target was a heavily armed St. George chapterhouse, filled with active soldiers dedicated to making my race extinct. They understood their part in this war; they knew exactly who they were fighting.

Whatever you have to tell yourself, Cobalt. Let's get this over with.

As smoothly as I could, I placed the bomb on the tile floor and slid it beneath one of the towers. It glimmered dully in the shadows, silent and deadly, and for a moment, I hesitated, staring at the device. Press a button; that was all I had to do. Press a button, and get out. The most dangerous mission of my life was nearly done. I was almost home free.

I shook myself, then reached down and firmly pressed the small red button on the side of the case. There was a faint click, and glowing numbers flashed across the tiny black screen on top. They blinked for a moment, then began counting down.

15:00
14:59
14:58

Swiftly, I rose, my steps heavy as I headed toward the door. Fifteen minutes. Fifteen minutes before this place exploded in a hellish firestorm and turned everyone inside to ashes.

These are soldiers, I reminded myself again as my hand closed on the knob. *They've accepted the risks. For every one of them you kill, more dragon lives will be saved. This is for the good of us all.*

So why did I feel like I might puke if I thought too hard about it?

I opened the door, stepped out of the room…

…and came face-to-face with a girl.

I froze. The human looked up at me, green eyes appraising in a round, pale face. She wore a simple yellow dress, and curls of white-blond hair tumbled down her shoulders. She seemed completely unafraid, and for a split second, we stared at one another.

Then the girl blinked her somber green eyes. "You're not supposed to be in there," she said softly.

Instinctively, my muscles tensed, ready to spring forward, cover the human's mouth and yank her back into the room. I knew I couldn't let her run away and alert the rest of the base to my presence. But as she gazed up at me, bold yet curious, I faltered. She was a kid, no more than six or seven in human years. Not a soldier, not even an adult. If I grabbed her now…I'd probably have to kill her.

The girl cocked her head as I struggled with my decision. "What are you doing?" she whispered, her voice furtive, as if she was in on the conspiracy. "Are you hiding from someone?"

"Uh…yeah." I had no idea what the hell I would even say to her after that. If the kid screamed, my chances of survival were basically zero. But the thought of killing her, feeling her small neck snap under my fingers, made my insides curl. Even though I knew she would grow up to hate my kind and want us extinct. Because she was part of St. George, and that's what they did. Took people as normal and innocent as this girl and turned them into dragon-hating zealots.

The little human blinked again. "Why?" she asked, still keeping her voice soft. "Who's looking for you? Are you in trouble?"

Oh, definitely. "No," I whispered, giving her what I hoped was a careless grin and shrug. "I'm…uh…playing hide-and-seek with some of the soldiers." Even as I said it, I winced inside at how stupid that sounded. But I couldn't stop now. "It's…a…a new exercise," I went on, as she frowned. "They have to find me before time runs out, or I win. But if I'm caught, I have to wash everyone's dishes for a month."

The girl's frown deepened, bordering on outrage. "That's not fair!" she whispered indignantly. "There's a lot of them, and only one of you. Not fair." She put her hands on her hips, and I shrugged again, giving her a "what can you do?" look. Her nose wrinkled, lips pursing in annoyance. "Do *they* have to wash dishes if you win?"

"Um…no," I said, wondering how I had been drawn into this crazy conversation, and how I could leave it without being discovered.

"Why not?"

"Because…ah…"

"Madison?"

A new voice drifted from another hallway, and I cringed. This was it. I was going to be caught, because I'd been stupid and softhearted, and hadn't silenced this kid when I had the chance. But the girl turned her head, eyes widening, then glanced back at me.

"You better go," she whispered. "Before they see you."

I stared at her, stunned, and she made shooing motions as she backed away. "Go," she whispered again. "Hurry up and hide! I won't tell anyone where you are, I promise."

"Madison!" The voice sounded annoyed, and closer. The girl grinned and, before I could do or say anything, turned and scurried off, vanishing around a corner as quickly as she had appeared.

Just like that, I was alone.

"There you are," said the man's voice, as I pressed against the door frame, listening with a kind of numb anticipation. "I thought I might find you down here. What do I keep telling you about wandering off? Who were you talking to?"

"Nobody," Madison drawled, way too sweetly I thought. "I wanted to see if Peter was down here. He promised he'd show me the server room if I was good." My heart pounded, but the man, whoever he was, simply grunted.

"You and your computer fascination. Well, come on. I have to finish one last report, and then we'll go get breakfast."

And their footsteps faded down the hall in the opposite direction. A door slammed shut, and silence fell once more. I let out my breath in a rush and collapsed against the wall.

Waaaaay too close, Cobalt. Still a lucky SOB. Now get out of here, before that bomb goes off...

Shit. The bomb.

I started to move, to hurry back into the shadows and make a beeline for the gate as quietly as I could, hoping to somehow avoid both the soldiers and the deadly explosion *minutes* from going off.

Then...I hesitated. In the middle of a St. George chapterhouse, surrounded by enemies who would kill me on sight, with my seconds rapidly ticking away, I hesitated, unable to make myself take another step. If I left now, if I finished the mission and walked away, everyone on this floor would die.

Including that kid. Madison, the girl I'd met for only a couple minutes, would die. She was human, she was part of St. George, but she wasn't a soldier. And without even knowing it, she had saved my life.

I raked my hands through my hair. *So, what are you going to do, Cobalt? Not complete the mission? Go back to Talon and admit you failed? You know they won't accept that.*

No, they wouldn't. So that left me with exactly three options. Return to Talon having failed the mission. Accept their punishment, whatever it was, knowing they would never trust me again, knowing they would consider me tainted and incompetent and somehow corrupted. Talon had little use for dragons who failed; my future with the organization was assured only if I continued to be valuable. It was career suicide, but I could kill the bomb, return to Talon and face the consequences of my decision, whatever they might be.

Or, I could finish what I came here to do: leave the bomb and get out, knowing more people would die. Knowing that kid would burn to death like everyone around her, because she had let me go. And I might never sleep again without seeing her face, staring up at me from my dreams.

Then, of course, there was the final option.

My chest felt tight, my stomach twisting into painful knots. Everything, it seemed, had come down to this moment. Run, or stay? Continue with the organization, or take my chances on my own? Hunted. Hated. A traitor to my own kind.

A rogue.

My hands shook, and fear spread through me as I realized the truth. I couldn't do this anymore. I couldn't go back to the organization knowing some little kid had died...no, that *I'd* killed her, and Talon wouldn't think twice about it. Why should they? She was only human, and human lives meant nothing to dragons. If a few mortals died so that our race was preserved, then the sacrifice was worth it.

But they never had to see the faces of those they destroyed; the *sacrifices* they spoke of, the consequences of our war, never touched their desks. They had me. I was doing their dirty work for them.

No. No more. That ended right now.

Numbly, I went back into the server room and walked to the place the bomb sat, tiny and ominous, red numbers ticking down. Looking down at it, everything inside me went cold.

2:33
2:32
2:31

Two minutes? What the hell? Even after the conversation with Madison, there was no way that much time had elapsed. Though the reason for it was immediately clear: the timer was moving twice as fast as a normal clock, eating away the seconds at a frightening speed. Even as I stared, they seemed to go faster, until the seconds were nothing but a red blur against the screen. My head spun with the implications. I'd never make it out in time. If I hadn't come back, I would've died with the humans when the building went down.

Horror flooded me. Dropping to my knees, I pulled out

my wire cutters and stared at the tangle of wires surrounding the bomb. Red, blue and yellow. My hands shook, and I clamped down on my resolve. If I chose wrong, none of this would matter, except my death would arrive a few seconds earlier than planned.

I clenched my other fist. Without thinking too much about it, I jammed the blades around one of the red wires and, before I could second-guess myself, snapped them shut, severing the line.

The device gave an ominous beep...then stopped. Nothing exploded in a blinding cloud of dragonfire, and my heart started beating again.

Dropping the snips, I ran my hands down my face, everything inside me twisting into knots as the realization of what I'd done—what *they* had done—hit me full force. Maybe the bomb had malfunctioned, maybe there had been a glitch to make the countdown accelerate like that. But I knew better than to think this had been accidental. Talon had never intended for me to come back.

In a daze, I rose from the tile floor and stumbled toward the exit. Fear clawed at me, dark and crippling. Talon was my whole life; my entire existence had been spent serving the organization. I knew what would happen once they figured out I hadn't died like I was supposed to. I was fully aware of what they did to those who went rogue. But there was no turning back. This had been coming for a while now. I knew it, my trainer knew it...and Talon had known it, too. My days of spy missions, sabotage and blowing up buildings full of innocent humans were over.

That's it. I remembered Madison's face, the way she'd smiled up at me, and my resolve grew. *No more. Do you hear that, Chief? I'm done. This is Agent Cobalt, checking out for the last time.*

Crossing the room, I opened the door and melted into the shadows. I still had to get free of St. George, but even if I escaped, the organization would have accomplished at least one thing. A Talon operative had died in this building tonight. As of this moment, Agent Cobalt no longer existed.

EMBER

My hands wouldn't stop shaking.

I couldn't stop them. My heart was racing, and my nerves felt charged with electricity. My trembling fingers were still curled around the smooth handle of the gun in my lap. The gun I'd used to shoot someone.

My stomach heaved, and I closed my eyes, but it didn't help. I could still see him, the slack face and the sightless, staring eyes. The bullet hole in his skull, oozing blood. I didn't even remember pulling the trigger. The moment I'd seen him through the attic opening, aiming his gun at Garret, I'd reacted. Without thinking, just as I had in the St. George compound—quick and lethal, almost instinctive. Now, because of me, a man was dead. I'd become a killer, an assassin, just like Talon wanted.

Lilith would've been proud.

"Where are we going?" Garret's voice echoed beside me, calm and composed. He didn't sound remotely anxious or freaked out, as if being targeted by snipers, breaking into a house and taking out two fully armed soldiers was a perfectly normal day for him. Business as usual. For a moment, I resented his perfect composure. I'd just killed a man, one of his former brothers in arms; you would think he'd be slightly upset by that.

"Downtown," Riley answered without looking back. He sat in the front seat, both hands on the wheel, and drove like he rode a motorcycle: fast and with purpose. Beside him, Wes hunched over his laptop, not looking up when Riley took a corner without slowing down, making the wheels screech. "Near the Strip. I have a friend there who can hide us."

"And the vehicle?" Garret looked out the back window, maybe searching for flashing lights. "I assume the original owner isn't going to be happy about us hot-wiring his car."

Wes snickered. "Hot-wire a car," he scoffed. "Please. Is that how you do things, St. George? How very primitive." He tapped two fingers against his skull. "Modern cars these days have lovely computerized brains that you can turn on with a phone. Makes them fairly easy to hack into, if you know what you're doing."

Great, I thought, crossing my arms. The gun dropped onto the seat beside me. I didn't want to look at it, much less touch it anymore. *So now we're murderers and car thieves.*

A soft click made me look up. Garret had reached over and taken the pistol from where it lay between us, then smoothly flicked on the safety. He turned the weapon around and offered it to me again, his gray eyes solemn as they met mine.

"You had no choice," he said, holding my gaze. "Those soldiers would've killed us both if they could. There was no other option, you did what you had to do."

The lump in my throat got bigger, and I eyed the weapon like it was a giant venomous spider. But I made myself reach out and take it back, closing my fingers around the now warm metal. "I know," I whispered, setting the gun carefully on my leg. "But that doesn't make it all right." I shot a wary glance at the front, where Riley and Wes were talking in low voices. Wes was pointing to a map on the laptop screen, where a glowing blue dot approached an intersection. Riley swore, gunned the engine and ran an aging yellow light. Neither seemed to be listening to what was happening in the backseat, but I lowered my voice anyway. "I don't want to be like them," I murmured. "Either of them. Talon *or* St. George. If I start killing without a thought, if it becomes instinct, why did I leave Talon at all? What makes me any different than the Viper they wanted me to become?"

The blare of a siren made us jerk up. A cop car passed us, going in the opposite direction, lights flashing blue and red, speeding toward the distant column of black smoke curling into the sky. The soldier leaned back, gazing out the window, and didn't answer my question.

★ ★ ★

The sun had set over the distant mountains, leaving only a fading orange splash on the horizon, when we reached the inner city, or the Strip, as Riley called it. My misery was temporarily forgotten as I pressed my nose against the car window, gaping at the wonders looming overhead. I'd never seen so many cars, lights, people. The streets practically glowed; hotels, casinos, massive signs, monuments, all blazing with neon luminance against the darkening sky. An enormous cartoon cowboy waved to us as we drove past, and a miniature sultan's castle boasted a colorful rainbow of lights across its domed roof. I caught a glimpse of the Eiffel Tower, shimmering gold against the night, rising above the streets like a beacon. Not *the* Eiffel Tower, I realized; as far as I knew, the real one was still in Paris, so this was obviously a replica. But it was still huge, and impressive, and blazing with light, like everything around us.

"Close your mouth, Firebrand," Riley remarked with a smirk in his voice as we cruised down the street, passing buildings and people and an endless string of cars. "You're fogging up the windows."

I tore my gaze from the massive buildings surrounding us, sliding back in my seat. "Are we going to stop soon?" I asked, hoping the answer was yes.

Riley snorted. "Not here," he said, and all traces of amusement fled. He shot a grim look out the window at the glittering structures lining the roads. "Definitely not on the Strip. Vegas is a huge cash flow for the organization. They have their claws in basically every vice you can imagine—gambling, drugs, strip clubs, you name it." Riley pulled a disgusted face, curling a lip. "Thankfully, there aren't many actual dragons in Vegas. Just *one*, really. But he's a temperamental bastard who makes even Talon nervous, and he owns nearly all the hotels and casinos on the Strip. We step into the wrong building, we might as well be walking around with glowing signs above our heads."

"Then why are we here?" Garret asked, voicing my own question. "If this city is so heavily influenced by Talon, why are we risking exposure by staying?"

"Because I want to know what Talon is up to," Riley snapped, glaring back at him. "I want to know why my safe houses keep disappearing, and if Talon is doing anything shady. More shady than normal, anyway. I want to know how the Order knows about me, knows who I am, when they didn't have a clue in the past. If my entire network is in danger, I want to know why, and what I can do to stop it." He turned back, gripping the steering wheel, eyes narrowed and hard.

"I have a contact here," he said at length. "One who keeps tabs on any movement between St. George and the organization for me. Nothing happens in Vegas without him finding out. If anyone knows what's going on, he will."

We turned off the Strip, leaving the mega hotels and dazzling lights behind. Several minutes later, Riley pulled the car to the side of the road and killed the engine.

"All right, let's go. The hotel we want is two blocks down, but we're ditching the car here. I'm sure it's been reported as stolen by now." He turned in his seat to look back at us and glanced at the pistol I still held. "Stash the guns," he ordered, and Garret immediately turned and pulled the duffel bag from the backseat. "Last thing we need is for someone to call the cops on us. Everyone keep your head down. We do this quick and quiet. Oh, and one more thing. Wes, you got them IDs, right?"

The human mumbled something and held up two plastic cards without taking his gaze from his computer. Riley snatched them from his fingers and held them out to us. "Cover identities for the hotel," he explained as I took my driver's license and peered at it curiously. My face smirked back at me, familiar and baffling; I had no idea where he'd gotten the photograph. According to the license, my name was Emily Gates, and I was twenty-one years old.

Curiosity and excitement flickered. What could I do with

a fake ID in Vegas? I wondered. I could definitely think of a few things.

"Those should hold up to most background checks," Riley went on, as Garret slid his own license into a pocket then continued stashing the guns. "But we don't want to draw attention to ourselves. So no ordering from the bar or wandering the casino floor. Those IDs are just to get us past the door. Firebrand…" Riley's gold eyes fixed on me, appraising. "Are you listening to this? We are here to *lie low*, understand? Shall I explain the meaning of the term?"

I wrinkled my nose at him. "I know what it means. Smart-ass."

His lip quirked. "Just keep that in mind, and try not to get distracted by the shiny."

I rolled my eyes. Garret finished zipping up the bag, swung it to his shoulder and opened the door. A dry breeze ruffled my hair as I stepped out onto the warm, crowded streets of Las Vegas.

Riley took the lead, striding purposefully down the sidewalk, with Wes, Garret and I trailing behind. And the rogue's warning was instantly forgotten. I couldn't stop staring at… well, everything really. Crescent Beach had been a small, sleepy town, with few highways and not many large buildings. Vegas was like another world. I'd never seen rows of buildings so high they were like canyon walls, or so many glowing lights that I couldn't see the sky through the haze, or an endless river of cars, red brake lights stretching on to the horizon. Unfortunately, navigating bustling sidewalks while trying to look at everything didn't really go well together. I kept bumping into passersby, muttering apologies and getting annoyed looks in return.

"On your six," a voice muttered, as I slowed to gaze at a building across the street. Confused, I turned...and someone barely swerved around me with a muffled curse. Blinking, I looked up at Garret, who shot me a half amused, half exasperated look before going back to scanning the crowds.

I offered a weak grin and fell into step beside him. "On your six?" I asked. "Is that soldier talk for 'pay the hell attention to what you're doing'?"

"We *are* in enemy territory." Garret watched a pair of thuggish-looking guys approach, relaxing only slightly when they passed. "Talon and St. George are both searching for us. They might have agents on the streets right now. A little situational awareness is probably...prudent."

Feeling chastised, I followed him, trying to stay close. Garret moved through the throngs like a fish through water, metallic-gray eyes constantly scanning, watching. I remembered his discomfort with crowds in Crescent Beach, that hyperalertness, as if a ninja could come leaping out at us from a potted plant. Back then, in the lazy little beach town, it had seemed odd. Now, I understood. That paranoia had probably saved his life more than once.

Finally, Riley took us across a huge parking lot and through the doors of a smaller, though still impressive, building. Nero's Garden Hotel and Casino, the sign read as we approached the front. A pair of marble lions guarded the entrance, though I saw someone had drawn a tiny mustache below one lion's nose. Then the doors slid back, and we stepped into a brightly lit lobby with green tile, fake marble columns lining the room and statues of half-naked Greek people in alcoves along the wall. A huge check-in desk ran the length of the back wall, and off to the side, through a fake marble arch, the casino floor buzzed, twinkled, chimed and flashed like a sprawling neon circus.

"Well, here we are," Riley said with false grandeur, and offered a sarcastic grin as he gestured to the glittering casino. "Welcome to Vegas."

DANTE

From the air, the city looked like an island of stars in the center of a black void.

"Can I get you anything before we land, sir?" the flight attendant asked, showing perfect white teeth as she smiled down at us. Or, more accurately, at me. At my side, Mr. Smith didn't look up from his phone, and across from us, Mr. Roth made a vague gesture with his hand, waving her away. I made a point of returning the smile as I shook my head.

"No. Thank you."

"Of course, sir." The human regarded me through lowered lashes. "Please, let me know if you need anything." She wandered toward the back of the jet, where a second attendant glared at her with stony eyes.

Mr. Roth chuckled.

"Do you see your protégé, Mr. Smith?" the VP said, as my trainer put his phone away and looked up. "You'll have to keep a closer eye on him. If we're not careful, we'll have humans clawing each other's eyes out for his attention."

I stayed quiet, not knowing if this was praise or a reprimand. Mr. Smith gave a small laugh that could have meant anything, but he didn't comment. I took a furtive breath and settled back in the plush leather seat, trying to calm my nerves. Normally by this time, my trainer would be going over Talon rules and protocol, grilling me on etiquette, making sure I knew what I was doing. But he couldn't now, or he wouldn't, not in front of Mr. Roth. There were no other passengers on Talon's elite private jet; it was just the three of us. My trainer, one of Talon's senior VPs and me. A sixteen-year-old hatchling who was keeping company with some of the most powerful dragons in the organization. A hatchling who, just yesterday, had been standing outside the door of an office in Los Angeles, waiting to be acknowledged.

★ ★ ★

"I believe we found them, sir," I'd announced, when Mr. Roth finally waved me into the room. I stepped through the frame, closing the door behind me. "We think they're in Vegas."

The VP arched one slim, elegant eyebrow at me over his desk. "Vegas, you say," he repeated. "That's unexpected. One of our biggest operations is in Vegas. That Cobalt would flee there is unusual." His gaze sharpened, brows drawing together. "How did you come to this conclusion, Mr. Hill?"

I handed him the folder Mist had given me; her report and the satellite pictures of the Order chapterhouse sat inside. "We've been monitoring St. George ever since Ember and the rogue broke into their western chapterhouse, sir," I said, as Mr. Roth flipped it open. "We believe St. George is looking for them as well, and recently, we've seen a lot of Order activity in and around Las Vegas. They appear to be converging on the city. We think Ember and the rogue are hiding somewhere close, maybe near the Strip."

"I see." Mr. Roth closed the folder and laced his hands under his chin. "Reign's territory. Of course, they would have to make this complicated."

My heart beat faster. Ember was in Las Vegas, I could feel it. Just a few hours' drive away, in the middle of a huge, dangerous city with St. George closing in on all sides. "Sir," I began, "if Ember *is* in Vegas, I believe I should be the one to bring her back. If we can find her, I would like to go. She'll listen to me. I just need to talk to her."

And if I can bring her back, Talon will know how valuable I am to the organization.

"Of course, Mr. Hill." Roth glanced up at me and smiled. "Of course you are going to retrieve your sister, that was never a question. However, there are protocols that we must observe, if we want the best chance of finding Ms. Hill and Cobalt. Before we do anything in Las Vegas, there is someone we must speak to first. I'll arrange the meeting."

★ ★ ★

Mr. Roth hadn't wasted any time. I'd been driven back to my apartment with orders to pack for a few days' trip, and this morning I'd been taken to a small airport, where Mr. Smith, Mr. Roth and a private jet awaited me. Everything had happened so quickly, I hadn't had time to reflect or feel nervous, until now.

Crossing my legs, I leaned back, affecting a pose of professional nonchalance. This anxiety wasn't like me, but everything, it seemed, hinged on bringing Ember back. *Everyone is watching you, Dante*, I reminded myself. *Talon is watching you, even closer than they did in Crescent Beach. This is your chance to prove yourself. To start building a future in the organization, to do great things for Talon. You have to impress them. You have to do better than anyone expects.*

"Sir," I ventured, making Mr. Roth glance up and raise an eyebrow at me. "Our contact in Las Vegas—his name is Reign?"

"That is correct," Mr. Roth replied.

"Is there anything I should know about him?" I went on, careful to keep my tone deferent. "Anything special I should be aware of before the meeting?"

"Ah yes, our good friend Reign." Roth smiled, though his tone was brittle. "Only know that he is one of the oldest dragons in the organization," he said, making my stomach drop to my toes. "He was around when the Elder Wyrm rose to power, so that should give you an idea of who you're dealing with. He is also very, shall we say…old-fashioned? He prefers things a certain way, and the Elder Wyrm allows him his small idiosyncrasies. He is crucial to the organization, as most of Talon's assets in Las Vegas come through his casinos, but Reign himself can be…challenging to deal with." Mr. Roth gave me a scrutinizing look and leaned back in the seat. "My advice to you, Mr. Hill? Be polite. Reign is loyal to the organization and will not risk the Elder Wyrm's wrath, but he is not fond of having other dragons in what he considers his territory. It is always good to be cautious when dealing with self-proclaimed kings."

The jet landed at another private airport on the edge of town, and a limo stood waiting to drive us into the city. Once inside I leaned back against the cold leather seat and crossed my legs, deliberately not looking out the tinted windows. I was resolved to appear as cool as possible, and not like a gawking, starstruck tourist who had never seen the glamour of Las Vegas.

I nearly broke that resolve when the limo pulled up in front of the biggest hotel I'd ever seen in my life. It soared above us, blazing with millions of lights, so bright you could barely see the sky overhead. Inside, it was even more difficult not to gape at the enormous foyer tiled in gold and black, ringed with silver-threaded onyx columns, a marble fountain in the center of the opulence. A retinue of well-dressed humans greeted us in the glittering foyer, with instructions that "Mr. R." was waiting for us, and to please follow them.

We did, trailing the escorts across a crowded casino full of flashing lights, bells and, of course, people. The place was enormous. The gold tile we walked on reflected the millions of lights, and the whole casino had an air of fantasy and surrealism, where time didn't exist and you could lose hours, or even days, without knowing it. Humans sat at tables with columns of colored chips, or fed bills into the rows of flashing machines that lined every aisle. Everything screamed wealth, riches, luxury, and for a moment, I felt a glimmer of envy through the fascination.

I wanted this.

The humans led us to the elevator bay, escorted us into a box and bowed as the doors slid shut. They did not, I noticed, press any buttons, and neither did Mr. Roth or Mr. Smith. But, after a moment, the elevator shuddered and started to move. Down.

It continued down for a long, long time. No one spoke, and I concentrated on remaining still and keeping the calm, serene expression on my face. When the elevator finally stopped and

the doors opened, I saw a short cement corridor, a lone florescent light and a single door at the end of the hall.

I caught Mr. Smith's eye as we stepped out of the elevator. His gaze was a warning, cold and ominous. This was it,
I realized. The moment where all my training, everything
I'd learned about Talon and its inner circle, came together. It
was either sink or swim, impress or disappoint. Through that
door, my future with Talon hung in the balance.

I met my trainer's stare and gave a short nod. I was ready.
Today was the day I started making a name for myself. Mr.
Smith watched me a moment longer, then turned away, fol-
lowing Mr. Roth toward the end of the hall.

We stepped through the door into a massive, dimly lit cavern. A huge, yawning chamber that soared up into the darkness, hiding the ceiling from view. The floor was cement,
but the walls, as far as I could see, were of natural rock and
stone. The air in the cave was unnaturally warm, surprising
for being so far underground, and smelled faintly of smoke,
though I couldn't see any fires. There were also no overhead
lights, no florescent bulbs or lamps, or even candles. In fact,
the only light came from a group of enormous flat screens
near the back wall. Over two dozen televisions, bolted to a
network of steel frames, formed an immense, flickering semi-
circle of noise and images. Each huge screen showed something different: sports, world events, news stations in several
different languages. A few of them appeared to be casino security, cycling through different areas of the hotel. More than
one screen showed nothing but the Dow, tracking the rise and
fall of stocks. Horses sped down a track, police sirens wailed
and an attractive Asian reporter babbled at me in Japanese.

It was a chaotic flood of imagery, a hundred different things happening all at once. So I didn't immediately notice what lay beneath the circle of screens. Then Mr. Smith put a warning hand on my shoulder, stopping me from advancing any farther into the room, and I dropped my gaze from the televisions.

My mouth nearly fell open, and I bit my cheek to keep from gasping in shock. An enormous pile of gold lay sprawled on the floor beneath the screens, the light glimmering off the metallic surface. In the darkness and shadows, it was difficult to see how big it really was, but I guessed it was at least forty feet long and fifteen feet high, a virtual mountain of gold in the middle of the cavern. So *this* was why Reign was so touchy about other dragons being in his territory. He was sitting on a literal treasure hoard. Old-fashioned indeed.

And then, the mountain moved.

The bottom dropped out of my stomach, and my mouth did fall open this time, as the entire hoard shifted, unfurled two colossal leathery wings and sat up. A head rose on a long, snaking neck, and a tail uncurled to double the length, as an eighty-foot golden dragon turned with a scraping of claws and scales and fixed us with a massive yellow eye.

My legs were frozen. I couldn't move. I could only stare at the creature before me, torn between awe and utter panic. Besides my sister, I'd only ever seen one other of my kind in its real form, an adult who wasn't even half the size of this dragon. He had to be a Wyrm, one of three dragons in the world who had passed the thousand-year mark, who had survived so long that they were the size of buildings. Everyone in Talon knew of the Elder Wyrm, the oldest and most powerful of us all, but the identities and locations of the other two were a jealously guarded secret. Reign was ancient, a lesser god gazing down at three tiny insects scurrying around his feet.

I suddenly realized why Talon allowed him his...idiosyncrasies, as Mr. Roth put it. Who would dare to tell him no?

"Well." The deep voice reverberated through the cavern like thunder, making the walls tremble. "Here you are, then." Reign pulled himself to his full impressive height, dwarfing everything in the cavern as he stretched, before sinking back and curling his tail around himself. His scales, like antique coins, glittered as he lowered his head to regard me with a blood-chilling smile. "Welcome to my casino," he continued, giving me a clear, terrifying view of his fangs. "I trust the accommodations are acceptable?"

He was talking to me, I realized, not my trainer or Mr. Roth. Which struck me as very odd. Why would one of the most powerful dragons in Talon take the time to address me and not my superiors?

Be polite, Mr. Roth had said. Always a good plan when staring down an eighty-foot dragon who could swallow you in one bite. "Yes, sir," I managed, grateful that my voice didn't shake. "You've been more than accommodating. Thank you for seeing us on such short notice. Your hotel is very impressive."

Reign sniffed, but he seemed pleased. "I see they've trained you well," he rumbled, and raised his head to observe the other dragons, standing patiently to either side. "Though I wouldn't have expected anything else. But I have little time for pleasantries. Let us talk business."

His eyes glittered, and he folded his front claws before him like a cat, the curved talons lightly raking the floor. "So the other little hatchling has run away," he said, sounding amused and impatient at the same time. "And now, you think she is somewhere in my city." He snorted, sending a billow of smoke into the air. "I find that highly unlikely. Nothing happens here without my knowledge. No one comes or goes unless I know about it. I have eyes in almost every casino, every hotel on and off the Strip." He angled a horn at the bank of screens surrounding him. "If this girl has entered my territory, what makes you think she can hide from me?"

"She's not alone, Reign." Mr. Roth's voice was cool as he stepped forward, though I noted he didn't stare directly at the other dragon but kept his gaze off to the side. "We believe she is with a former Basilisk operative who went rogue several years ago. He knows about you. He would know which hotels to avoid, and in which areas you might not have as large a presence." Reign's gold eyes narrowed dangerously, showing his obvious displeasure with the contradiction, though Mr. Roth did not relent. "He'll know how to stay hidden and out of sight, even from you."

Reign growled, not loudly, but I felt the vibrations through the cement. "A rogue Basilisk," the dragon king mused, tapping his claws against the floor. "I've heard of this upstart, Cobalt." His voice took on an annoyed edge. "I suppose he is also the reason St. George has suddenly appeared in my city?"

"Yes. We believe the Order is searching for them, as well."

Reign's nostrils flared. "So why should I risk exposure when the Order is swarming around out there, thanks to your wayward agent?" he asked. "Helping you with your rogue problem could expose my operations to St. George.

I've avoided the Order for a very, very long time. I intend to keep it that way."

My stomach turned. Ember was close, I could feel it. We were in the same city, the same territory. I just had to reach her before St. George did. Or before she left town with the rogue, and we were back at square one. Determination rose up, and I took a deep breath. I could not let anyone, even the ruler of Las Vegas, put my sister or my plans in danger.

"Sir," I began, and Reign peered down at me in amused surprise. I felt Mr. Smith's incredulous gaze on me as well and knew I was probably breaking protocol, a hatchling daring to contradict an ancient Wyrm. This was a gamble, but it was too late to back out now. I faced the ancient dragon, keeping my voice calm. "Forgive me, sir, but it's in your best interests to help," I said evenly. "You have a lot of resources at your disposal, and the sooner we find Ember, the sooner you can get St. George out of your city. Surely that is enough reason to assist us."

Reign cocked his massive head, the hint of a smile crossing his muzzle. "Is that so, hatchling?" he mused in a soft, deadly voice, making a cold sweat break out on my neck. "You're awfully confident about that."

"She's my sister," I replied. "No one knows her like I do." Those primeval eyes continued to watch me, unblinking, and I stifled my fear. "I just need to find her. If I knew where she was, I could reach her. I can bring her back to Talon."

"The boy has a point, Reign," Mr. Roth broke in. I wanted to glance at him but didn't dare take my attention from the Wyrm glaring down at me. "Once we retrieve Ms. Hill and deal with the rogue, the Order will have no reason to stay in

Vegas. They will leave, we will return to the organization, and your assistance will be much appreciated once it gets back to the Elder Wyrm."

"I'm sure it will." Reign hadn't looked away from me the entire time. "But let me ask you this, little hatchling. Let us say your sister is truly lost, that she refuses to return to the organization. What then?"

I swallowed, realizing he was testing me, seeing how far I would go. "Everyone has something that they want, sir," I replied. "Everyone has a price that they are willing to pay. Ember is with the rogue dragon, Cobalt, and even he has weaknesses. If we can find them, exploit them, we'll have them both."

Reign blew out a long, rumbling breath, filling the air with the smell of sulfur. "Spoken like a true dragon of Talon. Very well," he growled, and shifted upright, making my pulse skip at how big he really was. "I have several agents who might be able to track them down. One in particular has been very helpful, keeping eyes on the parts of the city I cannot. I'll have my people contact him. If the hatchling and the rogue *are* here, he'll know where to look." The tip of his tail thumped the ground, and he blinked slowly. "Will that be sufficient enough for you, Mr. Hill?"

Again, he wasn't looking at Mr. Roth, but at me. I bowed my head, letting gratitude seep into my voice. "Yes, sir," I said. "Thank you, sir. Talon will not forget this."

"I'm sure they won't." He shook his massive head. "Though I might have to have a talk with the Elder Wyrm about too-clever hatchlings who overstep their bounds. I assume you have a plan for dealing with this girl and the rogue, once you find them?"

My mind was already spinning. Bring Ember back, and make sure the rogue could never take her away again. That was all that mattered. Talon was watching me; I would not fail them. "Yes," I answered, setting my jaw. "I do."

RILEY

Come on, you bastard, I thought, glaring at my phone. *You know we're here. Text me back already.*

The device in my hand remained obnoxiously silent. Sighing, I shoved it into my jacket pocket and tried not to pace, feeling time ticking away from me. At least the room was large, airy and luxurious, though a bit on the gaudy side. I could've done without the shiny gold curtains and bright purple carpet. And the painting of the barely clad Greek woman lounging by a pool.

I snorted in derision. *Caesar's Palace, it ain't.* This wasn't a casino the high rollers and professional gamblers would set foot in, or come within a hundred yards of, really. Which suited me fine. No one from Talon—no one important, at least—would be caught dead here. And I wouldn't have to share the queen-size bed with anyone else; Ember was in the room next door and the other two—Wes and the soldier— had their own individual quarters across the hall. Money had never been an issue; during the years I'd worked for the organization, I'd racked up quite the nest egg. When I had gone rogue, those accounts had been frozen, but not even Talon's security was a match for Wes after he joined my team. The

money was now hidden in overseas accounts under false identities so that Talon couldn't trace it back to us. Not to mention, having an elite hacker around was pretty helpful for
those times I needed *other* things: bank codes, fake IDs, false
reservations and the like. Most times, I didn't even have to
touch my own accounts.

Now, if only my other contact would be as helpful.

As if on cue, my phone finally buzzed. I yanked it out
and stared at the message on-screen, short and to the point. I
smiled grimly. Time to get to the bottom of things, or at least
have some questions answered. Making sure I had my wallet and fake ID, I left the room and stepped into the green-
and-gold corridor.

I met Wes in the hallway, bottle of Mountain Dew in hand
as he headed back to his room. "Griffin finally get back to
you?" he asked, lowering his voice as he paused beside me.
I nodded.

"Heading down to meet him now. Where are the others?"

"In their rooms, last I saw them." Wes pointed the green
bottle down the corridor. "One sulking, the other doing bug-
ger all. Hope the blasted hatchling doesn't wander off. She
looked quite put out when you told her not to leave the floor."

I groaned inwardly. Boredom and following orders were
two things that Ember did not excel at. And below us was an
entire casino full of flashing lights, games, shiny objects and
other things that could tempt a curious dragon.

"Keep an eye on them," I said. "Make sure Ember stays
put, but watch the soldier, too. He might've broken from the
Order, but he's still St. George, and that will never change.
If he moves or leaves the room, I want to know about it."

Wes smiled grimly. "Want me to stick a bug in his lamp when he's asleep?"

"No." I shook my head. "I doubt he's in contact with the Order. They're hunting him now, same as us. But if he goes off alone, or gets within twenty feet of Ember, let me know. If everything is too quiet, let me know. Hell, if the St. George bastard sneezes or takes a piss, let me know. I have no idea why he's still hanging around, but if he stays with us much longer, I want to know what I'm dealing with, and why."

"Fabulous," Wes muttered. "Thirteen years of being the best hacker in this circus, and now I'm a bloody babysitter." He sniffed and took a quick swig from his bottle before ducking his head and lowering his voice even further. "Where are the guns, if you don't mind my asking?"

"In my room, of course. You think I'm going to let St. George anywhere near them?" The black duffel was sitting inconspicuously beside my bed, two 9 mms and a Glock wrapped neatly in my clothes. The do-not-disturb sign already hung from my doorknob, and I intended to keep it there. The last thing I needed was a curious maid tripping over a bag full of guns, but it would be worse if I was caught wandering the casino floor with an unlicensed firearm. Even in a place like this, security was trained to look for and spot anyone concealing a deadly weapon, not to mention the thousands of cameras watching your every move from the ceiling. Which meant I wasn't going to be armed while I was here. But at least the soldier wouldn't be carrying, either.

"I'm off," I said, stepping away from Wes. "Call me if the room explodes."

"You know, that'd be funny if I wasn't terrified it could actually happen."

Smirking, I entered the elevator and descended into the madness.

As usual, the casino floor was a chaotic sea of milling people, garish lights and clanging bells. Slot machines stood in endless rows throughout the room, blue-haired old ladies and men in suits alike feeding coins or cards into the machines with glassy-eyed determination. Crowds of men and women clustered around roulette tables, cheering wildly or groaning in turns. Dealers flipped cards at blackjack tables, smoothly picking away at players' stacks of chips until there was nothing left. *Humans and their wealth*, I thought with equal amounts of pity and disdain as I maneuvered through the crowds. *You fight and kill and work so hard to get it, only to throw it away like it's nothing. I'll never understand.*

I finally spotted the person I was looking for at a blackjack table in the corner, sitting calmly with his hands resting against the lip. A dark-skinned human in a bright red suit, matching hat perched atop his head. His gaze was riveted to the pair of cards in front of him: three of spades and nine of clubs. Crossing my arms, I leaned against a nearby column to watch. The human in the red suit tapped the table edge. The dealer flipped a card, a five of clubs, bringing the total to seventeen. The human paused, then very deliberately tapped the table again. The dealer flipped one more, turning up a five of hearts. Twenty-two and bust.

The man in the suit sniffed, rose from the chair and turned to face me.

"You threw that hand," I said. "You knew perfectly well it was going to go over."

He gave me a brilliant smile. "Oh, sure, please announce it to the whole casino," he said in a low voice, holding my gaze and grinning the entire time. His gold tooth glimmered in the artificial lights. "Blackjack isn't really my thing, but since I was meeting you tonight, I figured I didn't have time for an honest game of Texas Hold'em. Funny thing about blackjack, though. Win too often, and they start watching you. Keep winning, and they'll accuse you of card counting, which is perfectly legal in the grand state of Nevada and will get you banned from every casino on and off the Strip for life. That's the number-one rule in this town. The House always wins. Always." He continued to smile, but it had an edge now, and the eyes above the teeth were hard. "So I'd be ever so grateful if some cocky lizard didn't blow my cover and force me to change identities again. Now, laugh, you son of a bitch, like I said something hilarious."

He threw back his head and bellowed with laughter. I managed a chuckle, shaking my head. "Haven't changed at all, have you, Griffin?"

"Only my name," he responded with another grin, this one genuine. "And my face. And my personality. Helping *you*, if I remember. And I'm about to do it again, aren't I?"

"Who's the guy who got you out in the first place?"

"Touché." He gave me a rueful look. "What do you need, Riley?"

I shot a brief, wary glance at the numerous black globes on the ceiling, the cameras watching our every move. "Is this a safe place to talk?"

"Not in the slightest," he replied cheerfully. "Do you need a drink? I feel like I need a drink. Come on."

And he started across the casino floor, weaving through the crowds like he'd done it all his life. I followed him, keeping a wary eye out for anyone who might be watching. No one seemed to pay us any attention, except casino security, who eyed my dusty boots and black leather jacket with the same bored suspicion as they did everyone else. Clearly, they'd seen far stranger. Or thought they had, anyway.

We left the casino floor, and ducked into a crowded restaurant with dim lighting and dozens of flat screens lining the walls, all playing sports of various kinds. Humans sat like pigeons along the bar or clustered around tables, laughing, talking and oblivious to the world around them. Griffin and I took a booth in the corner. A group of college-age guys sat behind us, but with all the noise and chaos, I wasn't worried about eavesdroppers. The waitress took our drink orders and hurried off, leaving us in peace.

Griffin eyed me over the table. "So," the human began, folding his hands together. "Here we are. What brings you to Vegas, Riley?"

I sighed. "What do you think?"

"Hmm. Well, considering all the hubbub around the city of late, I'm guessing nothing good. I assume *you're* the reason St. George has moved in recently?" Griffin went on, making my stomach tighten. "Seems like they're on the warpath, and mighty pissed about something. Word on the street is that Talon is not happy with the Order being in their territory and are scrambling over each other trying to figure out what's going on. I'm thinking you poked a stick down a wasp nest and stirred it up a bit. Then kicked it for good measure."

"You could say that." I paused as the waitress returned with our drinks, then tossed the alcohol back, finishing the Scotch in two swallows. I didn't drink very often; it was tough to get a dragon wasted, even one in human form, so I didn't see much point in it. Tonight, though, I'd make an exception. Griffin drank his bourbon slowly, watching me over the glass rim, waiting for an explanation. I gave him a faint smirk. "Someone might have...snuck into their western chapterhouse and broken a prisoner out last week."

"Holy shit, Riley." The human lowered his glass with a look of disbelief and horror. "The Order chapterhouse itself? So, what you're telling me is you've gone insane."

"Very likely," I muttered.

"One of your hatchlings?"

"No." I scrubbed a hand through my hair. "One of *them*."

He stared at me, then used both hands to point at himself. "Okay, see this face? This is my what-the-hell face. Seriously, Riley. What. The. Hell. You snuck into enemy territory, dropped a figurative wasp down their pants and then brought that mess *here*, so I have to deal with it? Are you out of your freaking mind? *Why* would you do such a thing?"

"It's...complicated." He continued to give me his what-the-hell expression, and I scowled. "Look, I don't need you to understand or approve of what I did. What I need is to know why my safe houses keep disappearing, and how St. George suddenly knows *exactly* who I am and where I'll be. If there's a mole in the network, I want to know about it. And I need to find out what Talon is up to, where they are, if they know

I'm here. Think you can grease a couple palms and dig up some dirt for me?"

"On Talon *and* the Order?" Griffin scratched his eyebrows. "Probably, but it could take some time. I'm going to have to be very, very careful about whom I talk to."

"Please. I know the kind of people you work with. I don't think you have to do too much greasing. If they need incentive, you know I'm good for it."

He sniffed and sipped his drink. "Actually," he mused, looking thoughtful, "there is this one thing that came up recently. Something I heard just this morning, in fact."

I rubbed my eyes. "That didn't take long."

"Oh, trust me. You'll want to hear this." He paused as the waitress returned, asking if we needed anything else, and waved her off with a smile. "I don't know how credible the story is," he went on, "but my contacts seemed to think it's legit. It's actually quite amusing. Apparently, some poor bastard saw *something* in an abandoned hotel that freaked him out of his mind. A 'fucking huge lizard' I believe were his exact words."

I straightened quickly. "A runaway hatchling?"

"They seemed to think so." Griffin shrugged, swirling the ice in his glass. "I can't do anything about it, of course, but this sounds like the type of thing you'd be interested in. Might be worth checking out."

"Dammit." I sighed, knowing I couldn't ignore this. "Fine, send me the info. I'll check it out when I can. It's not like I have a million other things to do, like keeping Talon *and* St. George off our backs." I glared at him over the table. "This place is still off their sights for the time being, right?"

"Of course, idiot. You think I'd be here if it wasn't?" Griffin rose, tugging his suit jacket into place. "Give me a couple days," he said. "I'll see what I can find. And for God's sake, don't try to contact me until then. I'll call you."

I smirked. "Don't keep me waiting too long. Wouldn't want some cocky lizard sitting down at your table and ruining your perfect game, would we?"

"You're a bastard, Riley." Griffin gave me his most brilliant smile yet and turned to leave. "Thanks for the drink. Tell Wes I said hello."

I paid for the drinks and wandered back upstairs, hoping nothing had exploded while I was gone. And that a certain stubborn redhead had stayed put, or at least out of trouble.

Apparently, that was too much to hope for.

As the elevator doors opened and I stepped into the hallway, I caught sight of Ember's lean, slight form slipping across the hall and into the room on the other side.

EMBER

Nice place. Too bad it was driving me nuts.

The room was too quiet, too empty and still despite the paintings of naked Greek people on the walls and the bust of some square-jawed guy staring at me from the corner. Now that we could finally slow down enough to breathe, there was nothing to keep me distracted, no life-threatening situations to divert my attention. I flipped on the television, just for the noise, but that didn't stop all the images shifting around in my head. Memories I couldn't shut out. Everything that had happened in the past two weeks flooded my brain in a rush, pounding against me like waves. I could see the red dragon hide hanging on the wall of the St. George office, a lifeless trophy that had once been a hatchling like me. I remembered the look in Garret's eyes as he'd stared at me through the bars of his cell as if I were a ghost. The memory of his skin under my palm, his fingers curled gently around my wrist. The flight across the desert with him on my back, and that red-hot blaze of pain as the bullet had slammed into my body.

The enemy soldier, crumpling to the floor of the abandoned house, glassy eyes staring back at me. And Lilith's voice, telling me I was born to become a Viper, a killer like her.

Shivering, I rose from the bed and walked to the window, gazing down at the city. Las Vegas sparkled with a million neon lights, massive hotels and casinos standing tall and glowing against the horizon. Talon's territory. Going rogue hadn't been what I'd thought it would be. Riley hadn't mentioned this part—the running, the fear, being chased and shot and having to kill to survive. If I'd known what would happen after I'd left Crescent Beach, would I still have chosen to go with him?

Of course you would. A little voice, my dragon, perhaps, sneered in my head. *You know yourself better than that. Riley made it very clear what being rogue was like—you heard exactly what you wanted to hear. And if you had to do it again, knowing what you do right now, your choice would be the same. You're too stubborn for anything else.*

Angrily, I stalked back to the bed and flopped down again, putting a pillow over my face. I wouldn't regret my decision. I'd seen the dark side of Talon, knew what they really wanted, beneath the facade of "protecting our kind." And I refused to be a part of it. I just wished I could talk to someone, sort out these crazy, unfamiliar emotions that tried to drown me whenever I was in my own head. I wished I had someone here, just so I wouldn't be alone. Not the boys. They were part of the dilemma, part of the chaotic, confusing mess inside me. I couldn't talk to them.

I wished...

I wished Dante were here.

Dante betrayed you. I didn't know which voice this was, mine or the dragon's. But it continued with ruthless logic and disdain. *He sold you out to Talon. Lilith would've killed you and Riley that night, because Dante told her where you'd be.*

"No," I growled into my pillow. My throat felt tight, and I swallowed hard. "He didn't know what she would do. Talon lied to him, just like they lied to me, and everyone. It wasn't his fault."

Great, now I was talking to myself. Nothing crazy here. Throwing off the pillow, I stood once more and gazed aimlessly around the room. Everything was unfamiliar, and even with the television babbling, the silence seemed to press down on me. A lump caught in my throat. I was homesick, I realized. I missed my friends, my town and my old life.

I missed my brother.

"Dammit," I whispered, and felt my eyes prickle. I wanted Dante back. I wanted him to be with me, on the side of the rogues and away from Talon. Talon was using him, like they did everyone in the organization. I wished I could tell him, right now. All Talon's dirty laundry, all their secrets, the true price of staying with the organization. Dante needed to hear it. If he only knew the truth, he would never stay with them.

Maybe I *could* tell him, somehow.

Hope flickered, and I paused to think. I didn't dare call him; if Talon was looking for us, they'd be watching my brother closely, maybe even tapping his phone. The same went for texting and email. The organization had eyes everywhere; normal methods of reaching my brother could put us all in danger. Me, Garret, Riley and all the rogues under his watch. I wasn't going to risk that.

But, there *was* someone who was an expert at getting past Talon's radar unseen.

I crossed my room and opened the door a crack, peeking out. The long corridor was empty. I was probably being overcautious; Riley had said this hotel was safe enough, from Talon at least. But if there were strange humans wandering about who looked like they might be armed, I wanted to see them before they saw me.

Slipping out, I took three steps across the green-and-gold carpet and knocked on the door across from mine.

A moment later, it swung back, revealing Wes's haggard, unkempt face. His shaggy hazel bangs hung in his eyes, and his jaw and mouth were lined with stubble. He scowled when he saw me, clearly expecting someone else—probably Riley.

"Oh, it's you." His gaze flicked up and down the hall before returning to me. "What do you want?"

"Hey, Wes. I have a question." I offered a smile, making an attempt to be friendly. I knew Wes didn't like me, but maybe I could change his opinion. He just stared blankly, and I sighed. "Can I come in? I don't want to talk out in the open."

"Bloody hell," Wes muttered, but he stepped back, letting me cross the threshold into his room. It was much like mine, gold curtains, queen bed, pictures of Greek people in compromising positions on the wall. His bag had been tossed on the bed and forgotten about, but his computer sat open and glowing on the desktop.

Wes shut the door and turned to watch me with wary eyes. "Well?" he demanded as I hesitated, wondering how to convince him. "Whatever this is, can you make it quick? I really don't have time to faff around with hatchlings right now."

"Faff around?"

"What's the bloody emergency?" Wes snapped. I took a

deep breath, wondering how best to put it, then decided on the direct approach.

"I want to get a message to my brother."

The human's eyebrows shot into his hair. "Your brother," he repeated in disbelief. "I'm sorry, you mean the bloke who sold us out to Talon? Are you off your rocker? You want to let Talon know exactly where we are?"

"He didn't sell us out," I snapped back. "Talon lied to him. He didn't know what would happen when he told Lilith where we were. He didn't know she would try to kill us." Wes gave me a look of supreme disbelief, and I narrowed my eyes. "I know Dante. I've known him all my life. He wouldn't willingly do anything that would put me in danger. Talon used him, like they used all of us."

"Be that as it may," Wes said, "he's still part of the organization, or have you forgotten they're the ones sending Vipers after us? Even if your brother is being manipulated, it doesn't change anything. Talon will still use him to get to us. So, sorry, can't help you there. I like our status as is — alive and breathing."

Anger and despair rose up, and my chest squeezed tight. Half of me wanted to threaten the stubborn human before me with fire and fangs, the other half knew he was right, that he was only protecting himself and the rest of us. But still, Dante was my twin, my only family. I knew Talon didn't approve of such things; the organization was our "family," and we weren't supposed to need attachments to anything, or anyone, else. But growing up, it had always been me and Dante against the world. I wouldn't abandon him, even if he had turned his back on me in favor of Talon.

"Please," I said quietly, making the human blink. "Wes, please. He's my brother. I don't know what's happened to him, if he's okay, if Talon is making him do something awful." Wes thinned his lips, looking annoyed but hesitant, and I pressed forward earnestly. "I won't tell him where we are," I promised. "Or give him any information that can be traced back to us. I just need to know if he's all right."

Wes sighed. "Even if I wanted to do this," he said in a softer voice, "which I *don't*, let's make that very clear—I'm not going to risk it without Riley's approval. You haven't really seen the blighter lose his temper yet, and as I am not fireproof, I'm not going to sneak around behind his back. You'll have to take that request up with him."

"Fine," I said, backing toward the door. "Then I'll find him and ask him myself."

"Ask me what?"

I whirled. Riley stood in the doorway, watching us, and my dragon perked at his arrival. "Everything all right?" he asked, his amber gaze flicking past me to Wes, then narrowing slightly. "What are you doing in here?"

Wes snorted before I could answer. "Bloody hatchling wanted me to send a message to her brother," he replied, already back at his computer. I scowled at him over my shoulder, but his eyes were on the screen. "I told her that before she brought the whole of Talon and St. George down on our heads, she'd have to take it up with you."

"Ember." Riley's voice, furious and horrified, made my stomach clench. I quickly moved back as he stepped through the frame and swiftly closed the door, glaring at me. "Tell me you didn't try to contact Dante," he growled, backing me into the room. "Do you want the organization to know exactly where we are? Do you *want* to wake up surrounded by Vipers? What were you thinking?"

"He's my brother!" I protested.

"He's part of the organization!" Riley shot back. "He was in direct contact with Lilith herself. Did you not learn your lesson last time? You gave him a choice—Talon or blood—and he chose Talon. He'll do it again if given the chance."

"I don't believe that." The tightness in my throat was back, and the corners of my eyes stung. I'd already had this argument with Wes, but it was harder with Riley. "I don't believe Dante would willingly hurt me," I said, steadying myself under his accusing glare. "I think Talon is using him, and he doesn't understand who they are, or what they're capable of. If I could just reach him, make him see—"

"How?" Riley demanded, stepping forward. "What are you going to say? How do you think you're going to convince him?" He poked his chest, glaring at me. "I've been on the inside, I know how the organization works. Every second he's there, Talon's influence on him gets stronger. They'll smile and pat his back and promise that he's doing the right thing, that this is for the good of us all, and he'll believe them. He'll accept everything they say without question, because *they* believe it, too. And even if you could somehow change his mind, how do you think you're going to get him out? He's too deep within the organization to risk contact." Riley shook his head, giving me an exasperated smirk. "I'm *not* storming Talon headquarters, Firebrand, even for you."

I briefly closed my eyes against the angry stinging. "He's my brother," I said once more, raising my chin to stare Riley down. "I won't give up on him. There has to be a way. And if you won't help me, then I'll do it myself."

"Ember," Riley began, but I brushed past him and stalked from the room. He didn't understand. He didn't have a sibling. None of them did. Dante and I were the only pair that had been raised together, the only dragon siblings in existence. Riley couldn't understand because he didn't have one, but Dante was family. Talon couldn't have him.

"Dammit, Firebrand. Hold up."

Strong fingers grabbed my wrist just outside the door, halting my angry storm-out. Bristling, I tried yanking out of his grasp, but Riley pulled me back into the room with him and slammed the door behind us.

"Just wait a second," he snapped, but I was full-on pissed now and punched him in the arm. "Ow! Will you stop? Listen to me." Grabbing my arms, he pinned me against the door, glaring down with angry gold eyes. My instincts flared, rising to the challenge, nearly bursting through my skin as he shoved me back. I barely clamped down on the impulse to Shift right then and pounce on the dragon in front of me.

Riley took a deep breath, as if he, too, was struggling to hold his dragon down. "Look, I'm sorry about Dante," he said. "But we can't help him right now. We can barely help ourselves. If you try contacting him now and Talon finds out where we are, we'll be dead. Even if he doesn't give our location away, the organization will be monitoring his every move, because he's connected to *you*. They're watching him, Firebrand. They know Dante is their way to you, and if they find you, they find all of us. I do not want to wake up in the middle of the night surrounded by Vipers." His fingers gripped me tighter, his face intense. "It's too dangerous to send Dante any kind of message, Ember. Promise me you won't try to contact him."

Defiance rose, egged on by the dragon, the surging heat inside. Of course, he was right, but... "I'm getting him out, Riley," I said, meeting that intense gaze, almost seeing Cobalt peering out at me. "One way or another. I can't leave him there."

"I know, Firebrand. I do understand. Trust me, I would take them all away from Talon if I could." Riley straightened, sliding his hands up my arms. "But slow down for me a little. I know you want to save the world, but there are only three of us. We can't take on Talon, or St. George, by ourselves. We'd need an army for that, and they're not just lying around for the taking." One hand rose to the side of my face, brushing a curl aside with his thumb. "Just trust me a little longer, okay? Let's figure out where we're going, what we're doing next, before we go charging the organization's front door. Can you do that, without burning the hotel down in the meantime?"

I swallowed, then took a slow breath. It didn't cool the heat of the wild surging flames within. "I guess so," I muttered, relinquishing the fight for now. He exhaled in relief, and I gave him a faint smirk. "Though I can't promise not to set anything on fire, especially if St. George kicks my door down."

Riley grimaced. "At least there are extinguishers by all the exits," he said, rolling his eyes. "I can see the headlines now, though. Vegas Casino Mysteriously Ignites on Twelfth Floor. Strange Creatures Seen Flying out Window. That wouldn't catch Talon's attention at all." He shook his head. "You certainly keep my life interesting, Firebrand."

"You love it. Just think how boring life would be without me."

A grin tugged at one corner of his mouth. "My old trainer gave me a bit of advice once," he said. "Not that I listened to his ramblings most of the time, but this one stuck out. He said, 'A flame that burns twice as bright lasts half as long.' Any idea what that means?"

"Um. That you're a secret philosopher who writes poetry between car heists and jailbreaks?" I guessed.

He snorted. "Normally I don't break out the metaphorical crap, but I thought I'd make an exception." One hand rose, knuckles very lightly brushing my cheek, searing and tingly. My heart leaped, and warmth bloomed through my stomach. "You remind me of that flame, Firebrand," Riley murmured. "You burn so hot, and so bright, you set everything around you on fire. And you don't even realize what you're doing."

"I'm a dragon," I said, trying to catch my breath. He was so close; part of me wanted to pull away, though my back was still against the door and there was nowhere to go except through Riley. The other half wanted to step closer, to press my body against his until our combined heat became an inferno. "I'm supposed to set things on fire. What's the point in lighting a candle if you're going to hide it away so it doesn't help anything?" His brows arched, and I grinned. "Ha, see? I can be philosophical, too."

Riley's smile turned grim. "Just be careful that the people around you don't get singed," he said in a low voice. "Or that you don't burn too hot, too quickly. The brightest flames are usually the ones that are extinguished first." His eyes went dark for a moment. "I know what I'm talking about, Ember. I've seen it before. I don't want that to happen to you."

"It won't," I promised.

He paused, as if he wanted to say something more but thought better of it. For a moment, we stared at each other, both our dragons very close to the surface. Riley's fingers still gripped my arms; I could feel the heat of his body as he stood there, gazing down at me.

Wes cleared his throat, very loudly, from the corner.

Riley blinked, as if just realizing where he was, what he was doing, and let me go. Disappointment rose up, but what surprised me was the fact that I didn't know whose it was, mine or the dragon's.

"It's been a long day. Get some rest." Riley didn't look at me again as he turned and walked toward Wes. For a second, I had the crazy urge to grab him and pull him back, but he stepped out of my reach and the moment was lost. "Go watch TV, or download a movie or something. Order room service if you want. We're not going to be doing anything tonight."

I wrinkled my nose at his back. "How long are we going to be staying here?"

"Until I figure out what's going on with the Order." Riley reached the back of Wes's seat and peered at the screen over his shoulder. "And when I decide that it's safe to move out," he added. "Until then, we sit tight. Stay in your room. Don't go down to the casino floor. There are cameras everywhere and according to my contact, St. George is on the warpath and Talon is pretty pissed, too. It's a good idea to lie as low as we can right now. Think you can do that, Firebrand?"

"I'll try not to set the room on fire," I promised, and

walked out of the room. But as the door clicked behind me, I paused. Going back to my silent, empty room with only the television for company sounded depressing. I could stay in Wes's room, but the human didn't want me there, and besides, I wasn't sure I could face Riley again. My dragon was still writhing and coiling beneath my skin, frustrated at being contained. If I went back in there, I might really break my promise about not setting things on fire.

Spinning around, I crossed the carpet to the door right beside Wes's. Garret's room. Putting my ear to the wood, I listened for movement, voices from the television, anything to tell me he was awake, but there was only silence. I hesitated a moment, then tapped softly on the wood.

"Garret? Are you in there?"

Nothing happened. No footsteps shuffled toward me, no movement, sound, or voice came from the other side. The door stayed firmly closed. I hovered in the frame a moment, debating whether or not I should try again, louder this time. But if he was asleep, or worse, ignoring me on purpose, I really didn't want to disturb him.

Finally, I turned around and padded back to my door, feeling restless, lonely and slightly depressed. My room was quiet, and though the city twinkled and bustled outside the window, never still, the silence on this side of the glass made me feel very alone. I showered, turned up the television for noise and spent a good ten minutes figuring out how to order room service from the kitchen downstairs. When the food came I scarfed down the slightly overcooked burger in less than a minute, not having realized how ravenous I was until the first bite.

I guess gun battles and car chases work up quite the appetite. Not to mention nearly being shot to death.

My stomach turned, and my appetite vanished as quickly as it had come. Shivering, I left the fries to harden on the tray and crawled beneath the covers of the huge bed, pulling the quilt over my face. Curling into myself, I listened to the babble of the television filling the suffocating quiet, wishing I could just turn off my brain for a few hours. Garret, Dante and Riley all crowded my mind, each pulling at different emotions until I was a tangled knot of feeling inside. I finally drifted off, but kept jerking awake throughout the night as their faces, and the face of the man I'd killed, continued to chase me through my dreams.

RILEY

"You've gone mad for the girl, haven't you?" Wes remarked.

I glared at him from across the room. He sat on the bed with his computer in his lap, finishing off his bottle of soda. Lowering his arm, he raised a shaggy eyebrow at my expression.

"Don't try to deny it, mate." He gestured at me with the bottle, sending a spatter of Mountain Dew across the white bedcover. "I saw the two of you in the doorway, and you were a half second away from a full-on snog fest."

"Dragons don't 'snog,' idiot."

"Oh, sod off. You know what I mean." Wes shook his head, half closing his laptop to stare at me over the lid. "You're losing it, Riley," he said. "Ever since that bloody hatchling crashed into our affairs, your priorities have been screwed to hell and back. For Christ's sake, we have a bloody soldier of St. George following us around! I still don't know why you haven't told the blighter to shove off."

"He's useful," I argued. "Since he's here, I figured we might as well take advantage of having the enemy with us. If we can get him to give up secrets about the Order—"

"Bull. Crap." Wes glared at me. "That's not the reason

and you bloody well know it's not. Don't lie to me, Riley. I've known you too long for that." He narrowed his eyes, his scruffy jaw tightening in anger. "It's because of *her*. Everything we've done, everything that's happened to us since Crescent Beach, is because of her. And now we're holed up here, with Talon *and* St. George on our tail, and you're making promises you have no way of keeping. Dangerous promises. Promises that will get us all killed. If anyone else suggested we contact someone in the organization, you would've either laughed in their face and told them to sod off, or punched their bloody lights out."

"I have no intention of sending Ember's traitor brother any kind of message," I said, rolling my eyes. "So you can relax. I didn't promise her anything, and I'm sure as hell not giving that Talon clone another chance to turn us in. Once was enough."

"You're missing the point, mate." Wes rubbed the bridge of his nose, sounding tired. "Listen to what you just said. Once was enough?" He shook his head. "It should never have come to that. You *knew* that brother of hers was bad news. You knew he would sell us out to Talon, and you still let her go back for him. And what happened? Fucking Lilith, the organization's best Viper assassin, tracked you down and nearly killed you both. Because that hatchling has you so twisted around her little claw, you don't know which way is up anymore."

I took a breath to cool the sudden rise of heat in my lungs. "How about I worry about running this circus, and you worry about keeping enemy forces from sneaking in the back door?" I suggested in a flat voice. "What I do with Ember is none of your business."

"It's my sodding business if it gets us all killed!"

"I've protected this underground for years!" I snapped in return. "Before Ember even knew what a human was, I've been fighting to get my kind out of Talon. I've worked for it, bled for it, nearly died for it more times than I can count. I'm not going to throw that away, and I'm certainly not going to lose it now. You should know me better than that."

Wes slumped against the pillow. "I know," he murmured. "I know you'd do anything to keep those kids safe, just like I'd do anything to screw with Talon and throw a wrench into their plans for world domination, or whatever it is they're planning. But I've never seen you like this, mate. We've worked too hard to build this underground, to get dragons out of the organization, to weaken Talon however we can. I just want to be certain your priorities are still the same."

"No," I said, making him frown. "Weakening Talon, screwing with their plans, plotting to overthrow the evil empire, that's always been *your* objective. One more hatchling that I get out of Talon is one less dragon they can use in the future. *I* go after hatchlings because I want my kind to be free. *You* go after them because you have this crazy notion that someday Talon will fall because of us. Because of what we're doing right now."

"Everyone has their dreams, mate." Wes's voice was low, his eyes hard. "I know you don't believe it will happen, that Talon is too big, but I've seen giants crumble and empires brought down. It has to start somewhere. And if you don't think that what we're doing now will matter, even if it's beyond our lifetimes, then what is the bloody point of all this?"

An ominous beep from his laptop interrupted us. Wes

jumped and pushed the lid back, bending low. His fingers flew across the keyboard as he hunched forward, his nose only a few inches from the screen, brow furrowed in concentration. I moved up beside him, feeling tense and slightly sick, hoping that alarm didn't mean what I feared it would.

"What happened?"

Wes's fingers froze. His face blanched, and he slumped back against the headboard with a hollow thump. His face was blank with resignation as he looked up, and I knew what he would say before he opened his mouth.

"We've lost another nest. St. George is moving in."

GARRET

Why am I still here?

I tilted my face to the hot stream of water, letting it pound my forehead and sluice around me, trying to drown the question that had been plaguing my mind for the past three days. The water ran into my ears, muffling all sound, to no avail. I was used to long periods of inactivity, waiting for orders or for missions to begin, but I couldn't escape my own thoughts.

This afternoon had passed in silence; television had no appeal, and since I wasn't allowed to leave the floor, I'd leafed through random travel magazines or just lain on my bed, staring at the ceiling. Finally, needing to do *something*, I'd spent the rest of the afternoon working out in my room, pushing my body to the limits of its endurance, hoping that fatigue, at least, would provide a much-needed distraction. But the second I'd walked into the shower, it returned. The whisper that still haunted me, that nagging sensation of uncertainty and doubt, when before I'd always been so confident. Why was I still here? Why was I, a former soldier of St. George, choosing to remain in the company of dragons? I wasn't a prisoner; though the rogue dragon hated me—with good reason—he wouldn't try to stop me if I walked out the hotel door and vanished into the night. On more than one occasion, he'd encouraged me to do just that.

So why hadn't I?

The obvious answer—because the Order was hunting me—was a stall at best. I was resourceful enough to evade their notice for a while. And while St. George paid their soldiers only a small stipend each month, they also provided us with everything we needed, so I had a sizable amount sitting in an account I rarely touched. It wouldn't last forever, but it was enough to start over, to begin a new life.

The real question was: Could I pass for normal? I'd lived my whole life within Order walls, only venturing out when there were dragons to be slain. I had little experience of the real world beyond that brief summer in Crescent Beach and, truthfully, with no one giving me commands, telling me where to go, I felt slightly lost. My existence until now had been habit and structure and routine—the life of a soldier—and I'd welcomed that order, knowing exactly who I was. Left to my own devices, I felt I was wandering aimlessly, waiting for something to happen.

But fear, even fear of the unknown, had never stopped me before. I didn't need a command to walk away, to leave my strange new companions behind, to fade into anonymity. I was a trained soldier, and survival was one of my strong suits; even with a price on my head, I could manage the real world if I had to. What was stopping me?

With a sigh, I placed my palms against the tile wall and bowed my head, letting the water beat my shoulders and run down my skin. I knew the answer, of course, why I hadn't left. It wasn't because of St. George, or Talon. It wasn't because

I owed these dragons my life, or that I felt I could fight the Order that raised me. It wasn't even the guilt, the memories of blood and death that kept me up at night now. It wasn't any of those reasons.

It was Ember.

I shut off the water, toweled briefly and pulled on my last pair of semiclean jeans, one of two pairs to my name. I'd need new clothes soon. Wes had gotten me the essentials while we were holed up in the abandoned house, waiting for Ember to recover, but I couldn't count on him or Riley now. Especially since I suspected something had gone down with the rogue's network; last night, he and Wes had been talking in low, angry voices, and this morning, when I'd ventured out for a soda, Riley had stalked past me down the hall, his face like a thundercloud. He hadn't looked like he was inclined to share what had happened, and I'd known better than to ask.

Shirtless, I wandered to the window and stared at the glittering sea below. The sun was setting behind the distant mountains, and a haze had settled over the urban sprawl of Las Vegas. Where was St. George? I wondered. What was happening in the Order? Were they still out there, hunting for me?

And what am I supposed to do now?

A sharp rap on my door had me automatically reaching for a gun that wasn't there. With a grimace, I snatched a T-shirt from the bed and pulled it on while walking across the room. Peering through the eyehole, I felt a strange flood of both tension and relief wash over me, before I pulled back the lock and opened the door.

"Ha. There you are." Ember grinned at me, making my

stomach knot. She wore shorts and a loose tank top, and looked perfectly normal standing there in my door frame. Like any other human girl. "I was afraid you might've snuck out the window or something. Didn't you hear me knocking last night, or were you already asleep?"

My heart beat faster as I faced that familiar smile. She was a dragon, I reminded myself. Not evil or soulless as I'd once believed, but an alien creature nonetheless. Not human. I stifled the urge to touch her, to reach out and ease the worry in her eyes, the exhaustion she was trying to mask. A memory of another room, another time when it had been just the two of us, rose up to taunt me. I ruthlessly shoved it back.

I shook my head. "No, I didn't hear you. But I might've been in the bathroom." Truth was, I hadn't slept at all the night we'd arrived, and only a couple hours since. Not that I'd expected to. I'd been trained to survive on very little sleep, but more important, it was difficult to relax when there was a price on your head. And since the rogue dragon had all the weapons and I was currently unarmed, sleep was out of the question.

Ember looked at me expectantly, green eyes shining beneath her bangs. I sighed and took a step back. "Do you want to come in?"

She beamed and scurried across the threshold, gazing eagerly around as I closed the door and locked it out of habit. I heard a snort, imagined her shaking her head.

"Jeez, Garret. Two days, and your room doesn't look like it's been touched. Are you making *your own* hotel bed? You do know there's a maid service here, right?"

I managed a tired smile as I turned around. "Where I come

from," I told her, "if they ever discovered you let an old lady clean up your mess, you'd never live it down."

"Whatever. I'll take any excuse not to clean my room." She hopped onto one of the neatly made beds, rumpling it nicely. "If I can see my floor through all the clothes, I consider that a win. Besides, didn't you know, Garret? A messy room is a sign of genius."

"I've never been inside your house," I reminded her in a grave voice, "but if that's true, I have the feeling I'm talking with the smartest person on the planet."

She reached back and threw a pillow at me. I dodged, hearing her laughter ripple up, wicked and bright and cheerful. A strange lightness filled my chest, and I found myself smiling, too. Snatching the pillow from the floor, I prepared to hurl it back.

And caught myself, a cold chill driving away the amusement.

Too easy, I realized. Too easy to relax around her, to slip back into that role I'd adopted over the summer. A normal civilian, unguarded and carefree. Which was extremely dangerous, because this situation was anything but normal. I could not afford to drop my guard, even for her. Perhaps she'd come here to escape, to forget the reality of our situation. Maybe she wanted to pretend everything was normal for a while. But I couldn't be that person she wanted, that ordinary boy from Crescent Beach. I was a soldier of St. George; I'd killed too many, hunted her kind with the sole intention of driving them to extinction. My hands were stained with the blood of countless dragons. No matter what my feelings, I could never escape that.

Stone-faced, I replaced the pillow, not looking at her. "Why are you here, Ember?" I asked. "Did you need something?"

"Actually, yes." I looked up and found her watching me with a certain maniacal glee in her eyes. "You can come downstairs with me," she announced. "Right now. I swear, if I have to watch one more pay-per-view, I'm going to set something on fire."

"Downstairs?" I repeated, and she nodded eagerly. "To the casino? Why?"

"Because it's Vegas!" Ember exclaimed, throwing up her hands. "Because we're here. Because I'm literally going to start climbing the walls if I don't get out and *do* something." She raised her chin, and her eyes glinted. "And because I went to Riley's room to see if he has any new information on Talon and St. George, and he had already left."

I straightened quickly. "He's gone? Where?"

"No idea. I tried asking Wes, but he just said Riley had 'important things to do'—" she put air quotes around the phrase, rolling her eyes "—and wouldn't tell me what. Of course, he left without telling us, or leaving any hint as to where he went or when he'll be back. So much for trusting me, I guess."

With a sniff, she hopped off the bed, grinning up at me. "So, come on, Garret. We're in Vegas, the night is young and we have fake IDs. Even you must realize what we could do with those."

"We aren't supposed to leave the floor."

She actually growled at me. "If you want to stay here and mope and be boring, I can't force you to come," she said. "But *I* am going downstairs. The hotel is safe enough. Riley said so himself. Talon and St. George don't know where we are, and even if they see me, they're not going to shoot me in the middle of a crowded casino with guards and cameras and people everywhere." She bounced past me, heading toward the door. "I won't be long. I just need a change of scenery before I go completely nuts. If you see Wes, tell him I'm looking for Riley."

I grimaced. "Wait," I said, and caught up to her in the doorway. This was not a good idea, and I knew this wasn't a good idea, but I didn't want Ember to be alone down there. If something went terribly wrong, at least I would be there to help.

She grinned as I exited the room, and I shook my head. "Just for the record," I told her as the door clicked shut, "this is the exact opposite of the term 'lying low.'" She shrugged, waving it off, and I followed her down the hall. "Doesn't gambling cost money?" I asked as we neared the elevators. "How are you going to pay for anything?"

"I have a little cash," Ember replied. "Enough for penny slots, anyway. It's not like I'll be playing roulette or poker with the professionals, not unless I score really, really well. But who knows?" Her eyes sparkled as the elevator doors opened and we stepped inside. "Maybe I'll get lucky."

RILEY

I was not in the best of moods.

The taxicab reeked. Badly. Normally, I didn't mind the smell of smoke, but the patron before me had either lit three or four cigs at the same time or had been wearing a cologne called Essence of Ashtray. It smelled, it was annoying, and I was already tense enough. Of course, the irony of a dragon nearly gagging on smoke was not lost on me, but it didn't make me any less irritable, either. The memory of last night, when Wes had announced that yet another nest was gone, made me want to punch something. Dammit, what was happening? *Who* was giving us away? And could I find them before my entire underground was lost?

A guy in nothing but a Speedo, openly carrying a beer bottle, distracted me through the window and made a lewd gesture with his hips. I gritted my teeth, imagining what would happen if I set his Speedo on fire.

Clenching a fist against the door handle, I watched the lights of downtown fade in the rearview mirror and wished the cabbie would step on it. I hoped Ember was okay. I didn't like leaving her alone, especially with St. George close by, but I had no choice. This meeting was important and, like it or not, I had to follow through. Griffin had sent me the information an hour ago, saying the contact wanted to meet face-to-face, away from prying eyes, and had refused to come to the hotel. Which meant I had to go to him, and, annoying as that was, I couldn't say no. Nor did I want the other three trailing along while St. George was in town. Better for me to go alone; I was used to this type of thing, and if the Order jumped me, at least it was just my neck at risk. I'd told Wes to keep an eye on both the girl and the soldier; he was instructed to contact me immediately if he suspected there might be trouble.

I hoped it wouldn't come to that.

The taxi pulled up outside a skeevy-looking diner several blocks from the glittering brilliance of the Strip. The sidewalk wasn't well lit, and a couple thuggish-looking humans argued with each other near the entrance. Keeping an eye on them, I wrenched open the glass door and stepped inside.

The interior of the diner was dim and smelled like grease, smoke and too many humans packed into a small space. A couple Hell's Angels eyed me as I made my way across the floor, and I hoped my boots and leather jacket wouldn't offend them enough to pick a fight. I wasn't here to toss bikers through windows, amusing as that sounded. I needed to find that contact.

A dark figure in a corner booth caught my eye, and a thin hand twitched in a beckoning motion. Easing around a waitress, I walked over and slid into the seat across from him, trying not to curl a lip. The human was pale and unnaturally thin, with sallow cheeks and lank, greasy hair hanging to his shoulders. The huge sunken eyes, glazed over and unfocused, told me everything I needed to know.

"Griffin said you'd be able to hook me up." The human's voice was a raspy whisper, greedy and hopeful. He feverishly scratched at his arm, like he had spiders crawling on it. "Fifty bucks to tell you what I know, that was the deal." He scratched his other arm, leaving thin red welts down his skin. "You got the cash?"

"If the information is good," I replied, thinking I was going to kill Griffin when I got back. How in the hell was this a "reliable contact"? "Let's hear what you know, and I'll decide if it's valid."

"No way, man." The human shook his head, making his hair whip back and forth. "That wasn't the deal. Cash first, then info. Take it or leave it."

"Fine." I stood, dusting off my hands. "I don't need info this badly. Enjoy your nothing. I'm gone."

"Wait!" The human half rose from his seat, flinging out a hand. I paused, glancing back with cool disinterest. "All right, all right," he hissed. "I'll tell you what I know. But I'm not crazy, okay? I know what I saw." He squirmed, casting wary looks around the diner as if someone was listening to us. No one was; the whispered rambles of a junkie in a dark corner didn't merit a second glance here. I sat down, waiting silently, while he assured himself no one was lurking in the shadows in the next booth. Finally he hunched forward across the table, his eyes even wilder than before.

"My buddies and I, we have this squat several miles past the Strip, right? One of those big, half-finished hotels that was abandoned when the recession hit. It's been empty for years, and we don't bother no one, okay?" He sounded defensive, as if he thought I would care what he and his friends did on other people's property. I didn't say anything, and he dropped his head, his voice becoming a harsh whisper.

"So, a couple nights ago, we come back to find these two chicks in our squat, right? Pretty ones, not from around here. We thought they were runaways."

That piqued my interest. "How old were they?" I asked, making the guy flinch.

"Um." He scratched at his arms. "Fifteen? Sixteen? It was hard to tell, man. It was dark. Plus, they bolted when they saw us. We, um...*followed* them to the upper floors." He must've seen the fury in my eyes, because he jerked back, holding up his hands. "Just to talk. Hey, they were in our room, man. Two chicks show up unannounced in your squat, you wanna know why. If they in trouble with the cops, you need some sort of *insurance* to keep them hidden, you know?"

I took a furtive breath to keep from incinerating this low-life on the spot. "So what happened?"

The human blinked glazed brown eyes. "Uh, right. So, anyway, we followed them to the top floors. To talk to them." He emphasized *talk*. "You know, because it was dangerous up there, all unfinished and shit. We didn't want them stepping on a nail or falling off the edge, right? We were worried they'd get hurt."

Right, I thought furiously. *And I'm a were-newt.* "You're wasting my time," I warned, glancing at the window as if I was bored. "And not telling me anything worthwhile. You have about five seconds to make this interesting. Four. Three."

"Chill, man, chill. I'm getting to that part." The guy's

face turned the color of old glue, and he leaned forward, his voice a reedy whisper. "So, we went up there, looking for those girls," he rasped, while I contemplated how satisfying it would be to break his nose. "And we were poking around these half-finished floors. It's like a maze, right, but we knew they couldn't have gone far. But then, we looked up into the rafters and…" The human trembled. Shook violently, like he was in desperate need of a fix. The water glass on the table rattled, and the utensils clinked together until the guy took his arms from the table, putting them into his lap.

"And?" I prodded.

"And, I swear to God, man. There was this big, scaly *thing* looking back at us."

My stomach dropped, but I fixed a grimace of contempt on my face and leaned back in the booth. "This is the info Griffin promised was reliable?" I sneered. "Some user's drugged-out hallucination?"

"Man, it wasn't no hallucination!" Flecks of saliva spattered the table between us at the outburst. "I swear there was this fucking huge lizard in that room. Or maybe not a lizard, but *something*, okay? It was big, and black, and made this hissing sound when it saw us. I even think smoke came out of its nose."

"What did you do?"

"What do you think we did? We pissed our pants and ran. Haven't gone back since."

"Huh." I quirked a brow at him, though my heart was racing. "Sure you didn't see a big scary bat and think it was a monster?"

"Whatever, man." The human scratched his arm, glaring mulishly. "I know what I saw."

I slid to the edge of the booth, my thoughts whirling. Two new hatchlings in the city. Were they mine? Wes hadn't gotten any messages from our safe houses; could these two have escaped the recent Order strikes sweeping the country like the plague? I'd have to find them, and quickly, before St. George did.

Glancing at the human, who watched me with a greedy, hopeful expression, I held up a couple bills. "This was worth about twenty bucks, if that," I said, watching his face fall. "But I'll bump it to fifty if you can do two things. Stay away from that hotel, and don't tell anyone about this, ever. Think you can do that?"

"Sure, man." The junkie shrugged. "Whatever you want. No one else believed me, anyway."

Alarm flickered, and I narrowed my eyes. "No one else? How many did you already tell?"

He cringed and scratched his neck. "No one, man," he mumbled, not looking at me. "I didn't tell no one."

He was lying, but I couldn't dwell on that now. Throwing the cash on the table, I rushed out and looked around for a taxi. If there were hatchlings in this city, rogues or runaways, I had to find them. Especially with St. George on the move, looking for me. They could easily get caught in the cross fire, and then it would be on my head if more innocent kids were murdered by the Order.

I had to get to them first. But as I stood there on the corner, cursing the taxis that cruised blissfully by, my phone buzzed, making me wince. The only people who had this number were Ember and Wes, and I'd told them to call only in emergencies.

Bracing myself, I pulled the phone out of my jeans and held it to my ear. "Ember?"

"Not quite, mate." Wes's voice was taut with anger and disgust. My gut churned, and I closed my eyes.

"What happened?"

"Your bloody hatchling," was the peevish reply, "is what happened. I can't find her, or the soldier, anywhere. You'd better get back here, Riley. Before something else blows up in our faces."

EMBER

You're not supposed to be doing this.

I shoved the little voice aside as I descended the final escalator to the casino floor. It was truly another world down here: colored lights, ringing bells, an air of chaos and excitement that was lacking in my empty hotel room. Just what I needed to take my mind off...everything. I didn't want to think about Talon or St. George. I didn't want to remember Lilith's training, or Dante's betrayal. I didn't want to think about Riley, or this sudden, crazy longing for the human standing beside me. I didn't want to feel any of that. For a few hours, I wanted to turn off my mind and forget everything.

Garret, looking even less enthused as we stepped off the escalator onto the carpeted floor, did his normal crowd-scanning thing while talking to me. "Where to first?"

Good question. I'd never been to Vegas before, though I'd seen plenty of commercials and several movies that featured the famed City of Sin. They all showed Las Vegas in the same light: an almost mythical city where you could make your fortune in a few hours, or lose everything just as quickly. To our kind, that concept of instant wealth was intriguing, almost intoxicating. I might've been a hatchling, on the run from the organization and St. George, but I was still a dragon.

Spotting a row of bright slot machines along the wall, I smiled and tugged Garret's sleeve. "This way," I told him and started toward the twinkling lights. "That looks easy enough. Let's see how fast you can lose a dollar to penny slots."

★ ★ ★

Answer: about thirty seconds, the first ten spent figuring out how to make the machine work. Modern-day slot machines, I discovered, didn't require you to pull the "arm" on their side down. In fact, the arm was just for decoration now. Everything was automatic, which meant you pressed a button and watched the pictures of apples and bells and sevens spin around for a few seconds before they came to a stop—always unmatched—and the screen announced that you had lost.

"Dammit," I muttered, after I'd fed a third dollar into the side of the machine and lost it almost as quickly. "That was my last single." I looked to the soldier, standing vigilant at my side like an alert guard dog. I didn't think he'd taken his eyes off the crowds once. "Hey, Garret, you don't happen to have any loose change weighing you down, do you?"

He gave me a split-second glance, the corner of his lip curling up as he went back to surveying the floor. "I thought dragons liked to hoard their wealth," he said in a low voice. "Not throw it away at slot machines."

"I'm investing." I wrinkled my nose at him. "That last spin was almost triple sevens. I'm gonna get lucky any second now."

"Right."

I poked him in the ribs. He grunted. "Fine," I muttered,

digging in my shorts pocket. "Guess I'll have to use that five instead."

But before I could stick the money into the machine, Garret abruptly pushed away from the stool and took my hand. My pulse jumped, and a tingle shot up my arm, even as the soldier pulled me away from the aisle and into the crowds.

"Garret." I almost had to jog to keep pace with him. "What are you doing?"

"Security," he replied, and I looked back to see two men in uniforms pass the row we were just in. One of them caught my eye, frowned and angled toward us through the crowds. I squeaked.

"He's following us!"

"Don't panic." Garret's fingers tightened around mine. "And don't act nervous. Just keep walking, and don't look back."

Squeezing his palm, I faced forward and followed his lead. We "fast-ambled" through the casino, weaving through crowds, circling around roulette tables, trying to appear nonchalant and move quickly at the same time. I didn't dare look back, but Garret, without stopping or turning his head, somehow knew exactly where the guard was and what he was doing.

"Still following us," he muttered as we strolled through a slot machine aisle hand in hand. "I think he's waiting to see if we try to play a game. I believe that's illegal here, right? You have to be twenty-one to gamble?"

"I *am* twenty-one," I protested, and he shot me a quizzical glance. I raised my chin. "According to the ID of Miss Emily Gates, I turned twenty-one this January."

His lip twitched. "Do you really want them checking up on that?"

"Um. No."

"And do you really want *Riley* finding out that they checked up on that?"

I grimaced at him. "Right. Point taken. How do we ditch the rent-a-cop?"

"Just be ready to move when I do."

I nodded. Garret made a meandering left turn down a slot machine aisle, but as soon as we were out of sight of the guard, lunged forward with a burst of speed. I scrambled to keep pace. He pulled us around another aisle, and I followed, clinging to his hand and biting my lip to keep a maniacal giggle from slipping out. We wove through a couple more slot machine corridors, melted back into the crowd and circled a noisy, cheering roulette table. Abruptly, Garret pulled me to the edge of the table, somehow squeezing us between a pair of half-drunk guys and their girlfriends. They jostled us, their attention solely on the spinning roulette wheel and the little ball bouncing within, but then Garret wrapped his arms around me from behind and leaned in close, and I forgot about everything else.

"Keep your head down," he whispered, his voice low in my ear. "The guard is still following, but he's lost sight of us now. Don't make eye contact, and when he passes, we go back the other way and lose him for good."

"Got it." I held my breath, keeping my eyes on the table but hyperaware of Garret's arms around my stomach, holding me against him. I could feel his breath, the slow rise and fall of his chest, the taut coil of muscle in his arms.

After a tense, yet still far too short moment, Garret pulled away, looking back over his shoulder. "Clear," he muttered, as I risked a glance in the direction he was facing. The guard was moving away from us, following the crowds as they ambled through the casino. I couldn't see his face, but from the way he was turning his head from side to side, he was still looking for us. I let out a breath and started to relax.

But then, he turned and came back our way. With a squeak, I quickly faced forward as Garret did the same, pressing close. His heart beat crazily against my back, and I suspected he could feel mine pounding away, too. Thankfully, the guard passed us by once more, and this time continued through the casino until he was lost from view.

I exhaled, then collapsed into helpless giggles, leaning against Garret. He looked down with that amused half smile on his face, as if he didn't quite know what to do with me.

"Well." I peered down the aisle, making sure the guard was really gone, then looked back at Garret. "That was exciting, wasn't it? I think next time we should try the poker tables." He raised an eyebrow, looking alarmed, and I laughed again. "Sorry," I offered. "I suppose we should head upstairs before Riley comes back and bites our heads off. I'm sure dodging casino security wasn't exactly what you signed up for tonight."

He chuckled. "I've had to lose a couple tails in my life," he admitted. "Not all pursuers have been large angry reptiles. Tristan and I once spent the night dodging security guards in a museum warehouse. Nothing like huddling under a tarp with a family of cavemen to give you perspective."

I blinked at him. "Did you have a few drinks before we came down here?"

"No. Why?"

"You realize you just made a joke."

A cheer went up from the roulette crowd, and one of the drunk guys jostled me, knocking me into Garret. He quickly put out his hands, steadying us both, and my annoyance at Rude Guy was instantly forgotten as I glanced up and met those steely gray eyes.

Garret blinked. His hands lightly gripped my arms, rough, calloused fingertips warm on my skin. Slowly, he slid them up my shoulders, raising goose bumps and leaving a trail of heat. "Maybe you're rubbing off on me," he mused, serious again. "Or maybe...I've come to the realization that everything I know is wrong, and I'm starting not to care anymore."

"Is that a good or bad thing?"

"I don't know." He drew closer, looking thoughtful. His gray eyes were still intense, piercing, as his fingers brushed a strand of hair from my cheek. "But I'd be willing to find out."

My heart turned over. He was giving me that look, the look of the boy from Crescent Beach, the one who had danced and surfed and kissed me in the ocean. The boy who didn't know I was a dragon, not yet, who saw me only for me.

I swallowed hard. Ever since the night we'd faced each other on the bluff, dragon to soldier, I'd known that whatever we had over the summer was gone. Garret was part of St. George, the Order who saw all my kind as evil, soulless monsters. He might not believe that anymore, but I was still a dragon. Very much not human, despite these crazy humanlike emotions urging me forward, to reach up and pull his lips down to mine. I'd never thought we would be here again, face-to-face, with Garret watching me like I was the only person in the entire world. A ripple of doubt filtered through the happy longing. If I Shifted now, if I stood here in my real form, wings, scales, talons and all, would he still look at me like that?

The crowd at the table erupted once more, this time with loud groans and gestures of disgust. I swallowed a growl as Rude Guy hit me in the ribs with an elbow, and saw a dangerous light pass through Garret's eyes as his attention shifted to the oblivious human. I didn't *think* Garret would knock Rude Guy on his ass right here, much as I'd love to see that, but it was definitely getting crowded. I suddenly didn't want to be surrounded by bright lights and mobs of humans. I wanted a nice dark corner to see this—whatever *this* was— through in peace.

"Come on," I told Garret, backing away from the table. He followed me, that same bright, intense stare making my insides dance. "Let's find someplace quieter."

GARRET

What are you doing, Garret?

I followed Ember through the casino, keeping a wary eye out for security, and one guard in particular. The soldier in me operated on instinct, scanning the floor, constantly alert for hidden threats. I knew it was unlikely that St. George was here, and even more unlikely that they would attack us in the casino, but a lifetime of war and fighting had made me paranoid; I couldn't turn that off even if I wanted to. Which was good, because my emotions had become somewhat... distracting.

You know what she is. You can't plead ignorance anymore.

I knew that. Ember was a dragon; it was impossible to forget that now. I remembered the groggy red creature staring at me from the bloody floor of a van. I remembered the way she spoke in the abandoned house, the hurt on her reptilian face when she thought I was afraid of her, that we were enemies. Even then, she'd still sounded like Ember, like the girl I'd met in Crescent Beach, though her outside form had changed. It was strange; not long ago, dragons had been monsters. Ruthless, cunning and intelligent, but monsters nonetheless. Ember wasn't human, and maybe I was being profane, but the line between girl and dragon had somehow blurred, and I didn't see either of them as monstrous anymore.

You're a soldier of St. George. A dragonslayer. She should hate you, and everything you've done to her kind.

I winced. That was true, as well; I could never erase the years I'd fought with St. George, killing dragons, driving them toward extinction. That Ember had rescued me, risked her own life to save mine, was still hard to believe. She had to realize how dangerous it was, crossing into St. George territory, just to find me. Had it been a sense of obligation, the fact that I'd helped her and the rogue escape Crescent Beach, that made her risk everything to break into the Order chapterhouse? A debt that needed to be paid? Or could it be… something else?

Could I hope for something else?

I shook myself, trying to clear my head, calm the storm of confusing thoughts and emotions that battered me from within. I was still unsure what I was going to do, what was going to happen tonight, as Ember pushed back a door and led us outside. A rooftop pool glowed in the center of the space, and a few civilians lounged in a nearby whirlpool, despite the heavy desert heat.

Ember led us across the roof to an isolated corner surrounded by planter boxes and fake trees, where the bright lights of Vegas glimmered beyond the rails. The space was empty, but the soldier in me scanned the area out of habit, making sure it was safe, that we were alone. Ember gave a low chuckle and shook her head.

"Relax, oh paranoid one. I doubt there'll be Talon agents hiding in the potted plants."

"You never know," I returned, feeling strangely light and flippant, not like myself at all. Being around Ember had that effect on me, I was discovering. "It could be a brilliant Talon plot. Instead of humans, dragons Shift into benches."

She laughed. "Oh, great. Now I'm going to be paranoid every time I sit down. I hope you're happy." She turned and rested her elbows on the railing, gazing out over the city. I mimicked her pose, leaning against the rails, our arms almost touching. I was acutely aware of her body next to mine, radiating warmth, especially when Ember let out a sigh and leaned her head on my shoulder, making my pulse spike.

"Thanks for this," she murmured, as I told myself to keep breathing. "I needed to get out, to do something, or I was going to go crazy. Staying in that room alone, there were just so many memories. I can't be in my own head right now..." She paused, giving herself a slight shake, as if to drive those memories away. I didn't move, afraid that if I did it would break the spell and she would pull back. Instead, Ember pressed closer, causing all my nerve endings to stand up, and we stared out at the city lights for several silent heartbeats.

"Does it ever get any easier?" she whispered at last.

She didn't have to explain what she meant. "Yes," I told her. "Unfortunately. You have nightmares for a few weeks, and you question yourself for a long time—did you do the right thing, was there anything you could have done differently— but after a while, if you keep at it, pulling the trigger gets easier and easier. Eventually, it becomes routine, something you do without thinking." I glanced at her, hoping she didn't think I was bragging. "It's not something to be proud of," I said softly. "And it's not something you should strive for, not if you want to be anywhere near normal. I've been a soldier all my life. St. George taught me how to kill, but that's all I can do. It's the only thing I know how to do." Ember didn't answer, her gaze far away and dark. Maybe she despised me now, a soldier who took lives so easily, who killed without thinking. I wouldn't blame her if she did. "You don't want that, Ember," I said, not adding what I really thought, my own selfish desires. *I don't want that for you. I kill when I must for survival, but I wish you didn't have to be part of this war. If I could take you away from all of it, I would.*

"I know." She shivered and pulled away, hugging her arms as if cold. "That's why I left, after all," she went on, her voice barely audible. "Because they wanted to turn me into a killer, an assassin for Talon. They wanted me to slaughter people, not only in the war with St. George, but to silence anyone who wasn't loyal to the organization. They expected me to take out my own kind, rogues like Riley, if they ordered it."

I nodded, remembering an earlier conversation with Riley, how he'd said not all dragons wanted to be a part of Talon. And while he hadn't actually come out and said what happened to the rogues who left the organization, it had been strongly implied. Suspicion rose up, mingling with the guilt. Before this summer, it had never occurred to me that there were dragons who rejected Talon's ambitions, who wanted to be free of the organization. Dragons like Riley and Ember. Rogues hunted by their own.

I wondered how much St. George really knew about their ancient enemies. Were they truly ignorant of the rogues and the dragons outside of Talon? Or did our superiors choose to hide certain things from the rest of us?

"My old trainer, she was teaching me to be just like her," Ember continued, interrupting my dark thoughts. "Ruthless and completely unmerciful. Someone who would kill a defenseless hatchling in cold blood if Talon gave the word. She wanted me to strike fast and never question why, to execute people without thinking about it. She wanted me to become a killer." A shudder racked her body, and she gripped the railing, her voice a low rasp. "And now, I am."

I moved beside her and rested an arm on the railing. She didn't look at me, continuing to gaze at the streets below. Her posture was stiff, but I saw the grief, the helpless anger, the fear that she was becoming what she hated. The Perfect Soldier scoffed in disgust; this was a war. It was either kill or be killed. Pull the trigger before your enemy did, that was the only way to survive.

Before Crescent Beach, I would've agreed. Second-guessing yourself was dangerous. I had killed because the Order told me to, and I hadn't thought twice about it. But this summer, I'd met a daring, cheerful, fiery dragon girl who had turned my world upside down. Who showed me things I'd never seen, imagined or experienced. And it might've been selfish, dangerous even, considering where we were now, but I didn't want her to ever change.

"I know about the Vipers," I said, which made Ember glance at me sharply, perhaps surprised that I knew the name of Talon's infamous assassins. "I know what they do. I've seen what they're capable of."

"You have?" She blinked rapidly, her voice surprised and a little awed. "I mean, you actually saw one? And...lived?"

I gave a solemn nod. "Yes, but everyone in the Order has

seen this particular Viper," I said. "Not firsthand," I added quickly, as her eyes got huge. "No one who was there that night survived. But we've all seen the footage. It's from a se-curity camera the Order managed to recover from the area. They make us watch it as part of our training. To fully real-ize what we're dealing with."

Ember wrinkled her nose. "That's morbid."

"Yes." I paused, remembering the fuzzy, black-and-white images: a warehouse aisle, a flickering overhead light, four soldiers creeping forward with guns raised. A blur of shadow as something dropped from the ceiling, into their midst. Screams. Gunfire. The light swinging wildly back and forth.

And then silence, as the lamp swayed over a blood-streaked floor and the sprawl of blackened, shredded bodies, the killer nowhere to be found. "They didn't have a chance," I said, re-membering the horror I'd felt when I first saw the footage. I was eleven years old, and for weeks afterward, I couldn't walk into a dark room without scouring the ceiling for dragons. "There was no hesitation on the Viper's part. It knew exactly what it was doing."

Ember was still watching me as if she could see the scene play out in my eyes. "That dragon from the video," I went on, my voice just a breath between us, "the assassin, the killer… you're not like that, Ember." I paused, then said, very softly, "You're not like *any* dragon I've seen before."

"What am I, then?" she whispered.

My heart was pounding again. Slowly, I reached for her arm, turning her to face me. If she stiffened or pulled back in disgust, I would let her go. But her gaze rose to mine, di-rect and unafraid, and my breath caught.

"You're the girl who taught me to surf," I said, holding her stare. "And shoot zombies. And dance. And to never make you angry, even in human form, or risk being kicked where the sun don't shine." She snorted, not quite smiling, but her eyes lightened a shade at the memory. I smiled and eased closer, feeling the heat pulse between us, even in the stifling Vegas air.

"You're the dragon who chose not to kill a soldier of St. George when you had the chance," I went on in a softer voice. "You risked your life to break into a compound full of enemies who would slaughter you on sight, to rescue someone you should hate." Unbidden, my other hand rose, brushing a fiery strand of hair from her eyes, and she shivered. "I don't know what that makes you, exactly, but from where I'm standing, I'd say it's pretty amazing."

Her eyes gleamed, and a smile finally tugged at the corners of her mouth. "Okay, now I *am* worried," she murmured in a teasing voice. "Who is this smooth-talking, nonuptight normal person and what did you do with the real Garret?"

I shrugged. "I've been told I need to loosen up," I said, and kissed her.

She made a tiny noise of surprise, and then her hands were in my hair, holding me close, and my arms were around her waist, pressing us together. I closed my eyes, feeling my stomach twist, feeling her lips against mine, eager and insistent, her arms wrapping around my neck. She tugged on my bottom lip, and a groan escaped me as I let her in, clutching her tighter. There was no disgust. No regret. I stood on this roof, openly kissing a girl who was really a dragon, and I wasn't sorry at all.

"Ember!"

The shout cut through the quiet, and my nerves leaped in warning. I jerked back to see the rogue dragon striding across the roof toward us, a murderous gleam in his eyes.

RILEY

I'm going to kill her.

I stood in the center of the casino floor, surrounded by surging, babbling, oblivious mortals, and tried to ignore the temptation to turn the whole place into an inferno. Where was she? I'd already gone upstairs and pounded on the door to her room but, as Wes had said, she was gone. She and the soldier both. I'd called the throwaway phone Wes had given her and had been sent to voice mail both times, which meant she had either left it in her room or was deliberately ignoring me.

The urge to blast something to a smoldering ash pile grew stronger, and I started moving again, scanning the throngs for bright red hair and green eyes. Normally, Ember was impossible to miss, even in a crowd. But a Vegas casino, with its blinking lights, aimlessly wandering humans and deliberately confusing floor plans, was one of the worst places to pick someone out of a crowd. That was why we'd come here, to hide from Talon and the Order, but now that ploy was working against me. Which was ironic, annoying as hell and doing a great job of pissing me off.

Dammit, Ember. Where are you?

With a growl, I circled the casino once more before heading upstairs. I didn't have time for this. I had to get to that abandoned hotel to look for runaway hatchlings before St. George got wind of them. For every minute I wasted here, the Order could be drawing closer. There didn't seem to be any St. George activity around the casino, so I doubted Ember and the soldier were in trouble. I suspected the defiant red hatchling had gotten bored and had either bullied or convinced the human to come with her. That she was missing annoyed me. That she was missing and alone with the soldier pushed me a little closer to murderous rage, which I knew was unreasonable. She wasn't mine. I didn't want this attachment, despite every instinct telling me otherwise. I had more important things to focus on; my hatchlings, my underground, keeping everyone in my network safe from Talon and St. George. Wes was right; ever since Ember had come into my life, I'd been distracted. There was something about the fiery red dragon that I couldn't ignore, and that was stupid and dangerous and could very well get us all killed, but I couldn't help it. Like it or not, Ember had buried her claws in deep, and I was either going to have to accept it and give in, or find a way to live with it, because I'd be damned if I pushed her away now.

After searching the casino, the restaurants and the myriad stores with no success, I finally made my way to the roof. There were a couple humans floating around a brightly lit pool, but no Ember. I circled the edge and made my way toward the far wall, where the tops of the Vegas skyscrapers loomed against the night sky.

And there they were, both of them, by the railing. I saw

Ember mutter something, her eyes downcast, saw the soldier turn her to face him. He said something that made her smile...

...and then he kissed her.

Something inside me snapped. My dragon gave a shriek of outrage and reared up, filling me with fire and hatred, tinting everything with a red haze. I felt myself moving across the roof, heard myself shout something just before I reached them. The soldier glanced up, and I threw a savage right hook at his face.

He dodged, jerking his head back, my fist missing him by inches. Ember yelped in shock. St. George swiftly backed away and raised his fists, a clear invitation to fight, and the dragon roared acceptance.

Snarling, I tensed to lunge, but before I could go for him again, something grabbed my arm from behind.

"Riley, what the hell are you doing? Stop!"

I seethed, wanting to attack, to Shift to my true form and rend the human to little pieces, then char those pieces to ash. My dragon howled, violent and enraged, wanting to set something on fire. The soldier was now too far away, and on guard for an attack. I turned my anger on Ember, instead.

"What am *I* doing?" Spinning around, I yanked my arm from her grasp and glared down furiously. "What the hell are you doing, Firebrand? I leave for an hour, *one* hour, and come back to find you..." My voice caught on the words, and I curled my lip in disgust. "He's a human," I spat. "And not only that, a soldier of St. George. A dragon killer! I thought you were done with this idiocy when we left Crescent Beach."

Her eyes flashed, and she lifted her chin to face me. "You have no right, Riley—"

"You're a *dragon*," I interrupted, making her scowl. "Have you forgotten that part? Never mind that he was part of St. George. Let's ignore the fact that he's killed who knows how many dragons before his miraculous change of heart. Let's not ask how many hatchlings he's shot in the back, while they were running away." I sneered at the human before turning on Ember again. She stared me down, defiant; I growled and turned us away from the soldier, lowering my voice.

"Listen to me, Firebrand," I said, attempting to calm my anger, though my dragon still raged up and down my veins, wanting retribution. "You're not thinking straight. He's a human, with a human life span. How long do you think he's going to stick around? Where do you think you'll be sixty years from now? A hundred years from now? Have you even thought about that?"

"Of course not!" Ember snarled. "Right now I'm still trying to keep up with the present. Right now, staying alive and getting Dante out of Talon is keeping me pretty occupied. What about you?" Ember challenged, glaring up at me. "Have *you* thought about the future at all?"

"Every single day," I retorted, making her blink. "Every day, I wake up thinking about my safe houses, if they're secure, if the hatchlings I get out of Talon will survive another year. What will happen to them if *I* bite the dust, because I don't know how long I can keep getting lucky. But this isn't about me." I shot another glance at the human, wondering if he could hear us, then deciding I didn't care if he did. "Humans and dragons aren't supposed to be together," I insisted. "Their lives are a heartbeat compared to ours. What kind of future do you think you could ever have?"

Her eyes narrowed. "Don't give me that, Riley," she growled. "That's BS. Admit it—you don't want me with Garret because he was part of St. George."

I ground my teeth at her stubbornness. "I have *no* problem admitting that, Firebrand," I snarled. "What I don't understand is how you can let that murdering dragon killer anywhere near you without wanting to rip his head off!"

"Hey." The soldier had come forward again, eyes narrowed, his body tense and ready for a fight. "Leave her alone," he said evenly, as I gave him a dangerous look. "It's not her fault. I started this. Take it up with me if you have a problem."

I would love to, St. George, I thought viciously, but Ember beat me to it.

"Don't, Garret," she snapped, and I didn't know if the anger in her voice was directed at me, the soldier or us both. "I'm not afraid of jealous rogue dragons, and you don't have to step in front of him for me." She turned from the human then, looking me right in the eye. "I can take care of myself."

Jealous? I took a deep, cooling breath and stepped back, shaking my head at them both. "I don't have time for this," I said, which was true. The runaway hatchlings were still a question, and I'd wasted enough time already. "I'm supposed to be somewhere else right now," I went on, "and I'm done talking to the pair of you. Might as well beat my head against a wall."

"You're leaving?" Ember narrowed her eyes. "Again? Where are you going this time?"

"Out," I retorted, feeling mulish and immature. "Somewhere important, if you have to know." Her expression darkened, and I knew she was on the verge of demanding to come along. I took a step back. "Come or stay," I growled, "it makes no difference to me. I'm done here."

I spun on a heel, then strode across the roof without looking back. I heard them start after me, and controlled the urge to spin back around and lay the soldier flat on his back. It was my dragon talking, but what troubled me wasn't the anger, or the disgust, that Ember had forgotten everything St. George had done. She was still young. She didn't know the Order like I did, hadn't seen the true face of St. George, not yet.

No, what bothered me most was that, even after everything, my fiery red hatchling had still chosen the human... instead of me.

DANTE

The meeting room was frigid.

I didn't like the cold. Maybe it was growing up in deserts and sunny beach communities, where much of my free time was spent outside. I liked the feel of the sun on my skin, the heat blazing down on me, seeping into my bones. I didn't know what it was with Talon's executives, but all their office buildings had the AC cranked up so high you could almost see your breath. Even in Reign's opulent hotel, where the carpets were thick and gold and the leather chairs probably cost over a thousand dollars each, it was still cold enough to make my skin prickle. It certainly wasn't my place to tell Talon how to run things, but a few degrees of warmth would make things less uncomfortable. I hoped I could get through this without my teeth clacking together. I was already nervous enough.

Beside me, Mr. Smith leaned back and rested a foot on his knee, looking perfectly comfortable and at ease. As if reading my thoughts, my trainer shot me a glance, dark eyes appraising. "Breathe, Dante," he ordered. "It's a good plan. It will work."

I smiled. "I know it will."

"Good." Mr. Smith narrowed his gaze. "Don't *hope*. Know.

Hope will not bring your sister back. Hope will not impress Mr. Roth, or anyone in the organization. You must be confident of this plan, you must believe that it will work, otherwise you have wasted everyone's time."

"I'm aware of that, sir," I replied, still smiling. "And Ember will return to the organization before the night is out, I swear it."

Mr. Smith nodded and turned away, breaking eye contact as the door opened and Mr. Roth entered, followed by two more dragons. One, a slender man with slick dark hair and a goatee, I didn't recognize. He took a seat across from me and nodded, and I ducked my head in respect, but it was the second dragon that caught my attention. Lilith seated herself beside him, crossing long legs beneath the table, and smiled at me.

"I'm looking forward to seeing your plan in action, Mr. Hill," she said.

Her words were almost a threat. As if she, too, needed this plan to succeed, and there would be terrible repercussions if it did not. My blood chilled, but at that moment, Mr. Roth took the seat at the head of the table, facing us all.

"It is almost time," he stated, glancing at his watch. "Mr. Hill, have your agents contacted you?"

I breathed deep and nodded, putting my phone on the table in front of me. "Yes, sir. Everything has been set up. They're ready to move forward with the mission."

"Excellent." Mr. Roth leaned back, watching me with those cold dark eyes. "Then all we have to do now is wait. I look forward to seeing your success, Mr. Hill. Good luck."

I swallowed, glancing at the phone lying innocently on the

table, and my heart began pounding against my will. *Ember,* I thought, staring at the device as if I could sense her on the other side. *Please, don't do anything stupid. This is your last chance to choose the right thing.*

Folding my hands on the table, I waited for the phone to ring.

PART III

Leap of Faith

EMBER

You could cut the tension in the cab with a knife and serve it on a plate.

No one, of course, wanted to sit up front. Riley refused to have me and Garret in the back by ourselves, Garret wouldn't leave me alone with Riley, and I certainly wasn't going to sit up front so the boys could murder each other in the backseat. So we sat there, the three of us, myself in the middle, Garret and Riley flanking me on either side. And the silence was deafening.

Riley still looked murderous. He didn't look at me or Garret, but stared out the window, one arm on the sill. I could feel his anger radiating from every part of him, as if the dragon hissed and raged just below the surface. It prodded at my own dragon, riling her up, making me twitchy and restless. I felt guilty, and at the same time, I was angry about feeling guilty. Riley was way out of line; we hadn't done anything wrong. But his words still echoed in my mind, harsh and accusing, as if I'd betrayed not only him, but my entire race.

How long do you think he's going to stick around? Where do you think you'll be sixty years from now? A hundred years from now? Have you even thought about that?

He was being unreasonable. Of course I wasn't thinking about the future; what sixteen-year-old—of *any* species—did that? I hadn't been trying to piss Riley off tonight. I was just feeling bored, guilty, homesick and frankly pretty miserable, and somehow, Garret could bring me out of it. He made me forget the bad things for a while, just like he had in Crescent Beach. When I was with him, I could almost pretend I was normal.

My dragon snarled at me, disgusted. *You're not normal,* she whispered, an insidious worm in my brain. *You're not human, and the soldier won't be here forever. Riley will.*

A slight brush against my leg jolted me out of my dark thoughts. I peeked over and met Garret's eyes, worried and questioning, red neon lights washing over his face. His hand lay between us, the back of his knuckles resting against my jeans. A warm glow spread through my stomach and I gave him a furtive smile, even as my dragon recoiled with a hiss.

The cab took us away from the main flow of traffic, moving away from the Strip and the glittering behemoths on either side of the street. We drove for several more silent minutes, going deeper into the fringe neighborhoods, until the taxi pulled up to a curb seemingly in the middle of nowhere and lurched to a stop. A tall chain-link fence ran the length of the sidewalk, and beyond the metal barrier, a flat expanse of nothing stretched away into the darkness.

Riley shoved a bill into the driver's palm and exited the cab without speaking. Garret and I followed, and the taxi sped off. Leaving us on a deserted sidewalk many blocks from the lights and crowds of the Strip.

"What is this place?" I asked, peering through the fence.

There were no lights, no roads or even pavement. The ground was dusty and flat, an odd field of dirt surrounded by concrete. Though in the distance, I could see the uneven, skeletal outline of some huge structure hiding in the shadows.

"It's a hotel," Riley said brusquely, shoving his wallet into his back pocket again. "Started but never finished due to the recession, most likely. It's abandoned now."

"Why are we here?" Garret added, observing the area with a wary, practiced eye. The paranoia had returned; he was a soldier once more, and every shadow could hide a possible threat.

Riley gave him a cold look, as if debating whether to explain or not, then shrugged. "I got word of a couple runaways tonight," he said, making my stomach leap to my throat. "Possibly mine. They're supposed to be here, somewhere, hiding from Talon. I figured with all the St. George activity in the city, I'd better get to them first. Before the Order shows up and blows them to pieces."

Garret frowned. "You didn't think it important to tell us *before* we left the hotel?"

"I don't owe you any explanations, St. George," Riley said. "You're not here because I need you to be. We're going in, grabbing a couple hatchlings and getting out as fast as we can. If that flies in the face of your dragonslayer convictions, feel free to take the next cab back to the hotel. No one here is stopping you."

I bristled at Riley's assholey-ness, but Garret's voice was calm when he answered. "This could be a drug den," he said. "Or a gang hideout. At the very least, there will be homeless people and squatters wandering around. If we're going to extract two dragons without opposition, one or more of us should be armed."

Riley snorted. "Against a bunch of humans? What are they going to do, babble me to death?"

"They could have weapons."

"Then we'll be really careful and not attract attention," Riley snapped. "I didn't have time to grab anything, thanks to your and Ember's little disappearing act, and I didn't want to risk carrying a duffel bag of guns through the casino. So no, we don't have any weapons this time. Get used to the idea."

"And the Order?"

"Wes is hacked into a couple traffic cams around the block," Riley answered, making a vague gesture at the street. "He'll let me know if there's trouble. Don't worry, St. George." He gave Garret a cold smile. "I've got it all figured out."

Before either of us could protest further, he turned and leaped gracefully to the top of the fence, then dropped noiselessly to the other side. Without a word, he spun and strode away into the darkness. Garret and I exchanged a glance and then hurried after him.

It was eerie, being on this side of the fence. My shoes raised small poofs of dust as we walked. Stacks of rotting wood, iron and huge cement tubes were scattered about the barren landscape, like modern skeletons in the dirt. There were no signs of life. Even the eternal sound of traffic faded, red taillights becoming distant mirages, leaving us in a bubble of darkness.

The entrance of the hotel loomed ahead, the strangely elegant front marred by a crown of jagged beams and unfinished upper floors. Again, I was struck by the eerie silence as we approached the shattered lobby doors and stepped carefully over the threshold into the darkness of the dead hotel.

The first thing I noticed was the heat. The second was
the smell. The air through the doors was hot and stale, and
reeked of piss, sweat, puke and general human disgustingness.
I gagged and pressed closer to Garret. Who, of course, seemed
unfazed by it all. Damn soldier unflappability. Riley, clicking
on a small flashlight, wrinkled his nose, then turned to us.

"Stay close." His voice, though soft, echoed in the emptiness of the lobby. "Looks like there are people here after all."

"Ya think?"

There was a shuffle in the darkness, and Riley swept the
flashlight around, pinning a thin, almost skeletal figure in the
glare. A woman, her shirt nearly falling off her bony shoulders, gave us a glassy, deer-in-headlights stare before shambling away. My skin crawled, and I crossed my arms to hide
my fear.

"Oh, that's great," I whispered, as the shuffling footsteps
faded away in the darkness. "We're in a zombie movie. I
swear, if I see any walking dead, I don't care who's around—
they're all getting a fireball between the eyes."

Riley gave an amused snort, as if he couldn't help himself, and eased forward, sweeping the beam around the barren lobby. "Try not to burn down the hotel, Firebrand," he
warned, as the light slid over the front desk, which was covered in several layers of dust and cobwebs. "This place is a
tinderbox. One spark, and it's likely to explode." Something
small and furry darted across the floor and vanished into a
crack in the wall. Riley shook his head. "Actually, that might
not be a bad thing, but if an abandoned, multimillion-dollar

hotel suddenly goes up in smoke, it'll tell Talon and the Order exactly where we are. So no fireballs."

"Oh, fine," I whispered back, as we ventured farther into the hotel, following a wall as it curved away into the dark. "That's okay. If we are attacked by zombies, I don't have to run fast. I just have to run faster than you."

Garret's hand suddenly closed on my arm in a grip of steel, pulling me to a stop. At the same time, Riley froze. I looked past the thin beam of light from Riley's hand and tensed.

We'd reached the edge of what was probably the casino floor, had the hotel been finished. The room beyond was large and open; I could see the aisles of carpet where slot machines would go, the long strips for blackjack tables. Though the space was vast, it was even hotter here than in the lobby, and the smell was so bad it nearly knocked me down. I didn't know how anyone could stand it, but the small clusters of ragged, unwashed people scattered about the room didn't seem to notice.

A few yards away, a trio of humans sat huddled on a stained, threadbare mattress, giggling as they passed something small and bright between them. The glow of a lantern washed over their slack, pale faces and staring eyes. Nearby, another human glanced up from where he sat on an ancient sofa between two human girls. The girls stared at us, expressions slack and far away, but the guy's face hardened and he rose quickly.

"This ain't a public party, friends," he said with a menace-filled smile. He was tall and lanky, his torn jeans just barely clinging to narrow hip bones. A filthy red hoodie covered his head, even in the heat, and his eyes were bulging and eager. "I think you're a little lost. That's too bad, ain't it?"

Riley crossed his arms. "You mean this isn't the Palazzo?" he said, his voice echoing through the bare beams overhead. "Well, don't I feel silly. Especially since I blew all my cash on the penny slots." His voice changed, becoming slightly more ominous. "I don't suppose we can skip the pleasantries and get to the part where we walk through unmolested?"

The human snapped his fingers, and a trio of equally thin, ragged guys uncurled from the floor and shuffled forward to flank him. A knife suddenly gleamed between long dirty fingers as he raised his arm, and I went rigid. "Gimme your wallet," the junkie demanded. Garret tensed and stepped in front of me, his body like a taut wire. "And your phone. And whatever cash you have. Put it on the ground, and step away. Them, too," he added, jerking his head at me and Garret. "Jewelry, purses, whatever. Leave everything you have on the floor, and you can walk out still breathing."

Riley sighed. Raising his hands like he was thinking it over, he took a half step back, standing next to Garret. "How many?" he murmured in a voice almost too soft to hear. I frowned in confusion, but apparently, the query wasn't directed at me.

"Three here, another two on the wall behind us," Garret replied in an equally quiet voice.

"Armed?"

"No."

"Good. I'll let you take care of them. Firebrand, watch your back."

"Hey." The junkie leader stepped forward, raising the knife. "Didn't you hear me? Gimme your stuff, man, or I'll start cutting off body parts."

"I told you, I don't have anything," Riley insisted, lifting his arms in a placating gesture. "We came for the weekend and are now completely broke. I'm sure you hear that a lot here."

"Phones, then." The human turned and brandished the knife at Garret. "Gimme your phones."

"Sorry." Garret gave a helpless shrug. "Dropped it in the pool."

The junkie's gaze shifted to me, and I smirked at him. "Left mine in the cab."

"Rotten luck, huh?" Riley added.

"Man, do not fuck with me!" The junkie stepped forward, jabbing the blade at Riley's face. "Do you *want* me to gut you like a pig? Is that—"

Garret's hand shot out, grabbed the hand with the knife and wrenched it sideways, making the junkie yelp with shock and pain. His cry was cut short as the soldier moved in with a savage elbow to his temple, dropping him like a sack of stones. Before the others even registered what was happening, Riley lunged and drove a fist into one's jaw, snapping his head to the side. The junkie reeled away, toppled over the sofa to the shrieks of the two girls and lay still.

Something moved in the corner of my eye. I spun, dodged the arm grabbing for me and kicked the human's knee out as he passed, making the junkie crash to the floor. Garret blocked a fist from the second one and responded with a nasty right hook that rocked his opponent sideways. A third charged in, swinging a length of rebar, and my heart leaped to my throat. Garret ducked under the first swing and got out of the way, as Riley whirled around and smashed a fist into the human's jaw. He reeled back into Garret, who grabbed his wrist, twisted the rebar from his hand and swept his feet out from under him. As the human hit the ground on his back, Garret tossed the rebar to Riley, who turned and whacked a junkie across the temple, sending him crashing into a pillar.

As I grinned, watching the unconscious display of team-work, something grabbed me from behind and pinned my arms to my sides. Another junkie, reeking of smoke and body odor, tried to lift me off my feet and drag me away. I snarled and jerked my head back, cracking my skull into his nose. He yelped and released me, but threw a hard backhand at my face as I spun to face him. I dodged, but it clipped my cheek all the same. Pain flared across my eyes, and the dragon surged up with a roar of outrage. As the human groped for me again, I brought my foot up and kicked him between the legs as hard as I could.

His eyes bulged, and he staggered, mouth gaping. I kicked him once more for good measure, then shoved him back. He collapsed in a groaning heap on the floor, knees drawn to his chest, and didn't get up.

I curled a lip at him, then turned to find Riley and Garret. They stood back-to-back, surrounded by cringing, writhing junkies, while the rest of the den looked on from a safe dis-tance away. Riley held the length of pipe casually at his side as he gazed around the room, grinning. Garret hovered be-hind him in a ready stance, protecting his flank, scanning the area for threats.

"Anyone else?" he asked calmly.

No one came forward. The junkies on the floor crawled to their feet and staggered away, and the remaining humans suddenly seemed very interested in other things. Riley snorted, tossed the rebar away with a clank and looked around for me.

"Hey, Firebrand," he said as I walked up. "Sorry I couldn't get over to help. You okay?"

I shrugged. "Don't worry about me. Feel sorry for the guy who tried to slap me."

Garret, stepping out from behind Riley, gave me a faint smile. "I notice you managed to kick him in your favorite spot," he observed.

"Twice."

Riley winced, then looked at Garret. The other boy regarded him coolly, and Riley smirked. "See, St. George? We don't need guns. You're actually fairly competent at disabling people without them."

"I'll keep that in mind," Garret said drily, "the next time we face a dozen soldiers with assault rifles."

Riley shook his head. "Hopefully not tonight," he muttered, and turned away, observing the room once more. "So now the question is, how do we find two scared runaways in this mess?"

Soft footsteps interrupted us. I glanced over to see a skinny, zombielike figure shambling toward us from the shadows.

RILEY

The human edged into the light, shoulders hunched, watching us like a stray dog who wasn't certain if you would toss it food or kick it. A woman, I saw as she got close. As humans went, she might have been pretty once, maybe even gorgeous. But her blond hair was lank and stringy now, her skin pale and wasted, glassy blue eyes sunk into her face. She looked like a bony marionette as she eased forward and stopped just out of reach, the hollow expression and thousand-yard stare making my dragon stir restlessly.

"Angels," she whispered.

I frowned. My adrenaline was up; the fight had made me edgy and restless. I was not in the mood for this. "What?"

"The angels," she murmured again, and I saw she had only a few teeth left in her head. "The ones you want. The one's you're looking for. The pretty ones." One hand rose like a limp fish and pointed behind her. I squinted across the floor. A door sat against the far wall, barely visible in the shadows, looking like the entrance to a stairwell. "Near the sky," she whispered, as if in a daze. "The angels. They have to be near the sky."

"Upstairs?" Ember asked, but the human turned and shuf-

fled back into the darkness, muttering to herself. I listened to
her footsteps fade away, listened to her babble softly to herself, until the sounds were swallowed by the blackness, leaving us alone.

"Crazy humans," I muttered, and resisted the urge to brush
imaginary loony off my jacket. "Well, at least we know where
we're going."

Sick-looking, emaciated people gave us blank stares as we
crossed the open floor, giggling uncontrollably, or talking to
themselves in hushed voices. No one tried to stop or harass us
again, except for some crazy old guy who grinned and made
a lewd comment to Ember. She whirled on him, bristling.
The soldier quickly grabbed her, stopping her midlunge and
halting whatever she was planning to do, which was probably
kick the old codger in his withered jewels. I snickered, almost
sorry he'd stopped her, but by that time, we had reached the
other side of the room and I pushed open the door.

A wave of dry, stale heat billowed through the opening,
and a rusted metal staircase ascended into utter darkness.

"How far do you think we should go?" Ember asked once
we had all stepped through the door, crowding the bottom
of the stairs. It was even hotter here than the casino. My hair
stuck to my neck, and even though I didn't mind the heat, I
could feel sweat running down my back through my shirt.

"All the way," I answered, shining the light up the tube.
"As far as we can."

So we climbed. Up several flights in blistering, oven-like
temperatures, Ember and the soldier trailing behind me. We
met no one else; it was just our footsteps echoing up the shaft.
I assumed the heat and utter darkness kept most junkies out

of the stairwell at night, though the tube still reeked of piss and garbage and other things.

And then, quite suddenly, we couldn't go any farther. The stairwell ended at another simple metal door that creaked as I pushed it back, shining the light through the opening.

We'd reached the end of the hotel's construction. Beyond the door, half walls and rotting wooden frames created a labyrinth of metal and iron. Carefully, we eased inside, brushing aside ragged plastic sheets that hung everywhere, fluttering in the hot wind. I glanced up, and saw that the roof was open to the sky, though it was impossible to see the stars through the haze of the city. I could breathe easier, though, just being this close without the stink of human filth and craziness clogging my nose. If I were two runaway hatchlings, this was where I would go.

"What are we looking for?" St. George asked as we maneuvered our way across the floor. The wood groaned under our feet, and I stepped lightly over beams and rusty metal screws. Hopefully nothing would give way beneath us; the floor looked pretty rotten.

"Two kids," I told him. "Hatchlings. Probably no older than either of you." I brushed aside a sheet and ducked under a low-hanging beam, poking the light into dark corners. "If you find either of them, let me handle it. They're going to be terrified of strangers, of anyone who could be from Talon. I don't want them running off before I—"

Something lunged from around the corner, swinging a metal pipe at my face.

I jerked back. The pipe missed crushing my skull by about an inch but hit my arm instead, knocking the flashlight from my grasp. It went spinning across the floor in dizzying circles, as the attacker raised the weapon and came at me again.

"Wait!" I dodged and backed swiftly away, ducking around a beam. The pipe smacked into the wood a microsecond later, raising a hollow thud and a billow of dust. "Wait just a second," I said as my attacker followed me around the beam, holding the pipe like a baseball bat. It swung at me again, and I dodged out of the way. "Will you relax? I'm not here to hurt you. Just listen to me."

The others started forward, and I gave them a sharp look. "Don't move!" I snapped, and thankfully, they froze. "Stay right there, both of you," I insisted, holding out an arm, the universal gesture of *let's all calm the fuck down*. "Everyone relax."

The person with the pipe hesitated, shooting fearful looks between the three of us. A girl, I realized. Lithe and graceful, even as dirty as she was, with big blue eyes and silver-blond hair to the middle of her back. She wore a ratty T-shirt and baggy cargo jeans, and looked like she had slept in them for a while.

And she was definitely a hatchling, a teenager in human form. A little older than the ones I normally saw, wide-eyed and fresh out of training, but a hatchling nonetheless. The tightness in my chest eased a little, and I let out a furtive breath of relief. We'd found her before the Order did. That was all that mattered.

Panting, the girl backed up, still holding the pipe out in front of her. "Who are you?" she asked in a trembling voice. "What do you want?" Her voice, though it shook with fear, was low and cool, her words clear. Raising the pipe again, she gave us a fierce look. "I swear, I am not going back."

"Easy." I edged forward with one hand still outstretched, keeping my movements slow and unthreatening. "Take it easy," I said again. "You're safe. We're not from Talon."

She eyed me warily but visibly relaxed. The weapon hovered between us, dropping a few inches, but didn't lower completely. "If you're not from Talon, who are you?" the girl demanded. "How did you know about this place?"

"My name is Cobalt." I offered my real name without hesitation. More people knew Cobalt, who he was and what he'd done. And even if this girl didn't, Cobalt was a dragon name, subtly reminding her that we were alike. "And I'm sort of in the business of finding people like you. People who want out. I can help," I went on, easing forward again. "I can take you somewhere safe, someplace Talon won't be able to find you. But you have to trust me."

This time, the weapon dropped swiftly, and the girl stared at me with wide, stunned eyes. "You're Cobalt," she whispered, and all the tension left her, replaced with relief. The pipe fell from her fingers with a clank and rolled across the floor, but she didn't give it a second glance. "You're really here," she whispered, grabbing a beam as if to steady herself. "We heard you might be in the city, but we had no way to contact you."

I stared at her in surprise. "You were looking for me?"

She nodded. Taking a deep breath, she seemed to regain her composure. "Sorry about before. I'm Ava. A friend and I escaped the organization maybe two weeks ago. There were rumors that you were in Las Vegas, and we heard that you could help those who got out of Talon, so we came here to find you. But we had to hide as soon as we arrived in the city. St. George…"

I nodded. "You mentioned a friend," I said, hoping the worst had not happened, that St. George had not already found them. "Are they still alive?"

Ava nodded. "Yes, she's here. One moment." She walked a few steps to peer around a wall. "It's okay," she called into the shadows. "You can come out. They're not from Talon." She gave a short, breathless laugh, as if she couldn't believe what she was saying. "It's actually *Cobalt*, of all the lucky breaks."

"Cobalt?"

Another hatchling emerged around the corner, edging shyly into view. She was shorter than Ava by several inches and looked even younger than Ember. Her skin was pale, almost porcelain colored, and a mass of jet-black curls tumbled down her back and shoulders. Enormous dark eyes peered out at us with a mix of curiosity and fear.

"This is Faith," Ava introduced, holding out her hand to the other girl. Faith blinked as she came forward, pressing close to the other hatchling. Ava put a protective arm around her, though she still spoke to me. "The day before she completed assimilation, she discovered that Talon was going to send her to 'the facility,' because she was unsuitable to be a Chameleon, which is what they had originally planned for her."

I clenched my jaw, trying not to let the rage show. "The facility" was Talon's term for the place they sent dragonells to become breeder females, whose only job was to produce eggs for the rest of their life. Talon liked to start their breeder females young, because, like everything else in a dragon's life, producing offspring took a long time. Nearly two years to lay the egg after the dragonell had been mated, and another year for the egg to hatch. When I'd still been part of Talon, there had been dark rumors circling the organization that the number of fertile eggs was in sharp decline. An alarming one in three eggs simply never hatched, and no one could figure out why. What happened to the "dud" eggs was also a mystery; they disappeared, sent off to places unknown. I didn't know what the real story was, or where the eggs vanished to, but one of my bigger goals was to find the facility, free all the dragonells there and burn the place to the ground.

Later, I told myself, as rage heated my lungs, making the air taste like smoke. *Someday, you'll be able to save them all, but not tonight. Don't get distracted.*

"How did you know about me?" I asked the hatchlings.

"Everyone in the organization knows about you," Ava said. "The executives try to deny it, but we've all heard rumors of a rogue dragon who helps those wanting to leave Talon. You just have to find him—or hope that he finds you—before the Vipers catch up."

Ember blinked. "Wow, look at that," she said, grinning at me. "You're famous, or at least infamous. A real-life Robin Hood."

I stifled the urge to rub my eyes. My defiant little Firebrand might think it was great news, sticking it to the organization, but I did not want that much attention from Talon. That they talked about me meant they were thinking about me, which was never a good thing. I'd always been careful to lie low, especially after getting a hatchling out. We'd survived this long because I knew how to disappear, to vanish into obscurity without a trace. Talon was far too big to challenge head-on. As much as I hated them and would love to see them brought down, I knew that my tiny, ragtag underground could never stand against the massive force that was Talon. Right now, I was an annoyance at best. I did not want to reach the point where the organization brought its full might against me and my network, because we likely would not survive.

Faith's dark gaze abruptly shifted to my companions. "Who are they?" she whispered.

"I'm Ember." Ember stepped forward before I could say anything. "I just got out of Talon, too. You can trust Riley, uh...Cobalt. He knows what he's doing. He'll keep you away from them."

Faith blinked. "What about him?" she asked, glancing at the soldier standing a little behind us. "He's not a dragon. Why is he here?"

Ember stiffened, and I quickly jumped in. "He's all right," I said smoothly, and ignored Ember's raised eyebrow. "You can trust him. He's here to help." I nearly choked on the words, but getting the hatchlings to trust us was more important than the truth now. I couldn't have them freaking out if they discovered what he really was. The soldier's expression remained neutral in the face of such blatant lies, and Faith finally seemed to relax.

I turned to Ava. "Are you two ready to go?" I asked. The night was fading quickly, and I was uncomfortable standing out in the open like this. Once we got back to the safety of the hotel, I'd figure out what we were going to do. "You'll have to stay with us for a bit, until we can leave the city. But after that, I'll find a safe place for you both."

She nodded tiredly. "Yes, please. Anywhere is better than here, waiting for Talon or St. George to catch up."

"No arguments there."

The phone buzzed in my jeans pocket, making me jump, then whisper a curse. There was only one person would call me now. For one reason.

No. Not now. With dread blooming through my stomach, I put the phone to my ear and snapped, "Wes. Tell me you're not going to say what I think you're—"

His hissed words interrupted me. I listened to the frantic voice on the other end, lowered the phone and turned to Ember and the soldier.

"They're here."

GARRET

"The Order?"

The rogue glared at me, anger and loathing crossing his face, as if I had summoned my former brothers here with my presence alone. "What do you think?" he spat. "Of course it's the Order. They always seem to appear these days, like magic, wherever we are." He shoved the phone in his jacket and raked both hands through his hair. "Dammit, of all the crappy timing. How the hell do they keep finding us?"

It was immature and vindictive, but I couldn't help it. "*Now* do we need guns?"

"St. George?" The dark-haired girl, Faith, shrank back, her eyes huge and terrified. "The Order is here?" Her gaze darted to the entrance of the stairwell, as if armed soldiers could burst through at any time, then flickered to the edge of the building. "We have to fly," she whispered, edging away from the other girl, toward the sudden sheer drop at the end of the floor. "They'll kill us if we don't—"

"No!" Riley whirled around. "No flying. We don't know where St. George is, or what they have out there. They could be watching the building right now, waiting for us."

"I'll risk it." The girl stopped, but looked on the verge of panic. "It's the Order! We have to fly. It's better than dying."

"Faith, stop." I didn't dare step forward, lest I scare her into plunging off the roof right then. "Listen to me. That's what they want. This is one of their tactics, send in the ground team to force the targets into the air. Like hunting quail." She blinked at me, glassy-eyed with fear. I wondered if any of this was getting through to her. "There's probably a team of snipers scanning the roof right now," I continued, gesturing to the buildings around us. "If you fly, they'll shoot you down—"

The whirl of helicopter blades interrupted me, a guttural whine in the silence. Faith flinched, her gaze going to the sky, but Ember darted forward, grabbed her around the waist and yanked her back...just as a spotlight beam sliced over the floor, passing inches from where they'd been standing. The rest of us ducked down and pressed against the walls, melting into shadow, as an unmarked black chopper circled the building once, then wheeled lazily away.

Ember glared after the helicopter, eyes flashing, as Faith whimpered and huddled close to her. "Well, there are the snipers," she said. "What now, Riley?"

Shoved against a wall with Ava, Riley growled a curse and looked at me. "Any brilliant thoughts on getting out of this?"

"Back through the building," I said. "It's a big hotel. They'll probably have more than one unit sweeping the floors, coming in from different angles. If we can get past the ground teams, we'll have a chance of making it out unnoticed."

"And if we can't?"

"Then we go through them."

Riley swore again. "All right," he growled. "Go, then. We'll be right behind you."

The helicopter swung around again, and we held our breath as it went by, spotlight crawling over the walls and floor. I waited until it passed, watched it glide around a corner, then darted for the stairwell entrance. I heard the others scramble after me, and hit the door handle without slowing down, bursting through the frame into the building.

We quickly descended the stairs, myself in the lead, Ember close behind me. Ava and Faith followed, and Riley brought up the rear, watching our backs. Our footsteps echoed throughout the stairwell, unnaturally loud in the stillness. Each time we passed the entrances to other floors, my nerves jangled, wondering if this time the door would burst open and a squad of soldiers would step in to kill us.

A body suddenly rounded the corner and lunged up the stairs, making Faith shriek. Not a soldier, but a civilian in a white tank top, a baseball cap perched sideways on his head. He stumbled, nearly running into me, and I barely stopped myself from driving a fist into his throat.

"Shit, man!" The civilian glared at me wide-eyed, then shoved past, lurching up the steps. "Move, a-holes! Fucking SWAT team is everywhere." He scrambled past Riley, who gave him a disgusted look, then continued up the stairs, his footsteps fading into the darkness.

Ember took a deep breath and let it out slowly. "They're in the building," she breathed as we started down the steps again. "How close do you think they are, Garret?"

Two floors beneath us, a door opened.

I jerked to a stop and whirled around as flashlight beams

pierced the darkness below. "Go back!" I ordered, hearing booted feet ascending the steps behind me. "Everyone, get back! They're here."

Shots rang out, sparking off the walls and railing, and Faith screamed. We fled back up the steps, hearing the soldiers give chase, spatters of gunfire echoing up the stairwell.

"This way!" Ahead of us, Riley paused at the entrance to the twelfth floor and wrenched the door back. "We're sitting ducks in here. Everyone get out. Go, go!" Ava and Faith quickly ducked through the open door, and the rest of us followed, emerging into a narrow, unfinished corridor with empty rooms lining the walls. A maze of hallways, dark and empty, stretched out to either side.

The soldiers were still coming. Without hesitation, we ran, rounding a corner just as the door behind us opened and our pursuers followed us into the labyrinth. I heard a soldier calling for backup, informing the rest of the squads where we were, and knew the entire strike force would be swarming the floor in a matter of minutes. The rest of them would be sent to guard doors, exits, stairwells; anywhere we might try to escape, they would be waiting for us. A cold lump settled in my stomach. Getting out of here was going to be difficult, if not impossible.

After a minute or two of running, when it appeared the soldiers weren't right on our tail, Riley ducked into an open room, and the rest of us followed. "Okay," he panted, leaning against a wall, "this whole thing has gone completely FUBAR. We need a new strategy, quick." He looked at me. "Suggestions, St. George? What are they doing out there?"

"Right now, all squads will be converging on this floor,"

I answered, peering into the hall to make sure the soldiers were not close by. My mind raced, trying to think of a plan, to counter whatever they were going to do. "They're going to try to cover all the exits," I went on, ducking back inside, "but if we find another stairwell before they have a chance to get here, we could possibly slip past them and get to another floor. It'll buy us some time while they're searching for us up here. The challenge will be finding an exit that isn't guarded."

"One problem at a time," Riley muttered tiredly, and pushed himself off the wall. "First thing, let's try to get off this floor before the rest of the bastards arrive. Any ideas?"

"There's another stairwell at the west end of the building," Ava said, surprising us. She stood beside Faith, looking pale but calm in the face of approaching death. Unlike the other hatchling, who was frozen in absolute terror, her eyes huge and staring. "I saw it when we first came here. We could try to reach it before St. George does."

A hollow boom echoed from an adjacent hallway, followed by a gruff "Clear!" The soldiers behind us were kicking in doors, systematically checking each room before moving on. Riley winced.

"Stairwell it is," he whispered, beckoning Ava to the front with him. "Let's go."

We raced for the end of the hall, Riley and Ava leading this time, me bringing up the rear. I didn't know if the soldiers heard us and were giving chase, and I didn't pause to look back. We fled down narrow concrete hallways, ducking beams and scrambling over rubble, praying we wouldn't turn a corner and find the way blocked by soldiers and guns.

As we approached an intersection where two hallways

crossed, the hairs on the back of my neck stood up. Four
armored, masked men rounded the corner at the far end of
the corridor we'd been moving down. Hissing a warning to
Riley, I grabbed the two closest bodies—Ember and Faith—
and yanked them into the cross section of hall, just as the
scream of M-4s filled the corridor.

Faith wailed, hands flying up to cover her ears, as the roar
of gunfire tore through the air and bullets ripped chunks of
wood and plaster from the walls. Pulling her back from the
edge, I looked up to see Ava and Riley on the other side of
the corridor of death, streams of bullets zipping between us.
The soldiers were advancing, firing short, continuous bursts
as they marched forward in unison. From the sound of the
guns, they would reach our position in a few seconds.

I met Riley's gaze, and he gestured at us frantically. "Split
up!" he shouted over the howl of carbines. "Take them and
get out of here, St. George. We'll meet back at the hotel. Go!"

I nodded and turned to the girls. "Come on," I said, and
Ember stepped toward Faith, still huddled against the wall.

"Faith." She pried the girl's arms away from her head. "Hey,
we have to go."

"No!" Faith looked up, gaze frantically searching for the
other hatchling. "What about Ava? We can't leave them."

"We can't help them now!" Ember growled and pulled the
other girl off the wall. The chatter of gunfire was getting
closer, as were the footsteps of the squad. "She's with Riley,
she'll be fine. But we have to get out of here, right now."
Faith took a breath to argue, and Ember snarled at her with
the fury of a fire-breathing dragon. "Move!"

Faith gave a desperate sob and stumbled past me down the

hall. I started after her but Ember paused, shooting one final glance at Riley and Ava, who were already sprinting in the opposite direction.

"Be careful, Riley," she whispered, before spinning and catching up to me and Faith. We rounded a corner just as the squad reached the intersection, sending a storm of bullets after us, and whatever feelings I had about Ember and the rogue were quickly replaced by thoughts of survival.

RILEY

I might not get out of this one.

Angrily, I banished the thought as I led Ava through the maze of corridors, the echo of gunfire and soldiers' voices ringing behind us. I couldn't start thinking like that. I'd survived worse than this, and besides, I had too many who counted on me; I couldn't die now.

"Riley, wait," Ava said, bringing me to a halt in the middle of the hall. The pale-haired hatchling shot a quick look around, blue eyes searching, then jerked her head at an open doorway. "This way," she announced, and darted into the room. Frowning, I followed, hearing the soldiers close behind us, wondering what she was planning. We couldn't afford to be trapped.

"What are we doing?" I hissed, as the hatchling hurried to a pair of balcony doors. "We can't fly, Ava. They've got snipers out there—"

"We're not going to fly." Ava unlocked the frame and pried back the glass doors, glancing over her shoulder at me. "I know what I'm doing," she said to my dubious look. "Trust me, Cobalt."

Shouts echoed from the hallway, making my skin crawl.

"Looks like I don't have a choice," I growled, and followed her onto the balcony. She didn't launch herself into the air but hurried to the railing and swung over, making my heart jump to my throat. For a half second, she dangled over a lethal drop, feet swinging out over nothing. Then she pumped her legs twice and let go of the rails. My heart gave another violent lurch as I leaned over and watched her drop onto the balcony directly below us, landing in a graceful crouch.

Straightening, she looked up at me, as I told my heart it could start beating again. "Hurry!" she urged, just as the glass behind me shattered. Bullets sparked off the railing, and I scrambled over the edge, taking a half second to swing my legs forward as I released my grip.

I hit the concrete and rolled, distributing some of the impact, though it still clacked my teeth together and sent a flare of pain up my arm. Ava pulled me to my feet and dragged me away from the balcony railing just as the soldiers stuck their guns over the edge and fired down on us. We fled the room into another series of darkened corridors. This one without the swarms of soldiers, at least for now.

I leaned against a wall to catch my breath, and Ava did the same. Panting, I looked at her, at the slender body and the calm, young face. "How many times have you done this before?" I asked. She shrugged, pushing long pale hair behind her shoulder.

"I was trained for this," she said as I wondered what Talon had her pegged for before she ran. Basilisk, Gila and Viper were the operatives that received special combat training. "My final exam was supposed to be this month," Ava went on, staring at the wall, her eyes dark with memory. "But I knew I couldn't do what they asked. The new management was especially unbearable." An unexpected look of disgust broke through her composure. "Hiding what I felt was getting harder and harder. I'd been planning to leave for a long time, ever since I heard about you." Her gaze flicked to mine, then away just as quickly. "I'm not usually this disorganized," she admitted, hunching her shoulders as if embarrassed. "I was going to run when my test came around, but then I heard about Faith and…things happened a little faster than I origi-nally planned." She sighed, squeezing her eyes shut. "I hope she's all right," she whispered. "I promised I'd keep her safe."

I brushed her arm. "She'll be okay," I said, allowing a small grin to tug at my mouth. "You don't know Ember. She'll burn the building down before she'll let anyone hurt her. And the soldier…is a bastard, but he knows what he's doing. Trust me, she'll be fine."

Ava regarded me with solemn blue eyes. "You have a lot of faith in them," she said. "It's been so long since I've been able to trust anyone but myself."

"Hopefully that'll change." I pushed myself off the wall. "But right now, we have to worry about ourselves. Come on, we're not out of here yet."

We slipped through the empty corridors, keeping a close ear out for voices or footsteps, until we reached the elevator hall. Ava frowned as I walked up to a pair of metal doors and forced my fingers between the tightly sealed crack. "What are you doing?"

"Forget the stairwell." I grunted, gritting my teeth as I pried the doors back. They resisted, stubborn with rust and disuse. "The Order probably has them all guarded. Or are

using them right now. I don't want to run into any more soldiers on the stairs, so we're going the unconventional route."
She watched as I wedged my shoulder between the crack and
looked back at her. "You're not claustrophobic, are you?"

A door slammed somewhere in the maze of corridors, and
my blood froze. Claustrophobic or not, we were out of time.
With a growl, I shoved the doors as hard as I could, ram-
ming them with my shoulder. They gave a last rusty groan
and reluctantly slid back a few inches. A gust of hot, stale air
billowed out of the opening, and a long, pitch-black tube
plunged down into darkness.

I eyed the distance from the edge to the maintenance ladder on the wall, then looked back at Ava. "After you."

Flashlight beams scuttled along the wall, and the sound of
booted feet echoed through the hallways. Without hesitation,
Ava leaped into the shaft and grabbed the ladder's rungs with
easy grace, then started down the tube. I followed, gritting my
teeth as the ladder trembled under my weight. If it snapped,
we were in trouble; a fall here would kill us as surely as if the
soldiers stuck their guns through the opening and filled the
shaft with lead.

Let's hope my luck holds.

Together, we descended into the pitch blackness.

EMBER

A hail of bullets erupted behind us as we turned another corner, and Faith screamed.

"Garret!" I panted, as flashlight beams scuttled over the walls ahead of us, and the soldier stopped abruptly in the center of the corridor. I stopped behind him, shivering as harsh voices drew closer from different directions. "They've surrounded the floor," I whispered, feeling my heart pound in my ears. "We're trapped."

Garret scanned the hall, his gaze falling on a pair of open doors at the end of the corridor. "This way," he ordered, and we sprinted through the doors into a large conference-type room. It was only half-finished; scaffolding stood everywhere, and large iron beams marched down the center of an aisle, creating a tangled web of iron and steel. It was very dark in here, and the air was thick with the smell of dust and mold.

Garret pulled us behind a cage of scaffolding and iron beams. "Faith," he said softly, bringing the girl's attention to him. "Look at me." Faith's eyes were huge and liquid, and tear tracks stained her dusty cheeks as she glanced up. "Listen to me. I want you to climb to the top of the scaffolding tower, lie flat and don't move. Don't look up or make a sound, no matter what you hear. Can you do that?"

She stared at him. "What…what are you going do?" she whispered, looking between us fearfully. "You won't leave me here, will you?"

He shook his head. "We're not going to leave you," he said, with that quiet intensity that made my skin prickle. "But you have to get out of sight. I can't worry about you if I'm going to do this." She blinked in confusion, but he didn't explain. "Get up there," he said gently, nodding toward the scaffolding. "If the worst happens, wait until they're gone, then get out any way you can. Go."

With a final sniffle, Faith turned and scuttled up the ladder, vanishing from sight.

Voices echoed outside, and flashlight beams pierced the blackness beyond the doors. The soldiers were converging on the room. Garret took my wrist and pulled me farther back into the shadows.

I stepped close, resting my palms on his chest, feeling his heart race. "What's the plan?" I whispered, surprised that my own voice was so steady.

He took a deep, furtive breath. "There'll be two teams," he murmured, glancing at the entrance and the lights getting closer. "Possibly more, if they called for backup. Six soldiers at the very least, with M-4s, a sidearm and a pair of stun grenades. That's standard procedure for this type of strike." His voice was cool, unruffled, as he calmly analyzed our odds of survival. "We should split up," he said gravely. "I'll get in close, take one or two out, then you hit the others from a different angle when they respond. Try to surprise them. If they see us coming, it'll be over."

I shivered, closing my eyes. "All right," I muttered, clenching my fists in his shirt. "No problem. It's just like training back with Scary Talon Lady." *Just with real soldiers, and real guns. No paintball bullets this time, Ember.*

Garret gazed down at me, and for the first time, a shadow of fear crossed his face. Not for himself, I realized, but for me. "Ember…"

"Don't you dare tell me to stay up top and hide, Garret," I warned, narrowing my eyes at him. "That's something Riley would say, and I'll tell you exactly what I'd tell him. I'm not letting you fight them by yourself."

"I know. I mean… I wasn't going to." His hands rose and gripped my arms as he stepped close. "But…be careful, Ember," he said, his intense gaze searing into me. "They'll be searching for a dragon. They know how dangerous one is when it's cornered and trapped. Remember, this is the type of scenario they train for, what we've *all* trained for. Do what you have to do…" One hand pressed to my cheek. "Just stay alive," he whispered.

I swallowed the lump in my throat. "You, too."

Figures appeared in the doorway, freezing us in place, as six soldiers stepped through the frame, guns held in front of them. Fanning out, they advanced cautiously into the room, sweeping their weapons in tight arcs, the tactical lights on the bottom of their guns piercing the darkness.

Garret drew back. His eyes were hard, that blank soldier's mask slipping into place as he melted into the shadows and out of sight. I darted behind a scaffold, then hunkered down as thin beams of light swept the opposite wall, making my heart pound.

Okay, how was I going to do this? I took a deep breath to slow my heartbeat, and gazed around the room. Despite its vastness, it was quite cluttered. There were a lot of tight quarters and places to hide, where the soldiers would be at a disadvantage if I could get close. In fact, this was *a lot* like my training with Lilith, having men with guns chase me around a crowded warehouse while I figured out how to "kill" them. Of course, I'd "died" most of those times, too, shot down with paintball guns, as the soldiers had become increasingly aware of attacks from up top.

Up top...

Crouching down, I stripped out of my clothes and left my shorts, top and underwear at the base of a pillar. Any modesty or embarrassment I might've felt was swallowed by the need to stay alive, and besides, no one could see me in this darkness, not even Garret. In another circumstance, I might not have worried about ruining my clothes, but I didn't have my Viper suit on, and if we did make it out of here, I did not want to run through the streets of Las Vegas stark naked.

The soldiers were halfway into the room now, their lights creeping ever closer as they eased forward. Hurrying to the nearest scaffolding tower, I began to climb, feeling cold iron, rust and cobwebs under my fingers and the soles of my feet. When I reached the top, I crept silently along the wooden planks, keeping my head low, until I was almost directly above a pair of soldiers and could peer down at the tops of their heads. I couldn't see Garret, but I knew he was close, waiting for the perfect moment to strike. I would be ready when he did.

As I held my breath, muscles coiling and tingly with the energy right before a Shift, my foot brushed a loose nail on the edge of the wood. It fell and pinged off the cement, a tiny sound that might as well have been a gong in the silent room. The soldiers below immediately swept their beams straight up the scaffolding. My heart lurched, and I ducked down, pressing my cheek to the boards, as my perch was illuminated in light.

"Did you hear...?"

"Yeah." The flashlight swept back and forth along the plank. I took shallow breaths and thought invisible thoughts. "I think it might be up there—"

A muffled shout rang out from another corner of the room, followed by the sound of a scuffle, a body being slammed against a wall, a burst of gunfire. The light vanished as the two soldiers whirled their guns in the direction of the noise, and I leaped to my feet.

Here we go, I thought, and plunged off the scaffold, feeling my body explode midpounce. I landed on one of the soldiers in full dragon form, driving him into the concrete, and turned on the other with a roar, blasting him with fire as he spun around. He cringed back, tongues of flame snapping around him, but apparently his armor was fire resistant because the flames didn't stop him from raising his gun and firing. I ducked behind a pillar, sparks erupting around me, and bounded into the shadows. The soldier backed away, firing short bursts and shouting to his companions, his light sweeping wildly back and forth. His armor still burned, though the flames were slowly dying, and he looked like a torch in the darkness.

Something emerged from the shadows behind him, a pistol pointed at his back. My heart jumped as Garret deliberately paused, then lowered the gun and fired once, at the soldier's legs. The man shrieked and whirled around as he fell, raising his weapon, but Garret darted forward, smashed the butt of the pistol into his face and wrenched the rifle away as he collapsed to the cement.

More shots boomed out, the deafening roar of assault rifles making my ears ring as the rest of the squad converged on his location. Garret dived behind cover as they approached, not seeing me in the shadows.

I snarled and lunged, pouncing on one from behind, clamping my jaws around his leg and dragging him across the floor. He shouted, clawing at the ground, and his friends immediately aimed their rifles at me.

A blur of motion, and Garret hit them from behind, striking one behind the ear with the pistol and grabbing the other's weapon as he turned. The soldier beneath me tried flipping onto his back to shoot, but I pinned him down and slammed his head into the floor. He shuddered and went limp, the gun clattering to the cement. Tensing, I looked up just as the second soldier swung wildly at Garret and clipped him in the jaw with an elbow. Garret staggered, and the human immediately struck him in the head with the assault rifle, driving him to a knee, then raised the gun to fire.

I leaped with a roar, slamming into the soldier just as he pulled the trigger. He recovered, swinging the muzzle around at me, and I blasted him in the face with fire. Screaming, he reached up, tearing away the flaming helmet and mask...as Garret surged to his feet and punched him in the jaw as hard as he could.

The human reeled back, fell into a pillar and slid to the ground, his head dropping to his chest as he went limp. Silence fell, the echoes of screams and gunfire fading into the black. Still shaking with fury and adrenaline, I looked at Garret, wondering if we had really won. If it was really over.

He stood cradling his hand, gazing at the soldier slumped against the beam, his expression torn between relief and guilt. A trickle of blood ran down his face from his temple, crawling down his cheek, and my stomach knotted. "You're bleeding!" I exclaimed, jumping over the body of one of the soldiers. My claws clicked anxiously over the floor as I trotted up. "Are you all right?"

He nodded painfully. "Just a cut," he said, lowering his arm as I reached him. "It's not serious." Wincing, he looked down at his hand, clenching and unclenching a fist. "Think I burned myself when I punched the last soldier, though."

"Let me see," I said, reaching for his arm. He stiffened, and I froze when I saw my scaly foreleg, curved black talons hovering close to his skin. Claws that could easily rend and tear and rip right through him. His eyes rose to mine, and I saw my reflection in his steely pupils: a huge horned lizard with claws and wings outstretched, looming over him. For half a heartbeat, we stared at each other, dragon and soldier, surrounded by the bodies of his former brethren.

Garret moved first. In the moment before I would've pulled back, he raised his arm and held it out to me, placing the back of his hand gently in mine. Heart lurching, I very cautiously curled my talons around his wrist. He didn't move, didn't flinch or tense up, though a patch of his skin was red with the telltale shininess of a burn. I swallowed hard.

"Sorry about that."

"I've had worse." He held my gaze, gray eyes intense. "Besides, it's hard to be angry at something that saved your life."

"Garret? Ember?"

Faith edged into view. She held a length of rebar in both hands, and it shook as she gazed around at the fallen soldiers. "The shooting…stopped," she whispered, her body poised for flight, as if the bodies might leap up and attack again. "I didn't know if you were still alive, or if they had…had…" Her voice trembled, and she trailed off. I huffed a cloud of smoke at her.

"So you decided to come look for us? You're supposed to be hiding—"

One of the soldiers from earlier, the first one I'd taken down, suddenly lunged out of the shadows, gun held before him. Faith shrieked, swinging the rebar wildly as he appeared, catching him right in the face. He crashed to the floor again and lay still, while Faith scuttled behind Garret, breathing hard.

"Is he dead?" she squeaked, as I forced myself to exhale and relax my muscles, releasing the air that I'd sucked in slowly, and not in a violent explosion of fire. Garret walked to the fallen soldier, knelt and rolled him onto his back. His head flopped, blood streaming from his nose and mouth, and I couldn't tell if he was breathing or not.

"The others will be on their way," Garret muttered, not looking up from the body. He started rummaging through the soldier's stuff, checking for guns and ammo, most likely, anything to help us get out of here. "We need to hurry. Ember…" He glanced at me, narrowing his eyes. "Can you Shift back before we leave the hotel?"

I cringed. *Not without my clothes.* "Gimme two seconds," I said, and hurried to where I'd left my belongings, then changed back and slipped into them as quickly as I could. When I returned, Garret stood waiting for me, gun in hand, the soldier's belt now looped around his waist. Faith hovered beside him, watching his every move with starry eyes. All her fear of the former St. George soldier seemed to have vanished, and I bit down a snort of disgust.

Garret tossed me a pistol as I came up, and I caught it grimly. "Let's go," he ordered, and we fled the room, knowing the rest of the force was still out there, swarming the building. I suspected we weren't safe yet, and I was right.

As we turned down one last corridor, two soldiers looked up from where they guarded the stairwell at the end of the hall. The carbines blared, and we ducked back around the corner as bullets peppered the walls and floor. One of the soldiers called for backup, alerting the rest of them, and I snarled in frustration. So close; if we could just get past these guards, we were home free.

Raising the gun, I tensed to dart out of cover and fire, when Garret grabbed my arm.

"Wait." Drawing me back, he crept to the edge of the hallway and pulled something from the stolen belt at his waist. A small metal cylinder with a ring at the top. Glancing at me and Faith, he narrowed his eyes. "Look away," he ordered. "Close your eyes and cover your ears. Both of you." And he hurled what was in his hand around the corner, toward the soldiers.

The boom rocked the corridor, and even through my closed lids, I saw the brilliant flash of light, as if a star had exploded in the hall. The gunfire ceased, and Garret took my hand, pulling me to my feet with a brisk "Let's go!" We sprinted past the stunned, gaping soldiers, hit the stairwell at top speed and didn't stop running until we reached the very last door and burst through it into the hot Vegas night.

RILEY

We finally reached the end of the elevator shaft.

I heard Ava hit the bottom, the quiet thump of her feet on solid ground echoing faintly up the tube. Relieved, anxious to be done with tight spaces and lethal falls in utter darkness, I descended the last few rungs and hopped off the ladder, before realizing we weren't home free just yet.

The floor under my boots swayed slightly, as if hovering a few inches off the ground. Clicking on my flashlight, I saw we'd hit the metal roof of the elevator box, thick cables coming out of the center and rising up the tube. A small square hatch sat in one corner, and Ava crouched next to it, her hair a ghostly silver in the pale light.

"It's stuck," she whispered.

Putting the flashlight on the floor, I knelt across from her and grasped the handle at the top. "On three," I muttered, as her fingers wrapped around mine, slender and cool, and I tightened my grip. "One…two…three!"

Together we tugged. The hatch, like the elevator doors, resisted a moment, then opened with a rusty screech that made my teeth vibrate. I poked my head through the opening, shining the flashlight around, then pulled back with a nod.

"Clear."

We dropped into the elevator box, Ava landing as lightly as a cat. The doors were partially open, and I could see an empty hall beyond, dark and silent for now.

"First floor," Ava whispered, gazing at the brass number in the door frame. She sounded relieved. "We're almost out."

"Not quite." I eased into the hall, gazing around warily. "The doors will be guarded for sure, and there's no telling how many snipers they've got watching the exits. And of course, that damn chopper will be circling around, making things difficult."

"So we can't go through the doors." Ava followed me, pragmatic and as cool as ever. "How will we get out, then?"

"Easy." I grinned at her. "We use a window."

Voices echoed down another hallway, making us both tense. A moment later, the sound of boots started toward us, marching ominously closer. I switched off the flashlight, and we ran.

Ducking into an office, Ava closed and locked the door while I raced to the window and peered cautiously through the glass. The empty construction zone stretched away into the black, but past the barren lot I could see the lights of civilization in the distance, tantalizingly close. Question was, could we get across that flat, open plain without taking a bullet to the forehead?

"Cobalt!" Ava hurried to my side, her voice a warning growl. "They're coming."

Shit. Out of time. "Stand back," I told her, and grabbed an abandoned fire extinguisher from the floor. Raising it over my head, I smashed it against the window, feeling the impact jar my teeth together. Cracks appeared on the first hit, spread out on the second, and on the third, the glass finally shattered. I bashed the window a few times more, making a large enough hole, then threw the extinguisher down and beckoned to Ava. "Go!"

A heavy blow rattled the door behind us. Ava sprinted three steps and dived gracefully through the glass, then rolled to her feet like an acrobat. I followed, hunching my shoulders as I plunged through, feeling shards catch on my leather jacket. But then I was on the other side, scrambling upright, and we were running across the empty lot, hearing shots fired as we fled into the concealing night. Nothing hit us, but we didn't stop running until we reached the edge of the pavement, scrambled over the fence and darted across an empty street. Into the safety of civilization and away from the Order at last.

Taking refuge behind an auto repair shop, I slumped against the brick wall, sucking in deep, gasping breaths while I waited for my heart to slow down. Ava leaned beside me, head back, silver hair spilling over her shoulders.

Damn, we made it. Edging to the corner of the building, I peered back at the hotel, making sure we weren't being followed. Past the streetlights and the fence, I could just make out the helicopter, still circling the empty lot, and smiled grimly. *Still a lucky SOB. Now, if only Ember and the others made it out.*

"Okay," I muttered, hearing Ava step up behind me. "Looks like we're in the clear. We'll lie low for a bit, see if the others got out okay. If we don't hear from them in ten minutes, you go on to the hotel. I might have to go back for Ember and Faith."

"No, Cobalt," Ava said, her voice low and grave. "I don't think you will."

There was a sharp pain in the side of my neck, like a hornet's sting, hot and piercing. Alarmed, I started to turn, but the ground swayed, tilted beneath me, and everything went dark.

COBALT

Twelve years ago

The door swung open without a sound, and the figure in black eased into the room. On noiseless feet, it stole over the carpet, the long, straight knife glimmering in the shadows as it drew alongside the bed. The lump beneath the covers didn't stir, as a slender gloved hand reached down to grasp the corner of the quilt. In one smooth motion, the shadow flung back the covers and plunged the knife into what lay beneath.

The pillow gave a muffled thump as the blade stabbed into it, but otherwise made no sound.

"Nice try."

The assassin spun, raising her knife as I stepped out of the closet, my pistol already trained on her. She froze at the sight of the gun, and I gave a sad smile.

"Hello, Stealth," I greeted softly, moving around the other side of bed, keeping a large obstacle between us. It would at least slow her down if she decided to lunge. She watched me with dark, impassive eyes, and a lump caught in my throat. "I knew Talon had to send someone eventually," I said, my voice tight. "I wish it didn't have to be you."

The Viper continued to regard me without expression. I stayed where I was, every ounce of my attention focused on the other dragon. I could not let it waver, even for a millisecond. Because that was how long it would take the Viper to leap across the bed and put a knife in my throat.

Stealth blinked, seemingly unconcerned with the gun pointed in her direction. She was lithe and slender, and the black Viper suit looked like a spill of ink across her skin. Straight black hair had been pulled into a tail, and her pale, slightly rounded face seemed to float in the darkness of the room. "They were going to send Lilith," she stated quietly, making my skin crawl at the name. "I convinced them that it should be me. It's the least I could do…for old time's sake."

"Yeah." I sighed, feeling an ache begin in my chest. "I could see how you would think that. You did save my life once. Only fitting that you should correct that mistake."

Her eyes narrowed a bit, but that was all. "How did you know I was coming?"

I gave a small snort. "You know me better than that," I said, grateful that, for all their lethality, Vipers did not have the same skill set I did. Or the paranoia that came with being a Basilisk. The hidden camera pointed down the hallway was synced to my phone, set to alert me whenever there was movement outside. It was annoying to be woken up by every drunk shambling down the hall at three in the morning, but a few hours' sleep was a small price to pay when it came to this.

Stealth didn't press the question, standing calmly with her hands at her sides, still gripping the dagger. "Are you going to shoot me, Agent Cobalt?"

"Not unless I have to."

Her jaw tightened. "If you don't," she warned, "I'm only going to come after you again. You know that, right? We were colleagues at one point, and I respected you, Cobalt. I still do, so consider this your only warning. Next time, there will be no words."

I nodded tiredly. "I know." This was a courtesy call. A formality between two agents who had fought on the same team. Once I left the room, that civility ended. The next time I saw Stealth, one of us had to die.

The Viper's lips thinned and, for the first time, a hint of anger crossed her cool face. "Why did you do it, Cobalt?" she asked in a harsh whisper. "You had just succeeded Blackscale. You were on your way up. There were even rumors that the Chief Basilisk wanted to make you his second. Why did you throw all that away?"

"You wouldn't understand," I told her, and she wouldn't. The Vipers were trained for ruthlessness, to take lives without question. I knew Stealth; if Talon told her to slit the throat of a seven-year-old human girl, she wouldn't even blink. "And it doesn't matter now, does it?"

Stealth shook her head. "No," she whispered, and I heard the resolve in her voice, the knowledge that when we did meet again, she was going to kill me. "I guess it doesn't."

I swallowed hard and gestured at her with the gun. "The knife," I ordered, my voice firm. "Toss it to me, now." This might be a courtesy call, but there was no way I was letting an armed assassin follow me out of the room. I might not make it to the parking lot.

Without argument, Stealth flipped the blade in her hand and arced it toward me over the bed. It hit the edge of the mattress right in front of me, hilt up, and I grabbed the blade without taking my eyes from her.

"You'll never escape us." The Viper's voice was quiet, matter-of-fact. "Even if you kill me, someone else will take my place. Talon will never let you go, and sooner or later, we're going to catch up. You're living on borrowed time, Cobalt."

Ice settled in my gut, but I sheathed the knife at my belt and gave her a half smile. "You don't have to parrot the mono-logue at me, Stealth," I said. "I was part of Talon just as long as you. You're not telling me anything I don't already know."

"Go, then." The Viper eased a few steps aside, away from the door. "Run, traitor. I won't be far behind."

Keeping the pistol trained on her, I slid around the bed and edged toward the exit. Stealth didn't move, only watched me with flat, expressionless eyes, as I pushed back the door and left the room.

The second I stepped through the frame, I began to run.

EMBER

Made it.

The taxi pulled up to the curb, and I scrambled to the sidewalk and raised my head to bask in the artificial glow. I'd never been so relieved to see the bright neon lights of the Strip and the crowds wandering the streets in the middle of the night. Light meant visibility, and crowds meant lots of witnesses, and no matter how much they hated us, the Order of St. George was just as secretive and paranoid of discovery as Talon. They preferred to do their killing in dark alleys and abandoned buildings, where they could murder us in peace without having to worry about silly things like questions or the law. They would not risk gunning us down in the middle of a busy street.

At least, I hoped they wouldn't.

"Stay alert," Garret warned as the taxi cruised off after leaving us on the curb. Every bit of him was tense, gray eyes sweeping the crowds and sidewalks, constantly on edge. "The Order could still be here." Faith whimpered and edged close to him, clutching his shirtsleeve. Annoyance flared, sudden and unreasonable, but Garret didn't react to the girl's pawing.

"Keep calm," he said without looking at her. "If you're scared, you'll be easy to notice. Try to act like nothing is wrong."

"Easy for him to say," Faith whispered to me. In the glow of the street lamps, she was pale and thin, with dark smudges beneath her eyes, and my irritation faded somewhat. Poor kid wasn't trying to be overly clingy; she really was terrified.

"You'll be fine," I told her, as Garret motioned us toward the hotel. "We won't let anything happen to you. Just stay close to us."

Cautiously, we ambled toward the entrance. Okay, so maybe *ambled* wasn't the right word; Faith was way too frightened to act normal, and her casual walk was more of a rigid march, eyes glued straight ahead. As we neared the doors, Garret casually reached down and took my hand, lacing our fingers together and making a knot form in my stomach. I stared up at him, and he offered a smile, squeezing my palm. I relaxed, even managing to smile at the bellboy who opened the door for us, like we were just three ordinary humans here for a good time. Faith, having relinquished her grip on Garret's shirt, glued herself to my other side and clung to my arm as we swept through the doors into the relative safety of the hotel.

Once we were past the lobby, Faith relaxed a bit, uncoiling from my arm and staring at the casino floor in awe. Before, I'd been entranced by all the lights, bells, crowds and movement; now I understood Garret's suspicion. There were so many people; any one of them could be an enemy, a soldier of St. George or a Talon agent in disguise. How many were watching us right now, gauging our movements, waiting for the perfect moment to strike?

I'd never accuse Garret of being paranoid again.

"Come on," Garret murmured, and gently tugged my hand, leading us across the floor toward the elevators. Faith trailed us doggedly, trying to look at everything, until we reached the elevator hall. Garret hit the button, then stepped aside, back to the wall, keeping his eye on the crowd behind us.

I edged close, leaning against the wall and lowering my voice. "Did you see Riley anywhere?" I whispered. Now that we'd escaped the hotel and could finally breathe, my thoughts went to the two companions we'd left behind. I'd texted Riley once when we were in the taxi, but hadn't heard anything back. Of course, that could mean any number of things, and I was trying not to assume the worst, but the hollow feeling in my gut continued to grow with every minute that passed with no word from the rogue.

Garret shook his head, not taking his eyes from the crowds. "No, but I wouldn't expect him to be on the floor," he murmured back. "If he's here, he'll be upstairs with Wes."

I nodded, trying to ignore the knot of dread uncoiling in my stomach. *He'll be all right*, I told myself. *He probably got out long before we did, and hasn't contacted us because he's afraid we're busy running from the Order. Or he's been too busy to check his phone. Of course, he should have texted one of us, just to let us know he made it out. We should have heard something by now. Dammit, Riley, you'd better be all right. You can't have gotten yourself killed by St. George.*

The elevator dinged, and I pushed myself off the wall to move toward the doors. They slid back just as I reached them, and a man in a bright red suit stepped out, nearly running into me. I dodged back with a scowl, barely catching myself from snapping something rude. Much as I wanted to tell him to watch where he put his feet, now was not the time to draw attention to ourselves.

But the human caught me looking at him and his eyes widened, like he was seeing a ghost. Ducking his head, he sped past me and vanished into the crowds.

Huh. That was weird. For a second, I hesitated, wondering if I shouldn't go after him. They way he'd looked at me...it was like he knew what I was.

"Did you know that man?" Garret asked at my shoulder, making me jump. Of course, his suspicious hawk eyes had caught everything. I shook my head as we entered the elevator, Faith close at our backs.

"No, I've never seen him before," I said, relieved as the doors closed and the elevator began to move. Had anyone else gotten on, I would have half expected them to pull a gun or a knife as soon as the doors shut. The soldier had made me completely paranoid. "Should we follow him?" I asked, as the numbers climbed steadily toward our floor. "Do you think he's with Talon or the Order?"

"If he is, there's nothing we can do about it now," Garret answered, far too calmly. "We have to get to Wes, see if he's heard anything from Riley or Ava. Maybe they're already here."

I clung to that small flicker of hope as the elevator doors finally opened and we stepped onto our floor. I made myself walk, not run, to Wes's door and rap on the wood.

It swung back almost instantly, and Wes peered out with wild hazel eyes, making my heart sink. "About bloody time you got here!" he hissed, stepping back to let us in. His room was disheveled, torn apart…and empty, as I'd feared. "Where the hell is Riley?"

"Not here," I answered, as the hollow feeling in my stomach opened into a dark, yawning pit, swallowing me whole. Garret locked the door and stood against it, gazing through the peephole, and Faith hovered anxiously, looking confused and lost.

Wes shot me a glare full of venom. "I bloody well see that! That's not what I asked," he snarled. "*Where* is Riley? I've been trying to contact him for hours. Is he all right? Is he dead? Where is he?"

"I don't know!"

"What do you mean, you don't know?"

"We were separated." Garret eased back from the door, apparently satisfied that we weren't followed and that no one lurked in the halls. "The Order swarmed the building. We had to take different routes back to the hotel."

"Well, that's bloody fantastic," Wes snapped, throwing up his arms. "So the Order is out there, hunting him down, and you two blighters went and left him to die."

At that, Faith burst into tears. Wes jumped and looked at her strangely, as if just realizing she was there. Covering her face with her hands, the girl turned into the corner and shook violently with sobs.

"My fault," she gasped, her voice muffled. "This is my fault. Ava knew I was unhappy in Talon. She convinced me to run with her. We wouldn't be here if it wasn't for me." Her voice trailed off into more muted sobbing, and Wes ran a hand down his face.

"Bollocks," he muttered, sounding both annoyed and sympathetic, which surprised me. "I didn't even see her there. I suppose this is one of the hatchlings you went to rescue?"

"Her name is Faith," I said, as Faith didn't look like she could introduce herself at that point. "There's another one out there, too, with Riley."

"Ava," Faith supplied, her voice small and choked with tears. "Her n–name is Ava. And if she dies, it'll be my fault." Turning into the corner, she collapsed into helpless sobs again.

Garret watched the crying girl for a moment, then looked at me, clearly lost. Sighing, I stepped forward, put an arm around her shoulders and drew her away from the wall. She sniffled and turned into me, hiding her face, her whole body shaking against mine.

"There was a man in the hotel," Garret went on, looking at Wes, while I rubbed Faith's back and waited for her to calm down. "We saw him at the bottom of the elevators. Dark, tall, wearing a red suit. He looked suspicious. Any reason we should be concerned?"

"Red suit?" Wes rubbed the bridge of his nose. "That's just Griffin, one of Riley's contacts. And yes, the blighter is shady as hell, but I don't think we have to worry about him. I'm more concerned about Riley at the moment." He looked at Garret, narrowing his eyes. "Did you say the Order was waiting for you?"

"They ambushed us at the hotel," Garret replied. "We had to split up."

"That's bloody suspicious," Wes muttered, crossing his arms. "No one knew where you were going. The only ones with that information were me and…" He trailed off, the color draining from his face. "Bloody bastard," he whispered. "I'll kill him. If Riley doesn't, I'll shoot the blighter myself."

"Can you get a lock on Riley's phone?" Garret asked, before I could ask who Wes meant. Apparently, that information was obvious to everyone but me. The human shook his head.

"What do you think I've been doing the past hour, mate?" he snapped. "No, I can't get a signal. It's either turned off or dead. Which could mean all sorts of things, but I don't like the implications of any of them, do you?"

Faith hiccupped, still shaking, possibly from the effort not to burst into tears again. I grimaced, feeling sick and tense and frayed myself. I wanted to know what had happened to Riley, too, but the amount of stress and tension in the room wasn't helping Faith and was driving my own dragon crazy. If I didn't step away soon, I was going to snap.

"I'm taking her to my room," I told the boys, pushing back the lock and pulling the door open. "You two stay here, girl talk only." Garret watched anxiously from the room, then followed us into the corridor. "Garret, we'll be all right," I said as he frowned in protest. "Keep waiting for Riley. I'll be right across the hall if anything happens."

He shook his head. "No, we're not separating anymore tonight. Take care of Faith, or whatever you have to do. I'll be right outside the door. If St. George or Talon does show up, I'll see them coming."

I nodded, too exhausted to argue. We crossed the hall, and I slid the key card into the slot then pushed the door open, letting Faith into the room before looking at Garret. He leaned beside the door frame with his back to the wall, his eyes scanning the corridor in both directions before fixing on me. I gave him a tired smile.

"Thanks," I whispered. "I won't be long."

"I'll be here."

My stomach fluttered. He was so close, gunmetal eyes intense, watching me with that protective stare. I wanted to lean up and kiss him, but Faith waited for me in the room, and now really wasn't the time. I reached out and squeezed his arm instead, before ducking through the frame.

Faith stood in the center of the floor with her arms around herself and a dazed look on her face. "Sorry about Wes," I told her as the door clicked behind me. "He's a little uptight, if you couldn't tell. Wish I could say that he's not usually such a bastard, but…well, he is."

The other hatchling didn't answer. Or even look at me. Her face was streaked with tears, her eyes huge and glassy beneath the tangle of curls. She looked very young, barely a teenager, though I knew she had to be at least sixteen.

Or maybe not. Maybe she hadn't even started assimilation, that period when hatchlings were placed with guardians in the mortal world, to learn to "blend in" with humans. It was after assimilation that Talon decided where you fit within the organization. Maybe Faith hadn't even gotten that far, and Talon was all she'd ever known.

I hoped she hadn't gone into shock and shut down completely. I didn't know what I was going to do if she'd hit zombie mode.

"Are you hungry?" I asked, figuring that was a good place to start. I knew *I'd* be hungry if I'd gone through what she had. Come to think of it, I *was*. Faith blinked at me, still looking dazed, and I tried again. "Hey, are you hungry? I don't know about you, but I'm starving. There's snacks below the television stand, or we could order room service."

She shook her head. "I'm not hungry," she whispered. Well, at least she was talking. "But thank you."

"Not hungry?" The idea was unthinkable. "Are you sure? Check this out." I opened the cupboard to display the wealth of snacks. No hatchling I'd ever heard of could resist chocolate. After a moment's hesitation, Faith edged forward and plucked a Snickers bar from the shelf, making me sigh in relief.

Grabbing a bag of peanut M&M's for myself, I hopped onto the bed and crossed my legs, motioning Faith to the other side of the mattress. She sat carefully, like she was afraid of wrinkling the covers. I leaned against the headboard and watched her, feeling a weird prickle of déjà vu. It was strange, having another dragon in my room, especially another female. It reminded me a bit of the sleepovers at Lexi's house in Crescent Beach, where the two of us would stay up all night, eating junk food and talking about various human things, usually surfing and boys. I'd missed that, and her.

I missed a lot of things, actually.

"So, how do you know Ava?" I asked, before those memories got too painful. Faith gave me a wary look, and I shrugged. "You can tell me. It's not like I'm gonna report you for treason or anything. If you want to know why I left, it's because they had me slotted to be a Viper." Faith's eyes widened; she knew what a Viper was, apparently. "Yeah. And I had a small problem with hunting down and killing my own kind. So I ran. Left town with Riley, and I haven't looked back since."

"Just like that?" Faith asked, as if she couldn't quite believe it. "No hesitation? Nothing you regretted leaving behind?"

"Well, yeah, of course there was. I had friends, and family, and…" A lump caught in my throat, and I looked down at my fingers. "Dante," I muttered. "My brother. I miss him the most. When I left, he decided to stay with the organization. He doesn't know…what they're really like." I squeezed the M&M's bag, clenching my jaw. "I'll get him out, soon," I whispered, more of a promise to myself than Faith. "Stupid twin. I'll make him see, even if I have to tear down Talon's walls to reach him."

"You're braver than I am," Faith whispered, picking at the wrapper on her candy bar. "If it wasn't for Ava, I'd still be there, even though I hated it."

I shook myself from my sudden dark mood. "How'd you get out?"

She hesitated a moment longer, then sighed, as if she was tired of holding back. "I knew Ava from way back," Faith said, nibbling at the bar. "We were in a clutch that grew up together, until they separated us for Human Training. I didn't see her face-to-face afterward, but somehow we always kept in touch. Even though it was frowned upon. Talon didn't want us to have any previous attachments once we entered Human Training."

My insides curled, remembering the long years of schooling out in the desert, and how it was just barely tolerable only because I had Dante. Growing up, he was my best friend; we had each other's backs, and no matter how miserable things got, Dante was always there. I couldn't imagine going through that by myself, how lonely it had to be. Maybe that's why I didn't fit into the organization. Maybe I'd formed too many "attachments," when my only loyalty was supposed to be to Talon.

"Ava…had been planning to run for months," Faith went on, unaware of my musings. "She'd heard rumors about Cobalt, that there was a dragon who would help those wanting to leave the organization. Her first real assignment was coming up, and she told me she was planning to go rogue then. I was too scared to tell her I wanted to leave, too."

"Was that before you found out what Talon had planned for you?"

"Yes." Faith nodded. "And when Ava found out, she offered to take me with her, even though that would make her escape even more dangerous. I almost backed out, but she convinced me to run. That it was better to be hunted and free than a slave the rest of my life." She sniffed, curling into herself on the bed. "She was the brave one, the one who was trained for anything. I was only going to slow her down. And now she's out there, being hunted by St. George and Talon, maybe dead, and it's all my fault."

"Hey." I crumpled the empty M&M's bag, making her startle and look at me. "Beating yourself up isn't going to help her," I said firmly. "She made the choice to go rogue. She had to know the dangers. Besides—" I shrugged, feigning a confidence I didn't feel "—she's with Riley, and he's been doing this for a long time. If anyone can get away from St. George, it'll be him. Don't give up on them just yet."

She cocked her head. "You think so?"

"Yeah. So try not to worry. We don't know anything yet." I felt like a hypocrite, telling her not to worry when there was a yawning hole in the pit my stomach, threatening to devour me.

I slid from the bed, managing a smile as I headed toward the bathroom. "Be right back," I told Faith as she looked up. "Feel free to grab more food, or use the bed, or whatever. I don't know what we'll end up doing after this. You should rest while you have the chance."

She nodded but didn't say anything, fiddling with the wrapper of her candy bar, and I slipped into the bathroom.

Alone, I sat on the edge of the tub and dropped my head into my hands, breathing deep to keep the fear from swallowing me whole. Riley was out there, with Talon and St. George. What if he *wasn't* all right? What if he was dead? I didn't know what I'd do if the cocky, infuriating rogue was really gone, but my dragon was torn between curling into a ball and keening her loss and ripping something's head off.

Pushing myself upright, I splashed cold water on my face and ran wet fingers through my hair, making it stand on end. I was hot, sticky, and I desperately wanted a shower. But there was no time, and besides, if Garret or Wes burst into the room, I did not want either of them to catch me naked. I did, however, find my Viper suit where I'd tossed it on the floor. I pulled it on, then yanked my regular clothes over it. The outfit sucked greedily at my skin like it was eager to have me back, making me squirm. But if we were going to head back out for Riley and face St. George, at least, this time, I'd be prepared.

Faith had fallen asleep on the bed when I emerged from the bathroom, her breathing deep and steady. I smiled, tiptoed around the bed and shut off the lamp, plunging the room into shadow. The girl didn't even stir, soft snores coming from her open mouth. I watched her sadly for a moment, wondering if she would be all right. If anyone needed to get out of Talon, it was her, but I hoped she could handle being a rogue. It wasn't the easiest life, that was for certain. Come to think of it, *I* wasn't doing such a stellar job, myself.

I drew back, slipped quietly across the room and cracked open the door.

Garret stood there, leaning with his back against the wall and his arms crossed, vigilantly scanning the hallway. When the door squeaked open, he immediately pushed himself off the frame and turned to me, eyes questioning.

"Any word from Riley?" I whispered.

He shook his head. "Wes still hasn't been able to get a lock on his phone. How is Faith?"

"Sleeping," I replied, and took a step back. "Come on in, just be quiet. I don't want to leave her, and who knows when she'll get another chance to rest."

He eased through the frame, glancing warily around the room to make sure we were still alone, that no one had climbed in the windows or from under the bed when my back was turned. When he was sure the shadows were empty, he relaxed and followed me to the sitting area, where the huge curtained window showed off the glittering Vegas cityscape. I peered through the crack at the glowing carpet of lights, and my insides churned with worry. Riley was somewhere down in that mess, dodging St. George, fighting his way back to us. *Still alive*, my dragon insisted. He had to be. I wouldn't let myself think that he wasn't.

"Where are you, Riley?" I whispered to the haze of neon

lights. "Don't you dare die on me." A lump caught in my throat, and I clenched my fists. "Dammit, I hate this," I growled, feeling my dragon raging inside. "I feel so helpless. I wish I knew what to do." Garret watched me, silent and grave, and I slumped against the window. Las Vegas stretched out below me, dazzling and bright, but I couldn't see the luminance anymore. Now all I could see was a war zone.

"People are dying, Garret," I whispered. "Riley's out there. Ava is out there. And I'm just…" *Scared. Lost. Completely unprepared for what being a rogue actually means.* I leaned my forehead against the cool glass, staring at the streets until they blurred and ran together. "I don't know what I'm doing," I admitted. "I thought I did, but I was wrong. I have no idea what to do now. I…" *I don't want to lose anyone else. Especially him.*

Garret moved close, and then two strong arms enfolded me from behind, drawing me close. My pulse skipped, and my heartbeat sped up, echoing his own. I felt his quiet presence at my back as he leaned in, lips close to my ear.

"Riley's a pro at survival," Garret said in his soft, low voice, making my insides flutter. No reassurances, no empty promises, just simple facts. "He's been doing this a long time, longer than either of us. I know St. George. I know how they work." He paused then, his voice becoming just a little lighter. "I'm not too proud to say that he's smarter than most everyone in the Order. If anyone can get through this, he can."

I turned and slid my arms around his waist, hugging him to me. My fingers brushed the smooth metal of the gun beneath his shirt, and I wasn't afraid. He was a soldier, a former dragonslayer, but I felt safe with him. I trusted him completely. It wasn't the fierce, fiery longing my dragon had for

Cobalt. It was…simple. Easy. When I was with Garret, it was like we just clicked.

Riley's voice echoed in my head, angry and accusing. *Humans and dragons aren't supposed to be together! Their lives are a heartbeat compared to ours. What kind of future do you think you could ever have?*

I tried to shove it down, even as part of me agreed. I was a dragon; what was I doing with this human? My instincts raged at me, edgy and restless. I shouldn't be here; I should be with Riley right now. Why did I keep resisting? Cobalt and I were the same, split down the middle. Not only in species, but in everything that mattered. His dragon called to mine, and I knew he felt the same about me. If Garret wasn't here, it wouldn't even be a question.

But, Garret is here, I thought rebelliously. *He chose to be here. We gave him the chance to leave, and he chose to stay.*

For how long? the dragon whispered back. How long did I think a former soldier of St. George would remain in the company of his enemies? How long before he realized we had no future, that a dragon and a human were two vastly different creatures, and had no business being together?

"Garret?" I asked, making him shift to look down at me. In the face of those solemn gray eyes, my throat went dry, and I swallowed to clear it. "Is this…? Are we…?" I exhaled and pressed my face to his shirt in embarrassment. Garret waited patiently for me to go on, his arms still looped around my waist. I ducked my head, closing my eyes so I wouldn't have to look at him. "Us," I whispered. "What we're doing… Is this wrong?"

Garret went very still. I counted his heartbeats, listened to the rise and fall of his breath. "I don't know," he finally said, his voice just a whisper between us.

I gave a bitter chuckle, stifling my disappointment. "That's not exactly the rousing assurance I was hoping for."

"I know," he murmured, sounding resigned, though he still didn't let me go. "But I'm probably the last person you should ask." He rested his chin gently atop my head, his voice thoughtful. "All my life, I was taught that dragons were evil, that they had no souls or emotions or real feelings, that they were just imitating humans in order to blend in." His hand traced my back, making my skin prickle. "And then, I met you. And discovered that everything I had learned, everything I thought I knew, my entire way of life, was wrong."

The pain in his voice, the underlying bitterness, clawed at me. "I'm sorry," I told him. "I never wanted you to regret this."

"I don't." Garret pulled back to look at me, his metallic gaze intense. "Maybe I would've been happier if I'd never come to Crescent Beach," he went on, making my stomach knot painfully. "If I was still with St. George, I'd still be killing dragons, because that's what they expected of me, and I wouldn't know any better. Maybe ignorance is bliss, but that doesn't make it *right*." His face tightened, eyes going dark. "I think back to who I was, what I did, before we met, and it sickens me. I'd rather die right now than return to the Order. I'd rather be hunted like the very ones I used to kill than revert to the ignorant soldier I was. That life is done. I want no part of it anymore. All because I met a dragon on a beach, and she refused to be what I expected." One hand rose, pressing against the side of my face, stroking with his thumb.

"Ember, meeting you is the most important thing that's ever happened to me," he said in a quiet voice. "I wouldn't change it for anything."

"Really?" I smiled, feeling my chest squeeze tight. His words made my heart soar, but the intensity of his gaze was too much. "Even after everything? Being shot at and chased and followed around the casino by a security guard for underage gambling?" I asked, trying to ease the tension.

"Even then," Garret replied, his eyes shining silver in the darkness. "I think...I'm in love with you, Ember."

GARRET

Did I really just say that?

Time had frozen around us, the echo of my confession hanging in the air, impossible to retract. Ember blinked at me, looking as stunned, and almost as panicked, as I felt. What had come over me? Was I losing my mind? I had absolutely no experience to draw on. Nothing like this had ever happened to me before. Tristan would've laughed at my idiocy. I had been a soldier of the Order; our love affairs involved weapons—machine guns, pistols, sniper rifles. Instruments of death, not people. The Order itself cautioned about divided loyalties, saying our hearts should belong to St. George and the mission before all else. Marriage was infrequent among soldiers; most of us died young, and dedication to the cause had to take precedent over everything else, even family. The bond we shared with our brothers, our comrades in arms, was stronger and far purer than the weak desires of the flesh. I'd known that, believed it wholeheartedly, once. I was what they made me: a weapon. The Perfect Soldier. What did I know about love?

For a second, I balked, my heart going cold in my chest. Why *had* I said anything? I knew she wasn't human. Though she looked and acted and sounded like a normal girl, Ember was, at her core, a dragon. A creature that, according to the Order, could only imitate emotion. I no longer even remotely believed that, but I barely understood human emotion; I knew nothing about the hearts of dragons.

The soldier pressed forward, blank and emotionless, ready to numb all feeling. To shield me from pain and humiliation and fear. This had been a mistake. I'd left myself open, vulnerable, but there was still time to withdraw, to retreat behind a wall of indifference and—

No. I hardened myself, steeling my emotions in a different way. No illusions this time. No doubts. I knew exactly what was happening, that the girl in my arms wasn't human. The Order would call me profane, a blasphemer, a demon lover. I was selling myself to evil. I was joining the devil's own and damning my soul to hell. Ember might not return my feelings, not in the human sense. I didn't know if dragons were even capable of love.

All of this went through my head in a heartbeat, and between one pulse and the next I decided, once and for all, that I didn't care. Ember was a dragon. She was also beautiful, fearless, kind and ironically more human than the very people who wanted her whole race extinct. I didn't know if most dragons were as the Order said they were ruthless, conniving, power hungry—but I did know not *all* dragons were like that. Ember was different. Riley was different. I'd seen it firsthand. And the hatchlings I'd met, Ava and Faith, they weren't the savage monsters St. George claimed them to be, either. The Order had lied. Talon had lied. I didn't know what to think anymore, or who to believe. I was aware of only one thing: I was done fighting this. I no longer cared what anyone thought.

I was in love with a dragon.

Let the Order condemn me, I mused, perhaps my first truly rebellious thought in a lifetime. *Let them call me a traitor and hunt me down.* For thirteen years, I had followed commands, lived by the rigid code of St. George, become their perfect soldier, only to discover the Order I'd dedicated my life to was wrong. Everything I'd thought I knew was a lie. The only real thing was the girl in my arms.

"Garret," Ember whispered, her eyes huge in her face as she stared at me. I felt the acceleration of her heartbeat, thudding rapidly against mine, felt a tremor go through her, and held my breath. And I waited, everything frozen inside, to see if the dragon I loved would leave me unscathed, or shred my heart to ribbons in front of me. "I... I don't..."

A phone rang loudly in the darkness.

EMBER

I jumped, leaping away from Garret, as a tinny melody shattered the quiet, coming from the bed. He let me go, turning toward the sound as well, his expression shutting into that remote blankness. My heart raced, thrilled, relieved, absolutely terrified. I didn't know what to feel; I didn't know what I wanted. I only knew that the tangle of confusion, worry and dragony rage inside was threatening to pull me apart.

Later, I decided, between one muffled ring and the next. I would sort through everything later. I couldn't think about... what Garret had said right now. First, we had to find our missing dragons.

Faith stirred. Rising groggily from the mattress, she fumbled in her pocket and brought the phone to her ear with a mumbled "Hello?"

Instantly, she bolted upright, eyes going wide. Gazing across the room, she spotted me and swung her legs off the bed, holding out the phone. "It's Ava!"

I lunged and snatched the device from her hand. "Ava, are you all right?" I asked, putting it to my ear. "Is Riley with you?"

"Ember?" The voice on the end was a gasp, and cold fin-

gers clutched my insides. "We couldn't…make it back," Ava
panted, sounding frantic and breathless. "St. George followed
us from the building and have spread out. They're not letting us leave the area." She took two deep, ragged breaths,
her next words laced with fear. "You have to come quick.
Riley's been hurt—"

The blood froze in my veins. "Where are you?"

"Some old rail yard a few blocks from the hotel. Please,
hurry. We don't…" She trailed off, and in the distance, I
thought I heard the sounds of gunshots.

"Ava?"

"They're coming," the other dragon whispered.

The line went dead.

"Ava! Dammit!" I yanked the phone from my ear and stood
there, trying to calm the fiery urge to Shift and crash through
the window after them. What did I do now? Riley was out
there, wounded, maybe dying, and St. George was closing
in. Panic raged inside, the dragon flaring up and down my
veins, screaming at me to do something.

"What happened?" Faith asked, her eyes bright with terror. "Are they all right?"

"Riley's been hurt," I said, clenching the phone so that the
edges bit into my palm. My skin felt tight, the air in my lungs
simmering with heat. "They've been trapped, and can't get
back to the hotel. We have to help them."

"Where are they?"

Garret's cool, steady voice broke through the rising panic.
My dragon snarled at him, impatient and wanting action, not
this sitting around to chat. *Stop it*, I told her. *We can't just charge*

through the window and wing off to find Riley. We need a plan. I took a deep breath to calm us both and forced myself to think.

"Ava said something about a rail yard a few blocks from the abandoned hotel," I told the soldier. "But she didn't give me any street signs or numbers. And I didn't see any railroads when we were running from the building, did you?" Frustration reared up again, and I rubbed a hand across my face. "They could be anywhere, and we don't have time to guess. St. George is almost there."

"We won't have to guess. Come on." And Garret strode purposefully from the room, leaving me and Faith to scramble after him. We crossed the nearly empty hall, not pausing to look for would-be enemies, and Garret banged twice on Wes's door.

It swung back, and the gangly human glared out at us, looking exhausted. Dark circles crouched under his eyes, and his hair stuck out in every direction. "What do you—"

"Ava contacted us," Garret interrupted, making the human's brows shoot up. "St. George has them cornered in a rail yard a few blocks from the building we left. Can you pull up a map of the city?"

"Shite," Wes muttered, and ducked back into the room, hurrying to his laptop. We followed, crowding around the chair, as his fingers flew across the keyboard and his shoulders hunched in concentration.

"All right," Wes muttered, his nose very close to the computer screen, making it hard to see around him. "A rail yard, you said? That shouldn't be terribly hard to find." He typed a few more things, and the screen flipped to a large map of Las Vegas. "Okay," Wes mumbled, zooming in until street names

appeared on-screen, "this is where we are now. And here—"
he scrolled over the map "—is the site of that abandoned hotel.
So, now we're looking for a railroad... Wait, that must be
it." The mouse arrow circled a confusing jumble of lines and
squares on the map. "About five blocks east from the hotel
site," he said. "Right on the edge of town. Bollocks, Riley,
what were you thinking? You don't run *away* from the lights
and crowds if the Order is chasing you. Certainly not to an
isolated warehouse in the middle of nowhere." Sitting back,
he eyed us over the chair back. "If they're down there, that
place will be crawling with dragonslayers. You'll be walking
into a death trap."

"We don't have a choice," I said. "Riley's in there, and he's
hurt. Besides," I went on, glaring at him, "I thought this was
what you wanted. It's my fault he's in trouble, isn't that what
you implied?"

"That doesn't bloody mean I want you to rush into a trap
and get your stupid head blown off," Wes snarled back. His
eyes flashed, staring me down, before he sighed and scrubbed
a hand through his hair. "What do you think Riley will do
if you get yourself killed?" he went on in a softer voice. "He
nearly lost his mind the last time you were hurt. If anything
happens to you now, he'll never be the same. Riley is the
beating heart of this underground, but if you die, the resistance might very well die with you. Because he might not
have the will to care anymore."

I blinked in shock. Wes sighed, rubbing the bridge of his
nose, his face taut with pain. "I just want you to *think*, hatchling." He sighed. "To come up with some sort of plan, otherwise you'll *all* be killed."

"Don't worry about that," Garret broke in, and Wes turned to eye him wearily. "I know St. George," he added. "I know their tactics, and what they'll be doing. We're not going in blind. I'll get them out."

"I'm coming, too," Faith said.

Surprised, I looked at her. She stood a little ways behind us, pale and terrified but resolved. "Ava saved me," she insisted. "I wouldn't have gotten out of Talon if it wasn't for her. I want to help, however I can."

Garret shook his head. "You're not trained for this," he stated. "I can't effectively search for the others if I'm worried about protecting you, Faith. It's better if you stay here."

"Please," Faith whispered, and turned to me. "Don't leave me here," she pleaded. "I can't stay behind, doing nothing, not knowing if you'll come back. I swear I won't get in your way or slow you down. And I'll do whatever you tell me to do." Her eyes went glassy, even as she took a deep breath, composing herself. "Ava is like a sister to me," she said, making my stomach knot. "I won't abandon her. I might not be trained for this, but two dragons stand a better chance against St. George than one. Please, I have to come."

I looked helplessly at Garret, who nodded. "All right," he agreed, sounding reluctant. "Just stay close, and try to hide if things get dangerous." He turned to Wes, his voice cool. "They'll need weapons," he said. "Both of them. If St. George is down there, we can't take any chances."

Wes nodded, rising from the chair. "I suppose there's really no other way to do this," he said, pulling a duffel bag from the corner and setting it on the bed. Unzipping it, he stepped back as Garret rummaged inside and pulled out a handgun.

Turning, he offered it to me. I took it without hesitation this time, checking the chamber for rounds before shoving it into the waistband of my jeans and pulling my shirt over it, as I'd seen Garret do. No being squeamish now. I was a soldier, and this was a war. If we were going to save Riley and Ava, I had to accept that.

Faith paled when Garret held a pistol out to her, but she took it without hesitation. Wes watched the soldier with hooded eyes, his expression torn between dislike and cautious hope. "Get Riley out," he told him, as Garret checked his own gun for rounds, then snapped the cartridge back into place. "Nothing else matters. You're not just saving him, you're saving everyone in his underground. I can't do what Riley does. If he dies, all the dragons and humans he rescued from Talon are as good as dead."

"We'll bring him back," I told Wes, feeling a fiery determination spread through me. There was no way I was going to let him die. He was my other half; without him, I felt incomplete. I wasn't sure if this was my dragon talking or me, but I couldn't imagine a world without Riley. I looked to Garret, meeting those solemn gray eyes, and took a deep breath. "Ready?"

He nodded once. Together, we walked through the casino, out the doors and into the hot Vegas streets.

Back into the war zone.

GARRET

This place was a tactical nightmare.

The rail yard was separated from the rest of the city by a rusty chain-link fence and a strip of industrial desert that marked the end of civilization. Tracks stretched across the open, dusty ground, and aisles of freight containers created a labyrinth of cover and tight quarters. If I were to stage an ambush, this would be the perfect spot.

"Stay alert," I told Ember as we crouched behind a metal container on the edge of the yard. The place looked deserted, but that meant nothing. St. George knew how to stay hidden. "Watch the aisles, they'll be the most dangerous. If you see anyone, don't try to take them out. The Order never does single patrols. If there's one, there'll be more nearby. Just get out of sight."

She nodded, eyes determined. "I'll follow your lead," she whispered, raising the gun. "Tell me when to go."

Behind her, Faith trembled and pressed close, her gaze darting around the yard like a trapped deer. I felt a stab of apprehension; Ember could take care of herself. Or at least, she had faced St. George before, and she wasn't afraid to fight. Faith, despite her insistence on coming along, was not prepared for this. If we ran into the Order and had to fight our way free, I hoped I could protect us all.

I motioned us forward, and together we darted across the open yard, staying low and keeping to the shadows, until we reached the first train sitting idle on the tracks. Hugging the walls, I edged toward the front, peeking between cars for any hints of movement on the other side. Ember stayed close; I could feel her heat at my back, her steady breathing whenever we paused. For a moment, I had a distracting sense of how surreal this situation was. Again. Here I was, a former soldier of St. George, on the other side of the war with two dragons at my back, trying to rescue one of their own from the Order. It was a fleeting thought; I couldn't let myself be distracted now. I had to stay focused on the mission and our surroundings, the tactics that would keep us alive. But it crept in all the same, dark and taunting. Would this ever feel normal? And who was I? I didn't even recognize myself anymore.

"Where are they?" Ember whispered as we crept into an open boxcar after making certain it was empty. "This place feels completely deserted. Where could they be hiding?"

"I don't know," I murmured, peering out the other side of the car. The space between the narrow aisles was dark and still. Too still. No bullet holes, no footprints, no signs of a fight or struggle. I hadn't seen any telltale spatters on the ground, either, which made me both relieved and nervous. The Order was trained to strike hard and fast and to vanish without a trace when the job was done, but they would at least leave *some* signs of passing. There was nothing here. Ember was right; this place felt completely deserted.

"What about that building?" Faith said, pointing to a large

rectangular structure beyond the maze of tracks and containers. From this angle, it looked like the freight warehouse.
"Do you think they could've gone in there, to hide at least?"

I shook my head. "That would be one of the first places
the Order would search. If they are in there, they're either
trapped, or..." I didn't voice what I was thinking, but Ember
went rigid at my back, drawing in a short breath. She knew
what I was going to say.

"We have to check it out," Ember said, her voice tight
with anger and fear. Not fear for herself; I recognized that
steely look on her face, and knew nothing would frighten her
away now. It was for Ava and Riley, and what would happen
if we didn't find them. Or worse, if we *did*. I remembered
the aftermath of a successful raid; the smoldering ruins, the
charred, blackened husks that were once people, the lifeless
dragons lying in pools of blood. My stomach turned. I didn't
want Ember to see that, to really see what St. George did to
her kind. What I used to do.

"Let's go," Ember told me, rising swiftly. "If St. George is
here, we have to help them. They could still be alive. And
if they're not, if the Order killed him..." Her eyes flashed,
and I caught a split-second glimpse of an angry red dragon
below her skin. Her lip curled, and the air around her shimmered with heat. "If St. George wants to fight a dragon, I'll
give them one."

"Ember, wait." I caught her arm, felt the faint outline of
scales rising to the surface before they vanished. She turned
on me, and I met the furious glare of the dragon. "Stay calm,"
I murmured. "Don't go charging off by yourself, not with St.
George. This is *not* a good place to fight the Order." I nod-

ded toward the warehouse. "There'll be a lot of narrow aisles and tight quarters, places where it's easy to become cornered or trapped or lost, and St. George is trained to take full advantage of that confusion. If we're separated, they'll pick us off one by one. We can't help Riley if we become hunted ourselves." She stubbornly set her jaw, and I raised my other hand, pressing it to her cheek. "Do you trust me?" I asked.

"Yes," she whispered. No hesitation. Not even a heartbeat of silence. It made my heart turn over, that blind faith in a former dragonslayer, but I shoved it down. We had to stay focused.

"I promise," I began, even as a part of me cringed inside. I never made promises to anyone; it was impossible to know if you could keep them. But the way Ember was looking at me, I wanted to give her some kind of assurance. "We'll get Riley out," I continued. "And Ava. I'll do everything I can to keep them safe, but I also know what can happen if we're not careful. The Order has us at a disadvantage. This is their ideal location for a strike, and if they surprise us we don't stand a chance."

"You seem to have forgotten that I've done this before."

"I know." I almost smiled at her indignant look. As if I could forget what she really was, what she had done. "But this is still the Order, and they'll still do their best to kill us. I can't help Riley and be worried about you and Faith at the same time."

Ember was stiff for a moment, then nodded. "All right," she said quietly. "I trust you, Garret. What do you need me to do?"

"Just follow my lead," I replied. "We stay together at all

times. And don't Shift unless it's a matter of life and death. Faith?" I glanced over my shoulder at the other girl. "Are you all right? Can you do this?"

"I'm…good," Faith whispered, though a tremor went through her voice at the end. She took a deep breath and straightened grimly. "I'm okay. Lead on. We're right behind you."

We crept silently across the deserted train yard, weaving between cars and hugging the shadows, always on guard for the Order. I kept my eyes trained for movement, footprints in the dust, spent bullet casings or drops of blood. Nothing.

"Are you sure Ava said they were here?" I asked, glancing at Ember as we crouched behind a row of shipping containers a few yards from the warehouse. She nodded vigorously.

"I'm sure. Old rail yard a few blocks from the abandoned hotel." Ember scanned the open space between the tracks and the warehouse, frowning. "She said Riley was hurt and they had to hide because the Order was coming."

Unease gnawed at me. It didn't make sense. If I wasn't sure that this was the only rail yard this side of the city, I would think we were in the wrong place. Still, we couldn't go back, not until we were certain. If Ava and Riley were here, we had to find them.

There was no movement or sound as we approached the warehouse and sidled along the outer wall, looking for a way in. Several windowpanes were out, the glass shattered and broken, but they were filthy and covered in grime and cobwebs. Nothing had gone through them in a while. Beyond the filmy glass, the interior of the warehouse was dark, with aisles of freight stacked nearly to the ceiling. Again, my soldier's instincts recoiled. Another maze of narrow halls and tight quarters; I was liking this situation less and less. The large metal doors, where freight was presumably taken and dropped off, were closed and locked tight, and nothing short of a blowtorch or a pack of C-4 was going to force them open. My hope that Ava and Riley were here was fading fast, when Faith gave a sudden gasp and surged forward.

"Ava!" she cried, making me jerk up. "Wait!"

Before I could stop her, she sprinted forward, toward an open door I hadn't noticed, and vanished through the frame.

"Dammit," Ember growled, and started forward, as well. "Come on, Garret, before she gets herself killed."

I gave a silent curse and hurried after her, ducking through the opening into the enormous shipping room. The shadows of the warehouse closed around us, smelling of dust, wood and iron, and the maze of crates and shipping containers loomed overhead. Faith was nowhere to be seen.

Grimly, I raised my weapon and motioned Ember behind me. Hugging the walls, we edged around the stacks of crates, searching for the girl while staying on high alert. Light footsteps pattered across the floor, fading into the darkness, but it was impossible to tell which direction they were coming from.

"Dammit, where did she go?" Ember muttered.

A scream cut through the darkness, turning my blood cold. It was followed by a crash and the sound of a scuffle somewhere in the maze. Ember snarled something in Draconic and rushed past me, her eyes flaring green in the darkness. Gripping my weapon, I followed. The aisles of freight abruptly ended in a large open area, cement floor bare but for a few stacked pallets and a forklift.

"Faith!" Ember hissed, creeping forward with the gun raised. "Where are…"

A figure melted out of the shadows, dragging something into the light, and my stomach dropped. Faith met my gaze, her eyes huge with fear, as a man in a black suit yanked her forward, one arm around her neck, the other pressing a gun to her temple.

The lights came on, driving away the shadows, and a half dozen armed men stepped into view, muzzles of their M-16s pointed right at us.

RILEY

"Comfortable, Cobalt?"

Ava lowered the phone and turned, smiling at me across the table. Without waiting for an answer, she reached over and flipped on the spotlight, beaming it right in my face. I squinted but refused to turn my head. "Anything you want to say before we get started?"

"I'm good, thanks." I tried to shrug, which was harder than it looked, being tied to a chair with my arms behind the metal back. The plastic cuffs dug into my wrists as I turned, pretending to look around the room. "Though the service in this place sucks. I ordered a glass of 'Screw you, Talon bitch' an hour ago."

Ava smiled.

"Vulgar bravado will not save you, I'm afraid." The girl walked around the table, regarding me like she might a particularly tricky math problem. Plucking a needle and syringe from the table, she held it up and turned back to me. "I assume you already know what I stuck you with."

"I'm guessing Dractylpromazine," I replied. Developed in Talon labs using a mix of science and old magic, "Dractyl" was a powerful tranquilizer that essentially put the dragon side of us to sleep, preventing Shifting and locking us into a human form for a short time. One of Talon's more terrifying weapons against their own kind, it was a jealously guarded secret, given to agents only in rare, special circumstances. I'd attempted to Shift earlier, as soon as I'd woken up and realized where I was. But the dragon had barely stirred, sluggish and groggy, as if coming out of a long hibernation. That was when I'd known this wasn't an ordinary kidnapping, that whoever had captured me knew exactly what I was and how to counter my most potent weapon. Which meant only one thing.

Talon had finally caught up. I was in trouble.

"Yes," Ava agreed, putting the syringe back on the table. "So you know escape is impossible. That dose is good for at least three hours, and I have several more where that came from. None of your friends know where you are, and I disabled your phone so that your human hacker friend won't be able to track it. No one is coming for you." She stepped in front of the table and faced me head-on. "This doesn't have to be hard, Cobalt. You know I'm going to get what I want, sooner or later. How quick, and how painful, this is going to be depends on you."

I smirked. "Is that your best opening? Take away all hope, make the victim think he has no options left, that you're always one step ahead of him. If he has nothing left to cling to, nothing will matter to him, and he'll be much more pliable to suggestion." She blinked, and my smirk grew wider. "Psychological Warfare 101, hatchling. I've *forgotten* more about Talon mind games than you'll ever know. If you think you're going to out-psyche me, give it your best shot. I can do this all night."

"Insightful," Ava said, sounding reluctantly impressed. "You do remember your Basilisk training, after all. When we first met, I thought you were just a thug who kept getting lucky. I'd forgotten you were one of Talon's best."

"I was," I agreed. "Though I must not rate *too* high on Talon's threat meter, if they're sending hatchlings to do a Viper's job. So, what's your *real* name? If we're going to go through the dance tonight, you can give me that much, at least."

The girl regarded me for a moment, then shrugged. "I suppose it doesn't matter now," she mused. "My real name is Mist."

"Mist, huh? You're awfully young to be doing this with no backup." I curled my lips into a sneer. "Is this your exam, hatchling, or are all the real agents off murdering defenseless kids in their sleep?"

She offered another faint smile. "Trying to anger me into letting information slip is not going to work, either, Cobalt. Besides, you know the answer to that as well as I do."

I did know, which made the organization's interest in me all the more insidious. Talon couldn't send one of their real agents after me because I knew them all. If someone like Lilith or another Viper showed up in town, I'd be gone the instant I got word of it—unless I was trying to convince a stubborn, red-haired hatchling to leave with me, that is. It didn't even have to be a Viper; *any* dragon from my old life, be they Viper, Basilisk, Chameleon or Gila, I was instantly wary of. Talon knew I'd never trust one of their agents. They had to send a hatchling, someone I'd never seen before and would want to help, to lower my guard.

I should've seen this coming. I knew Talon was getting irritated with my high jinks; losing even one or two hatchlings a year was a big thing when your numbers were small. I'd thought I could handle whatever big nasty Viper they sent to take me out. But Talon was also devious as hell, a master of manipulation, of finding your weaknesses and using them against you. They'd baited me with the one thing I couldn't ignore: a couple hatchlings in trouble, and I'd fallen for it like a moron. I'd been overconfident and was paying for it now.

Fortunately, I had a couple tricks up my sleeve, as well.

"Pretty clever," I admitted, looking at Ava, or *Mist* now, I supposed. "The soldiers of St. George were a nice touch. That ambush felt completely real." Mist didn't answer, and I sighed. "We can play these games all night," I said, subtly reaching my fingers into one of my jacket sleeves, feeling around the cuff. "But I'm tired and sore and kind of cranky, so can we get on with it? What do you want from me? Or, rather, what does Talon want from me?" Mist raised her brows, and I rolled my eyes. "Don't act so surprised. If the organization just wanted me dead, I wouldn't be here now. They wouldn't go through all this trouble to set me up. What does Talon want?"

Mist pushed off the table, serious now, her eyes hard and cold. "The location of your safe houses," she said, making my stomach lurch. "All of them. Where they are, how many dragons live there and the number of humans you have working for you. Give us the information, and we promise that most of the hatchlings will survive."

I barked a laugh. "Really?" I sneered. "That's all Talon wants? Me to betray every dragon and human I spent years protecting from the organization? That's not completely in-sane at all."

"Think of what you're doing to them, Cobalt." Her voice changed, becoming low and soothing. "Think of what their existence means for us all. All Talon wants is for their hatch-lings to return to the organization, where they belong. Where we can protect them. You can't really believe they're better off with you. Constantly in hiding, always on the run? Liv-ing in fear that the Order will come for them in the middle of the night? What kind of life is that?"

"A free one," I returned, curling my lip in disgust. "One that isn't dictated by the organization's demands, or what Talon wants them to be. One where they can actually breathe without Talon looming over their heads, ready to pounce if they set one claw out of line. Where they can actually have thoughts of their own, and choose their own future, instead of being forced into the role that would benefit the organi-zation." I gave her a grim smile. "I'm sure *you* didn't have a choice tonight. If Talon gives the order to betray, capture and interrogate your own kind, you don't get to question why."

Mist cocked her head, looking truly baffled. As if she couldn't imagine how this was a bad thing. I sighed. "Not all of us want our lives run by Talon," I finished, knowing I was wasting my time. Mist was too deep in the organization, fully indoctrinated to Talon's way of thinking. She wouldn't understand. "Some of us would rather be free. To at least be afforded that choice."

"Free?" Mist gave me an incredulous look. "At what cost? Our extinction? Is this so-called freedom so important that you would risk the existence of our entire race? How many

have you lost to St. George? How many hatchlings have died
because you took them from the organization and threw them
into the world with no experience, no knowledge of what
they were doing? Without Talon and its resources, they're exposed not only to the Order, but to all of humanity. Even you
realize that we cannot let the humans know about us. Your
rebellion is endangering us all. Something had to be done."

"Why now?" I asked. "I've been doing this for years, and
Talon didn't seem to care much, other than a couple half-
hearted Viper assassination attempts. Why are they so interested in me now?"

"I'm afraid you don't get to know that."

"Well, we're at an impasse, then," I said, leaning back in
my seat as best I could. "Because I'm not giving up my nests
to Talon, no matter what you say. Especially since I know
you're going to kill me right after. Doesn't give me a lot of
incentive to cooperate."

Mist shook her head.

"I was hoping it wouldn't come to this," she said, turning
to the table behind her. "I was hoping you would see reason,
and realize this is for the survival of us all." Leaning forward,
she dragged a rolling cart out from under the table. It had
been draped with a towel, and a shiver went through me as
she pulled it into the light.

Mist walked around the cart and faced me over the toweled surface. "This is your last chance," she said, fingering
the corner of the cloth. "No one is coming for you. No one
will hear you. I *will* get what I want, make no mistake about
it. How long it will take depends on you." She reached beneath the towel, drew forth another syringe and set it next to

the Dractyl on the table, where it glimmered wickedly. My blood chilled at the sight of it. "This can be quick and painless," Mist went on, "or we can drag it out, all night if we must. It's up to you. What is your answer, Cobalt?"

I took a deep, steadying breath, feeling my heart pound through my veins. "I don't think you have the stomach for this," I said, looking her right in the eye. "What's more, I don't think you *want* to do this. It takes a certain mind-set for this kind of work, and you're not like that. Not the girl I've seen tonight, anyway." Her brow furrowed just slightly, and I pressed forward. "You can walk away, Mist," I said earnestly. "This doesn't have to be your life. Talon doesn't have to control it. Come with us, and I can show you how to be free."

For just a moment, she hesitated, a flicker of uncertainty crossing her face. I leaned forward, ignoring the cuffs digging into my skin. "You know you don't want to do this," I cajoled, my voice gentle, and she scowled. "Mist, listen to me. You don't belong with them. You're resourceful, quick-thinking and one of the most intelligent dragons I've ever seen, hatchling or otherwise. Your talents are being wasted. Think of what we could do for our kind if Talon wasn't in the picture. Cut me loose, and we can leave together."

"You're wrong," Mist answered, and a steely note had entered her voice. Straightening, she narrowed her eyes to icy blue slits and pushed the cart back. "I am what Talon requires," she said, all hesitation gone. "The organization entrusted me with this task, and I will not fail them. I need that information, but if you refuse to cooperate, then you leave me no choice."

She grabbed the second needle from where it lay on the

table, turned and plunged it into my neck. I jerked, clenching my jaw as my fingers fumbled further with the cuff of my sleeve and the thing I was trying to get at slid away. Mist injected the syringe's contents into my veins and stepped back, replacing the needle on the table.

"What was that?" I growled.

"Sodium thiopental," Mist said, wiping her hands on the towel. "Only, this is a special version, produced in Talon labs, specifically for our kind. Our scientists have been mixing science and magic to great effect lately. It's still in its experimentation phase, but the results have been very encouraging."

Sodium thiopental. Truth serum. Dammit. As a rule, dragons were fairly resistant to modern drugs and their effects. Much like alcohol, the amount required to get any kind of reaction from a dragon would kill a normal man. But we weren't immune. Pump us full of enough shit, and we'd feel the effects, same as a human. "You're very forthcoming suddenly," I said, renewing my efforts with my sleeve cuff. Where was that stupid slit? I had to find it again before I got too loopy to do anything. "Sure *you're* not the one who got stuck with the needle?"

Mist regarded me with a practiced blank expression. "I'm telling you this because I want you to know that fighting is useless," she said, "and it would be better in the long run to give me the answers quickly. Holding out is only going to make it worse. I *was* going to interrogate you the old-fashioned way, but I suspect you have a fairly high pain threshold, and Talon wants the information as soon as possible. We'll give that a few minutes to work, and then we'll see how you feel about cooperating."

"I didn't think Vipers did this sort of thing," I said, buying time as Mist leaned back, regarding me blankly. "Isn't your shtick more murder and assassination? Is Lilith finally deciding to branch out?"

Mist paused, the hint of a smile tugging at her lips, turning my insides cold. "What makes you think *I'm* a Viper?" she asked. "I was trained to be a Basilisk, just like you. Don't worry, though," she went on, and settled back against the table, crossing her arms. "I'm not the only agent Talon sent. The Viper should be finishing up shortly."

EMBER

"Drop your weapons."

The human's voice echoed in the empty space, low and commanding. I tensed, eyeing the men surrounding us. Not soldiers of St. George; they wore black business suits and no armor, looking more like bodyguards or FBI agents than military people. Their guns, however, were all too real, pointed unerringly at me and Garret. My heart seized with the realization.

Not St. George. Talon.

The man holding Faith cocked the hammer of his weapon and shoved it harder against her temple, making her gasp. "I won't ask again," he warned. "Put your weapons on the ground and your hands on your head. Now."

"Dammit." I glanced at Garret, who lowered his gun, looking resigned. Bending down, he set the pistol on the cement and rose, clasping his hands behind his skull. With a growl, I did the same, tossing the weapon to the floor and lacing my fingers behind my head. The half circle of men closed in, motioning us forward, keeping their guns trained on us. They also kept a safe distance away, I saw as we were herded toward the front. Wary and alert, offering no opportunity to be pounced on by a dragon. They knew what they were dealing with.

The man in the suit didn't smile as we were brought before him, didn't move a muscle. His grip on Faith didn't lessen, though he kept his gaze trained on us. My mind raced. Talon was here for me. Not Faith or Garret. Just me. I didn't know how I knew this, but I did.

Faith met my gaze, pale and terrified, her eyes pleading for me to do something. Setting my jaw, I took a step forward.

"Let her go," I said, as all the guns came up, pointed at me. I stopped, keeping my hands raised, meeting the impassive stare of the human in front of us. "Leave both of them out of this," I insisted. "They're not important. Just a runaway and a human nobody. You're here for me, right? I'm the one you want."

The agent didn't reply. He continued to stare at me, expressionless, and my desperation grew. "Please," I continued, taking one more step toward him. "You don't need them. Let them walk out, and I...I'll come quietly. I'll go back with you to Talon. Just let them go."

And Faith started to laugh.

"Oh, Ember." She chuckled and slid easily from the human's grip, smiling at me. "You *are* naive, aren't you?"

RILEY

I slumped forward, feeling sweat run down my face into my eyes, my jaws aching from clenching them so hard. I knew if I relaxed an inch, I would start babbling like an idiot, but at the same time, my inclination to care was getting smaller and smaller. I knew the drug was working its way through my brain, suppressing inhibition and my ability to think straight. I had been completely, utterly trashed exactly once in my lifetime, having consumed enough alcohol to drown a football team. This felt very much the same.

"It doesn't have to be like this," Mist said in a gentle voice. "Tell us what we want, and this can be over. You know you're going to break sooner or later."

"Probably." The word slipped out before I could stop it. *Damn. Stop talking, Riley.* "Though I don't see why I shouldn't drag this out as long as I can," I went on, as my mouth refused to cooperate. "You're going to kill me as soon as this is over."

Mist didn't answer, which told me everything I needed on that front. Deliberately, I jabbed myself with the item between my fingers, and the instant flare of pain cleared my head for a moment. "Just tell me one thing," I gritted out, meeting the other dragon's cool gaze. Hoping she wouldn't notice the blood dripping from my hand to the floor. "Since I'm going to be spilling my guts here shortly, I think I deserve at least one straight answer. How much was Griffin paid to sell us out?"

Mist's slender eyebrows rose. "Enough," she replied, her gaze almost impressed. "Mr. Walker's deal with the respective parties is not important right now, but I am surprised you know about him."

"I didn't," I said, making her blink. "I was guessing a second ago. You just confirmed it."

Mist's gaze hardened. Crossing her arms, she leaned back and watched me, saying nothing more. My vision grew blurry, and everything became dreamlike and surreal. I felt like I was floating, and strange images filled my head, hazy and fragmented. Where was I? How did I even get here?

"Are we ready?" A clear, quiet voice cut through the drunken fog. I didn't know what it meant by that, but another question followed before I could wonder about it. "What is your full name?"

"Depends on who you ask," I heard myself saying, though my voice sounded slurred and detached, like it belonged to someone else. "I've had a lot of names."

"Your real name, then. The one given to you when you were hatched."

"Cobalt," I replied. That was an easy answer; no use in trying to hide it.

"And how many humans do you have in your network right now, Cobalt?"

"I don't know, exactly." I shrugged. "I've lost count. Maybe a few dozen?"

"All from Talon?"

"Yeah."

"Excellent." The girl looked pleased. She placed a chair in front of me and sat down, then leaned forward to peer into my face. I stared blankly at the floor between us and felt cool fingers against my sweaty cheek.

"Cobalt, listen to me," the voice cajoled, and I raised my head to meet those intense blue eyes. The rest of her face blurred in and out, and I blinked hard to clear my vision. "Where are your safe houses located?" she asked in a firm, direct voice. "Your resistance has been admirable, but you will answer me, now. Where are Talon's hatchlings? Tell me where you hide your rogues."

EMBER

"Faith?"

I stared in disbelief as the other girl smiled and stepped away from the man in the suit, brushing at her sleeves like she was trying to wipe away filth. The human didn't even glance at her, keeping his gun pointed directly at me. The six men behind us didn't move, either.

"What's going on?" I asked, my voice sounding small and weak in the vast chamber. Faith dusted off her hands, tossed back her curls and shot me a look of supreme disdain.

"Oh, I think you know the answer to that," she replied, with a smile that was completely different from the shy, terrified girl of a moment ago. "You're smart enough to figure it out. You wouldn't be one of *her* students if you weren't. By the way, do you like where I staged this little encounter?" She raised her arms, as if showing off the room around us. "I thought it would bring back memories."

And everything hit me with a jolt. The warehouse. The maze of crates and shipping containers. The armed men surrounding us. I stared at Faith, horror and rage creeping over me. "Lilith," I growled, making her smile widen. "You're one of her students, aren't you? You're a Viper."

Faith chuckled. "Her *only* other student. Before you came along, anyway." For a second, her eyes glittered, a flash of hatred crossing her expression, before she shook it off and smiled again. "She told me to tell you hello, and that she fully expected you and Cobalt to fall for such an obvious trap. A beginner's mistake, if you ask me. If you had only completed your training, this never would have happened."

"Where's Riley?" I snarled, making the men surrounding us raise their weapons higher. "You know where he is, don't you? Tell me!"

"He's dead," Faith replied offhandedly. "Or he will be soon. Mist should be nearly done."

"Mist?"

"Oh, sorry. That's Ava to you."

The floor dropped out from under me, and for a moment, I couldn't breathe. Not only was Faith a Talon operative, Ava was one, too. This whole thing was an elaborate plot by the organization. If they had sent a Viper, Lilith's other student, of all people, I must have really pissed them off. And Riley... might already be gone.

I clenched my fists as my dragon snarled in defiance. "No," I said, as Faith's eyebrows rose. "You're wrong. You don't know Riley. He's more than a match for any Talon agent." He had to be; I refused to believe anything else. If he was dead...I would know. My dragon would know. "It's Mist you should be worried about," I told Faith.

Faith shrugged. "Regardless," she said, seemingly unconcerned about her partner, "he's not here. And he isn't the one *you* should be worried about right now."

Her gaze shifted away from me, turning calculating and

cruel as it fixed on Garret. "A soldier of St. George," she mused, and my blood chilled. "How very…interesting. You *have* fallen quite far, haven't you?" She shook her head and glanced at me with obvious contempt. "Consorting with the enemy? Allying yourself with a soldier of St. George?" She *tsked*, a mock-sorrowful look crossing her face. "For shame, really. What would Lilith say? What would *Talon* say?"

My throat felt tight with panic. I didn't know what was happening with Riley, what Mist was doing to him, but I did know what would happen to Garret. Talon would kill him, right now, for no other reason than he had been part of St. George. It didn't matter that he was on our side now. It didn't matter that the Order itself was hunting him. They would show a soldier of St. George no mercy, unless I could somehow change their mind. Fighting right now would be suicide. With half a dozen guns trained on us, even if I survived, that first volley would kill the soldier.

We were trapped. Riley was gone, we were outnumbered and outgunned, and the Viper had us right where she wanted. This was checkmate for us, but I had to save Garret, at least. I could endure going back if I knew the soldier was still alive out there. And then, when I had returned to Talon and discovered who was responsible for this, I would take my revenge. For Riley, Dante, Garret and all the rogues Talon had crushed. If I couldn't be free, I would make them suffer for it.

But keeping Faith from putting a bullet through Garret's skull was the important thing right now.

"Let him go," I told Faith, who raised her eyebrows. "He's not part of the Order anymore. You've been around us. You know he's not one of them." Her lip twisted nastily, and my voice hardened. "He saved your life from St. George, remember that? They would've killed us all if he hadn't been there."

"Ember," Garret said quietly, a motionless presence at my back. "You don't have to do this."

I ignored that, continuing to stare at Faith. "Let him go," I said once more. "I'm the one you want, right? Trust me, you don't want to kill him."

"And why is that, exactly?" Faith smiled, eyes gleaming. I wondered how I'd ever thought of her as some innocent kid. "I've seen the war," she continued. "I know what St. George does to our kind. Who cares if the human doesn't hunt dragons now? He was still part of the Order, which means he's killed before. As a loyal member of Talon, I'm not only expected but required to take out their enemies whenever I get the opportunity. Why should I let him go?"

I swallowed hard. "Because," I whispered. "If you let him go, I'll come back to Talon willingly. I'll become a Viper, or whatever they want from me. Let him live and I...I won't try to leave again, I swear."

"No," Garret said, stepping forward. "Ember, don't—"

Two men closed on him, weapons raised. Garret stopped, lifting his arms again, but his gaze sought mine. "Don't bargain for me," he said in a low voice. "Not with Talon. They don't accept compromise. It's either all or nothing...and my life isn't worth your freedom."

I met his gaze. "Yes, it is."

"Ember—"

"Don't argue with me, Garret," I almost hissed, feeling my throat tighten. "There is no way I'm going to stand here and watch them shoot you. Just shut up and let me do this, okay?"

My voice was starting to tremble; I swallowed hard and took a quick breath to steady it. "I already lost Riley," I whispered. "If I have to go back, at least I'll know you're still alive."

"Well, this is all very interesting." Faith's cool, amused voice made me bristle. I turned back to find her watching me, that chilling smile on her face. "You are correct," she told me. "We *do* want you to return to Talon, that's why they sent me, of course. But there is a small problem with your proposal. You see, you've already confirmed your disloyalty to the organization, and they are somewhat reluctant to take you at your word. If you want to come back, you're going to have to prove that we can trust you again."

I clenched my jaw. The thought of having to prove anything to Talon rankled. But if it would save Garret's life… "How?" I asked through gritted teeth.

Faith nodded to the men behind me. As I spun, two agents stepped forward, one on either side of Garret, and forced him to his knees. The others formed a line behind the soldier, keeping their guns trained on the back of his head. I started toward them, but Faith grabbed my arm in a grip of steel.

"You want to prove your loyalty to Talon?" she asked, and pressed a cold black pistol into my hands, making me freeze in horror. Faith didn't smile as she let me go, nodding toward the kneeling soldier.

"Kill him."

My heart stood still. I stared at the weapon in my hands, torn between hurling it away and shoving the muzzle in the Viper's face. Not that it would do any good; Faith could probably disarm a person fairly quickly, and neither choice would help Garret, kneeling in front of what I knew was an execution line. Any aggressive move on my part might trigger them to blow his head off. Gripping the handle of the gun, I looked up at Faith, shaking my head in disbelief.

"You're crazy," I told her. "Did you not hear me at all? I said I'd come back to Talon if you let him go, not murder him in cold blood. You can't possibly expect me to do this."

"I don't think you understand the situation you're in," Faith replied, and made a vague gesture at Garret. "The soldier is dead," she said flatly, making my heart drop. "Either way, no matter what you decide, we're going to kill him. There is no argument that will convince me to spare an agent of St. George. I am not here to make bargains. I'm here to bring you back to Talon, and this is the final test to see if you can be trusted. If you refuse, then you will share the soldier's fate."

"Then you'll have to kill us both," I said, feeling my lungs heat, the dragon rising up for a final, desperate battle. *I'm sorry, Garret. I wanted us to be free of Talon. But if they won't let us go, I'll fight as hard as I can.*

"Really?" Faith gave me an evil, knowing smile. "So, you would sacrifice not only the human, but Dante, as well?"

RILEY

"Phoenix."

Mist cocked her head, regarding me intently, as if trying to determine whether or not I was lying. I growled a curse and hunched forward, panting, feeling the other dragon's gaze on the top of my skull.

"Phoenix," she repeated in a slow, clear voice. "That's where your safe houses are located?"

"One of the locations," I replied.

"There are others? Where?"

"All over the place. Austin, Phoenix, San Francisco. There was even one in Mexico for a little while." I listened to myself ramble on, unable to stop. "I thought about moving some of them overseas, but that would require me to travel more. I can't be on two continents at once."

"No, you cannot." I heard the triumph in her voice. "And how many hatchlings are you hiding, right now?"

"Twenty-three."

She blinked, the only outward sign of surprise. "You *have* been busy, haven't you?"

"I've been doing this awhile."

"Indeed." Mist leaned farther forward, her gaze intense.

"Where can we find them, Cobalt? Tell me exactly where they are."

"You'll never find them," I slurred, smiling up at her with the knowledge. "If I disappear, Wes will give the signal for everyone to move. They'll be gone before Talon ever gets there."

"It doesn't matter," Mist said. "Once we have them on the run, they'll be easy to track down. You're only delaying the inevitable." Her voice dropped, became soothing again. "Stop fighting, Cobalt. Where are they? Tell me the closest safe house from here."

Fighting. Why was I fighting? That seemed hard right now, too much work. "The closest safe house from here?" I shrugged. "That's easy. I have one right in the city."

Mist frowned. "Here?" she asked. "In Las Vegas?"

"Yep." I nodded, tilting my head back. The inside of my skull felt full of cotton; a weird sensation. "We were just there a few days ago, in fact."

"Who was there?"

"All of us. Me, Wes, the soldier of St. George, Ember…"
Ember.

Deep inside, the dragon stirred, rousing sluggishly at her name. It struggled into consciousness, growling defiantly, before sleep overcame it and it sank into the void again. But that brief rush of heat and fire burned away the fog and, for just a moment, my thoughts were clear.

"Was there anyone else in that safe house?" Mist went on, her voice closer now, not seeming to come from a great distance away. "Any hatchlings that could still be there, right now?"

I clenched my fist, curling my fingers around the item in

my palm. It bit into my skin, and I exhaled in relief. Still there. I hadn't dropped it. "No," I muttered, almost before I knew what I was saying, and winced. The damn truth serum was still in full effect. "There was no one else. Just us."

"All right." Mist slid off the table, coming to stand in front of me. "Enough of this," she said, and a note of impatience had crept into her voice. "You know what we want, Cobalt. You know you cannot hide them from Talon any longer. I will make this as clear as I possibly can. Where—"

"Before you ask," I interrupted, making her frown in surprise, "there's something you should probably know. Well, a couple things, really. One, you're either very inexperienced at this, or overconfident. Or both. You realize you left that second dose of Dractylpromazine sitting on the table there, right?"

"Yes," Mist said, glancing at the syringe. Her brow furrowed in wary confusion as she turned back. "But I'm in no danger. The dose I gave you is good for another hour, at least. Why?"

"No reason." I shrugged. "Only, you forgot one of the prime rules of interrogation training. Never leave possible weapons like that lying within the prisoner's reach. Because if they ever escape their plastic cuffs, that's the first thing they'll go for."

Mist jerked back, eyes widening…as I surged to my feet, snapping the weakened plastic restraints, and lunged for the syringe.

EMBER

"Dante?"

The flames within sputtered and died as I sucked in a horrified breath. Faith smiled, looking pleased, and I clenched my fist, glaring at the other hatchling. "Where is he?" I demanded. "What have they done to him?"

"He's safe with Talon," Faith went on. "For the moment, at least." She paused to let that sink in, before continuing, "You don't quite realize what's at stake here, do you? This isn't only *your* final exam. It's also Dante's. The organization is testing him, making sure they can trust him, the brother of a rogue and a traitor. This plan, well, most of it anyway, was his idea. If you fail and refuse to return to the organization, *he* fails, as well." Faith smiled evilly. "And you know how Talon feels about failures."

I felt like I'd been punched in the stomach. Dante was in charge of this. He'd sent Mist and Faith after us. He was responsible for Riley's disappearance and, if things continued down this road, Garret's death. Did he know what he was doing? Was Talon coercing him, forcing my brother to go along with their plans? If I didn't return to the organization tonight, Dante would fail. I might never see him again. But to go back, to make sure my brother would be safe…Garret had to die.

"So, you have to ask yourself—" Faith's voice was a croon, low and dangerous "—who is more important to you? Who are you going to save? The soldier of St. George? The greatest enemy of our kind? The human whose pitiful life span will be over in the blink of an eye?" She glanced at the kneeling soldier, a look of contempt crossing her face, before turning to me again. "Or will you choose Dante, the twin you've known all your life? The dragon whose only concern, from the moment you ran away from Talon, has been your safety? He's waiting for you, Ember. Everyone is. We all want you to come home."

I was suffocating, struggling to breathe, to make an impossible choice that wasn't really a choice at all. I couldn't shoot Garret—there was no way I could do that. But if I didn't, they would kill us both anyway. And who knew what Talon would do to Dante.

I looked down at the weapon in my hand, then back to Garret, kneeling on the floor in front of the firing squad. His expression was blank, carefully guarded, though his eyes were bleak as they met mine.

Faith eased closer, her dark gaze burning the side of my face, as her voice dropped to a soothing murmur. "You can start over," she said. "Everything you've done will be erased, all your crimes against Talon will be forgiven. You belong with your own kind. But, if you don't pass this test, you will die. And Dante will suffer for your failure." She leaned back, her expression confident, as if everything had already been decided. "I think you know what you have to do."

And suddenly, I did.

I shivered and closed my eyes, willing my hands to stop shaking. "If…if I do this," I whispered, "can you promise that Dante will be safe? That none of this will impact his place in the organization? And that we'll be able to see each other again, without consequence?"

Faith's voice was full of triumph. "You have our word."

"Okay." My voice came out choked. Raising my head, I met the gaze of the soldier in front of me, knowing he hadn't glanced away from us the whole time. Garret watched me, gray eyes resigned, the look of someone who expected to die.

"I'm sorry," I told him in a shaking voice, and felt my stomach wrench sideways at the look on his face. Betrayal and disbelief glimmered from his eyes, a split-second reaction, before his expression shut down and became a blank mask. Taking a deep breath, I stepped forward. "This is my brother," I went on, my voice pleading and defiant at the same time. "My twin. Dante has always been my first priority. I'll do anything to keep him safe, even this."

Garret didn't answer. I spared a glance at the men behind him and found they were watching me, not the soldier. Clearly, the dragon girl with the gun was the bigger threat, though they still kept their weapons trained on the back of his head.

My heart was pounding in my ears as I stopped a few feet from the kneeling soldier. I could feel Faith's eyes on my back, the hawk-like stares of the men behind him, but my gaze was only for Garret. He was still watching me, though his eyes were distant now, almost glassy. Like he was staring right through me, at something I couldn't detect. A lump caught in my throat, and my stomach twisted so hard I felt sick.

With trembling hands, I raised the gun, aiming it at his forehead. Garret closed his eyes, bracing himself. For a split second, with my finger curled around the trigger, everything held its breath.

"Look at me," I whispered. He didn't move, and I hardened my voice. "Look at me, Garret. I want to see your face when I do this. Open your eyes."

For a heartbeat, the soldier remained motionless. For an agonizing moment, I thought he would refuse. But then he opened his eyes and his dark, tormented gaze met mine. I stared into those gray eyes and mouthed a single phrase, hoping he would understand.

Trust me.

He blinked...and I opened my fingers, dropping the weapon at my feet.

The second the gun left my hands, I Shifted, exploding into dragon form with a roar, my wings snapping behind me as I reared onto my hind legs. The Talon agents instantly raised their weapons, sighting down the much bigger threat, but I sucked in a breath and blasted them with fire, sending two of them reeling back. Still, I couldn't catch all of them, and the chatter of assault rifle fire echoed through the room. Bullets whizzed by me, sparking off my horns and chest plates, and at least two punched through my wing membranes, making me shriek with pain.

A gun barked and two men fell. Garret had lunged forward, snatched the fallen pistol and fired with deadly accuracy into the line of Talon agents. The rest of them scattered, diving behind cover, as Garret leaped upright, still firing his weapon, and I tensed to attack.

Something slammed into me from the side, knocking me away from Garret and sending me tumbling across the floor. I caught myself, looking up just in time to see a lithe dragon, its scales a dark indigo, lunge at me with the speed of a cobra. I managed to scramble back, and Garret raised his gun to shoot it, but a hailstorm of bullets caused him to duck behind a stack of crates, hunkering down as the shots tore into the wood and peppered the wall behind him.

Ignoring the preoccupied soldier, the purple dragon turned to me, eyes gleaming yellow in the dim light. She was a little smaller than I was, with an elegant tapered head and a long, graceful neck and tail. Her scales were so dark they were nearly black, her chest and belly plates a lighter indigo, as were the wing membranes. A mane of curved black spines ran down her back from a narrow, hornless skull as she raised her head and hissed a challenge, needlelike fangs flashing viciously in my direction.

"Come on then, *Viper*," she called, raising her voice to be heard over the cacophony of shouts and gunfire around us. "Let's see who's the better student. Just you and me, no friends, no interference." She half spread her wings, giving me an evil smile. "Of course, if you want to know about your brother, you'll have to beat me first."

She launched herself into the air, soaring over my head, to land somewhere in the maze behind us. I tensed to spring after her but paused, looking back at Garret. He was still crouched behind the stack of crates, pistol in hand, bursts of gunfire tearing splinters from the barrier in front of him. Our gazes met across the room.

"Garret—"

"Go," he called, motioning with his free hand. "I'll cover you, and I'll catch up when I'm done. Go!"

He turned, firing twice at a cluster of pallets. There was a cry, and a Talon agent fell into the open, his gun clattering to the cement. I winced, then spun and bounded into the maze.

RILEY

Mist hit me hard, side-kicking me in the ribs just as I reached the table, knocking me back. Grunting, I staggered, and she followed with a nasty roundhouse kick to the temple that, had it connected, might've knocked my lights out. But she'd taken the bait, left herself open, and I caught the foot as it came in, spinning and throwing her into the corner. She crashed into the wall and slumped to the floor, dazed, though not for long. I snatched the syringe and bolted out the door.

Bursting through the frame, I hit the railing of a flight of stairs and stared into the dark, open expanse of a warehouse, aisles of containers and crates spread out below. Of course, it was the perfect place to stage this little encounter. Silent, empty and isolated—no one around to see an interrogation, a murder or a huge mythological creature chasing someone through the aisles.

Speaking of which…

There was a low growl behind me, raising the hairs on the back of my neck. I leaped over the railing, dropped the eight or so feet to the ground and sprinted behind a stack of crates as the door burst open and the roar of a pissed-off dragon echoed through the room. Ducking into the nearest aisle, I pressed back into a corner and tried to Shift, hoping that the tranquilizer had worn off.

Nope. Couldn't do it. My body stayed locked in human form, the dragon barely responding. Cursing, I looked around frantically, searching for anything that would help me even out this fight. Crates, containers, random boxes. Unless I found a hidden stash of guns, or maybe a couple grenades, this was going to go poorly for me.

My hand throbbed, and I clenched my fist, gritting my teeth. Thank God Mist hadn't removed my jacket before the interrogation; she might've discovered a few other precautions hidden within the lining, as well. A lifetime of close calls had taught me to be ready for anything: capture, imprisonment, being abandoned behind enemy lines. I'd learned to rely on myself and to always have a backup plan. Case in point: having to cut myself free with the razor blade hidden in my jacket cuff. The thin lacerations across my wrists were shallow and would heal quickly, but they still stung like the world's most obnoxious paper cut.

A large, ghostly shadow soared overhead, landing atop a nearby crate, and I froze. In her true form, Mist was as slender and poised as her human counterpart, her scales a glittering blue-white, her ivory horns curling back from her skull. Sinking to her haunches, the pale dragon folded her wings, curled a long, diamond-tipped tail around herself and peered into the darkness with slitted blue eyes.

I didn't move, holding my breath as that piercing gaze swept the warehouse. This was bad. The white hatchling was graceful, elegant and probably one of the prettier dragons I'd seen in my long existence, but I was still human, and she could turn me inside out with one claw.

Abruptly, Mist raised her hair, nostrils flaring, to sniff the air. And I winced, realizing my mistake.

She can smell your blood, idiot. Move!

I bolted from the corner just as Mist turned her head sharply, blue eyes narrowed in my direction. With a hiss, she leaped gracefully atop another aisle, then another, following me as I sprinted through the labyrinth of crates. I could hear her talons scraping over metal and wood, and didn't dare look back as I fled through the aisles, searching for anything that would save my hide.

As I hurried down a dark, narrow corridor, stacks of plywood on either side, there was a blur of motion from above. I skidded to a halt, tensing to run back the way I'd come, as the white dragon landed in front of me with a snarl. Raising her head, she drew in a breath, the fire gland below her jaw swelling, and my pulse spiked. I dived aside, toward a narrow gap between piles of wood, and squeezed through as a massive firestorm erupted behind me, setting everything ablaze. Wrenching myself through the space, I scrambled upright, feeling the immense heat at my back, searing through my clothes. Panting, I tensed to run again, when I spotted a gleam of yellow in the corner of the aisle, half-hidden in shadow, and my heart jumped.

Oh, please let that work.

An angry roar echoed behind me. Without looking back, I bolted to the corner, swung into the forklift seat and grabbed for the key, praying it would be there. It was still in the ignition, and the engine sputtered to life as I wrenched the key up and threw the machine into Drive.

A white dragon landed in the aisle with a snarl, hellish firelight playing across her scales. She had just enough time to glance up and hiss in alarm…as the forklift slammed into her, the metal prongs catching her on either side. Shrieking, she was dragged across the cement floor, ripping and tearing at the forklift, until I drove full speed into the opposite wall. The impact rocked me forward, nearly throwing me out of the vehicle, and several large crates tumbled free and crashed around us, spilling their contents everywhere.

Mist slumped against the prongs, trapped between the fork-lift and the wall. Her legs moved weakly, and she raised her head, dazed, as I dropped from the seat and stepped around to her side. Crystal-blue eyes opened, trying to focus as I fished in my jacket and pulled out the syringe.

"Wait," she muttered, trying to struggle free. Her wings fluttered, pinned against the wall, and she clawed feebly at the metal prongs. "Cobalt, stop. You don't know what you're doing."

"Sorry, kid," I muttered, and drove the needle into her neck, angling up to slide it between the scales. She snapped at me, and I dodged back, watching as her struggles grew weaker and weaker. Eventually, her eyes rolled up, and she collapsed against the forklift. I sighed, stepping away, as the white hatchling gave a final twitch and lapsed into a drugged sleep.

"I do know what I'm doing," I told the unconscious dragon. "I've always known. I just wish you could have seen it, too. I wish you could see what Talon is doing, to all of us." Shaking my head, I watched her for another moment, then took a step back. "I would have shown you everything, if you had let me."

Raking a hand through my hair, I turned and sprinted out of the aisle, back to the office to search for my phone. I had to contact the others, let them know I was okay. Let them know they were probably walking into an ambush. Alone.

With a Viper.

EMBER

Well, isn't this déjà vu?

I crept through the shadowy labyrinth of metal containers, all senses alert, searching for any hint of the other dragon. Of course, it reminded me of my training sessions with Lilith, stalking through a warehouse maze just like this one, hunting those who were hunting me. I was sure that was exactly Faith's intention; she seemed to emulate her trainer flawlessly, taking sadistic pleasure in my pain. But she wasn't going to win this time.

There was a ripple of movement above me, a shadow darting from other shadows. I tensed, craning my neck up, wary for an attack from above. For the indigo dragon to suddenly pounce from the ceiling. I had used that tactic many times my—

A blur of motion from the side, and something hit my front leg, tearing through scales and skin to the muscle beneath. I snarled, fangs bared, but all I caught was a brief glimpse of a long, slinky tail vanishing around a corner. Already gone.

Wincing, I glanced at my shoulder. Four straight, narrow gashes cut through my scales, already starting to well with blood. They weren't very deep; my armor had absorbed a good bit of the attack, but they still hurt like hell.

A scraping sound came from the corner Faith had vanished around and I whirled, ready for the attack. It came from a different direction altogether, talons ripping into my flank. Roaring, I loosed a blast of flame that seared the container behind me, leaving a black spot in the metal, but Faith had already vanished.

Growling, I turned in a slow circle, trying to watch every angle at once. "Is this what Lilith taught you?" I challenged, feeling hot blood trickle down my shoulder and back leg, dripping to the cement. Both wounds throbbed, but I refused to show pain. "How to hit someone in the back? What's the matter, scared I'll kick your ass if you face me head-on?"

A sibilant chuckle echoed from the darkness around me. "I don't know what they saw in you," the disembodied voice stated. Impossible to pinpoint which direction it came from. "For the life of me, I can't imagine why Talon chose Lilith to be your instructor. What a terrible waste of her time and talent. It's certainly not her fault you were completely un-suited to be a Viper. No discipline, no killer instinct at all." A disgusted sniff followed, though I still had no idea from where. "I heard the Elder Wyrm was hoping to ingrain some of Lilith's ruthlessness into you, that's why she was chosen as your teacher," Faith continued, "but then you went rogue and disappointed everyone. Your brother is much more sal-vageable, I hear."

"Where's Dante?" I snarled, my voice echoing through the warehouse. "I don't believe he set this up, he wouldn't do that do me. You're lying."

Another soft laugh. "I suppose the hatchling in the meeting with Mr. Roth—the one who looked just like you—was just there to discuss politics," the voice said, finally resolving itself in a direction, directly in front of me. "Of course, you could always ask him yourself. If you survive tonight!"

I spun around with fangs and claws bared to face the dragon charging in from behind. With a triumphant snarl, I lunged, thinking I had her. Quick as a snake, she changed direction, leaped over my head and soared up to land on the container aisle behind me.

Dammit, she's fast. Hold still already.

Growling, I sprang after her, using a shove from my wings to launch myself off the ground. This time, the other dragon didn't run away but smiled as I landed on the edge of the container. Somewhere in the labyrinth, a flurry of gunshots rang off the rafters; Garret and the remaining Talon agents still going at it. I hoped he was okay, but I couldn't help him now.

"No more games," I said, glaring at Faith, who watched me with her tail curled around herself, that insufferably smug grin still plastered across her muzzle. She was faster than me, and she knew it, but I wasn't going to let her get the upper hand. "That's twice now that someone has mentioned the Elder Wyrm," I went on. "What does the CEO of Talon, the most powerful dragon in existence, want with us? And how does Dante fit into all of this?"

Faith sneered. "You think they'd tell me? If you're so very curious, go back to Talon and ask him yourself. Or better yet, I can call him right now and ask him." She jerked her slender muzzle at the ground, smiling. "I left my phone right over

there when I changed. There's only one number on it. Call
him yourself and see what your precious twin has been doing."

Without thinking, I glanced in the direction she pointed.

And Faith lunged.

I jerked up, realizing what she was doing at the last second,
and the other dragon slammed into me, knocking me off the
edge. I tumbled to the floor, hitting the cement on my side,
the impact driving the breath from me. Gasping, I struggled
upright as Faith hit the ground a few yards away, landing as
lightly as a cat. Her grin was cruel as she turned to face me,
lashing a slinky tail against her flanks.

"You wanted me out in the open, *Viper*," she taunted, as I
growled and staggered forward, trying to ignore the dull ache
in my side. "You wanted to face me one-on-one. Well, here
I am. Are you ready?" She gave a weird little sidestep, her
lithe body rippling like ink across the cement. "Here I come."

And she surged forward, a dark blur over the floor. I barely
had time to register she had moved when something hit my
shoulder and sent a flare of pain up my leg. I snarled and lashed
out with my claws, but Faith was already gone, skipping back
out of reach, then darting in again. I managed to dodge the
blow to my neck, feeling the tips of her claws rake along my
scales, and sprang forward to sink my fangs into her throat.
She sidled away, quick as a shadow, and slashed me across the
face, rocking my head to the side. I stumbled, disoriented,
felt something hook my front leg and yank it sideways. I lost
my footing and crashed to the floor again, a breathless grunt
escaping me as my chin struck the unforgiving concrete.

Ow. Crap, I'm getting my ass kicked here. Panting, I clawed
myself upright, searching for the other dragon. She stood a

few yards away, watching me with that amused smile across her narrow face, making my temper spike. She was toying with me, just like Lilith had.

"What's the matter, Ember?" Faith asked, cocking her head like a curious dog. "I thought this was what you wanted. Are you saying you expected to be able to take on a Viper without finishing your training? If you had only stayed with Lilith, you might actually have had a chance." She shook her head, narrowing her yellow eyes at me. "Are you ready to stop this, kill the soldier and return to Talon? Or am I going to have to tear you apart bit by bit?"

Dammit, she's so fast. *How do I counter it?* Angrily, I thought back to the fight with Lilith, trying to think of anything that I could use. *She's quick, but she's relying on speed to keep her out of danger. If I could get close, I might have a shot.* I took a deep breath, bracing myself. *Okay, then. Let's do it. This is gonna hurt.*

Raising my head, I met the other dragon's smug grin with one of my own. "You're making the same mistake she did," I told her, making her blink. "She thought I was beaten, too. Overconfidence must run in the family." Faith's smile faded, and I bared my fangs defiantly. "Talon's best Viper did her best to drag me back to the organization, and I'm still here. What makes you think her slimy little apprentice will do any better?"

Faith slitted her eyes. "You know what?" she said, gliding closer, her body nearly invisible in the shadows. "I think I'm done playing with you. It was fun, seeing you and the soldier stumble about, completely oblivious. It was *highly* amusing, watching the pair of you dance around each other like skittish goats." Her muzzle curled back, showing rows of needle-sharp teeth. "But you crossed the line. You have feelings for that human, that soldier of St. George, and that's something no true dragon would ever allow." She sank into a crouch, her lean body coiled like a snake, ready to strike. "You're a disgrace to Talon," Faith spat, lashing her tail. "An embarrassment to us all. And I think Lilith would congratulate me for getting rid of you!"

She lunged, a streak of darkness over the cement. I snarled and leaped forward to meet her, lashing out with my claws as she got close. Like quicksilver, she sidled away, leaving a stinging gash along my neck as she did. I turned, lowered my head and plowed forward, pursuing her across the floor. She dodged and twisted away, slashing me with her talons, trying to fall back. I took the blows, gritting my teeth with every gash and cut ripped across my scales, and slammed into her like a bull.

My horns struck her chest, bowling her over with a startled gasp. She hit the floor on her back and instantly kicked out with her back legs, catching me in the stomach and ribs with her back claws as I pounced, tearing me open. I ignored the pain and went for her throat. Snarling, we rolled across the floor, tails and wings lashing, trying to pin the other down.

Shrieking with fury, we rolled into a pair of steel drums in the corner, tipping them over with a crash. Liquid spilled everywhere, sharp and acrid, stinging my nose and burning my eyes. I was instantly drenched, choking on the fumes that rose around us, but I couldn't take my eyes off the Viper beneath me. As the drums clanged to the concrete, there was a split-second hiss...

...and a firestorm erupted around us. Flames shot into the

air, running up my back, spreading over my wings. It engulfed the Viper, surrounding her with fire, until she looked like a snarling, bat-winged demon from the pits of hell. Shrieking, she raked her claws down my neck, then slapped me across the muzzle with a flame-wreathed talon. Before, the gashes had merely stung; now it felt like a hot poker was being jammed up beneath my scales, then doused with acid. Pain exploded behind my eyes, snapping the final threads of clear thought, and I roared.

Pinning the Viper to the floor, ignoring the claws that slashed at me, I bared my teeth and aimed for that slender neck. My jaws clamped shut on the dragon's throat, right below her chin, and Faith screamed, thrashing wildly. All four talons beat and slashed at me, back legs kicking my stomach, front claws trying to shove me off. I closed my eyes, braced myself and began to squeeze.

"Stop!"

I paused, jaws still clamped around the slender throat, as the dragon's frenzied cry rang out, echoing off the rafters. "Wait, please!" Faith went on, her voice strangled. "Don't kill me! Stop!"

Relief, swift and sudden, spread through me, making my legs tremble. I hadn't really been planning to kill her, not like this. Viper or no, I couldn't stand here and ever-so-casually tear someone's throat out. No matter what Talon said, I was not Lilith, and I never would be.

I eased up a bit, though not enough to let go. "Why not?" I growled through my teeth. "Why should I trust anything you say?"

She writhed helplessly, tail beating frantically against my

legs. "Because I'll tell you about Dante," she wheezed. "I'll tell you whatever you want to know, just let me live." She swallowed hard, wings trembling. "Let me Shift back to human form," she offered. "I can't hurt you like that, right? And I won't be able to run. I'll Shift, and then I'll tell you whatever you want. Your brother, Mist, Riley. Anything."

I thumped my tail, as if I was considering a moment longer, then sighed. "All right," I muttered, and carefully opened my jaws, letting her slump to the concrete. I needed that information on Riley and my brother, and I didn't have the will for any more fighting. Not that I would've killed her anyway, but it was getting hard to move without sharp stabs of pain shooting all up my body. Turned out fire in open wounds was a bad idea. If she ran now, I didn't think I could catch her, even as a human.

Faith crawled out from under me and, as the flames around us burned low, started to shrink. Tail and neck retracted, scales disappeared and wings pulled into her body, until only a human in a black Viper suit remained sitting on the floor. She hugged herself and gazed up at me, looking like that scared, innocent girl I'd first met, though I knew better now. I folded my wings and sat down, clenching my jaw to keep from hissing in pain. No showing weakness in front of the trained Viper assassin. The last of the flames had finally flickered out, burning off with whatever flammable goo was in those drums, and now that the adrenaline was gone, I ached. Badly. The outside of a dragon might've been fireproof, but the numerous gashes I'd taken blazed with agony, burned and seared around the edges.

Great. I'm probably the only dragon in history who will ever suffer from third-degree burns.

"Riley," I said, my voice a low, dangerous growl. "Where is he? Why were you sent for us? Tell me everything you know."

Faith took a deep, shaky breath and exhaled slowly. "Mist and I were commissioned by Talon to find you and the rogue," she began. "My orders were to bring you back alive and kill anyone else involved. Mist was to go after Cobalt, extract certain information from him and then dispose of him. Divide and conquer, then return to Talon with our objectives, that was the plan."

I felt ill, but tried not to show it. "What information do they want from Riley?"

"I wasn't privy to that part of the assignment," Faith replied, and shrank back as I curled a lip at her. "Mist was the only one with that information," she added quickly. "I had my orders. That's all I was required to know."

"So you have no idea where Riley is right now. Or what Mist is doing to him."

"No."

I growled in frustration, scraping my talons across the cement. The girl flinched, but I ignored her. Still no information on Riley, where he was, if he was still alive. We were no closer to finding him than we were when we left the hotel. Mist and Faith had set us up perfectly.

And then, I remembered something else.

"Where is Dante?" I asked, narrowing my eyes at the other dragon. "You said you had his number on your phone. Or was that another lie?"

"It wasn't." Faith rubbed her arm. "Dante...is the one in

ROGUE

393

charge of this operation. He and the rest of the board are standing by. I'm supposed to check in with him as soon as I take care of you, one way or another."

My stomach dropped to the pads of my toes. "I don't believe you."

"Believe what you want." Faith's gaze didn't waver. "But Dante was the one who set this whole thing up. This was part of his test, coming up with the plan to bring you back to the organization."

My throat was suddenly dry. "And if I refused to come?"

"Then I had orders to kill you."

Reeling, I shook my head, still unwilling to believe. Dante had truly done this? My own brother had sent a Viper after us, with orders to kill me if I didn't return? That couldn't be right. He wouldn't do that to me. We might've argued, fought, disagreed on a lot of things, but Dante wouldn't give the order to take me out if I refused to cooperate.

Or would he? Was he so invested in Talon's doctrine that he'd really believe he was doing the right thing? I remembered something Riley had told me once, and it made my stomach twist. *Talon has him now. He'll betray his own blood if they give the order.*

Faith curled an arm around her side, her face creasing with pain. "What are you going to do with me?" she asked in a tight voice.

I stood up, wincing as the movement pulled at the charred, blackened cuts on my body. The Viper flinched, as if expecting a sudden attack, but I was just about done with this. My mind was spinning, I ached and I felt nauseous in more ways than one. "Take a message back to Talon," I growled at the

Viper. "And Dante. Tell them to stop sending people after me. They're just wasting their time. I'm not coming back." Faith still eyed me warily, like I might pounce on her as soon as she moved, and I bared my fangs. "Get out of here!"

She scrambled to her feet, holding her side, and staggered into the darkness. I watched until she slipped down an aisle and vanished, then I slumped to the cool cement.

"Ow," I whimpered, wishing I could just lie here and not move for a few minutes. I hurt all over, but at least I had won. I'd actually won a fight with a trained Viper. A small Viper, but a Viper nonetheless. I guess I should be thankful I was alive; Lilith's prize student certainly wouldn't have spared me if the situation were reversed. She didn't know how close she'd come to beating me, that I wouldn't have been able to kill her if she hadn't surrendered. *I guess I'll never be a proper Viper after all*, I thought, and felt nothing but relief at that notion. *And if Faith had realized that, I don't think I would've won.* But I didn't have to worry about her now. My bluff had worked. She was gone.

Though Mist was still out there. And Riley.

My stomach turned over. Setting my jaw, I pushed myself upright and started to limp back down the aisle. Find Garret, find Riley, deal with Dante. Those were the items I had to focus on now, in that order. And not passing out before we could leave; that was on the list, too.

A sibilant chuckle behind me froze me in my tracks.

"Oh, Ember," Faith crooned, as the ripple of a Shift went through the air. "Haven't you learned anything? What did Lilith teach you about showing mercy to your enemies?"

I spun painfully, knowing I wouldn't be fast enough. The

Viper was already in midleap, jaws gaping, talons fully extended to tear me apart.

A shot rang out, slamming the dragon aside. The Viper collapsed to the cement and rolled into a pile of crates, screeching in pain as she came to a halt. Heart pounding, I looked over to see Garret, pistol raised, step out of the shadows between aisles, keeping the dragon in his sights. His eyes were hard and dangerous, his expression a flinty mask as he aimed the gun at the fallen Viper.

Faith screamed in rage and defiance. Tail thrashing, she tried clawing herself upright, but a second shot followed the first, jerking her to the side. The Viper struck the crates and crumpled to the floor, leaving a bright crimson smear across the wood. Her wings twitched, frantically at first, then growing slower and slower, as a trickle of red seeped over the floor from her body. Her jaws gaped, gasping for breath. Her eyes glazed over in pain and fear.

"No," I heard her whisper. "Not yet. Not like this. I can't die...like this."

I felt sick. My legs wobbled, and it was uncertain whether they could hold me up much longer, but I gritted my teeth and staggered toward the dying dragon. She was a Viper, she'd been sent to kill us, but she was still part of my race, someone who had been just like me, once.

The Viper stared vacantly as I stepped up beside her, trying not to glance at her heaving sides. At the two round holes seeping blood right behind her foreleg. A perfect shot to the heart, from someone who knew exactly how to kill a dragon. Faith blinked, and I caught my reflection in one golden eye that was slowly turning to glass.

"I wanted…to be her best student," she whispered, as a thin line of red trickled from her nostril. "Her…only…student. I wanted to make her proud. To prove…I could be like her."

A lump rose to my throat, and I swallowed hard. "You are," I told her, my voice a ragged whisper. "You were a true Viper. Lilith would've been proud."

Faith didn't answer. Her wings had stopped moving, and her gold eyes stared up at me, fixed and unseeing. She was dead.

And the soldier who had killed her was standing right behind me.

GARRET

I lowered the gun, watching as Ember stepped away from the body, feeling some of the tension leave me as I gazed at the dead dragon. It was over. She was the last; the others, the Talon agents, were scattered behind me in the warehouse. They had fought stubbornly and persistently, down to the last man. As if they had nothing to lose. Maybe they didn't. Perhaps Talon's policy was return victorious or don't return at all. Regardless, it didn't matter. No one would be returning to Talon tonight.

Abruptly, Ember staggered, catching herself with a grunt, and my alarm flared up again. Holstering the pistol, I hurried toward her, scanning the lithe, scaly body for wounds. Her crimson scales made it difficult to see if there was any blood, though by the stiff way she was moving, I suspected she'd been hurt. I'd never witnessed a full-on dragon fight, but I had seen firsthand what their claws and teeth were capable of, able to crunch through bone and rip doors off vehicles. Their scales might be fireproof, but I imagined two warring dragons could still do a lot of damage to each other.

My hunch was confirmed when I drew close and saw the glimmer of open wounds on her back, four long claw marks that had been raked across her scales. But the edges around the narrow cuts looked *burned*, blackened around the edges, the flesh inside a raw, painful pink.

"Ember," I said, lightly brushing a wingtip as I circled around. More wounds came to light, all in the same condition, claw marks scored by flame. The faint scent of smoke and chemicals lingered in the air, seeming to come off the limping dragon, and I frowned. "What happened?"

"Bad decision that seemed a good idea at the time." Her voice was tight, and she turned to face me fully. Four thin, seeping gashes scarred her muzzle, red and painful looking, and my stomach clenched. "You killed her," she whispered, not quite accusing, but her eyes gleamed angrily. "You didn't have to kill her."

"Yes, I did." I met the dragon's gaze, saw my reflection in those slitted green eyes. They narrowed sharply, but I didn't feel one inkling of fear. Strange now, that I could stand this close to a furious, wounded dragon and know, beyond any doubt, that she would never hurt me. "I had to use lethal force," I told her. "You know that. She wouldn't have stopped until you were dead."

"I know. Dammit." Ember slumped, glancing at the lifeless body against the wall. A pained expression crossed her face, and she let out a gusty sigh, smoke curling from her jaws. "She was still one of us," Ember murmured. "She was like me, once. Who knows what she might've been if Lilith and Talon hadn't gotten their claws into her." A shudder went through her, and she turned her head, closing her eyes. "I wish it didn't have to be this way."

I reached out and put a tentative hand on her neck, feeling

warm scales under my palm. My heart jumped, still thrilled by the idea of touching a dragon. "We need to take care of those," I said, mentally assessing her wounds, wondering how serious they would be in human form. "Can you Shift back?"

"No." Ember shook her head, staggering away from me. "I mean, yes, I can, and I will, but what about Riley? He's still out there. We have to find him."

"Ember, you're hurt. Badly, by the looks of it." I sidled around to face her, blocking her path. "We need to get you back to the hotel and let Wes know what's going on. Maybe he's heard from Riley by now."

"He would've called us if he had!" Her tail lashed, and she raised her head in defiance. "I'm fine, Garret. We have to keep looking."

"Where? We still don't know his location. He could be anywhere in the city by now. Where are you planning to search?" Ember slitted her eyes, and I kept my voice calm, knowing that if a five-hundred-pound reptile wanted to walk right through me, there was little I could do to stop it. The strangeness of standing in a dark warehouse arguing with a dragon did not escape me, either.

"We have to regroup," I said, hoping she would listen to reason, that her worry and eagerness to find Riley would not override logic. Some dark little part of me bristled with anger at the thought, but I shoved it down. "Let's go back to the hotel, get you taken care of, and see if Wes has heard any-thing. That's the most reasonable course of action right now."

Ember lashed her tail, taking a breath to argue, then frowned. "Wait," she muttered, cocking her head. "Did you hear that?"

I fell silent, pulling the gun from my belt and stepping around to her flank. For a moment, we stood there, a soldier of St. George and a dragon, guarding each other's backs. Strangely, it felt no different than the hundreds of times I'd done this with Tristan.

A faint, familiar jingle sounded, somewhere in the maze. Ember gasped.

"My phone!"

She started forward, stumbled and nearly fell, hissing in pain. Hurrying to her side, I gently caught a wing joint, making her pause and look back at me. "Hold on a second," I said, wishing I knew a trick to get a dragon to lie down, especially *this* dragon. "Ember, wait. You're going to hurt yourself." She snorted and glared at me, and I sighed. "Stay here and don't move," I said, holding out an arm as I backed away. "Lie down if you have to. I'll find it. I'll be right back." And I jogged into the maze without waiting for a reply.

I sprinted back to the place we'd first been ambushed, passing the bodies of several Talon agents, slumped in corners or behind crates. The majority of the group lay sprawled on the cement where the line had been, torched with dragonfire or shot with the gun Ember had tossed me.

The weapon she was supposed to kill me with.

My jaw clenched. For a bleak moment, I'd really thought she would. I knew she and Dante were close, that they shared a bond unheard of between their kind. Dante was a dragon, her brother and her only family; I was a human soldier she had known only a few weeks. She'd told me herself, she would do anything to get him out of Talon.

Why had she chosen me over her twin?

The ringing had stopped by the time I reached the area, but after only a few seconds of searching, it sounded again. I discovered the phone lying beside a pallet and snatched it up, bringing it to my ear.

"Wes?"

"Oh, goodie." The voice on the other end, though heavy with sarcasm, was not Wes. "You're still alive."

"Riley." I felt a strange mix of both relief and disappointment. Relief because, no matter what his feelings toward me, the rogue dragon was a competent leader and strategist, a soldier in his own right. And he obviously cared about the rogues in his underground, the hatchlings he got out of Talon, something I hadn't thought dragons capable of a month ago. I hadn't wanted him dead; I was glad he survived.

But at the same time, I'd seen how Ember looked at him sometimes, and I'd caught the protectiveness on his face whenever they were close. He was a dragon; long-lived, intelligent, and able to understand Ember in a way I never would. Jealousy was not something I'd experienced before. I despised how it made me feel. But it was there all the same.

"Where's Ember?" Riley asked, making resentment flare up again, stronger than ever. I stifled my anger, knowing it was unreasonable right now, and answered calmly.

"She's fine. She's wounded, but she'll be okay. We...ran into some trouble with Talon."

"Yeah, no shit." Riley sighed, sounding angry and weary all at once. "I guess you know by now that Faith is a Viper," he continued, sounding like he really didn't want to know the answer.

"Yes," I answered simply.

"Is she…?"

"She's dead," I replied, making him sigh again.

"I figured. Fucking Talon." The pain in his voice surprised me. "They were just kids. Sending Vipers after us is one thing, but they weren't even juveniles yet. Dammit." There was a muffled thud, as if he'd slammed his fist into something. "Sending dragons to kill dragons. It makes no sense."

"Where are you?" I asked.

"Heading your way now. Old rail yard, right? I was there when Mist gave you that false information." Riley paused, then asked in a quieter voice, "How is she?"

Of course, he could mean only one person. "She sustained a few surface injuries when she was fighting the Viper," I answered, making him mutter another curse. "The wounds themselves don't look too deep, but the edges are burned fairly severely. Third-degree if I had to guess." I stifled a wince, knowing from personal experience just how painful third-degree burns were. Though I continued to hear myself speak with clinical detachment. "Other than that, from what I can tell, her injuries are minor."

"Dammit, Ember," Riley growled. "Taking on a Viper yourself, you idiot hatchling. Where is Faith now?" he went on, sounding faintly hesitant now. "Did Ember…kill her?"

"No. I did."

"Good." He hesitated again, longer this time, as if struggling to make himself speak. "Look, let's make one thing clear," he finally muttered. "I don't like you. I think you're a murdering bastard, and the fact that you've recently had a change of heart doesn't erase all the blood on your hands, and it never will. I also think you're an idiot for believing

Ember would ever choose a human over her own kind. She's a dragon, and even if she hasn't figured it out yet, dragons and humans don't belong together. You should know that, St. George. And if you truly care for her, you'll let her be with her own kind. For both your sakes.

"But," he went on, as my insides twisted painfully at his words, "I know what Talon is capable of. I know what the Vipers are capable of, even their hatchlings. Ember might be too softhearted to destroy one of her own, but I know that Faith wouldn't have hesitated to kill her. If you put that Viper down, much as I hate you for it, then you probably saved Ember's life. And for that..." He sighed. "You're not as much of a bastard as I thought."

"Thanks," I said drily, knowing that was the closest to gratitude I'd ever get from the rogue.

He snorted. "Don't get me wrong. If the Viper had ripped your throat out instead, I wouldn't lose any sleep tonight. Where is Ember now?"

Soft footsteps made me whirl around, just as a slight figure in a black suit emerged from the maze. Ember had, of course, followed me, her jaw clenched in pain and determination as she limped doggedly across the floor.

"Riley?" she asked as I hurried over, catching her by the arm just as she staggered. Four angry red gashes scored her cheek, making me grimace. But her eyes shone with hope, even through the pain. "Is that Riley?"

For just a moment, I considered lying, turning off the phone and claiming it was Wes. For a moment, I hated the fact that Riley had lived, that he could make her face light up like that. It cast a dark uncertainty over my thoughts, and all the confusion and doubt I had pushed down rose to the surface once more. Was I just fooling myself? Would Ember ever see me in the same way as the rogue dragon?

"Garret?" She looked up at me, eager and confused, her eyes searching. "Did you hang up? Who were you talking to?"

Wordlessly, I handed her the phone.

RILEY

"Riley?"

Heat flared through me at the sound of her voice, nearly making my breath catch. The dragon rose up, shaking off the grogginess, burning away the tranquilizer. And maybe I was still under the influence of the truth drug, but suddenly everything became a lot clearer. Ember was mine. I needed her. She was impulsive, reckless, infuriating...and I couldn't imagine my life without her.

"Hey, Firebrand." I sighed. "Good to hear your voice. You okay?"

"Oh, you know." I heard the tremor that went through her, the breathless relief. "A little burned, a little sore. Nearly died a couple times. The usual. You?"

"The same." I staggered through a metal door and paused outside the building to get my bearings. Some old warehouse district on the edge of town, isolated and unremarkable, as I expected. Still, I scanned the area carefully, not putting it past Talon to be watching this place, via satellite or something else. I had to get out of the area quickly. Now that my phone was back on, Wes would be able to find me; he was supposedly on his way now. "Though I am a tad confused by one part," I went on, hurrying across the dusty yard toward a chain-link fence surrounding it. "Did you just say you were burned? You're a *dragon*. How does that happen?"

"Um, I might've set myself on fire."

I closed my eyes. "Ember…"

"But look on the bright side, I managed to avoid being shot this time."

"I need you."

A very long silence followed. Long enough for me to slip through the fence and step onto the sidewalk. Gazing up and down the street, I picked a direction and started walking, toward the glow of distant lights that, hopefully, marked the edge of the city. A warm breeze blew against my face, smelling of dust and pavement; I breathed it in and smiled to myself. It was good to be free.

"Riley." Ember's voice trembled slightly, though I couldn't tell what she was feeling. "What…what are you talking about?"

"I think you know what I'm talking about." I raked a hand through my hair, feeling dangerously light and uncaring. "However, I'm probably still under the effects of a truth drug," I went on, with the same easy nonchalance I'd felt while talking to Mist. "And it made me realize something, about us. But, if you don't want to hear what I'm really thinking, I'd hang up right now."

"Do you want me to?"

Yes. Say yes, Riley. "No."

Ember took a deep, shaky breath. "Tell me, then."

No turning back now. Ah, screw it. I officially don't care anymore. "I realized something while I was in that session with Mist,"

I began, hoping to tell her everything before Wes showed up. "She's a Basilisk, you know. Talon wanted the locations of my safe houses, and they sent her to retrieve them. She was supposed to kill me after she got the information."

"Bitch," Ember growled.

"Wasn't her fault," I said, feeling a small twinge of regret that I couldn't save her, too. "You know what Talon is like. You know what they're capable of. I would've brought her with us if I could."

"Is...is she...?"

"No," I murmured. "I didn't kill her. She's sleeping off a tranquilizer that would put down an elephant, so she won't bat an eyelash for at least a couple hours. But that's not the point." I paused as a taxi cruised toward my corner but then sped by without slowing.

"I would've told her everything," I continued, feeling my stomach twist at how close I'd actually come to revealing my entire network. "I almost betrayed my entire underground. All my hatchlings, all the humans I got out. But something stopped me, kept me from spilling my guts and telling Mist everything she wanted to know."

"What was it?"

"You, Firebrand." I stopped at an intersection and leaned against a crosswalk sign. "I saw your face, and I knew I had to keep it together." A human passed by, giving me a smirk as he crossed the street, and I didn't even care. "You kept me grounded, Ember," I said quietly, resting my head against the metal pole. "You're the reason I was able to resist. I just kept thinking about you.

"I don't know what you want from me," I hurried on,

knowing this would be the only time I'd have the guts to actually say it, "or what you feel for the soldier, but I'm letting you know right now… I'm done fighting this. From now on, I'll be fighting for both of us."

"Riley," Ember said again, her voice almost a whisper, "I can't… I mean. This isn't…" She broke off, and her voice dropped even further, becoming nearly inaudible. "I can't promise anything," she whispered. "I don't know what I feel."

"That's fine, Firebrand." I looked up as headlights pierced the darkness, and a taxi pulled to the curb. "But when you figure it out, when you remember that you're still a dragon, I'll be right here. I'm not going anywhere, that's *my* promise."

The cab window lowered, and Wes's shaggy head poked out, thin arms gesturing frantically. I grinned and started toward the cab, surprised at how relieved I was to see him. "I'm heading your way now," I told Ember, sliding into the backseat, ignoring Wes's I-told-you-so glare. "Hang tight, we'll be there in a few minutes."

"Riley?"

I paused, stopping myself from clicking off the phone. "Yeah?"

"I'm glad you're all right." The voice on the other end sounded defiantly embarrassed. "You scared us there for a while. Don't do that again."

"You mean don't get captured and interrogated by Talon's double agents? No promises, but I'll do my best." I smiled, hearing her snort into the phone. "See you soon."

"Well," Wes commented as I hung up. "Don't you look like hell."

COBALT

Twelve years ago

I don't know how he tracked me down, but he did.

A human was waiting for me in the latest dump I'd rented for the night, sitting at the desk in the corner, watching as I came through the door. I tensed, going for the gun I always carried now, and he quickly held up his hands.

"Relax, mate! I'm not here for trouble. Just hear me out."

I recognized him then. The kid who had been in that meeting with Roth and the Chief Basilisk, so long ago, it seemed. His brown hair stuck out in every direction, hanging in his eyes, and his clothes looked rumpled and dirty, like he'd spent a few days in them. I racked my memory for his name, then realized it had never been given.

"Okay." I did not lower the gun, keeping it aimed at the kid's scrawny middle. He might've been human, and unarmed as far as I could tell, but I'd had a hell of a week and wasn't going to be taking any chances. "You have my attention. What do you want?"

"Uh, could you maybe put the gun down? I told you before, mate, I don't want any trouble. I'm here to help you."

I smirked. "Really? I find that a little hard to believe. One, you're human. What can you possibly do that would help me? And two, more importantly, I saw you in that meeting with Roth. You're part of Talon."

"Not anymore."

I faltered and gave him an incredulous look. "Not anymore? What do you mean?"

"I mean, I left, mate. I'm out. Went rogue, dropped off the grid, gone AWOL, whatever you want to call it."

"How?"

"I've been planning this a long time," the kid explained, a flash of anger and resentment crossing his narrow face. "If you wanna lower the gun, and not make me so bloody nervous, I'll tell you everything. Including some things about *you* that you might not know."

Sighing, I dropped my arm. "Fine," I muttered, and he relaxed. I did not need this right now, having some strange human show up on my doorstep like a lost cat, but if the kid really had gotten out of Talon, it could be worth listening to him. He might know what Talon was up to, if they had any more plans involving me and another Viper. I'd managed to avoid Stealth so far, but that wouldn't last. She was still out there, looking for me. The least I could do was hear him out. "Although," I warned, with one last jab of the pistol, "if Talon unexpectedly shows up while we're talking, you're going to be the first one I shoot. Just so you know."

He paled, but nodded. "Fair enough. Though if the bastards do show, it might be better to shoot me." Resting bony elbows on his knees, he sighed, sounding suddenly tired, and far older than I first took him for. "I think…I might actually rather be dead than go back."

Shoving the gun into the waistband of my jeans, I stepped farther into the room. "Who are you?" I asked, pausing at the foot of the bed, watching him. "How'd you find me?"

"My name is Wesley," the human said, leaning back in the chair. "Wesley Higgins, or just Wes, if you like. Not that it matters, I officially don't exist in any system anymore. And there's no need to introduce yourself, Agent Cobalt. I already know who you are. I know a lot of things about you, actually."

"Do you, now?" I said in a flat, dangerous voice. "And what exactly do you want for this information? Is the deal I give you everything I have, or you go back to Talon to turn me in?"

"That's not it at all! Look, I'm not trying to blackmail you or anything. I just…ugh." Wes scrubbed both hands through his hair. "Bloody hell, I don't want a fight. I'm on your side, okay? Let me start from the beginning. Can I do that, without you blowing my head off?"

I shrugged. Maybe I was being paranoid, but again, hell of a week. "No promises," I growled. "Get on with it."

"Right," Wes muttered, and took a deep breath. I leaned against the wall, crossing my arms, and waited.

"I've been in Talon nearly five years," the human began, eyeing me warily. "Before that, I lived in London, with my folks. I didn't have any siblings, and both my parents worked long shifts, so I was alone most of the time."

"What does this have to do with Talon?"

"I'm getting there, mate." Wes paused to gather his thoughts before continuing. "Like I said, my folks were absent most of the time. They didn't know what I did. They weren't aware that I was an...um...anonymous independent computer specialist."

"You were a hacker," I said.

"And a bloody good one, too. Still am." Wes looked faintly smug, then his eyes darkened. "Of course, that's what got me into this mess. I was home alone one day, minding my own business, when there was a knock at the door. I opened it, and two uniformed policemen were standing there on the stoop. Said I was under arrest, and that I already knew why they were taking me in. I was terrified. I was fourteen, alone and being dragged from my home in handcuffs." He smiled grimly, completely without humor. "Of course, it wasn't the police. It wasn't anyone in law enforcement. But you already know that, don't you?"

It was my turn to sigh. "Talon."

"Bloody Talon," Wes repeated. "Though I didn't know that at the time. They took me to a room, sat me in front of a computer and said that if I didn't do what they wanted, not only would they expose me, they would ruin my family, as well." Wes shook his head. "I was a stupid bloody teenager. I believed them. So I did what I was told. For three years, I worked for Talon, wondering about my parents, wondering when the organization would let me go home. And you know what I finally realized?"

"They wouldn't," I muttered.

Wes nodded slowly. "When I was sixteen, I attended my first meeting with Adam Roth. They brought me into a secure room, no windows, no other humans around. And they showed me Talon's secret. They showed me who I was working for." Wes gave a short, bitter laugh. "A gift, they said. A reward for my brilliant service and talents. Bloody bastards. I realized then they would never let me go. I was in for life."

"That's when you decided to get out?"

"They bloody kidnapped me." Wes's lip curled in a snarl. "Took away my freedom, my family, everything. I was a bloody slave to the lizards for five years. I'd be damned if I was going to stay there."

"Getting away must've taken some work," I said, amazed that the kid had pulled off something so risky, and that he'd avoided Talon even this long.

"Yeah, well, like I said, I've been planning this awhile," Wes repeated. "I had to set everything up so that when I did leave, I'd be out of their systems forever. And I had to scrape together enough secrets and blackmail to keep my family safe. When I ran, I made it very clear that if they ever threatened my folks in an attempt to get to me, there are some very interesting files on Talon's businesses that would go public."

I smirked. "Playing dirty with Talon. I'm impressed."

The human snorted. "Right. There's just one small snag," he said, lowering his brows. "I can't do this on my own. I can hack my way through just about anything, but I don't have the survival skills you do, the ones that will keep me alive and away from the organization. If I run, eventually, they'll send someone to kill me, or drag me back. Some Viper will slit my throat in the middle of the night." He shuddered, giving me a grave look. "Honestly, I've been waiting for someone like you for a long time now. When I heard that you went rogue, I knew it was my chance. I'd probably never get another one."

"So you tracked me down hoping I'd protect you from Talon?" I shook my head. "I don't need a human tagging along, slowing me down. I work alone, that's how it's always been." His face fell, making me feel like an ass, but I hardened my voice. "Do you even know what you're asking? What going rogue means to the organization? They'll never stop looking for you. They will never give up, or forgive, or accept any compromise. And they'll never forget, because dragons have insanely long memories and will hold a grudge forever. You go back now, sure, Talon will lock you away and you'll live a very sheltered existence until you die of old age or boredom. But at least you'll be alive. You come with me, and your life is going to be uncertain, violent and probably very short."

His eyes narrowed. "I don't think you quite realize the opportunity here, mate," he said, making me frown. "I'm not just some stupid kid in need of protection. I can help you, too."

"How?"

He smirked. "For starters…you know all those accounts frozen by Talon when you went rogue? I can open them again, and make it so they'll never be traced back to you."

"What?" I stared at him, and his smirk widened.

"I told you, I'm one of the best, mate. You need something, some file stolen or code decrypted, I can do that. In fact…" He reached into his pocket and pulled out a strip of black plastic. "A goodwill offering," he announced, tossing it to me.

"What is this?" I asked as I caught it.

"All of Talon's files on you. Everything you've done for the organization, all their information on where you've been, where you've stayed, your case files, your assignments, your hatching date, everything. Congratulations. You are now truly a ghost to them." I gazed up at him, stunned, and his smile turned hard. "You know you were never supposed to come back from that mission, right? According to your file, you were becoming a 'liability' and 'suspect to corruption.' Which is Talon's way of saying they couldn't control you anymore. So they decided to stage an accident, have you killed in the line of duty." He shrugged. "But, since you're here and not buried under a ton of bricks and mortar, I guess you already knew that."

"Yeah," I muttered, glancing at the thumb drive in amazement. My whole life, on this tiny strip of plastic. And now, it was mine alone. Thanks to this human, tracking me down had just become that much harder. "I guess that 'file' they had me steal from St. George was bogus, too," I said, slipping the drive into my jacket. "Just an excuse to get me into the compound."

"Oh, no, mate. That was very real." Wes grinned again as I looked up. "Talon took a very important file from St. George that day. They already had an agent inside the base, why not use him one last time? Only problem? It seems to be missing now. Like it was never there. Funny how that works."

"You have the file," I said, and he shrugged. "So what is it?"

"You're asking me? I thought you worked alone."

I glowered, but it was a mostly empty gesture. The human was right; he was far too useful not to keep around. Still, something nagged at me. "Let's say I accept your offer," I began, making his brows rise. "Why do this? What do you get out of it?"

"Besides staying alive? I would think that's a sodding good

reason right there, but…there is something else." Wes leaned back in the chair, his face suddenly hard. "The bloody lizards stole my life," he muttered. "I'll never be normal. I'll never be able to see my family, get married, have kids, anything like that. Because of Talon."

"So this is revenge?" I asked, and shook my head. "And you think you'll…what…bring them down? This isn't a single company you can infect with a virus. This is a worldwide corporation, an empire. We're only two people."

"What if there were more like us?"

"Even if there were," I said, "how would we find them?"

The human's eyes gleamed. "How indeed," he said, and opened his laptop, bending over the keys. "You want to know what that file you took from St. George was?" he said, as I edged forward and peered over his shoulder. "Check this out."

I squinted at the image that popped onto the screen, frowning in confusion. It was…a list. There was no title, no header, nothing to indicate what it was actually for. But the first line read: "Carson City, NV. Talon activity: Moderate. Sleeper agents discovered: 1."

Sleeper agents? *Sleeper* was the Order's word for the hatchlings ready to complete assimilation, when they were sent to human towns to blend in with humanity. I scanned the list, amazement and awe growing with each line. Each row held the name of a town, the level of Talon activity discovered there and one or two possible sleepers. My heart beat faster in excitement.

"This is…" I muttered, and Wes nodded.

"All the places St. George thinks Talon will send their hatchlings," he finished, and shrugged. "It's probably not accurate, some of those places might not be in use anymore, especially with Talon's paranoia. But…"

But it was something. And now that we had a list of possible sleeper locations, the wisp of an idea began to creep into my head. A crazy, impossible, terrifying idea. If we could find these hatchlings, be there when Talon planted them into a town, I could show them the truth about the organization. They needed to know, before Talon sank their claws in too deep, before they were brainwashed completely. They needed to see what Talon was really like. And, if they decided they could no longer be a part of the organization, they needed someone to help them escape, to show them how to be free.

I could show them how.

Wes noticed the change, and a slow smile crossed his face. "So, what'd'ya say, mate?" he said softly. "Partners?"

"You realize this is going to take a long time," I warned. "The type of network we're talking about, it will take years to build, decades even. We'll constantly be on the run, from Talon *and* St. George. Our lives are never going to be safe, or anything close to normal. Sure you're up for it, human?"

"Hey." Wesley Higgins leaned back with a shrug. "I'm being hunted by a bloody dragon empire that won't stop unless it's completely destroyed or taken down. What else am I going to do?"

"All right." I looked down at the screen, at the first place on the list, and nodded. Carson City, Nevada, was our first stop. "Let's get this resistance started."

EMBER

I lowered my arm, feeling my heart pound, my emotions raging everywhere all at once. Riley was okay; I couldn't express how relieved I was to hear his voice, to know he was alive. The past few hours had been a nightmare; I hadn't even realized how much Riley meant to me until he was gone.

And my dragon, surging like molten lava through my veins, was acutely aware of Riley's promise, was relishing it, even. She couldn't wait to see him again. She recognized her other half, had always recognized it. Cobalt called to her. She felt the other dragon's pull as surely as I felt the need to fly or sleep or breathe. And Riley wasn't holding back anymore.

So what was holding *me* back?

"We should move." Garret's voice echoed at my side. I glanced up and found him watching me, his face shut into that blank, expressionless mask that made my insides shrink. "Talon is probably aware by now that their ambush failed," he went on, gesturing to the carnage around us. "If they aren't, they'll find out very shortly. We should leave the premises before they send in the cleanup crew."

"Right." I nodded and pushed myself off the crate stack,

but pain shot up my leg and I nearly fell, barely catching myself on the edge. "Ow. Dammit. Ow."

"Are you all right?" Garret hovered at my side, his remote expression cracking a little with worry. I waved him off.

"I'm fine." I took another step, clenching my teeth as my leg, back, ribs and shoulder throbbed. I didn't know if it was from dragon claws, or just general aches and bruises from my fight with the Viper, but dammit I was sore. Of course, the stupid magic Viper suit didn't show rips or tears, so I couldn't even see how bad the wounds were. "Right behind you," I gritted out, wishing I could Shift to my real form again. The human body didn't deal with pain as well as a dragon's. "Just moving…a little slower than normal. Keep going."

Garret hesitated, then stepped beside me, putting a hand on my back. Surprised, I glanced at him as he bent, scooped an arm under my knees and lifted me off my feet. I gasped, wincing as the motion tore at the open wounds beneath my suit, but then he shifted me gently in his arms, and the pain receded.

"Garret." My heart pounded, my stomach tying itself into knots at being so close. I put a hand on his chest, feeling his own heart thudding beneath my palm. "You don't have to do this," I said, torn between exhilaration and embarrassment. "I'll be okay…"

I trailed off at the look he gave me. Sorrow, regret and longing glimmered in his eyes for just a moment, before they blinked and became remote once more. "Let me do this one last thing," Garret said quietly, and offered a faint smile when I frowned in confusion. "You carried me to safety once. Now it's my turn."

He sounded sad for some reason. Like this was the last thing he would do for me. Wanting to ease the tension, I looped an arm around his neck and smiled. "You know, if you really wanted to impress, I could Shift right now and you could carry me out like that."

The corner of his mouth twitched. "Somehow, I don't think I'd get very far. Riley would walk in and see a dragon lying on top of a crushed soldier. He'd probably take a picture to remember it, always."

I chuckled, feeling some of the awkwardness subside. A soldier of St. George carrying a dragon to safety—what was next? Sighing, I leaned my head on his chest, as Garret walked easily through the maze with me in his arms. His heart beat steady and sure against my ear, and I relaxed. We were okay, all of us. St. George had come for us, and we'd survived. Talon had sent two deadly double agents to force me back to the organization, and I was still here. Riley was alive. Garret was alive. We'd taken the worst Talon and the Order could throw at us and had come out on top.

But the casualties were high, even if they weren't on our side. I didn't have to look up to see the dozen or so Talon agents, sprawled throughout the warehouse. More dead humans than I'd seen in a lifetime. Dead humans that would probably show up in my dreams for weeks to come. And of course, somewhere in that mess of blood and darkness was the lifeless body of a purple dragon. A girl who, at one time, had been just like me.

Anger burned, and shockingly, I felt my eyes stinging. It was a waste. Such an awful, stupid waste, and for what? Faith didn't have to die. Talon didn't have to send her. Why couldn't they just leave us alone? Why was it so important that I return to the organization? Now a hatchling and a dozen humans were dead, because someone in Talon had ordered my assassination...

"Garret," I whispered, clenching a fist in his shirt, "wait!"

He stopped and gave me a puzzled look. We were almost to the exit; I could see the open door to the rail yard dead ahead. Riley and Wes would be here soon, and we had to get out of here before Talon, the Order or the authorities showed up. But something still nagged at me, and if I didn't resolve it now, I'd drive myself crazy wondering.

"I have to go back," I told Garret, whose puzzled look deepened to a frown. "You don't have to come. Put me down and go wait for Riley if you want. But I have to go back. There's something important I forgot to do."

DANTE

She should have called by now.

The clock on the wall was too loud, every ticking second like a miniature drill in my brain. The senior dragons did nothing, said nothing, sitting around the table with the patience of mountains, their blank eyes on me. Occasionally, they would speak to me, or each other, their voices cool and remote, but for the most part, they waited, silent and unmoving. I mimicked their positions, trying to remain calm and patient, staring at my folded hands until the image was seared into my retinas.

The phone buzzed on the table.

I jolted in my seat like I'd been stung. Without waiting for Roth's approval, I snatched it up and put it to my ear, my voice low and grave.

"Faith? Is it done?"

"It's not Faith."

I froze. The room froze. I sat rigid in my chair, the eyes of four senior dragons on me, as *her* voice echoed in my ear, low and unmistakable. They couldn't hear the conversation, but from the looks I was getting, it was clear they knew something wasn't right. Heart pounding, I closed my eyes, knowing it was useless to hide it.

"Ember," I said, and felt the attention in the room sharpen to a razor's edge. I swallowed hard and forced myself to speak calmly. Maybe I could salvage what was left of this assignment. "Where are you?"

"I think you already know that, Dante." Ember's voice was icy. She'd spoken to me that way only a couple times in her life, and I had painful memories of one, and a tiny scar from the other. "Considering you were the one who set this up."

The weight of the combined stares was becoming unbearable, four senior dragons pinning me with hard, intense eyes. "Where is Faith?" I asked.

A heartbeat of silence. "She's dead."

The ground dropped out from under me. I sat there, unable to believe what I'd just heard. I'd always known Ember was rebellious, reckless and stubborn, but I'd never thought her capable of this. "She's dead?" I choked in disbelief. "You killed her?"

"I didn't kill her."

"The soldier, then," I guessed. "St. George. You're with him now, aren't you? And you let him kill her." There was no answer on the other side, and my voice hardened. "How could you let him do that?"

"You've got some nerve asking me that," Ember hissed. And though she sounded furious, her voice cracked on the last word. "Don't play innocent with me, Dante. You were the one who sent her, after all. You set this whole thing up, didn't you?"

"Yes," I admitted, not knowing where this absolute rage

was coming from. "I did. To bring you back. You belong here, Ember. You belong with Talon." There was a squeak, as someone in the room rose from their chair, but I barely heard it. "I'm trying to keep you safe," I said, suddenly furious myself. "I'm trying to make a future for both of us, but you insist on tearing it down! I can't believe you let that human kill Faith, just because you didn't want to come back. What is wrong with you!"

I was almost shouting into the phone now, and a second later, it was smoothly plucked from my grasp by Mr. Roth, who gave me a blank, chilling smile before putting it to his ear.

"Ms. Hill," he said cordially, "this is Adam Roth, senior vice president of Talon's western operations. How are you tonight?" He paused, smiling faintly, his sharp face giving nothing away. "Well, I'm sure you don't mean that literally."

I buried my head in my hands, raking my fingers through my hair, not caring how it made me look. I could only imagine what Ember was saying to Talon's senior vice president. My stomach turned, shocked at how badly this had turned out. Faith was dead. Where was Mist? I wondered. Had she been killed, too? The two hatchlings had been our best bet to find Ember and the rogue; as the newest agents of Talon, they wouldn't be recognized by Cobalt or his network, so they'd be able to get close without arousing suspicion. Originally, I'd wanted Mist to talk to Ember, convince her to come back, but she'd later informed me that Talon had other plans for her. I'd been annoyed—this was my operation, after all, and Mr. Roth had put me in charge. But then I'd spoken to the second agent, Faith, who'd assured me that she would bring Ember safely back to the fold. Before talking to her, I'd had serious doubts that the quiet, delicate-looking girl was a good fit for this assignment. Cobalt was a dangerous rogue, and calling Ember stubborn was putting it mildly. But it took only a few minutes of discussion to know that Faith was more than she seemed. And when she'd told me she would get the job done, I believed her, though I had made it clear that she was not to harm my sister in any way.

"Bring Ember back to Talon," I'd told her. "Use everything at your disposal to convince her to return, but do *not* hurt her. If she refuses to come back, do what you must. But I want my sister returned alive and safe. Do you understand?"

"Of course, sir." Faith had smiled at me, confident and professional. "Your sister will not be harmed in any way. I will make certain of it."

And now she was dead. Faith was *dead*. Because I had sent her after my wayward twin, and Ember had let her be killed rather than return to the organization. How had this happened? How could she have resorted to that, after everything we'd gone through together? Apparently, I didn't know my sister at all.

And now, because of her, I had failed. I had failed Talon.

My hands shook, and I flattened them on the tabletop, trying to steady myself. Above me, Mr. Roth continued with polite coolness. "I'm afraid I cannot tell you that, Ms. Hill," he said evenly. "If you wish that information, you must return to the organization." Pause. "No, Mr. Hill is in no danger. He is a valued member of Talon, and we appreciate his cooperation." Pause. "No, our policy on rogues is very clear. Cobalt is a criminal who has caused irreversible harm to the organization. We must protect ourselves from his extremist views." One last, lengthy pause, and Mr. Roth's voice grew hard. "I'm sorry you feel that way. But if you would only agree to return and speak with us, you would see that…"

He trailed off, lowering his arm. "Well. It appears Ms. Hill will not be joining us tonight." Turning, he rested his fingertips against the table and spoke to the rest of the room. "We will adjourn for now, until we can come up with a new strategy to retrieve Ms. Hill and deal with Cobalt. As Ms. Anderson has not yet reported in, perhaps she will give us better news. But it can wait until tomorrow." He looked over the table with cold black eyes. "Dismissed."

Everyone rose at once, keeping their eyes downcast as they began to exit the room. I stood as well, but suddenly Mr. Roth's long steely fingers gripped my shoulder, making me freeze.

"Mr. Hill. You will come with me."

EMBER

"Only you, Firebrand." Riley sighed.

I grimaced at him over the table, where an open first-aid kit, bandages, burn cream and disinfectant wipes sat scattered between us. My Viper suit lay discarded on the bathroom floor of the hotel room, replaced with shorts and a loose top that didn't rub against my skin. Riley leaned forward in his chair, winding the last of the gauze around my arm. His long fingers occasionally brushed my hand, sending a pulse of heat up my arm every single time. Garret had left the room a few minutes ago, saying nothing as he slipped out the door, presumably to stand guard or check the parking lot for "suspicious people," leaving me and Riley alone.

Well, alone except for Wes.

"There." Fastening the gauze, Riley looked up with a rueful smile, shaking his head. A bandage square covered my left cheek, right below my eye, and it felt weird and tight against my skin. "Don't pick at the bandages, Firebrand," Riley ordered. "Hopefully those will heal in a day or two, though this is the first time I've had to treat another dragon for burns. Like I said, you are one of a kind."

"Thank God," Wes muttered from the bed, laptop perched

on his knees. I ignored him, which was getting harder to do in the tiny room. After meeting Riley and Wes in front of the rail yard, we'd fled downtown Vegas and the Strip, putting as much distance between us and the massive glittering casinos as we could. This tiny hotel on the outskirts of town had more roaches than slot machines, and the four of us were currently packed into one room like sardines in a can, but Riley wasn't planning to stay long. According to Wes, there was a used-car lot two blocks down that would sell you anything, no credit history, no questions asked, and Riley planned to be there as soon as it opened in a few hours. I had no idea where we were going, but I knew Riley was in a hurry to leave Vegas. And after tonight, I was more than happy to say goodbye, too. Goodbye to the City of Sin. Goodbye to Talon and the Order...and Dante.

A lump caught in my throat, and I swallowed it with a growl. I refused to mourn my traitor brother, no matter how sick it made me feel. Dante was part of Talon now. Part of the organization that wanted me dead. He'd sent a Viper after me and a Basilisk after Riley, with orders to kill us both. I didn't know him anymore. Riley had been right all along.

"There." Wes tapped a final key and looked up. "I've sent instructions to all our nests, telling them to relocate immediately and not contact anyone until they've heard from you. They're on emergency evacuation until further notice."

"Good." Riley stood up, wiping his hands. "Hopefully that will buy us, and them, some time until we can figure this out. See if we can't find who the hell is leaking information to the organization and shut them up for good. If Talon wants to kill us, I'm not going to make it easy for them."

I was only half listening, still brooding over Talon and Dante and the whole screwed-up situation, so a gentle touch on my shoulder surprised me. I glanced up into Riley's intense golden eyes.

"Firebrand? You okay? Are you in any pain?"

"No," I whispered, as the now familiar heat surged up again, pushing me toward him. Gingerly, I stood, testing my range of motion. My various cuts and burns throbbed, but they were slowly going numb with salve and painkillers. The real hurt wasn't physical, and no amount of aspirin would make it go away. "Just...thinking about Talon," I told Riley, who hadn't taken his eyes from me, "and St. George and what a bastard my brother is. You can go ahead and say *I told you so*—"

Riley stepped close and very carefully pulled me into his arms, making me freeze in shock.

"I'm sorry about Dante," he murmured, keeping one hand on my waist, the other in my hair, avoiding my many bandages. My cheek was pressed to his shirt; I could feel the heat of his skin through the fabric, his voice rumbling in my ear. "I wish we could have taken him, too. But he made his choice, Firebrand. And now you have to make yours. Are you still going to stand with me, against Talon? Even though you might be fighting your brother again one day?"

Putting my hands on his arms, I pulled back to face not Riley but Cobalt peering down at me. The human veneer was still there, still in place, but the dark blue dragon stared out through human eyes, ghostly wings outstretched, casting us both in their shadow. I swallowed hard to keep my own wings from breaking free. "Why now?" I whispered.

"I told you, I'm done fighting this," Cobalt rumbled, and one hand was suddenly against my cheek, hot and searing. "I almost lost you today. I won't make that mistake again." His fingers traced my skin, brushing my hair back, and I shivered. "You don't have to make a decision tonight," Cobalt said. "I have time." The corner of his mouth quirked, and he stepped back, looking more like Riley. "I'm a dragon, after all."

"Bloody hell." Wes's disgusted voice rose up from the corner. "Will the pair of you please stop before I yark all over the room? Riley, you might want to come see this."

Rolling his eyes, Riley pulled away. I stood there, watching them for a moment, my heart thudding in my chest and my dragon surging beneath my skin. The temperature in the room was suddenly too hot, stifling, and the walls seemed too close. I had to get some air.

With one last look at Wes and Riley, still deep in conversation, I slipped out the door into the warmth of the night. I told myself I needed to be alone, to clear my head, but that was a lie. And I didn't have to search far. A lean, pale form stood in the outdoor hall with his elbows against the railing, gazing out over the parking lot. I started toward him, but as I did, my steps faltered and I hesitated, suddenly torn between saying something and going back inside. Why was I afraid? This was Garret.

Swallowing, I forced myself to move, knowing he'd heard me come out. "Hey, you," I greeted as the door clicked behind me. I kept my voice light, a stark contrast to the uncertainty within. "Spot any ninjas yet? Maybe a secret agent hiding in the cactus?"

"No," he said quietly, still watching the pink glow over the horizon. "But there is a suspicious-looking bench near the parking lot that I'm keeping an eye on. Just in case."

Smiling, I joined him at the railing and mimicked his pose, and we stared at the distant mountains for several heart-beats. In this quiet moment before dawn, the world was silent, peaceful. I wished I could feel the same, but the raging storm of questions inside made that impossible. I wondered where we would go next. I wondered where Dante was, what he was doing, what he was planning now. I wondered if there would come a time when I could stop running. If someday Talon and St. George would just stop killing each other, if the war would ever cease.

"Ember."

Garret's voice, soft and hesitant, broke the predawn still-ness. He kept his gaze on the horizon, but his whole posture was stiff, tense. "You never answered me last night."

My stomach turned inside out, and everything around us froze. Garret straightened and turned, keeping one hand on the railing, to face me, metallic gaze burning the side of my head. A little flutter of panic bloomed inside. I kept my gaze on a distant street lamp, watching it flicker against the com-ing dawn, and felt the silence stretch between us, brittle and terrifying. My heart pounded, screaming at me to say some-thing, to give him the words he was waiting for. But I didn't know if I could...feel like that. When I was with him, I was happy. When we touched, my heart beat faster and my stom-ach did crazy cartwheels. When we were apart, I thought of him constantly, and when we were together, I was content. But I didn't know if that was love.

And how could I love him, when a part of me longed for Cobalt, standing in the very next room?

"What do you want me to say, Garret?" I whispered at last.

Garret didn't answer for a moment, then took a quiet breath, as if bracing himself. "I just want the truth," he said, and his voice wasn't angry or cold or demanding, just resigned. Sad. "I have never felt...anything like this. And I know that I'm the last person in the world that deserves it, but...I meant it when I said that I'm in love with you." His voice wavered on the last sentence, then grew stronger, almost defiant. "I love you, Ember," he said again, and I closed my eyes. "I'm not ashamed, and I'm not afraid of what it means. But I...I need to know if you feel the same."

He was putting all his cards on the table, leaving himself wide-open, and I was probably going to rip his heart out. I wanted to tell him. I wanted to say I felt the same, but at the same time, I didn't want to lie to him. My emotions were a chaotic swirl of confusion and doubt. Garret. Cobalt. Longing. Love. Which was stronger? How did people even know if they were in love?

"Garret," I stammered miserably, "I...I don't know. I'm not human. I don't even know if we're capable of...those kinds of feelings."

"I don't believe that," Garret said. "I might have once, but not anymore. I've seen you, Ember. From the very first day we met in Crescent Beach, I've watched you. You've made friends and formed attachments, and you miss them, even now. You're angry at your brother because he chose Talon over you. You refused to be what your trainer wanted, a Viper that kills without emotion. You're the one who taught me that dragons aren't really that different than us, and I abandoned everything I believed in because of you." He paused then, his voice becoming quietly desperate. "Don't tell me you're not capable of it," he almost whispered. "What's really holding you back?"

I sighed and looked up at him, finally admitting the truth to us both. "Riley."

He didn't look surprised. He just nodded once, slowly, as if I'd confirmed what he'd always suspected. I finally turned to face him head-on, needing him to understand. "Garret...I like you. I really do. When I'm with you...I feel more human than I have in my entire life. I don't know if I'm supposed to feel that way, and I don't know if that's a good or a bad thing, but at this point, I really don't care. I want to be with you. Sometimes...sometimes I wish that I wasn't a dragon, so we could be normal together." I gave a tiny, bitter chuckle. "Of course, if I was human, we would've never met, so it's kind of a catch-22, isn't it?"

Garret didn't reply. He still watched me, those solemn gray eyes making me want to drop my gaze and hide. I stifled the impulse and continued to face him.

"But," I went on, "I can't ignore what I feel for Riley. And I don't want to lie, to either of you. I honestly don't know what's going on between the three of us, and until I'm sure... I can't give you a real answer. I'm sorry, Garret." I couldn't take the way he was looking at me any longer, and I turned away. "I think...I need some time to figure this out."

"All right." His voice surprised me. I was expecting anger, contempt, accusations for leading him on, not this quiet resolve. "Then I guess that makes this easy."

I looked back at him quickly. "Makes what easy?"

This time he turned away. Only then did I notice the backpack, propped beside the door, already packed, and everything went cold inside me. "You're leaving?"

"There's no reason for me to stay." Garret's voice was calm as he swung the pack to his shoulder. "I've paid my debt, to you and Riley at least. And it's not safe for me to stick around. Sooner or later, St. George will come after me again. Better if I'm far away when that happens."

"Where will you go?"

"I don't know yet." He glanced back at me, eyes shadowed. "England, maybe, if I can get there. Something is wrong in the Order—that ambush with Mist and Faith wasn't a coincidence. St. George knew we were coming, and I don't like what that implies." His gaze narrowed, expression going dark. "If there is a connection between Talon and the Order, it will change everything St. George has believed for hundreds of years. Everything we thought we knew will be a deception. Now that I've seen both sides, I need to know if there's something more to this war than either faction is letting on." He sighed, and for the first time a shadow of doubt crossed his face. "I hope I'm wrong," he murmured. "But I have to be sure." One last pause, barely a heartbeat, one last chance to tell him to stay, before he stepped back. "Goodbye, Ember," he said, as something shattered inside me. "Thank you...for everything." And he walked away.

"Garret, wait."

He turned around, eyes widening with surprise, as I flung myself against him, wrapped my arms around his neck and kissed him. His arms circled my waist, pressing us together, as I buried my fingers in his hair. He groaned, backing me into a pillar, his mouth at my jaw, my neck, searing a path down my skin. Our lips met again, hungry and eager, sending the pit of my stomach into a wild swirl. A low growl escaped me as I locked my body to his, wanting to feel him with my entire being.

Abruptly, Garret pulled back, breaking the kiss, and set me gently on my feet. I glanced into his eyes and saw the confusion, the uncertainty and the wary hope shining through, and my heart stuttered. The soldier watched me a moment longer, then closed his eyes.

"Tell me to stay," he whispered, his voice a low, husky rasp, "and I will."

Cold flooded my body. I took a breath to answer...and nothing came out. I knew the words that would convince him...but I couldn't say them, even now. Especially now. That would be even more cruel on my part, telling him what he needed to hear, just to get him to stay with me, when I wasn't certain myself.

Sickened, I drew back, sliding from Garret's arms. He opened his eyes but didn't move, watching as I backed away from him. The look on his face was devastating, but only for a moment. Then that blank, remote soldier's mask slipped into place, his eyes turning cold and flat.

Spinning on a heel, he walked away again, and this time his stride was confident and sure. I watched, heart in my throat, until he hit the stairs on the other side and started down, not looking back once.

And then he was gone.

I swallowed, blinked rapidly until the stinging in my eyes went away and went back into the room.

Riley and Wes were still at the computer, but they had moved to the table now, with Riley standing behind the chair as the human hunched over the screen. Wes didn't move, but Riley looked up as I came in and leaned against the door, still coming to grips with the fact that Garret was really gone forever.

"Firebrand? You okay?" Riley stepped toward me, frowning in concern. "Where's St. George?"

"He...left," I answered, making Riley's brows shoot up. "Just now. He said he was going to check up on the Order or something. He's...not coming back."

"Huh." As expected, Riley didn't seem terribly heartbroken at the news. "Well, I'd say that's too bad, but then I'd just be lying. Don't glare at me, Firebrand," he went on, crossing the room. "You knew this was coming as much as I did. He's a human and a soldier of St. George. Did you really expect him to stick around a bunch of dragons for the rest of his life?"

"No," I whispered, my voice breaking a little bit. Of course not. Garret was human. He belonged out there, with the rest of humanity. Maybe now he could finally live a normal life. "I knew he had to leave sooner or later," I admitted. "I just... I'll miss him, that's all."

Riley stepped forward and, without hesitation, pulled me close. My pulse skipped, and warmth bloomed through my stomach, burning away the grief, at least for now.

"Forget him," Cobalt murmured, bending his head to mine. "You don't need the human. You have me. And when you're ready, when we reach a spot where we can both be ourselves, I'll show you exactly what that means."

Yes, my dragon agreed, as I closed my eyes, basking in the warmth. This was right. This was what I wanted. I didn't need humans or their tangle of confusing emotions. I was a dragon; it was time I finally accepted that.

Pulling back, I looked up at Riley, saw myself in that bright gold gaze and tried to smile. "So," I asked, as Cobalt peered back at me, eyes glimmering, "where to now?"

"Now?" Riley said, his voice full of dark promise as he turned away. "Now we're going to hunt down a traitor."

EPILOGUE

DANTE

I stood in another small, cold elevator, Mr. Smith and another Talon agent flanking me, as the tiny box descended into what felt like the bowels of the earth. Gazing at my blurry reflection in the metal door, I thought back to the past two days and allowed myself a small smile.

After the disastrous meeting and phone call with Ember, Mr. Roth had escorted me into his office and closed the door, inviting me to take a seat. I had obeyed with a numb sense of dread, knowing I had failed, both the organization and my sister. Sinking into the seat before the desk, I waited for the ax to fall, to be reamed out for my failure.

"First off, Mr. Hill, I'd like to congratulate you."

I had stared, unsure I'd heard him right. Why was he congratulating me? Surely this was a joke, though I hadn't known any of the senior executives to kid around. "Sir?"

Mr. Roth smiled. "This operation with your sister was a test, Mr. Hill. It was the reason we put you in charge of returning Ember Hill to Talon. We wanted to gauge your loyalty to the organization, as well as your ingenuity and commitment to doing the right thing."

"But...I failed, sir. I didn't bring Ember back."

"No, that failure was not yours, Mr. Hill." Roth's eyes glittered, though it wasn't directed at me. "You performed exactly as we hoped, and suffice to say the company is pleased with the results. There will be…repercussions. Reign is not going to be happy with the loss of his people, but that is Talon's concern, not yours. You've proven you can be trusted, that your ideals are in line with Talon's, that you value the safety of the organization above all else." He leaned back in his leather chair. "So again, I offer my congratulations, Mr. Hill. You have passed your final exam.

"Now," he continued as I sat there, reeling from the announcement. "We have business to discuss. As a full-fledged member of the organization, you now know how serious the rogue threat is. Your own sister committed a heinous act against one of her own kind, allowing her to be slain by a soldier of St. George. Such is often the case with dragons that go rogue. Without structure, they become violent and unpredictable, a danger to themselves and to the organization. Your sister has started down a very dark path, but we believe it is actually the rogue dragon Cobalt who is influencing her. He is an extremist whose hatred of Talon is well-known, and his tactics against the organization border on terrorism. Cobalt and his network of criminals must be stopped at all costs. How dedicated are you to bringing this about, Mr. Hill?"

Rage burned, and I clenched a fist on my leg, careful not to let Mr. Roth see. *Cobalt.* The rogue dragon who had lured my sister away, turned her against me, was my personal enemy now. He had almost cost me everything and would pay for what he had done. "Whatever it takes, sir," I said evenly. "Whatever Talon needs me to do."

"Even if it means working against your sister?"

I took a deep breath. "Ember made her choice," I said. "She has to live with the consequences of her actions. My hope is that she'll realize her mistake and return to the organization willingly, but if she doesn't, I will bring her back by force if I have to." Mr. Roth raised an eyebrow, appraising, and I spoke firmly, confidently. "The rogue movement must be eliminated, for the good of us all. I'm fully committed to seeing that happen, sir."

"Excellent." Mr. Roth beamed. "Then I do believe you are ready." He stood, extending a hand to lead me out of his office. "Rest up, Mr. Hill," he announced as he escorted me to where Mr. Smith stood waiting in the hall. "Tomorrow morning, you have a plane to catch."

★ ★ ★

The elevator slowed, and finally stopped with a faint ding. As the doors slid back, revealing a sterile white hallway and a pair of guarded metal doors at the end, Mr. Smith turned to me.

"Keep in mind, Dante," he warned as we stepped into the hall, passing humans in white lab coats scurrying from room to room. "This is one of Talon's greatest secrets. That you are even allowed to be here shows the amount of faith and trust the organization has in you. Do not abuse that."

"I won't," I promised, and meant it.

We came to the doors, and the Talon agent flashed a badge at one of the armed guards, who nodded briskly and waved us through. We stepped into an even smaller room, barely larger than the elevator box, where the guard pressed his hand to a small sensory pad by the door. It lit up, green lines scanning his palm and fingers, before it beeped once, and the light above the metal door turned green.

"Remember, Dante," Mr. Smith warned again, and pushed back the door.

My eyes widened. I stumbled forward in a daze, hardly believing what I saw. Steam billowed through the frame, and the air was hot and humid, as if I'd stepped into a rain forest. I was almost instantly drenched in sweat, but I barely felt it. I couldn't tear my gaze from the wonders of the scene before me.

Dragons. Hundreds of them. In rows of huge cylindrical vats marching down the aisles. They floated in translucent green liquid, eyes closed, wings and legs folded neatly to their bodies. Tubes jutted from their necks and stomachs, snaking to the tops of the canisters, where they disappeared in a tangle of machinery. From their size, most of them were hatchlings, some barely out of the egg, but there were a few near the end that were larger, older.

And they all looked the same. Through the glass and the green-tinted murk, their scales were a dull metallic gray, with no hint or spark of color at all. They all had the same ridge of ivory horns over their eyes and along their jaw. The same bony spikes jutting from their backs, shoulders and forelegs. The similarities were more than coincidence, more than sharing the same bloodline or parents. They were identical. Down to the same crooked horn on the left side of their head.

I smiled, as I realized what Talon had been planning, all this time.

"Behold, Dante Hill," Mr. Smith said, walking up behind me, his deep voice full of triumph. "Welcome to the future."

★ ★ ★ ★ ★

Thank you for reading ROGUE,
Book Two of THE TALON SAGA.
Look for Book Three, SOLDIER, *coming soon.*
Only from Julie Kagawa and MIRA Ink.

ACKNOWLEDGMENTS

Thank you to my parents for your prayers and guidance, and for encouraging me to go after my dreams, no matter how crazy they were. To the people at MIRA Ink for your continued hard work, amazing support, jaw-dropping covers and so on. A massive thank-you to my wonderful editor, Natashya Wilson, who continues to be Superwoman in everything that she does. To my agent, Laurie McLean, who asks the questions I cannot, without whom I would be completely lost. Also to Brandy Rivers, for championing my books and making the impossible happen.

And, of course, to Nick, my other half. My love for you burns hotter than dragonfire.

QUESTIONS FOR DISCUSSION

1. Two dragon lifestyles are contrasted in *Rogue*; that of the dragons in Talon and that of Riley's rogues. What are the advantages of each and which does Ember seem best suited for? Why does Dante want to stay with Talon? Point to evidence in the story.

2. Ember and Riley have different ways of seeing Las Vegas. How does each of them describe the city, and how do you account for the differences in their points of view?

3. Garret has spent most of his life in the military-esque Order of St. George. In what ways is he equipped to live on his own, and what challenges might he face as he learns to survive outside the Order?

4. Cobalt had become disillusioned with Talon prior to his mission to break into the St. George chapterhouse and blow it up. What experiences pushed him to leave, and what might have happened if Talon had not tried to kill

him back then? Where might Cobalt/Riley be now if Wes had not joined him?

5. In *Rogue*, Ember begins to feel a greater split between her dragon and human selves, mainly caused by her different reactions to Garret and Riley. Why does each character appeal to a different side of her, and what does that show about a dragon's ability to feel emotions?

6. Garret does not understand why Ember saved him from being executed. Ember has learned that Garret has killed many of her kind. Why is Ember so determined to save Garret, despite knowing what he is? Point to evidence about her character in the book to inform your answer.

7. Dante believes he has failed his mission to bring back Ember and is shocked when Mr. Roth congratulates him and welcomes him as a full member of Talon. Why, in Talon's view, did Dante succeed, and who do you think will take the fall for the failure of the mission?

8. Exploiting your enemy's weakness is a running theme in *Rogue*. What makes each entity—the rogues, Talon, the Order of St. George—weak, and in what ways might those weaknesses also be strengths? In what ways is the author hinting at a potential future solution to this ancient conflict?

9. Madison and Stealth both have minor parts in *Rogue* but each has a big impact on Cobalt. How is he changed by his encounter with each of these characters? How might

his actions toward each of them impact those characters in the future?

10. Dante is trusted with an incredible secret at the end of *Rogue*. What do you think Talon is planning? Discuss.

For your reading pleasure
Julie Kagawa and MIRA Ink
are proud to present
this exclusive excerpt from the final novel
of THE IRON FEY *series,*
THE IRON WARRIOR.

The rulers of Summer and Winter stood at the head of the table, watching us as we came in. I'd never seen either of them before, but they were instantly recognizable. Oberon, the King of Summer, stood tall and proud at the table edge, silver hair falling down his back, his antlered crown casting jagged shadows over the surface. A pale, beautiful woman stood a few feet away, dark hair cascading around her shoulders, a high-collared cloak draping her armor of red and black. Piercing dark eyes stabbed me over the table, and my insides curled with fear. Mab, Queen of Winter, was just as dangerous and terrifying as I had imagined she would be. The only good thing was that Titania, the Queen of Summer, appeared to be absent today. The queens' hatred for each other was well-known, and the situation was volatile enough without two immortal faery rulers throwing down in the middle of the war council.

"Iron Queen," Mab stated in a cold, flat voice as Meghan and Ash stepped forward. "How good of you to join us. Perhaps you would like to hear the reports of what your son has been doing of late?"

"I am aware that Keirran is with the Forgotten," Meghan

replied, far more calmly than I would have expected. "I know they have been scouting the borders of Arcadia and Tir Na Nog. They have not, to my knowledge, harmed anyone or made any hostile overtures toward the courts."

"Yet," Mab hissed. "It is obvious they plan to attack, and I refuse to be besieged in my own kingdom. I propose we take the fight to the Forgotten now, before they and their mysterious Lady set upon us en masse."

"And how do you plan to do that, Lady Mab?" Oberon asked, his voice like a mountain spring, quiet yet frigid. "We do not know where the Forgotten *are*, where the rest of this army is hiding. Whenever anyone tries to follow them, they disappear, both from the mortal realm and the Nevernever. How do you propose we find something that does not exist?"

Mab glared at him. "They cannot simply vanish into thin air," she snapped. "An entire race of fey cannot simply will themselves into nothingness. They have to be somewhere."

"They are," I answered. "They're in the Between."

All eyes turned to me. My heart stuttered, but I took a deep breath and stepped forward, meeting the cold, inhuman stares of a couple dozen fey.

"King Oberon is right," I said, moving beside Meghan, feeling the chill of a Winter knight to my left. "The Forgotten can't be found in the mortal world or the Nevernever because they're *not* here anymore. They're slipping in and out of both worlds, from a place called the Between. It's—"

"I know what the Between is, Ethan Chase," Mab stated coolly, narrowing her eyes. "Most call it the Veil, the curtain between Faery and the mortal realm, the barrier that keeps our world hidden from mortal sight. But the ability for fey to go Between has been lost for centuries. I know of only one who has accomplished it in the past hundred years, and she has not seen fit to share her knowledge with the rest of Faery."

Leanansidhe. I nodded. "Well, it might've been lost to the courts, but the Lady—the Forgotten Queen—remembers how," I said. "And she taught the rest of the Forgotten, too. You haven't been able to find them because they're all hanging out in the Between."

Mab's icy black gaze lingered on my face, seeing far too much. "And the Iron Prince?" she asked in a soft, lethal voice, making Meghan stiffen beside me. "Does he have this special talent? Has the Lady taught him to go Between, as well?"

I swallowed.

"Yes," Meghan confirmed before I could say anything. "Whatever old knowledge the Lady brought with her when she awoke has passed to her followers. Keirran can move through the Between like the rest of the Forgotten."

Oberon raised his head. "Then it seems the Lady has chosen her champion," he stated in a low, grave voice. "And so the prophecy comes to pass. Keirran will destroy the courts unless we stop him. Iron Queen..." He gave Meghan an almost sympathetic look. "You know what you must do. Declare Keirran a traitor and cast him from your court. Only then may we stand united against the Forgotten and the Lady."

"What? Whoa, wait a second." I leaned forward, feeling the frigid edge of the table bite into my hands. "You don't know what they want. Keirran is only trying to help the Forgotten survive. Yeah, he did it in the most ass-backward way possible, but maybe you should try talking to them first before declaring all-out war."

"And what do you know of war, Ethan Chase?" Mab inquired, as her cold, scary gaze settled on me again. "You are the reason we are here, the reason the prophecy has come to pass. It was your presence that allowed the Forgotten to invade, your blood that tore away the Veil, even if it was for but a moment. You and the Iron Prince have brought nothing but chaos to Faery, and now you dare to tell us that we should be merciful?" Her lips curled in a terrifying smile. "I have not forgotten your hand in the destruction of my Frozen Wood," she said, making my blood chill at the memory. I tried to draw back, but I suddenly couldn't move. My hands burned on the edge of the table, and I looked down to see ice had crept up and sealed my fingers to the surface. "You are lucky that the impending war demands my attention for now," Mab hissed, "but do not think for a moment that I will let that slide. You and the Iron Prince have much to answer for."

"Lady Mab." Meghan's cool, steady voice broke through the rising fury. "Please stop terrorizing my brother before I take offence." My hands were suddenly free, and I yanked them back, rubbing them furiously to start circulation. "I am aware of the prophecy," Meghan went on, as I stuck my frozen fingers under my arms. "I am aware that, misguided or not, Keirran has done terrible things. But I beg you all to consider what we are really dealing with. This is my son and your kin. Both of yours," she added, looking to the Summer King and the Winter Queen in turn. "Are we going to declare war on our own blood without knowing the details? We are still uncertain as to what the Forgotten and the Lady really want."

"I can tell you what she wants," said a new, familiar voice behind us.

The blood froze in my veins. I spun, as did the rest of the table, to face the entrance of the room. The double doors had been pushed back, and a figure stood in the entryway with a pair of shadowy sidhe knights flanking him.

Keirran.

IN JULIE KAGAWA'S GROUND-BREAKING MODERN FANTASY SERIES, DRAGONS WALK AMONG US IN HUMAN FORM

Long ago, dragons were hunted to near extinction by the Order of St George. Hiding in human form and increasing their numbers in secret, the dragons of Talon have become strong and cunning, and they're positioned to take over the world with humans none the wiser.

Trained to infiltrate society, Ember wants to live the teen experience before taking her destined place in Talon. But destiny is a matter of perspective and a rogue dragon will soon challenge everything Ember has been taught.

www.miraink.co.uk